LUMINESCENCE TRILOGY

Complete Collection

J. L. WEIL

Dark Magick Publishing, LLC

ALSO BY J. L. WEIL

THE DIVISA SERIES

(Full series completed – Teen Paranormal Romance)

Losing Emma: A Divisa novella

Saving Angel

Hunting Angel

Breaking Emma: A Divisa novella

Chasing Angel

Loving Angel

Redeeming Angel

LUMINESCENCE TRILOGY

(Full series completed – Teen Paranormal Romance)

Luminescence

Amethyst Tears

Moondust

Darkmist – A Luminescence novella

RAVEN SERIES

(Full series completed – Teen Paranormal Romance)

White Raven

Black Crow

Soul Symmetry

BEAUTY NEVER DIES CHRONICLES

(Teen Dystopian Romance)

Slumber

Entangled

Forsaken

NINE TAILS SERIES

(Teen Paranormal Romance)

First Shift

Storm Shift

Flame Shift

Time Shift

SINGLE NOVELS

Starbound

(Teen Paranormal Romance)

Dark Souls

(Runes KindleWorld Novella)

Casting Dreams

(New Adult Paranormal Romance

Ancient Tides

(New Adult Paranormal Romance

For an updated list of my books, please visit my website: www.jlweil.com

Join my VIP email list and I'll personally send you an email reminder as soon as my next book is out! Click here to sign up: www.jlweil.com

PART I
LUMINESCENCE

CHAPTER 1

I was pissed—body shaking, steam-coming-out-of-my-ears kind of pissed.

And that only meant one thing: extreme trouble. Even in my heightened anger, I was frightened—scared not for *myself*, but for anyone who got in the path of the fury just past my control.

A ripple of heat flowed through my veins, bubbling and sparking. It scorched my skin, causing a haze of crimson to swirl in front of my eyes. So hot, it felt like a dragon's flames licked at the back of my throat, threatening to lash from my mouth if I dared speak. Clamping my teeth together, I avoided my lips in the process. The thought of tasting blood, even my own, didn't bode well at this very moment. Not with the intense tingle radiating everywhere within me.

"Let it go, Brianna." I faintly heard Austin's nervous voice. He might have touched a hand to my arm, but I was too far in depths for reasoning.

Early on, I learned my temper was something to avoid at all costs— all costs. I went to serious lengths to keep it under wrap. Deep breathing and the whole find your center of balance thing. Yoga. Meditation classes. I learned to control my breath, but my emotions were another story. But it didn't stop me from trying to protect others from myself. It had been ages since I'd been hit with such intensity, and I'd forgotten what it was like; I had forgotten it was wrong.

Experimenting with my odd, peculiar, and volatile temper was something I never did. Trying to pick it apart and find out the particulars to why it initiated such bizarre and often harmful results wasn't a good idea. The sensations it induced made me uncontrollable, wild, and reckless. Like there was nothing and no one that could stand in my way. I felt invincible. Then after I'd seen the results of what I'd done, I was consumed with guilt and shame. A freak. What normal person inflicts the impossible with just a flare of anger?

Most of the time, it wasn't an issue. I made sure of it. I kept mostly to myself, with a small handful of close friends. Even they didn't know the violence that lived within—no one knew. Not my friends, not my parents —when they were alive—not even the one person I trusted and loved most in this world—my aunt.

Part of it was shame, and part of it was fear. What if someone found out? I'd no doubt be branded a freak. The nuthouse would surely be my new home.

None of it made sense. No doctor or meds could help me.

Regardless, I tried not to reflect about my freakish attributes, and how different they made me. What I wouldn't give to be free of whatever curse or hex I'd been born with. That was how I thought of it: a curse. Nothing like this could be good. I refused to allow myself to get mad or even on the verge of angry. I walked away.

Until today.

I would have walked away today if only Rianne had let it go. If she hadn't pushed me further and further, until there was no other response but to react. If only she hadn't chosen this day to harass and bully one of my best friends. And maybe if I hadn't already been in a shitty mood. There was an underlying headache, hammering at my skull, that wouldn't quit gnawing away. Or if Tori, Austin and I had stayed another minute at our lockers, fooling around, we wouldn't have passed Rianne in the pit.

Today was turning out to be the day from hell.

But as it turned out, we did pass Rianne, and she *had* bumped intentionally into Austin, knocking him down and spewing vile words at him in her skanky cheerleader voice. A voice which begged me to tear her into shreds and rip out her wicked tongue. She had no regard for the hurt she caused others.

Austin wasn't a big guy. He might be a few inches over my five-foot, two-inch frame, putting him almost at equal level with Rianne. His weight wasn't much more than her either. If only I had his metabolism. He ate like a starving horse and still looked like a stick figure. Today he had on skinny jeans, which emphasized his scrawny legs. Hair, product styled, was still perfectly in place, framed by his bottle glass green eyes, now bright with humiliation. He had the whole GQ thing going for him.

Regardless, it wasn't how Austin looked or how he dressed that had Rianne yelling those choice words out over the pit. It wasn't enough that she'd purposely rammed into him while we were making our way through the crowd. If it had been anything else, I would have been able to maintain the thread holding my anger in check.

"Get out of the way, *faggot*." She shrieked over the bustle and commotion of the circular room deemed "the pit". The crowd was making their way to final period. With both palms spread, she took advantage of his unsteadiness and shoved, sprawling him over the mascot in the center of the pit, where practically the entire school congregated between classes.

Yep, Austin was gay.

My control snapped like a rubber band. The combination of hearing my friend being called that ugly name, and seeing him tossed ass first on the school's dull gray carpet caused the first kindling of my temper.

Momentarily stunned, I just glared at Rianne while the assault of emotions snuck up on me. Somewhere in the smog, I remembered Tori speaking to Austin.

"You okay?" she whispered, giving Austin a hand up.

If he had given her a reply, it was lost by the bursting flood of rage consuming me.

Recklessly, I reached out in front of me and grabbed Rianne's arm, stopping her from turning and walking away. Her sneering golden eyes pierced into mine with disgust, like little spears of hate. She couldn't believe I had the gall to touch her. I was normally quiet and very non-confrontational. This was so out of the norm, it hit a home run off left field.

With a tug, she attempted to shake off my grasp, but my hold held like vise grips. "L-E-T go of me," she hissed through clenched teeth, drawing out the threat. But her anger was nothing to match my own. Right then my fury spiked. Fervor raced in my blood, tumbling into my fingertips. My hand trembled under the tight clutch I had on her arm.

When I spoke, my voice sounded nothing like my own. It quivered with potency. "Like hell. You should watch what you say," I spat.

There was a falter in her expression when she'd felt the burn, the sting radiated from my fingers. Again she tried to wiggle out of my hold. When she failed a second time, her gaze turned to mine and widened in astonishment, skepticism, and a touch of fear.

"Your eyes," she accused, staring intently into mine. "What's wrong with your eyes?" her voice cracked, giving away the shock she must have felt. Appalled, her feet scrambled to back up.

I stepped forward, my heart accelerating. Thumping heavily against my chest, her admission put anxiety into my stomach. I let go of her arm with a quick jerk. She stumbled once, unsteady on her feet, but never took her eyes from mine. They bore into me with fear and repulsion, branding me like the freak I felt.

My breath came in quick pants as I averted my gaze and closed my eyes tight, trying to get a handle on the rage still pumping in me. Calming the quick pants to longer slower ones, I recalled one of the meditation techniques I'd learned. I didn't know what Rianne thought she saw in my eyes, other than extreme anger, I tried to remind myself. Even if her fear had been real, it was hardly out of Rianne's character to make a fool out of others in front of the whole school. Hell, it was what she did on a daily basis.

I continued to mentally talk myself down, and slowly the anger receded. The warmth faded from my skin, and the overwhelming urge to punish Rianne drifted with the loss of contact.

"Brianna, are you okay?" Tori asked behind me over the retreating buzz in my skull.

Shaking my head, I tried to clear the rattled outburst, berating myself for the enormous slip in front of the entire school. If I wasn't thought of as odd and weird before, this just put me on the front page of weirdos attending Holly Ridge High.

"What did you do to me?" Rianne screeched, her tone simultaneous contemptuous and fearful.

Saying nothing, I opened my eyes to see her clutching the arm I had grasped. Dread sunk to the soles of my converse- covered heels. *Had I really done that? Was I capable of inflicting that kind of harm with just my fingers?*

Swollen, cherry red marks lined Rianne's arm in the spots my fingers had clasped. The wound looked like imprints or burn marks from a flatiron that had penetrated her flesh, except my fingers had been the branding iron.

There was no doubt of the horror now blistering Rianne's forearm. Embarrassment, regret, and shame swarmed my gut, twisting it heavily with sour guilt. I couldn't answer questions I didn't have answers for, so I quickly turned to leave.

Like a gust of wind, I became acutely aware of the large audience my spectacle had created. They stood circled around Rianne, Tori, Austin and I, some chanting and jeering our names, encouraging a fight.

Without a second thought, I pushed my way through an opening in the awkward sea of people. I rushed forward before someone could stop me, and the need for escape steamrolled over me.

There were too many eyes.

Too many questions.

Too much emotion.

My mind seemed to have temporarily abandoned me. There was no explanation for my actions, or for my legs carrying me not to my last class, but to the exit doors of the school. I'd never, in three years of high school, ever ditched out on a class.

I know, unfathomable.

However, I'm among the select few who like school. Okay, maybe not so much school, but learning. Being shy and mostly socially challenged, books were more my friend than my peers—Tori and Austin the exception.

My actions today were so out of character for me, I began to doubt who I thought I was. I hated confrontation. I never caused trouble. And I don't attack people in the hall, burning the fuse on my temper.

Never.

Right now, all I knew was, I had to get out of here, run from what I had just done. The walls of the school suffocated me in their confines.

CHAPTER 2

As I stepped out the front door of school, a soothing breeze whipped through my tousled dark hair, washing over my flushed face. It cooled the heat that had crept up on me during my rage. The balmy air was scented with just a taste of the ocean in the distance. It never seemed far away.

Holly Ridge, North Carolina, had been in the midst of one of those dreamy, sun-drenched days. But now gray clouds were rolling across the sky, the ground was drenched from a downpour of rain, and a crackling of lightning lit in the distance, followed by a gentle rumble of thunder. Whatever storm had passed through was on its way out. Ironic. It fit my mood—dreary and unpredictable.

I peered around at the lush landscape, a sight I often took for granted. The overhang of trees and grass met the sandy shores, and then plunged into depths of expansive, sparkling turquoise sea. Blades of grass began to glisten as sunbeams tried to break through the storm clouds.

Inhaling a deep gush of sea-flavored misty air, I rounded the corner to the backside of the building, rushing toward the parking lot. A strange prickly sensation climbed over me, like clashing with a cactus. I brushed it off and took the corner faster than planned, speeding up my retreat. Unfortunately, I wasn't the only one who apparently skipped out of school early today.

Leaning comfortably against the wall was an unfamiliar face, and in my rush, I smacked into him. Literally. The front of my face connected with the solid front of his chest, hands clutching on the muscle of his biceps. In an impossibly quick gut-reaction, he caught me in his arms. We wavered a tad, but he managed to keep us upright, instead of mortifying me further and tumbling to the grass.

Damn. What else can happen today?

I forced my glance upward from the black cotton tee that conformed to his chest, ready to apologize for my clumsiness. His hands tingled on my arms, still holding me. It should have been too intimate for comfort, but I found the opposite to be true. A sense of safety came over me, probably because he had just saved me from falling all over him.

My hands released their grip and flattened on his chest. His heart quickened under my fingers. The scent of him drifted to my senses, smelling of the woods, wild and untamed. The apology on my lips got stuck in the back of my throat, and in that blinding moment, I tripped into a set of sapphire eyes. My own heart picked up speed, thumping wildly in my chest—uncontainable, like stallions roaming the plains. Nothing like the trepidation I felt previously. This was racing excitement.

He raised a perfectly arched brow, accented with a studded bar. His eyes sparkled with amusement, assumingly at my gaping stare. I, on the other hand, was unaware I'd stood stunned, feet planted, with no attempt to move from his arms. In retrospect, I could only hope he didn't find me as stupid as I later felt.

My gaze wandered from his eyes, down the planes of his cheeks, to lips donned with yet another piercing. This one was a hoop in the center of his lower lip. Those silver-studded lips upturned into a lazy smirk. I was fascinated by the curl of his mouth. An intense string of butterflies flew in my stomach. They felt more like fireflies, due to the warmth that swirled with the exhilaration. I wondered if there were any more parts of him that were pierced.

Then his mouth lowered the tiniest fraction closer to mine, and I stopped thinking at all. The breath I held caught in what I never would have imagined—anticipation. I actually wanted this strange guy to press his lips to mine. Right now, it was all I wanted—his kiss. The gentle tendril of his breath fanned my senses, making me dizzy with the scent of him. My mind must have taken a complete detour between eighth and ninth period.

A gentle stroke of his thumb on my bare arm sent a shudder down my spine, knocking me out of my spellbound gape. I jerked out of his embrace, immediately missing the contact. What was wrong with me? I don't encourage strange guys to kiss me, really *any* guy, for that matter.

"What are you doing?" I demanded, sounding harsher than intended.

He arched his pierced brow again mockingly. "Looks like I'm not the only one ditching last period."

His voice was an extension of his look. Dark. Sexy. Edgy. Mysterious. And dangerous.

Not precisely the kind of guy you'd want to meet alone in an alley, or behind the schoolyard, for that matter.

He was dressed from head to toe in black: dark denim jeans, with a T-shirt, combat boots, and a thick leather band around his wrist. This guy wasn't shy about jewelry. He had a James Dean quality, a *Rebel Without a Cause* ambiance.

Now that I wasn't so enamored by his eyes, I could appreciate the whole package. His hair was layered around his face with flirtatious slashing strands, also black as sin. He was a mouth full of eye candy. Yummy and delicious.

"I—I don't normally ditch," I stammered, running a frustrated hand through my tangled hair.

The look he gave said he found me entertaining, but didn't buy into the whole "not ditching" thing. He shrugged his shoulders. "Well, that's a damn shame."

My eyes narrowed, and I slung the bag that had slipped back over my shoulder. "I've never seen you before. Are you a new student?"

His eyes caught mine again, and they seemed to laugh. "Umm, yeah —it's my first day."

"You ditched on your first day?" My voice sounded as perplexed as the idea was to me.

"Sure. It seems worth it, now." His voice held sex appeal. Husky and dark. "I'm Gavin," he introduced, shoving both hands in his pockets now that he wasn't holding onto me.

"Brianna," I replied. The last warning bell sounded, reminding me I shouldn't be loitering. "I should go," I mumbled hastily.

He leaned back casually against the brick wall, one leg propped up behind him. "I'll be seeing you, Bri." He shortened my name, as if we were acquainted. His husky voice held promise.

I couldn't tell if I was flattered or insulted. "Sorry about...running into you," I muttered and turned toward the parking lot, not waiting for a response. I couldn't get to my car fast enough.

When I got inside my aging Mustang, I wasn't sure what to do next or where to go. Everything inside me was muddled. An inability to get a handle on the rattled emotions overcame me. The lingering exhaustion from my anger slowly faded and was now accompanied by a burst of excitement in my chest. All of it was too much. The need to unwind and smooth my frazzled nerves was too great to ignore. The first thing that came to mind was my aunt and her shop, *Mystic Floral and Gifts*.

MY AUNT WAS like no other—she was amazing. Her small floral boutique was located in the heart of downtown Holly Ridge, and it was also my part-time job. The short ride from school had done little for my frayed emotions. I felt as if I had just been bungee jumping, flying from pissed off to shamed—a giant drop. Then to a confused excitement that, if I didn't know better, resembled attraction. Gavin wasn't my type, not that I really had a type. I would've had to have dated to know what my type was. My inability to find my niche in life was no doubt contributing factors to my confusion.

My aunt's shop was enchanting and potent. The second I walked, in I was dazzled with the serene smells of lilies, lavender and freesia. She has this impressive window display that captivated people, pulling them in, showing off her flair for the dramatic. Cornflower velvet was draped over stands of various heights, her floral arrangements cascading over like green waterfalls, clusters of rainbow crystals sparkling like magic in the morning sun.

I'd always been at complete ease here, and had a sense of belonging. The atmosphere she created was what I identified with. Otherworldly. Fantasy. An escape from reality.

Right now, I needed all of the above.

Walking into the shop, I noticed my aunt behind the glass counter with a customer. Her long, silky, caramel-colored hair lay softly over her shoulders, such a contrast to my own dark strands. Her smooth and creamy skin looked flawless in the sunbeams from the storefront windows, and her soft mahogany eyes twinkled.

My Aunt Clara was my legal guardian. She and my mom had been twins. Sometimes it was peculiar having my aunt look and sound exactly like my mom. When I was younger, it had been much more difficult.

At age five, I came to live with my aunt. I was orphaned after a drunk driver killed both my parents on New Year's Eve. Gwynn and Andrew Rafferty had been on their way home from a business event with my dad's firm, when the tragic accident occurred. I don't have clear memories of that day, only a snapshot in my head of the way they looked before they left. They were elegantly dressed, and I can still recall the smell of her perfume, like roses, as she hugged me good-bye.

I do remember the empty confusion after the fact. My aunt cried with me through our pain, kissed the salty tears from my eyes, and held onto me at night when I was frightened and alone. She became my rock.

Even now, years later, when I caught the scent of a rose in full bloom, I would ache and wonder what life would have been like. The what-if game... I detested playing those wishing games. The loss of my parents wasn't something I reflected on often; although, it snuck up on me occasionally and squeezed the place they held in a corner of my heart.

Mostly, I deluded myself into believing I was nothing but an average teenager. After today, my doubts skyrocketed. What I needed was confirmation that I wasn't an oddity or needed to be locked up in the loony bin. Maybe I did need therapy, but right now, I wanted my aunt.

Passing by one of the mirrors used on display, I caught a glimpse of my reflection. A loud sigh escaped my lips. How I yearned for the elegant grace and classic beauty of my mother and aunt. In truth, there were none of those traits within me. Instead, I was graced with unmanageable auburn hair and, my skin was dusted with freckles that went over the bridge of my dainty nose. I scrunched it in the reflection just to prove my point.

My aunt said I have a unique look. What did that mean? Did she mean unique as in appealing, or unique as in odd? Probably she was trying to keep my self-esteem from reaching an all-time low. I had a hard time looking at myself and visualizing anything uncommon. Just the same face. The one I've seen for the last seventeen years.

Ordinary.

I'd admit I did have an odd feature. One I guessed you could call *novel*—my eyes. They are a true violet, like an amethyst.

I trailed a finger along the shelves, as I strolled through the shop, trying to distract my mind. Nothing worked.

Mystic Floral was my aunt's heart and soul. She was divorced, and the store had become her saving grace. Being the owner did take up an extensive amount of her time. She often felt guilty that I spent much of my time alone and taking care of myself. When I was younger, I would spend my afternoons in the shop until closing. This place had been as much of home as the house on Mulberry.

I admired my aunt's gift with plants, and her artistic ability to make something beautiful. It was in this place I could breathe. The smells were so alive and aromatic, the environment spellbinding. I traced my nail along some of the new colored decorative bottles she had arranged, glistening against crystal stones.

"Brianna." Her voice was like a warm hearth, filled with security. I turned to face her. "You're early, is everything okay?" She checked the time on her wrist.

Swallowing hard, I didn't know whether to cry, laugh, or hug her. Instead, I lied, something I don't do very well. "I got sick before last period." I kept my eyes averted to the tiled floor, silently praying she wouldn't see through my ruse.

She pursed her lips, looking concerned. "Why don't you go home and take the night off? You look a little... peaked." Her caring suggestion only made me feel guiltier than I thought possible.

"It's not as bad now," I assured. "Would it be all right if I stayed?" I asked hesitantly. I really wanted her company, the calm reassurance of love.

"Yeah, honey, if that's what you want." She totally didn't buy my flimsy excuse, but she wouldn't hound me until I was ready to talk.

I nodded my head.

"Why don't you help me set out some of these arrangements I just finished," she encouraged, knowing I needed a distraction to help ease my mind.

An hour into my shift, I headed to the back room in hopes of occupying my thoughts with homework. Mister Dark and Dangerous seemed to find a way to slither into my head. Something told me I hadn't seen the last of Gavin. He was going to shake things up in Holly Ridge.

CHAPTER 3

T he shop had a bell on the door that chimed at the arrival of a customer.

I found my aunt sitting at her work table, crafting a display with flowers. She cut the ends on their long stems. "Feeling any better?" Concern fed her tone.

I took a seat beside her, picking up the discarded stems. "Some."

"Good. You want to talk about it?" She could tell that something was bothering me. I sucked at hiding my emotions. And lying.

I sighed. "I just had a horrible day." Horrific was more like it. "I had a headache that wouldn't quit. Then a girl at school was bullying Austin and—" I paused, not sure how to tell her.

"Did you say something to this girl?" She clipped another stem from a pretty, blush-colored flower.

"I kind of grabbed her arm. Hard." Admitting what I done was tougher than I expected, and I kept my eyes locked onto the grain of the table.

She put the flower down and eyed me. "Did it go further than that?" she asked, obviously wondering if we'd exchanged blows in the halls. The whole hair-pulling and nail-scratching deal or if she was going to be getting a call from the principal.

I shook my head, lifting my gaze. "I left school right after and came here. I wanted to punish her for all the crap she's been giving Austin, but I didn't want to physically hurt her." Well, if I was being honest with myself, at the time, it was exactly what I wanted to do. I brushed a strand of stray hair behind by ear.

She eyed me with worry. "I know it's challenging, dealing with those who have no care for others feelings. You did nothing wrong by defending your friend."

Then why did I have so much guilt? She was trying to calm my inner turmoil, but I wasn't sure there was anything she could say that would absolve it from me.

"I know that in my head, but it's my conscience that doesn't agree. I feel like I lost myself somewhere during the day. Like my control just snapped," I begrudgingly admitted and slumped in my seat.

"What happened may be uncharacteristic for you, but everyone has a breaking point. Maybe you found yours." She gathered the fresh cut flowers and began slipping them into a crystal vase.

"Yeah, I guess." I was unconvinced.

Pushing the abundantly-filled vase aside, she faced me. "You have always had a soft heart. It's something to be proud of."

Her words recalled a memory of me at nine, caring for a baby bunny lost from its family. I took it in, swaddled it in blankets, and fed it baby formula with an eyedropper. For weeks, I doted on this tiny bunny, afraid he wasn't going to be strong enough on his own, willing with all my might that he would survive. He did. The day I released him back into the trees bordering my yard was a mixture of gratified happiness and an achy sorrow, but I knew he was going to thrive.

"You're right." I attempted a half-smile for her sake. Propping my elbows on the table, I placed my chin in my hands and exhaled. "Now all I have to do is deal with the gossip tomorrow."

"You're stronger than you can imagine," she said, engulfing me in hug filled with unconditional love. Her hair brushed against my cheek and smelled of lilacs.

I leaned my head on her shoulder and took a second to appreciate what she meant to me.

By the time my shift ended at the shop, I was physically spent. I pulled into our driveway, and my eyes roamed over the house of all my childhood memories. The two-story pearly white colonial trimmed in black. A veranda swept off both sides of the house. In the center was a massive cobblestone fireplace. Here and there the stone was accented throughout. My aunt, of course, landscaped the yard, and it looked like something out of *Better Homes and Gardens*.

My favorite part of the house had always been the large pear tree sitting off the garage. I loved when the tree blossomed in the spring, stuffing its branches with the white flowers. The waxy petals ended up blanketing the yard in a cloud.

My aunt inherited the house from my Grandma when she declared there was too much unused space for just her. Gran wanted something low-key and less work, a maintenance-free townhome. The house had been a part of our family for generations. It was very old, but well kept.

I walked inside and headed to the kitchen. The house was quiet and creaked in certain spots underfoot. There were leftovers from last night I planned on having for dinner, but my stomach was unsettled from the day's events. I went for the caffeine instead. Grabbing a can of soda from the fridge, I headed upstairs to my room.

Moving out of habit, I changed my clothes and discarded the old ones in the hamper. By nature, I was tidy, and liked things in order. I went to the window and cracked it, letting the twilight breeze into my room, cooling the humidity. I pulled back the covers, fluffed my pillow and climbed into bed.

That night I found the restlessness had returned, and I was unable to sleep, in spite of being exhausted. My mind raced with images, darting from Rianne to Gavin and back to Rianne. What had happened to me today? I didn't even recognize myself.

Fighting.

Ditching class.

Engaging with a troublemaker.

Wanting to kiss the troublemaker.

I covered my face with my hands, mortified at just the thought of how I'd acted. I was a basket case.

Snippets of Rianne's cherry rash on her arm, and the terror and accusation in her face, kept me up. My mind over exaggerated the incident. There had to be a rational explanation for what I'd done, and more importantly, how. So I grabbed her arm, but tight enough to leave marks like that? It was the only plausible solution my mind could come up with, and nowhere near made me feel better.

In the late hours of the night, my body succumbed to the rest it sought. My dreams however, were anything but peaceful.

❧

THE DREAM WAS one I had many times before. Maybe not the same dream per se, but always of him. The blond-haired boy with emerald eyes that beckoned me.

Lukas Devine.

He was as *divine* as his name indicated. With his boy-next-door, clean-cut looks and athletic built, Lukas had a charming smile. The random dreams of him have existed for as long as I can remember. They'd become such a part of my sleep that I welcomed his arrival.

The fact that I converse with a hot guy in my dreams was another sad aspect of my so-called life.

He had been the most exciting part—pitiful I know—until my run-in with Gavin. I chalked it up to being the stuff dreams were made of. Perhaps that feeling only existed in the fantasy my mind created. Other than this made-up guy of my dreams, no one had come close to making me feel the heat rushed exhilaration I'd experienced with Gavin.

The dreams started when I was very young, five or six. He always appeared to me at the same age I was. We sort of grew up together. He'd been a friend, confidante, and playmate. Lately, the pull of attraction seemed to heighten each time I dreamed of him. And because it was a dream, I could be everything I wasn't in real life.

I was lying under a weeping willow, mile-long branches swaying overhead. A babbling brook flowed over scattered bedrock, sounding in the distance. The ambrosial smell of sweet pea sweetened the air: A suitable surrounding for dreams made of fairy tales.

The sun was cast above, gleaming rays of light like spears through pockets in the willow tree. Lukas lay next to me on his side, fiddling with strands of grass. He eyed me coolly, waiting for me to turn toward him.

"Brianna." His honey smooth voice spoke my name.

"Hey," I replied lamely. Even in my dreams, I couldn't master being anything other than me.

He smiled brightly, his entire face beaming with a golden glow. "Long time, no see." He was lying beside me on the grass, propped up on the willow's trunk. Months had gone by since my last dream of him.

"I know. I was beginning to think you had forgotten about me."

He had one leg spread alongside me, and the other one bent up. "These are your dreams, remember?" he teased lightly.

He was always so carefree and happy, nothing seem to get to him. I had no idea how that felt. Responsibility seemed to be bred into my genes.

We spent much of our time doing things I wouldn't dare do in my real life, and divulging parts of my life I was afraid to tell anyone else.

Today was no different.

"What's wrong?" he asked, his bright smile losing some of its shine.

Sitting up beside him on the trunk, I sighed. "What isn't wrong is the question."

He chuckled and brushed a stray hair from my eyes, tucking it behind my ear. His touch surged a blooming of warmth over me. "It can't be all that bad." Always the positive outlook for Lukas, his world was a cup half full.

Picking at the grass growing near the base of the willow, my problems came to the forefront of my mind. "In my case, it is," I grumbled, refusing to let go of my somber mood.

He looked amused by my discomfort. What is with guys suddenly being amused by me? I couldn't figure why my thoughts continued to drift to Gavin. There was an extremely gorgeous guy in my dreams, and I was thinking about the rebel with the piercings. The problem with Lukas was, he wasn't real, and I wanted something real.

Even with the familiarity of Lukas, there had always been an awareness of caution just under the surface. It never made much sense to me, so I ignored the warning. He was a dream, after all. What harm can he possibly cause? Not to mention, he drew me to him like a bee to a flower. The more I dreamed of him, the more I felt the pull. He was easy to be with.

I should have just kissed him already. *It's not real*, I rationed. Better yet, I should have kissed Gavin when the chance presented itself—a real possibility.

"Spill. I want to know what troubles you," he said.

I looked out over the green valley. "I lost my temper today. It was bad," I revealed bleakly.

"Are you sure it was as bad as you think?" he asked, knowing I occasionally exaggerated a situation.

"I don't know. I guess if you consider grabbing a girl's arm and leaving burn marks not bad then...yeah, it wasn't bad," I replied dryly.

His lips upturned at my melancholy disposition. "That's bad." He was trying to hide the smile that wanted to surface.

Playfully, I smacked him on the chest. "It was," I admitted. "She deserved it, though," I defended, feeling the need to justify my actions.

"Of course she did. You wouldn't do anything someone didn't deserve," he blithely teased.

Looking into his face, I immediately thought about what a contrast he was to Gavin, like the sun and the moon. Lukas was the boy next door, with his wholesome good looks and lighthearted sense of humor. He had the kind of smile you had to answer in return. Gavin made me think of shadows, starlight nights and werewolves.

As soon as the thought fluttered through my head, the dream took a drastic change.

CHAPTER 4

My head was so filled with thoughts of Gavin and Lukas; it took a few moments for me to realize the shift.

The air surrounding us began to transform, covering the sun in murky clouds as darkness descended. Winds screamed and howled, whipping the branches in a war against us. It all happened so fast. I shivered in the gloomy intensity.

Lukas grabbed my hand, pulling me sharply to my feet. "Hurry," he yelled over the deafening winds. Using himself as a shield from the slashing switch of tree limbs, he guided us out from underneath. As we reached the edge of the covering, the willow's limbs transformed into venomous snakes, seething in a chorus of hissing tongues. The clatter of rattling tails echoed off the valley walls. At this point, it was clear my subconscious was wacked.

We had almost broken away from the tree when an overpowering tug stopped me in my tracks. Something was attached to my leg, squeezing with deadly pressure— it was a snake, coiled around my leg. A piercing scream ripped from my lungs, ringing over the valley.

Lukas spun around, expelling a hushed string of words over the chaotic noise.

I couldn't make out what he said over the racket and fear roaring in my blood.

With a snap of a finger, a ghostly silence erupted, followed by an eerie ambiance filling the valley. The push and pull of my breath thundered in my ears over the muteness. Lukas pulled me protectively to his side, keeping his arm around me.

"Are you hurt?" He hastily looked me over from head to toe, searching for blood.

Before I had the ability to answer, a smothering, ash-like fog engulfed us. I reached for Lukas, but I wasn't fast enough. My hands filled with nothingness. Panic started to rise in my chest.

"Lukas!" I yelled. My voice held the prickling of hysteria as it rang out. "Lukas...where are you?" I listened for his response, but it wasn't his voice that echoed through the thick air of mist.

"Bri!" it called in a dark huskiness.

A quivering of dread threatened to paralyze me as my head thrashed back and forth, searching. I took one step in retreat, and then another, looking for an opening in the impenetrable haze. My eyes burned as I scanned for a face.

There was something familiar about the voice. It tugged at my mind... then it clicked. If I had not just heard the voice earlier today, I wouldn't have been able to place it. As recognition seeped through, my pounding heart began to slow.

"Gavin?" I whispered, half to myself, in confusion.

Turning in circles, the toe of my shoe bumped into a rock embedded in the ground, sending me sprawling. I landed with a groan, barely catching my face before it splattered into the forest floor. As I lay there, stunned, a band of arms wrapped around my waist, pulling me carefully to my feet. Even without looking, I knew it was Gavin. His scent assaulted my insides.

I rubbed my hands over my scraped and throbbing forearms. Fireflies spread through my stomach like wildfire at his proximity. Those pesky fireflies were present in dreams, as well!

"What are you doing here?" I asked, dumbfounded. This was a dream— it didn't need logic— but his presence puzzled me. Never has there been anyone else in the dream other than Lukas and me. His appearance startled me, along with the creepy scenario. Nightmares weren't normally part of the deal. Today was full of bombshells.

Gavin's eyes, alert, scanned beyond me. I wasn't sure how he was able to see past the smog. Obvious tension in his back caused a frisson of unease to sprinkle along my spine.

"What is it?" I asked.

He never had a chance to answer, because that was the moment it ended.

I awoke with a sharp headache, and a lump lodged in my throat. Swallowing to relieve the pressure, I was shocked to find it scratchy, as if I had been screaming. I shoved the bed covers aside, rolled off the bed, and switched on the lamp, chasing the dark shadows from the walls. My body was trembling.

Facing the oval mirror on my dresser, an unfamiliar reflection stared back. My skin was pale, covered with a sheen of sweat, and my eyes were surrounded by dark circles. The violet irises filled my glossy eyes. Running an unsteady hand through my hair, I forced myself to take deep, even breaths.

"What the hell was that?" I mumbled, startled by the shakiness of my tone.

Leaving the light on, comforted by its soft glow, I crawled back into bed. With my back braced against the headboard, I hugged my knees to my chest and forced the tense muscles to relax. I'd never had a dream with such clarity and devastating effects. My mind swirled around the dream, the sense of reality still with me. I wasn't prone to nightmares, even as a child; this exceeded anything I'd experienced.

"Something is seriously wrong with me," I murmured. I must be getting sick. Lifting a hand to my forehead, I expected a temperature, but was met with clammy skin that seemed perfectly normal.

I tried to lie back down, to close my eyes, hoping sleep would take me. To my utter dismay, it proved impossible. Sleep was beyond my control, so I surrendered and lay there with the lamp shining, waiting for the first signs of dawn.

As tired as I was in the morning, I forced my body to pay attention to my mind. *Must get up*, I chastised and rubbed the sleep from my eyes. I zombie-walked to the shower and cranked the heat with hope to chase the chills. Thank God it was Friday. The weekend was within reach, not that I had a life to boast about. My weekends were usually spent at the shop.

I lived a wild life.

The steam from the shower massaged my taut nerves as the memories of yesterday started flying in my head. This day couldn't end fast enough.

I dressed in my favorite outfit, a plum-colored tank and my most flattering skinny jeans. Comfort was key on days like today. And maybe everyone would stare at my ass, instead of the bags under my eyes.

A girl could try.

I gave one last longing look at the bed before walking out. Better to face your problems head on than to run and hide. I don't know who said that, but they definitely didn't have my problems.

❦

THE TOP WAS down on my very used black Mustang, its engine roaring like a big Herculean cat. To drown the noise and my nerves, I turned the radio a few octaves higher than comfortable, One Republic's *Apologize* crooning from the speakers. The seats vibrated in time with the bass. My hair was tied in a loose ponytail, the wind whipping strands on my cheeks. The skies dejected clouds hung overhead in a display of chaos.

Just like my mood.

The middle of October had an aura of fall creeping closer. More storms would threaten the oceans as hurricane season started to settle in. I focused my attention back to the road as the Mustang effortlessly hugged a gentle curve. I pulled into the parking lot of Holly Ridge High, and reached in the backseat for my messenger bag. This was my senior year, and something told me it might just be a year I wouldn't forget.

CHAPTER 5

The school's structure reminded me of an odd shaped S, with its faded red bricks reflecting the wear and tear of decades. There was a sweeping pink dogwood in front of the main office, with wooden benches flanking either side. A large cougar was mounted over the front of the building where the school's motto stretched across the top in bold, black letters.

Maneuvering my slightly rusting car into a parking space, the lot was packed with second-hand vehicles like mine. There was the occasional glimmer of something flashy, like the silver Infiniti next to me. I deliberately avoided it. The last thing I needed was to dent the luxury car with my peeling black paint.

I tossed my bag on my shoulder and headed toward the lockers. As I arrived at the rundown row of metal compartments, I started shuffling my books for my first class, pulling out my U.S. History book with subdued enthusiasm. I was acutely aware of the murmuring hum from the students around me. The hall sounded like the swirling buzz of mosquitoes after a humid rainfall. So much for hoping the events of yesterday would be old news. It was only a matter of time before my classmates found some other gossip to spread.

Resigned to whatever fate was in store, I numbly headed to

homeroom.

My first two classes went as expected. Nothing life threatening, just more of the hushed whispers I barely noticed anymore. Or maybe I didn't care.

Before third period, I stopped at my locker to switch books. As I flung my chem text into my bag, the locker beside mine squeaked open. In no mood for company, I hiked my bag over my shoulder, ready to make a quick exit. My hand slammed the locker shut, and I averted my gaze, avoiding the body next to me. As I spun around, the scent of reckless woods washed over me.

Silently I groaned. *What is with this guy?*

I rolled my eyes, angling toward him, not expecting to fall into the depths of his sapphire eyes. Was I supposed to breathe when he looked at me like this? My annoyance was momentarily forgotten.

He smirked, moving the hoop in his lip slightly. "Hey, Bri." The shortened name sounded so intimate when it came from his mouth, suggesting he knew me on a more personal level.

If I stayed another minute with him, I was going to make a complete fool of myself. Who knew what idiotic thing would come out of my mouth. Then there was his smirk, which I couldn't figure out. Was he laughing at me? Was he amused by me, or did he just have an annoying smirk I found charming and maddening all at the same time?

I took a step to the side. He shifted his unlaced boots in front of my path, obstructing my escape.

"What's your deal?" I asked, sharper than intended. I ran a nervous hand through my hair. My emotions around him reminded me of a pinball machine, bouncing from one side to another. Up. Down. Left. Right.

His smile only widened. "You're the only person I know." He had an arrogant confidence about him, in his stance, the way he was sure of himself. Of course, I would find that endearing as well. "I figured you could be my guide, help me find my next class," he replied at my confused look.

I snorted. "You're actually going to class today?" My disbelief was real. I wasn't sure what to expect from him, or if we'd even meet again. My school was the only high school in town, and fairly large; there were plenty of kids I didn't know. Not only that, but I didn't have the best social skills.

He moved a little bit closer to me, shutting out more of the activity in the halls. "It seemed like the best way to see you again, unless you're planning to skip..." His voice had dropped, but lost none of its huskiness.

Did he just say he wanted to see me again? My brain couldn't process the idea. Skirting over what my mind couldn't believe, I asked the obvious question. I cleared my throat. "What's your next class?"

"Umm..." He pulled out a crumpled slip of white paper from the back pocket of his jeans. It was impossible not to notice how good he looked in them. He was dressed pretty much the same as yesterday, in dark clothing that looked impeccable on him. "What period is it?" he asked.

"Third," I replied, perplexed by his lack of interest. If he didn't know what period it was, what was he even doing here? He smoothed out his class schedule, looking for third period. I leaned in to peer at the printout.

Big mistake.

I couldn't help but notice how a stray lock fell over his eyes when he bent to read the slip. My fingers itched to brush it back from his face. "Looks like I have chemistry. Room C102." He read off the schedule, ignoring the midnight strand of hair.

"*Great,*" I replied, a tad sarcastic. Wasn't that just my luck? It also happened to be my next class.

He raised a studded brow.

"It's my next class." I echoed my own thoughts and turned toward C hall

He followed in step beside me, not missing a beat. "Chemistry...this should be interesting."

I glanced sideways, my eyes narrowing. He held my gaze, a smile on his lips, and the promise of a secret he was unwilling to divulge. There was no doubt he understood my irritation. The longer I stared at the blue of his irises, the faster my heart sped, and the zooming fireflies multiplied in my stomach.

"You have such unusual eyes," he finally stated. The husky dark texture of his voice lulled over me and seriousness shone in his eyes, a contrast to the teasing quality I'd gotten use to from him.

I was stunned. Was that another compliment? Odd. I'd been admiring his eyes. We more or less had the same thought. My tongue was tied in knots, and he had yet to break eye contact.

As fate would have it, he ended up saving me from yet another disaster. My focus was entirely on him, and in rationalizing the incident, it boiled down to really being his fault. Fortunately for me, he was more aware of our surroundings.

I all but walked into one of the pillars edging the entrance to C hall. Gavin casually placed a hand at the small of my back, and, gracefully on his part, glided me around the pillar. The contact of his hand broke the staring spell and incited an all-new set of excitement. Tingles, like tiny shooting stars, burst throughout me, and the intensity of it snapped me back a second before I whacked the column. My feet miss-stepped, and I stumbled on the frayed carpet.

I wasn't extremely graceful, but around him, I was downright klutzy. Afraid to meet his eyes, I kept my head straight. "Thanks," I muttered under my breath, trying to hide my mortification.

"Is this going to be a habit? Me saving you?" There was amusement lining his words.

I just rolled my eyes. Relief huddled over me now that he was back in teasing form. His flattery wasn't something I knew how to handle.

We walked into Mr. Burke's class side-by-side. The majority of the class was already seated, and all eyes were on us. Gavin left my side, walking up to where Mr. Burke sat at the front of the class. He handed Mr. Burke a pink slip as I made my way over to my table. He looked to me and winked. A murmur of chatter zigzagged down the rows of desks. It wasn't enough that I caused a spectacle yesterday, now I had some new mysterious gorgeous guy flirting with me. Sinking further into my chair, I scowled at him.

By the time lunch rolled around, I was in the need of some serious girl time, Austin included. I hadn't talked to either of them since I skipped out of school early. I had turned my phone off last night, hell bent on shutting myself off from the world.

Winding through the cafeteria, the smell of milk cartons, fries and all things greasy enveloped the room. I spotted Tori at our table with Austin.

"Hey," I greeted, throwing my bag over the back of my chair while taking my seat. I'd been prepared and primed for the interrogation coming my way. They were both concerned about me, and would want to know what crazy juice I'd drunk yesterday.

I barely had my butt in the chair, when the seat in front of me pulled out and was filled by none other than the dark and mysterious Gavin.

My heart thumped at the sight of him. "What are you doing?" Having him suddenly appear every time I turned around was grating on my already frazzled emotions. There was no downtime to calm the effect he enticed.

At his arrival, Austin and Tori both froze mid-bite and gawked. I hadn't been given the time to fill them in on the events of the soap opera I was living. My plan to spill my guts at lunch was now nixed.

"Eating lunch," he responded, meeting my glare with a mischievous grin. He held my eyes longer than comfortable, but I couldn't look away. It was Gavin who finally turned to Austin and Tori. "Hey, I'm Gavin," he introduced, dazzling them with a smile.

Austin still had his mouth agape, looking star-struck. Tori, thankfully, had the decency to smile in return, instead of looking like a goon.

"Sorry," I mumbled. Why did he make me forget myself? "Austin, Tori, this is Gavin. We met, umm..." I stumbled to find a reasonable explanation without sounding like a dork, "...ran into each other yesterday in the parking lot," I managed. The admission caused a faint blush to crawl on my cheeks as I remembered our meeting. So much for not sounding like a dork.

Tori's inquisitive gaze burned at my side. I shifted fretfully in my seat. No doubt there would be a lot to answer for when the two of them got me alone. Gavin was not the kind of guy you forgot to tell your best friends about. Gavin's husky voice broke me out of my thoughts. "It was sort of a hit and run." His twinkling eyes met mine as an uneasy cough escaped my mouth. As bad as the joke was, it felt wicked, sharing in something only the two of us understood. I found it impossible to be irritated with him. But it didn't last long.

The moment was ruined by none other than Rianne. She strolled by, trailing a finger on the table and angled at Gavin. "Hey hottie." She all but purred her words. "Sure you don't want to join me?" she invited, batting her fake lashes. If I had to guess, I would say that just about everything about her was fake. Her obvious flirtations made me want to gag. Lucky for her, I hadn't eaten yet.

"I'm good here." He didn't even spare her more than a polite glance, which she couldn't possibly understand. Boys didn't ignore her. Not that I blamed them, she did look like Barbie's slutty twin. Her fire-engine red skirt barely covered her ass, and the black top was low enough to be outlawed at Hooter's.

"You'll change your mind." Her utter confidence made me nauseated. I'm sure she couldn't imagine what Gavin saw in me and my friends. She was popular and probably thought she was doing him a social favor, a once in lifetime opportunity. She teased her honey blonde hair between her fingers. Rianne had been bullying kids at our school far too long.

Looking directly into my eyes, he replied, "I doubt it."

A genuine smile broke out over my face and was mirrored in his. Next to me, I could hear the low snickering of my friends. In an attempt to slam me, her sweet flirty tone turned down right sour and nasty. "You better watch yourself," she threatened. Apparently, being rejected didn't bring out her bright side.

I really didn't want her to destroy the mood we had going again, but I couldn't let it go. "Suck it," I cheerfully snapped. Classy, I know. The damage was done, best to just go for it. Never do anything half-ass —my new outlook on life.

Rianne flipped her hair over her shoulder and sauntered to her clique of followers. A glimpse of her black thong peeked over the top of her skirt as she swayed her hips with more oomph than necessary.

Gavin laughed low in his throat. "That was fun."

I had to fight the urge to roll my eyes. His idea of fun and mine didn't even come close.

"Is your life always this entertaining?" There was a hint of expectancy in his voice.

My friends sneered. Okay, I was prone to weird things happening around me, and I did have what I would call an explosive anger issue, but that didn't mean my life was a freaking side show.

I glared their way. "Hardly," I muttered.

By the time lunch ended, I'd picked my way through what food I had. My appetite was on the fritz. Tossing the remaining in the trash, I glared at Gavin and took off after my friends.

Walking side-by-side, both Austin and Tori's interest was piqued beyond control now that we were alone. They stared at me, gleaming, waiting for me to dish.

I rolled my eyes. "It was nothing. I ran into him when I left yesterday. Literally. End of story."

"Wait...he ditched yesterday?" Tori asked, putting together the facts.

"I guess." I was reluctant to admit.

"He oozes trouble," Austin commented like it was hot.

"You're telling me," I grumbled under my breath.

"You better not let *that* slip away, babygirl," he hollered as we split off to our separate classes.

The final bell sounded, piping into the classrooms during my French lesson and interrupting my traveling thoughts. Shuffling into the halls, I weaved my way between the cluster of eager kids ready to kick start their weekend.

Gavin was leaning casually up against the wall by my locker, one leg over the other. His stance was lazy and relaxed. Shifting my gaze to his face, I skimmed the sharp angles that defined his jaw line. His black hair was edgy, with strands framing his searing sapphire eyes. Those eyes were thickly fanned by dark eyelashes. Gazing into the pools of blue, he was staring at me, his mouth upturned in a smirk. Mesmerized, he played with the ring glittering at his lower lip.

"So you made it through the whole day." His lips split into a knee-shattering smile.

I stared hard after him as he walked away, and I was left with a bewildered expression on my face.

"Damn," I murmured, silently praying I wouldn't behave like a blubbering idiot the entire school year.

Dazed, I stumbled my way to the parking lot.

CHAPTER 6

E very other Saturday, I went into the shop at noon and stayed until closing. With Halloween around the corner, the displays and floral coolers were abundantly filled with the vibrant colors of fall—burnt oranges, deep reds and golden yellows. Tiger Lilies, marigolds, chrysanthemums and pansies showcased the majority of the collections.

There were the traditional spooky arrangements in shades of black and orange, sprinkled with glitter or ghostly accent pieces. The shop also stocked specialty items. Scattered between the floral designs were mystical figures, seasonal decorations, and artwork from local artists.

Homecoming just so happened to be this weekend. The orders for corsages and boutonnieres over the week had piled up and were ready for pickup. With everything going on the last few days, the school event never even crossed my mind. In my distraction I had missed all the décor and posters littering the school. Not that it made a difference.

Homecoming, or any other school function for that matter, really wasn't my thing. It was no surprise I was relieved to be working.

The commotion of the event made the day fly by, especially, the last few hours before the dance began. I manned the counter, helped with customers and rung up sales. There were also two other part-time employees besides myself who helped out. Today it was just the two of us, and I had about reached my limit of baby's breath, roses, and dyed carnations. I was clueless to why my peers matched the flowers to the exact shade of their shoes or dress. Sadly, very few actually knew my name or that we attended the same school.

Missy Walters was one of the last to come in. Her sun-bleached hair was curly and cascading prettily over her exposed shoulders.

"Are you here to pick up a corsage?" I sweetened my voice like I hadn't uttered the phrase a hundred times before.

She nodded, sending her bouncing curls for a wild ride. "For Walters," she added, unaware I already had her corsage in hand. She wasn't the brightest crayon in the box.

"Do I know you?" Her voice was fit for a little girl, all cutesy.

"Umm...yeah, I think we have Interior Design together, fifth period," I replied offhandedly as I tied a ribbon on the box of her corsage.

She popped her pink gum and giggled. "Oh yep, that's it. You sit in the back row."

Correction. I sat in the second row, but for her it was close enough. I don't how she heard herself over all the snapping of gum, so I nodded in agreement.

"Well, thanks for the flowers." She smiled when I passed her the package.

"Have fun tonight," I called as she headed for the exit, unsure she heard me over the gum smacking.

"Sure thing, you too." Her voice was over bubbly, like her gum.

Oh loads, I thought mockingly. I had big plans for tonight that involved the snugness of my bed and the current Nora Roberts book I was reading.

The chime on the door rang near the end of the night while I was wiping down the counter. We had an hour left before the shop closed, but most everything had been cleaned, straightened and restocked. I stopped what I was doing to greet the customer, absently tucking a hair behind my ear.

"Hi, is there something—" The rest fell from my lips. Tingles danced down my back, and then I realized who came through the door.

Gavin, in his dark jeans, strolled across the room to where I stood behind the glass counter. The clatter of his half-tied boots echoed at his approach.

"There is something you can help me with." He reached the counter and stood in front of me, leaning a hip against the glass.

I ignored his words. "Are you stalking me?" I was stunned by the fact he was standing in front of me.

"Not precisely the greeting I was hoping for." He leaned in, smiling at me with teasing eyes.

"So you are stalking me?" I smiled back. I hadn't the first clue how to flirt. Instead I was left with lame responses.

"No, actually..."

And that was all I needed for my mind to go off on a tangent. What if he'd come in to buy something? I assumed he was here for me, but what if he wasn't. Maybe he was here to pick up flowers for home-coming. It was late—but not enough so he couldn't still go to the dance. My heart sunk at the image of him dancing with another girl. He might be new here, but he would have no trouble finding a date. Hell, it was possible that Rianne had asked him. She made her interest overtly clear at lunch.

He watched me as my mind ran through the entire horrible scenario before finishing. "...I wanted to ask you something."

I swallowed back the large lump that suddenly formed in my throat. "Sorry, long day." I pasted on a smile, yielding. Internally, I scolded myself to be as polite as I could be. "Are you picking up an order?" I assumed, trying to keep my voice even and the disappoint-ment from it.

He played with the hoop on his bottom lip—absently twirling it. "No." His brows drew together at my assumption. "But I was hoping you were almost done here?" There was a touch of hesitancy to his voice, completely out of character for his normally cocky attitude.

Wide-eyed and tongue-tied, I went all spacey. He had to stop doing that to me.

"I was hoping you could show me what people do for fun around here," he continued, after I failed to have a coherent response. I never even heard my aunt return from the backroom in the middle of his invitation.

She smiled brightly over his shoulder at me as she made her way around the counter. Gavin straightened slightly at her approach. His gaze went from mine to hers.

"Hi, I'm Clara—Brianna's aunt." She grinned at him sincerely. "Are you a friend of hers?" She was fishing for information, more specifically if he was something more than a *friend*. I couldn't blame her inquisition. A hot guy in the shop asking me on what could be misconstrued for a date was a rare commodity. Or in my case...unheard of.

Not giving him the opportunity to give her false hope, I quickly recovered and cut in. My aunt didn't have a judgmental bone in her body. Everyone got an equal chance until you deserved otherwise. But I think her genuine acceptance caught Gavin a little off guard. Well, I assumed that was why he looked at her cautiously, like she might toss him out at any moment.

"He just moved here," I lamely answered with more volume than I meant to. I took a quick breath. "We met a few days ago at school." This time I lowered my tone but raced my words. The whole situation was making me jumpy.

"Hmm..." My aunt pursed her slightly grinning lips, no doubt picking up my odd behavior.

This wasn't going at all as I would have hoped. Not that I had even a second to think about what was happening here.

"I was just asking Bri if she would be willing to show me around town. That is, if you don't mind?"

She raised her brow at the nickname, and I could see her internal mind making all kinds of wrong assumptions. "*Bri* would love to." She excitedly agreed on my behalf.

"I could drop her off at home afterwards. I'll make sure it's not too late," he added.

"Perfect, she'll be ready in a few." She took my place behind the counter, gently nudging me into action.

What?

I will?

How had everything had spun out of my control? They were talking as if I wasn't there or didn't have a say in the matter. Maybe I didn't want to go. Totally not true, but at the least, I should be the one to say yes or no. I mean, the idea of spending an entire evening with Gavin was both elating and frightening. The fireflies in my belly began their dance.

"I haven't finished—"

"Don't worry. I got it covered. Go. Have fun," she rebuked, interrupting my protest.

I wasn't against going out with Gavin; I didn't know anyone who would be. I was just slightly infuriated about being sneakily maneuvered.

I eyed her, letting her know I wasn't happy about being finessed. "I'll be ready in a minute," I mumbled.

Surrendering my fate, I headed to the backroom. I did what I could with what I had. With haste, I ran a brush through my hair, reapplied my eyeliner and mascara, and coated on my favorite strawberry-flavored lip gloss. Thank God we don't have uniforms at the shop. I just wore whatever. Today, it was a black halter and jeans. At least they made my butt look good. *Halle-freaking-lujah for small favors*! Digging through my bag, I pulled out a pair of silver dangling earrings and fitted them in the holes.

This was the best I could do, under the circumstances.

Walking back into the shop, I saw he was casually chatting with my aunt. They both looked toward me at my approach.

"Ready?" He lifted the brow with the sterling bar in it.

I nodded and waved good-bye to my aunt. She mouthed *have fun* and grinned from ear-to-ear.

He led me to a sleek and shiny car that probably cost more than my aunt's and mine combined. Coming around to the passenger side, he opened my door. The gesture was completely sweet, unexpected, and made me extremely self-conscious.

"Thanks," I muttered.

He drove an old-school black '69 Charger. At least that was what he told me. It looked like it was straight out of the showroom. It wasn't the kind of car I imagined he would drive. I'd envisioned him on a motorcycle, something more daring, but once the engine roared to life, thundering with the powerful rumble, I got the appeal. I buckled in for what proved to be a very fast ride.

The radio was on low, pumping an alternative band. His interior was clean and smelled of leather and exotic woods. If someone had told me last week I would be going out on a Saturday night with an extremely drool-worthy guy, I would have asked them what kind of crack they were smoking. Honestly, I figured I wouldn't date until I got to college. There would be a fresh batch of hotties who wouldn't know me, a whole world of opportunities.

Look at me now— I was on my first *almost* real date. Hold the presses.

"Where to?" He looked over at me for direction.

He was so asking the wrong person. "There really isn't anything fun to do here," I reluctantly admitted. I didn't want him to know how boring my life was.

"In that case, I guess we'll have to make our own fun." He smiled devilishly at me from across the seat. "What's open late?"

That grin was going to get me in trouble. I was sure of it.

CHAPTER 7

We ended up at a little coffee shop near the edge of town that I went to often. Caramel macchiatos had become a self-indulgence I took at every opportunity. Taking a seat in a quiet section near the back, we sat opposite of each other. The place had a scattered array of patrons sipping on steaming mugs, tapping away on laptops, or sucking on frozen concoctions, gossiping.

There were multi-colored hanging lights casting a low glow, giving a secluded atmosphere. Each table had three tea light candles flickering in unruliness.

Upon sitting, we were greeted by a young girl— Carla, according to her nametag. She couldn't have been much older than me, and her eyes were glued on Gavin. Invisibility wasn't a foreign feeling. Her uniform was a little tight, and I was afraid she was going to fall out of the top.

I folded my hands on the table, watching her soak up the sight of him. Stealing a glance, I noticed a strange spark about Gavin's eyes. They were normally pools of deep blue, but this was something else. Blinking to clear the glare of the soft light above, he turned and asked what I would like. Whatever I thought I saw was gone.

"Caramel macchiato," I said on auto-response, still wondering what just happened.

Smiling, he gave Carla my order and his, black coffee. Of course. Carla scurried to get our drinks. I didn't remember the service being this good. The coffee was great, but the service was usually crap.

"So is it just you and your aunt?" Gavin inquired, bringing my focus back to the present.

"Yeah, my parents died when I was five," I confessed and glanced around the room. My paranoia must be setting in, it was either that or everyone was staring at us.

"That must have been hard." There was sincerity and compassion in his expression.

I shrugged. "I don't really remember it much. It's always been the two of us." I kept taking a peek to see if anyone was looking our way.

"And what about your other relatives? Do you see them?" He was just full of questions.

I hadn't thought about my family in some time. My aunt was mostly it. I did have a grandma on my mom's side that I visited, but I couldn't picture one face from my dad's side. "I have a grandma not far from here, but no one else really," I admitted, slightly sadden by the lack of people in my life. "What about you?" It was time to turn the table. "Do you have any siblings?"

He relaxed his posture and smirked. That said everything. He adored his family. "I have an older brother and a younger sister. Jared is in college, and Sophie is a sophomore in high school."

"At our school?" I was taken by surprise. I hadn't seen her yet.

He nodded his dark head. "I'm sure you'll see her around. She's eager to meet you."

"You told her about me?" My tone was skeptical.

He laughed. The huskiness of it flooded over me and packed my belly with the heat of fireflies. "It's kind of unavoidable. She has a way of pulling information out of you without you knowing. A small talent of hers. You'll see what I mean."

Carla returned with our drinks and asked Gavin pointedly if there was anything she could do for him. I fought the urge to kick her from under the table, anything to get her attention elsewhere.

"That will be all, thanks," he said graciously, dismissing her.

"Is your sister psychic or something?" I teased.

He grinned. "Not quite."

"Okay, now I'm intrigued and a little afraid." I took a sip of my macchiato and closed my eyes as the sweet and acrid flavor hit my tongue. Swallowing the hot liquid, I opened my eyes to find Gavin staring intently at me. They lured me into unexplored territory.

"You are not at all like I thought." There was a low, husky strain to his voice.

His admission caused a powerful flush that had nothing to do with the coffee and everything with the way he looked at me. Absently turning the cup in my hand, I tentatively asked, "I'm not?"

He stared at me as if I was a mystery waiting to be solved, ironic considering, I was trying to do the same with him. Neither of us could figure the other out.

"No, you have my mind spinning in circles. I can't figure you out," he admitted, not entirely happy about it.

"What's there to figure out? I'm just a girl from a small town."

He sighed. "I don't know. It's more complicated." He tugged on his lip ring, looking lost in thought. "Come on... I should get you home," he said, before I could ask him what was so complicated. I wanted to press the subject, but the confusion in his expression stopped me.

The car ride to my house was death-defying. He drove at speeds I had never ventured to. Yet, somehow I never felt like my safety was threatened. Everything about this guy screamed danger, but I only felt safe in his presence.

The porch light glowed its welcome as he walked me to me to the front door. I shuffled my feet on the sandy wood planks. That was one of the downfalls of living by the ocean; there was sand everywhere.

He held out his hand. "Let me see your phone."

I eyed him warily, but gave it over. Our fingers touched for a split moment, and a static shock tingled at the spot where our fingers met.

If he had felt anything, he never led on. Scrolling through the menu, he punched on the keys. There wasn't much of a glow from the porch light, so I couldn't see what he was doing.

"There." He handed the device back.

"Thanks, I think." I stood in front of him, uncertain how to say goodbye. When he traced his fingertips alongside my face, tucking loose strands behind my ear, a bolt of shock and something more caused my head to snap up.

His eyes glimmered, but I swear behind the twinkle was a hint of regret. "Sweet dreams, Bri."

I walked inside and leaned up against the closed door. The roar of his engine rippled through the night, and I sighed, with a smile on my lips.

THE NEXT MORNING I woke up mystified. On one hand, I was ecstatic about spending time with Gavin. On the other hand, he was a puzzle. I was pretty good at puzzles, so the idea of trying to figure him out was appealing. As I lay there staring at the ceiling, I tried to sort out the little I already knew about him. I couldn't let go of this nudge that there was something peculiar about him. Call it a hunch or whatever, but it gnawed at the back of my mind.

Sundays were lazy. I didn't work at the shop, and mostly spent the day catching up on household chores, finishing my homework, and watching my DVR. Growing bored of staring at the ceiling, I got up and pulled a hoodie over the tank I slept in, padding my way downstairs.

My aunt was at the breakfast bar with her morning coffee, the aroma tempting. "Morning," she beamed between sips of her steaming mug.

There was a hint of something sweetening the air, mixed with the bitter coffee grounds. I plopped my but down on a burgundy stool, running a hand through my tousled hair and grumbled an incomprehensible response.

"Coffee?" She spun around, going to the pot still on the warmer.

Our kitchen was ornamented in cranberries and ivy. They were woven around the chains of the chandelier and intricately staggered above the dark cherry cabinets. The whole ensemble had a country living vibe.

Nodding my head, she set a steaming cup in front of me. I placed my hands on either side of the mug, letting the warmth soak into them.

"I made cinnamon rolls, if you would like one," she offered, leaning her elbows on the counter, grinning at me.

It was killing her, waiting for me to say something about last night. She was all but bursting with fervent impatience. I glanced over at the clock and noticed there were only a few more minutes before she needed to leave for the shop.

"You're killing me." She echoed my thoughts.

I rolled my eyes. "It was nothing," I insisted.

She didn't believe me. "He sure didn't look like nothing."

You're telling me. "I know...this is so bad," I whined, shoving my face into my hands.

She laughed. The sound was like home. Comfort. Security.

"I think he wants to be *friends*," I scoffed. The last word was said with annoyance.

"The way that boy looked at you was anything but *just friends*. Give it time, you'll see. For now, be yourself. He won't be able to resist."

Who was she kidding? How was I supposed to be myself when I barely even knew who that was?

Exhaling, I said, "I think I'll take one of those cinnamon rolls now."

She placed a sticky bun on a plate and handed it to me. "I can't believe my angel has a boyfriend." She had a silly grin on her face.

Groaning, I laid my head on the countertop. "He is not my boyfriend." The words were muffled by the granite.

"See you by five," she sang out over her shoulder and headed to the garage.

THE DVR WAS CURRENTLY PLAYING the previous week's episode of my favorite series. I had my feet tucked beneath me, a blanket wrapped around my legs, and I still wore the hoodie from this morning. The bad reality show on screen only had part of my attention. Before I could prevent it, the memory of last night with Gavin came back to taunt me. What was it about him that caused my hairs to stand up and get my blood pumping, all at the same time?

He struck a chord in me, and I started to regret not pressing him on our *complication*. Maybe that was part of his angle, to remain aloof and mysterious to keep me interested. Little did he know, I was way past interested. I might have just slammed into what I was sure was an unhealthy obsession. Why couldn't I get him out of my head?

Halfway into the show, my phone vibrated on the cushion beside me. I unlocked the home screen, the text icon blinking with a new message.

What are you doing? It read, popping up Gavin's name next to the message. He had added himself to my contacts last night.

Nothin. Did you steal my number also? I sent the response with a squiggling smiley face.

The phone hummed again seconds later. **One of my many tricks.**

Oh, I'm sure it was. Grinning, I tapped away on the keys. **I would have given it to you.**

Not as much fun!

And you're all about fun... I replied.

There's nothing wrong with a little fun. You going to school tomorrow?

I rolled my eyes after reading the last text. **Where else would I be?**

Somewhere with me?

Funny... See you in Chem.

Ugh... Fine. If that's the only way I can see you. I could almost hear the aggravation in his text.

Returning my attention to the last half of my show, the night wore on. And on. And on.

Finally, out of sheer boredom, I climbed the stairs to the sanctuary of my room. My homework was done and the laundry washed.

God, I was so lame.

My bedroom walls were glistened in lilac frost, accentuated by the silvery moss comforter that spread across my bed. There were always fresh flowers in the vase at my nightstand, a perk of having an aunt who owned a floral shop. I believed the current flower was hydrangea, filling my room with its sugary aroma.

I whipped my hoodie off and tossed it into the corner, heading to the small desk housing my ancient, barely functioning laptop. Flipping the power switch, I waited for it to boot up as my mind wandered, his dark, poetic features clearly impressed into my memory.

A deep sigh heaved from my chest, and I shook my head, mentally trying to erase his hotness.

The homepage on my computer loaded, and I logged into my email. Nothing significant: a bunch of spam, a few jokes from Austin, and one from school reminding me to sign up for email updates on my grades. I sifted through the junk, read Austin's and sent most to my trash folder. Frustrated with the snail speed of my internet connection, I shut the computer down and closed it with a satisfying snap.

This day was dragging butt.

I grabbed my iPod, flung myself on the bed, and scrolled down the long menu of songs. Within seconds, Alanis Morissette was singing at the top of her lungs. I was determined to drown out all images of Gavin Mason, steaming ones included.

The dream hit me faster than ever. One instant I was listening to Alanis belt '*You, you, you oughta know*', and the next I was in a clearing, enclosed by fields of lavender. The transition was normally gradual, but not this time. It was like being sucked down a waterslide.

CHAPTER 8

L ukas was sitting next to me, close enough that his arm brushed mine. It was easy comfort with him. The sandy blond of his hair moved slightly with the gentle breeze that mixed with the lavender essence. His emerald eyes sought mine.

"Hey." The warmth of his breath flushed my cheeks.

"Hi," I replied. "I didn't think I'd see you so soon."

He smiled charmingly, illuminating the golden boy face. "Me either... I'm not complaining, though."

At times he seemed too good to be true, or in this case dream about. I was pretty sure my mind wasn't that ingenious.

"Earth to Brianna," he called mockingly.

"What?" I startled from the random thoughts.

He was eyeing me coolly. "You were a million miles away."

I huffed. "Sorry, it's been a hectic week," I apologized.

Taking both my hands in his, he pulled me effortlessly to my feet. "Good, let's do something." The head rush caused a little hitch in my breathing. "Come on," he said, a second before taking off into the meadow of lavender, his golden hair bouncing with his hurried movements.

Not missing a beat, I bolted out after him. "Lukas!" I shouted. "You better not lose me." Forgetting he was way more athletically built than most guys at my school, he could have been a track star. Yet this was a dream, so how far could he really go?

Well, it seemed pretty far, because it wasn't long before I lost sight of him, or he was in a great hiding spot.

Reaching the edge of a pond immersed with lily pads, I paused in my search. My lungs were ragged from chasing and then losing him. Maybe it was time I hit the gym. Before I caught my breath, he snuck up behind me. Encircling his arms around my waist, he spun me in dizzying circles. His arms felt amazing. Real or not, I still appreciated being held by him. I collapsed us to the ground. He took full advantage of his position and tickled me until I couldn't breathe. I choked on my laughter.

"Stop," I sobbed between giggling gasps.

His fingers were hitting just the right spots to make me curl in tickled torture. "What did you say, more? It's hard to understand you when you're laughing so hard," he teased in his honey-smooth voice.

"For real—can't—breathe," I spit out between gasps.

"Okay, okay...I'll stop," he conceded, but grinned impishly. He rocked back into a sitting position, swiping grass off his clothes.

Smiling into his emerald eyes, a huge boulder lifted from my back. A few stolen moments of childish pleasure relaxed my body. I felt weightless.

"You have no idea how special you are." His dreamy voice had softened.

Who doesn't dream of a guy saying those exact words? The problem was... it was a dream. I fleetingly pictured Gavin's dark looks, and his smirk that was becoming all too sexy.

"I'm really not," I protested. "I'm just some girl."

"Not just any girl—trust me."

Trust him. Did I, trust him? How could some mysterious guy show up in my life and I trusted him uncomplicatedly, but I couldn't decide if I did indeed trusted Lukas, who I've dreamed of for virtually my entire life.

Our feet dangled over the pond's edge. He sighed, the carelessness gone. "Who was the guy that showed up last time?" There was a disapproving edge to his tone. He tried to hide it.

Strange, only a moment ago Gavin had been on my mind, and now Lukas was asking about him. I shrugged, my fingers wringing together. "No one."

He arched an eye.

"Okay, he's a new guy at school," I confessed.

His lips thinned in a straight line. "Is he something more?" There was a disapproving quality about the way he asked, like a bad after taste.

"No," I said shaking my head. "Just a friend. Why?" I wanted to know why he even cared.

"It was just...weird."

I assumed he was referring to the nightmare ending from our previous encounter. Weird was an understatement. I was still unclear how my mind came up with these dreams. "It was weird. I don't understand any of this." I threw my hands in the air on a whim of aggravation.

"Were you thinking of him while you were with me?" he asked, a speck of jealousy lacing it.

I didn't like the insinuation behind his tone, like I'd done something wrong. Chewing at the bottom of my lip, I contemplated my answer. No matter that Lukas was being unreasonable; I didn't want to hurt him. Was it possible to hurt a dream's feelings? Because that's what I was afraid would happen.

Craziness.

"I don't know... I guess I was," I grudgingly admitted. "Does it make a difference whether I was or not?"

The expression in his face fell, and it sunk my heart. "Not really. I'm just not used to sharing you. You've never brought anyone else into the dreams."

True, I hadn't, but I never really realized I could. It hadn't been intentional. I thought about Gavin, and somehow my subconscious had thought it was a good idea to include him into the mix, regardless that it ended in a very hot mess. My mind was playing tricks with me.

I'm sorry," I said sincerely. "I'll try not to do it again." Was I really apologizing for something I couldn't control? I wanted to appease him, to see the lightness in his emerald eyes. Not the heavy emotion that shone. It didn't feel right upsetting Lukas. I mean, what harm could it do appeasing my imagination. He seemed satisfied with my apology —for now.

Our fingers entwined, he played with the ring on my hand, twisting and turning it. "I believe you."

Well, that only made one of us, because I wasn't so sure I could stop thinking about Gavin any more than I could stop dreaming about Lukas. Gavin's name alone was enough to have my heart racing, even while I was sleeping. As guilty as it made me feel when I was dreaming of Lukas, I couldn't stop my mind from drifting to Gavin. Lukas used to be all I dreamed of. I didn't know what changed, which made it worse, because Lukas was also aware of the shift. The whole situation stunk like yesterday's garbage. It bothered me more than it should, considering none of it was real.

As if my dream was sudden angry from my straying thoughts, a growling roar erupted, long and vicious.

I awoke with the sound still ringing in my ears.

৩৯৫

THE FOLLOWING WEEKS at school were different. I was actually excited about school. Don't get me wrong, I loved to learn, but I also really loved sleeping in. Somehow, I didn't mind the early wake up calls if it meant I got to see Gavin.

His mysterious presence in my daily life was becoming something I depended on. My friends accepted the newcomer as part of our group as easily as he'd fit into my life. Austin found him extremely sexy, like a magazine cover he could ogle and appreciate. Tori was more watchful. She was aware there was something between us, but couldn't figure it out what.

That made two of us.

There was no denying the sparks that crackled over my skin whenever he was near, yet both of us tried to tamp it down.

I wasn't sure how long I could go on ignoring the connection between Gavin and I. However, I was no closer to figuring out his angle, and meeting his sister only amplified my inkling that something was different about them, and it had nothing to do with his dark and dangerous looks. I couldn't pinpoint what it was. Something inside me demanded that there was more to him than he let on.

I met his sister in the parking lot Wednesday morning on my way into school. She had caught a ride with Gavin, and I got my first glimpse of the youngest Mason as I stepped out of my car. Gavin had whipped his car in beside mine. Each morning the rumble of his engine sent my innards on a roller coaster. I wouldn't be surprised if I started getting ulcers from the amount of activity my stomach went through around him. It couldn't possibly be healthy.

Stepping from the passenger side, she wasn't at all what I expected. I pictured a hardass with purple hair, raccoon makeup and Goth wear. What I got was an eyeful of an intimidating beauty. She had the shiniest midnight hair that blanketed her shoulders and framed her delicate face. Her eyes were the same piercing blue as Gavin's, but outlined with thick lush lashes. The floor-length dress she wore had a hippy vibe, and contoured to her perfect body in a way I envied. She was downright stunning and immediately inviting.

"You must be Brianna." Her voice sung in the morning air like a hummingbird. "I've heard so much about you," she shared before Gavin jabbed her playfully in the side. "What?" She batted her lashes innocently. "You're all he's talked about since we moved here," she softly added as we walked toward the lockers.

"Sophie," he growled low in warning.

She was unfazed by him. "I'm Sophie." She smiled with genuine warmth.

"Wow, you're really pretty," I lamely complimented and cringed inside. Sometimes things shot out of my mouth that I could thump myself over the head for. This was one of those times.

She tossed her head over her shoulder at Gavin. "I like her already." He trailed behind us. Glancing back at me, she enclosed me in her live-liness. Sophie was such a disparity to Gavin's dark and brooding looks. I wouldn't have guessed them brother and sister, if it weren't for the eyes. "I don't know how you stand this brute's company." Her musical tone was lit with bantering affection.

"It's a gift. I'm irresistible." Gavin smirked.

We both snorted, and then smiled at each other over our dual action.

"Please, don't flatter yourself," she countered. Their sibling repartee was amusing and reminded me how much I missed out on not having a brother or sister.

Her hand causally looped my arm with hers, spurring a zing comparable to the one I occasionally felt with Gavin. Yet, not exactly, because with Sophie, it didn't have the essential tension. It lacked the zeal of intensity. Everything with Gavin was intense. Her familiar eyes quickly sought mine, judging my reaction. I knew the energy, or whatever it was, meant something. I kept my face blank. I didn't want to let on that I thought something was amiss. We walked side-by-side into the school.

"I don't know many people yet, and I know you're a senior, but... maybe we could hang out sometime? My family would love to meet you."

"Sure, I would like that." And I was being sincere. I initially thought her beauty would intimidate me, but just as quickly, there was a kinship I rarely felt, something in her hummingbird voice I had an affinity with.

Her smile twinkled in excitement. "See you later." She gave me a quick hug. Sophie was impossible not to like. I sucked with people, but hopefully, I'd just made an ally and a friend.

"I'm going to kill her," Gavin half-heartedly threatened when Sophie was out of reach.

Walking next to me, his arm brushed mine occasionally. "Why?" I wondered aloud. He smelled like heaven.

"Why? Because that was embarrassing," he confessed, grinning.

I laughed at his uneasiness. "Hardly...she's amazing."

"Amazingly annoying."

"She's your sister. What does that make you?"

He smirked recovering his insolence. "Dashing."

So true. I rolled my eyes as he opened the door to my first class. "See you in Chem."

"Wouldn't miss it," he assured, and then strolled across the hall to his class.

Chemistry, for obvious reason became my favorite class, and it had nothing to do with atoms, molecules or particles. I always thought of myself as an English buff, but how quickly that could change. Gavin managed to find a way to finagle his way into becoming my lab partner. I haven't the slightest idea how. Before he moved to Holly Ridge, my partner had been Adam Joyhart. Gavin should have been added to a group. Instead, Mr. Burke moved Adam to another pair and assigned Gavin as my partner. I was tempted enough to ask Gavin if had bribed Mr. Burke or had resorted to blackmail.

We walked into class together and took a seat at our table. He made a habit of showing up at my locker each day and walking me to class—a gentleman behind the badass.

No sooner did my butt hit the seat and Mr. Burke started in on his lesson about Conversion of Mass. I glanced down at my notes for the last week. They were practically non-existent. I had found that with Gavin beside me, my note taking abilities sucked. He clogged my brain cells. Even with the extra studying at my house, I'd be lucky to pass this class. A hard concept for an almost straight-A student.

"You want to hang out tonight?" he whispered, leaning in close to my ear. His breath tickled the back of my neck, causing the tiny hairs to spike. If I turned my head a fraction in his direction, it would be incredibly simple to press our lips together. Failing this class was proving to be worth the risk.

Focusing my thoughts on inhaling and exhaling and not on his pleasurable proximity, I softly replied, "Sure."

At this point, I'd completely checked out of the lecture, my dilemma clear. Mr. Burke shoved his glasses back up the bridge of his nose and rambled on in monotones about isolated systems. No idea.

"Better bring your notes," Gavin smirked, gesturing to the blank page in front of me.

Groaning, I laid my head on my arms. How had he woven his way so intently in my life?

CHAPTER 9

C hemistry always ended too soon, and it had absolutely nothing to do with the topic. The remainder of my schedule dragged, compared to third period. I should be thankful he was only in one of my classes. I couldn't imagine how my grades would suffer.

In the middle of my ninth period French lesson, I started to daydream. I don't know why Lukas came to mind, yet as in most of my thoughts of Lukas, I couldn't help smiling and imagining his boyish, charming looks and the sunny warmth I'd always found with him, not like the eruptive feelings Gavin gave me. Lukas was calm, steady, and confident... Everything I wasn't.

Our conversation the other night started playing through my head. The way things had ended tugged at my heart as I remembered the hurt and disappointment swimming in his eyes. I'd never in my wildest dreams (no pun intended) thought my day life would compete with my night life, so to speak. The fact that Lukas knew about Gavin, but Gavin didn't know about Lukas, in some bizarre and misplaced way made me feel dishonest and regretful. Like I was cheating on one of them, or both of them, which was completely insane, since in reality, I wasn't dating either one of them. Not that I wouldn't if I was given the opportunity. Maybe that was it? Maybe somewhere deep inside my messed up head, I was holding out for one of them. Again, how any of this made sense was beyond my comprehension. It was inhumanly possible for me to even have a *normal* relationship with Lukas. Why did I continue to torment myself with possibilities that weren't there?

My impractical internal struggle was interrupted by the familiar buzzing of my phone. I carefully snuck it from the front pocket of my jeans. We weren't allowed to text during class, but that hardly stopped anyone. The trick was to not get caught.

Tori's name blinked under new messages. **Mall on Friday?** It was followed by a line of smileys.

We hadn't hung out in a millennium. My life lately had been divided between Gavin and the shop. He'd come over on the nights I didn't work, under the disguise of doing our chemistry assignments. Homework aside, there was always a few tense moments that heated my blood. Our friendship, or whatever we had going, progressed rapidly. I didn't want Tori to feel ignored. And the blame weighed heavily on my decision.

I inconspicuously texted back as my French teacher lectured on about our upcoming vocabulary.

Sure...I'll pick you up after school.
Great. I'm in need of some retail therapy.

I grinned at my phone. Only Tori could think of spending her dad's money as therapy.

⚜

THE MALL on Friday night wasn't exactly my venue of choice. I enjoyed shopping like most girls; I just preferred to do it without crowds. Tori was a shop-a-holic. While I spent most of my time window-shopping, she needed a valet to help her to the car. My part-time check only went so far. But if I had a credit card with daddy's infinite limit on it, I might enjoy the experience at a whole new level.

For someone who never had to worry about cash flow, Tori was the least snobbish person I knew. She shopped—I read. Somewhere between quiet time and peanut butter and jelly sandwiches during first grade, we became friends.

High-end shops lined the shopping center on two floors, the kind where they pumped perfume or cologne throughout the store, so when you walked by, it tempted you with the fragrance of seduction.

Located at the heart of the mall was the food court. Tonight the overpriced stores were jammed with teenagers causing a ruckus. Guys scoping out desperate girls with too much make-up, wearing clothes two sizes too small. Rianne totally came to mind. I gave up on the whole mall scene while Tori found it mildly amusing. The lack of entertainment was evident in my peers' choice of hangouts.

"Check out the buns on Mr. Abercrombie," she said, nodding to a guy we passed on the escalator.

I elbowed her in the side. "Focus."

"Oh, I get it. Now that you have a hot guy to drool over, the rest of us have to suffer without. Let me at least check out the merchandise."

I laughed. She could be so dramatic when she wanted to be. I always felt like I needed to be the responsible one when we were together. She had a careless air about her. "You can look, but no touching."

Tori pouted. "What fun is that? Austin wouldn't mind."

I shook my head. She could get me in so much trouble. *Trouble* should have been her middle name. "Fine," I conceded. "Let's look."

"That's more like it," she purred and had me laughing. "Check out blondie over by Aeropostale. I bet you could eat off his abs." There was practically drool foaming at the side of her mouth.

Laughing, I turned to check out the edible abs. Blondie had his back to me, but when he turned to the side, walking to the next store, I choked on air. From this angle, he looked like a spitting image of Lukas. It wasn't until he got close enough that I could see that his eyes weren't right, and he lacked Lukas's carefree smile. Breathing again, I regained my composure.

"See I told you, but I didn't expect you to get all choked up about it."

"Shut up," I grinned at her after I hacked up a lung. I was seeing things my subconscious wanted to see. What other explanation was there?

She smiled back. "Fine, let's do some damage. Where to first?"

"You tell me. You're the one with the bank roll."

"Touché...let's start wherever edible abs is going," she said, taking after the Lukas look-a-like.

Tori hauled me to store after store, pillaging through the racks. With an arm loaded with clothes, we made our way into the dressing rooms. I sat on one those chairs they leave outside the changing rooms, waiting for her to try on the first of fifty outfits.

"What's up with you and Gavin?" she called from behind the door.

Tori had one volume. Loud. "Nothing," I replied, picking at my nails.

"Really? 'Cuz it doesn't seem like a whole lot of nothing," she retorted.

"We're just friends." There was a defensive edge to my voice.

"Friends, my ass," she muffled, pulling on an articles of clothing. "That guy looks at you like he's afraid you'll disappear. His eyes are always watching you."

"Whatever, you make it sound creepy," I scoffed.

"I wouldn't call it creepy—intense, maybe." She stepped out with a pair of skinny jeans and an off the shoulder tee. She was taller than me and carried it mostly in her legs. Her brown hair was pulled back into a ponytail, emphasizing her chocolate eyes. She was quite pretty, and I didn't understand why she didn't attract more guys. Tori surpassed me in the looks department. Her body was pretty killer, too, curvy in all the right places and pencil thin.

I glared at her in full-pestered disbelief.

"Fine—don't believe me, but I'm serious." She turned in the three-dimensional mirror, checking out her butt. "So have you kissed him yet?"

A sigh escaped. "No," I sadly admitted.

"What are you waiting for, an invitation? Gavin is nuts about you. He even rejected Rianne for you," she insisted.

Point well made. There was nothing really standing in the way, which didn't explain why at that moment Lukas came to mind. Was I so enamored by Mr. Dreamy that I was scared by what was right in front of me? Why the hesitation with Gavin?

"I don't know, maybe you're right," I agreed.

"Of course, I'm right. Are you seeing him this weekend?"

We hadn't discussed it, but I kind of assumed we were. "I think…" There was skepticism tracing my words.

"Good, there's your chance." Everything in Tori's mind was so cut and dry. You wanted something—you went for it.

A part of me was being guarded. He was hiding something from me. I felt it. And until I found out what it was, I couldn't take the chance. That didn't mean I didn't want to. But what was the rush?

Five outfits later, we made our way back into the mall. Packages in hand, we strolled to the food court for dinner. I ended up ordering a slice of cheese pizza, and Tori got a taco salad. The great thing about food courts was there was a little everything for all taste buds.

After finishing up our calorie-lavished meal, we hit a few more stores, including Victoria Secret. Being surrounded by underwear and bras made me nervous.

I was picking through a bin of panties and thongs all priced far more than I was willing to pay for such skimpy material, when Tori's mind turned to sex. And since she didn't have a current boyfriend, and Austin didn't have a boyfriend, I became the closest thing to sex-worthy gossip. Complete shit, because I didn't have the first clue about sex.

"I think you need a pair of these," she declared holding a thong that consisted of three strings and a dangling charm.

"Why would I need those? They look like floss," I sneered.

Swinging them on her finger, she sweet-talked, "Because, I bet Gavin would love them."

"I think I should take it a little slower…like maybe getting him to kiss me first."

"A girl can never be too prepared. At least, that's what my step-mom always says." Tori's step-mom, Mariah, wasn't the kind of person I would take advice from. She was twenty-some years younger than Tori's dad, and this was her third marriage. I was sure Mariah was prepared for all *kinds* of scenarios.

"Tori, my sex life isn't up for discussion. It's nonexistent."

"Look, one of us needs to have sex, and since you have a phenomenally hot guy chasing you, it's a sure bet that someone is going to be you. I'm just trying to help out a friend."

I tossed the butt floss back into the bin. "Thanks for the thought, but no. Besides, if we were going to have sex, I'd get these," I replied, picking up a lacy purple pair.

She laughed too loud, drawing unwanted attention our way, but it was too hard to resist joining her. "I knew it. You want him."

I rolled my eyes. "I'd have to be dead to not want him. I'm just saying, we aren't even remotely close to being there."

"Yeah, I know, but it's a hell of a lot of fun to talk about."

She had me there.

When I pulled into the driveway, a text message rang in my purse. Unlocking the screen, the message lit the dark interior of the car. It was Gavin. My heart hammered in my chest as I read the text, inviting me to meet his family tomorrow.

I groaned. The idea of seeing his family was scary, but my curiosity overruled the fear.

I sent him a quick acceptance reply, before I lost my nerve. My head dropped on the steering well, forehead hitting the horn in a long chorus of honks.

What did I just do?

CHAPTER 10

S aturday came, and with it the fear. Today was the day I was going to Gavin's for the first time. This was my weekend off from the shop, and I was currently in panic mode. I had changed my outfit at least a dozen times, the evidence littering the floor of my room.

I settled on a pair of skinny denim, a back-tie tank and boots. Primping wasn't my forte. My makeup basic, eyeliner, mascara and lip gloss. I left my auburn hair straight and tumbling down my back. With a quick smack of my lips in the full-length mirror, I was out of time. This was going to have to do.

The Masons only lived a few blocks down the road from my house, and the short drive did very little for my freaked-out nerves. I don't know why I felt like a lamb going into the lion's den. Sophie was incredible and Gavin was...well, I hadn't figured that out yet. How could his family be anything other than fabulous? *Not scary at all*, I tried to assure myself.

My brakes squeezed as I came to a stop outside of the Masons' new home. It appeared as if the house had recently been repainted in a fresh coat of soft yellow, trimmed in cottage white. A full, wrap-around porch covered the perimeter, with a glider swing on the left. The landscape was alive and vibrant in color; a garden of floral variations weaved about the porch. My aunt would have been in pure heaven. Most impressive was the entryway, which featured two large, etched-glass paneled doors inviting you in. A massive chandelier, visible from the outside, hung in the foyer, sending a rainbow prism glittering on the glass doors.

Everything about the house made me think of fairytales. I could almost visualize the fairies dancing under moonbeams, with their fluttering fragile wings and childish secretive giggles.

I gathered my courage and walked up to the porch, and I was bombarded with a wave of dizziness. It hit me out of nowhere and with a force that left me unsteady. My hand shot out, grabbing the rail. I was nervous, but this was ridiculous. When my head cleared, I took a deep breath and rang the doorbell. The crashing of ocean waves sounded from behind the house as I waited.

Sophie answered the door with excitement shining in her eyes. She pulled me into the house. "I'm so glad you came," she bubbled.

I was at a loss for words.

The grand foyer was just that—grand. Rows of windows flanked the walls on both sides of the room. To the left was a living area with thick, plush carpet decorated in hues of turquoises, blues, and gold. The room reminded me of feathers on a peacock.

On the right was a study, and the voracious reader in me sighed in appreciation at the rows upon rows of bookshelves lining the walls from floor to ceiling. Some filled, but many of them waiting to be housed with novels. Boxes of books were scattered along the room. It often escaped my mind that the Masons had moved in only a few weeks ago.

Overhead, a massive mural was in process on the ceiling. I wasn't able to make out the entire scene from the angle where I stood, but from what I could see, it was a portrait of an extraordinary woman with flaming hair, like the sky at sundown. She was gracefully posed in a long white dress that whipping out around her. Power emitted from her, through her, and about her. She wallowed in confidence, and determination shone her stunning eyes.

I was mesmerized.

Tearing my gaze from the ceiling, an enormous circular staircase stretched out before me. It was there I noticed Gavin's parents waiting to greet us.

My palms were damp.

God, was I nervous.

The staggering beauty of Mrs. Mason struck me speechless. Straight, silky raven hair ran down the length of her back, like Sophie's. She was tall, slender, and graced with curves. Something about her heart-shaped face and magnetic cobalt eyes reminded me of mystical Celtic myths. A welcoming smile touched her lips.

At her side was Gavin's father, with a light hand on the small of her back. He was tall and lean, with sandy brown hair that curled just above his hazel eyes, which were behind horn-rimmed glasses.

"You must be Brianna," his mother greeted, in a voice as lovely as her daughter's. She embraced me in yet another hug. Apparently, the females in this family were not shy with their affections. I didn't think the same could be said for the men, at least not the one I was acquainted with. "I'm Lily, and this is John." She gestured to Gavin's father.

"We are so happy to finally meet you," John said, in a tone timbre and male. He smiled my way.

"Thank you. Your home is absolutely beautiful," I complimented.

"It's coming along; there's still so much to do. Moving is never an easy task." Lily took both my hands in hers. At the touch, a blue spark passed between us. I let out a small gasp and raised my startled eyes to hers. She continued with barely an acknowledgement of what we both felt. "Which is why we are so happy that Gavin has met you." Her voice was thick with feeling and sincerity. She was impossible not to adore, and her demeanor did what I hadn't been able to do all day— calm my frazzled nerves.

At the mention of his name, Gavin strolled down the spiral stair-case. My gaze irrevocably sought his, and any calm I felt dissipated. Fireflies tangoed in my belly, and a flush dusted my cheeks. I lost all sense of everything in the room.

"Hey." His husky voice rolled over me, filling me with warmth.

"Hi."

He stood in front of me, and I couldn't think of anything else to say. Had I been acutely aware that I was unabashedly staring, I would have been mortified.

Luckily, Lily filled the silence before it became extremely awkward. "Gavin, why don't you give Brianna a tour?" she suggested, breaking the thick silence permeating the air. "I'm going to finish dinner, with Sophie's help," she said, turning to her daughter.

"But I was going to show Brianna around," Sophie protested.

"I think Gavin can handle it." Lily arched a brow at her daughter, and glanced back at me. She had such an air of maternal instinct about her. "Brianna, we would love for you to stay for dinner, Sophie especially." Her smile only brightened her features.

"Sure, thanks," I replied.

"Come on," Gavin said, lacing his fingers with mine. "Let's go before Sophie swindles her way out of kitchen duty."

I had already seen most of the main floor, so I followed him up the winding staircase.

"This is Sophie's." He indicated to the first room on the left.

Her room was bohemian chic. A wrought-iron bed stood in the center of the room, draped with bold, jewel-toned bedding. A crystal embellished teal canopy tailored the corners of her bed. It felt like walking into a gypsy camp.

Down the hall and to the right, we came to another bedroom.

"Jared should be here shortly. This is his." His voice was like music to my ears. I was pretty sure I could listen to him ramble about the weather patterns, and I would be enamored.

Messy summed up Jared's room in one word, and it smelled similar to a fraternity. I wrinkled my nose.

Our hands were still joined as he led me around. I loved the feeling of our entwined fingers, and I wasn't willing to give his up anytime soon. There was an underlying spark of awareness.

"And this one is mine." He walked into the doorway angled at the end of the hall.

Gavin's room wasn't at all what I expected. I figured he'd have black walls and heavy metal posters. I was surprised by the neatness, a contrast to his brother. He did have a black framed bed with a book shelf as the headboard, lined with black and white photos. Across from the bed, a large stereo and TV shared space with CDs, DVDs and an. The scent of him was everywhere—taunting me.

It felt naughty being alone in his room. Not like the time we spent in mine. This was suddenly more intimate.

"Let me show you the best part." He opened a set of French doors, exposing a circular balcony with a spectacular view of the ocean, just steps from the house.

I leaned over the railings and inhaled the fresh air of the evening tide. "This is amazing," I said in awe. "To wake up to this view every morning..." My voice trailed off, taken away by the crashing waves.

"You want to check it out?" he asked with excitement.

I nodded.

While we waited for dinner, he took me for a walk along the ocean's rocky shoreline. "What do your parents do?" I had removed my shoes earlier, and my feet buried in the sand as we walked.

"My dad is a historian, and my mom is an artist."

"Did she paint the mural in the library?" I looked up into his face. Our arms swung together as we strolled on the beach.

"She did. It's not done yet," he explained. "She paints a lot of mythology and folklore."

"It's stunning," I praised. Stopping, I bent down to grab a glittering shell that caught my eye.

He looked out into the indigo vastness of the ocean. The sun was setting, casting an assortment of oranges and purples at the horizon. "It's a depiction of Morgana le Fey." His glance returned to me. "She reminds me of you."

I snorted. "You're kidding, right? That painting was beautiful."

Nibbling on his lip ring, he considered what I said, looking sinful and serious. "So are you." His tone had lowered.

I swear I heard him wrong. Maybe that was just what I wanted to hear. Right then, I wanted more than anything for him to kiss me, with the lapping waves and sea salt teasing my wits. Maybe if I thought about it hard enough, I could somehow have what my heart desired.

He took a step closer. The heat from his body infused mine, and a sharp gasp escaped my lips. My head was lost on a turbulent of raw emotions. *Kiss me now*, my mind demanded.

The depths of his eyes darkened, and his mouth crushed over my mine in an assault of power. Excitement rippled inside me like chain of lightning. His hands gripped my sides, pulling me in and steadying my swirling head all at once. He tasted of dark promises and pleasure beyond what I could imagine. My entire being filled with flames, and I encircled my arms around his neck. With nothing between us, our bodies collided. My mouth traveled lavishly over his, loving the feel of his cool hoop rubbing against mine.

As first kisses went, this was unworldly. The flavor of him was an addiction I wasn't able to fulfill. He made me dizzy, weak, and feel exactly what he claimed—beautiful.

The kiss ended, to my utter dismay, as fast as it began. He pulled away, keeping me at arm's length. I moaned at the loss of his lips and opened my eyes. Gavin gazed longingly at my swollen mouth, before shutting his eyes again. He laid his brow on mine, and I breathed in the familiar scent of him, mixed with the misty spray. Our quickened breathing synchronized in heavy rhythm.

Dropping his hands from my lower arms, he broke the spell. "We better get back inside." His voice was thick with huskiness.

I had to fight every muscle in my body not to pull his mouth back to mine. His self-control was staggering, which was both annoying and admirable.

I nodded. No longer touching, we turned back toward the house, walking back at a slower pace that barely gave me enough time to control my thrashing heart.

As we got closer to the kitchen, a slew of animated voices bantered back and forth. Gavin and I stepped into the dining nook, where I was greeted with smells of spaghetti sauce and garlic. My stomach rumbled in response. I hadn't had an appetite earlier, and my stomach was in serious protest. The remainder of his family was gathered, including the brother I yet to meet.

A hush fell over the room as we stepped in. Sophie smiled beside her eldest brother.

"Jared, this is Brianna. Be nice," Sophie warned him.

A laugh snickered from his chest, a wolfish grin spreading across his face that looked similar to Gavin's, but without the seriousness. He had a boyish charm, the devil's smile, and irresistible dimples.

Jared pulled out his chair and walked to stand in front of me, smiling the entire time. "It's a pleasure to meet you, beautiful Brianna." His voice was almost as seductive as his brother's, but it failed to send my heart sputtering in overdrive. Instead, his smile was contagious, and I found myself answering his devilish grin.

"You, too," I said, my voice having yet to recover from the emotional onslaught.

"Here, I saved you a seat." He pulled out a chair beside him.

Gavin growled, eyes darkening and brewing with a violent storm.

"Jared," Lily warned in a stern tone. I wasn't exactly sure what was going on, but Gavin was not happy. There was a thick static in the air, suffocating the room. No one else seemed to notice, but they felt it.

"What?" he answered in mischievous laugh. "I'm just being a good host," he defended with charisma.

Dinner was delicious, and it felt so nice being included in a family dinner. It was so full of commotion, laughter, and so opposite of my own dinners at home. I never realized what I was missing in not having a large family.

"It's Saturday night. Let's go out," Gavin suggested over the chatter.

"There must be a bowling alley or something in this town," Jared added in exasperation to my left. He didn't seem like the kind of soul to sit idly around. He screamed action.

"Yeah there is, but—" I was cut off.

"Great. Let's get out of here," Jared swiftly interrupted my rebuttal. I sighed. I sucked royally at bowling.

CHAPTER 11

H olly Ridge Bowl was no sight to behold. There were ten bowling lanes, a small arcade, and a bar in the corner that served only beer and frozen pizzas. As we walked through the alley, just two of the lanes were occupied. I couldn't believe I'd let them talk me into this. It was going to be so humiliating.

The four of us went up to the register, and Jared requested a lane.

"We should play on teams," he suggested. "A little competition, what do you say?" A gleam hit in his eyes.

"Jared and I against Gavin and Brianna," Sophie suggested.

Gavin turned to me. "You okay with that?"

"Sure. If you're prepared to lose," I mumbled under my breath.

"Have a little faith, Bri. With me by your side, we can't lose," he assured, oozing confidence.

I hoped it was contagious.

"We'll see, little brother," Jared countered, loving the banter.

We gave the guy behind the register our shoe sizes and set off for lane six.

"Any chance we're using bumpers?" I asked as we wound our way down.

Jared laughed, but I wasn't being funny. I would have totally used

66

bumpers. "Not a chance," he replied still grinning. "Trust me. We won't need them the way we bowl."

Great. Was that supposed to make me feel better? What were they, bowling fanatics? I had no idea what the heck I had gotten myself into. "Lovely," I retorted sarcastically.

I set off in search for the lightest ball possible. Maybe they would let me just watch? I picked up the different colors balls, testing their weight, finally settling on a blue one. At least it was a pretty color.

Sophie was setting up the order into the computer when I came back with my sparkling ball. I took a seat next to her and waited with dread for my turn.

"Thanks for coming with us," she said. "This is the first time we've been out since we moved."

Her words penetrated through wall of dismay I'd been building inside me, making me feel remorseful for wallowing in self-pity. They were new in this town. I should be making them feel welcomed.

"Sure, no problem." I attempted to muster up some enthusiasm.

Jared was up first, eldest and all, and in perfect form, threw a strike. There was no doubt in my mind; Gavin and I were going to get slaughtered. Jared strutted off the lane, giving Sophie a high-five as he took his seat.

I frowned.

Gavin was up next. He looked adorable in his t-shirt, black jeans and the multi-colored bowling shoes. Gavin answered Jared's strike with one of his one, and I sunk lower in my seat. The Masons were serious about their bowling. This was going to be a long game, I thought miserably.

Being the good sport that I am, I grinned at my partner. "Nice work. At least one of us will score points."

He sat beside me smirking. "It's all in fun."

"Wait until you see me bowl," I said somberly.

Sophie, at least, didn't get a strike. She knocked eight of the pins the first time, and on the second wasn't able to pick them up.

It was a nasty split.

"Your turn, Brianna," she called after her last throw.

"Here goes nothing." Literally.

I walked up to the lane and grabbed my blue ball. Fitting my fingers in the holes, I aligned my feet with the triangles on the floor and said a quick prayer before sending the ball sailing down the lane. Halfway down, it started to curve, riding on the line. I backed up, afraid to look, but even more afraid not to. A lonely crack sounded as the ball knocked over only one pin. My shoulders sagged a little.

"At least you have great form," Jared razzed.

He was rewarded with a punch in the arm from Gavin.

"What?" He pretended innocence, then winked at me while I waiting for the ball to be retrieved.

My next throw was slightly better. I was able to take down three more pins.

"Don't let them get to you," Sophie encouraged. "It's really just a brotherly competition, a power struggle between the two of them. I don't know why they enjoy it so much."

"Are they always like this?"

She nodded. "They are forever trying to outdo each other. It's all in fun, as frustrating as it is for the rest of us."

"Yeah...I can see that," I agreed.

"It's so nice to have another girl around. I'm always caught in the crossfire. You balance the scales now."

"I'm not all that graceful," I jested.

"You're a lot of things you don't believe." There was a prophetic knowledge behind her words. As friends went, Sophie was pretty uplifting to have around.

My next few turns where no better. If possible, they were worse.

Gavin leaned in closer beside me. "Let me give you a tip. Think about what you want the ball to do, visualize it before you throw and keep the image as you release. Works for me every time," he swore, grinning.

"You're joking," I said in disbelief.

He lifted his brow.

"Fine."

My next turn, I thought, what could it hurt, and gave it a whirl. What did I have to lose? I did exactly what he'd said. I envisioned the ball gliding down the middle of the lane, hitting it dead center.

Ignoring everything I thought I knew about bowling, I let the ball soar down the lane, the whole time, keeping my focus on the ball. I hadn't expected much, but when the ball thundered the pins, I was stupefied. All the white pins fell.

Holy shit.

I jumped in the air and bounded down the lane straight into Gavin's arms. He twirled me once before setting me back on my feet.

"See, I knew you could do it."

"Beginners luck," Jared joked beside me.

I stuck my tongue out at him, and he hooted with laughter.

The strikes kept on coming, and the competition never let up. Something about the way they played struck a chord with me. I started to *really* pay attention. No one was that good, not without some help, my skeptical mind rationed. It wasn't the way they bowled, or their form. What made me leery were their eyes.

Each time Gavin or Jared bowled, they would line up and eye the pins. It was then I noticed the bizarre glow in them, the same glow I saw at the coffee shop. Before they released their throw, the gleam shined brightly. Over the last few frames, I came to expect to see it. I considered the possibility it was a trick of the dimmed lights, but the moment Sophie went to bowl, her eyes remained the same. No glint, no glimmer, no unearthly glow.

I was being ridiculous.

When the night ended, Gavin offered to drive me home. We had dropped my car off earlier, before going out. The prices of gas were outrageous, and I needed to save a buck where I could.

The night was late, and the moon was mostly hidden. Gavin's shadowy form was outlined by the neon blue of his interior lights. I shifted in the leather seat, laying my head on the back of the headrest and watched him.

This was the first time we had been alone since we kissed earlier, and I wasn't really sure what to say. So of course, I complicated matters by saying what had been on my mind the better half of the night. A part of me thought I was making a gigantic mistake by bringing it up. He could very well think I was a lunatic. And probably would.

I didn't want to admit how much that would hurt, but there was no way I was going to let this go, especially, if there was an off chance I was right.

"You're different." My quiet voice broke the silence through the steady purr of his engine.

"What do you mean?" He had both eyes on the road, but he wanted to look at me. His jaw tightened ever so slightly.

"I don't know, just different." I had such a way with words It was uncanny.

"Different how?" he asked, his voice had stiffened, and I knew I hit a nerve.

I heaved a sigh. "I just feel it. There's something different about you." I explained warily.

He gave in and looked at me with a perplexed expression.

"Tonight...I saw your eyes glow. Jared's too. I've seen it before." I rushed the end of the confession—absurd as it was. "What are you?" I asked.

Cutting his gaze back to the road, he was silent. "I've been too relaxed with you," he mumbled, chastising himself. Or at least, that was what I thought I heard.

"Are you a werewolf or something?" I was only half-joking. Though a part of me actually thought he might just be a werewolf.

"Bri, do you really think I turn into a wolf and howl at the moon, or that I am any different than you?"

I bite my lip. "I don't know," I admitted, more unsure than ever.

His lips thinned. "I'm not."

It was hard not to believe him. Maybe this whole thing was just me. Maybe I was the one who wasn't *normal*. Right now, I didn't even know what *normal* meant. I regretted asking.

We didn't talk at all the remaining way home, each caught in our own thoughts.

When he pulled up to my house, I hadn't the first clue how to undo the tension. "Gavin—"

He cut me off. "Bri, just let it go." He tried to sound lighthearted but failed. I could still hear the strain in his tone. "I'll talk to you tomorrow."

I nodded and got out of the car without another word, no matter that I had a hundred more questions and an apology I badly wanted to utter on the tip of my tongue.

Later that night, I laid spread on the bed, hands propped under my chin and feet dangling in the air. The television was on low while I artlessly riffled through the channels, not really paying attention to the screen.

I was mentally trying to dissect the puzzle of Gavin and his family, or the possibility it was all me. There was the crazy way I felt about him. He caused elevated emotions, and I was drawn to him in an irrevocable pull, both terrifying and confounding. Uncontrollably compelled by him, I was taken in by the sultry sapphire of his eyes.

Then there was humming vibration I sometimes got when he or Sophie touched me. Or the strange light of his and Jared's eyes, like at the coffee shop or tonight. He might want me to drop the suspicion, but my mind was having a difficult time of it.

How had I let any of this happen? It was stupid—absolutely stupid to fall for someone like Gavin. He could be so grating, and his smirk infuriating. Those seemed petty and insignificant excuses compared to the sputter of my rapid heartbeat. He made my head spin and left me feeling breathless when we were together.

I fell asleep with the television flicking in the background, the barely audible voices drifting with me in dreams. And like most of my dreams, they were of Lukas, a detail that ate at my guilt. Only seconds ago, all I could imagine was Gavin. How messed up was that?

CHAPTER 12

"**I** missed you," were the first words out of his mouth as soon as he saw me. We were in a park, sitting on a marble bench, an elaborate stone fountain bubbling at the heart. Robins and blue jays sang from the treetops, chasing each other through the branches.

"Me too,"

I agreed. I had really missed him.

"We've seen more of each other the last few weeks than we have...

ever," he commented. "Not that I'm complaining."

We had. It made me wonder if something had changed. I shrugged. "Who knows how my mind works."

He laughed and put an arm around the back of the bench, encompassing me in his nearness. "I like the way your mind works." Grinning, he inched closer. The air outside was comfortable and sunny. A flock of robins picked at the grass in front of us.

If I didn't know better, I'd think the golden boy was flirting with me. "That's just sad," I retorted, unable to believe anyone liked my mind.

He laughed. "Oh Brianna, when will you see what I see?"

I had no idea what he saw, but I doubted in the *real world,* it would make a difference. "I think you need to get your eyes checked," I suggested.

He ignored my comment. "So have you seen the new guy?" Although, he tried to sound nonchalant, I could hear the underlying disapproval.

"It's impossible not to. He's my lab partner." I was a little annoyed by the fact he brought up Gavin. Something in his tone rubbed me the wrong way.

A warning?

A scream of caution?

An accusation?

I couldn't figure it out. "Does that bother you?" I absently kicked the dust under the bench.

"Just curious about him."

Oh, it seemed like a whole lot more than curiosity bubbling under the surface. Didn't anyone ever tell him that curiosity killed the cat? "Why?" I couldn't resist questioning him to prove it a point. I didn't believe him.

Lukas gazed out into the park at an aging statue of a horse with a warrior on its back. "I can see he means something to you," he finally admitted.

How was I to respond to that when I wasn't even sure what I was feeling? He was accurate Gavin meant something to me, but it wasn't any of his business. And how exactly did he know that? Was it because

I thought about him when I was here with Lukas? My brows muddled in confusion. I couldn't deny my feelings for Gavin and lying was an option. He would see it in my face. I was a sucky liar.

"We're friends." I was trying to be evasive.

"I can make you forget him," he pledged, emerald eyes locking with mine, and he saw the stunned expression on my face. I didn't want to forget Gavin, but that didn't stop Lukas from taking full advantage of my speechless shock.

He leaned toward me, pressing his lips lightly to mine. And, I let him.

I didn't pull away.

I didn't stop him.

If anything, I wanted it.

This kiss was something I'd wondered about too often to let slip away.

His lips were soft, smooth, and dreamy, as they moved expertly over mine, drawing out each heavenly sensation and causing me to forget any doubts. The tips of his fingers moved lazily on the small of my back, gently coaxing me closer. He tasted of golden honey and sugary spice. Degree by slow degree, I submerged into the kiss, letting it carry me to ecstasy. He cupped the sides of my face, hands tender, keeping us locked together. His thumb stroked my cheek with affection. He made my head feel like it was flying with the clouds, floating on desire that felt endless. The kiss was perfectly sweet.

Perfect, except it lacked the punch my kiss with Gavin had, or the passionate desperation—like my last breath depended on him. Lukas's kiss was nice, gentle and wistful. I've been kissed twice in one evening, and I had no reason to complain. This was only a dream.

Then why did it feel so real?

As sure as this kiss would end, I would feel overwhelming guilt. His lips lingered for a moment before leaving mine, and his pure green eyes opened slowly. Our faces close enough, and he traced a feather-soft finger over my thoroughly kissed lips.

"I've wanted to do that for so long," he murmured, his voice like silky honey. "Something for you to think about."

I didn't need anything else to think about, and my body must have agreed as the dream started to drift slowly away. I could feel myself being sucked back into my sleeping form. His emerald eyes and the sunny scent of him wafted with me.

Before I was completely tossed out, a woman's raspy voice slipped in through the journey. "Be careful what you trust. Dreams aren't always what they seem," she warned, her voice fading off in the distance.

When I woke up in my dark room, the taste of his honey smooth lips lingered on mine, and my body was humming and electric. I lay there the rest of the night, too wired to fall back asleep. The woman's voice and her warning played over and over in my head. Who was she? What did she mean?

⚜

WHEN I GOT to school on Monday, I was in a zombie-like state. Yawning endlessly, my eyes were heavy, like there were weights pulling them down. The extra effort it took to keep them open proved to be too much during first period, when I feel asleep on my desk.

Not my finest moment.

Mrs. Schwab's voice echoed in ears, and I hadn't fully realized she wasn't talking in my head.

"*Brianna...Brianna*...would you like to join the class?"

I jolted upright, wiping the drool with the back of my hand. "Sorry," I barely managed to mumble.

She eyed me with disdain, before giving me her back and continued her lecture. Austin caught my attention a row over and gave me a, *what-the-hell* look. I sighed, my shoulders slumping in exhaustion.

He walked out with me after class. "Hey, babygirl. Is that hot piece of boy candy keeping you up at night?"

I snickered. "Not exactly."

"You okay?" There was a touch of worry shadowing his forehead.

"I haven't a clue. Just tired I think."

"We still on for Friday right?" he asked, reminding me of our plans.

Friday was Halloween. Tori, Austin, Gavin, Sophie and I planned on going out. It was all Austin's idea. I loved Halloween. We were going to the Haunted Trails at Morris Landing. Sophie, Tori, and I had decided to dress up. The three of us were getting together later this week to shop for our costumes. I was actually looking forward to shopping, for once.

"Of course. I am so excited!" I assured.

"I know. It's going to be a scream." His sense of humor was so lame. I adored him.

Today however, everything went over my head. I couldn't even muster up a grin. "Funny," I replied.

"See you at lunch," he called as we broke off in different directions.

By the time third period hit, I was finishing my second cup of coffee and hoping for an adrenaline boost. Gavin caught up with me as I knocked off the last of my caffeine and tossed the evidence in the trash.

He arched his brow lifting the silver bar in query. "Why so glum?"

A yawn escaped the second I opened mouth. "There is something wrong with me. I shouldn't be so tired after the amount of caffeine I just inhaled," I admitted.

He studied my face as we walked. "Didn't sleep well?"

I shook my head, stifling yet another yawn "It's my dreams that are keeping me up, if that makes any sense." Neither of us mentioned the previous night, or what I had accused him of. I was too tired to even care at this point. He could be a zombie or a werewolf, and I wouldn't have blinked an eye. I was glad there wasn't any weird tension between us. However, I could also be so out of it, I just didn't pick up on it.

"Are you fantasizing about me? I could see how that could be disrupting."

I choked at his words. "Maybe." I teased, but in the back of my mind, I was thinking about Lukas and the kiss we shared. *God, if he only knew*. Better yet, I was glad he didn't.

"If they're really keeping you, try tea. I think my mom has a recipe that might help."

"Thanks. I just might take you up on the offer." I fumbled with my books. This topic was making me uncomfortable. The last thing I wanted to do was dwell on Lukas with Gavin.

As we walked, my mind started dissecting my relationship with

Gavin. There were a hundred girls at Holly Ridge that were prettier than me. What was it about me that made Gavin interested in me? I didn't think his type was dorkish with a dash of sarcasm. Surely, I wasn't his first choice. What was so special about me? He had once told me I was special, but I didn't see it. I was just some girl. The next thing, I knew I blurted out, "Why did you pick me?"

Gavin gave me the side eye. "What do you mean?"

I wanted to crawl under a rug. Why did I have to open my big mouth? Why couldn't I just let things be?

We were in a good place after last night, so this was just asking for trouble. Was I sabotaging something before things got serious?

I sighed. I'd already started this conversation, why not see it through? "There are hundreds of girls at this school, why did you pick me?" I repeated. A few students passed us by.

"Is it that hard to believe?" He raised his voice an octave.

A question with a question. I found that nerve racking. I shrugged, feeling more exposed than I thought possible, and defeated. What kind of admission had I been expecting? That he was madly in love with me and couldn't live without me?

"It just is," I argued.

He ran a frustrated hand through his midnight hair, the leather cuff on his wrist shifting with the movement. "Besides being gorgeous and insanely attracted to you, we have something in common," he said.

"What?" I asked, taken by surprise. I wasn't expecting a declaration of love, yet my heart faltered a tad.

"Isn't it enough that I am attracted to you?" He disputed. His evasiveness wasn't lost on me.

I don't know, was it? His words affected me, giving me a river of thrilled sensation. I stared at his eyes, waiting to see some form of deceit. They were clear, blue and honest.

The bell sounded through the hall, announcing the beginning of third period. For now it would have to be enough, because we were both late for class, and I was too exhausted to continue.

I don't know how I made it through the whole day. But as soon as last period ended, I went home and slept like the dead.

Dreamless.

CHAPTER 13

After school the following day, Gavin came over to study for our chemistry group test we had tomorrow. By group test, I meant Gavin and me. While I planned on studying, Gavin had another idea entirely. Honestly, I would have preferred to study without him sitting across the bed from me. He was a distraction from even the simplest thoughts, let alone an entire chapter of science. But the study session had been his idea, and I had yet to refuse him anything.

I had the textbook open and a spiral notebook with minimum notes spread out around us on the bed. Biting the end of my pencil, I flipped through the study guide Mr. Burke had given us. It outlined the points in the chapter we would be tested on.

"Are we really going to study?" he asked, complaining.

"Yes," I replied, exasperated. "I have to pass this class. So do you."

He grumbled beside me, doodling on the notebook.

I yanked it out from underneath his pen. "Hey," he protested. "I wasn't finished with that."

"Chemistry, remember...we are supposed to be studying."

"You are a slave driver," he stated, fumbling with his pen cap.

"And you're a slacker."

"Ouch. Can't we take a break?" He was bordering on whining, and I felt like I was babysitting a two-year-old.

I laughed. "We just started. Here look up question ten in the text." He needed a task to keep his mind busy and on other things.

A few minutes later, I peered at him over the top of our study guide. He was flipping through the pages of the textbook, looking sexy as sin. It was hard to believe that he was here in my room with me. When I imagined dating, I never pictured someone like Gavin—dark, edgy, or with so many piercings. But now, I didn't want any other boy at my school. He ruined all other prospects for me.

Yesterday's tizzy in the hall had been forgotten. We couldn't seem to stay upset with each other.

I bite the end of my eraser, and he looked up, catching me staring at him. My cheeks stained pink. He smirked, and I quickly averted my gaze back to the study guide. My concentration had been shot to hell.

"You're not studying," he playfully scolded.

I kicked him lightly from across the bed. He grabbed ahold of my leg before I had the chance to escape his reach.

"Hey!" I screeched.

"Just remember that you started it." He pulled me by the leg toward him. I was laughing and squealing at the same time. As soon as he had me in his grasp, he picked me up effortlessly and tossed me to the other end of the bed on a pile of pillows. My laughter pealed out over the silence of the empty house. So much for studying.

Sometime later, I looked over at the clock on my nightstand. My stomach rumbled in response as I thought about dinner. My aunt wasn't due home for a few more hours, and it was my turn to cook. Even with her gone most of the time, she insisted on trying to make sure I had a balanced diet and was well taken care of. It grated on her that I was alone so much. On her nights, she usually had something in the fridge ready to be heated up

Tonight the menu was Italian.

"I'm starving." My stomach agreed, growling. "Do you want to stay for dinner? I'm making lasagna." I didn't really want to eat alone, and there was always so much, no matter how many nights I ate leftovers.

"You're cooking?" he asked, and scrunched his nose.

I tossed my pencil good-naturedly at him. "I'm a good cook, I'll have you know."

He caught the pencil mid-air before it had a chance to hit its target and smirked, pleased with himself. "Sure, under one condition."

"What?" I replied, narrowing my eyes cautiously.

"You let me help."

I grinned. "Deal. Let's go before I pass out from hunger." I climbed off my bed, the litter of notes forgotten.

We walked into the kitchen, and I preheated the oven, before going to the pantry. I pulled out the ingredients I needed: pasta sauce, noodles and spices.

"What do you want me to do?" He took a seat at the island.

"You can make the salad," I suggested, setting down the stuff from the pantry. I went to the fridge, gathering hamburger and vegetables and placed them on the counter. I handed him a knife from the butcher block. "Can you handle this?"

He lifted his brow. "You haven't seen anything."

I went to the stove, put the hamburger in a pan and set a pot of water to boil. Turning on the burner, I began breaking apart the ground beef and browning it. I glanced over my shoulder to check on Gavin, see how he was faring with the salad.

My mouth dropped.

What had it been? Two minutes?

"You did not just cut up all the vegetables," I declared, mystified by the impossible. How had he made an entire salad?

"I told you not to doubt me," he said grinning, so sure of himself.

"What, you're a chef? You're practically failing chemistry, yet you can create a salad in under a minute. What gives?"

"Talent. Do you need help over there?"

"Yeah, boil the noodles smarty pants."

We worked together in a seamless rhythm. It was harmonious and completely domestic. There was something so homey about having him in the kitchen with me. Maybe it was from growing up without a male figure, or maybe it was that he was so familiar with cooking, either way, it was nice to not be alone. Cooking for two was not only boring and lonesome, but lacked the sense of family I missed.

With the lasagna baking in the oven, we sat at the table, kicked back, with the radio on low.

"Where did you move from?" I asked.

"We lived outside of Chicago, until my dad got the job offer in Jacksonville."

I was surprised. I didn't know how many job opportunities there were for a historian, let alone exactly what a historian did.

"What was it like there?"

"Busy. Windy. Cold." He grinned.

I rolled my eyes. Those were all things I already knew about Chicago. "Do you miss your old friends?" I secretly wondered if he also had an ex-girlfriend there as well.

He slouched back in his seat and smiled. His whole face relaxed. "Yeah, sometimes I do. Chicago was where I was born. It was really hard to leave. My friends understood me in ways people here won't be able to." His smile drooped, and he looked a little lost in the past.

My heart went out to him, I couldn't even think about leaving Holly Ridge, starting over somewhere foreign and having to make new friends. But there was no denying how glad I was that he was here with me, instead of in Chicago, were we would have never met.

Buzz. Buzz. I jumped at the sound of the timer. Dinner was done. I got up to pull the dish out of the oven. It was so strange having a guy over for dinner—just the two of us. If I wasn't careful, this was something I could get used to, and want more of, time alone with him.

"What makes the people so different here?" I asked, setting the plates on the table. And did that include me?

He shrugged, forking a heap of lasagna into his mouth. "Culture, I guess, except you. I felt this connection with you the first day we meet. I remember thinking, *finally, someone who will get me.*"

I bit into my garlic bread and thought about the first time I saw him. Maybe I judged him too harshly that day for skipping class. I never really thought about what he must be going through being the *new* kid. Or what he had to leave behind. My heart beat a little faster at his admission of the connection we both felt.

"Is that why you ditched your first day?" I blew on a forkful of steaming lasagna, before popping it into my mouth.

"Partly," he admitted. "Mostly, I was pissed at my parents, but running into you that day changed my mind about small towns. It's one of the reasons my mom was so happy we met, helping her angry son make the new town slightly more bearable. You wouldn't have recognized me had you seen me before that day. I was rebelling every way possible. I don't think my mom could've thanked you enough. She absolutely adores you," he said, polishing off his food in record time.

The feeling was completely mutual. "I'm sorry it was hard for you. I can't imagine leaving the only home I've ever known."

"I think it worked out for the best."

I smiled.

When we finished dinner, I walked him to the door. "Thanks for staying."

"Anytime."

"You know that we are going to fail that test tomorrow," I told him. Group test or not, we were doomed.

"Have a little faith, Bri. I'll get us through it," he smugly assured.

I rolled my eyes and shut the door after him.

I didn't want to know what kind of tricks he had up his sleeve.

CHAPTER 14

Madame Cora's Wardrobe was a costume establishment in Wilmington, packed with plenty of flair. Austin decided to tag along for the thirty minute trip and was riding shot-gun, with Sophie and I in the back. Tori convinced him it would be fun if they dressed in coordinating costumes.

Both Tori and Austin had adopted Sophie as one of our own. They absolutely loved her. No doubt that grated on Gavin's nerves a tad, to have his younger sister hanging around all the time.

Walking into Madame Cora's Wardrobe was like being transported back in time. A tall woman with long, curly, cinnamon hair sat on a stool behind an enclosed glass case. She was decorated in more dangling silver jewelry than I thought one woman should wear. Or own. Her every move jingled in music. She had bold red lips—an extreme contrast to her ivory skin and hazel eyes. She smiled at us as we walked through the front door, a whimsical chime resounding through the shop, announcing our arrival.

The shop had mannequins dressed up in full gear—wigs, shoes, makeup, masks. You name it, she had it. Jack Sparrow, Medusa, Queen of the Nile, the guy from Saw. He still gave me nightmares. A Halloween mix pumped in the store from speakers near the doors.

"Well hello, my lovelies," she greeted in a voice of a seductress. I don't know who she thought she was going to seduce, since Austin was the only guy, and he definitely didn't swing her curvy way.

"Hi," the four of us said in unison.

"Is there something I can help you look for?" she offered, never losing the deep, sexy quality to her voice.

We had started to look around the store, poking through the racks near the entrance. "We're looking for Halloween costumes," Sophie said. She eyed Madame Cora coolly, measuring her with bright sapphire eyes. There was just a hint of that strange glow.

Round racks housed costumes of every variety. Sexy. Scary. Slutty. The three S's. She had it all. The best part was the quality of the materials. They weren't the cheap, mass-produced ones you found at Wal-Mart. The detail was spectacularly crafted. I realized that the most difficult part of shopping here was going to be which costume to choose.

"If you need any help, you let me know," she offered, returning Sophie's inspection. Her blood-red nails taped on the glass.

Tori and Austin took off to a row on the back wall filled with companion costumes, while Sophie and I stayed at the center racks.

"Do you have an idea what you want to dress up as?" I asked, pulling out a black kitty cat bodysuit. So not my style. I put it back in with the others.

"I haven't dressed up since junior high." That was only two years ago, but I figured she didn't need me to point that out. "I don't know... maybe a French maid or a fairy?" she suggested, pulling out an extremely short and barely there black and white skirt with a matching, even smaller, top.

I couldn't really see her as either. "That is pretty darn short," I commented as she held up the skirt. I am sure she would look freaking amazing in anything she wore, with those legs oh hers.

"I know...that's the point right? The chance to dress slutty without the usually backlash," she pointed out.

She had me there. I wasn't so sure her brothers would agree, but since I didn't have any... "You think Jared and Gavin would let you wear that?" I was trying to avoid a potential situation. They were both overly protective of Sophie, as much as they teased her.

She snorted. "Please. My brother has a thing for you. He could care less what I wear. He will be too busy staring at you." She was wrestling through a rack of angel costumes. Sophie was a get-to-the-point kind of girl. No beating around the bush.

"Excuse me." She completely caught me off guard. I was not entirely comfortable with her banking on him being too distracted by me. She couldn't possibly be serious.

"Gavin," she responded, grinning at my growing discomfort.

I kind of figured that part out, captain obvious. "Define *thing*."

"He is totally into you."

"Really?" The disbelief was thick in my tone. Okay, so we kissed once and we hung out a lot, but I had a hard time believe he felt even half of the way I did.

She rolled her eyes, the ones identical to the brother in question. "You have no idea the amount of power you have there, do you? We really need to have a girl-to-girl talk."

This was her brother we were discussing; she was not my first choice to gossip with about my womanly wiles. Or lack of, in my case. Not to mention, it was sad that she apparently had more experience in this department than I did. "I don't have any *power* over your brother," I argued.

She rolled her eyes. "Here, wear this one." She handed me a revealing gypsy costume. The skirt was violet with an extremely large slit up the leg. There was a wrapper bejeweled with chattering gold coins. The top was white with flared sleeves and showed a little midriff.

"You're kidding right?"

"Absolutely not. This is the one," she insisted.

I did really like it. What the hell. The goal was to be someone else. Well I wanted to be hot. Smokin' hot. And this number was sizzling.

Sophie settled for a skanky angel outfit, which in my mind kind of defeated the point of being an angel. Tori and Austin, the nuts that they were, decided to go as Brad and Janet from *Rocky Horror Picture Show*, the best Halloween musical ever.

Yeah, I was that girl.

I was the last in line as I waited to pay. Laying down the gypsy costume near the register, I waited for Madame Cora. I glanced down the glass counter case, admiring the jewelry as it sparkled under the light. She had so many beautiful pieces, with raw cut stones and silvery charms. While I was admiring a certain necklace that had caught my eye, Madame Cora had come to stand on the other side of the counter.

"Do you dabble in crystals?" she asked me.

I shook my head. "No. I just think they're pretty."

"No... hmmm, I would have thought you did," she admitted, looking at me oddly.

I don't know what made her think I knew anything about crystals and magic.

"Here, let me show you. Each has its own unique properties. This one here—" She indicated to the bauble around her neck. "Is for clear sight and open-mindedness." Her voice enthralled me.

She unlocked the glass case, pulling out an intricate silver chain with a milky iridescent stone and a purple crystal. My eyes were spellbound by the necklace that I had only moments before been intrigued by. I don't know how she figured out that it was that specific piece I was interested in. My fingers itched to touch the smooth stones. They weren't raw cut like some of the others, but flat and polished. She laid it on the counter, and I ran my fingers over the crystals.

"This one is made of moonstone and amethyst," she informed. "The moonstone is said to strengthen intuitive power. Placed under a pillow alongside an amethyst can allow for a more peaceful sleep. The amethyst protects against evil sorcery. Something tells me you are in need of some."

I picked up the necklace and let it dangle from my finger. The stones glinted off the lights, and her words affected some deep part of me locked away. This necklace was made for me. I didn't know if it was coincidence that the properties of the stones were incorporated so close to my life. I was starting to believe I should leave nothing to chance.

So, of course, I added it to my purchase. Not to mention, it would look great with my costume.

She rang up my items and handed me my bags. A tingling shot down my arm as our fingers touched. It was more commanding than what I had gotten accustomed to with Gavin and Sophie. Her hand snaked out and grabbed my arm, holding me. I lifted my head and saw the eerie glow in her eyes, almost as if she was possessed. A gasp escaped my lips, and I tugged at my arm. Before I had the chance to feel freaked out beyond my control, Sophie was at my side.

"Ready?" she asked, staring intently at Madame Creepo, who was giving her the stink eye.

Madame Cora released my arm immediately at Sophie's arrival. I couldn't have been more grateful. "Yeah, let's go," I swiftly agreed.

"May safety find you...Brianna," Madame Cora called as we walked out of the store.

CHAPTER 15

O nce we were in the car, I allowed myself to breathe. And to think. That woman had given me some serious voodoo vibes.

"That was weird," Austin commented as Tori started reversing out of the parking space.

"No kidding," Tori agreed. "I guess Halloween started a little early for some. Or maybe never ends in her case."

Sophie and I sat in silence. I took out the necklace and ran my fingers over the stones. It was very pretty, and there was this gentle hum that danced along my fingertips.

Sophie occasionally eyed me warily. She was checking to make sure I was okay, that I wasn't creeped out by what happened. In truth, I didn't know what to make of it.

HALLOWEEN NIGHT WAS MY FAVORITE. The moonlit air was infused with the scent of damp leaves and wet moss. Fall had moved in like an artist's brush, painting the trees in vibrant colors of gold, burgundy, rust, and tangerine. I stood on my porch dressed in my blatantly revealing costume, toying with the necklace, and anxiously waited for Gavin to arrive. I looked pretty damn good, thanks to Sophie. We were meeting Austin and Tori at Morris Landing.

The Trail at Morris Landing was like a haunted house outside. They had hayrides, bonfires, and held costume contests each year. At the guests' own discretion and risk, they wound along the trail, preparing to get the shit scared out of them. Different sections of the trail had its own interactive scene or scenario to haunt you. From the guy chasing you with the chainsaw, to the headless woman hanging from a tree, it was like being in your own personal horror film.

Gravel crunched under the tires as Gavin's car approached. Before his car came into view, fireflies rocketed through me in anticipation. Sophie was hitching a ride with us, much to Gavin's chagrin. He was like a grizzly bear when things didn't go his way. I found it cute.

When the Charger came to a stop, Gavin got out of the car to open my door. He looked good enough to make me wish we could at least drive alone, in spite of how much I adored Sophie. I just felt as if we hadn't been alone since the night we kissed.

"Hey," I greeted, smiling with happiness. Just the sight of him made me giddy.

"Wow...you look great." His eyes roamed over me in a way that had my entire body reacting.

The night air was balmy, but I instantly felt overdressed... and I was practically wearing nothing. Thank God, my aunt was at the shop. I wasn't sure she would have let me leave the house tonight, looking as I did.

"Thanks," I replied. His gaze was making me self-conscious. I had to fight the urge to cover up as I got in the car.

Sophie was in the back, grinning like a fool. "I told you," she smugly said before Gavin got back in the car. "This is going to be fun. You do look great, by the way."

"So do you." And of course she did. She looked better than great, actually. She looked celestial in her angel costume, her long raven hair curling over her shoulders, sprinkled with glitter. Her eyelashes were decorated with rhinestones, and her sapphire eyes were dotted with a tiny star in the middle. She could have just flown down from the heavens.

"How did you get your eyes like that?" Thinking she must be wearing contacts. I couldn't help but stare at them, trying to see the lenses.

"Magic," she said, with twinkling eyes.

Sometimes I swear I couldn't get a straight answer from either one of them.

Tori and Austin were waiting for us as we pulled up to the trail, engine roaring. The sign at the entrance dripped in blood, the black letters bold and written with a shaky hand. *Don't get left behind, or you might not come back.*

As we got out of the car, an ear-splitting scream hit the air. The three of us laughed.

"Looks like the fun as already begun," Gavin said, as we walked toward Tori and Austin. The place was overflowing with the sounds of chatter, spooky music, and creepy chuckles, along with the scent of buttered popcorn and apple cider. Halloween.

"I feel sick," Tori moaned.

"You guys look so cute," I remarked on their costumes.

"Who are you supposed to be?" Gavin asked.

"Janet and Brad from *Rocky Horror Picture Show*," Austin informed him. "Tell me you have seen that movie."

"And if I haven't?" Gavin countered.

Austin's mouth dropped open. "Oh man, we have got to seriously educate you on films."

The five of us paid for our tickets and got into the weaving line. When our turn came to enter the trail, Sophie, Tori, and Austin went in first, with Gavin and I picking up the rear.

"I think I'm gonna faint," Tori complained. Haunted houses weren't her thing, but she didn't want to miss out on the fun. Nothing with her ever made sense. She loved to watch the goriest films, yet couldn't handle the haunted woods.

The first guy we came across on the trail was decked in rattling chains and covered in gooey fake blood. If I hadn't been preoccupied with walking so close to Gavin, he wouldn't have given me a fright. I jumped like ten feet in the air and grabbed onto Gavin's arm. He found the situation hilarious. It had a domino effect. Tori jumped due to my jumpiness, which then made Austin flinch and so forth. Before long, we were all laughing.

"Do I need to hold your hand?" Gavin whispered in my ear, and caused me to shiver for entirely different reasons.

Somewhere along the trail, Gavin and I had fallen behind. There was a group in front of us, and I think Tori, Austin, and Sophie had wound up walking with them. We must have taken a wrong turn. There hadn't been a single sign of anyone.

No Freddy Kruger.

No gruesome blood.

No Jack the Ripper.

I don't know how else to explain the fact that I was pretty sure we were lost.

"This can't be right," I argued. "We're lost." The first inklings of concern weaved within me. I hoped the entrance sign wasn't prophetic.

"Come on," Gavin said, reaching for my hand. "Let's see if we can find the trail again and get us the hell out of here."

For the next fifteen minutes, we walked and walked in what felt like endless circles. A layer of clouds had rolled in above the treetops, and the wind started to pick up. The trees offered little comfort in the descending blackness.

I pulled out my phone and glanced at the screen. "Damn it. I have no service," I swore, deflated. Fingering the stones on the necklace, I nibbled on my lip.

"Something is wrong." Gavin was on guard, shining the flashlight over the trees surrounding us. "I can feel it."

My anxiety hitched with each step, and the wind whipped against our backs, picking up speed. Dried up leaves covered the ground, crunching underfoot.

Gavin came to stand beside me, scanning the woods. "Bri, it's going to be all right," he assured in a steady voice.

A twig snapped behind us, and I jerked around, expecting the worst.

A faceless, horrid monster.

A bloody zombie

A thirsty vampire.

Fear lanced through me, while the winds yowled in the distance. "There's something out there." My voice was shaky, and there was no doubt in my mind that we were being watched. Or worse...hunted.

This is a haunted maze, I reminded myself. Of course there were nasties out there.

"Nothing is going happen to you. I won't let it." He squeezed my freezing hand. The night had been fairly warm, but with the abrupt change in the wind, it added a bite to the air.

I clung to him, seeking solace. "How are we getting out of here?" My hair blew around in crazy circles, constantly hitting my face. I gave up trying to control the skirt that was whirling in the wind. The metal coins clattered together in a chaotic musical array, and the more I seemed to fret, the stronger the wind blew.

He must have noticed the chill in my hand. Pulling off his hoodie, he handed it to me. "Here put this on."

"Thanks," I murmured, slipping it over my arms, the sleeves falling past my fingertips. At once, I was enclosed by his scent. I savored the security and warmth instantly. When he went to grab for my hand again, he got a handful of cotton. Grinning at each other, I pushed the end far enough for us to lace fingers.

"Lucky for you, I was a Boy Scout...more or less."

I gave him a doubtful look, but if I trusted anyone to get me out of these confounded woods, it was Gavin. "Do you think the others are okay?" I was worried about Tori, Austin, and Sophie.

"They have Sophie. She is better at this stuff than me. They're probably waiting in the car, wondering where the hell we are."

I was wondering that, as well.

I glimpsed at my cell phone again, hoping to see a change in the reception bars. Nope. No service at all.

Of course it couldn't be that easy.

The only light now was the gleam of blue from the moon. It cast intimidating shadows in all directions. We walked to the right, looking to see if we could spot anything familiar, other than trees, trees, and more trees.

Then out of nowhere, a deafening sound reverberated through the woods. It was followed by the rapid smacking of branches.

"Bri!" Gavin screamed.

CHAPTER 16

His eyes were pumped with fear, and my heart accelerated in triple time. I was in trouble, but the threat hadn't hit me yet. Literally.

My eyes went over my head. A big mistake. The blood in my veins turned blue, my legs paralyzed. Above me was an enormous tree, falling straight at me and knocking away everything in its path. It was only a matter of seconds before it hit, trapping me under its trunk. A scream tore from my lungs, ripping through the forest, the back of my throat burning from the power.

I don't know how he managed to get to me as fast as he did, but he knocked the scream right from my lips. I landed on the ground with an oomph and Gavin on top of me. My eyes were squeezed shut, waiting for the monstrous impact of the tree. He was breathing hard above me, winded, his head resting on my shoulder. My back was pressed into the pine-needled forest floor.

As the seconds went by and nothing happened, I cautiously opened my eyes, afraid of what I would see. The image above me was unexplainable and gravity defying. Maybe I was dreaming, or was seeing threats that weren't there, because the tree was no longer falling.

It was suspended in the air above us. Just floating.

I blinked. A gasp of shock sprung from my mouth

What the holy hell?

Gavin stared into my frantic eyes. A gush of rash wind blew through the forest around us, throwing leaves and debris in a whirlwind. The sapphire of his irises burned with a flaming blue more intense than I've ever seen before.

With a sweep of his hand, the hovering tree disintegrated into thousands and thousands of tiny pieces of confetti. The particles rained down on us, sticking to our clothes, tangling in my hair, and sprinkling in our eyes. The wind continued to protest in anger, pounding with the beat of my heart.

"Make the wind stop," I demanded, utterly freaked.

Gavin wasn't God. It was irrational to think he could do something as control the weather. He bit his lip as he watched me on some internal struggle. He sighed. "I can't until you calm down."

I didn't question him or why I was the one who needed to calm down, besides the fact that I was the only one hyperventilating. Right then, I just wanted to go home. I focused my breathing, taking slow, steady breaths until my heartrate stabilized.

He ran a hand over my hair, sending the confetti of leaves tumbling to the ground. His finger trailed along the side of my cheek to just below my jaw line, before he tipped my face up. And just like that I was caught in a sea of blue, awareness seeped inside my body. He was still on top of me and every contour of him pressed against me. Perhaps it was the near-death experience that had the blood pumping in my veins, but I had a feeling it was just him. He studied me, marveled by something I didn't understand.

I wanted him to kiss me. I bit my lower lip to keep it from trembling. He sensed the change, and his finger moved to outline my lower lip. I had the deepest urge to drag his finger inside my mouth and taste him. I might have, if we hadn't been jerked out of the trance.

Thunk.

A branch fell from the tree, landing just shy of our heads. The winds had finally died down and were nothing more than a gentle breeze. Gavin stood and held out a hand to me.

"Thank you for saving me." I internally cringed at the breathy sound of my voice.

"You will always be safe with me."

I believed him. There was no one else in the world I felt safer with than Gavin.

THE TRIP out of the forsaken woods was unmemorable. No joke. We were able to find the trail without a hitch and make it to an exit.

Tori, Austin, and Sophie were leaning against Austin's car as we came out of the trees. They were all right and by the look of it, overwhelmed with worry. I doubted the sight of our mud-stained clothing and leaf-strewn hair helped our cause.

"What the hell happened to you guys?" Tori blurted.

Wincing, I didn't know what to say. Any explanation that came to mind sounded ridiculous. Gavin and I had talked about what happened, so I kept my trap shut. Someone else could handle this. I wasn't even sure I could handle what I'd seen.

"We took a wrong turn, and then Bri tripped on a tree." Gavin summarize, staying as close to the truth without giving away his secret.

Sophie's eyes bore into her brothers. She didn't look like she bought a single word that spewed from his mouth.

"I should really get her home," he added.

"Good idea." Austin agreed, keeping his eyes focused on my face. I hadn't the foggiest idea of what he saw when he looked at me.

"Austin, would you mind giving Sophie a ride home? I need to talk to Bri," Gavin said with a don't-ask edge to his voice.

Austin looked between the two of us, trying to judge what was going on. "Sure, no problem. You guys have a fight or something?" he asked.

I could tell he was worried about me, and my silence wasn't helping. "No, we're fine," I reassured. My voice came out too high-pitched.

"Gavin," Sophie called as my friends turned to leave. "You're sure this is a good idea?" She gave him a hard look.

"I don't have a choice." A look passed between them, and Sophie was content with whatever she saw. She nodded her head and slipped into Austin's car.

"Let's go, Bri," Gavin commanded.

I mechanically got in and sunk into the plush leather seat of his car. He turned the heat up, chasing the chill that had settled over Holly Ridge. The ride to my house was awkward and quiet. I didn't know what to say to break the silence. My mind was still having trouble believing and processing everything that had occurred tonight. In the dim glow of the dashboard, none of it seemed real. If it wasn't for the awkwardness, it might be all too easy to convince myself it never happened.

We pulled up my driveway, and the little light was radiating on the porch. My aunt had left it on like she always did. That small action made it all rush back to me in a flood of alarm.

Should I be afraid? The unknown of what he was, and what he might be capable of, hung in the air between us. If there was one thing I concluded, it was that Gavin wasn't like me. He was different.

I studied his profile. This was Gavin. My body screamed that he would never hurt me, no matter what he was. Fear wasn't an emotion he evoked. I couldn't feel the way I did about him if that wasn't true. Those feelings alone validated that I would never turn away from him. No matter what I learned. Sorting through those feelings restored a flow of calm.

He turned the key in the ignition, cutting the engine. The keys jingled, slicing through the dead air, followed by his voice. "I don't know where to start. This is all so much harder than I ever thought possible," he admitted. His hands tightened on the steering wheel as he fought to find a way to tell me what was on his mind

I bit the inside of my cheek, clueless how to make it any easier. My eagerness was bubbling at the surface. I couldn't take my gaze off his form, but he kept his eyes averted. I waited patiently. It was all I could do.

He broke the silence again. "Screw it. Here goes nothing. My family wields magic, and has for generations," he revealed in a rush. He knew I would need more than words; I would need proof. He flicked his wrist, and the silver woven ring I'd been wearing on my middle finger was suddenly in the palm of his hand.

There had been a ripple in the air. My eyes tapered as I stared at the ring in his hand, then back up at his face. I heaved as understanding started to sink in. "Are you telling me that you're a...a witch?" My mind tugged back with reluctance, even with everything I had seen with my own eyes. All of it was impossible to believe.

"I am," he admitted, keeping his eyes focused on the silver ring.

"What do you mean, you're a witch?" My voice caught. I still couldn't get myself to accept what he was claiming. If I let go of the disbelief, it made sense. And that scared the hell out of me.

"You know what I mean," he rebuked, twirling the hoop at his lip, reminding me this was hard for him also.

Of course, I did. That didn't mean I believed him. Exhaling, I stared up at all the luminous stars dotting the night sky. There was so much out there I'd probably never understand. The universe was filled with the unexplainable. Life. Death. The deep stuff. But witches? Magic? My life wasn't a Harry Potter book. "Is it just your family? Are there other witches?"

"No, witches are everywhere, and have been around for centuries. There is an entire organization," he informed, slipping the little silver ring back onto my finger. A spark ignited on contact.

Whoa, an organization? Like a cult? For the moment, I decided to play along. "How does it work? Your magic?" My gut said he was telling me the truth. The guy I was absolutely head-over-heels crazy about was a witch.

He finally looked me in the face, and a sigh of relief escaped. "It's hard to put into words. Mostly, it's control over energy. Everything around us pulses with a life force. Witches are just more in tuned with those energies." He absently toyed with the leather cuff at his wrist.

"Is that why your eyes glow?" I recalled the unusually fiery radiance to them sometimes, like tonight.

He nodded. "The stronger the spell, the more power it requires. The deeper I give myself over to a spell, magic pulses from within me."

"How do you conjure a spell? Do you do so with just a thought?"

"For experienced witches, it can be as easy as breathing. For me it is a little more complex. I have to concentrate on the spell and keep it in line with the energy, whether it is my energy, or someone else's energy."

It sounded complicated, not just a swoop of the hand or blink of the eye (Bewitched totally came to mind).

"Some spells come easier, depending on what kind of witch you are," he continued.

"Wait, what? There are different kinds of witches?"

His lips upturned a little at the corners. "Yeah...I would need all night to tell you everything I know. We should probably stick to the basics tonight."

Point taken. "What kind of witch are you?" I asked. That was basic, right?

He shrugged. "Defense spells."

"Defense spells? Like what you did tonight? Saving me?"

He looked out the windshield again, focused on some hidden shadow I couldn't see. "Yeah." His normally husky voice was harsher. "That never should have happened. I should have been able to stop it before it even came near you," he said, obviously berating himself.

I hated hearing it. What he had done was save my life. "Hey," I said, touching his arm and forcing his attention back to me. I tried to ignore the zap that always came. "Are you kidding? What you did was beyond amazing. You're always saving me."

"That may be, but it was close...too close. I should have been more aware of what was going on," he scolded himself.

"I am fine, okay?"

He nodded, yet his eyes betrayed him.

Gavin blamed himself, making me grind my teeth in frustration. My heart thumped at his protectiveness.

There was one more question I had to ask, just to make sure. "What about vampires and werewolves? Do they exist as well?"

He laughed under his breath, chasing some of guilt from his eyes. It was music to my ears. "No...not that I know of." His stance was more relaxed now that I hadn't bolted from the car, and he wasn't down on himself.

"That's a relief." I reached my hand up to my neck, searching for the necklace. My eyes widened as I glance down. Nothing. Closing my eyes, I dropped my head against the back of the seat. "It's gone," I groaned, disappointed.

I'd lost the necklace.

CHAPTER 17

"What's gone?" Gavin asked, brows drawn together.

"My necklace, the one I was wearing tonight," I hastily replied.

"The one with the moonstone and amethyst? Are you sure it's gone?"

The fact he knew which one was impressive. Talk about attention to detail. I nodded. "It must have fallen off in the woods." And my disappointment sunk in my gut. There was no way I was getting it back.

"I'll look for it; don't worry about it. You'll get it back," he vowed. I could see the determination in his eyes. Everything about this guy was intense.

"I don't want you going back there. It's fine. I'm sure I could try to replace it."

I didn't convince him. The gleam of stubbornness was in his eyes.

Yawning, I decided I had enough excitement for the night. "Text me tomorrow," I said as I reached for the door handle. On a whim, I leaned in close to Gavin and pressed my lips softly to his. "Thanks again for saving me," I whispered against his mouth.

His head rested against the seat, and I'd be lying if I didn't admit to myself how much I wanted more than a kiss. His eyes were still closed as I forced myself to get out of the car.

WHAT A FREAKY NIGHT.

Walking into my room, I half-expected some monumental change, proof that life as I knew it wasn't the same. Instead, everything was just how I'd left it. My shoe rack still hung over the door, the bed was messy but made, and clothes were scattered haphazardly all over the floor. I peeled off the muddy and torn gypsy costume, tossing it on the floor with the others.

Moonlight streamed through my curtains, and I went to the window, cracking it to let in the night air. I grabbed a tank and cotton shorts from a pile on the floor and slipped them on before throwing myself on top my cluttered bed. Buried under the covers, the evening's events played through my brain like a film. The weight of everything came crashing down like a meteor. Before I could stop, unexplainable tears were streaming down my cheeks. A patter of raindrops pelted the windowpanes in a sad harmony.

Gavin had saved my life, and the price for it was I knew he was a witch. The innocence of the unknown was long gone. I would have to deal with wonders of the world that I was far from ready to handle. Then there was the fact Sophie was a witch. We had gotten so close. She was like the sister I didn't have and a good friend. I didn't have many of those, and now two of them were witches. Way to balance the scales.

And where in all of this did I fit?

The gentle rainfall mixed with my salty tears and uncontrollable emotions, eventually lulling me to sleep.

Lukas's distant voice penetrated my slumber. He was calling my name, calling me to him. Sometimes it would fade out, nothing but a hush. Then it would grow, beckoning me. It was as if his voice was playing tug of war, pulling me from one side to the other.

He caught me in his arms as I tumbled into the dream. I didn't have to look up to know it was Lukas. He was as familiar to me here as Gavin was in the real world. Or what I thought was the real world. I wasn't sure of anything anymore.

Lukas held me at arm's length, studying my face. After everything, it was good to be held. Being in his arms, even briefly, was like being encompassed in the sun's solar rays. I had to fight back the tears that threatened to consume me again. The emotional outlet left me drained and exhausted. Even here.

"Okay, what's going on?" he asked at the sight of my puffy eyes.

I don't know why it never occurred to me to make myself look hot in these dreams and not like I cried myself to bed with ugly tears. It was absurd that Lukas looked like a golden angel, and I looked like a train wreck.

"You have no idea," I muttered.

"I would if you tell me what has you so upset," he encouraged.

"Where do I start? How about this? I was almost killed tonight by a tree that came out of nowhere, only to be saved by that new guy you are so fond of," I began to ramble out of control, pacing in circles. "And then of course he can't be like any other guy. No. He's a witch—"

"The new guy is a witch?" he interrupted, scowling.

"Yeah, that's what I just said." I was waving an agitated arm in the air.

He ran a hand through his sandy hair. "Unbelievable," he muttered.

"I know, right." *Yes*, someone to share my disbelief.

"Brianna, listen to me. You must be careful. Witches are unpredictable and treacherous," he warned.

He was telling me to be careful? Lukas was a figment of my imagination. And here I thought I had an ally in my astonishment of witches roaming the world. Guess not.

"He could be dangerous," he insisted, when I didn't respond and just stood there, glaring at him.

What did he know of danger?

I couldn't help it. I snorted, which was definitely a mistake. Gavin had done nothing but protect me from trouble. I doubted it would have made a difference to Lukas. Narrowing his eyes at me, he knew I wasn't taking him seriously. The annoyance rippled through him and sent a wave of caution down my spine. He had decided to hate Gavin from the get-go. Nothing I could say would change that. His opinion was set in stone. It was written in his stance. However, the need to defend Gavin was quick and on the tip of my tongue.

I stopped myself, before I said something I would regret. I shouldn't have brought it up. *What had I been thinking?* That Lukas was a friend, and I could confide in him. I couldn't trust anything anymore.

"Brianna, I am serious," he said, his jaw clenched. The veins in his neck had started to pulse in annoyance. I've never seen Lukas get upset. Prior to today, I wasn't even sure he had a temper. I guess he did, which made him seem more real than he was. The darkening of his green eyes happened so fast I was taken aback.

"I know you are. I'm sorry. It's just that I can't see Gavin hurting anyone," I said defensively.

"Look, there is a lot you don't know." His voice was stern with an underlying of impatience.

And apparently he did. Now that I thought about it, he wasn't the least bit surprised when I told him Gavin was a witch. "What do you know about witches...other than they are dangerous?"

He sighed and sat down on the floor of sand. , I looked around. We were on a small island surrounded by nothing but the midnight waters, exotic flowers, and palms. The moon's reflection glowed over the rippling waves. His voice interrupted my inspection of the island.

"More than you know. They aren't all dangerous. There are good and evil, just like in the human race. Not all witches use their gift with respect and understanding. Many abuse the privileges they were blessed with, or get caught up in the power."

Okay, that all made sense. Good and evil always existed. I kind of expected that. What I didn't expect was for Lukas to know so much about the inner workings of witchcraft.

He must have seen the emotions flickering in my eyes. "Brianna, I'm not trying to hurt you, just the opposite. I'm trying to look out for you," he argued.

I sunk into the sand next to him. "I don't know about anything anymore. I feel as if I've lost my grip on reality," I admitted, sifting grains of sand through my fingers.

"You haven't." He bumped his shoulder lightly with mine. "This is just beginning."

That's what I was afraid of.

CHAPTER 18

I sat behind the counter at *Mystic's*. My aunt was changing the window display for the next season, while I organized a list of stock that threatened to make me cross-eyed. I took a break, sipping on some sweet tea. My aunt had her sleeves rolled up as she worked, draping bronze fabric over the sill. Kicking back in my stool, she caught me watching her and grinned.

"How was Morris Landing last night? Did you guys have a good time?" she asked, popping a pin into her mouth.

"It was definitely terrifying," I mumbled, thinking about my near death experience and eliminating that little tidbit. The last thing I needed was her worrying about me every time I left the house.

"I don't know how you guys find that trail fun. It still gives me the heebie-jeebies, and I haven't been there in years."

She had me there. That was going to be the last time I went to Morris Landing voluntarily.

"Though with Gavin there, I doubt you had much to be frightened of," she commented, smiling at me mischievously.

"You have no idea," I muttered under my breath, her insinuation hitting so close to home.

"Now that I'm thinking about it, I haven't seen Tori or Austin in here for a while. How are they?" she asked.

Tori and Austin often popped into the store when I worked to keep me company...and bug the hell out of me. What were friends for? The guilt that we were drifting apart somehow made me sick and for my aunt to notice, made it worse. "Umm, they're good. You are never going to guess what the two of them dressed up as last night." My aunt was very fond of them both and found them humorously entertaining.

"I can only imagine," she said over her shoulder as she started to stack some items on the display.

My aunt wasn't the biggest fan of musicals, but I was, so she suffered through them more times than I could count. "Brad and Janet," I told her and aimlessly played with the straw in my sweet tea.

She was shaking her head, smirking. "I should have known it was going to be from *Rocky Horror Picture Show*. The three of you watched it every Halloween."

True, we had, except this one. Again with the guilt.

I picked back up my inventory list and started reconciling the items, trying to not think about what a horrible friend I was.

❧

THE BELL never rang above the door, but it didn't matter. Where he was concerned, I had an internal alarm. It alerted the moment he opened the door, his reckless scent fanning my senses and making me slightly dizzy. He wore jeans and a white tee that hugged his chest.

"Did you use magic?" I whispered when he reached me.

He smirked. All the answer I needed.

"Are you trying to sneak up on me? Aren't you afraid someone will see you?"

"Most people are too preoccupied to notice something so small," he replied, excitement brewing in his face. He was up to something.

I guess that meant I didn't count as *most people*. "Oh, I forgot. I have your hoodie. If I'd known you were coming, I would have brought it in."

"Keep it," he replied, flash me a brilliant smile. "I brought you something."

I narrowed my gaze.

"Hold out your hand," he prompted.

I laid my hand palm open on the glass counter and looked into his smiling eyes.

"Now close your eyes."

I glared.

"Close them," he laughed.

I let my lashes flutter down over my eyes and waited for whatever surprise he had in store. A cool, small object touched my skin, followed by the weight of something more. I didn't need to open my eyes to see what it was. Just like I knew he had stepped into the shop, I knew he had found my necklace.

My fingers closed around the stones, the gentle hum reassuring. "You found it," I said, grinning, and opened my eyes only to be swallowed by pools of shimmering sapphire.

"I told you I would."

"And I told you not to..." I scolded. "Thank you. I'm really glad you did."

He took the necklace from my grasp. "Turn around."

This was one time I wouldn't argue. Spinning around, I lifted the hair off the back of my neck. He unclasped the necklace and settled it around my throat. His fingers grazed the sides, spearing alertness in every tingling nerve. I shuddered involuntarily and silently mourned the loss of contact. Turning back around, I touched the stones.

"They'll help you sleep," he said, reminding me of the peculiar lady from the shop.

It just occurred to me that she could have very well been a witch. I made a mental note to ask Sophie next time I saw her. "Do they really have properties like that?" I asked curious. "The lady who sold this to me said the same thing," I admitted.

He came around the counter, pulled up a stool close to me, and sat down. The fireflies started buzzing. "They do. Crystals and stones each have their own function. Some work stronger than others, depending on how well they are received. These two together, the moonstone and amethyst..." he paused and fingered the stones at my neck, causing an all-new set of thrills to swirl in my belly, "...work harmoniously together, especially for you. If I had to pick, these are the ones I would have chosen for you." He let the cool silver chain fall back on my throat.

My knee bumped his casually. "What about you? What are your stones?" I was utterly caught in the tone of his voice and his words. He might as well have spellbound me; I was so enamored by him.

Gavin reached behind him and pulled two crystals from his pocket. "Mine are onyx and obsidian. Protection against black magic," he stated, losing a little of the glint in his eyes.

"Is there a lot of that? Black magic?" My thoughts turned to my dream last night. The warning.

"More than I want to admit. I don't want to scare you, Bri. Magic can be wonderful and exhilarating, but with everything there is a price. It isn't meant to be misused. And there are plenty of people out there willing to do that. Just as there is light in this world, there is dark."

This conversation was beginning to eerily mirror my dream.

"Have you ever done dark magic?" I hesitantly asked, afraid what the answer might be. Lukas had to be wrong. Gavin wouldn't hurt me.

His eyes roamed to the tile floor in the shop, and for a second, I held my breath with the possibility I might be wrong. "No, I've never given myself over to darkness...but I know some who have." His expression was filled with pain and hurt as he spoke. "And lost them because of it."

"I'm so sorry Gavin." I enclosed his hand with mine, offering him comfort.

He stared down at our joined hands, toying with a ring I wore on my right finger, twirling the knotted silver band. "I like hearing you say my name," he softly spoke.

Gravitating toward him, I wanted to close the distance between us. It didn't matter that I was working or that anyone could come strolling through the door. The only thing that mattered was him. I was absurdly disappointed when he pulled back, and it showed all over my face. I had to suppress the groan that formed at my lips. I should have been thankful that one of us was thinking clearly. Instead, I pouted.

Why couldn't he lose his control, his focus, like me? Why was I the only one suffering?

Just as I was about to voice something stupid, my aunt came through the back door. "Hi Gavin, I didn't hear you come in." She smiled at him.

"Funny neither did I," I muttered.

"I should probably let you get back to work," he said as he got up from his seat. "It was nice seeing you again, Clara." My aunt had insisted that he call her by her first name. He paused as he got around the glass counter and looked back at me. "You want to hang out after work tonight?"

He caught me off guard, but I jumped at the chance to be with him. "Sure, pick me at my house?" I wanted to go home and freshen up.

Watching him walk out the door, I sighed.

CHAPTER 19

I raced home after work to quickly jump in the shower. With less than an hour before he showed up at my door, I had driven like a madwoman, beating my aunt home.

Scrubbing my favorite shampoo into my hair, I rinsed, conditioned, and then made a last-minute decision to shave my legs. The nights were still warm, and since I didn't know what we were doing, I was going to be prepared for any scenario.

I slathered on some lotion and padded to my closet to find something to wear. His hoodie lay on the back of the chair, bringing a smile to my lips. The scent of him lingered on the material.

On a sigh of excitement, I turned to my closet. Five minutes went by and I was still staring. There was only one way to solve this wardrobe dilemma. I closed my eyes and grabbed. It was a thigh-length simple white dress, somewhere between dressy and casual. Perfect.

I plopped in front of my vanity to fuss with my hair. Adding a quick layer of mascara, eyeliner, and lip gloss, I finished just as the roar of his engine sounded outside my opened window. The fireflies began to dance in my belly. A quick mist my favorite perfume and I was running down the stairs. It was a wonder I didn't break my neck.

The doorbell rang when I was halfway down the stairs. My aunt's voice slowed my haste as I rounded the corner. He was standing in the entryway with her, looking dark and dashing. I found it hard to believe that out of all the girls at school, he wanted to go out with me.

"You ready?" he asked me, his eyes finding mine.

I nodded, sweaty palms gripping the banister. "Where are we going?" I asked as we walked to his car.

Gavin slipped behind the steering wheel and started the car. He put the car in reverse and punched the gas, the engine thundering into the dark. "You'll see," he responded with a smirk.

I sat back in my seat, wondering what Gavin had up his sleeve.

The lights of Wilmington lit the night as we approached the River-walk. A tint of blood orange hit the coastline, spreading shadows over the quaint shops. Trees twinkled with decorated strands of lights along the plaza. This little coastal place was a slice of history, with its canopied vendors, planked walkways, and charming historical buildings.

"I love the Riverwalk. How did you hear about this place?" I asked.

"Your aunt told me how much you like coming here."

"It's so pretty at night." I couldn't help but be flattered by his thoughtfulness.

"Are you hungry?"

"Sure. There is a really great place right on the water," I volunteered. "They have the best chicken scampi."

"Sounds perfect."

The restaurant faced the ocean, back-dropped by the lights of downtown Wilmington. At this time of night, the restaurant was filled with plenty of night-goers. We only had to wait a few minutes to be seated at a table, and the view from our booth overlooked oceanic boardwalk. The restaurant was a cozy, with a warm atmosphere filled with laughter and decadent scents.

The waiter took our drink orders, and Gavin played with his fork. "So I've been meaning to ask you...we haven't had a chance to talk. Are you okay with me being a witch? I haven't scared you off, have I?"

I smiled. It wasn't possible for him to scare off the insane feelings I had toward him. "No. If anything, I think I'm more intrigued by you."

"Good." He returned my smile.

The waiter came back with our drinks, and we gave him our dinner orders, two plates of chicken scampi. My mouth watered in anticipation. The food here was famous.

I took a sip through the straw of my coke. "Since you brought up the topic, I have a few questions."

"Of course, you do. Shoot."

"Are there any other witches in Holly Ridge?"

"Not an overwhelming number. Only one or two that I have seen." He appeared a little uncomfortable, and it made me wonder if maybe I knew them.

"Is there anyone at our school who is a, you know, witch?" It still felt funny to form the word.

He shrugged, divulging nothing.

"Oh, my God. There's a witch at our school. Other than you and Sophie, I mean." He had my attention now. I jutted my straw in and out of my glass as I wracked through my brain, trying to figure out who it could be. My bet was on Rianne. "No hints?" I implored Gavin with a look, but he wasn't going to give away any details.

So frustrating. There was nothing worse than someone teasing you with a secret, and then not sharing the details.

I sighed and slumped back the booth. Our food arrived, and the smell of garlic and pasta was enough to derail my mind and remind my stomach how hungry I was.

Dinner was phenomenal, and no matter what I promised, begged, or threatened, Gavin never did reveal the name of the other witch at school.

We stepped outside into the glittering balmy night. "Do you want to go down the Riverwalk?" Gavin asked.

I slipped my arm through his. "I would love to."

A gentle evening breeze teased the ends of my dress as we strolled along the boardwalk. I imagined this was what a perfect date felt like. For all his dark and brooding qualities, deep down there was an extremely great guy, nothing about him that didn't make me feel good and safe. I was content to walk by his side all night, with the sound of the ocean rising and falling on the shore. I was the luckiest girl in the universe. The other girls at school could keep their homecoming and proms. I had a witch.

We walked to the end of the dock, and I leaned against the railing, inhaling the crisp ocean mist. I gazed out into the endless waters, watching the moon's reflection glistened in the quiet surf. Gavin's elbow brushed up against mine as he came to stand beside me.

"It's so peaceful. I can't imagine not living near the ocean." I'd grown up with it practically in my backyard. It would be like not having a park or a playground.

We sat there enjoying the music of the splashing waves, and the company of each other. Lost in the moment, I felt the air shift with a tingling of magic. I looked at Gavin, unsure how I knew he was using his gift. Something awoke within me and wondered what he was up to.

He stared into my violet eyes. "Your name is written in the stars," he said, pointing to the sky over the tranquil waters.

I tilted my head up, expecting a cheesy gesture. The air caught in my lungs. Millions of twilight stars dotted the sky, spelling out my name. It was an impressive sight that struck a chord in my romantic heart.

"Incredible." There was no downplaying the awe in my voice.

With a wave of his hand, the stars scattered, reshaping into a perfect single-stemmed rose.

Mesmerized, I met his eyes. "I guess being a witch has its high points. That was...magical." I didn't have any other words to describe it.

"I wanted to show you the fun part of being a witch. We're not finished yet."

The sky before us broke out into a spectacular firework display worthy of Fourth of July. Colors exploded against the black night, and his hand closed around mine as we watched the booming spectacle.

"What is everyone going to think?"

He shrugged. "That the city put on an impromptu show."

Hanging out with a witch was really raising the bar on my expectations for an evening out.

When the fireworks came to an end, we began the walk back to his car, hand in hand. Most of the shops were closed, and only a few bars remained open. We took a shortcut down an alley just adjacent from where his car was parked. There was a stupid grin plastered on my face. Never in my wildest expectations had I imagined a night like this. I could ride on the emotional high for months.

Lost in blissful happiness, I was confused when Gavin stiffened and suddenly stopped. Before I could ask what had caused his abrupt alarm, I heard the clanking of multiple footsteps, followed by sporadic laughter. Not a pleasing, happy laughter either. It made my skin crawl and my stomach lurch in fear. I snuck a quick glance over my shoulders, and my heart raced. Three shadowy figures were trailing us.

"Keep walking," Gavin whispered in my ear, drawing me closer to him.

Their footsteps echoed from one wall of the alley to the other. I squeezed Gavin's hand, repressing the urge to run, and kept moving forward.

The creepers were catching up, and I started to pant from fear and trying to keep up with Gavin's long strides.

"Hey waittt upp," one of the guys called out from behind us, slurring his words. "We only wantsss tooo talk."

They had obviously been drinking, explaining their inability to form coherent words.

"Stay behind me," Gavin ordered.

My hand grasped his forearm, and his muscles bunched under my fingers. "Gavin don't," I pleaded when I realized his intent. I got that he was a witch, but three-on-one were not good odds. Witch or not, I didn't want him getting hurt.

"Bri. I am serious." His tone was one I'd never heard before. Hard. Unyielding. "Stay out of the way. You got that?" He looked quickly over at me to make sure I got his point. His eyes were pools of blazing blue fire. They radiated with danger and something darker.

It was the something more that frightened me.

I gulped and nodded.

"Hmm, what do we have here?" The one with light hair spoke up as they stopped in front of us. "Isn't she something?"

I shivered.

Gavin had a different reaction. He flicked his hand and big mouth was thrown up against the brick wall by what appeared to be thin air. The impact knocked him unconscious, and his body crumbled to the concrete ground. I flinched at the sound.

"What the hell?" One of the other two swore, staring, confused by his unmoving buddy. A moment later, the two of them charged at Gavin.

A scream ripped from my throat, the sound bouncing off the narrow brick alley. Before either of them got the chance to throw a punch, they were withering on the floor, gasping for air. Their hands flew to their necks, eyes bulging, and fear of imminent death in their eyes. Gavin stood over them, the space surrounding him crackling with power.

I didn't know what to do, but if I didn't do something, he was going to kill them both. I couldn't let their blood be on his hands. Not even to save me.

CHAPTER 20

"Gavin," I said. He didn't budge, so I took a step closer, repeating his name. The two guys were gurgling as the last few breaths began to leave their body. I put my hand on Gavin's arm and yelled. "Gavin, stop!" The second I touched him, I was jolted with a nippy shock. My hand jerked away.

And just like that, he dropped the spell, his glossy eyes burning in an eerie glow. It was as if he didn't see *me*.

"Gavin, it's okay."

Ever so slowly, his eyes cleared, focusing on my face. A sideways glanced revealed all three of the guys were lifeless, but I didn't think any of them were dead.

"We need to go," Gavin said, some of the coldness leaving his tone. He put his hand under my elbow, guiding me toward his car

There was no protest from me, and I obediently got into the passenger seat and buckled my seatbelt. This was going to be a bumpy ride, based on his current mood.

He tore out of the parking lot, peeling his tires, and the car fish-tailed, before zooming down the street. It wasn't until we were safely speeding down the road that the effects of what had happened hit me like a bulldozer.

I told myself I wasn't going to cry, not now, and forced my lip to remain stiff. When I was alone I would have myself a nice ugly cry, but right now, I was going to hold it together.

He had both hands gripping the steering wheel, his knuckles white from the pressure. "Are you okay?"

I ran an unsteady hand through my hair. "I'm fine."

"I'm sorry I lost control. I..." He paused and took a deep breath. "I couldn't let them hurt you."

"It's okay." His expression left me under the impression that he didn't believe me. "Really, I'm okay. I promise." And it was true. I was going to survive another day, and I was pretty sure those guys weren't dead.

He pulled up to my house, and I was never so happy to be home. The perfect date had ended as the date from hell. There was an entire side to Gavin I had never witnessed before, his darker side. It should have frightened me. It should have sent me packing. It should have concerned me. The only thing it did do was soften my heart.

"Come over tomorrow? I know Sophie would love to see you," he added. He was worried I was going to fall apart.

"Um, sure." I just barely hesitated, but it was enough for him to notice. Could he blame me? I'd gotten a glimpse of darkness that lived inside of him. Lukas might have been right after all. Gavin may be capable of evil things when pushed too far.

Yet, I thought the same could be said for me, thinking of my own anger issues.

None of it stopped my heart from wanting him.

"I DIDN'T THINK you were ever going to get here," Sophie said the moment I went to rang the door. My hand was still in the air when she ripped the door open. Apparently, her patience level was thin, and she was really excited to see me.

Sophie was like the gorgeous sister I never had and always wanted. "Sorry, Gavin never told me when. He just said to come anytime."

She rolled her eyes. "He's such an idiot."

"Is he here?" I asked, worried about him and slightly disappointed he didn't answer the door.

She started down the hall, with me at her heels. "I think he's upstairs, brooding or something. He's been in a mood all day, but he knows you're here. It's a witch thing."

"Oh. Okay." I followed her into the kitchen, her floral skirt swishing as we walked. The Mason's kitchen would make Martha Stewart sigh. I wasn't that much of cook, but I found this kitchen intimidating. There were more appliances and gadgets than I knew what to do with. I'd probably end up losing a finger in the process.

The kitchen was decorated in beiges, golds, and dark blues. Impressive paintings hung on display around the room, and I assumed they were all made by Lily.

Speaking Mrs. Mason, she was standing behind the island, nibbling on a feast of snacks. A spread of salsa, guacamole, and some kind of cream cheese dip, along with a few others I couldn't identify. It looked like the *Food Network* in here. I hoped she hadn't done this all for me, but my stomach thanked her.

"Hi, Brianna." Lily smiled warmly at me. I couldn't help but grin back. "Have something to eat," she offered. "We've got plenty."

I took a seat next to Sophie and wasted no time digging in. "Thanks."

"Can I get you something to drink? Sophie?" she asked us. Setting two cans of soda in front of us, she mixed a bowl filled with what looked like spinach dip. "So, Gavin mentioned that he told you about our abilities," Lily said as I was putting a pretzel in my mouth.

Crap. I'd completely forgotten. With everything that happened last night, it had completely slipped my mind. This was the first time I'd seen his family since he told me their secret. They were witches. Thank God it hadn't occurred to me earlier, or I would have stressed myself out like crazy.

I swallowed the chip. "Umm, he did," I replied, feeling a little uncomfortable. I didn't want them to think I'd tell anyone.

"I just want to make sure that you are okay, and to let you know that if you have any questions, any questions at all, you can ask me.

Any of us," Lily offered in a soothing motherly tone. "I can't imagine what you are thinking. It has to be an enormous shock."

It had been, but I'd gotten over it, and now I was intrigued. "I'm fascinated."

"I'm surprised he told you," Sophie said. She was swinging her feet under the bar chair. "Don't get me wrong, I am glad he did. I wasn't sure how much longer I could keep it from you. I don't keep secrets very well from my friends," she confessed.

"Honey, you can't keep a secret at all. Remember that, Brianna. Sophie is the last person you tell if you want a surprise to be a surprise," Lily said with a joking twinkle.

Sophie rolled her eyes.

How did I tell Gavin's mom that her son exposed himself to save my life? Not once, but twice? I didn't think there was any easy way to put it. "He exposed himself to save my life," I warily revealed, waiting for some kind of astonished reaction.

"Ahh, my brother the hero." Sophie bit into a tortilla chip.

Something about Halloween night popped into my head. Sophie had known Gavin was going to tell me, I remember seeing the odd exchange. It hadn't made sense then, but now... "How did you know he was going to tell me?"

She shrugged. "Magic. Part of my ability is seeing the future. I always knew he was going to tell you, but the timing was different. The future is always changing. I don't what changes, only certain outcomes. I also knew you and I were going to become fast friends."

Okay, that was a more than a little weird. "You can see the future?" I asked, completely dumbstruck by the idea.

"Sort of. It isn't black and white. There is a lot of gray."

Nothing ever was.

"I see images, places or people. They are never clear or precise. The future is always evolving based on decisions and circumstances. Nothing is set in stone, which makes it so hard to decipher. I only get glimpses," she explained.

All right, that sounded far more complex than I realized magic could be. There was so much I didn't know or understand. I was beginning to feel afraid I wouldn't be able to fit in or belong in this world. If I couldn't exist here, what hope would I have with him?

Sophie shook her head. "Stop worrying. You will always be a part of this world, and magic will be a part of your future."

I stared at her. She had read my mind or gotten inside my head. I remember what Gavin had said about his sister, the night we had coffee. I wasn't sure I liked her in my thoughts. The more I thought, the less safe my random thoughts felt. "Did you just read my mind?" I accused.

"No, I can't read your mind, but I can see your aura, and you project your feelings very loudly. Auras are my specialty." You could see the passion on her face. She truly enjoyed her powers.

I gave her a, *what-are-you-talking-about* look.

"Very loudly," Lily grinned, echoing Sophie's words.

Just great. Even in magic standards I was odd.

Sophie reached in the guacamole dip bowl. "Everyone has an aura that is dependent upon moods and feelings. Some people are more difficult to read than others. This is my realm of magic. Auras. More so than the little glimpses of the future I sometimes get. I think my ability to see the future opens the channel to tap into people's auras. The closer I am to the person, the easier they are to read. Each emotion is identified by a color. Sometimes colors can blend if there are conflicting or multiple feelings. Your emotions are such a part of you, that you not only show them, you project them. Loudly."

Great. I needed to work on that somehow.

A movement from the doorway caught my eye and in sauntered Gavin. "Hey Bri," he said and sat down on the other side of me, carefully eyeing me. He plucked a chip from one of the bowls and popped it in his mouth. His lip ring moved with the movements of his chewing, and I found it extremely sexy.

"Hey," I answered, smiling. I toyed with the pop tab on my can, anything to distract myself. I wanted him to know I was okay, and he didn't have to tiptoe around my emotions.

"Right now your aura just went through the roof," Sophie giggled.

I wanted to bury my head in mortification, and I seriously hoped she was the only one in the family with that particular ability, or I was in big trouble. They were all grinning at my obvious discomfort.

"Sophie giving you a lesson in auras?" he asked, as he reached in for more chips.

"I'm getting a crash course. What about you, can you see auras?" I asked, praying he would say no.

"Nope, unfortunately that's never been one of my talents. Just Sophie."

Well thank God for small wonders. I turned to Lily, who was now cutting up pieces of bread. She was the example of what I envisioned a stay-at-home mom to be. "What is your gift?" I asked, caught up in the phenomenon of it.

"I'm so glad you asked. I am healer of sorts. I dabble in herbs, potions, and remedies." She was proud of what she could do. I could hear it in her tone, honest respect for such a powerful gift.

"And Jared and John?"

Gavin laughed. "Jared will have to show you. And my dad and I share the same defensive energy."

"Where's Jared?" I wondered aloud, beyond curious about the eldest Mason.

"He's at class," Gavin informed me, loving that he was instigating my impatience.

"You're going to make me wait, aren't you? That's cruel."

He chuckled. "It's way more fun to see in person. Trust me."

Fun for whom? If I had magic right then, I would have turned him into a toad. It was hopeless; I knew a losing battle when I saw one.

We sat around a little longer, snacking, and me listening to their stories about magic. All of which sounded mystical and electrifying. I was convinced that being a witch was utterly kickass.

As the day slipped away, I left before it got too late. Tonight I promised my aunt I'd cook dinner, and I was meeting up with Tori and Austin tomorrow to hang out. My social life was jam-packed, a truly unusual thing.

He walked me out to my car, and again asked about my wellbeing. "You sure you're okay?" There was guilt tracing his words.

In my eyes, he had nothing to feel guilty for. I took his hand. "I'm fine. You're always saving me. One of these days you're going to get tired of coming to my rescue."

He smirked, looking a little more like the confident Gavin I knew. "I'm not so sure about that."

I grinned back at him. I didn't want any awkwardness or guilt lying between us.

"Are you busy tomorrow?" he asked.

I silently groaned and wished more than anything that I wasn't busy. Relishing in the few moments we had alone together, I stalled. "Sorry, it's movie night with Tori and Austin."

His face fell slightly, but I was sure it was all in my imagination. He reached around me to open my door, brushing my body in the process. My belly jumped on contact, and I don't know what came over me. Maybe it was the near-death experiences. Maybe it was because he never let me down, and no matter what might lurk inside of him, he made me feel incredible, like no one else ever had.

I leaned into him before he had a chance to pull away and put my hand on his waist, steadying myself. He smelled like the woods at night, and I wanted time to cease. I didn't know if it was him or me who made the move, but if I had to guess, it was me.

His lips melted to mine in a searing kiss that whisked my head to the clouds. Both his hands went on either side of the car, boxing me in. His hands never touched me, but I swore they were everywhere.

Our lips rushed over each other, caught in a pleasure like I felt never before. The silver hoop from his lip danced with my tongue, and I loved the coolness against the heat in my mouth. Toying with his mouth, I tempted him to take the plunge.

His lips broke from mine to trail down my throat and over the pulse that hammered there. "You taste like strawberries," he murmured against my neck, causing a shudder to rack through my body. Our mouths met again. My nails dug into his silky hair, his name tumbling from my lips, and with the moonlight overhead, I gave into him. Where Gavin was concerned, I had no control.

We were so wrapped up in each other that at first neither of us noticed the beam of headlights. They came out of nowhere, shooting across his driveway and putting a spotlight directly on us. Gavin and I sprang from each other's arms. Shaken, Gavin ran a hand through his messy hair and jammed both hands in his pockets. I sunk back against the car, hugging my arms over my chest.

Jared walked up, dimples on display. "That was hot," he said as he passed us on his way into the house.

The moment was broken, even while my insides were still humming.

"See you Monday," Gavin said huskily as I got into the car.

I gave a little wave and he shut the door.

My heart pounded the whole way home, and it wasn't until I got in the driveway that I realized I'd missed my chance to ask Jared what his ability was. My mind had been too muddled with the addicting taste of Gavin.

CHAPTER 21

Movie night with my best friends was never without its drama. I really wanted to get our friendship back on track. It was never my plan to suddenly get boy crazy. We hardly did any of the things we used to, and it was eating at me. So I was on my way to Tori's, where she and Austin were no doubt picking some horrid slasher movie. We'd been doing this exact thing since we were in grade school.

Tori had a theatre room on the first floor of her big house. It was seriously large. Her Tudor-style brick home was on the other side of Holly Ridge, and the driveway was like a mile long, equipped with a gated entrance. I let myself in through the double front doors. The house echoed as my shoes clattered over the tile. Tori's stepmother was probably at some outrageously priced spa, and her dad lived at work.

I could hear bickering coming from down the vast hall, and I smiled. Just like old times, arguing over which movie. I kicked off my shoes and headed down the hallway. The smells hit me the closer I got. Popcorn. Butter. Brownies. They were our signature snacks, and we were creatures of habit. She had one of those old-fashioned popcorn makers; I could hear the *pop-pop-pop* noise as I pushed open the door.

The two of them were standing in front of the towering shelf that housed movies of every genre lining the back wall. "What did I miss?" I said, drawing their gazes toward the doorway. Tori had lit the pillar candles around the room. Their sweet aroma mixed with the savory smell of buttery popcorn.

"Good, you're just in time," Tori replied, the bangs of her light brown hair hanging over her chocolate eyes.

"So, what are we watching?" I asked, dropping into one of the huge leather recliners.

"It's a toss-up between the new *Saw* or *Final Destination*. Tori's being a diva," Austin answered, giving Tori the side eye, hand on his hip.

They were always on each other. They enjoyed squabbling, like an old married couple.

"I am seriously not the only diva in this room," Tori retorted, pushing the hair from her face.

"How about I pick the movie this time?" I suggested, thinking I could end this before it got out of hand.

"No," they unanimously bellowed.

"*Final Destination* is fine," Tori conceded, pulling out the case.

Predictable. If there was one thing Tori and Austin could agree on, it was that my taste in films sucked. Whatever. As long as we got to hang out, that was all I cared about.

Tori popped in the movie as Austin and I grabbed the snacks and settled in our preferred seats. When the movie began to play, Tori hit the lights.

Austin reclined his seat beside me, and handed me a bowl of popcorn with a brownie on top. I settled in, grabbing a handful of popcorn as the credits rolled.

"You better not jump in my lap," Austin warned. It was a known fact that I tended to flinch during scary films.

"Funny, just remember *you* sat next to me. It's not my fault if you lose an arm." I couldn't help it, scary movies made me skittish.

"Sometimes you're more fun than the movie," he teased, but I'm sure there was truth to it.

I threw a piece of popcorn at his head and then shoved a handful in my mouth.

"You're going to regret that later," he threatened. It was only a matter of time before he got me back. "Where's dark and sexy tonight? You should have brought him along. He could have been dessert." Austin practically drooled at the prospect, and I was right there with him. I hated to admit it, but I missed him. A ton.

I shrugged. "I don't know. I didn't think about it." Not completely true. I always thought of him.

"Does he taste as good as he looks?" Austin purred.

"Better," I assured, both of us grinning wickedly. I refocused my attention back into the movie, which was difficult now that I'd pictured Gavin.

Halfway through the film, I had managed to only attack Austin once, and his arm survived. But he started to lean out of my reach. It was around then that I began to get a chill. Not the kind where I was cold, but the creeping, hair-raising kind. I tried to convince myself that it was just the movie, but my body wouldn't listen. My concentration was blown, and I couldn't shake the ghostly feeling that someone was watching me, like those moving eyes in a painting. The images on the projection screen long forgotten, I scanned the candle-lit room, trying to find the source of my discomfort. I made a mental note to ask Gavin about ghosts. In the meantime, I was going to pretend this paranormal activity was a hoax.

"Austin, knock it off," I whispered, even though I knew he wasn't the responsible party.

"What?" he asked, confusion flickering in his eyes.

"Nothing," I grumbled, incapable of shaking the negative vibes that had started to crawled over my skin like centipedes. It was like being trapped on my own horror set. Even scarier, no one else knew it. Real evil existed, and it made me more on edge.

The vibe permeated the air and slithered along the floor, insinuating itself between the recliners. There wasn't anything visible to be seen, but I could picture it all the same. My eyes ran over the row of recliners behind us, and I tucked my feet underneath me. No way was that creepy thing tugging on my toes.

"What are you staring at?" Austin whispered, eyeballing me in the dark.

He rattled me out of my trance. I had to pull my eyes from the floor. "Nothing," I mumbled, not wanting him to think I was off my rocker, a valid consideration.

"Are you sure? No offense, but you look pale and your eyes are weird." He was watching me oddly.

Tori leaned out over her chair. "What is going on?"

A sweeping wind came barreling across the room. I studied both of their faces, waiting for the astonished look. It never came. Conclusion: only I could sense the voodoo that was happening in this room. The breeze had given me goose bumps, and the instinct to run. It prickled at the back of my neck, making the room cold. Moments later the room was engulfed in darkness, the flames from the candles extinguishing.

That got their attention.

Tori gasped.

"What the hell," Austin complained.

"That was bizarre," Tori added, pausing the movie.

An understatement and she took the words from my mouth. Movie night was over for me. I needed to get out of here before I did something completely irrational and stupid, like tell Tori that her house was haunted by ghosts, or that we were being hunted by some supernatural being. My mind could come up with about ten other crazy concoctions, none good.

Instinct told me it was time for me to leave. Never mess with instinct. I sat up. "I'm sorry, guys, but need to go home. I'm not feeling well." My excuse wasn't totally bogus, if you factored in my mental health.

"You need to get home before your ass faints on us," Austin proclaimed. "You look like you've seen a ghost."

A hysteric laugh escaped my lips.

"Are you sure you can drive?" Tori put on her mother hat.

"I'll be fine." I got up to grab my things. "I'll text you when I get home."

As soon as I shut the front door, I raced down her driveway and slammed myself into my car. Quickly locking the doors, I turned the key and shifted in reverse. The need to escape was wild inside me. I needed distance from whatever *that* thing in Tori's house had been. I was convinced it was definitely a *thing*.

The moment my wheels came to stop outside my house, I shoved my free into my purse, digging for my phone.

He answered on the second ring, "Are you okay?" It was as if he could sense my panic. No hello or what's up.

"Are there ghosts?" My voice pitched even as I tried to keep the psychotic from leaking out.

"What are you talking about?"

"I don't know. I mean, I do know. It's just..." And here came the crazy rambling. *Get a hold of yourself.* I took a deep breath and started again. "I was wondering if there are ghosts here...with us?"

He was silent on the other end, not a good sign. "There are some spirits that walk this plane. Where are you? I'm coming to get you," he demanded.

"I'm at home, sitting in my driveway," I told him.

"I'm on my way over." He hung up, never giving me the chance to object. Typical.

The dial tone rang in my ear. I looked at the clock. It was late and by the look of the house, my aunt was likely asleep. I never snuck a boy into my house before, but there was a first time for everything. "Great," I mumbled, gripping the steering wheel.

Killing the lights, I grabbed my phone and purse from the passenger seat, and made a mad dash across the yard.

Ugh. My house key. I should have had it ready, instead of sitting somewhere at the bottom of my bag with loose Tic Tacs and gum wrappers. I rummaged for my house key, turning toward the house and bumped into something solid.

"Shit!" I yelped, looking up into to Gavin's shadowy face. "You scared the hell out of me." My hand flew to my chest as my heart stuttered.

He put a finger to his mouth and hushed me. "You're going to wake up the whole block."

"Me," I said. Glancing at the rear of my car where a little white Jetta parked behind it. "That's not your car."

He raised the eyebrow with the silver bar. "I know. I borrowed my mom's. My car would wake the dead, and I figured that wasn't such a good idea this late."

He was killing me here. I ran a hand through my hair and leaned back against the door. "How did you get here so fast?" He didn't live far, but it had been a minute since we got off the phone.

"Have you seen me drive? Though the Jetta doesn't have the greatest pick-up."

I rolled my eyes. "Whatever. Let's get inside." I was still freaked out, but I was feeling better with Gavin here.

Cracking the front door, I peered inside, checking to make sure my aunt was indeed sleeping. The coast looked clear. All the lights were turned off except for the one above the kitchen sink. I weaved my fingers with his and slowly walked through the hall and up the stairs to my room.

I closed the door carefully behind us and turned the lock with a tiny click. He'd been in my room before, but never in the middle of the night.

My clothes smelled like popcorn and probably had butter stains smeared on them. "I need to get out to these clothes. I'll be right back," I whispered. "Don't move."

He grinned devilishly at me.

This was going to be a long night.

A small bathroom was connected to my room. Convenient, especially in times like this. I rushed to change into the first thing I found, a tank and shorts, and ran a comb over my hair before I brushed my teeth. For the final touch, I applied a coat of strawberry lip gloss.

He was sitting on my bed when I emerged, looking sinful and a bit impatient. I stood at the door for a moment, feeling nervous, jittery, and energized all at once. His gaze flew to my face as I walked across the room and sat cross-legged on the bed beside to him.

"Tell me what happened?" he asked, keeping his voice low.

The room was dimly lit by an ornate desk lamp. "I don't know. It's probably nothing."

"I can tell you're upset. If it was nothing, you wouldn't have called me," he reasoned.

He was right. All true. I sighed. "I was at Tori's, and we were watching a movie in her theatre room. I started to feel this... presence, I guess. It was as if we weren't alone. The room got cold, and a gust of wind blew through. It's hard to describe." I bite my lip. "I couldn't see anything, but I felt it. Does that make any sense?"

He nodded, his eyes glowing in the lamplight. "Yeah, it makes perfect sense. You're a magnet for trouble."

I grabbed the nearest thing I could find and chucked it at his head. He caught the pillow midair and grinned at me. "So not funny. I thought you would take this seriously."

"I am. Sorry, I couldn't resist. Go on. I swear I'll behave."

I gave him a sideways glance before I continued. "And then, I started thinking about ghosts. Tori had a lit a bunch of candles earlier, and they all went out at the same time. It was so strange." What I didn't say was, how *bad* whatever *it* was had made me feel.

"I leave you for one night and you start hanging out with the wrong crowd." He was making light of the situation to ease my nervous, but I caught the tone of caution under the teasing. "I'm sure it was a spirit. What I don't know is if they were seeking you specifically or something in Tori's house."

My fingers tugged on the bedding. "It felt personal," I grudgingly admitted.

"That's what I'm worried about." There were lines of apprehension lining his forehead.

"I don't understand," I groaned, lying down on the bed.

He followed, lying next to me, our faces no more than a breath away. We both stared up at the ceiling. He swirled his hand in the air. "You should get some sleep. We can worry about it another day."

I watched as sparkling stars shot and danced over the ceiling. Their tails left stardust trailing behind them, scattering above our heads. He knew just how to distract me.

"Don't leave," I said softly. The idea was wild and reckless, but I couldn't let him go. For reasons beyond my control, I needed him. My safety depended on it. My sanity depended on it. My heart depended on it.

He twined our fingers together. "I won't leave you, Bri," he promised, opening up his other arm.

I moved into his embrace, laying my head on his chest, and listened to the even, rapid beat of his heart. His free hand played with the strands of my hair, sending a different kind of shooting stars down each tendril. There was nothing in my world that came close to the experience of being in Gavin's arms. I doubted there ever would be.

CHAPTER 22

I cornered him first thing in the morning at school. "Hey, what happened? You were gone when I got up this morning." I leaned my shoulder up against his car, trying too not sound irritated. But I was. I was looking for a fight when I woke alone, and by God, he wasn't going to disappointment me.

He shut the door to his Charger. "Calm down, Bri." His controlled tone only increased my annoyance. I was anything but calm.

The sky was sunless and gray when I'd left my house, and those dark clouds seem to grow with my anger. Teeth clenched together, a surge of fury rushed me. "Don't tell me to calm down." Each word layered the streaming heat pumping in my veins. It was slipping out of my control again, and there was nothing I could do about it.

People began to take notice of us in the parking lot, but they were the least of my concerns.

"Okay. I won't," he answered to composed for my liking.

"Don't patronize me," I hissed. The sky darkened and clouds rolled in turmoil above.

A small crowd had stopped and glanced our way. "I think we should go somewhere else to finish this," he advised, lowering his voice.

Throwing my arms in the air the, wind started to howl, picking the ends of my hair. "I don't care about them," I barked.

He took a deep breath, trying to figure out how to best handle me. "Look Bri, I had a good reason for leaving. I was looking out for you."

"How was that looking out for me?" I yelled at the same time the sky opened up and crackled with lightning, then exploding with thunder. The oncoming storm fed the anger I was feeling, feeding it with its electrifying currents.

His eyes went skyward, eyeing the violent show above and took a step toward me. "I thought it would be best if I was gone before your aunt found us," he explained.

The mention of my aunt weakened a chip in the cyclone of rage spinning inside me. In the rational part of my mind, he had a valid point, but that still didn't absorb the illogical disappointment, turned insane anger bubbling within me. I was treading on dangerous ground and becoming irrationally dependent on him. One night with him had spoiled the rest of my nights forever. His scent still lingered on my sheets and would taunt me for nights to come, I was sure.

"You said you wouldn't leave," I argued, the root of my hurt.

His arm reached out tentatively for my hand.

Lightning lit crazy patterns in the sky. "Don't touch me!" I snapped, stepping out of his reach. The haze of red behind my eyes had not entirely receded. I was afraid I would hurt him. And hurting him would kill me.

"I'm sorry, Bri," he said, looking sincere.

The last bell for first period rang, and the parking lot was mostly empty except for a few stragglers who were hurriedly trying to seek shelter from the impending storm.

Tears started to burn my eyes, spilling over my flushed cheeks. They were washed away by huge raindrops that had begun to pour from the ominous clouds. With the back of my sleeve, I wiped under my eyes. I was ashamed of the violence inside me, ashamed that I was crying, and most of all, scared that I loved him. Unable to speak, I turned and walked away.

"Bri!" he called, and I knew it was only seconds before he caught up with me. I wasn't prepared to go up against a witch, but I had to get away from him. Taking off at a full run, the rain pelted me in the face, mixing with my own tears drenched and blurred my eyes.

I managed to reach my car without slipping or falling on my face.

"Bri!" my name sounded behind as I fumbled with the lock.

It clicked open and I got in, slamming the door shit. Two seconds later, the engine was revving as I peeled out of the parking lot. My eyes were glued to his as I sped by. His blue eyes were glowing with magic. There was only a very slim window of opportunity to escape what he was brewing, but I had to try. Pressing down hard on the gas, I floored the poor aging Mustang. *Please let me through. Please let me through*, I repeated over and over again.

It wasn't until I reached the main road and the school was in my rearview mirror that I eased up the gas and exhaled.

I kept driving, and the realization that I ditched school *again* hit me. Where the hell did I plan on going?

My aunt was at the shop. That was not an option. Home was out of the question. I didn't want to be in my room with the reminder of what started this whole terrible day to begin with. There was only one place I wanted to be right now.

The one place I went to when I wanted to be alone.

And knowing Gavin, he wouldn't be far behind, which meant I needed to hit the gas. My car had no chance at outrunning his Charger, not in its present condition, and there was no doubt in my mind he would be at my wheels.

Every few minutes, I checked in my rearview mirror, expecting to see his black car trailing me. My face was salt-streaked from my dried-up tears, and the storm looked to be passing on, but still left the sky darkened from the aftermath. It wasn't until I pulled up to a secluded section of Topsail Beach that I relaxed.

I loved the beach, the crisp, clean ocean air, the gentle sound of waves crashing, and the feel of warm sand in between my toes. There was peace and harmony, and it settled my mood. I walked down the boardwalk, glad to see only a few people wandered the beach this morning. Stormy weather tended to keep people inside. If there was anything I wanted, it was solitude. Now if only I could get rid of those pesky seagulls. A flock of them dive-bombed the churning waters in an attempt for a fresh catch.

Trotting down onto the beach, I sat just far enough from the shoreline to not get wet. I hugged my knees to my chest and lost myself in the rippling of tides washing over the sand. With each pass, seashells were uncovered from the depths of the ocean floor. As a little girl, my aunt took me here every weekend during the summer. We spent hours gathering shells, playing in the unpredictable waters, and making up stories about the mermaids who lived below those rapid waves. I'd always had a fascination with mermaids as a kid, thanks to Ariel.

The memory made me miss my aunt in a way I hadn't in a long time. An ache bloomed in my chest. Solitude no longer appealed to me, and I wished she were here. My eyes closed as I laid my chin on my knees, basking in the sounds. I didn't know how much time had passed when I felt him.

"How did you find me?" I whispered.

He sat down beside me in the sand, his shoulder touching mine. "Magic."

It hadn't occurred to me that he might be able to track me. The idea was both disconcerting and relieving. He'd always be able to locate me. "I bet you're no fun to play hide and seek with," I said. My heart swelled. I was glad he found me.

His lips upturned at the corners. "Sophie never thought so."

"Sophie couldn't track you?" She was a witch. I assumed she could use magic to find him as well

"No, and it drives her nuts."

"How does it work?" I asked.

He shrugged. "It's a defense spell. Easier to follow when it's someone I care about," he explained.

I swallowed thickly.

"It's a locating spell. The closer I am to the person, the faster I can locate them, but I can find anyone if I have something personal of theirs. Though that kind of spell takes time," he finished.

That had me thinking. "How long have you been here?" I asked, holding my breath and waiting in anticipation.

His sapphire eyes held mine. "I watched you walk down the boardwalk. I wanted to give you space. You seemed like you needed a few moments to yourself. You were safe. I didn't see a reason to crowd you."

I exhaled and warmth spread in my chest. Gavin somehow knew what I needed before I did. "You got a spell for getting out of detention?" There was going to be consequences for leaving.

"Don't worry, I took care of it," he assured me.

I assumed he did a kind spell to excuse me from school for the day. Regardless, I was grateful. He was handy to have around. My eyes wandered out over the vast ocean. "I'm sorry about earlier. I don't know what came over me. You did the right thing by leaving," I admitted. "I overreacted." It also never even occurred to me that his family might have been wondering where he was all night. How selfish. I hoped that I hadn't gotten him into any trouble.

"We need to talk. There's something I think you need know." His mouth set into a straight line, telling me this was a serious talk. What other secrets could he possibly have bigger than wielding magic?

My mind spun trying to figure out what this was about. The events of today seemed to somehow have triggered this *talk*. And that frightened me.

"Okay," I said tentatively, not really sure what was going on or what to expect.

"Since we have the day off...what do you say we go to my house?" he suggested, grinning. "Then we can talk."

"Okay, but you're scaring me. Your parents won't care?" I asked, thinking that his mom was usually at home.

"Nah, but Sophie is going to be pissed when she finds out that I did this without her."

I gave him a blank look.

CHAPTER 23

I followed him in my car to his house. He kept it to a reasonable speed for my slow-chugging mustang. By the time we arrived, my stomach had wound itself into a thousand pretzel knots.

What did he want to *talk* about?

Was it about my behavior?

Did he not want to see me anymore?

We weren't official, but we'd sort of been dating. The last thing I wanted was losing what we had.

Gavin's mom poked her head out of the study when we walked in. She looked from him to me and back to him. "Gavin?" Her expression wasn't angry or upset, as I had pictured. There wasn't even surprise. I had a feeling Lily knew we were coming.

She had a brush in hand and paint splattered on her hands and apron. I imagined if the situation had been reversed, and we had walked into my house, my aunt would already be driving my butt back to school. The Masons definitely had a different policy about attendance than my family.

"Bri and I had an altercation at school this morning," he began.

I shifted my feet, feeling uncomfortable. Talk about the understatement of the year. The mention of our fight this morning caused my cheeks to bloom red. I wasn't proud of what happened and had hoped to keep it between us. Guess not.

"Which led to a little bit of unexplainable magic," Gavin continued. "I covered my tracks, but I thought it would be best if I had that *talk* with Bri now."

Whatever he wanted to tell me, Lily knew what it was.

"Hmm, I see. I wondered when you would get to this," she stated, wiping her paint stained hands on the front of her apron.

The fact that she knew what was going on, and I was clueless, unnerved me, to say the least. It was as if I was walking blind into a busy highway.

"I don't have much choice. She needs to know," he said.

"She does," Lily agreed and looked over at me. "Brianna, remember that if you need anyone to talk to I am a great listener."

I nodded, and more confused than ever, I followed Gavin to the backyard. It was fenced beautifully with decorative framing and offered privacy between the house and the beach. I could hear the water spraying over the rocky shores, infusing the air with salty surf.

He turned around and faced me, biting the bottom of his lip. His sapphire eyes searched mine. "When I first met you, I recognized something of myself in you. It's what drew me to you. I spent the first few weeks waiting for you to acknowledge you felt it, too. And when you didn't, it puzzled me. I thought maybe you were playing a game. I couldn't figure you out. It was my mom who brought it to my attention that you didn't know. And I thought, how does she not know? Truthfully, I still don't know how it came to be that you weren't told, but if I had to guess, it has something to do with losing both your parents at a young age."

What do my parents have to do with anything?

What is he talking about?

He ran a hand through his dark hair and exhaled. "I want to show you something. It will be easier to show you than tell you. Give me your hands," he instructed.

I eyed him with hesitancy and concern, my heart thumping wildly in my ears. Nothing he said made sense, and my fear was written in the lines of my face. If there was anything I knew about

Gavin, though, it was that I trusted him. So, I placed both my hands of top of his, palms up. A spark of power ignited, but I'd come to expect it.

He eyes locked onto mine. "Relax."

Easier said than done; my brain was on overdrive. I inhaled the moist air and tried to calm my anxiety. The feel of his hands under mine were reassuring.

"I want you to think about the warmth and glow of a light, any kind of light. Envision it inside your head," he encouraged in a husky voice, making it difficult to concentrate on anything else.

"I don't understand. Why am I doing this?"

"Indulge me."

Fine. I did what he asked, bringing the image of silver starlight, shining brilliantly behind my eyes. The beams surround the star, lighting up the sky, each giving off their own natural light. I'd always been fascinated with stars.

"Keep the image in your mind. Don't let it go, and say the word *Luminescence*. Repeat it."

My gaze was locked on to the depths of his blue eyes, and I swore I could see the twinkling of starlight in them. I felt detached from the rest of my body, an underlining hum buzzing along my arms and traveling through my veins, like an IV of power. I could feel it mixing with the heat of my blood—an elixir.

"Luminescence. Luminescence," I murmured, my eyes never wavering from his. My body began to sing with an intoxicating high, the taste of something pivotal on the tip of my tongue.

A gust of flames erupted at the center of my palms, a soft glow of dazzling silver light. My lips parted, and a gasp slipped from my mouth as the light pranced over my hands. There was no pain; the magical fire didn't burn, but tickled. My skin tingled where I could see the magic fluttering. It was illuminating and invigorating.

Looking through the flickering silver luster, my lips curled. Gavin was watching my reaction. "It's beautiful," I said.

"This is one of the most basic spells. To make light," he whispered. "Can you feel the energy feeding the magic?"

There was a zing dancing down my arm. Was that what he was

referring to? It was similar to the spark when we touched, but more prominent. "I feel something," I admitted.

We grinned at each other. What he could do was breathtaking, and I admired his gift. "This is amazing," I told him.

He took a step backward. "Don't move. Just stay where you are." Carefully, he removed his hands from underneath mine, so I was flying solely.

"Oh, my God! You can share magic." My eyes stared down at my hands. I turned them from side to side, watching the flames follow my movements.

He shook his head. "No, I can't. This—" he indicated with his arms. "Is all you."

"W-what?" I stammered, eyes wide. The light in my hands flickered.

"It's your magic," he said softly.

My head shook in denial. He was crazy. I didn't have magic. "That can't be. I don't have magic," I said, adamant. The glow dropped from my palms, but there was still a faint hum under the skin.

"You're wrong," he stated. "I've been aware of the power in you from the second we met. What I didn't understand was how you didn't know. I thought for sure you recognized me for what I was— A witch."

I was still shaking my head in denial. Refusing to believe anything he said. "That's crazy?" my voice bordering frantic.

"If you stop and let yourself thing about it, you know I'm right. Witches can always identify each other. The energy we wield is like a signature."

"Why are you doing this?" I tried to keep the disbelief and anguish from my voice. He was turning my whole life upside down, and I didn't want to hear it.

"Because it's the truth. I thought it would be easier to show you," he reasoned.

"Easier?" I shrieked.

"I'm trying to help you, Bri."

I believed that he thought he was. It hurt nonetheless. "I'm not a witch."

He looked exasperated, his shoulders slumped. "You used magic earlier today to get out of the school parking lot. I was shocked that you were able to overpower my spell without really knowing you could. And that wasn't the first time. Have you ever noticed how the weather mirrors your moods? You can weathercast. I saw it the day we met, Halloween night when you were scared, and today, the storm. Indirectly, you've been using magic."

Everything he said sort of made sense, however, it wasn't enough proof I was a witch. How much of it could be considered coincidence? He might have been able to put a seed of doubt in my mind, but I wasn't ready to start calling myself a witch.

He saw the uncertainty begin to ease into my eyes. "You're not only a witch, but there is something different with your energy, something unique, extra. I've been trying to pinpoint it. I just don't know what it is."

Freaking great. Was that supposed to make me feel better? Not only was I supposed to be a witch, but I was some super mutant witch on steroids.

I crossed my arms, hiding my tingling fingers. "I know you think I'm a witch, but I'm not." Even as the words left my mouth, I was beginning to discredit everything I thought I was or knew about myself. Doubt wiggled its way in.

My uncontrollable anger. The little things I always brushed off. The welts I'd left on Rianne's arm. How could I be a witch and not know?

"I'm not the only one," he countered, running a hand through his hair. "My whole family knows. If you don't believe me, ask Sophie."

I didn't want to ask her, for fear she would only tell me what I wasn't ready to hear. My whole world felt like it had just tumbled down on top of me like a nuclear bomb, the damage irreparable.

"Look, I know this is a lot to take in, but I want you to know I am here for you, and I want to help," he said, closing the space between us.

I took a step in retreat and watched as his eyes flickered. The only thing I wanted was to get out the hell out of there. I didn't want to be bombarded with questions, sympathy looks, or admit what they all believed. The Masons might be ready to call me a witch, but I was far from ready or eager.

"I've got to go," I said and turned, walking toward the gate. Away from the one guy I thought got me. Away from a family I admired. Away from the possible truth.

I looked over at him, before I opened the iron door. "And don't follow me...please," I pleaded.

His eyes fell, causing an ache in my chest. It didn't stop me from walking out the door and getting into my car.

CHAPTER 24

When I reached the shelter of my car, I laid my head on the steering wheel and gave up trying to sort all the scrambling thoughts. I concentrated on getting home; doing simple tasks like putting the key in the ignition, hitting the gas, and making sure I stayed on my side of the road. By the time I pulled into my driveway, I was a wreck. My entire body was numb, and my brain fuzzy. I couldn't feel anything.

In my zombie-state, I let myself into the house, tossed the keys on the entry table and went to my room. I shut the door behind me before climbing into bed fully clothed, my eyes affixed on the ceiling above. I started getting flashes of myself, each time in a different form, and all of them depicted me as a witch.

In a black dress that whipped around me in violence. Another with me in the same dress, but in red, and this time I was standing at the edge of cliff, my hands thrown in the air. I even saw myself Salem-style, burning on a stake.

I was having a mental breakdown. There was an underlying evil in the visions I was having of myself. It got to the point where I didn't close my eyes anymore. I laid there clutching the moonstone and amethyst necklace, praying it would chase away the images.

I don't know how long I lay there, but it was the sound of my phone vibrated on the nightstand that roused me. I ignored the buzzing and continued to stare at the ceiling, falling in and out of reality. There was no concept of time. No sense of the room around me. No desire to move. Just the numbness I came to depend on, to shut out the truth.

When my aunt got home, she came to check on me. I mumbled something about not feeling good. In a way, I *was* sick. The bowl of chicken noodle soup she fixed me before going to bed sat on the nightstand, and remained untouched all night.

By morning, I was in the same position, in the same trance-like emotionless state.

I blinked, beams of sunlight hurting my eyes.

A knock sounded on my door, before it squeaked opened a crack. "Brianna?" Aunt Clara called, peering inside.

I was still tucked in bed. I rolled to my side and watched her walk across the room. She sat on the edge of my bed beside me, pushing the hair back from my face, eying me warily. Her floral perfume hit the room and soaked into my soul, breaking it a little. I was afraid she was about to open the floodgates I'd been numbly holding back.

"Hey, honey, still not feeling well?" she asked.

"No, not really," I croaked. I needed water. My throat started to close up, courtesy of the overwhelming emotion rising within me.

She studied me another moment. "Okay, I'll call the school to let them know you won't be there, and I'll check on you later. If you need anything, you know where to reach me." Leaning over, she pressed a kiss to my forehead, and picked up the still-full soup bowl. She paused at the doorway. "You should really try and eat something."

I nodded.

And the tears started pouring as the garage door shut. Noisy, gut-wrenching sobs tore from deep inside me. The kind that gave me hiccups in an effort to breathe and cry at once. I'd held them off all night, but they couldn't be contained any longer. My body, mind, and soul needed the emotional purge.

I curled the blanket around me and hugged myself in a ball. The windowpanes in my room pounded with giant raindrops that made me cry all the more. It was like the universe was telling me what I didn't want to hear, a justification of my uncontrollable magic—magic I didn't want.

My blanket was soaked with my tears, and my chest heaved. I glanced out the window, unable to believe that I was somehow causing the storm. I didn't know what to do. It seemed like a huge responsibility to be able to control something as immense as the weather.

I snatched my phone off the nightstand. There were two missed calls for Tori, one from Gavin, and a string of text messages. Everyone wanted to know the same thing. *Where are you? What's wrong? Why are you ignoring me? I'm about to report you missing.* And so forth.

And so my day went. When I finally dragged my butt out of bed, my body felt achy and weak, as if I'd just gotten over a bout of the flu. It never occurred to me before how lost and alone a person could feel. I'd never been so unsure of anything in my life. There were two options here: I could go on with my life, pretending Gavin never mentioned the word *witch*, or I accepted that I could be a witch, as Gavin claimed, and ask for his help. What I couldn't do was stay in this room and hide from the world.

Downstairs I nibbled on some crackers, trying to settle my empty stomach. I made a mental pro-con list. To be or not to be a witch. It sounded like a snappy book title.

If I ignored what I was, I could potentially harm others by not being able to control my magic. I could disappoint those who cared for me. Most of all, I could lose Gavin.

If I were a witch, I would have to lie to my friends, to my aunt. I could lose my only friends.

It all boiled down to being scared. Scared to be a witch. Scared of failing. Scared to lose the guy I was probably in love with. Scared to lose my friends and potentially my aunt. I wasn't sure I could risk all that.

I spent the rest of the day going over and over the same questions with no answers. When night fell, I was in bed again before my aunt got home. Much like the previous night, she came in to check on me. This time I forced myself to eat a little of the soup she brought, and wished I could tell her what was eating at me inside.

There was only one person I could talk to about this whose opinion didn't really matter. He was, after all, a figment of my imagination.

I unclasped the necklace, and laid it on the nightstand. Since I'd starting wearing the amethyst and moonstone, I hadn't had a single dream of him.

His name whispered from my lips. My eyes fluttered close as I slowly went under. *Lukas.* His name echoed in my mind as I drifted off to sleep.

The darkness gave way, and when I opened my eyes, the first thing I saw were the lilac frosted walls of my bedroom. *Hell, it didn't work.* Frustrated, I tossed the covers aside and turned on my bedside lamp, running a hand through my unwashed hair. Mental note: shower tomorrow. Just because my life was falling apart, didn't mean my hair had to suffer.

I sat up in the bed and yelped. There was a figure sitting at my desk chair. His grin was one I knew well.

Lukas.

"Holy crap! You scared me to death," I exhaled.

"You look like hell." He leaned back in the chair, grinning from ear-to-ear.

I tossed a pillow at his head and missed, making him chuckle. "What are you doing here?" ...in my bedroom, I added in my head.

"You brought me. As always," he answered, looking at me like I lost my mind.

Maybe I had.

"I'm dreaming?" This was a first. I've never dreamed of my own life, nothing this personal, and certainly not my bedroom. And again, why does my subconscious continue to make me look like I just rolled out of bed? If I was a witch, at least I should be able to spell myself hot.

"Pretty sure," he commented. "Nice room." His smile was infectious. "I always wondered what it would look like."

He got up from his seat, the college t-shirt spanning his chest as strolled around the room, looking at the most intimate part of my life. There was a slight sting in my chest at having another guy in my room, even if it was a dream. He came across the necklace on the table beside me.

"So this is why I haven't seen you lately." He trailed a finger over the moonstone and amethyst gems.

"How do you know that?" I wondered aloud.

He shrugged and sat down on the bed next to me. The mattress shifted under his weight, and his blue jeans rubbed against my bare leg. "My mom."

We never really talked about his parents before, and it made me wonder about them. I always figured that my dreams didn't have a world outside me. I guess I could dream up parents.

"Remember the new guy, the witch I told you about..." I started getting right to why I had wanted to see him. His emerald eyes held mine, waiting for me to go on. "He told me that I'm a witch. Can you believe that?" I asked, expecting him to express the same outrage I'd felt.

"And you don't believe him?"

"Should I?" I retorted, baffled.

He regarded me, brows drawing together. "I can't tell you what to believe, but I have always thought there was something unique about you."

"And if I don't want it?" I argued.

"Do you really have a choice, if it is who you are? Do you really want to deny such a powerful gift?"

"I don't know," I sighed more discouraged than before.

"I think you owe it to yourself to find out if that is who you are," he advised.

Maybe he had a point. What would it hurt to try? Maybe I owed it to myself and to Gavin. "You might be right."

He put his arm around me in comfort, and I rested my head on his arm. "It doesn't have to change you as a person, if that's what you are worried about."

"How can it not?"

He brushed a piece of hair from my face. "Don't let it define you. You need to take control of the power if it is yours. It doesn't control you." His honey voice had softened.

Easier said than done, but he was right. "Okay," I agreed. "It might be worth a shot."

His dark green eyes smiled at me, highlighted by the blond of his hair. "Brianna the witch—has a nice ring to it."

Reaching behind me, I smacked him in the back of the head with my pillow, not missing this time. His laugh resounded off my bedroom walls.

"You'll regret that Lukas Devine. Just wait..." I playfully threatened him.

"I'm looking forward to it," he replied.

Laying my head back on his shoulder, I closed my eyes and was cloaked by his radiance. He brushed a light kiss on my cheek. When I opened them again, I was alone.

CHAPTER 25

B y the third day, I had got up to face the truth and the world. I couldn't hibernate in my room forever. My aunt was already worried sick about my state, and I didn't want to upset her further.

I had finally come to terms with my decision. Life was filled with choices, and if I had magic inside me, it wasn't going to just disappear. From what I'd already experienced, it didn't work that way. Already, magic had already found ways to weave into my life without my knowledge. Accepting it and learning to control it seemed a better solution, instead of letting someone get hurt.

What I planned on telling my aunt was another story. I wasn't even comfortable with the idea, and until I was, I would keep this part of myself a secret...for now. When the time came, if the time came, I would find a way to tell her.

My phone rang, and I was tempted to throw it across the room or flush it down the toilet. I checked the clock. School had just gotten out, and for three days I had been absent.

I cringed at the pile of homework that waiting for me on my return tomorrow.

The good thing about my decision: my appetite had returned with a vengeance.

I padded out of my room, on the hunt for something to eat. As I rounded the corner to the kitchen, a voice stopped me in my tracks.

"I was just about to drag you from your room."

I pitched a scream worthy of breaking glass, and a hand wrapped around my mouth, stifling the shout of terror. His scent hit me all at once. Wild woods. I stopped struggling and relaxed in his arms. He released me, turning me around so I could see his face.

Gavin.

"What are you doing here?" I screeched. My mind told me I should be mad at him for scaring the shit out of me, but it had been too long since I had seen him.

My eyes ate him up every inch of him. He was wearing all black, looking like the poster boy for a male model ad. And he smelled amazing. My pulse skittered as I stared into his eyes. I could be as angry or upset as I wanted to be, but it never changed the way my body reacted to him.

"I was worried about you. You haven't been to school in three days. You don't answer your phone. You don't text back. What am I suppose think?"

"I needed some time." I opened the fridge and grabbed us something to drink, trying to still my overzealous heart. "How did you get in here?"

He cocked a brow. "Do you think a locked door is going to keep me out? I was afraid you wouldn't see me," he replied, taking a seat across from me at the table.

"I wasn't fit for company." I popped the top on my can.

"Bri, I truly never meant to hurt you." So much regret and pain shone in his eyes.

The sight tore at my heart. I had indirectly hurt him. By rejecting what I was, I had, in a way, rejected him, and that had never been my intention. What a mess.

"I only wanted to help. I swear. I know this is scary for you. When I saw you struggling, I had to do something. If you let me, I can help you. Sophie, too. I promise."

I gazed into his eyes, wondering how I ever doubted he didn't have my best interest at heart. "I know. I was going to talk to you at school tomorrow. This whole witch thing is still... unreal to me," I confessed, letting the exasperation show.

"If you let me, I know we can figure it this out together. Or, at the very least, I can teach you how to block it, if that's what you want."

"I don't know what I want. Not yet, but I'd like to learn."

He exhaled. "Sophie has been dying to see you. She has been very difficult since she found out that I told you. She's not the easiest witch to deal with," he confessed.

I could only imagine. Sophie was stubborn when she wanted to be.

"She's quite mad at me, if it makes you feel any better," he added, leaning back against his chair, looking out of sorts.

"I'm not mad at you anymore. The shock has more or less worn off," I admitted. "To be honest, I am still not a hundred percent convinced I'm a witch, but I am willing to try. I need to know one way or the other so I can move on."

"Good, now I can tell Sophie to stop trying to hex me."

I gave him a half smile. "Not on my account."

He eyed me across the table with a hint of a smirk. "She was so mad at me for what I did, she refused to talk to me the rest of the day, and then when she was speaking to me, she was yelling at me about what an idiot I was."

"She's such a good friend," I said, sipping my drink.

He snorted. "Lately, I'd say your taste in friends is questionable. Look what you got yourself into." The smile he sent me was dangerous.

"You're telling me."

"Come over tomorrow after school?" he asked.

"I can't. I have work," I said, remembering I needed to resume my responsibilities, which included my shift at the shop.

"Fine, the day after that," he suggested, an obvious look of disappointment on his face.

"All right," I agreed.

"I'll pick you up after school."

I nodded. Witchcraft 101, here I come.

CHAPTER 26

My first day as a witch, well, potential witch, Sophie and Jared were waiting for Gavin and I outside, around back.

"This is going to be fun," Jared said, all geared up. His dimples winked on either side of his cheeks mischievously. "Don't worry, I'll go easy on you."

I rolled my eyes. The eldest Mason was trouble in a different sense than his brother.

"You didn't think we were going to miss out on your first day of boot camp, did you?" Sophie asked, smiling innocently.

Seeing Jared suddenly reminded me that I still didn't know what magic he could do. "Jared," I called, bringing his attention to me instead of whatever prank was running through his head. "Gavin promised me you would tell me what you can do."

Jared's eyes twinkled, but it was Gavin's voice behind me who answered. "Not tell, Jared, show her." He came to stand next to me, taking my hand.

"I'd be delighted to," he said, gleaming in roguery, dimples winking on either side of his cheeks.

Right before my eyes, Jared began to change, form shifting so quick to the eye that I almost didn't believe—or see the change. A gray and white coated wolf stood where Jared had been moments before, his eyes the same piercing blue as Gavin's. In a blink of an eye, Jared had transformed into a beautiful and fierce wolf.

My mouth dropped open.

A shifter? Jared was a shifter.

I needed to sit down before I fainted.

Kneeling to his level, I scratched the sides of his fluffy neck, feeling how real the wolf was. His fur was much softer than I expected. Jared the wolf closed his eyes in appreciation at the neck rub.

At this point, I was becoming good with weird. "Wow," I exclaimed. "You're a shift shaper. That is seriously wicked. Any chance I'll be able to do that?" I asked, standing back up.

Just as smoothly as before, Jared returned to his human form. The three of them looked at me as if I had grown horns. They had expected me to freak out again.

Who could blame them?

"You never fail to surprise me," Gavin grinned. "Just when I think I understand you, you blindside me again. Why is it you don't bat an eye when Jared shifts, but you lock yourself away for days when I inform you that you're a witch?"

I eyed him levelly and shrugged. Even I didn't understand how my mind worked. Why should anyone else? "Maybe I'm getting used to the unusual. I should, since I am one."

"At least you're starting to believe," Sophie replied. "Come on; let's see what you can do!" Her excitement was starting to become contagious.

"Where do we start?" I had no idea what in the world I was supposed to be doing. This wasn't exactly like learning how to play Battleship.

I sat across from Sophie on the grass, with Jared and Gavin behind us. Sophie's expression was suddenly serious. "You know that spark you sometimes feel?"

I nodded.

"That is your energy, the source of your power. By recognizing it, you should be able to focus the energy to command it."

Okay, sounded simple, which made me believe it was going to be harder than it sounded. Most things were.

"Close your eyes," she instructed. "Now relax your breathing. Gavin says your power is at its strongest when you are angry. It's connected to your emotions. I want you to find the energy source that feeds your anger. That is where you're going to pull your powers. You need to be able to access it at your whim, not just when your emotions are high."

"I don't know what I am looking for," I admitted, feeling a little defeated.

"Just like your heart beats, magic has its own sound, so to speak. For some, it's a vibration, for others it's a hum, but it's there in your blood, pumping inside your veins. Once you recognize the source you can begin to tap into it," she explained. "I want you to listen, find the energy within you."

With my eyes closed, I listened to the rolling waves of the ocean, keeping my breathing even with gentle ins and outs. Focusing deeper on myself, I picked up the stable rhythm of my heart, pumping strong against my chest. And there, keeping time with my heart, was a steady hum. It traveled throughout my body, warm and willing. I could follow its movements, extending from one side of me to the other.

I smiled and whispered, "I can feel it."

"Good. Now let's use it. Your powers seem to have an affinity with the elements, according to what Gavin has seen. Concentrate on something from nature."

Something from nature. The first thing that popped into my mind was a butterfly. I pictured the soft, pale yellow wings that sometimes hovered in the large tree outside my house. How its tiny wings sunbathed on the tree limbs during the summer.

A tingle started at the base of my spine.

I bite my lip and opened my eyes. Nothing. "It didn't work," I said deflated. She could see the disappointment in my eyes.

"There won't always be so much preparation. Just like anything new, the more you practice, the more in tune you will be with your powers." She looked above my head at Gavin and Jared. "You guys need to leave, you're distracting her. Especially you," she said, pointedly to Gavin.

I could feel him smirking behind me, but neither protested as they walked back inside the house. My cheeks bloomed in color at her insinuation. "Why was it so simple before with Gavin?" I groaned, thinking about the light we had produced together.

"Because you're fighting it. Before you didn't know what you could do. You opened yourself up on faith and trust, but you are unwilling to trust in yourself. It is holding you back. Believe," she told me.

Believe that I was a witch. Believe in myself. Take a leap of faith. That was asking a lot. But what choice did I have?

With a deep breath, I closed my eyes to try again. I gathered all my determination and attention into envision the single butterfly, except this time, I multiplied it by a dozen. Maybe the more I conjured in my mind would help boost my magic. Whenever I thought of spells before, I thought of hocus pocus rhymes. I couldn't decide if this was harder or easier, harnessing power this way.

The tingling tripled, expounding throughout my body and filling me with a heady feeling I craved more of. My mind wanted to get swept away in the sensation.

"Brianna," Sophie called. "Brianna!" It wasn't until the third or fourth time that her voice penetrated through my wall of concentration.

This time when I opened my eyes, a whole new sight beheld me. Hundreds of butterflies in vibrant colors danced in the air around me, purples, blues, turquoise, pinks. I've never seen such beautiful species before. Their delicate wings fluttered against my cheeks like tissue paper. I held out my hand, and a lilac butterfly with black spots landed on the tip of my finger. Laughing, I realized that magic didn't have to be scary, dark or unnatural. It could be wonderful.

I peered into the large picture window and saw Gavin grinning at me through the glass, his dark poetic features reflecting the excitement inside me.

"Holy crap," Sophie breathed. "I didn't think I was going to be able to reach you." There were butterflies in her hair.

"Did I do something wrong?" I asked. The butterflies had begun to spread out and take flight with the gentle breeze.

"Are you kidding me?" Her grin said it all. "You just blew the roof off that spell. There must be two hundred butterflies. Very impressive. He was right, you know. I've never felt so much untapped energy before, and you weren't even at full potential."

My smile lost some of its luster. The insinuation at me being powerful sent a stream of worried inside me. I'd barely accepted I had magic. The last thing I wanted was the kind of responsibility that came with having gobs of power. I didn't want to be different. For once in my life, I wanted to be like everyone else, or in this case, like other witches.

Gavin and Jared came back outside swatting at my butterflies. "You're a natural," Jared stated, his dimples making an appearance.

"Great," I muttered.

Gavin must have noticed the shift in my attitude. He came to my side and whispered, "Let's go to my room. I think we've had enough witchery for one day."

I stared into his eyes, and then nodded. "Thanks, Sophie," I called over my shoulder as we headed for the house. Most of the butterflies had taken off in flight.

"What's wrong?" he asked, the moment we stepped into his room. It was just as I remembered and smelled just like him.

I sighed. "Everyone keeps telling me how much power I have. I don't want it. I don't want to be some uber witch."

"You might not have much choice in the matter."

"That's just it. I'm scared. What if I can't control it? You've told me that I've used it before, and I never even knew."

"You used magic on me the first time we kissed," he revealed, taking a step closer to me. The air suddenly charged with my aggravation and his aggression.

I didn't know how that was supposed to make me feel better, because it didn't. If anything, I felt worse. "What are you talking about?"

"I felt it that night, under the moon. You demanded me to kiss you. Your eyes were glowing with this incredible dark purple, the moon reflecting in your eyes. I'd never seen eyes as beautiful as yours when under magic."

"Are you saying I made you kiss me?" Dread wove in my belly at the anticipation of his answer.

"No...it wouldn't have worked if I hadn't wanted you. It wasn't a compulsion spell, but a nudge," he said backing me into a corner.

I ran a frazzled hand through my hair. Would everything in my life be so complicated? "I can't believe I used magic to make you kiss me," I said in mortification, completely unaware that he had me cornered.

"You didn't *make* me Bri," he said, but I wasn't listening anymore.

"I'm sorry," I uttered and turned to leave.

He blocked my exit, fingers sliding under my chin and tipped my face up. "I'm not," he said, and then the world rocked on its axis.

He cupped the back of my head, bringing his mouth down on mine. Before I even registered that he was kissing me, there was a burst of heat gulfing every corner of my body.

My back pressed into the wall as he deepened the kiss, and I relished in his taste. Dark and delicious. The scent of him heightened every tiny, blissful tingle.

My world shattered.

Ravenously, my fingers curled into his dark hair, keeping him close him, but not matter how close we were, there still seemed to be too much space between us. I couldn't get enough of him. Even as the contours of his body molded to mine, it didn't satisfy the craving for more.

I sank into his lips, basking in the feel of his silver hoop teasing my mouth. The urge to tug on it was almost too much to resist. I'd waited for this moment for eternity— a guy who made me feel beyond amazing.

Moaning on an explosion of hunger, his hands roamed, skimming the sides of my breast. A shiver raced down my spine at the contact.

His mouth pulled just a breath away. "Tell me I didn't make you do that," I whispered.

"No, you didn't," he sighed. "I don't want to let you go," he confessed.

"Don't," I murmured.

"I don't know that I have a choice," he admitted, struggling with his emotions. "There is so much you don't understand... that I don't understand."

My eyes sought his. "What more do you need to know? I thought my being a witch was what you wanted. Now, you're telling me that you don't know what you want?"

And just like that, the mood was blown. I was tired of feeling misplaced and disconcerted. I wasn't a yoyo.

"It's not that simple, Bri," he argued.

"Nothing is with you. I think you should take me home," I stated, emotionally spent.

CHAPTER 27

After he dropped me off, I left his car without even a good-bye. I rushed inside, tiptoeing into my room, avoiding my aunt. I didn't want to be disturbed or talk. If she took one look at me, she would see the raw emotions I couldn't hide.

Closing the door softly behind me, the room was submerged in darkness. I reached for the light switch, fumbling along the wall, and miscalculated how far the switch was. Instead of my hand connecting with the switch as I expected, my head connected with the door of my bathroom.

Everything went black.

WHEN I AWOKE, I wasn't alone, and I was most certainly not in my room. There was giant-sized knot on the side of my head and a killer thumping at my temples. I raised a hand to the side of my head as I scrambled off the ground, catching a flash of red in the corner of my eye.

What the—?

"Hey!" I yelled after the figure.

What is going on?

I took off, my feet hitting the pavement at a dead run. Not precisely the smartest move. My head protested at the quick movements, slowing me down. But I didn't stop. Something was telling me I had to follow the figure.

As I turned the corner, a woman with flaming hair and burning violet eyes so like mine stood a few feet in front of me. She had a twisted smile on her lips, and I couldn't help think she looked like an enchantress. And then it dawned on me.

Holy Picasso.

She was the woman from the painting in the Mason's library. What had Gavin said her name was?

For the life of me, I couldn't remember.

It didn't matter. She was beckoning me forward. I didn't see how I had a choice. I had no idea how I got here, where I was, or what she wanted with me.

So, of course, I followed her.

As we walked, I studied her, fascinated by her presence and the amount of confidence she oozed. Stunning in a black dress, her hair whipped out around her, a striking contrast to the dark clothing she wore. I tore my gaze from her to look at my surroundings.

Sand squished under my feet, and in the distance, the shoreline came into view. I noticed the houses up on the embankment. We were in Holly Ridge. We weren't far from Gavin's house and only a block or two from mine. Somewhere in the middle was my guess.

But there was something unusual about this Holly Ridge. The houses seemed out of place— different— older, I guess.

A gentle breeze ruffled my hair, and for the first time, I looked down at myself. What the hell was I wearing? Where were my jeans and tank top? I was in a freaking dress, a white lacy one at that, similar in style to what the flaming-haired woman wore. The top cinched at my waist in an old fashion corset. And I was barefoot. Whose butt was I going to have to kick for putting me in such a frilly outfit?

Occasionally, the woman would glance over her shoulder at me to see if I was still following. Our identical eyes caught, and her name vibrated in my head.

Morgana le Fey.

Now I knew I hit my head a lot harder than I thought.

When we reached the shoreline, my feet sunk into the cool sand. The sky was dark and thickly layered in ominous clouds.

I'd grown tired of chasing after her. "What do you want?" I called.

My feet were tired and beaten from the lack of protection, and I didn't know how much longer I would be able to keep up with her. We were fighting against a wind that seemed to be getting stronger with each step, and I fleetingly wondered if I was the cause. Maybe I was unintentionally using my magic. Where my emotions were concerned, anything was possible. What I did know was, my body wasn't up to this long trek after being knocked unconscious.

Morgana never acknowledged my voice, but kept her steady, grueling pace down the beach. I hadn't the slightest idea what I was doing out here in the middle of the night following a dead and possibly fictional woman. The more I thought on it, the less smart it became. I wanted to deny the part of me that was pulled to follow her. I wanted to tell it to go to hell. My subconscious didn't care what I wanted, and I wasn't sure I could stop. I was beginning to think she had put a spell me.

We continued to trudge across the beach with the wind picking up speed at our approach. There was a connection to the air around me. It tugged in my core, urging me to take control of it, no matter that my body was exhausted and worn. I crossed my arms over my chest, tucking them under and refusing the pull.

Without the knowledge of the extent of my own powers, and the ability to govern them, it was best to avoid using them. Even as I thought that, another part of me highly disagreed. It fought to surface and demanded to break free.

When I thought this was never going to end, she stopped in her tracks, turning to me with a troublesome grin on her blood red lips. Her back faced the dark waters, crimson hair and dark dress twirling with the winds. "Brianna, my child, it is time for you to embrace your heritage," she said, her voice powerful. She threw out her arms, and the sky opened up in disorder at her command. Wow, and I thought I had temperamental storm problems. She made me look like an amateur.

What did she mean heritage? I didn't have time to dwell on it, because magic flowed from her to the storm brewing. The electrifying energy of her spell cloaked around me, summoning me to join her. The call was impossible to ignore, and as molten power flowed through my veins, I mimicked her movements, incapable of doing anything else. Together our spell intertwined, and became so dominant and forceful I felt as if we could easily destroy Holly Ridge with a flick of our finger. Nothing ever felt so wickedly good, like I was born for a purpose.

My head back fell back, thunder cracking in the clouds and bolts of lightning shooting from the sky. Her siren voice sounded in my head, encouraging me, not that I needed much motivation at this point. My magic recognized hers like they were long-lost friends. Our spells blended harmoniously and effortlessly together as one.

"Born of my magic and blood, you shall be mine," she belted over the turning seas and howling winds.

With each word came a bolt force, radiating power. If I had been in my right mind, I would have been frightened. As the richness of power engulfed me, a warning went through my head, whispering to me. Gavin's name echoed in the forefront of my mind. I remembered him telling me how my moods often dictated the weather because I was insentiently using magic; *weathercasting* was what he called it. Glancing at the ferocious storm concocting, I knew this wasn't me, but I didn't know how to break the hold the intoxicating spell had over me.

I didn't how to get out of here or away from her, but there was an internal urge that insisted I call for help in my single moment of sanity. Only one person made a habit of saving me and was on the tip of my tongue before I second guessed myself.

"*Gavin*," I yelled, over and over again.

I needed to wake from this nightmare, if it was indeed a dream. I prayed it was.

My faith sunk as nothing happened. No shift in the air. No fireflies. No Gavin. The energy I was projecting stumbled in my discouragement, yet I couldn't stop it. It was as if she was sucking the power from me.

Without him, I didn't know what hope I had of getting out of this perilous situation.

Just when I was about to give up all hope, a shadowy form appeared higher on the bank. He looked fierce, dangerous and pissed off. "Bri!" Gavin shouted.

Morgana's head whipped up at his voice. He started to make his way toward me and dread spilled into my belly. I didn't want her attention focused on Gavin.

I suddenly regretted bringing him in the middle of this mess.

"You cannot be here," Morgana hissed, displeased with Gavin's appearance. Her eyes darkened to the deepest shade of purple, a hint above pitch black. Fear stabbed at my heart. All I could think was *not him*. If she hurt Gavin because I brought him here, I would never be able to forgive myself. That much I was at least certain of. Damn. It looked like I was going to have to head-to-head with a bat-shit crazy witch.

Morgana shifted her energy at Gavin. I felt the alteration, as our magic was no longer joined. The release left me bewildered for a few seconds, and then without a second thought, I threw myself in between Morgana and Gavin.

The stream of magic came straight at me. The sheer force of it knocked me back ten feet, as I sailed like a doll in the air. I landed flat on my ass, the air knocked out of my lungs, and I was left gasping.

Gavin knelt beside me, brushing the hair out of my face. His touch made me realize I was still alive; the fireflies were still zooming inside me. I must not be dead.

"Silly girl," Morgana's voice broke through the pain. "He has no part in this." Her voice dripped with venom and spite.

And once again I felt the draw of her magic, pulling me. Bitch was relentless. She had started the spell again.

Could I just get a break already?

Severe winds, twice as strong as before, kicked up sand in our face. Visibility was out of the question, and I lost sight of her. Deep out in the ocean, a monster hurricane rose from the violent waters, groaning with sickening power. It spun in rapid circles, heading for shore. With each passing second, the whirlwind picked up speed and strength, ready to destroy anything in its path, including us.

"Bri!" Gavin called over the deafening winds, running his hands over my limbs, checking for injuries. "You need to wake up! You have to fight this and wake up. It is the only way to stop the storm," he screamed.

Wet sand plastered to my skin. "I don't know how," I admitted, my own voice sounding raspy and foreign.

"You do," he insisted. "Focus. Use your power to make yourself wake up. Break through the spell she has woven to keep you here."

He was right. I had to try. I had to save us. I closed my eyes and searched the hum of energy. The crazy chaotic circumstances made it way more difficult to concentrate. Somehow I was able to find the thread I needed. With every last bit of vigor I had left, the magic merged into my bloodstream, and I chanted, *Wake up! Wake up! Wake up!*

The world went silent. I could no longer sense Gavin beside me. Collapsed on the shore, the white dress was plastered against me my skin covered in sand. Morgana's temptress laugh ran in my ears, but she was nowhere to be found. Soaked to the bone, I laid on the beach, too exhausted to move.

A whizzing of water drew my gaze to the ocean, and I watched in horror as a hurricane was swirling out of control. My heartbeat pounded in my chest, threating to burst free. I'd traded one threat for another. No Morgana, but what was I going to do about that?

I had failed.

CHAPTER 28

L ying on the beach, I was resigned my fate over to the hurricane that would surely sweep me away. Not an ounce of stamina remained in my body. Even my magic was drained. I couldn't muster a flicker.

"Bri." Gavin's voice flittered from somewhere behind, distance and muffled. He called my name again.

How appropriate that his voice would be the last I heard.

When his dark features appeared in my vision, I thought I was hallucinating.

"Stay with me," he said as if I had a choice.

I didn't want to die, and I sure as hell didn't want him dying with me. "You need to leave," I muttered, using the last strength I had, my voice gravelly.

The sapphire of his eyes radiated with magic as he muttered a few hushed words. Silence erupted, dissolving the hiss of spinning water. The eye of the storm, and I thought *this is it*. All I needed was the bright light and a white angel.

He lifted me up into his arms.

"I love you," I murmured against his neck and inhaled one last sniff of the wild and reckless energy that could only be him.

"Keeping you alive is becoming more than I bargained for," he said, carrying me in his arms.

A moment later I blacked out again for the second time that night.

❦

DRIFTING in and out of consciousness, I awoke to bits and pieces of conversation around me. The voices all belonged to one Mason or another. It seemed the whole family was in attendance. I could safely assume I was in their home.

"Is she going to be all right?" I heard Sophie ask.

A cool damp cloth was placed over my forehead, and I became aware of the burning inside me. A fire blazed in my veins.

"She has a good-sized bump on her head and is banged up some, but I think she will be fine. Her body and magic need time to recuperate. She needs rest, lots of it," Lily said. Her hand brushed back my hair where beads of perspiration gathered at the hairline.

"What are we going to tell her aunt?" Sophie asked.

"I don't know. Let's just see when she wakes up. Hopefully, it will be soon," Lily replied.

The rest of the conversation was lost to me as I floated back into a deep sleep. A dreamless sleep. I didn't want to go back under, but my body had other plans and didn't care for my fears.

There was no concept of time in my fitful sleep. I repeatedly woke, but didn't actually wake up. I was more or less stuck in an in-between time warp of slumber. It was a journey I would like to take again.

"Is he okay?" Lily asked in one of my lucid semi-conscious moments.

"He will be. You know Gavin. He is beating himself up about not being able to pull her through sooner, and thinks he should have done something to prevent this," John replied, sounding strained.

Just like Gavin to blame himself, when there was no one to blame but the woman who cast the spell. If anyone was a fault for my current condition, it was her.

I was determined to stay awake this time. The seesawing between dream and reality was screwing with my mind. I needed to get home, before my aunt realized I was gone and panicked. I wasn't ready to explain what was going on with me.

I turned restlessly, trying to keep the blackness at bay when I heard Gavin's voice. "She can dreamscape."

"Are you sure?" John asked his son.

"Yes. It's how I knew where she was tonight. She's done it one other time before that I know of. The night we met."

Dreamscape? What did that mean? What had I done? It had something to do with my dreams, but that was all I gathered.

"Tell us what happened," Gavin's father demanded.

He willingly obliged. "I was sleeping when I heard her call my name. The next thing I knew, I was outside in a storm of magic, and Bri was standing on the shore in the middle of it all. I yelled her name and that was when I noticed Morgana."

"Morgana le Fey was there? You are sure?" Lily asked. There was disbelief and bewilderment in her voice.

"Yes, it was her, and she did not want me there."

"I don't doubt that. It would have messed up her plans, I'd imagine," John said.

"What does she want with Bri?" Gavin asked.

"Whatever she wants from Brianna, it can't be good. Nothing good can come from having the most powerful witch the world has ever known seeking you out in your dreams," Lily said.

Morgana the most powerful witch, echoed in my mind. Her power had been unparalleled, and yet I was certain that my magic felt so close to hers, like a twin. That couldn't be though, none of this made sense.

"How were you able to wake up, break the spell?" John asked.

"Bri was the one who broke the spell. I just guided her a bit, but not before Morgana threw a spell. I'd been her target, but Bri stepped in its path." He sounded tired, and my heart ached. "When I got to her after the spell hit, she wasn't moving, but she was awake. She found the strength to get us out of there." He struggled to keep the aguish out of his voice.

I moaned. My head felt as if it was splitting in half, the pain excruciating. Forcing my eyelids open, I blinked, the light hurting my eyes. I tried to lift my head, and instantly grimaced. Bad idea. Spears of pain radiated from the sides of my skull. My hand flew to my temple as I lay back on the pillow. Lily and Gavin were at my side instantly.

"Bri," Gavin breathed out a sigh of relief.

I groaned. "Sorry." My own voice sounded scratchy and hoarse.

There was soft concern in Lily's expression as she looked into my face. "Don't try and move too much. You need to gain your strength."

I wasn't sure how much I could move, even if I wanted to. Everything felt bruised, battered, and sore. "What happened?"

"How about you concentration on resting, and we talk after you get better? I don't think you are in much shape to have the kind of conversation this requires," Lily suggested. "I'll you two a few minutes." She touched my cheek, before walking out of the room.

"That complex, huh?" Like everything in my life lately. Gavin smirked down at me, a strand of his dark hair falling over the eye with the silver bar. "What fun would it be without a little excitement and a dead witch haunting your dreams?" He sat down on the bed beside me and took my hand. "How are you feeling?"

I closed my eyes for a moment. "I've been better."

His expression flickered with a flash of anger.

"Don't," I croaked, my throat so dry.

He handed me a glass of water and Lily came back into the room. She held a potion that I was sure was going to taste like bitter vinegar or worse. I scrunched my nose.

She laughed. "It's not as bad as it looks. I promise, and it will speed your healing. That kind of trumps the taste."

She had me there. At this point, I'd give up all my powers to relieve the pain and discomfort. Gavin helped me sit up as Lily propped a mound of fluffy pillows behind my back. I wrinkling my nose again, giving the seaweed-green mixture a look of repugnance. My stomached turned at the sight; forget about what it must taste like.

I took sniff, and was surprised the scent wasn't what I expected, but a cross between citrus limes and clover herbs. Not altogether bad, but I wouldn't drink it voluntarily if it wasn't a matter of easing my aches.

"Here goes nothing," I mumbled, taking a deep breath. I sucked it down in one giant gulp, but getting it down my throat was another matter entirely. I've always had a sensitive gag reflex, and if I hadn't been in someone else's home, I would have pinched my nose. I'd embarrassed myself enough for one do, so I forced it down and was pleased when it went smoothly.

"There you go, dear," Lily coaxed. "Lie back down for a little bit longer and you'll start to feel the effects." She smoothed the hair that stuck to my face unflatteringly.

"What time is it? Will I be able to get home soon?" I asked, my mind on my aunt. If she thought I was missing, it was only a matter of time before she sent out an Amber Alert, the very last thing I needed. The police at my house. My face on the side of milk carton.

"It's a little past one in the morning. I think we'll be able to sneak you home before morning," she said winking.

I smiled as best as I could in return and relaxed more deeply on the pillows.

Sophie replaced her at my bedside. "Hey, there," she said.

"Hey, yourself," I managed.

A tear slipped from the side of her eye, and she wiped it away with the back of her hand. "I'm sorry. I don't know why I'm crying... You really scared me tonight. When Gavin brought you inside—" Her voice caught on a sob.

"Sophie, I'm fine." I grabbed her hand. "Better after the stuff your mom gave. My mind is still a bit fuzzy, but I'm okay."

"I know. You're the only real friend I have here," she said squeezing my hand. "I can't lose you."

"You won't. I'm glad we're friends." And it was true. I might not be the most popular or the friendliest, but I was close to the friends I had and was lucky to have Sophie as one of them.

True to Lily's words, I started feeling better. Magic could certainly hurt, but it could also heal—quickly. Sophie lent me a change of clothes. The warm sweats made me feel like me again, or as close as I could come to feeling normal.

She gave me a long hug as I got ready to leave. "Be safe, little witch."

Gavin drove me home in his mom's car sometime in the wee hours of the morning, before the sun crested over the horizon. I was better.

Not a hundred percent, but alive. What a long night this turned out to be.

I studied Gavin at the wheel. What would I have done tonight without him? I felt more connected to him than ever. "About what happened—"

He cut me off, shifting his body toward me. "Don't say anything. This wasn't your fault."

"But it is," I insisted.

"Bri, you're different. I've never met a witch like you. There is something about your energy, something that Morgana recognizes."

"What does it mean?"

"I don't know...yet. What I do know is that you need to rest. I swear, I will do whatever I can to help you find out what it is she wants," he vowed.

The sun was barely beginning to rise behind the house, framing the yard in a halo. "I know you will. I'm not going to let her use me," I huffed.

He raised a brow, knowing very well this wasn't the last he'd hear of this conversation. "I never thought you would."

"How are we getting in?" I asked, yawning.

He smirked. "I got this."

I never doubted him, not when it came to breaking the rules. I didn't ask what spell he was weaving; all I could think about was my bed.

We made it upstairs without making a sound. Walking into my bedroom was therapeutic in ways I never thought possible. I collapsed on the bed. Gavin came over beside me, tucking me in. He brushed the hair from my face and pressed a light kiss on my forehead. "See you tomorrow," he whispered, and a sparkling tingle of magic spread over my body.

CHAPTER 29

I stayed home from school the next day. My aunt was hovering, and beside herself over the fact that I was sick again. It wasn't like me. I'd been a healthy child. These last few weeks, with everything going on, put me on her radar, not a place I liked to be. But there was no way I could tell her what really happened, or that Gavin was a witch, much less that I was a witch. I was afraid.

Her opinion mattered most to me.

Gavin was at my door the moment my aunt left for the shop. We hadn't said a word about what happened, which was a blessing in disguise, because the more I had the chance to think over what happened, the clearer I remembered professing my love to him. He hadn't brought it up, and I wasn't about to. In my heart, I loved him, but I wasn't yet ready to vocalize that love (except of course unless I was threatened with death). So making the mature decision, I decided to ignore whatever I said or thought I said. The events were still fuzzy.

"What are you doing here?" I asked. Fireflies frolicked at the sight of him, an indicator I was on the mend.

"Checking up on you." He looked at me from head-to-toe, and it had anything but an unhealthy effect on me. I'd say my body was pretty much healed.

My cheeks flushed, and I cleared my throat. "Aren't you supposed to be in first period?"

"You're more important."

Flattered as I was, he needed to go to school. It didn't stop me from smiling. "That's crap. Go to school. I can't have you failing."

He smirked, toying with his hoop. "I won't, nothing a little magic can't fix."

I gave him a stern look.

"It's only one day, Bri. I promise not to miss another day this..." he paused, reconsidering what timeframe he was going to commit to. "Until winter break. Satisfied?"

"I guess." There was a meow from under his jacket. "Why are you meowing?"

He grinned and pulled out a fluffy black kitten. "Every witch needs a cat." He held a wriggling bundle of fur in his arms.

I couldn't help the cooing and ahhing. This was, after all, the cutest kitten on the planet. I took the kitten from Gavin and holding him over my head, I looked into his sweet baby eyes. "You are absolutely adorable." My heart tumbled for this itty-bitty little guy. I never owned a pet. "You're giving me a kitty?"

"I talked to your aunt first, and she said it was okay. I have a trunk full of stuff for him." He watched me with amusement.

I snuggled him into my arms, burying my face in his dark fur. "He's purrrfect, but why the gift?"

Sapphire eyes sparkled. "I told you, every witch needs one. Now comes the important part of being a pet owner. What are we going to name him? I was thinking Merlin," he suggested.

I scrunched me nose. "To obvious."

"You might be right, Gandalf?"

"That was a great movie," I said smiling "But, I'm thinking something original." I stroked his tiny head, and noticed a small white crescent shape on the back of his neck, the only white spot on him. "Lunar."

"Lunar," he said, testing it out. Lunar let out the tiniest meow. "I guess he likes it." He scratched the top of Lunar's furry head, and the kitten purred on contact, the sound vibrating through his little body.

"Oh, I forgot. Your aunt asked me to pick up your homework assignments for you."

"And how did you manage that if you didn't go to school?"

He smirked. "Do you really want to know?"

I shook my head. "No, but I wished you'd spell it all finished."

"Already did."

"Gavin..." I groaned, giving him a look of steel.

"What? Your aunt just said to pick it up. She didn't say anything about you actually having to do it. Look, I was worried about you and your recovery. I didn't want you stressing and laboring over school work. You can't fault me for that."

I groaned. "You're impossible."

"So my parents tell me," he said, but not like he really was offended by it. "How are you feeling?" There was a mood shift in his eyes, concern replacing the light banter.

I walked to the couch, placing Lunar in my lap. "I'm fine. Stop asking." I stroked Lunar's back as he tried to attack my fingers with his baby paws.

Gavin sat down next to me, the couch sinking with his weight. "You look much better."

"I am," I insisted. "In fact, I'm going back to school tomorrow. Oh, tell your mom I said thank you again. What she did for me saved me a lot of trouble."

"She was glad to do it, but you know, Bri, you're going to have to tell your aunt sometime," he stressed.

Another topic I wasn't comfortable yet dealing with. At the rate my list of uncomfortable topics was growing, I was going to be swimming over my head in problems.

I shifted my eyes back down to a wiggling Lunar. "I know," I admitted softly.

"When you're ready...I'll be there to help you."

Lifting my eyes back to his, I replied, "Thanks, it means a lot having you here."

"You mean a lot to me."

My heart swelled, thumping wildly.

We hung the rest of the day on the couch, watching TV and just relaxing. He left right around the time school was got out, and I walked him to the door.

He trailed a finger along my cheek, lifting my chin with his thumb. His touch was soft and electric. I leaned into his caress, my eyes sparkling with out-of-control awareness. I was afraid to think about kissing him, in case I accidentally spelled him, but it didn't stop my body from moving closer to his. My mind or magic had little control over that. He bit on his silver hoop as his head lowered fraction by fraction to mine. I held my breath as I waited impatiently for his lips.

Lunar meowed between the two of us, ruining the moment. I internally moaned at the lost opportunity. He was smashed between us, looking up at me with those baby blue eyes.

"I'm picking you up tomorrow morning for school," he said in a gruff voice.

I hoped he would suffer as much as I would without those few minutes of bliss that I would inevitably be thinking about. I bit my lip, contemplating if I should grab ahold of him and lay one right on him.

Swallowing the lump in my throat, I nodded. "Bye."

Closing the door wistfully behind, I plopped myself down on the couch. Everyone was worried about my health, but I was going stir crazy. I needed to get out of the house, and a quick trip to the Riverfront Farmers Market for dinner tonight would be nice. My aunt wouldn't be home for a few more hours, still plenty of time left in the day to get there, shop around, and make it back to start dinner before my aunt got home.

I loved the farmers market in Wilmington, and the idea was too much to resist. They had more than the average fresh produce. There were vendors with everything from jewelry, arts and crafts and musical entertainment, to every kind of fruit, vegetable and herb you could imagine. Not to mention, the fresh air would do me good.

I twirled the moonstone and amethyst necklace at my neck, rolling the idea in my head while patting Lunar with the other hand. He was curled up next to me, taking a nap and feeling pretty snug. The decision was easy. I had to get out of this house. How dangerous could the market be?

Picking up a protesting Lunar, I placed him in my bedroom, near his food and litter in my bathroom. With him being so tiny, I was afraid to let him wander the house by himself.

After shutting him in my room, I grabbed my keys and headed for Wilmington.

The drive was easy and one I'd done a million times before. During the trip, Tori and Austin had each sent me a text on their way home asking how I was doing. I missed them and was ready to get back to my *normal* routine. When I got to Wilmington, the sun was shining, the sky was crystal blue, and I soaked up the rays after being cooped up in the house. I took my time, strolling leisurely from vendor to vendor, looking at all the merchandise. I had a deep, reflective mood going. I wanted to just enjoy the drama-free day and lose myself in the crowds.

My world might never be the same. Who I was had changed. Magic was a part of my life, and I needed to find a way to conquer the power inside before it destroyed me or hurt someone I loved. Unearthing answers to questions of the past and the future seemed my only hope at figuring out what was happening to me.

I didn't know where Gavin and I stood, or why he was reluctant to take what we had further. But I knew my heart and what I felt for him wouldn't diminish, something twined us together like vines to a trellis.

I hadn't decided what to tell my friends about my newfound magical powers. I don't even know if I should. This would be a helluva secret to keep from them, and I didn't know how long I'd be able to keep up the charade. They were smart. They knew me. And they were bound to notice I was different. Worst case, I could cast a memory spell, make them forget. Well, not really.

It was impossible to believe all that had happened, and my senior year had barely begun. I didn't have a clue what I was doing after high school, let alone next week. Winter was coming, and the last few days of fall were started to fade.

I was admiring an intricate design on a handwoven bracelet, when I looked up and caught a flash of sandy hair that reminded me of Lukas. Squinting, I tried to get a glimpse of his face, because the similarities were frighteningly familiar, and I'd too many weird things happen to me. The boy angled his face toward me, grinning at the girl behind the table, and the knot in my stomach released. He lacked Lukas's lustrous smile.

If I was seeing things, I was tired. I sped through the remaining vendors, grabbing what I needed. My last stop was the pepper stand. I riffled through, testing their ripeness, and I was suddenly saturated with a familiar energy.

I lifted my eyes over the stack of vegetables, searching for the source—another witch maybe? It was difficult with the number of people about.

Then across the booth from where I stood, emerald eyes smiled at me over the fresh produce stand. This time I knew I wasn't dreaming, and my eyes weren't deceiving me.

"Lukas?"

Ready for the next part of Gavin & Brianna's story?
Grab your next Gavin fix and continue reading book two, Amethyst Tears.

CAN'T WAIT to meet you back in Holly Ridge!
Thank you for reading.
xoxo
Jennifer
P.S. Join my VIP Readers email list and receive a bonus scene told from Zane's POV, as well as a free copy of Saving Angel, book one in the Bestselling Divisa Series. You will also get notifications of what's new, giveaways, and new releases.

Visit here to sign up: www.jlweil.com

Don't forget to also join my Dark Divas FB Group and have some fun with me and a fabulous, fun group of readers. There is games, prizes, and lots of book love.

Join here: https://www.facebook.com/groups/1217984804898988/

You can stop in and say hi to me on Facebook night and day. I pop in as often as I can: https://www.facebook.com/jenniferlweil/ I'd love to hear from you.

PART II
AMETHYST TEARS

CHAPTER 1

THE DAY BEFORE MY LIFE changed forever felt like any other day.

In a blink, my life went from unbelievable to completely messed up. How did this kind of stuff even happen to me? Wasn't it enough that I accepted there was such a thing as witches? Or that I accepted my fate as a witch? Now the universe had to go and throw me a curveball.

Un-freaking-believable.

I was a magnet for disaster, which appeared to not have changed. My life was exhausting. Not to mention, I was still recovering from a psychotic dream with a very old and very dead witch.

Lucky me.

I was glue for trouble.

And to think, I thought Gavin was the bad boy. He didn't have shit on me. And that brought me to my current predicament.

My eyes still couldn't acknowledge what was right in front of me, smiling with those heart-sinking dimples.

This had to be some kind of aftereffect or symptom from dream-scaping. I wasn't certain what the heck that was, but I had no other logical explanation.

"Lukas?" I heard the incredibility in my voice. Who wouldn't be more than a little freaked out at seeing a figment of their imagination come to life? I mean, this wasn't fiction, this was my real life.

Leaving my house for some fresh air at the Farmer's Market no longer seemed like it had been the smartest decision I'd made. I was known to have my ideas backfire on me. Hell, maybe I was still sick. I could always blackout again.

His breathtaking smile captured me from across the tomatoes, and he was not in the least bit shocked to see me. Whereas my jaw had literally dropped to the ground, and I had yet to pick it up. Sandy hair lazily flopped on one side of his forehead.

Seriously. This couldn't possibly be. I pinched myself, squeezed my eyes shut, and demanded that I wake up. How had I fallen asleep? It was the only rationalization I could deduce, even though I swore it felt so real. The only time I ever saw Lukas was when I was dreaming... In conclusion, I must be dreaming.

He walked in front of me, and my eyes ate up his easy strides, time moving in a slow-motion film. His carefree smile bloomed on his tan face when he reached me, deep dimples and all. He stroked a hand alongside my cheek, while I stood there frozen in place—dumb-founded.

The feeling was exactly how I dreamed, soft and tender.

"You're real," he said, his honey silk voice caressing my ears as easily as his hand on my face.

I leaned into his palm, the spicy warmth of his scent rocking my senses. *I'm real*, I thought. He was the one in *my* dreams. "Lukas...?"

I couldn't seem to get past his name, or past the fact that he stood in front of me for my eyes to feast upon. He was my best friend of another dimension, another realm—the realm of dreams. I had poured my heart out to him on numerous occasions. He was the closest I'd ever been to anyone because he wasn't real.

Lukas laughed, nodding, emerald eyes shining in the sunlight. "In the flesh. I always wondered if we'd meet somewhere other than your dreams—not that I mind being in them. It's the highlight of my night."

My head was spinning so fast, I was afraid it was going to twist right off. I could imagine it rolling down the market next to a runaway apple.

Okay, I was game. If we were going to pretend this was in fact real, and not a product of my dreams, then game on. "How is this possible?" I asked, unable to tear my eyes away. Who knew? He might vanish. Poof. Gone. I was back to wondering if I was losing my sanity.

His hand took mine in his, idly playing with our fingers. "Well, I am a freshman at the University of North Carolina in Wilmington. I guess fate decided we should meet," he said, completely dodging what I really wanted to know.

I wanted to know how he was even *here,* flesh and blood. How he was alive?

Fate wouldn't be so cruel as to have him practically under my nose all these years, right? I had even toured the campus during my junior year. That was the university I had chosen to attend next year.

Should I be angry? Should I be overjoyed? Or just awestruck?

If we were still playing the *is he real* game, then I felt all of the above and a gazillion other emotions I couldn't identify until my brain started functioning again. "Umm, that's not exactly what I meant. How are you alive?"

He looked at me liked I'd grown a third eye. "Don't you know?"

Duh. If I knew would I be asking? "Know what?"

"I just assumed you knew. You're a witch," he whispered, moving in closer to me, avoiding anyone overhearing our conversation. His breath tickled my ear.

I rolled my eyes. "I know I'm a witch. What does that have to do with this?" I asked, gesturing to the two of us standing in the middle of the Farmer's Market.

He shot me a funny look as if I was crazy. Maybe he wasn't that far off, because nothing in my world made sense. "You dreamscape, Brianna," he said calmly.

"Dreamscape," I repeated. "Yeah, I know. Am I dreamscaping now?"

His darker brows furrowed together. "No. This is real."

I shook my head. "It can't be." I was thinking he was feeding me a line of crap—teasing me—but I knew Lukas and the expression on his face was stonily serious. This wasn't a game.

He glanced around the Farmer's Market. "I think it's best we have this discussion elsewhere. We should meet tomorrow and talk. It sounds like we have a lot of catching up."

I was so aggravated by my ignorance that I wanted to scream. Why did everyone around me know what was going on but me? "I can't tomorrow. I have school."

He ran a hand through his highlighted hair. "Right, I forgot. How about this weekend? Saturday?" He smiled warmly.

I nodded my head. "Sure, I can meet you Saturday."

"How about on campus? I could show you around, and we could get something to eat."

"All right," I agreed. "That sounds fine." At this point, I would have met him on the moon, if he'd asked; my mind was so jumbled from seeing him.

Lukas put a hand on my shoulder. "Hey, are you going to be okay?" he asked, scanning my face, which was stripped of color.

I straightened my shoulders and met his concerned gaze. "I'll be fine. It's just been an overwhelming week. I-I can't believe you're real," I stuttered.

He grinned at me, with the sun shining at his back. "I've waited a long time to see you." His hand lifted my chin until I looked into his dark green eyes.

I gulped. A memory of us sharing a kiss in one of my dreams had my cheeks staining red. I guess best friends don't kiss, so maybe he was more. Maybe I had feelings for him. In my dreams, it has seemed so harmless, but now... I didn't know.

"Here, take my number." He grabbed an old receipt from his pocket, scribbling on the back of it before handing it to me. "Text me Saturday when you're on your way."

I took the wrinkly slip from his hand and felt the tiniest surge. Perhaps it was all my own doing, but something told me Lukas wasn't just a guy. He wasn't just a college student who I happened to drag into my dreams.

"Okay," I replied, on autopilot. My voice sounded drained and tired.

"See you soon," he said. "You could always dream of me." The grin on his face was playful as he turned and left.

He walked away, weaving around the booths of the market. "I don't even know how," I mumbled to myself.

I stared into thin air long after he was gone. A small, elderly lady with a bag of veggies and fruits bumped into me, startling me from my trance. Like a rush, the sounds of the noisy market came back at full speed.

"Pardon me," said the bird-like woman. "These bags are bigger than me."

"It's okay," I assured. "Do you need help to your car? I was just leaving," I said.

"Aren't you the sweetheart? But I'll manage." She waddled ahead of me.

I followed behind her, just in case, as we headed to the parking lot. When I got to my car, I put my purchase in the backseat and drove home. As I walked through the front door, I heard the faintest meow from upstairs.

"Lunar!" I exclaimed, my thoughts immediately turning to Gavin. How was I going to explain Lukas? Where did that leave us? I wasn't sure I wanted anything to change, yet I knew this was the kind of *thing* that changed everything—another thing that scared me shitless.

I set the bags down in the hall and jogged upstairs to my room. Lunar nudged out his moist pink nose at my entrance. I scooped him up and snuggled against his downy fur, scratching his head. Lunar, who was just as happy to see me, starting purring.

"C'mon on, stinker, let's go make dinner," I murmured against his fur, his ears perked up at my voice.

In the kitchen, I started washing and cutting the fresh vegetables I'd bought. Lunar wove in between my legs, making a nuisance of himself and attacked my shoelaces. I couldn't stop thinking about Lukas: about the kiss we'd shared and all of the intimate details I shared with him. At least I didn't have to explain Gavin to Lukas. He already knew, thanks to one of my blabbering moments.

How had I gone from having not a single guy look my way to two possible boyfriends? There was no way was I doing a juggling act. But I didn't know what else to do, for the moment.

Distracted by Lunar's antics and my mixed-up thoughts, I was being careless. In my absentmindedness, my finger slipped right as I brought the blade down. "Crap!" I stuck my bleeding finger in my mouth, trying to alleviate the sting. It wasn't the most sanitary action, but that was the least of concerns on my building mountain of problems.

I was lucky; it was just a nick. I ran the wound under the faucet, threw a Band-Aid on, and finished dinner just as Aunt Clara walked in.

"Hey, how are you feeling?" she asked, pushing the hair from my face. She needed to make sure I hadn't broken out in a fever.

"I'm fine," I insisted, shaking off her hand.

Lunar meowed at her feet. She bent down and picked up the little black furball, saving me from any more scrutiny. "And who is this little guy?" she asked in a baby voice. Lunar just looked at her with his big, blue eyes.

"That...is trouble. I named him Lunar."

"Well, Lunar, you are too cute." She rubbed his belly, and he closed his eyes in appreciation.

"Are you really okay with this?" I asked. I didn't want to burden her with any more stress or responsibility.

She nodded. "Of course, I thought it was a great idea." Her expression turned serious as she eyed me. "He cares for you. And I like him."

I swallowed. Guilt, there it was, swarming into my belly. "I know," I nodded, quietly keeping my eyes on the floor.

"Hmm, something smells good." She set Lunar on his feet, and he padded under the table, batting at a loose tie from one of the chair cushions.

Aunt Clara grabbed the plates, and I dished up dinner as we sat down at the table. It wasn't long before she picked up on my distractedness. I was unusually quiet and kept pushing my rice around my plate in aimless patterns. So much for trying to fake it until I could make it.

Halfway through, she set her food aside. "Brianna, are you going to tell me what's going on? You've been pretending to eat for the last ten minutes."

I stopped spinning circles with my rice and intentionally shoveled a forkful in my mouth. She lifted a brow, unimpressed by my grand gesture.

Sighing, I tried to find a reasonable explanation for my spacey-ness. "I'm tired. I think I might have overdone it today." What a lame excuse, but it was all I had. I forced myself to swallow. "I've got so much catching up to do at school tomorrow. I probably should get to bed early."

That she agreed on, and it got me out of the spotlight. "You go on up to bed; I'll take care of the dishes."

I nodded and scooped up a yawning Lunar. We'd both had an exhausting day.

Safely behind closed doors, I dropped the façade, no longer having to pretend I wasn't having a teenage crisis. It was more than teenage problems—witch problems, maybe. My anxiety was through the roof. Tomorrow was my first day back since the dream incident with Morgana. The loony witch had tried to flatten Gavin with a spell that I had stepped in, taking the full force of her wrath. It had knocked me unconscious, leaving my body battered and bruised. Lily, Gavin's mom, had given me a potion that had healed most of the aches.

I was going to have to face Gavin tomorrow, and I didn't know what to say to him. He would undoubtedly pick up on my scattered emotions, but since I wasn't ready to tell him about Lukas yet, I would have to be an exceptional actress. To make matters worse, his sister, who was also my friend, could read auras. I didn't even think there was a way to fake those.

I was up shit creek.

There was no way this situation had a positive ending, no matter how I looked at it. Either way, I was going to lose someone.

CHAPTER 2

G AVIN WAS WAITING FOR ME in the school parking lot. My eyes ran over the length of him, devouring his dark, yummy form. My dark witch. Dressed in his usual black jeans and gray shirt, one of his unlaced boots was crossed over the other as he leaned on his car—eyeing me from top-to-bottom. It sent a parade of fireflies in my belly. I couldn't help them. Just the sight of him made my heart flip-flop and sigh.

We weren't technically dating, but neither of us was seeing anyone else...well, sort of. The whole Lukas thing was confusing.

The timing couldn't have sucked any more. Just as things between Gavin and I were getting hotter, Lukas showed up. As much as we were seen together at school, everyone assumed we were a couple. And that was just fine by me. In fact, I preferred it.

I wasn't entirely sure why we weren't dating, and it was an issue I'd been thinking lately to rectify, meaning I was going to ask what the heck was going on between us. I was—until yesterday—before Lukas being *real*. Now, I wasn't sure of anything, except that Gavin still made my heart race and my breath catch.

He smirked at my approach, and I couldn't help but smile in return. I took the hand he offered. Even with the mixture of fireflies and anxiety, when I was with him, he was the only one I wanted to be with. Lukas seemed like a tiny blip in my life as Gavin's fingers caressed the skin over my pulse.

The flitting thought of Lukas brought all those doubts and nerves bubbling to the forefront of my mind, and I was glad Sophie wasn't around to see my aura fly all over the place.

"How was Lunar last night?" Gavin asked, his dark and sinful voice filling me with warmth and making the fireflies dance.

Lunar was like the devil on speed. "He was very bad. Kept me up half the night playing with my hair and knotting it."

He laughed, and the sound was bliss. "What a lucky kitty."

I rolled my eyes.

He played with our fingers as we walked toward school. "You look better." His eyes roamed over me in a way that had me flushing.

I glanced down at my feet. "I am better." If you discredit the crazy insane predicament I was in.

"Good, because we need to talk after school."

I gulped. *Oh no*, I thought. He knows.

He lowered his voice and leaned close, his soft breath tickling my ear as we walked into school. "About what happened in your dream with Morgana," he clarified.

I let out a sigh of relief. "Right, the whole dreamscape thingy." This was a good and way overdue conversation. Hopefully, it would answer some questions I had about Lukas. "One problem, though. I have to work tonight."

He shrugged. "No biggie. I'll just come by when you get home tonight. Your aunt will never know." He gave me that troublesome grin of his.

"Great," I muttered and pasted on a smile. I was horrible at lying and keeping secrets. The deception was already getting out of hand. Fast. And this was only the beginning.

I was doomed.

Usually, the idea of having Gavin in my room was exactly what I longed for. Now, being alone with him made me nervous. I might slip up and mention Lukas. I wasn't sure I could hold off until Saturday after I talked with Lukas.

The bell rang through the halls.

I swear he pouted. He wasn't a fan of school. We were so yin and yang. "Ugh. Guess that means we have to get to class. See you in chem," he grumbled, squeezing my hand.

I nodded, my skin still tingling from his touch.

Since the afternoon we met, any contact we had always brought this incredible zing. It was supposed to be from our magic because we were witches, but with him, everything was always...more.

Austin grinned at me when I took my seat in English. Mrs. Schwab began her lecture, chalk scribbling over the chalkboard, yet my mind was anywhere but on congruent verbs. It was worrying about getting through the rest of the day.

After class Austin walked out with me. "Hey, babygirl, we missed you." He looked so cute in his Guess jeans and gel-styled hair. Plus, he smelled incredible. Austin swung for the same team, and he took a ton of shit from idiots like Rianne at Holly Ridge High. Rianne was the absolute worst.

We'd gotten into an altercation a few months ago, and I sort of zapped her with magic, leaving some nasty cherry welts on her. In my defense, I didn't know at the time I was a witch or that I was doing magic. Not that it mattered. Rianne deserved it for being a bitch.

"Believe it or not, I missed you too. Anything happen?" I asked as we walked side-by-side down the hall, pretty much in our own little bubble.

He lightly bumped my shoulder. "Nah, just the same crap every day. I do think I heard that Rianne was dropped from the top of the pyramid during practice yesterday. Would have paid to have seen that."

"No kidding. Would it be too much to hope it knocked some sense into her?" She was definitely not one of my favorite people. The feeling was mutual.

"You sure you're feeling better?" he asked, lines of concern creasing his manicured brows.

Leave it to one of my best friends to see through my ruse. Neither Tori nor Austin knew I was a witch, or that witches were a thing. For now, it was best the truth stayed hidden, regardless that it was killing me having to keep something this huge from them. They were, after all, the only friends I had besides Sophie and Gavin...and I guess Lukas. I wasn't sure where I stood with him, but I would find out this weekend.

I nodded. "Yeah. Just stressed." That was an understatement, but at least the truth.

"You got this," he encouraged, thinking I meant catching up in my classes. If he only knew. His confidence was bittersweet.

"Thanks," I mumbled. "Catch you at lunch," I replied before we split off in different directions.

Our high school was like a giant octopus. All the halls stemmed off from a circular hub like tentacles. The approach of third period crumbled any confidence I might have gained from the comforts of routine.

Lost in my head, I never heard anyone sneak up behind me, not until his hands spanned my waist, and then I jumped like a fool in front of half my class.

"You nearly gave me a heart attack!" I shrieked, smacking Gavin on the chest.

He laughed in my ear behind me. "Wasn't hard. You were a million miles away." I hadn't been just a million miles away; I'd been in another galaxy. "What's on your mind, beautiful?"

It always embarrassed me when he gave me compliments, especially ones that weren't true. "Nothing," I shrugged. "Just the usual." For Gavin, the "usual" meant witchcraft and all the baggage that came with it. Or in my case, the strange and unexplainable happenings that occurred only to me. Any other witch my age didn't have to deal with half the crap I did.

His sapphire eyes were sparkling like stars, and the corners of his lips smirked. Lips I was well familiar with. Gavin was a good kind of distraction, and boy did I need to be distracted.

My heart constricted as I thought about what I was eventually going to have to tell him. With Gavin, I didn't want there to be anything between us.

No lies.

No hiding.

No secrets.

I have had enough of being left in the dark. From now on, I was going to take charge of my life. How else was I going to protect those I loved? And Gavin was at the very top of the list.

"I've just got a lot on my mind," I said, trying to convince him as much as myself. Every moment we were together, my guilt magnified. And that frightened me, maybe more than my unexplainable dreams.

Gavin and I took our seats at our table, and he scooted his chair closer to me. Warm tingles skated across the nape of my neck. Our legs brushed under the table, and I felt the flash of energy. It made my insides sing.

"I can't wait to see you tonight." His words hinted that there would be way more than just talking going on.

Lord help me. My pulse jumped. All too well I could recall the feel of his lips on mine, the cool steel of his hoop on my burning mouth.

As if he could read my mind, his eyes darkened to midnight, and I watched him twirl the ring at his lip. The class around me disappeared, and I leaned forward, bringing our lips even closer. He was like the most addictive drug. The closer we were, the more I needed him.

My brain was consumed with thoughts of how much I wanted to sink into him—how much I wanted him to make me forget my problems.

He wiggled his brow at me. "It's probably best if you wait until after class to devour me." Even his smirk was becoming irresistible.

His words were like a splash of cold water, shaking me out of the haze of desire. Being near him caused me to lose my head, my emotions going haywire every time.

I gave him a look of exasperation, putting some needed distance between us. His grin only widened.

I rolled my eyes.

By lunch, I was ready to call it a day. Tori, Austin, and Sophie were waiting at our usual table as I approached.

"Eeee! I'm so glad you are back." Tori's high-pitched voice was over-exaggerated, drawing way too much attention.

You'd think I had just come back from a year abroad. I had only been gone a few days, for goodness' sake, but I appreciated their concern nonetheless.

"You look better," Sophie whispered as she gave me a quick hug.

"How are you feeling?" We both knew there was an underlying question.

I nodded. "Fine. It feels great to be out of the house. I was literally going stir crazy at home."

"Where is that reckless brother of mine? I am surprised he isn't glued to your side." Sophie asked.

I shrugged. "I don't know, actually. He was here for third period."

She pursed her lips. "You know, you're the only reason he shows for third period anyway."

"Speaking of smexy and gorgeous, have you guys made it official?" Austin asked with a sly grin.

Everyone at the table was staring my way, waiting for me to dish some dirt on our relationship status. "I hate to disappoint you, but..."

Tori snorted. "You guys just need to get it on already." Sex—her answer to everything.

Sophie snickered beside me.

"I second that," Austin commented, adding his two-cents.

If I'd had food in front of me, I would have tossed it at the three of them. They were lucky my appetite was on the fritz. I took a sip through the straw of my chocolate shake, ignoring them.

Chocolate cured everything.

Most of the time.

"Should I give that bonehead brother of mine a nudge?" Sophie asked with just a bit too much enthusiasm.

I choked on the smooth shake. "Sophie! Don't you dare!"

She smiled in response, and I wasn't reassured.

"Sophie, I am serious," I warned.

"Fine. I won't say anything, but seriously, one of you needs to make the first move. Honestly, I'm a little floored he hasn't. Gavin isn't usually so cautious with girls. He must really like you."

It was like twisting a knife in an open wound. Her intentions were good; it was my guilt that was panging me.

After lunch, Sophie caught up with me in the hall as I headed to my locker. "Hey, I noticed your aura is off. It's a weird mixture of brown and pink. You know you can talk to me if something is bothering you, right?"

I could feel beads of sweat lining my brow. There wasn't much you could hide from magic. "I know." I was almost afraid to ask what the colors meant. I needed was an aura reference guide or something. "What does that mean?"

"Auras aren't always clear. Each color tends to have multiple feelings attached to it. In your case, brown can be confusion or deception and pink can be guilt or love. So what's going on in the pretty head of yours?"

"More than I think I can handle."

"Hey." She laid a gentle hand on my arm. "You're not alone."

I didn't have it in me to tell her this was more than self-esteem issues or coping with being a witch. This time it went outside my personal demons.

CHAPTER 3

O N MY DRIVE HOME AFTER WORK, I was filled with a
concoction of emotions: excitement, anticipation, and anxiety. There was nothing I wanted more than to be alone with
Gavin, doing all the wicked things my mind imagined, but I knew the
moment he found about my *secret,* we would lose something. The
longer I stalled, the bigger the damage to our relationship, and I so
wanted a relationship with Gavin.

Didn't I?

Then there was that, the purple elephant in the room. What were
my feelings about Lukas? Did I want something more than friendship
from him?

I was so frustrated with myself.

How could I possibly be so sure I loved Gavin, then turn around
and doubt those feelings?

I was a mess.

With my hip, I bumped open the door to my bedroom, and my
heart sighed like a sappy love song. Gavin was spread out on my bed,
a purring, blissful Lunar curled against his side. He looked like he
should be on the cover of Rolling Stones. Dark. Edgy. Killer eyes. The
two of them together looked like trouble and more trouble. He aimed

a downright sinister grin my way as if he could see the naughty images conjuring in my head. They would have made the devil himself blush.

I was drawn to him. Not just drawn—compelled might be a better word.

Just staring at him, I was filled with a boost of confidence. When it came to boys, I was more than a little inexperienced; I was downright clueless. It wasn't like there was a step-by-step manual on dating or a guide to teenage love. If there was, I probably would have memorized it.

Our gazes locked, and a surge of empowerment ribboned within me.

Maybe some part of me was tapping into my magic, or maybe it was because Gavin made me feel beautiful. Wherever my newfound confidence stemmed from, I wasn't about to let it slip through my fingers. I was going to take full advantage of it while it lasted. Meaning, I was going to take full advantage of Gavin.

I tossed the keys on my dresser and crawled into bed alongside him, propping my head on my hand. His eyes hadn't left mine since I entered the room. Neither of us said a word. Words weren't needed for what I had in mind.

We had at least an hour before my aunt came home, and I wasn't about to waste any more time. Without a second thought, I started what I had wanted since chemistry class.

Our lips met in one quick, fluid motion. The spark of our magic ignited as soon as our mouths touched. It was a fine line between pleasure and pain. For some insane reason, it felt like we hadn't kissed in years. I was starved for him—for his touch.

He fisted a hand into my hair, tugging me closer to him. I could feel the waves of heat coming off of him as our bodies collided. This was...crazy and wonderful, at the same time.

As if he wasn't satisfied with our closeness, I abruptly found myself lying on my back and Gavin's glorious weight sinking into me. Our lips never lost contact. Talk about skills. He tasted of summer nights as he deepened the kiss, smoldering and heady.

I slipped my hand under his shirt, running my fingers over the planes of his back. I was beyond thinking rationally. Beyond thinking at all. It was all need. Lust. Hormones gone wild.

Holy hot moonbeams.

Bunching my fingers at the hem of his shirt, I pushed it up and in a swift movement, it landed on the bedroom floor. My fingers couldn't have been happier. I traced patterns on his back and dark stormy eyes locked onto mine, holding me prisoner.

A strangled groan escaped before he took possession of my lips again, more potent than before, blowing off the hotness radar. My fingers dug into his already messy hair, and my lips greedily ravished his. I loved the texture and feel of him.

His knee shifted between my legs as I soared to yet another dimension. Nuzzling my neck, his lip ring left a cool trail behind the scorching heat. His body contoured to mine in all the right places. Inside me, there was a feeling I couldn't yet identify. Magic-y, I guess, a strand of energy that pulled us together. Being with him like this was beyond words.

It was unworldly.

I never wanted it to end.

When had I become such a hussy?

I loved the tingling sensation his hands left on my skin. It made me wonder if these were normal teenage reactions, or if our touch and feelings were heightened because of what we were—witches. I had to believe the latter. Being a witch changed the rules.

More than ever, I wanted to tap into my magic. It radiated under my skin, ready to be unleashed. The tingles launched from the center of my chest, splintering everywhere—building with each kiss.

If I could ever think intelligently again, I wanted to ask him about it. Right now, all I could think about was how heavenly Gavin's lips were. I was floating on a mystical cloud.

We shifted positions on the bed, and a very loud and angry hiss sounded through the room. Neither of us was prepared for the abrupt interruption.

Lunar was standing on the bed on all fours, with his fur spiked like an arched bow. He looked like a tiny panther. Ears low, he stared into the air, hissing at nothing.

I sighed and ran a hand through my hair. Rascally cat. *What has gotten into him?*

Gavin was still hovering above me and indecision ran through the depth of his ocean eyes. I could see the choice swimming in them. Did he kiss me again as he clearly wanted to, or do the sensible thing and stop things before they went too far?

Then he closed his eyes briefly, and I knew what choice had won.

My body was still humming like a live wire, but he was right. We needed to slow down.

I sat up as he reached down and grabbed his discarded shirt. My heart was racing, so I took a deep breath and hugged my knees.

Gavin settled back down beside me, both of us staring straight ahead. "Well, that was intense." His voice was gruff.

Boy was it ever. Intense might not be a strong enough description. "I'll say," I muttered under my breath, brushing my hair back into place as best I could. I wasn't sure how we were going to just *talk* when my body was thinking about anything but talking. "So..." I said lamely, breaking the sexual tension still vibrating in the air.

He leaned back against the bed beside me, leaving just enough space so our bodies didn't touch. A wise choice. "So..." he echoed, making me grin.

I turned my head toward him. "I missed you at lunch. Where were you?"

"I had some stuff to take care of," he replied nonchalantly.

"What kind of stuff?" I hated that I was being so nosey. It was not like I expected him to never leave my side. Or that I needed to know where he was at every second of the day. But, I had this inkling he'd been up to no good.

"The magical kind of stuff," he said evasively.

Smooth.

I let it go. He obviously didn't want to talk about it. And did I want to know? There was enough bouncing around inside my head without worrying about what kind of trouble Gavin was getting into. I'm sure it was plenty.

"How have you been sleeping?" he asked, studying my face, looking for any physical indication I was having restless nights.

What he really wanted to know was if I had any of those crazy dreams, the dreams where I summon other people. "I haven't had any of *those* kinds of dreams, if that's what you are wondering."

"What kind of dreams are you having?" he murmured, and I felt myself getting sucked in again.

I grabbed the nearest pillow and tossed it at his head. Gavin had reflexes like a ninja and magic. Before the pillow had a chance to hit him on the head, it met an unfortunate demise. Fabric and stuffing snowed all over the bed, Gavin's spell having destroyed it.

Lunar was going to go bonkers over the mess if he ever came out of hiding. I glared at Gavin in annoyance. "Was that necessary?"

He held up both hands smirking. "Hey, you attacked me."

Resting my head on the headboard, I chewed on my bottom lip. The mention of dreamscaping had flooded back all the emotional anxiety about Lukas.

Gavin angled his body toward me, sapphire eyes narrowing. "I can see a gazillion questions running around in that head of yours."

Boy, did I have questions. I started with the one that seemed to be the cause of all my trepidation lately: dreamscaping. What exactly was it, and how the hell did it work? "You said I dreamscape. What does that mean?"

"Dreamscaping is a merger of dreams. Usually it involves two people, but in some cases, if the witch is powerful enough, they would be able to summon more."

I gulped. One time I had both Gavin and Lukas in a dream together. Worse, I didn't even know *I* was doing it.

With a deadly smirk, his fingers plucked pillow stuffing strewn in my hair. "We've shared dreams, and as you know, they can be very real."

Uh, you could say that again. I absently played with pieces of stuffing on the bed. "The people I summon, can they refuse to dream with me?"

"Yes. The person you summon can accept or refuse. Although, there are witches with the power to take the decision out of their hands," he added.

Oh, God. Was I that kind of witch? Did I force them into my dreams?

He noticed the self-conviction that spread over my expression, lifted my chin with his finger until my eyes met his. "You didn't force me into your dreams."

"Well, at least that's comforting," I muttered. But what about Lukas?

"Bri, you're too hard on yourself. Give it time and *you* will feel more in control."

He was probably right. I needed practice, loads of it. Then I might feel more in my own skin and used to being a witch. Now would have been the perfect opportunity to explain about Lukas, except my tongue wasn't cooperating. Try as I might, I couldn't form the words.

Instead, I chickened out, like a total pansy. "You're right. It's just I've never felt so unsure or lost before." Not since I lost my parents.

"We're going to change that." Always the voice of reason, and he said just what I needed to hear. His confidence was like a shield.

I envied him for it. "This is so much more complicated than I bargained for," I mumbled.

"It might be, but the pay-off is huge. Plus you get to spend more time with me." His grin said it all.

"This is serious," I groaned.

His eyes sobered. "I know. I just don't like seeing you stressed."

Tucking my legs underneath me, I turned and faced him. I wondered if there was any chance that dream- and weather- casting were the extent of my abilities. Was that all the magic I had? "So, should I expect any other abilities to pop up?" As if dreamscaping and weathercasting weren't enough.

"Something tells me that exploring your magic will be anything but dull. It should be downright entertaining." His eyes gleamed with anticipation.

Gavin had a warped sense of entertainment. "Great," I replied, dripping in sarcasm. "I can't wait."

Just what kind of witch was I?

And who the hell was going to clean up this mess?

CHAPTER 4

S ATURDAY ARRIVED FAR TOO QUICKLY, and not soon enough.

My hands were unsteady, my palms were sweating, and I couldn't decide if I was going to throw up or pass out. It was like a giant mountain of emotions. Fear. Guilt. Excitement.

Sweet Jesus, I was a disaster.

All morning I fought with myself. Did I text him to cancel because I was chickenshit? Or did I grow some ovaries and get the answers I sought? These were the kind of questions that ran through my mind. Even if he didn't show up, I could summon him in my dreams, and get the answers I wanted. But if I was being honest with myself, I wanted to see him. I needed another visual to make sure he was real, that I hadn't imagined the whole encounter.

I hated that I was keeping Lukas a secret from the people that mattered most. My heart ached just thinking about Gavin, pinpricks of pain spearing my gut.

So why was I?

The answer was like trying to figure out the meaning of life.

What I did know was I needed the truth. And Lukas was somehow part of this. I needed to find out how he fit in, if he fit in, and what he knew.

I tossed another crumbled up shirt into the corner of my room and changed for like the zillionth time. Fed up with my wardrobe, I huffed and sent him a quick text before I changed my mind yet again. Then I headed for the door.

Well, here goes nothing. If anything, I hoped I would at least walk away from this with some kind of understanding of what was going on between us. Only then I could move forward to the next problem in line.

The University of North Carolina campus was a maze for a small-town girl like me. Even though I had been here before, suddenly it felt as if I was being swallowed up. I was Alice, lost in Wonderland.

We were to meet at a place called the Hawk's Nest, a large dining center on campus. There wasn't an abundance of students lounging around, probably because it was a Saturday. The wind destroyed my ponytail, and I brushed aside the flyaways as I scanned the sitting area and locked with a pair of emerald eyes I knew far too well. I would have even recognized him in my sleep.

Ha. Ha. Ha.

If I didn't find some form of humor in all this, I was going to lose my nerve. My legs were like Jell-O as I walked toward him, and I thought my heart was going to jump out of my chest. For reasons I couldn't explain, this wasn't like meeting Lukas in my dreams.

This was more...real.

Putting one foot in front of the other, I concentrated on each step. It was his sunny smile that finally set me somewhat at ease. That smile was familiar, with those deep dimples, and it would warm even the coldest of hearts. I was still anxious about what I would learn, but this was a guy I had spent more time with than any other.

This was Lukas. My best friend. The guy who knew all my secrets and every nitty, gritty detail.

It didn't have to be weird. I just needed to stop thinking about all the dirty laundry he knew, and I needed to stop thinking about the kiss and what it could have meant.

I slid into the seat across from him, giving him a sheepish grin. "Hey."

His smile brightened. "You're nervous," he said, hitting the mark on the head.

There he went, reminding me how well he knew me and how little I knew him. "Uh, I am. Is that weird?"

"In this situation, I don't think weird cuts it." He had on a UNC T-shirt, looking like just another college boy.

I took a moment to study him, see if there were any differences between dream-Lukas and the real version. He looked exactly as I could recall. A poster ad for the boy next door: sandy hair, football-player build, and a smile as bright as the sun, with the greenest eyes I'd ever seen.

"Do you want something to drink?" he asked.

A drink would be good, something to do with my hands and calm my jittery nerves. We could get to the heavy stuff in a minute. "Sure. Caramel Macchiato?"

The corners of his mouth lifted. "You would be one of those girls that drinks fancy coffees I can barely pronounce. I'll be right back."

I watched him stroll over to the Starbucks stand with carefree swagger. He filled out his jeans in all the right places and was hard to ignore. I didn't seem to be the only one who was looking—girls turned their heads as he walked past.

Who could blame them, when he aimed dreamy dimples their way? I'd have to be dead not to be affected.

Seriously, I totally shouldn't be checking out his ass. I forced my gaze back to the table, mentally scolding myself, and fumbled with the stones on my necklace. It crossed my mind that not too long ago, I was in a coffee shop with Gavin.

The thought weighed heavily on me.

A few minutes later, Lukas set a paper cup in front of me, bringing me back from my trip down memory lane. I was glad to have something else to do with my hands. Wrapping them around the paper cup, I blew off a stream of steam.

Silence stretched between us. Where did I even begin? Lukas took care of the matter, and I couldn't have been more relieved.

Stirring a cup of black coffee, he said, "So you finally figured out you have magic."

My eyes glanced around the room, and I realized that we were strategically situated in a far corner, away from anyone who might pick up pieces of our conversation. Wouldn't that have been an epic debacle? "Yeah. It only took me seventeen years." I took a huge gulp of my frothy drink.

Heaven.

He chuckled low.

"How is it that we practically live in the same city and have never run into each other before?" I asked what had to be on both our minds.

He shrugged, causally stretching his legs out under the table so they just touched mine. I couldn't tell if it was deliberate or not. "Honesty, I haven't got a clue. It's been running through my head since the market. I knew you were out there, I just—"

"How?" I interrupted. "How did you know that I wasn't just a dream?"

His eyes danced at my confusion. "Because we have more than just dream-sharing in common. I'm like you, Brianna—a witch."

"A witch!" I cried. *Christ almighty.*

He nodded his pretty-boy head. "I would have thought you would have figured it out by now."

He thought wrong. But now that he said it, I should have known. I should have seen the signs. Tingles. Bizarre crap. The fact that he knew more about witchcraft than I did.

There might as well have been a giant neon sign over his head flashing "I'm a witch." I could thump myself on the forehead. For someone so smart, I could be so dense sometimes. And to think, I wasn't sure anything could surprise me anymore.

Boy was I dead wrong.

The golden witch, that's what I saw when I looked at Lukas. It fit. He was as light as Gavin was dark. "It makes sense now, but I only just found out witches exist. So you knew that I was dreamscaping you?" I tripped a little over the word, still foreign to me. Actually, anything witchcraft-related felt odd coming from my mouth.

"I did," he said carefully like it was a trick question. "Is that a bad thing?"

I was feeling sort of cheated here. Why did I always have to be the utterly naïve one? Sighing, I replied, "No. I just feel like an idiot."

"I'm sorry." His eyes did that puppy thingy. On Lukas, it was impossible for my heart not to melt, even a tad.

I turned the cup in circles between my hands. "It's not your fault. I just wish I had known sooner. Before things suddenly became...hectic."

"Has something happened?" Alarm instantly broke out across his face. Leave it to Lukas to go all He-Man on me.

"I'm not sure yet." I was hesitant to tell him about the hellish dream I'd recently had, featuring none other than Morgana le Fey. It just didn't seem like the right time. My eyes kept shifting to the other people in the café with us, innocent to the world around them. I used to be that blind. There was a kind of bliss I missed in not knowing—less problems, for sure.

"Should we enchant them?" Lukas teased, noticing my wandering gaze. At least I hoped he was teasing. This might have been his way of trying to lighten the mood.

"You're joking, right?" He wanted *me* to enchant them? That was a laugh. I might be a witch, but I was pretty useless when it came to performing spells. Only recently had I begun to experiment with the energy that lay inside me. The results were often unpredictable. I would probably end up conjuring a storm inside the Hawk's Nest. Unless he wanted to soak everyone, I wasn't the kind of witch he needed.

Lukas's smile widened.

I shook my head. "No, I don't want to cast a spell on them. I was just remembering that I used to be like them. Clueless."

"And do you think you would be better off clueless?"

I stared at the cooling macchiato. "I don't know."

He moved from his seat across the table into the one beside me, closing the space between us. When he spoke, his voice held conviction. "What you have is power. Not just any kind of strength. Magic. It's whatever you want it to be. You have the world at your fingertips now, Brianna. Take advantage of it. Don't run from it."

Whoa. Who knew the college boy could have such inspiring words?

He leaned in, and all I could think was... *Oh, shit. He is going to kiss me.* His breath warmed my face, but instead, his fingers grazed over my necklace. The spot on my throat tingled. His touch caused the amethyst to illuminate and the moonstone to radiate, both glowing brightly against my skin.

"We have signature magic," he said in a low voice, his eyes holding mine.

Huh? What did he mean, "We had signature magic?"

I watched, stupefied, as his emerald eyes took on a mystic glow, probably a lot like mine did when I used magic. I could almost feel mine taking on the same iridescent hue. His fingers stroked the stones, and like a switch, a surge of pleasure ran through me.

"You have the most beautiful eyes." His tone had gone velvety and smooth.

There was no doubt in my mind that my eyes were lit up like the Northern lights. *Warning* screeched my internal alarm. This was stepping into a territory I wasn't willing to go. Not while my feelings were jumbled with uncertainty, and I hadn't had a chance to tell Gavin about Lukas.

I owed them both that.

There was something about Lukas's energy that mirrored mine, and before I did something stupid that I was going to utterly regret, I pulled back. The small distance was like a breath of fresh air.

"What was that?" I asked, with accusation in my tone. I didn't know if I could trust Lukas, or even if I could trust myself.

An air of disappointment reflected in his eyes, eyes that had lost their luster. With a heavy sigh, he reclined back against the seat. "I don't know exactly."

I narrowed my eyes at him. I wanted to call bullshit.

"It's the truth. There is something about our magic. It's like they're companions. One identifies the other."

"But don't all witches recognize one another?"

"They do, but this is different—on another level, so to speak. Sure, when we first met in your dreams, I knew you were a witch. I was young and didn't understand, but as we got older, I could tell that it was more than just us being witches. My power is drawn to you."

"And you never thought to tell me?" I couldn't hide the irritation.

His emerald eyes softened. "Do you honestly think you would have believed me? A guy in your dreams trying to convince you that you are actually a witch? You could barely believe that I was real the other day."

Fine. Sure, he had a point. That didn't necessarily mean I was okay with it. "I never would have believed you," I conceded. "In fact, I probably would have thought I was losing my freaking mind." Some days I still did.

He leaned forward on the table. "We could help each other."

I tilted my head to the side, wondering what he had up his sleeve. "How so?"

"I can help you learn to use and control your magic. There is something unique about our energies. They parallel one another. I want to see what they can do together." There were hope and curiosity in his face. He wanted to do this.

I thought about what he offered. I couldn't deny that I had felt something weird, more weird than usual. The few times I had done magic with Sophie or Gavin hadn't come close to the surge of power I felt briefly with Lukas, except in my vision of Morgana.

The idea was both intriguing and seductive.

That scared me.

"Are you game?" he asked after a few prolonged moments of me just staring at him with drawn brows.

There was another long pause as I contemplated his offer. "Why not?" I heard myself respond. What did I possibly have to lose? Somewhere, the back of my mind warned me that I might be risking more than I was willing to pay, but how could I ignore the opportunity to gain such knowledge, to control this gift? It wasn't like Lukas was a stranger. I would be safe with him.

All I had to do was tell Gavin. I couldn't hide Lukas forever.

This should be fun.

CHAPTER 5

S UNDAY, I HAD TO WORK. I had done a damn good job of evading Gavin all day yesterday, but I knew the time had come.

With the impending holidays, *Mystic Floral and Gifts* was in full swing. Strands of twinkling lights were strung around the shop like tiny crystals. The whole place smelled of pine, candy cane, and mulberry spice. Poinsettias, garland, wreaths, and lilies decorated every corner of the shop. Confetti snow dusted the counters and displays.

It was like walking into Narnia.

As the coffee pot brewed a holiday blend, I organized a plate of Christmas cookies for the customers. It might only be the middle of November, but Christmas in the shop started almost immediately after Halloween. There was still a small section dedicated to autumn and Thanksgiving, but primarily Christmas had taken over and would until the end of the year.

By that time, I would be ready to pull my hair out. The holidays were joyous, but they could also be frazzling. Carols pumped cheerily from the shop's speakers, although I was feeling anything but cheery.

Actually, I thought I might hurl.

The amount of coffee I had inhaled this morning wasn't helping my jumping nerves. My stomach was tied like a Chinese knot. I thought about my day with Lukas all night long. It plagued my mind.

The feeling was like being in a tangled web. It spun and spun out of my control.

I lost myself in the monotonous task of arranging the complimentary tray.

"Brianna." Faintly, I heard a familiar voice.

My name finally registered, and I lifted my head, turning toward the sound of my aunt's voice. I don't know how long she had been calling my name, but I hadn't been paying attention, my movements quick and jerky. In horror, I felt my elbow bump into something and watched the shiny porcelain faerie on the counter tumble to the ground and smash to smithereens. The sound boomed through the serene shop.

"I'm sorry. I don't know what is wrong with me today." *Liar,* screamed my conscience.

She put a steady hand on my arm as I went to bend down and clean up my mess. "It's okay, really. I got this. Why don't you take a break for a bit?"

Nodding, I took a seat on one of the stools.

She grabbed a broom and dustpan from the back room, her eyes brimming with concern when she returned. "You seem a little out of sorts. Do you want to talk?"

No matter how much I tried to disguise my emotions, no one knew me like my aunt. Everything inside me wanted to pour my heart out, all the dirty details. Finding out I was a witch. The dreams. Lukas. Gavin. Morgana. I could use some loving advice right now, someone to tell me how to handle this sticky situation, someone to help shoulder all the mounting stress.

How much could I tell her without involving her in trouble?

"I don't know. Maybe," I admitted, studying her as she effortlessly picked up the broken pieces. Too bad my problems couldn't be swept away so easily.

What was life without complications?

Peaceful.

Her light brown hair was secured in a low ponytail with a pen stuck in it. Some ribbon pieces were hanging around her neck. "I'm listening."

I might not be able to tell her about the spells, the magic, or the witchcraft, but boy troubles were common teenage problems.

I sighed. "Uh, there is this boy. A friend," I added.

She lifted a brow. "I see. Is he really just a friend?" There was no judgment, which was why it was so easy to talk with her.

Was Lukas only a friend? "It's complicated."

She pursed her lips. "You're afraid how Gavin will feel about this *friendship?*"

Ding. Ding. Ding. "Not only that, he doesn't know about him. I'm not sure he would understand."

She was probably wondering how I had suddenly become so boy-crazed. Honestly, I was too. "Well, you won't know until you tell him. You need to be honest here, to both of them. The longer you prolong the truth, the harder it will be to confess. Trust me. Secrets are never good."

And I did—trust her. I trusted my aunt more than anyone. She was not just my aunt. She was my friend, my guardian, my family. "You're right. I've already decided to tell Gavin. It just has me completely freaked out."

"Understandable." She brushed a strand of hair out of my face. "Whatever happens, Brianna, you can handle it."

I hoped she was right because the pit in my stomach wasn't so certain. Her unabashed confidence in me was a boost to my bruised esteem. I could always count on my aunt to make any situation less complicated.

After work, I knew that it was now or never. The sun was just beginning to set over the horizon, casting waves of purple and orange. The temperature had dropped, making the evening refreshingly cool.

I pulled into my driveway and took a deep breath, sending a text to Gavin before I lost my nerve. **Can you come over?**

His response was quick and short. **On my way**.

Just like that.

No questions, no demands for explanations. He was just that forthcoming.

It was hard to imagine my life before Gavin, or my life without him. We might have only met four months ago, but I felt as if I'd been waiting for him my whole existence. I'd never been boy obsessed before. One impulsive action led to my demise. Had I not skipped class that day, we might not be here. Together.

My heart hammered against my ribs. Surely, I was going to have a heart condition after all the insanity I'd been living with as of late. Knowing I had only a few minutes before his speedy arrival, I rushed into the house and bolted up to my room.

A sweep of the room revealed I needed to do a bit of damage control. The bras hanging over my dresser had to disappear. I shoved what I could under my bed, and waited for him, nibbling on my nails. What else could I do?

Lunar tottered under my feet, weaving in and out of my legs. He sat on the floor, looking up at me with those big, baby eyes and let out the tiniest, pathetic meow. Leaning down, I picked up the little furball and snuggled him under my chin.

"Lunar, you're such a little pest." His presence was a small comfort. Oh, the simple life. He just purred, loving any and all attention.

Tingles skirted on the back of my neck. Gavin had arrived. Lunar's ears perked up, and I lifted my gaze to meet Gavin's in the doorway. He engulfed the entrance. Gavin was many things.

Drool-worthy.

Dreamy.

Dangerously sexy.

A deadly combo. It was impossible to control the effect his presence had on my heart. Not to mention, the dancing fireflies in my belly.

He sauntered into the room, smirking, and I stared, memorizing the lines of his face. Every detail. His eyes were always the clincher for me, sealing the deal with just one glance.

"You couldn't manage one day without seeing me?" His smile was filled with cockiness that for some ungodly reason, I found attractive. He sat beside me on the bed, the mattress squeaking under his weight.

Gosh. Did he have an inflated ego much? I hated that I was going to burst his bubble. "Funny," I replied snarkily. I blamed it on nervous tension. Lunar scampered to Gavin, and I folded my hands together. "Actually, I need to tell you something." How was I going to get the words out? Where did I even start?

He raised his silver-studded brow. "Are you going to finally tell me what's been bugging you?"

And to think I thought I'd been fooling everyone. Apparently not. I dropped my head into my hands. "God. I don't know where to start." My voice cracked, and a giant lump got stuck in my throat. He heard the apprehension in my tone and tears suddenly welled in my eyes.

Emotional overload.

Reaching for me, he wrapped his arms around my shoulders, pulling me to him. "Hey, Bri, it's going to be okay." His fingers stroked my hair.

The last time we had been in my room, it had been an entirely different vibe, the steamy and hot variation. Now, it was dreadful and stifling.

He waited patiently as I clung to him like a lifeline, listening to his heart race. The zeal of energy between us was reassuring. I swallowed and forced myself to continue what I started. "It's about my dreams," I mumbled against his shirt, not wanting to let go just yet. I inhaled his woodsy scent, wishing I could bottle it up.

Then suddenly, I realized that a huge amount of my anxiety had disappeared, like a switch had been flipped inside me, a stream of warmth and tingles followed from Gavin's body. I pulled back to gaze into his glowing eyes, concluding he was using magic on me. "Did you spell me?" I asked.

His expression was unreadable. "I wanted to help you relax."

I pulled my hand from his, and his eyes sharpened. "I don't know why I didn't tell you this sooner," I said, bulldozing full steam ahead. "I should have realized it was important."

"Tell me what?" The glint left his eyes, and his expression turned stony.

Holy moly. This was so much harder than I envisioned. "I've dreamscaped before. A lot, actually. I just didn't know it." Now I had his full attention.

"What do you mean, a lot?"

I cringed and wiped my sweaty palms on my jeans. "Uh. I don't know, for as long as I can remember. I thought they were just dreams, nothing more. It wasn't until the Morgana thing that I realized it was more. Well, that and..."

"And what?" His tone indicated that he didn't like where this was going. I couldn't blame him.

Oh crap. Time to drop the bomb. I was sweating bullets. "The person I dreamscape...I-I saw them the other day. Up until that moment, I thought they were only a product of my imagination."

His dark brows drew together. "I don't understand. You dream with the same person? A person you've never met?"

I swallowed the cannonball- sized lump in my throat and nodded.

He ran a hand through his already messy dark hair. "Wow. That's trippy. Did she recognize you?"

Shit.

The long pause and panic in my eyes must have said it all.

His shoulders slumped. "It's a guy," he muttered. The shade of blue in his irises darkened.

"He's a witch," my voice squeaked.

A vein in his temple ticked. "You've dreamed of the same guy most of your life—a witch nonetheless—and you're just now telling me this?" Hurt and jealousy laced his voice.

Each word stabbed me in the gut, over and over again. "I know. I'm sorry. It didn't seem important at the time. I thought they were only dreams." Words rushed from my mouth as I tried anything to rectify this horrid situation.

"I can't believe this!" He stood walking to the center of the room, voice rising. "Do you have feelings for this guy?"

The question of the hour, the one I'd been hoping to avoid.

Searching his eyes, I felt myself drowning in pools of hurt. I guess because I had to think about it, it was enough in his eyes to say that I did. When in reality, my feelings for Gavin were way stronger, but that wouldn't cushion the blow. "It doesn't change how I feel for you. It couldn't."

He wouldn't even look at me. Giving me his back, he put a hand on the wall. For a split second, I thought that fist was going to go straight through the drywall.

Quietly, I got up and stood behind him, laying a hand on his arm. I called his name. "Gavin, I—"

He jerked away. "Don't," he said in a voice cold enough to freeze Hawaii.

My heart ripped to pieces—thousands of jagged, irreparable pieces. The hand he had against the wall flexed, and I watched, stunned, as it plummeted through the drywall spraying pieces in the air. Without another word, he walked out of the room.

It felt like a volcano had erupted inside me. Red-hot molten lava ran over my skin. I couldn't breathe at the pain that had been in his eyes. Surely, it was going to kill me.

CHAPTER 6

THIS WAS WORSE THAN I had ever envisioned.

The pain was unbearable.

As soon as the front door slammed shut, I broke apart. Sliding down the wall, I curled into a ball. It didn't help that simultaneously a wicked storm burst outside. Thunder exploded, lightning crashed, and the wind roared against the rattling windowpanes in a threatening war. I was responsible for the storm, but it didn't mean I could control it, and the knowledge only made me cry more.

Everything inside me felt fragmented.

I was sick and heartbroken.

My entire being wanted to run after him, to beg him to hold me until the tears stopped until the hurt stopped. But just as I knew it was too soon, it didn't make me want it any less. He was more than just a guy I had fallen hard for. He was my protector, my guide through this whole magic mojo. Without him, I felt lost and alone.

Hours had gone by before the tears mostly dried up and my chest stopped heaving. I picked myself up from the corner where I was huddled and plopped down on my bed, still fully dressed. Each breath ached inside. My head hit the pillow, and the moment I closed my eyes, I was being sucked into a dream. A dream that wasn't of my doing for once, but that didn't make it any less real.

Or any less unwanted.

Tonight of all nights was not a night I wanted to dreamscape.

A part of me hoped that it was Lukas summoning me in the dream, regardless that every bone in my body was telling me it wasn't. The hairs on my neck stood out, and the feeling of going under was different. I felt myself being pulled. This wasn't Lukas's doing. It wasn't Gavin's either.

It was her.

Morgana.

Sure as shit, when my eyes opened, there she stood. Beautiful. Prevailing. Intimidating.

What did she want with me? What could the most powerful witch want with *me*?

It just didn't make sense. How had I gone from quiet, plain, boring Brianna, to a witch who dreams of dead witches?

Well, on the bright side, maybe this time I could get some answers, instead of fighting for my life. I really wasn't up for going round two with Morgana le Fey. Of course, she showed up when was I feeling like I'd been kicked in the gut and defeated. If I called Gavin in my dream, would he even come?

Her timing was no doubt deliberate.

Staring into her vibrant shade of violet-colored eyes was like looking into a mirror. It freaked me the heck out. I tore my gaze from hers as I looked around. The only words that came to mind were "enchanted forest." Beams of colored fireflies zoomed in the air that smelled like fresh-cut grass and full-bloomed roses. Exotic and tempting—sort of like Morgana. The trees were filled with glamourous, glowing fruits. Moss carpeted the ground, climbing up the trunks of trees. Any minute now, I expected to turn around and see a unicorn.

I felt like Snow White, and Morgana was the evil queen, trying to tempt me with her wily ways.

I stood there like a statue and waited.

Dressed like a Grecian goddess, her flowing raven gown draped to the mossy bed. Nails the color of death twirled a flower as red as her cherry lips. Locks of dark red hair pooled over her exposed shoulders.

Paralyzed, I didn't know if I should run or attempt to cast an incantation. My spells usually worked best if I was mad, and right now, with my heart so dejected, I couldn't muster up any anger, not even toward the woman who had tried to kill me.

I should have been shitting bricks. There wasn't enough emotion left in me to feel anything but numbness. I was punishing myself for being such an imbecile and handling the Lukas situation poorly.

When Morgana finally spoke, her voice rang with authority. She expected to be heard and not taken lightly, as if anyone would disregard her. "Looks like there is trouble in paradise."

I flinched.

"I'm not here to hurt you. Come," she waved her hand, expecting me to fall in step with her.

Like I had a choice. Robotically, I moved my feet one in front of the other. Together our legs kept perfect time.

Weird.

"Where are we going?" I feebly asked. Maybe this time she might actually tell me what the hell was going on instead of leading me blind.

"Nowhere in particular. Just to talk." She angled her head toward me, scrutinizing me. "I thought it was past time I got to know my...let me see... I think, if I am right, it's great-great-great-great granddaughter." She ticked off each *great* on her hand.

Huh?

I tripped over my own feet as I felt the mossy ground fall out from under me. Holy Crapola.

This dream had taken a turn in a direction that I was entirely unprepared for. *Her granddaughter?* How the hell was I supposed to feel about that? It didn't seem real or plausible.

She had to be lying. It was impossible. Not me.

I'm just a small-town girl.

A small-town girl with extraordinary abilities whispered a voice in my head. I ignored that pesky voice.

One of her lips curved. "I can see that I've shocked you. Are you really that surprised to be my only living descendant?"

Only living descendant? At least that would explain why she was stalking my dreams as of late. I wasn't buying it yet. "D–did you say *only* living?"

Her cherry lips turned into a seductive grin. "The one and only, dearie." She was the kind of woman who thrived on drama and being the center of attention—the polar opposite of me.

How could we be related, and why should I trust her?

I paused from our walk, and she faced me. "Bri, my dear."

The sound of my shortened named caused my heart to twist. Only Gavin had ever called me such. She held out her palm and instructed, "Here, give me your hand." The look on my face must have shown my skepticism. She gave a dignified eye roll and reached for my hand.

Like the last dream, I felt an instant connection, a string of our energies linking together, harmoniously synchronized.

"Do you feel that?" she asked softly.

Did I ever.

It was the greatest high—pleasure so surreal—thousand times more potent than any spell.

The gleam in her eyes spoke volumes. She knew I felt it as strongly as she did. My eyes widened, and I started to believe. Just maybe, I was what she claimed.

"Our energies are naturally drawn together. They identify the link —our shared blood." I found myself caught in the enticement of her words. "Some bonds are love or friendship. Ours is family. Together, our magic is limitless. Through generations, it has thrived and flourished, and then slowly it began to die. Until you."

"How can this be?" I asked, picking my mouth off the ground.

"You know...the birds and the bees. Please tell me you know about—"

"Yes!" I cut her off before things got any more awkward. "I get the picture." *Fabulous*. My grandma was not only an extremely powerful dead witch, but she was also a smartass.

Did I call her Grandma or Granny? Neither suited her. She was far too stunning to be anyone's Gran.

The corners of her eyes laughed at my unease. I shifted on my feet. "Is this your dream or mine?"

"Hmm. So I see you have learned a thing or two since our last... visit. Well, since I no longer walk the earth, it's yours, dear."

"I summoned you?" I asked, finding it hard to believe.

"Not exactly. The planes between worlds aren't strong enough to keep me from pushing into dreams. It's one of my specialties. Yours as well, it seems." There was pride in her voice.

How much of her power had I inherited? "Will I be able to do everything you can?"

"That remains to be seen. In theory, your bloodline should be diluted, but what I feel under the surface suggests that you have more power than you should."

That was a frightening thought. "Why are you here? The last time we saw each other wasn't exactly on friendly terms."

Her expression flinched ever so slightly. "True. It definitely didn't go as planned. I underestimated you. My intention was never to hurt you."

I snorted. "Well, you have a funny way of showing it."

She reached above us, plucking what looked like forbidden fruit from a tree, golden and glowing. "On the contrary, I was hoping for some family bonding. I might have a slight anger problem, especially if things don't go my way." She twirled the mesmerizing fruit in her hand.

Wow, did that sound familiar, and I doubted her idea of *family bonding* was the same as mine. "That's your best defense? We could have been killed. Gavin could have been killed."

"Gavin? Is that his name? Your boyfriend, I presume?"

"Umm. Kinda. Maybe. It's complicated."

She bit the round fruit. "Oooh, this sounds juicy. Do tell." Her smile was sinister.

I slouched on a nearby ornate bench and sighed. Why was I even considering confiding in her? However, she was dead. How much harm could it possibly cause? And if I was lucky, she might have a solution. "Gavin, the guy you tried to dispose of, we're...close."

She tossed the half-eaten fruit aside and sat beside me. "You have the hots for him. Yeah, I got that part."

I narrowed my eyes at her. This might not have been the best idea I'd ever had. "Thanks to you, I figured out about the dreamscape thing."

Turns out, I've been doing the whole dream sharing for a long time. With another guy...Lukas."

"Ah, the plot thickens," she cooed. "Let me guess. Loverboy isn't overly thrilled that you have been merging dreams with another guy."

"Bingo. That and the fact I stumbled into the real Lukas," I added.

"Boys. They can be so irrational. Boy witches—worse. So do you having feelings for this other witch, Lukas?" She was totally loving my boy problems.

I shrugged. "I don't know. I never thought about him as anything other than the cute boy in my dreams. And now that he is real, I don't know what to do about him, let alone how I feel."

"Being a witch has its advantages. There is a spell for everything. If you want to know where your heart lies, it's simple magic."

Her advice sucked. "Simple magic, huh? It just so happens that I am not that educated in simple magic." I picked at the chipping paint on the bench arm.

She tsked her tongue. "We're going to have to change that." The smile she aimed my way reminded me of the Cheshire cat in Alice in Wonderland. Mischievous and full of plans.

Every witch in my life wanted to be my teacher. For seventeen years, witches were something only in fantasy books for me. Then in a just a few short months, I found myself surrounded by the real deal.

But could they all be trusted?

CHAPTER 7

I WOKE UP MONDAY MORNING before my alarm, with a mother of all headaches. The icing on the cake was the dark circles under my eyes. I swear it was if I'd been sucker-punched. This dreamscaping stuff sucked; it was as if I hadn't been sleeping at all, my energy depleted instead of rested. I might as well have been up all night partying and waking up with one killer hangover.

Not that I would actually know what a hangover felt like, but I figured this was pretty darn close.

Slowly, I forced myself upright as I waited for my head to stop spinning. I was convinced it was going to split open. I needed drugs. Strong ones.

I stumbled to the bathroom, black dots swirling behind my eyes. I braced my hands on the sink and took long deep breaths, praying the pain would subside for just a moment. Two aspirins later, I waited for the relief to kick in, but standing was most definitely not helping.

There was only one thing to do: crawl back under the covers. I threw them over my head, hiding the sunlight that began to stream through the windows. The darkness didn't seem to aggravate the pain as much, but it was only a matter of time before my alarm started buzzing in my ear.

Or Lunar purring.

No sooner had I pulled the covers over my head, did Lunar poke under them, snuggling against my neck. I groaned. His incessant purring was normally comforting. Today it was driving me absolutely nutty.

"Lunar, hush," I muttered.

Luckily for me, he was a lazy kitty. Before long his purring stopped and he was fast asleep. I, on the other hand, was counting the beating throbs drumming at my temples.

By the time my alarm finally rang, I was semi-functional again. The pills had worked a little magic of their own. There was still a dull ache, but nothing compared to earlier. With the pain mostly gone, the events of yesterday came rushing back, including the ache in my heart.

How was I going to face Gavin?

What did I say to him?

I needed to talk to him, if only about my dream last night, assuming he still cared. It hadn't been an ordinary dream, not even for my standards, but what she said...was it true?

Gavin would know.

Now all I had to do was figure out how I was going to get him to listen long enough for me to explain. I couldn't blame him for being pissed. Hell, I was pissed at myself, but eventually, he would forgive me.

Right?

Passing my reflection in my mirror, I gasped. Shit. I looked like death warmed over. What I needed to do was learn some beauty spells, something for washed-out coloring and the rings under my eyes. I was beyond helpless at this point. Sophie never looked like crap. I made a mental note to ask her to teach me and grabbed my bag off the floor.

My gaze passed over the circular hole beside my door, and my heart cracked all over again like the plaster on the floor. Damn. I was going to have to do something about that after school before my aunt saw it.

I arrived at school knowing this was going to be a hellish day. I wasn't sure I had it in me to see the condemnation in Gavin's eyes, especially while not in my best form. Even on a good day, it would have been difficult.

I slide behind my desk in first period, wishing I'd thought to wear sunglasses, something to hide my bloodshot eyes. Austin sat down at the desk to my right, looking swag and cheerful, everything I wasn't. It made me grumpier than I already was. I hated him.

Not really. Didn't the world know I was dying inside?

He gave me a once-over. Keeping his voice low he asked, "What were you and dreamy doing last night? You look like crap-balls." Leave it to Austin to be brutally honest and point out the obvious. Not to mention, kick me when I was feeling down.

"Not everyone can look like a diva all the time," I snapped.

"Ouch. Touchy and bitchy. Well, aren't you just a bowl of sunshine this morning. Did you forget your Wheaties?"

I gave him a withering look, but he was right. It wasn't his fault. He didn't need me taking it out on him either. "Sorry," I sighed. "Gavin and I had a fight."

"I see. The first *official* fight. Was it that bad?"

"The pits," I said, tapping my pencil on the desktop.

He pushed his chic glasses back in place, edging to the end of his seat. "I am just having a hard time imagining lover boy mad at you."

I propped my chin on my hands. "Believe it."

His eyes zeroed in on my face. "I don't like knowing that my friend cried herself to sleep last night without calling me." His eyes were brimming with worry. It was nice having friends that cared.

I started playing with my pencil just for something to do. "I was a sticky, hot mess. I just needed to be alone and wallow in my misery."

"Well, the heavens must have felt your sorrow. It poured all night. A big, scary-ass storm."

The pencil I'd been twirling fell out of my hand and shot across the aisle, smacking Dominic Jones in the back. *Just peachy.* Little did Austin know, that scary-ass storm had been *me*.

An aggravated Dominic turned around and glared my way. "Sorry," I mouthed.

Austin stared at me with sympathy and looked to be contemplating whether I needed an intervention.

By the time chem came around, I was fidgeting in my chair like a two-year-old pumped on sugar. Before third period I had been anxious to see Gavin. Time flew by. My stomach turned and I was plagued with questions.

Was he still mad at me?

Would he even talk to me?

Look at me?

None of it mattered; the seat beside me stayed empty like my heart. I felt hollow inside, knowing Gavin hadn't shown up for class. I guess I had my answer.

He was furious. He was hurt. Unable to resist, I snuck a peek at my cell phone. No messages. Rejection stung like a dagger.

The remaining of the class was a blurry muddle. I comprehended nothing and time stopped. A part of me wished I'd stayed at home. The only reason I was here was the chance to try and make amends with Gavin.

That was crushed to dust.

By lunch, I wasn't fit for company. Gavin had never bothered to come to school today. I wanted to hide away and lick my wounds, incapable of dealing with the crowded chaos of the lunchroom. Or the questions. Austin and Tori would be full of them, and regardless that they meant well, I couldn't face it.

So, I went to the one place I could be utterly alone. The library. At this time of day, the circular room was vacant. Holly Ridge High's library was small and used more for making out than reading.

A short while later, Sophie found me hidden in a corner, surrounded by the wonderful smell of dusty books. It was a relaxing smell. The room was quiet and deserted, just the way I wanted it. I knew it was Sophie without ever looking up. The tingle of magical fringed down my spine.

I was afraid to look at her—afraid she would be angry with me. There was only so much I could take.

"Everyone is wondering where you are," she said, her voice lyrical like a song. I couldn't detect any criticism. *Everyone* meant Tori and Austin.

I risked a glance up into her enchanting blue eyes. "Did Gavin tell you?"

She shook her head looking puzzled. "Tell me what?"

Awkward. Crap. Me and my big mouth.

"What's going on? Why are you in the library instead of sitting with us? And why is my brother skipping school? Something fishy is going on between you, and one of you better fess up." She put her hands on her hips, waiting. Her floral skirt swished with her movements.

Thank goodness there wasn't anybody here to overhear what I had to say. They wouldn't have believed it anyway. "Is he okay?"

"Define okay. All I know is my brother is in a mood. I assumed the two of you had a disagreement or that my brother was just being a jerkwad. It really isn't that uncommon you know."

Those troublesome tears welled in my eyes. I did that. I caused him pain. "I'm sorry, Sophie. I never meant to hurt him."

She sat next to me and wrapped her arms around me. "Hey. Don't cry. My brother's an ass. Whatever he's done, he doesn't deserve your tears."

That only made it worse. She had it all wrong. The roof of the library pattered with the heavy drops of rain. A strike of lightning lit the darkened sky, flashing across the floor. There I go again, losing my grip on magic—it was out of control. And a nuisance.

She looked outside the library windows. "Wow. You're like a walking weathervane."

I laughed on a sob.

"You ready to tell me what's got you so upset? I promise not to be biased." She smiled gently at me, her dark hair pulled back in a low ponytail. "He might be my brother, but you're my friend, too. And I hate that the two of you are having a tiff."

A *tiff* was putting it mildly.

The guilt didn't lesson once I told Sophie. I felt like I had betrayed one of my best friends, though I had to give her props. She handled it a thousand times better than Gavin, and she kept her promise. She didn't condemn me on the spot and looked at it from a less emotionally involved perceptive.

I needed that.

"Wow. I wasn't exactly prepared for that. There is more going on here. I can sense it. Did you wonder why he never told you what you were?" she asked about Lukas.

Sniffling, I wiped my nose with the back of my sleeve. "He said that he didn't think I would believe him. And he was probably right."

"But you believed Gavin," she countered.

"That's true, but he wasn't what I thought of as a figment of my dreams. I didn't think Lukas was real," I defended.

"Do you trust him?" she asked.

At one time I would have answered the question without hesitation, but I didn't know then what trust really was. Since meeting Gavin, I could say I trusted Gavin implicitly. *But you hadn't trusted him to tell him about Lukas*, nagged a voice in the back of my subconscious.

My subconscious was a real downer lately.

"I don't know," I finally admitted.

Her feet swung under the table. "Do you trust my brother?"

"Of course," I answered immediately. Didn't that speak volumes? "Sophie, can you just let him know that I'm sorry? More sorry than he will ever know."

"You know, he's just jealous. Once he realizes that you are interested in only him, he'll come around," she assured.

My eyes must have deceived me, as I didn't jump to agree. Truthfully, I was an emotional wreck. I nodded meekly.

She lightly nudged me. "Give him a little space. He'll miss you in no time. I guarantee it. He won't give up easily." She was a better friend than I deserved.

If the roles had been reversed, I would have probably lost my temper and struck something with a bolt of lightning. "I hope so," I said, sounding not nearly as convinced she was.

It turned out that Sophie might have underestimated his anger. I didn't see Gavin once all week. His absence left a gaping hole in my heart. He filled such a huge part of my life that I never knew was empty.

I missed him, desperately.

And I wanted to tell him about Morgana possibly being my great (however many greats) grandma.

CHAPTER 8

T HIS WAS MY WEEKEND OFF from the shop. It was also the first day I was going to practice magic with Lukas. That just sounded odd. Would I ever get used to him being real? Better yet, would I ever get used to using magic?

It was still foreign to me, this whole wielding magic business. I would be lying if I said I wasn't apprehensive. The fact that we were meeting at my house didn't help the spasmodic butterflies in my stomach.

I missed the fireflies. They were so much more warm and exciting. Not this crazy, irrational fluttering in the pit of my belly. I could probably account for more than half of my anxiety because I still hadn't talked to Gavin. He was evading me like I was an officer with a warrant.

Lunar and I both jumped at the sound of the doorbell. Exhaling the breath I didn't know I'd been holding, I stood from the couch, hugging Lunar in my arms. He was like a security blanket, giving me strength. *You want this*, I reminded myself. That I did. I definitely wanted to learn to control this gift, but I didn't realize all the people who would be involved, or the hurt I would cause.

Magic comes with a price. Well, so does withholding the truth. I always was a sucky liar.

I was greeted by a smile that would put sunshine to shame. His dimples winked on either side of his cheeks, and his emerald eyes sparkled. He had a day's stubble on his otherwise clean-shaven face. It made him look sexier, and that was the last thing I needed or expected.

He had both hands shoved into the pockets of his jeans. "Hey," he said, rocking back on his heels.

Oh, Lord. I was in trouble.

His grin spoke volumes. Maybe I could steal some of his happiness. "Hey," I replied, Lunar wiggling in my arms.

"Who is this little guy?" He reached out to scratch the top of Lunar's head.

The kitten was having none of it. He hissed in my arms, simultaneously extending his claws on all four paws. The tiny, needle-sharp nails dug into my arm, and I squeaked in protest before quickly putting the little booger on the floor. He promptly ran from the room. "I don't know what's gotten into him," I mumbled, staring in the direction he had taken off.

I moved aside, letting Lukas in the house. He brushed past me, and I felt the surge of magic. Tendrils of energy gathered at my fingertips. Apparently, I was more ready to do magic than I thought. If there was one thing I was learning, it was that magic couldn't be ignored.

"Nice house," he commented, not taking his eyes off me.

With the tingles coursing through my veins, I suddenly didn't feel like myself. "Did you want a tour?"

A mischievous gleam came into his Irish eyes. "I've already seen your room."

My cheeks instantly flushed.

Oookay, that wasn't awkward much.

"Right," I replied, more than a little embarrassed. Clearing my throat through the tension, I asked, "So what are you majoring in?" When I got nervous, I rambled.

His lips curled. "Can you believe I haven't declared a major yet?"

"Are you kidding? I am the queen of indecision lately."

He chuckled.

I walked into the family room, fumbling with my hands. "So um, how did you want to do this?"

He stood in front of me so I had to bend my neck to see his face. "Tell me what you *can* do?"

That was easy. "Pretty much nothing."

He wasn't put off very easily. "Good, a clean slate."

That was one way of looking at it. His optimism was staggering, considering who he was teaching. He must have seen the doubt in my eyes. It was evident how much self-confidence I lacked.

"Come on," he encouraged smiling. "Let's see what you got."

I looked at him blankly.

"Can you tap into the center of your energy?" he asked, finally realizing I wasn't doing anything.

That was about the only thing I could do and had practiced. I was more aware of the tingles flowing in my veins. I might not be able to always control it, but at least I recognized it for what it was.

Magic.

I nodded. "I can almost always find it now. It's more of knowing what to do with it."

"Command it."

He made it sound so simple, like riding a bike. "Easier said than done."

"It is," he promised, "once you know what you are doing. One of the first things I learned was levitation. Want to give it a go?"

"Why not?" I said dryly.

He scanned around the room, looking for what I assumed was something safe to levitate. His gaze landed on an item sitting on the fireplace mantel. Walking in front of the stone hearth, he said. "This will work."

The item of choice was an antique glass vase. I let out a loud gasp as he plucked it off the mantel. It had been part of the house since before my grandma had lived here. No doubt it was a priceless family heirloom, and I wasn't about to play Jeanie in a bottle with it. "You've lost your mind. My aunt would kill me if I broke that."

"Exactly the point. It is better if the item has importance. That way there is less a chance of you fumbling the spell."

His logic sounded like utter BS to me, especially if I failed. The odds of his theory working on me were probably one in a gazillion. I had a bad feeling about this, and it sat unsettled at the bottom of my stomach. It could have been just my nerves, but I wanted so badly to be able to control this so-called *gift*, and I was tired of the outbursts.

"You better not be wrong about this," I warned him, narrowing my eyes to slivers.

He hardly batted an eye at my not-so-sunny disposition. "Trust me."

Trust him. The words echoed in my head. Then there was that. Trust. How much did I trust Lukas? At one time, I would have said unequivocally. Now, I wasn't so...*confident* in that trust.

"Fine," I agreed, shoving my hands in my pocket. "The vase it is, but I am holding you responsible if anything happens to it."

"Deal."

I didn't like the stupid grin on his face. It was too charming. "You're sure I can do this?"

"Positive...well, pretty positive."

I shot lasers at him with my violet eyes, losing a notch of my assurance.

"Don't worry," he rushed to add before being seared by my laser beams. "I can fix whatever goes wrong. That's a promise."

His reassurance wasn't enough to smooth over my worries. Someday I was going to work on my self-confidence. Someday in the distant future—today I was going to just try and not fry my own ass. "Bring it on," I said in a voice both sweet and menacing.

He smiled, diving right into it. "I want you to put all your concentration into that vase. Then I want you to picture it moving, floating through the air toward you. Let the source of your energy guide it."

I took a deep breath, then another, and closed my eyes. Okay, all I had to do was move it to me. Easy peasy. Reaching inside to the sweet spot of magic, I welcomed the sensation that spread through me. It was amazing how just accepting what lived within me had suddenly become such a part of me.

There were no words to describe the feelings. It was empower-ment, a perfect blend of strength and spirit. I could lose my head, like the most potent drugs on the planet, but without the addiction. It was nearly as awe-inspiring as kissing Gavin.

I was a different person. Maybe not different per se, but a super-enhanced me.

I savored the awareness as it traveled through me—consuming me. I could feel it coursing from head-to-toe. When I opened my eyes, I was looking into Lukas's face. He was watching me, and I could see the surprise and something more shining in his emerald eyes.

He nodded once, encouraging me to move forward and not lose my grip. I focused intently on the very breakable crystal vase and pictured it moving into the air, floating effortlessly into my waiting, sweaty hands. With my luck, it would slip right from my grasp the second I clutched it.

Nothing happened.

I tried harder. And harder. Lines of concentration stretched across my forehead, but the vase didn't so much as whisper a movement. My head was starting to throb and the buildup of energy inside of me was bursting to be released, to the point that it was becoming painful.

I was about to concede defeat when shit hit the fan.

Like the sound of a hurricane, pressure built around the walls of my house, creaking and squeaking funnily. Then, as if it had reached its maximum, all the windows on the first floor shattered into lethal confetti. Glass rained down over Lukas and me from all directions, and my hands flew to cover covered my head.

Sweet baby Jesus, please let this be a horrible nightmare.

But nothing I could do or say would change what my eyes were seeing. We stood frozen. I couldn't say what was going through Lukas's head, but in mine, it sounded like a string of very colorful swear words.

"Holy shit!" I gasped. I was in so much trouble. How was I going to explain this to my aunt? It was bad enough that I had to patch a hole in my bedroom wall, but this...

"It might be safer if we practiced in your dreams," Lukas said, brushing diamonds of glass off his shoulders and shaking it out of his hair.

He was joking, trying to lighten the situation, but I was having none of it. I hadn't moved. I was too afraid to even blink. What an utter disaster.

I felt dejected.

I felt defeated.

I felt like a failure.

"Brianna," he called my name, but I was unresponsive. "Brianna!" he said again more forceful. "I can fix this." He did a wavy hand thingy, eyes glowing like polished glass in the sun. As quickly as I had destroyed the windows, he had them repaired as if it had never happened.

I blinked.

I should be feeling relieved, but I wasn't. I felt hazardous—a danger to everyone around me.

Stepping in front of me, he grabbed both my shoulders. "This isn't as bad as it looks. You think every witch doesn't have a few slips here or there? It's how we learn, from our mistakes."

"I don't think I qualify as your *average* witch."

His lips curled. "Maybe not, but you're still allowed mistakes."

"And if those *mistakes* cost lives? Then what?" My cheeks heated as I argued in frustration.

He wasn't the least put off by my bad attitude. "That's why you can't give up. You have got to keep practicing. You'll get it. Everything will one day click into place."

"If I keep practicing like this, I won't have a house to live in."

He snickered. "It's not power you lack, that's for sure. That wasn't even at full strength."

He *so* wasn't helping. I gave him a wry look. "Funny."

"Don't discredit yourself so easily. You can do this. Try again," he advised.

Too late. *I failed. Again.*

I had to be the worst witch in the history of time.

Even my crestfallen expression didn't deteriorate Lukas. "This time with a little less...*enthusiasm*," he suggested.

I shook my head. "It's your death sentence, buddy."

"I'll take my chances on you," he said, squeezing my shoulder.

I stared at him, dumbfounded. So be it. Lukas had faith in me; the least I could do was give it one more shot. If I leveled the house, so be it.

Nodding, I backed up, putting some space between us. The erratic tingles gathered inside me. This time, I didn't put so much effort into it. I relaxed and tried not to overthink what I was supposed to do.

Then, almost like a trick, it happened. The crystal vase slowly hovered in the air over the fireplace mantel. It shimmered in time and space.

Hope sparked.

I could feel Lukas behind me holding his breath—waiting. That made two of us. With careful precision, I kept a steady hold on the energy flowing from me as it guided the precious vase across the room and safely into my slightly shaking hands.

I took a moment to wallow in pure giddiness. Warmth and pride flooded me. Putting the vase safely back in its place on the fireplace mantel, I turned and jumped into Lukas's waiting arms. "I did it!" I squealed, grinning like a fool.

He spun me in the air, before setting me back on my feet. "Hell, yeah! I told you. It was in you the whole time."

"That felt amazing," I gushed. It helped take my mind off *other things*.

Gavin.

At the thought of his name, a tidal wave of emotions came roaring inside me. This was the kind of thing I'd imagined sharing with him. Disappointment laced through the excitement. Lukas noticed my immediate distraction. How could he not? My mind was having a hard time staying with the high of my accomplishment and swiftly tumbled down, crashing. This strife between Gavin and I was affecting my abilities, affecting my life.

"Does your boyfriend know that I'm helping you?" he asked, interrupting my wandering mind. His warm fingers brushed aside a strand of hair that had fallen over my face.

"No," I replied, hearing the sadness in my voice. Hard to tell him when he was not talking to me. "He's not my boyfriend, technically."

"Uh, you could have fooled me."

I sighed, tired and cranky. Doing magic always sucked the life out of me. "Sorry, I'm such shitty company right now. It's been a long week. I thought this would...help."

"It will help. What you need is somewhere to throw all the emotions you're feeling. There is no better way than in magic."

"At least one of us thinks so. I seem to be crying more than not the last few days," I revealed with more vulnerability than I meant to. There was always something about him that made me pour my heart out

"The skies have been filled with amethyst tears." He wiped away a single tear that streaked down my cheek.

More than he knew. I was probably responsible for every storm we had in the last few days.

Lukas gave me a sincere smile. "I think you deserve a break. What you need is a change in scenery. Want to grab dinner?" he asked as if it was the most natural thing in the world. And maybe it was normal, but somehow I felt like I would be betraying Gavin.

I was speechless. A date? Is that what he was asking? Or was I just jumping to all kinds of crazy assumptions?

He held up both hands. "No strings attached."

I rolled the idea around in my head, as I left him hanging. What I wanted was just a night to forget.

Forget who I was.

Forget what I was.

Forget my sorrow.

Before I could second guess myself or change my mind, I replied with a partial smile, "Sure, why not." Two friends having dinner; it didn't have to be any more than just that. *Right?* He said "no strings attached."

"Do you like Italian?" he asked, grinning ear-to-ear. His dimples winked on both cheeks. He was just so damn charming. Any girl in the world would be a puddle at his feet.

So why wasn't I? He was what dreams were made of, after all.

I tried to return his smile, but only managed a fraction of his eagerness. I couldn't fake it. Even though I had said yes, inside guilt gnawed at me. "Who doesn't like a little Italian?" I replied.

CHAPTER 9

I T SEEMED LIKE WE DROVE forever to get to the nearest Olive Garden. In reality, it probably wasn't that far, but there weren't a large number of Italian dining options in Holly Ridge.

My cheeks were flushed as I sat across the booth from Lukas. It had nothing to do with the fireplace beside our table and everything to do with him staring at me so intently. With the dim lighting, this suddenly seemed more intimate than I had bargained for. It was supposed to be innocent, just two friends.

Who was I kidding? Friends don't swap spit.

In our defense, it had only been once, and in a dream. I wasn't sure that even counted. Lukas and I weren't *just* friends. What we had experienced in my dreams forged a weird bond that I didn't know how to explain. And now, I didn't know how to act around him. Things weren't the same as they were in my dreams.

"So how long is this...strange vibe we have going to last between us?" he asked, flashing those lethal dimples at me. Leave it to Lukas to just lay it all there on the table.

I exhaled and smiled, trying to relieve the tension in my shoulders. "I'm glad it's not just me. It's so strange still seeing in the real world. My mind doesn't seem to be able to keep up with what my eyes see."

"Understandable. I look at you, and I can't believe how much more beautiful you are in person."

That did it. My cheeks deepened, and I tucked my hair behind my ear. I wasn't the best at receiving compliments, and luckily, our server saved me.

We placed our orders, and I used that short time to regain some of my lost composure. The conversation moved to a less awkward topic. I couldn't have been more grateful.

"Have you thought about what you're going to do after high school? What school you would like to attend?" His magnetic eyes shimmered under the dim glow of candles.

I shook my dark head, fiddling with the moonstone and amethyst at my neck. "School has been the furthest thing from my mind." And my grades were starting to show it.

"I know a really great school..." He let his words linger in the air. We both knew he was talking about *his* college. Like a seasoned frat boy, he tried to sweeten the proposal. "Just think how convenient it would be to practice magic, and I could always use someone to spar with. There aren't many witches on campus, so we would be doing each other a favor."

Chewing on my lip, I considered what he said. Before magic entered my life, the University of NC had been my school of choice. Now...I wasn't so sure I even wanted to go to college. "I'll think about it." It was the best I could do for now. I couldn't commit to anything while my life was so jumbled and unsteady.

Lukas grinned like he'd won a small victory. "That's better than no. And in the meantime, I will take every opportunity to convince you."

Wonderful. I'd just opened a can of worms.

Our food arrived and the air wafted with parmesan and tomatoes. Lukas dug right in. I, on the other hand, pushed my food around the plate in circles. I was having fun, but there was a strange tug in my belly. Being here with Lukas was nice, normal even, but...

He cleared his throat, pausing between shoveling monstrous bites of meatball in his mouth. "So this *thing* with..." he paused. "What's his name again?"

I looked up from my half-eaten plate of noodles, meeting his quizzical gaze. There was just the slightest light to them. He'd been watching me aimlessly play with my food. We both knew he remembered his name. "Gavin," I supplied.

He scratched his chin. "Right. This thing with Gavin is seriously bugging you."

I sighed heavily, leaning my elbows on the table. "To say the least."

"Do you want to talk about it?"

I made a face. "I don't want to spoil dinner."

"It might make you feel better," he countered, dangling the option like the last serving of tiramisu.

True, although I wasn't sure he was the person to be my sounding board. But really, who else did I have? My aunt, Tori, and Austin were out of the question, for obvious reasons. Sophie was his sister, and I could probably talk to her, yet it felt wrong. Lukas might be the only person out there.

But he probably had an agenda.

I gave in. "Let's just say that he didn't take it well when he learned I'd met the guy in my dreams."

He grinned wolfishly. "Clever. I like the sound of that. Hopefully, it didn't come out just so."

I snorted. "Hardly, but no matter how you twist it, I still deceived him. I should have told him the truth much sooner than I did, and in the process, I hurt him." I slumped against my seat, my food forgotten. This was not making me feel better.

"So what happened when you told him? Did he get mad at you?" A hint of irritation crinkled at the corner of his eyes.

I twirled my straw. "Something like that. I haven't talked to him since the night I told him. He's avoiding me like I'm carrying a deadly disease."

"Then he's an idiot." His eyes flashed.

I shifted in my seat. "It's not like that."

He arched a brow, clearly not believing me. "What makes you so positive? He hasn't called you. He's been avoiding you."

I shrugged. How could I make him understand that what was between Gavin and me ran deeper than just a teenage crush? It was more. There was some invisible thread stringing us together. "I can't explain it."

His gaze held mine with a glowing tint. "That's crap, and you know it."

Doubt bubbled up. Did I? I wasn't so sure anymore.

Crossing his arms he declared, "He sounds like an asshole."

"He's not, really. Actually, he's been nothing but supportive," I defended.

"That may be, but if I were him, I wouldn't have walked away so easily." There were passion and anger in his words.

Gulping, I believed him. The change in his eyes was swift, scarily so. I would be lying to myself if I didn't admit that there was a fraction of fear inside me. He must have noticed it, because a moment later he banked that fire, and sighed. "I'm sorry. I didn't mean to sound so harsh."

I frowned. I was probably being overly twitchy about this whole thing. I had nothing to fear from Lukas, never had before. "Let's just forget about it."

"Under one condition," he replied, stretching his long legs.

Great. I was almost afraid to find out what his one condition would be. I eyed him warily.

He smiled at me with his Lukas award-winning grin. "You share dessert with me. We need chocolate."

I snickered. "You're right. Chocolate makes everything better." At least if you were a girl.

He ordered a triple chocolate cake. Just one. And like that, there was a weight gone from the air again. I could breathe. Gone was the weird tension; he was the Lukas from my dreams. My golden witch. My friend.

I missed him.

"Here." He forked a bite of chocolate cake, holding it suspended over the table. "You've got to try this." He stretched across the table, the college T-shirt he wore spreading across the muscles on his chest.

Yum. And I wasn't just talking about the cake.

My mouth watered.

I kept my expression blank, knowing I was close to crossing a line, but it wasn't like I was kissing him. The candle on the table flickered, and I rubbed my hands on my jeans, leaning over the table. I took the bite he offered, the chocolate melting in my mouth. "God, that is good," I said after I swallowed the sugary goo.

"You bet your sweet ass," he said, his emerald eyes twinkling.

"Your way with words is staggering."

"I'm just getting started."

"That's what I'm afraid of." I seriously hoped that was a metaphor for something else, or I was going to find myself in a precarious situation with more guys than I could handle. Breaking hearts wasn't my forte.

Friends, I reminded myself. We are just friends.

Who would have ever imagined that at the brink of eighteen, I would find myself in such a mess? Certainly not me.

CHAPTER 10

ANOTHER WEEK WITHOUT GAVIN.
Depressing.
This was getting ridiculous. How was he going to keep his grades up to graduate? It wasn't like he could just spell his way through high school. Okay, he could, but he wasn't learning anything that way.

Enough was enough. I got that he was mad at me, that he refused to answer my messages, but there had to be a way we could co-exist in the same school. Of course, I wanted to do more than co-exist, but I would take anything I could get at this point, even a few glimpses passing in the halls.

To make matters worse, Rianne decided today was the day she was going to make me her target.

Goody gumdrops.

Between periods, she snuck up on me at my locker. I should have been able to smell her skanky scent. She gave me an evil grin, flanked by two of her cronies. "Well, if it isn't the school mutant. Where's your boy toy? Don't tell me he got tired of you already?"

I tried counting to ten in my head. It was a waste of ten seconds and did nothing to lessen the mounting anger within me. The more words she spat, the more intense the tingles ran through my body. I was going to burst. Or worse.

I clutched my fists at my sides and moved past her, trying the ignore route. It wasn't going so well.

"Wait," Rianne rambled on like I gave two shits. "Let me guess." She caught up beside me and tapped her blood-red nail against her lip. "He found out what a freak you are and ran for the hills." The smirk on her face was almost enough to make me lose it.

She had it coming; she really did. In my book, Rianne must be glutton for punishment. There wasn't any other explanation I could fathom, but I'd reached my limit with her, my fingertips surging with magic.

How much more damage could I possibly do? If she was already hell-bent on slandering my reputation, then what did it matter what everyone else thought of me? Why not add more fuel to the flames? In reality, it was not the best idea, but I couldn't think straight. I wasn't rational.

"Don't screw with me today." My whole body was shaking with the need to hurt her, and a haze of darkness swarmed behind my eyes.

"Ooh," she taunted, holding her hands up. "What are you going to do?" she sneered, the two insignificant girls behind her giggling.

I could smash her like a bug, crush her under my Uggs. "You could stick around and find out," I snapped.

There was just the tiniest flicker in her golden eyes. Fear. Under all that bravado, Rianne was afraid of me. I was small enough to admit that pleased me. She could say whatever evil thing came to her mind, spread all the nasty rumors she wanted, just as long as she knew, there was nothing she could do to destroy me. I wouldn't give her the satisfaction.

Hell-to-the-no.

Not today. Not tomorrow. Not ever.

A wicked gleam lit her eyes. "I just wanted to see your face when you found out I was banging your boyfriend."

That was it!

I was going to gouge her eyes with my short, chewed nails. "He wouldn't dare," I professed, barely keeping my cool.

She pursed her sultry cherry lips. "Maybe not yet, but I will." Leaning in close to my ear, she whispered. "I'm on to you, freak." She spun her stilettos, strutting away like she owned the runway, leaving me gaping after her.

Rage pulsated in my blood. "Bitch." A crack of thunder split outside with a violent wall-shaking-sound.

There was a hum simmering under my skin, not at all satisfied that it hadn't been unable to unleash its full wrath on the beast. Reining in the energy was harder than summoning it had been.

On a shaky breath, I wondered if I would ever get used to the direct connection between my emotions and the weather.

I had let Rianne get to me, playing right into her little game. She wanted nothing more than to hurt me. Unease snaked around my belly as I thought about her finding out what I was.

Utterly terrifying.

The more I pondered over the idea, the more enraged I became. Dark thoughts floated through my head. She was no match for me. I had the kind of power to destroy her, to silence her verbal assaults. Tendrils of shadowy magic coursed through my blood. It wasn't the heady kind, but more addictive, like a drug, enticing me to strike out now, while I still had the back of Rianne and her groupies in sight.

"Brianna."

Hearing my name, I whirled around. The edge of power still glowing in my violet eyes, I could feel them radiating.

Tori stood in front of me, watching me curiously. She looked like one of those private school brats gone wild, dressed in a plaid skirt, black knee highs, and a tied white button-up. Tori looked upon me with confusion, as if she didn't recognize me. "Are you okay? You look ready to commit murder."

Sadly, that was almost how I had felt. I nodded. "Rianne." Don't know how she found about my falling out with Gavin, but it was the only explanation I could come up with.

The one word was enough for Tori to understand why I was upset. "What a bitch. Someone needs to pull the G-string out of her ass."

My lips twitched. "I'd been thinking the same thing." But much more violently.

And that scared me.

Who knew what I would do next?

SOPHIE CAUGHT me at the end of lunch after everyone had left. I had been unusually quiet, and by the look on Sophie's face, she knew what was nagging me. What she probably didn't know was that I was more worried about my *almost actions* than I was at Rianne insulting me.

She shifted her books under her arm. "By the way, I heard what Rianne's been saying about you and Gavin. It's not true," Sophie said, her all too perceptive blue eyes studying me. I could only imagine what my aura revealed.

Rumors could be ugly and spread faster than chickenpox. I shrugged, trying to downplay what I was feeling. Mortified. "Yeah, well, she is Satan's spawn. If she isn't spewing verbal diarrhea about someone, her life would be useless. Better me than one of my friends."

"That's not fair," she argued. Tiny blue flames sparked into her eyes.

When was life fair? "It's no big deal."

"I don't think Gavin would agree."

"Sophie," I growled. "Don't even think about it." The last thing I needed was for him to go all macho like he had that night in Wilmington. Nothing good would come of it, I was certain. The warning bell rang overhead, cutting our conversation short. "I've got to get to class. Just drop it. For now," I added when she didn't appear convinced not telling Gavin was the best solution.

"For now," she agreed. "But it would better if he heard about it from you than the grapevine."

And that wouldn't be a problem if I could get the guy to acknowledge me. Or show up to a class. She had a point though—I didn't want to put anything between us again, and most certainly not Rianne.

Sophie laid a soft hand on my arm. "Brianna, you need to talk to him. And I don't mean just about the Rianne thing. He hasn't been himself. I'm worried about him. We all are. His aura has been dark, filled with jealousy and hurt. I think you're the only one who can break through to him. I am afraid of what he might do."

Every line in her face showed her concern, and that concern cut straight through me. My stomach sunk to my toes, and anxiety buzzed inside. Nodding, I agreed. "I'll try again."

I needed to talk to him, even if I had to use unusual methods.

AT THE END OF SCHOOL, I was kidnapped by Tori and Austin. Okay, not exactly kidnapped, but more like taken hostage for a girl's night.

Looping his arm through mine, Austin gave me his million-dollar smile. "Babygirl, you need some serious fun. We got just what you need."

Tori mirrored his action on the other side of me, securing me in their clutches and leading me to the parking lot. "Something to get your mind off Gavin."

"Off boys in general," Austin piped in.

I laid my head on his shoulder. He smelled like Giorgio Armani. What were best friends for? Mine apparently thought I needed some sort of intervention. They were probably right. I had been moping around for far too long.

Rolling my eyes, I could only imagine what these two conjured up. Someone shoot me now. "Guys, I appreciate—"

"Nope," Austin cut me off. "We're simply not taking no."

Oh, Lord. "Fine," I muttered, managing a small grin. They were just trying to help, after all.

"Hell, yes!" Tori screeched.

I scrunched my nose. "That was my eardrum you just ruptured." I guess I could always talk to Gavin tomorrow. How could I say no to Beavis and Butthead?

CHAPTER 11

S HUFFLING INTO TORI'S LITTLE VOLKSWAGEN
beetle, complete with eyelashes on the headlights, I sat in her
car, praying they weren't taking me to an underground rave. Or
worse, a nudie joint. With these two, I never knew what I was getting
myself into.

Tunes cranked, the three of us sang at the top of our lungs, off-key,
to an indie punk rock band. The elderly couple in the car beside us
shook their heads in disgust.

We burst out laughing.

I needed this, a night out with my besties. There weren't two other
people in the world that could drag me against my will into some
outlandish scheme and I would actually enjoy myself.

"I've been thinking about dying my hair turquoise," Tori stated,
fussing with her long, caramel strands. Tori driving one-handed was
dangerous. She needed to keep both hands at ten and two at all times.

I tried to ignore the fact that her front tire just skimmed over the
yellow line. "Seriously?" I asked.

"Sure, why not?" she shot back, overcorrecting the little car. It
tossed me to the other side of the seat.

I frowned at her in the rearview mirror.

Austin turned in his seat so he could see us both. "I say go for it. I am all about freedom of will, be who you are, and all that blah, blah, blah."

I hit him from the backseat. "Knock it off. Don't you dare encourage her. You know she will do it."

He smirked. "Isn't that the point? Besides, she would look posh in turquoise. It would complement her complexion."

I groaned in the back, thumping myself on the head. "Great," I muttered. "Next, she's going to be covered from head-to-toe in piercings and run off with a drummer from Oz."

"Whatever you say, Mother Goose," Austin smirked.

I glared at him. "Funny." How he could even think with all that gel in his hair was beyond my comprehension. There should be some kind of limit on the use of hair products.

"I live to entertain," he said, grinning over his shoulder.

Five minutes later, my destination was revealed.

They had hijacked me to the zoo.

I embarrassed myself by getting a little misty. My emotions were on overdrive today, and it wasn't even that time of the month.

The zoo was in every childhood memory I'd had of Tori and Austin. For as long as I could remember, we'd spent multiple days of our summer vacation at the zoo.

Stepping through the iron gates with Tori on one side and Austin on the other was like traveling back in time. It had been so long since the three of us had been here. Too long.

"You guys, this is awesome. Seriously." I couldn't help but think that life before boy troubles had been so much simpler.

"B, you know you can count on us to pull you out of your boyfriend blues," Tori vowed, pushing her light brown waves out of her face. The three of us stood in a circle just inside. "Let's make a pact. Today there will be no mentioning of boys. Period. Just us," she spread out her long arms. "And the wildlife."

On cue, a ferocious roar ripped over the massive grounds.

"Deal," Austin and I echoed, grinning.

I eyed Austin in his Michael Kors jeans and Dior shoes. "Are you sure you are dressed appropriately for the zoo?"

"Please." His hand touched the top of his dark head. "Don't you think animals appreciate quality too?" The lens of his round glasses glinted of the fading sun.

He was something else—one in a million. And that was putting it nicely.

We strolled from exhibit to exhibit, talking about nonsense, laughing at the animals, but mostly giggling at ourselves. I was having the time of my life and hardly thought of Gavin. Well, just a little.

As usual, venturing into the snake house gave me the willies, and it had nothing to do with anything unnatural, just my aversion for creepy, scaly, slithering things. They freaked me out.

"God. This place still gives me the creeps," Tori said.

Amen sister.

A huge python stared at us through the glass, and I couldn't help but think of Harry Potter. I was a witch; did that mean I could talk to snakes?

Hey, it was worth a shot.

Staring intently at the colorful python, I tried to get the creature to do something. Minutes past.

Nothing.

"What are you doing?" Austin asked.

I broke my awkward staring contest with the snake and glanced at my friends. They were both eyeing me with twin smirks. "Nothing," I muttered, casting my gaze to the ground.

"BS," he called me out. "You were wondering the same thing we were. If you could speak parseltongue."

My violet eyes widened. Holy shit.

"Admit it."

I glanced at Tori. She nodded her perky nose wrinkling. "Yep."

I grinned back. "I will admit to no such thing."

"Liar." Austin bumped my shoulder with his.

"I guess you'll never know." It drove them bonkers when I withheld anything, even something as stupid as talking to a python, which I couldn't do.

My mind leaped from Harry Potter to Gavin and the smile on my face slowly faded.

"I know we said we wouldn't, but you are my best friend, B. So I have to ask. Do I need to kick Gavin's glorious ass?" Tori volunteered, reading the crestfallen expression glittering in my eyes.

A short laugh escaped my lips at the image of Tori going up against a witch, her with her designer jeans and manicured nails. She meant well. "I wouldn't go that far," I assured, leaning against a railing.

Her hands went to her hips. "It's obvious he hurt you, and in my book, that calls for a good ass-whooping."

"So this fight is pretty serious?" Austin asked, his face sobering.

"Serious enough for douche to skip school. What?" Tori asked when Austin poked her in the ribs and I scowled in her direction. "He hurt you. Anyone who causes you pain is an automatic douche. It's like girl code. B, you couldn't hurt a fly."

"Tori, I am not a saint. Trust me. This isn't his fault." That belonged mostly on my shoulders.

Austin put his arm around me. "Whatever it is, babygirl, we still love you. That will never change."

I was counting on it. When and *if* they found out about my secret, I was counting on that devotion.

I needed it.

"By the way..." Tori nudged between us. I could tell by her grin that I wasn't going to like this. Not one bit. "Since we are getting all mushy, I need a favor."

I groan. Whenever Tori started a sentence with "I need a favor", I either ended up taking the blame for some harebrained idea of hers or...she was having a party.

"I'm throwing a Christmas party at my house after Thanksgiving. I expect you there," she finished, ignoring my extreme protest.

Bingo. Called it.

Ugh. Just once, couldn't she have a different kind of favor?

Tori could throw epic parties. No matter how stellar they might be, I hated parties. Just the thought of all the crowds, loud music, and the amount of groping that went on in the dark, made me shudder. Oh, and don't forget the dancing. An act of God couldn't get me there.

She laid her head on my shoulder giving me a look of pity. "It will be fun. I promise," she tempted like it was a piece of Godiva chocolate. "Everyone will be there. And what you need is to let loose, have a little fun. Let's show Gavin what he's missing."

The keyword in that sentence was Gavin. Wow. I couldn't believe I was thinking about suffering the agony of one of Tori's parties for Gavin. "Fine. I'll go. But don't expect me to enjoy myself," I muttered.

Her soft pink lips broke out into a generous smile, and she threw her arms around me.

CHAPTER 12

I T WAS SATURDAY NIGHT AND like the lame, lazy bum that I was, I was spending the evening on the couch with a sappy chick flick. The clunking of heels on the tile floor had me turning my head, and the remote control slipped from my hand.

There stood my aunt, looking sexy as hell in a little black number that made me blush. She set a glitzy wristlet on the counter before facing me. Smiling, she seemed pleased with herself. My eyes might have bugged. It wasn't every day my aunt looked like a sex kitten.

"Whoa. Where do you think you are going looking like that?" I asked, narrowing my eyes suspiciously.

"I have a date," she replied happily, looking a little dreamy.

A date? My aunt never dated.

My brows drew together as I assessed how this made me feel. It was pathetic that she had a hot date on Saturday night, while her teenage niece sat at home, pigging out on triple chocolate ice cream, looking homeless.

I licked the chocolate goo from my spoon, pondering. "With who?"

"Just a guy," she confirmed. "I know; it's unheard of." There was a luminous luster to her skin. She was glowing.

My rainbow knee-high socks padded on the kitchen floor, as I set the carton of ice cream on the counter and leaned on my elbows. "It's not that. It's just...unexpected."

"It is, isn't it? And probably long overdue." She brushed a hand down her short black shirt, wiping away at invisible wrinkles. "I must be crazy. Me dating? I don't even know what to do on a date."

A small smile crept on my lips. "Be yourself," I repeated back the words she had said to me a few months ago.

"Hmm. My own words coming to bite me back in the butt, even if it was good advice." She leaned a hip on the counter. "You're right. If he doesn't like what he gets, he isn't good enough for me."

"Any guy who isn't into you is just an idiot."

"Thanks...I think." She straightened up and asked, "So how do I look?"

I gave her a quick scan. "Like sex on a stick."

She gave a short laugh. "That's good, right?"

"In this case, it's perfect."

She let out a whoosh of air. "I can't breathe in this getup. And these shoes..."

"Beauty is pain," I quoted some jerk that was obviously male and didn't know squat about being female.

"Well, whoever designed these heels should be shot. It's like a Chinese torture chamber. I don't care how hot they look."

"They do look superb," I assured, assessing the black strappy shoes.

"Ask me again at the end of the night, *if* they even make it home with me." She fiddled with the straps on her evening bag, a sure sign of nerves.

I eyed the black cage shoes with a least a three-inch heel and fell a little in love. I might not be a dress and heels kind of gal, but I could still appreciate a sexy shoe. "If you plan on tossing those babies, just throw them my way."

She smiled at me. "Deal."

"So who's the lucky stud?" A part of me was happy; she needed this. It was healthy for her, but I couldn't deny I was surprised. She never mentioned anyone, so I was sort of thrown for a loop.

Securing a dangling earring in one ear, she replied, "Just someone I met at the shop. I should have suspected something when he started coming in every day. He took me by surprise and asked me out. I shocked myself even more by saying yes." There was a starry quality in her eyes and voice as she talked about him. This wasn't just some random guy. She was interested in him.

Why didn't I know about this? *Because you have been so preoccupied with your own drama,* my subconscious reminded me of my self-absorption.

Before I could question her further, the doorbell rang, announcing Mister Mysterious's arrival. Her eyes widened with both a mixture of excitement and worry. "Here goes nothing," she mumbled, walking toward the front door.

I gave her an encouraging smile. My curiosity was peaked, and I snuck off around the corner behind her. The voices of their pleasant but nervous greeting carried to where I stood. I wasn't exactly dressed for receiving company, let alone the first guy to take my aunt out. My rainbow socks, boxers, and tank weren't first-impression material. I didn't want him to think she was raising a hooligan.

There was a nice, gently deep timbre to his voice. A whiff of subtle cologne carried to the hallway. He had a mop of brown hair and towered a good foot over my aunt. At least he wasn't balding. He had a very distinguished yet casual quality to him. I could see at my quick glimpse what attracted her to him.

Go, Aunt Clara.

They looked very nice together, and the glint in his gray eyes mimicked what I saw in hers. She looked over her shoulder, giving me a tiny wave before walking out the door. I leaned against the wall feeling both happy for her and a little jealous and slightly weirded out.

Dragging my feet back into the kitchen, the ice cream melted and forgotten, I tossed myself back onto the cushiony couch. The TV was on in the background, but no longer of any interest to me. My mind was just catching onto the fact there wasn't another soul in the house, except the fast-asleep Lunar, curled in a ball.

Alone. Utterly alone at home, with nothing but my rambling thoughts.

And I knew at that moment I needed to talk to Gavin. Now was the time. The dream with Morgana had been weighing heavily on my mind, and her claim that she was my great-grandma haunted me. It was something I had been trying to ignore. She wasn't exactly trustworthy. How could I be related to her?

It just couldn't be.

Then why didn't everything inside me start to hum when I thought about her? That couldn't possibly be a coincidence.

I needed help.

I needed Gavin...

The distance and space separating us killed me. It was like an ocean spanned between me and what I wanted most, a turbulent, bumpy, rough sea. The more and longer I thought on it, the more my stomach churned.

I needed to see him. I needed to hear his voice. And I wanted this silence between us to cease.

Everything came rushing down on me like a tidal wave. Sure, I could have probably called Lukas, but that wasn't going to fix my lack of Gavin problem. If anything, it would only complicate matters more.

It was time to take destiny into my own hands.

CHAPTER 13

W hen the idea of hunting down Gavin popped in my head, I couldn't let it go. Before I knew it, I was up and off the couch, running to my room.

My mind was made up. He was going to see me, even if I had to wait all night. Even if I had to track him down and resort to desperate, devious measures.

Looking into the mirror, I readjusted the thin, black straps on my top for like the umpteenth time. Finally, I gave up. Nothing I did at this point was going to show any less skin. The top fit snugly and my jeans were just as tight, emphasizing my curves. My hair fell loose over my shoulders in soft waves of auburn.

I looked...hot, under short notice.

Good. That was the point, to make him suffer. And I wanted him to want me again if I was being honest. I wanted to be irresistible. Lukas might be fun to hang out with, and I might not understand all that was happening, but every fiber inside me ached for Gavin.

My fingers fumbled with the keys on my dresser as they slipped from my grasp, jingling to the floor. Lunar jumped ten feet at the jarring noise. He wasn't the only one who was acting like a scaredy-cat.

Holy smokes. I was a ball of jitters.

It was going to take more than the luck of the stars to get me through tonight. I was going to need a miracle.

Closing my eyes, I searched for that center of energy inside me, pulling from it to steady my pounding heart. I needed to collect my bearings. Keep my cool. It was amazing what I could do when I concentrated. The energy core was more than just power. It was...

Security.

Self-reliance.

Strength.

What I needed it to be when I needed it, or so I was learning.

I snatched my keys from the floor and drove over to the Masons. Their house was just as impressive as the first time I'd seen it. Magic oozed from the place, and not just from the witches that lived inside. I'd always envisioned faeries playing hide-n-seek in the bushes or mermaids swimming with dolphins in the ocean tides behind their house. I half-expected the characters of mythology and fairytales to be lurking around every corner.

I pressed the doorbell, before I lost my nerve, and shifted my feet as I waited. A part of me hoped it would be Gavin, though another part thought he might just shut the door in my face.

That would suck big time.

I let a small sigh of relief when Jared came to the door. His smile was disarming and lazy as if he had all the time in the world.

Now that I was here, I was losing my courage. Did they hate me? I didn't know if Gavin had told anyone, and if he had, I was feeling like the biggest fraud.

My cheeks grew red. What had I been thinking? I was about to bolt off the porch when Jared spoke.

"Hey." He stepped aside with a hand propped on the door over his head and waited for me to walk inside. "Do I dare hope you came to see me?" he asked. There was always a playful trouble to his voice.

I stood there a few seconds, chewing on my lip, before stepping over the threshold. My heart pounded, but I was going to force myself to see this through, no matter what the outcome. Feelings of love, family, and home washed over me. I gave Jared a halfhearted, apologetic smile. "Is he here?" I asked, unable to keep the tremor from my voice.

"Nope. Sophie either. It's just you and me, babe."

I gave him a glare that clearly stated I was no one's *babe*.

His grin only widened. "But he just texted me that he was on his way home if you wanted to wait." Jared was so less complicated than Gavin. He was more muscle than brains.

"Sure. Is it cool if I wait in his room?" I asked, wanting to escape anymore advances from meathead. And it would be harder to throw me out of the house without making a scene.

Jared smirked, and there was a gleam in his eyes. "Knock your socks off."

"Oh," I added, spinning around toward him. "Could you not let him know I'm here?" I fumbled with my necklace as I waited for him to answer, wondering if I had pushed my luck.

Crossing his arms over his broad chest, his expression lost a little bit of its playfulness. "Anything for you, but I am warning you. He is being a total asswad lately."

I swallowed hard. "Thanks for the heads up," I muttered and made a beeline upstairs. The last thing I wanted to do was hang around and get the third degree from Gavin's very flirty older brother.

Gavin's room was stamped into my memory. Every. Teeny. Detail. The French doors to the balcony were left open, a black hoodie was thrown over the back of a chair, and his bed was neatly made. It looked exactly as I remembered. Being here made me feel closer to him than I had in weeks, and I vowed at that moment to find a way to get him back into my life. It was just too drab and miserable without him.

The scent of him surrounded me, and I ached with the emptiness of his absence. Nothing smelled like Gavin. My magic missed him. The stirrings swirled inside me the moment I stepped into his room. It seemed to awaken, to recognize his scent, just like my heart did. Trailing a hand on his bed, I only thought about it for a second before I crawled in.

Five minutes, I thought.

I just wanted a few stolen moments to savor his lingering presence. His energy was everywhere in this room.

My head hit the pillow, and I drank in the feeling of being in the one place that oozed Gavin. My whole body relaxed, my muscles feeling weightless. I dozed off with the scent of him surrounding me like a blanket, lulled by the sound of the frothy ocean waves lapping at the sandy shore.

In my dream, Gavin caressed my cheek. Heat unfolded through me, and I stretched toward his warmth. His touch was far better than dreamscaping. It was better than doing magic. This was the best dream of my life.

Gavin.

He was lying stretched out beside me. Our legs touched, and he was propped above me on an elbow. Our faces close, he brushed a lock of tousled hair from my cheek, his touch electric. It charged through my body, separating dream from reality, and my eyes fluttered open.

I stared into his luminous sapphire eyes and wet my lips nervously —afraid to move—afraid to shatter the spell. His eyes settled on my mouth, and I knew he was going to kiss me.

It was what I wanted. Before I even thought about what I was doing, I willed him to kiss me, magic humming through my veins.

Memorized, I couldn't tear my eyes from his as his mouth descended to capture mine. The moment our lips touched, I knew I wasn't dreaming. No dream could be this real. This hot. This mind-blowingly glorious. It was all the encouragement I needed. I threw my heart and soul into kissing him, never wanting him to stop.

My arms stole around his neck, needing to keep him close; afraid it would end too soon. I sunk my fingers into his dark hair, and with each brush of our lips, magic shimmered to the surface. Not just mine. Ours. Swirling together.

His power swirled with mine just as I mirrored his kiss. Something was happening here, something more than just a heavy make-out session. And heavy it was getting.

In one fluid movement, I found myself spread across him, his hands burning through the back pocket of my jeans. My surprise and pleasure were swallowed in his kiss. The material of my jeans was so thin it felt like he was stroking my skin.

He had me spellbound.

Slowly, his lips left mine, kissing both my eyelids, before he stared down at me with eyes that glowed as brightly as the stars. His gaze dipped and he reached out, knuckles brushing my chest. "Does it still chase away the dreams?" he murmured, holding the amethyst and moonstone necklace in his fingers.

Only when I wear it, I thought, which hadn't been as often as I should. His question brought back the dream I'd had with Morgana. How could I have forgotten?

Simple.

When Gavin was near, it was impossible to think of anything else. "I wanted to ask you something about dreamscaping."

His brows drew together, sensing my distress. At the same time, a light of fury flickered into his eyes, turning them a menacing deep shade of blue. They were almost black. His lip curled into a snarl.

God, how could I be so stupid? Of course, he would immediately think of Lukas. The intoxicating mood between us snapped. I lowered my chin, blinking. "It's not about him; it's about Morgana," I rushed before he could send me from his room.

That got his attention, as I had hoped. Some of the hard lines on his face softened. Dropping the necklace back on my neck, he moved away from me and sat up on the bed. I followed facing him. "I had another dream with her," I continued.

He exhaled roughly. "When?"

I felt the heat creep into my cheeks and shifted my gaze to my fingers as they picked the stitching on his comforter. "The night I told you about Lukas," I replied in a barely audible whisper. I hadn't wanted to bring up his name, but I refused to lie. I felt the invisible force field being thrown up between us. Lukas's name brought fresh, painful memories into his dark blue eyes. Anger lurked there.

He pushed the darkness from his eyes. It was impressive, his control. If only I could wield that type of restraint over my emotions. "What happened?" he finally asked.

I shrugged. "It wasn't like the last time. She didn't threaten me or try to hurt me. Actually...she claims that she is my..." I counted in my head, "great-great-great-great grandma."

Gavin cracked his neck. "Interesting. Is that all she said?"

I narrowed my violet eyes. "Is that all? Why are you not surprised by that?" Where was the same outrage I'd felt when she told me?

He twisted on the bed toward me. "I always knew there was something...special about you."

The word *different* had been at the tip of his tongue; he knew how much I hated that word. "So you believe her? You think she was telling the truth?"

"I think what she is claiming is a very real possibility. It makes sense, but I don't trust her worth a damn. And neither should you."

"If I am her granddaughter, what does that mean for me?" I asked.

His dark worried expression wasn't helping. "I'm not sure, but for her to seek you out, it must be important. And the necklace isn't keeping her away?" he asked, again reaching out, touching the cool stones at my neck.

"No," I admitted, sounding a little defeated. "They don't seem to stop her. She bypasses their protection. She's too strong."

Staring straight ahead, his jaw worked. "All the more reason to be careful. You might need to learn how to block the dreams on your own."

"I miss you," I blurted, unable to keep what I was feeling inside.

He let a heavy sigh, rubbing his hands over his face, a face that was etched in my mind. "This doesn't change things, Bri. I'm still dealing with everything."

And just like that, my world tilted over the edge again. How could he keep doing this to me? "How long do you plan on ignoring me, punishing me?"

"I'm not punishing you. I just need space. I need to think some stuff through."

I was probably pushing my luck, but the words just tumbled out of my mouth. "Are you about done?"

"Bri," he growled. "Let's just focus on figuring out why granny dearest is suddenly interested in you. We can deal with...other stuff later."

It was a start, and far better than not seeing him at all. "Does that mean you'll be back in school on Monday, and you're talking to me again?"

He laid his dark head back and stared at the ceiling. "I guess Monday is as good as any."

A sprinkle of hope trickled within me. I would be able to see him every day again. There was nothing right now I wanted more than time with him, however, I got it.

He swallowed hard. "Have you seen him?"

Then my exhilaration came crashing down. I stared at my hands. "Yeah. He's been helping me learn to control my magic."

It was extremely difficult for him to hear. Lines of strain pulsed at the sides of his temples. "Is it working?" he asked, the words sounding forced.

I sighed. "Some. I was able to move an object from across the room." I tucked my legs up against my chest.

He ran the back of his knuckles down my cheek, and his eyes grew sad. I couldn't stop the shiver or the drop in my heart. "It really should be me." He pushed off the bed, and I was helpless to do anything.

I watched him walk out the door. I squeezed my eyes shut and swore.

He might be right. Maybe I was making a huge mistake with Lukas. I wasn't sure of anything anymore. Who was right? Who was wrong? Who to trust? I felt like my head was going to fall off.

So much for talking to him. I'd spent most of our short time together with my tongue down his throat. Not that I was complaining, it had been glorious. The problem was I didn't know if and when it would happen again.

And I so wanted it to happen again.

CHAPTER 14

I HAD MY HEAD PROPPED on my hands, daydreaming about nothing in particular when I heard the door to the shop chime. Smoothing my red turtleneck, I slapped on a smile and glanced up. A sprinkle of magic danced along my skin, announcing my guest was a witch. I was getting better at recognizing the feeling. The warm greeting I had on my lips never made it out. My smile lessened as I stared at eyes green like rolling plains.

Lukas.

This was unexpected. What was he doing here, at the shop nonetheless?

He sauntered across the shop until he stood in front of me with a saucy grin. It wasn't nearly as lethal as Gavin's, but still effective. He was fond of college T-shirts. This one was gray and stretched across his wide chest. I would have to be dead to not appreciate his hotness.

"Hey." My voice gave away my surprise. I wasn't going to lie; I was shocked to see him, but I had this coming. I'd been sort of avoiding him all weekend, and now looking at him, I was guilt-ridden. He found another way to catch me after I dodged all his calls and texts.

Sometimes I could be such a shitty friend. Procrastination should be my middle name. It was mostly the practicing that I had been eluding, not Lukas.

Well, maybe Lukas a little.

"I hadn't heard from you. I hope it's okay that I just popped in?" There was such a sincere and boyish charm to him.

I smiled. "Of course. I'm sorry I didn't return your calls. I've been super busy." I cringed inside. What a lame excuse.

His hip leaned against the counter, bringing our faces closer. "Busy with Gavin?"

Did I detect a hint of jealousy? Hmm. I wasn't entirely sure I liked his implication. Or that he in fact was spot on. Was I that readable? "Maybe."

He raised one of those emerald eyes at me. God, he was like a walking lie detector, and I stunk at evasion.

I stepped back putting space between us. "Fine. I had to talk to him, okay? I needed to make him understand," I defended, sounding slightly desperate.

"And how did that go?" he asked with a tint of sarcasm as if he already knew the answer. It put me on the defense.

I crossed my arms over my chest and tried to suppress the pout I could feel coming on. "Just fine if you must know."

"Liar." He smirked.

Grrr. He could be so infuriating. And perceptive. This time I gave him a full-out pout. "Why is my life so complicated?" I mumbled, mostly to myself.

Walking around the glass counter, he closed the distance between us. He trailed a finger under my chin, causing a tiny spark. "Because you skipped practice."

I rolled my eyes. Practice. Ugh.

I ignored the fluttering in my chest. He was right. I hadn't been making an effort. It was time to change that, especially after my new heritage discovery. His proximity was sending out the wrong signals. I wanted to be friends, and I needed to start lying down the ground rules. "You're right," I conceded and retreated a step.

He took a step forward, putting us back at square one. "You free after work?" He cornered me with his muscular body.

I had to stop avoiding this...magic. And it would give me the chance to tell him I just wanted to be friends. Nothing romantic. So I heard myself say, "Yeah, why not?"

He grinned like sunshine. It was startling and potent. I swallowed, trying not to get caught up in his smile. "Don't sound so enthusiastic. You know how to make a guy feel special."

"Whatever." I playfully pushed at his chest. He didn't budge. "You know what I meant. I'm not exactly a pro at this magic jazz." I lowered my voice over the last bit. I could never be too careful, especially with my aunt lingering in the back room.

And what perfect timing, as my aunt strolled through the work-room area into the shop. Lukas and I both turned our heads at the squeaking hinges. We were pretty close, our bodies almost brushing. His arm shot out to steady me as I practically gave myself whiplash at my aunt's sudden appearance.

There was inquisitiveness in her eyes as she assessed the situation. Oh boy, I was going to be answering a parade of questions after Lukas left. Running a hand through my dark hair, I cast my eyes to my feet. Lukas casually stepped aside and flashed my aunt a dimpled grin worthy of an award.

He turned the charm on and had my aunt laughing like a schoolgirl. She liked him but was confused by what was going on between the two of us. Numerous times I caught her glance volleying between Lukas and me as she tried to figure out our relationship. The ease Lukas and I had together were apparent. Obviously, that felt odd to my aunt, considering she'd never even heard of Lukas. It was clear we knew each other on a personal level.

Lukas bumped my hip with his, pulling me out of my own lost thoughts. "I'll see you later?" he asked.

My aunt raised a brow. Peachy. I nodded and watched him walk out the door.

She waited a whole two seconds before pouncing like a cat. "I guess I'm not the only one who has been keeping secrets," she said. I had that coming, I really did. "I take it that was the other guy."

Oh man, if she only knew that half of it. I shrugged. "It's no big deal."

Smooth. Real smooth. There was no way in hell she was going to buy a line like that. Not after the way she saw us together. It had been evident we knew each other on more than just a friendly basis. Not that I blamed her. I didn't even believe it wasn't a big deal.

"That..." she indicated to the door. "Was a *big* deal. Does Gavin know about Lukas?"

The dreaded question. "Yes," I replied like it should have been obvious they knew about each other.

"And is he okay with it?"

Did she have to ask all the questions I didn't want to answer? I leaned an elbow on the counter, drawing circles into the glass. "Define okay."

"Brianna," she scolded in a stern voice.

I hated that voice. It meant that I'd done something wrong. Immediately, I felt like I had let her down in some way. It was a horrid feeling. She was the one person I never wanted to disappoint. I dropped my head onto my arms. "I'm so confused," I admitted in a small, weak voice.

She ran her fingers down my hair. "When did this happen?"

I sighed into the cool glass, steaming it up with my breath. "Just recently. A few weeks." This was partly true if you discount all the dreams. Then suddenly boom...two guys. "I don't know what to do." At this point, I wasn't above whining.

"You've got yourself in quite the quandary. I can't tell you who to choose if that is what you are asking. That is entirely up to you."

She wasn't being much help here. Was it too much to ask her to make such a decision for me? I was desperate to get my life back to simpler days, with simpler problems.

Her fingers continued to stroke my hair offering me comfort. "I'm not sure I am cool with you seeing a college guy. And I am for sure not cool with you dating two guys."

I groaned, lifting my head. "First, I am not *seeing* Lukas. At least not in the way you think. We're...friends. And second, he is only a year older than me. I will be in college next year," I reminded her, assuming college was still on the agenda. It all depended on this whole witch thing, and if I made it through high school. "Third, technically I am not dating either of them." But a huge part of me wanted to—desperately, but which one? I was pretty sure I already knew the answer. I had known all along.

If my aunt knew about my after school curriculum, it would send her to an early grave. My senior year had been eventful. What other kinds of trouble could I possibly get myself into?

"Hmm," she said, totally sounding unconvinced. "If you say so."

Who could fault her? I was hardly that persuasive. But that was the end of the discussion, for now. I was sure I wouldn't be hearing the last of it.

After my shift, I left my aunt at the shop to close. That gave Lukas and me at least an hour to get some magic mojo in. Joy. I needed to get my game face on.

Even in the dark twilight sky, Lukas was like a ray of sunshine. He was leaning against my house as I pulled into the driveway. I killed my headlights, cut the engine, and sat there staring at his majestic dimples. My heart warmed. It was a slow, languid feeling, not like the thunderstruck stuff I got when I was with Gavin. This was gentle, soft, safe.

Our hour together went much smoother and faster than our previous practice. I'd gotten the hang of moving things, including the family room couch. No object too large or small, too heavy or too light.

Turned out, Lukas was a pretty darn good teacher. Or maybe it was that he understood how my magic worked. He claimed our energy was similar, and I couldn't deny his logic. There was something different in the air when we used magic together. I shuddered to think about what we could do if I actually knew how to be a real witch.

In all honesty, I was kind of anxious to test out the bounds of power. When I was with Lukas, there was a call inside me, begging me to answer.

"That was awesome!" I sounded like a geek, but there weren't any words I could come up with to describe the feelings of wielding magic. It was spectacular. I felt amazing, a rush of exhilaration that lit me up from the inside.

Lukas's eyes were bright and brimming with vigor. I could tell that his power was at the surface, ready to come out and play. He wanted to use magic with me. "You did amazing."

Suddenly he was a whole lot closer than he had been a second ago. I hadn't even seen him move. My cheeks were flushed from concentration, and my eyes mirrored the glow of magic. They shimmered like the aurora borealis on a cool autumn night. Splendid.

His hand slid across my back, curving around my waist. I held my breath for what I knew was to come. My mouth opened, but no words came out. A retreat should have been on the tip of my tongue, but there was just the need to lose myself, to go with this feeling of being on top of the world. Untouchable.

And maybe a little bit of anticipation.

Could the boy next door make my world burn like Gavin? Make me forget the loneliness and sadness? It was for all the wrong reasons, yet it still happened. Again. This time there was no dream as an alibi.

I closed my eyes, and Lukas whispered my name. His lips brushed lightly over mine at first, gentle, testing my response. With the slightest pressure at my waist, he inched me closer. I placed my hands on his arms, and his lips swept over mine, deepening the kiss. My fingers tightened on his muscles, overwhelmed by the elation. He kissed like his lips were born for kissing.

Yet, I kept waiting on the edge of his breathless kisses, waiting for anything but emptiness and restlessness. No matter how much I wanted to wash away the sadness, anger, and hurt, this wasn't the way to go about it. I was not only using Lukas, I was hurting myself more.

I broke our lips apart, and I stared up at his clouded, dark green eyes. He was breathing heavily, studying me. There hadn't been anything wrong with the kiss. Sure, it lacked the wow factor, but I could blame that on Gavin. The rest was all me. I was turning everything into a gigantic mess, making one bad decision after another, just so I could feel better. It was wrong, pathetic, and not me.

Guilt poured through me.

I had a funny way of attempting to make things better with Gavin. Kissing Lukas wasn't going to win me trust points, and I was leading Lukas on, both things I didn't want to do.

My heart hadn't been into the kiss, for one good reason.

I was hung up on Gavin. I was more than hung up—I was a goner, head-over-heels crazy about him. My heart had been lost to him the day I smacked into him while ditching school.

Lukas read the string of emotions galloping through my eyes. I didn't want to hurt Lukas any more than I had wanted to hurt Gavin.

Slowly he tucked a strand of loose hair behind my ear. "I'll call you later?" He left the question dangling in the air between us.

I nodded, head still swirling with recriminations and revelations.

CHAPTER 15

THANKSGIVING DINNER.

The holiday wasn't going to be dull, that's for sure. Not only was my aunt bringing the *new* guy, but she had also insisted that I invite Lukas. Once she found he was going to be spending the holiday alone, she had pressed me relentlessly, until even I felt guilt-ridden.

So here I was, preparing for a very awkward evening.

How do I even get myself into these situations?

Lukas and I had talked a little since the *kiss*, but never about the *kiss* itself. I was much better at ignoring things than I was at lying. Still, seeing him face-to-face for the first time since was going to be...challenging.

This past week at school had been short due to the holiday, so I still had seen very little of Gavin, to my heart's dismay. I'd been hoping to find time to talk, but the measly fifty minutes during chemistry didn't allow for deep conversations. I missed him terribly, and wanted to get things back to how they'd been, instead of this indecisive insanity I was always feeling.

As it turned out, my relationship with Gavin was in limbo. I wasn't sure what steps were necessary to repair the damage I'd caused. Not only did I need a guidebook on witchcraft, but I also needed one on boys.

Blow drying my soaking-wet hair, I sat in front of my mirror, wrestling with the tangles. My stomach was twisted in loops. This thing must be more serious with the *new* guy than I realized, for my aunt to have him over for Thanksgiving dinner. I wasn't entirely sure how I felt about it. Might sound selfish, and I am sure it was, but I was used to having Aunt Clara all to myself. I found that sharing her with a guy didn't exactly sit well in my belly. Not that I didn't like him. He seemed nice enough, and he made her happy. That should have been adequate.

I threw on a pair of jeans and a glitzy black sweater, only applying a light coat of makeup. I wasn't feeling the holiday spirit. My phone buzzed on the vanity as I finished my mascara. Unlocking the screen, it was a text from Sophie, wishing me a happy Thanksgiving.

I don't know why, but it made me sad. I guess thoughts of Gavin were never far from my mind. My fingers punched over the keys as I sent her a quick text back wishing her the same, and then shook the depressing thoughts from my head. This wasn't the time to be ungrateful.

Heading down the stairs, I heard my aunt whistling cheerfully in the kitchen. The holidays were one of the few days we were both at home, with no school and no duties to the shop. I treasured the holidays, even if this one felt a little funky.

She was at the sink, her caramel hair in a messy bun with a stylish apron tied at her waist. Well, as hip as an apron could be. She had the silly, spacey look of someone on the brink of love. I had that same look not too long ago. Still did whenever I saw Gavin. She seasoned the turkey unaware she had an audience. My heart warmed inside, seeing that lovely glow of happiness shine on her beautiful face.

Quietly, I stepped beside her and hopped up on the counter. "Hey. You need any help?"

She grinned, the dreamy look clearing from her eyes. "Sure, I would love some help. Think you can handle the table?"

Thousands of memories bombarded me. I rolled my eyes. "Please. It's only been my job since I was five." I jumped to the floor.

"Brianna?" she called my name before I stepped out of the room.

I spun around. "Yeah?"

"I know you said you were okay with having Chad over for dinner, but are you really...okay with it? This is your home too, and I don't want you to ever feel uncomfortable or put out."

I gave the biggest, best, most reassuring smile I could. Whether she would say it or not, I knew this evening was important to her—a monstrous step. I even believed the invitation to Lukas had been her small way of trying to make me more comfortable, so to speak, regardless, she hit way off the mark. It wasn't her fault I'd screwed things up so badly. "Of course it is. This is going to be the best Thanksgiving. Just wait and see."

She beamed at me, satisfied that I was truly cool with it. Something told me that this would be a memorable holiday.

My aunt was all about visual appeal. It was just as important that the table be beautifully decorated as it was for the food to be scrumptious. Spreading a glittery gold tablecloth on our dining room table, I put my mind to setting the places. Each seat had a deep cherry placemat with cream-colored china and a gold-rimmed glass goblet. I still wasn't sure why we needed so many forks, spoons, and knives. Why couldn't I use the same fork for my salad and dinner? I wasn't much for fancy, but it appeased my aunt. I should be thankful she didn't insist I wear a dress. That would have been a battle.

The centerpiece was from *Mystic Floral*, one of my aunt's deigns. Setting the table was a mindless chore. Just the kind I needed.

A tiny meow at my feet caught my attention. Some sneaky little kitten had escaped like Houdini from my room. He was forever doing that. If I didn't know better, I'd swear Gavin had given me a charmed kitty.

I scooped up the neglected-feeling Lunar in my arms just as the doorbell rang. Nuzzling his cozy warm fur, I walked to the door. "Here goes nothing. Let the fun and games begin," I mumbled sarcastically to Lunar. Then I hollered through the house. "I got it!" My aunt was still sweating it out in the kitchen.

My heart raced a little as I turned the knob on the front door.

Then it dropped to my socks as I saw the new guy with his shaggy, brown hair.

He had a name; I reminded myself— Chad something or other.

Stuffed with an armful of orange mums, yellow sunflowers, and deep red carnations, Chad peeked over the bouquet. How original. Flowers for a florist. Couldn't he have been a little more creative? This was my aunt, after all, and she was pretty darn awesome. She deserved some awe-inspiring awesomeness.

"Wow, uh, these are lovely. I am sure Aunt Clara will love them," I said, smiling and lying through my teeth.

"I hope so. You don't think it's too cheesy?" Chad asked, looking ready to abandon ship.

God, I hoped I'd gotten better at lying. "No. Definitely not." I brightened my already fake smile, giving him credit for trying, at least.

"Thank goodness." There were little beads of sweat on his brow. He was nervous, and I couldn't help feeling sympathy for the guy.

I closed the door behind him.

"This must be Lunar," he said, scratching the kitten's black furring head. Lunar, loving all attention, purred a mile a minute. Chad noticed my surprise. "Your aunt has told me a lot about you."

"And you still came to dinner?" I teased.

"I don't scare off that easily." He had a nice smile. I'd give him that.

How about a witch, I silently wondered. Tonight he was getting two for the price of one. Oh, goody.

Lukas arrived right behind the semi-dorky Chad. Lunar took one beady glance at him and made a mad dash upstairs. I rolled my eyes and ushered Lukas inside. Before we got to the kitchen, I cornered him in the hallway. "No funny business tonight," I warned in a hushed whisper, poking him in the chest. For some reason, I felt the need to lay down the ground rules.

He held up both hands claiming innocent and grinned devilishly. "I'll keep my hands to myself. Both of them, I promise," he added when I didn't look immediately swayed.

Somehow that smile didn't look reassuring. I probably should have added that he also keep his lips to himself. Technicalities.

Dinner was surprisingly normal considering. The conversation was light, funny, and entertaining. Lukas had a way about him. Charismatic. Likable. Electrifying. I couldn't help but think he used some kind of spell that made people fall in love with him. One flaw with that assumption—it didn't work on me.

I must be immune.

"Who wants dessert?" my aunt asked, standing up to go into the kitchen.

I slumped in my seat, feeling like a beached whale, overstuffed on turkey, mashed potatoes, and broccoli and cheese casserole. I'd left very little room for dessert, which was my favorite part of the meal. Somehow I was going to have to make room.

I should have probably gotten up and helped my aunt bring out dessert, but I couldn't move a muscle. Lukas sat across from me, smirking and chuckling. I was this close to kicking him under the table or unsnapping the top button on my jeans. I couldn't decide. "Stop laughing at me," I grumbled, trying to keep a straight face.

He leaned forward, elbows on the table. "You make it so easy."

I gave him a snarky glare.

Dessert arrived. I don't know how I managed to lift my spoon, but I had a bite of pumpkin pie topped with Cool Whip halfway to my mouth when I was interrupted by a burst of noise that sent my spoon clattering to my plate. One of the windows had blown open at crashing speeds, the shutters smacking the edge of the house. Everyone at the table jumped. The wind outside howled painfully, and the curtains flew around the room in crazy disarray of silk.

My eyes met Lukas's quizzical gaze across the table, and he arched a brow, silently asking if I was responsible. I shook my head. Storms and I sort of went hand-in-hand, so I could see why he would think it was me. I'd gotten pretty good the last few weeks at feeling my energy rise. This was most definitely not my doing, and if it wasn't Lukas...

I shot to my feet and jogged to the window, slamming it shut. There was an eerie ambiance in the room. I shivered.

"That was weird," Aunt Clara said, folding her hands in her lap. "The weather has been on the fritz lately."

Chad grumbled some response, but I had checked out of the conversation. My entire body knew the gust of wind hadn't been an accident. It had been magic. The tingle of magic was pulsing through the air, even thicker near the window.

I took my seat again and gulped. If anyone noticed my lack of participation, it wasn't brought to light.

Designing swirls with my uneaten pumpkin pie, I no longer had the desire to gorge myself. My stomach was whirling. I twirled the mushy goo around on my plate, trying to figure out what witch might be responsible. I couldn't shake the feeling that we were no longer alone.

The excitement of my bewitched Thanksgiving didn't end there. Nope. I couldn't be that lucky. Stuff like this wasn't just coincidence, and I needed to accept the cold truth.

Things were never going to be *normal* in my life again.

My aunt gasped beside me, and I turned to see what had her attention. Coughing, I choked on my water. *What the hell?* The flowers sitting at the center of the table, Chad's contribution, were shriveled, dried, and black as spades.

Dead.

The vibrant colors, the dewy petals, and the sweet aroma were gone. Even the water had turned a nasty shade of darkness, like poison.

"Wow, what was in that vase?" Aunt Clara mumbled.

This time I gave into my earlier urge and kicked Lukas under the table. He narrowed his eyes at me. Nodding in the direction of the sad flower display, I seared him with daggers.

He shrugged his shoulders, the lightheartedness gone from his bold, green eyes. He was just as innocent as I was in this fiasco.

The very second the dishes were cleared, I grabbed Lukas by the arm and dragged him into the hallway. I could hear the banter between my aunt and Chad in the kitchen. He had volunteered for kitchen duty —totally fine and dandy by me. I had more pressing problems.

"What the hell was all that?" I asked when I was sure the coast was clear. Even as the accusations left my lips, I knew Lukas wasn't responsible.

Lukas wasn't listening. And damn if that didn't boil my blood. His sharp gaze was scoping out the room.

"Lukas!" I yelled, much too loud.

"Hmm?" he responded mindlessly, still scanning.

I huffed. Then, of course, I didn't the most mature thing I could think of; I pinched him.

"Ouch!" he cried. "What was that for?"

"It wasn't that hard, you big baby. Focus."

"What do you think I have been doing? There is someone else here."

I rolled my eyes. Well, duh. "I kind of figured that out already, Watson." Admitting it out loud still didn't stop the spine-chilling tingle from coursing through me. "Who is it?"

His emerald eyes begin to shine. "I'm not sure it's a who. Maybe more like a viable source."

I blinked. "English."

He grinned and leaned his back against the wall, folding his arms. "You have a spirit."

I wiped my sweating palms on the legs of my jeans. "You mean a ghost?" This was worse. Way worse. It was a stupid question, but I couldn't fathom the idea of being haunted in my own house, for God's sake. And it screwed up Thanksgiving dinner, too.

I could only hope my aunt wasn't suspicious. The last thing I needed was her calling the Ghostbusters, or a priest.

But the joke was on me. Lukas and I never got any more solid information or answers that night. It remained another mystery.

CHAPTER 16

THREE DAYS AFTER THE STRANGEST Thanksgiving ever, I got a text from Sophie inviting me to hang out. My first thought was it would be a great way to possibly run into Gavin. He had kept his promise and returned to school, but it was hardly like it used to be. I think he went to great pains to avoid me. Chemistry couldn't be avoided, but all the other classes and in the passing periods—zilch.

So I jumped all over the chance to see him.

In less than an hour, I was standing on the porch of the Masons' house. A gazillion emotions were plummeting through me: excitement, fear, hope, nervousness. A roar of crashing waves could be heard over my bubbling feelings. It was a heartening sound.

The door opened, and my heart pitter-pattered right into over-drive. I didn't have to look up to know who stood in the doorway. Every bone, every muscle, every fiber in my being was humming.

Gavin.

My chest jumped for joy. Fireflies, like the beacon of the night, zoomed in my belly. I missed those pesky fireflies. When I raised my head, I was slammed into a pair of sapphire eyes, the same eyes that burned my steamy dreams night after countless nights. I couldn't stop staring at him. My tongue was stuck. My legs started to shake. My world hadn't felt complete without him.

A tendril of something inside me reached out to him, willing itself to attach to this one guy for all of eternity. The intensity startled me. I knew I loved him, but forever?

He leaned against the doorframe in a pair of ripped denim jeans, a T-shirt, and a lopsided grin. God, I missed that mouth. My eyes fastened onto his lips, and a flush covered my skin. His knock-your-socks-off lips were tempting. Once you have drunk from the fountain of ecstasy, you always want more.

Those dark sapphire eyes roamed over me slowly, and suddenly I was scorching hot. It didn't matter that it was November. My body was on fire. I could have thrown myself all over him in a matter of seconds.

It was that bad.

When I referred to jumping at the chance to see him, I hadn't meant literally, but geez, at this rate, it was a good possibility that I wouldn't make it off this porch without embarrassing myself greatly.

His grin only grew wider, the longer I stood there with my mouth hanging open, drooling at his feet.

It was his smirk that finally snapped me out of my trance before I made an even bigger doofus of myself. He stepped aside, waiting for me to come inside. Brushing past him, I cleared my throat uncomfortably. "Is Sophie here?"

He waggled that studded brow. "No, she is gone for the day with my parents."

I groaned. *Sophie.*

I was going to kill her, then hug her.

She could be conniving when she wanted to be. And I utterly fell for it. I had been smartly maneuvered. She set this whole thing up, so Gavin and I would be alone. Sophie was in deep shit. The next time I saw her, I was going to tell her she was a genius.

Understanding lit in his sultry eyes. "Sophie," he growled. "Don't let that innocent face fool you. She can be devious."

I noticed how quiet it was as I stepped inside. Not a peep. "Are you home alone?" I asked.

"Yep." He tucked his hand into his pockets.

"Oh. Uh, I guess I should go—"

"You can stay if you want," he said, cutting me off. "We could hang out."

I held my breath. "Sure," I expelled. "I'd like that."

We ended up watching a movie, *Zombieland*. Deciding on a movie with Gavin was nowhere near as problematic as it was with Tori and Austin. Side-by-side on the couch, everything clicked into place, just like that. There was no longer a brick wall between us. No Lukas. It was just Gavin and me, talking, poking fun at the movie, and being normal teens. I couldn't remember the last time my heart felt so weightless.

I wiggled my nose at a gruesome but funny part of the movie. Pulled by the sound of Gavin's chuckle, I peeked at the hot guy next to me and found him staring at me.

"I adore your freckles. They're cute." He flicked the end of my nose.

I made a horrible face. "Cute. I don't want to be cute."

His lips twitched. "They're sexy, okay? How's that?"

A small smile appeared on my lips. "Better."

"Uh, how's the magic coming?" His leg was pressed up against mine on the couch. Just the little contact did funny things to my belly.

My violet eyes twinkled. "I'll show you."

The whole moving object thing was easy as pie, but I hadn't factored in Gavin as a distraction. It took more concentration and focus to get a simple glass of water from the coffee table to move. Once I had it in the air, it was smooth sailing, more or less.

Just one small hiccup.

I had the glass balanced mid-air in front of him, right within his grasp. What I hadn't been prepared for was his whispered breath near my ear. His lips grazed my neck and that did it. My concentration was shot. I didn't know what he said, but the words didn't matter. The glass tumbled into his lap, splashing water all over him and soaking his shirt. Droplets of water sprayed my face and hair.

Stunned, neither of us moved.

Then like a dam had been broken, I busted into a fit of hysterics. I don't why it was so funny, but I couldn't stop the laughter. Falling back into the couch cushion, tears gathered at my eyes. I hadn't laughed so hard in a long time. It felt freeing until my stomach started to cramp.

"I swear you did that on purpose," he smirked, shaking the water from his hair. He stood up, and I slid to the floor, clutching my middle.

"You. Broke. My. Concentration." I blamed it on him, between giggles.

His eyes said he was secretly pleased. I just bet he was.

I held my stomach, rolling on the floor. He just looked so darn adorably rumpled. With a quick flick of his wrist, he pulled his soaking wet shirt over his head, and my laughter immediately died.

I gulped.

Holy hotness. Stop the broomsticks.

Sexy didn't even come close to describing Gavin shirtless.

I clamped my mouth shut to keep from embarrassing myself.

That was unexpected. Very nice, but I was completely unprepared for a half-naked Gavin. My eyes roamed over every glorious, golden inch. I've seen him without a shirt before, but we'd been too busy for me to appreciate it. Now that I had the chance, I wasn't wasting it. My eye gobbled him up, stopped short by a mark, unlike anything I'd ever seen.

It was a tattoo, but it wasn't. I mean, tattoos don't glimmer. The ink looked like a metallic rainbow, changing color with the light. It was more than just the unusual ink. I had to be seeing shit. How could it flicker like that?

"You have a tattoo?" I exclaimed, astonished, pushing to my feet. How did I not know this? Not that I really should have been that surprised, this was Gavin. The embodiment of a bad boy, he really could be one with a few scars and tattoos.

He twirled the hoop at the center of his lip, his contemplation habit. I wasn't going to let him get out of explaining this.

A tattoo that seemed to live...no way. "It is a tattoo, right?"

He watched me. "Of sorts. It's more of a rune. It's protection. The ink is spelled and bound to the witch."

I was entranced.

On their own accord, my feet moved until I could feel the heat radiating from his superb body. Later I might be mortified by my behavior, but right now, I wasn't thinking at all. My fingers lightly traced the lines of the shimmering rune, situated on the left side of his chest. I mean it literally shimmered, as if it was moving. Enthralled, I let my nails outline his hot skin. His muscles trembled on contact. Right. He wasn't wearing a shirt, and I was touching him. Uh, more like caressing him. His abs were freaking edible. I wanted just one nibble, and I stepped forward, brushing against him. Rune forgotten, I peeked up from under my lashes. His eyes gleamed. Dark. Sinful. Scrumptious.

He placed his hands on either side of my hips, and my entire being went up in flames. Leaning down, he whispered my name against my partially open lips. He tugged on my bottom lip, and I fought the need to sink my teeth into him. He had a way of bringing out the crazy-girl side of me.

Unable to move, I stood immobile, afraid to break the mood. I didn't want to do or say anything that would ruin this moment. His mouth outlined my jaw, leaving tiny, fiery embers behind. He made me sparkle from inside and out. With him, I felt like a better person, a better witch. He made everything seem brighter.

Our bodies fused, and my hands flattened against his bare chest. I tilted my head, giving him more access. His lips grazed my neck, my cheek, my chin. So lost was I on the crazy intensity of his kisses, I couldn't keep track of where his lips roamed. They were everywhere, and at the same time, it was not enough.

My fingers dug into his dark locks, and he finally gave me what I craved, our lips meeting in one fluid motion. And his lips were to die for.

Sweet Jesus, he could kiss.

I didn't know how I could go another day without one of his kisses, though one was never enough. Never.

His tongue swept over mine, tasting of the richest flavors. Sliding my hand down his back, I kissed him ardently back. Sparks flowed, cascading off our bodies. It was purely cosmic, moonbeams and shooting stars. Our hearts beat in time. Our magic purred together.

Sliding down the curve of my back, he cupped my backside. His fingers tightened, searing through my jeans, and pulled me closer, surging our bodies. Behind my eyes, flashes of silver and white light burst. We were seriously electrifying. I opened myself up deeper as Gavin pressed his lips more firmly against mine. I was lost to the world, lost to only him.

I couldn't catch my breath. It was amazing.

Need spread through me like wildfire. It was only a matter of seconds before we devoured each other, and I was going to enjoy each second.

We were both breathing hard as we surfaced for air. A huge part of me wanted to dive in for round two, and I was pretty sure round two would end up with fewer clothes, and further than we had gone before. It sounded divine. But a small fraction of me was still absorbed by the rune.

It won.

"I want one," I proclaimed, breathless. The idea was just suddenly there, and I knew to the bottom of my curled toes that I truly wanted one.

"No." He stepped out of our embrace, and I mourned the loss of his warmth.

I wrapped my arms around myself. "What do you mean, *no?*"

And just as quickly, his eyes flashed with stubbornness. "Do I need to spell it out for you? N. O."

Smartass. He most definitely was going to pay for that. "Why is it okay for you to have one and not me? If you say it's because I'm a girl, I swear I'll kick you."

He tried not to grin and failed miserably. "It's more than just decorative body art, Bri. It's magic. A different kind of magic. One bound beyond the rules of witchcraft."

"So it's like illegal magic."

His fingers combed through his hair. "Yeah. That pretty much sums it up."

I remained undeterred. "You don't get to decide what's best for me." The look on his face said he was going to fight me tooth and nail on this. Fine. Time to play dirty. "I had another visit from Casper the friendly ghost."

That got his attention. He frowned.

"I am going to do this with or without you," I declared, trying to sound like a hardass...and failing.

He remained an immovable force. "You can't go without me; you don't even know where to go."

True, I might not know where to go, but he wasn't the only witch in town. "I'll just get Sophie or Jared to take me."

His frowned deepened. I think the Jared thing pushed him over the edge. "Fine."

I grinned a mile wide. "Your car or mine?"

He sighed heavily. "I know I am going to regret this."

"Live a little." This coming from the girl who a few months ago would never have skipped school, never failed a test, much less contemplate getting a rune tattooed.

She also hadn't had magic or a mega-gorgeous boyfriend. Almost boyfriend. Things were looking promising.

He waggled his studded brow. "I'll drive."

"So how soon can we get there?" I asked, slipping into the passenger seat of his Charger.

He grinned wolfishly. My heart tripped. I was feeling wild and reckless.

It was fabulous.

CHAPTER 17

I MISSED THIS SO MUCH I ached like my heart had caught a fever. This easiness, silliness, and plain fun between us was cleansing, a breath of fresh air after inhaling nothing but smog.

"So where are we going?" I asked, snuggling in the plush leather.

He had both eyes on the road, a slip of hair flopped over one brow. "I know someone." His lips tipped at the corners.

Like I doubted him. "And *this someone* can do a rune like yours?"

"Yep." He looked like a dangerous little boy.

I narrowed my eyes against the setting sun. "How do you know *this someone?*"

"Jared." He gave me a lopsided grin.

"Figures." It was just like Jared to know everyone in a town he had barely lived in. There was just something about Gavin's older brother that attracted attention. The good and bad kind. And it was more than his ridiculous hotness. "Does *this someone* have a name?" It was getting kind of old referring to the artist as *this someone.*

He angled his gaze toward me, waiting to see my reaction. "Blaze."

He wasn't disappointed. I rolled my eyes. "Blaze? What kind of name is that? It sounds like a male stripper."

He cocked a brow at me. "You've changed."

I gave him a sassy grin. "No thanks to you."

"I really shouldn't take all the credit. When did you become so feisty? You're like a kitty cat with its claws out."

"I'm turning over a new leaf."

He grinned. "I like it."

I smacked him on the shoulder. "Why am I not surprised? Tell me more about the rune. Does it hurt?"

His eyes sobered. I didn't understand why he was set against me getting one. What the heck was the big deal? "It's a rapid needle and spellbound ink. Hell, yeah, it's going to hurt."

Hmm. He was going to make this difficult. I could see it in the hard-set line of his chiseled jaw. It was impossible to look at him and not have my heart somersaulting. "Why are you so against this?"

"A rune doesn't come without consequences. There are rules and responsibilities, just like anything with magic. If the rules are broken, it can change you, not only as a person but as a witch. It can warp your magic."

Nothing in this world came without a price.

"I just don't want anything to harm you. Runes can be very powerful, but they can also destroy you." His eyes were brimming with concern and worry.

Even after everything that had happened, he was still concerned about my welfare. It made my heart swell. I stared out the window, mulling over his words. I wasn't going to lie, it made me think twice, but not enough to change my mind. What would my aunt say if she found out or accidentally saw the rune? She would no doubt lose her shit. The key here was to make sure she didn't find out.

More secrets.

More lies.

The guilt gnawed at me.

She would ground me for eternity and probably ban Gavin from my life. But that brought on a new set of questions. "Can someone without magic see runes?" I recalled how it had been almost animated.

His hand effortlessly guided the wheel as we made a turn onto the highway. "No. Those without the gift see nothing but a tattoo. What did you see?"

I laid my head on the back of the seat and turned my body toward him. "It was stellar. Like nothing I ever could have imagined. The ink was a prism of colors. I swear it moved in waves, shifting in and out."

He nodded. "It's a symbol to ward off dark magic. Four crescent moons intertwined. The four elements of magic: earth, water, air, and fire. Those are the colors you saw swirling within the shapes, along with a fifth color—spirit. Spirit is more of an incandescent color. Once it is on you, you can never have it removed. Whatever spell is cast in the ink will follow you forever."

There was a foreboding ring to his words.

It was for protection, I rationed. It had nothing to do with the fact that Gavin had one, or that I wanted to share something with him. And definitely had nothing to do with making him think I was a cool chick.

No way. None of the above.

Who was I kidding? It was all those reasons and more. Everything told me that this magical body art would bring us closer. I needed to do this. For me. For Gavin. For us. I really couldn't explain it in any other way.

He drove us into a seedy part of Wilmington, the side of town I normally avoided. I focused on the road to keep my mind from thinking of other things. Thick trees lined both sides of the road in a blur of shadows, hiding the pale moonlight from our view. We were the only headlights on the two-lane road. He turned onto a barely visible road. There were no markings; nothing to signal that there was even a road. I wasn't even sure how he hadn't passed it by.

The car bumped along the dirt and gravel road.

"Well, this isn't creepy," I muttered.

"This was your idea," he reminded, not that my stomach needed the reminder.

This had been my idea, but it wasn't exactly what I had pictured. Were there no rune shops along the boardwalk? That seemed a much safer option. I guess maybe they didn't have the proper equipment that was needed. "It's safe, right? I'm not going to be butchered up and stored in a freezer, am I?"

He snickered. "You need to lay off the slasher movies. I promise nothing bad will happen to you."

And those were words I trusted from no one but him.

An old ranch-style house sat off to the right. Shingles were missing from places on the roof. He killed the lights and the engine, immersing us in darkness. A neon sign lit a small section of the house in bold, blue lights. It read *Divinity Tattoo*.

He reached for my hand as I stepped out of the car. My stomach went topsy-turvy, and my pulse picked up speed. I was doing this. I was going to puke. My nerves had settled in and were hammering against my ribs.

"Is there an age requirement?" Suddenly, I just realized I wasn't of legal age to get a tattoo. I didn't know if it worked the same way with magical art.

"I got you covered." He flipped his wrist, and a plastic card appeared.

"You made me a fake ID?" I asked in disbelief.

"Every teenager needs one, especially when breaking the law." His blue eyes sparkled in mischief.

I peered down at the plastic card. It looked flawless. "This looks so real."

He flexed his fingers. "Magic."

Taking my hand again, he guided us toward the creepy house. Everything was dark, with slivers of moonlight cutting across the yard. I couldn't see two feet in front of me as I cast an unsure glance to the tree line bordering the property and tripped. Damn pothole. Gavin's hand was there, steadying me before I ended up face first in the ground spitting dirt.

My eyes must have been wide as saucers. "We can leave if you want. You don't have to do this."

I just shook my head.

I can do this, I told myself. *You can do this. You want to do this.* It helped a little.

The door jingled as we pushed it open, and I was awestruck. The place was the complete opposite of the exterior. Two steps inside, and I was transported to a parallel universe. The walls were painted with mermaids and harpies that seemed to dance and sing. Everything in the spacious studio was touched by magic in some form.

My mouth must have fallen open, because he whispered in my ear, "It's glamoured."

I tried to ignore the little blip in my heart at his closeness. It was challenging. Glamour—made sense, I just had never experienced it firsthand. It was pretty kickass. I so needed to learn that trick.

A man in his thirties sat on a stool behind the counter with a half-dozen piercings on his face. Both arms were sleeved in ink that sparkled like Gavin's. It was mind-boggling to see so much of his body covered by mystic art.

Billy the badass—that's what I decided to call him—eyed Gavin in the macho way guys do when they size each other up. Then he turned his gray eyes on me. "What can I do for you, sweet thang?" He had a deep, gruff voice, like the kind you get from screaming too much, and a tinge of the Deep South.

In all honesty, he was pretty scary.

Gavin stepped in front of me, centering the attention back to him. "She's here to see Blaze."

Billy the badass looked from me to Gavin, and back to me. "You got ID, babe?"

The muscle in Gavin's jaw ticked. I don't think he took well to the casual endearments Billy threw around.

I tried to play it cool and reached into the back pocket of my jeans. I totally failed.

Gulping, I slapped my new ID on the counter. He slid it off the glass onto his huge palm. Rings decorated each finger.

"So..." He scanned the plastic card for my name. "Britney, you looking to get inked?"

I glared sideways at Gavin. *Britney*. He smirked, reading the flicker of spice in my eyes. He had changed my name on the ID. I just nodded my head, afraid to speak.

Billy must have taken my silence for nerves, which was partially true. "Looks like we got ourselves a virgin."

I choked on a horrorstruck laugh. Gavin's fist clenched at his side. This was going well.

"Don't worry, Blaze will take good care of you. Blaze!" he bellowed. "You got a customer."

A tiny woman with silver hair that traveled past her butt rounded the corner. She had it tied at the nape of her neck, and it swayed with her movements. Her features were enchanting, like a little pixie. As far as I could see, she didn't have an inch of ink on her.

This was Blaze. She wasn't at all what I had expected. She was a *she*.

Her smile was charming, reaching the depths of her aquamarine eyes. She was definitely a witch, yet she looked anything but human. An unearthly glow gleamed on her skin like her outline had been blended by an artist.

"You must be Jared's brother, Gavin. I can see the resemblance." She held out her dainty hand, unadorned with any jewelry.

He shook her hand, giving her a wry grin. "The one and only, and I'm the better-looking one." His ego had no bounds.

I rolled my eyes. Blaze caught the movement, and the corners of her shell-pink mouth turned up. "You must be his girlfriend."

Awkward.

He didn't deny or confirm, and she'd caught me off guard. Since the whole fiasco with Lukas, neither of us brought it up. "Brit wants to get inked," he informed her, letting Blaze make up her mind about us.

My chest swelled, and my heart skipped. It gave me hope, though I had to stop myself from rolling my eyes when I heard him call me by my fake name.

"Well, Brit, aren't you one lucky girl?" I wasn't entirely sure it was necessary to stroke his already-inflated ego anymore, but Gavin definitely didn't have any qualms with it. "Let's step into my office." She gave me a quick wink and then led the way down a narrow hallway.

As we turned around the corner, I elbowed him the ribs. "What was that?"

He grunted and scowled down at me. "Security. I don't want anyone tracking you," he whispered near the nape of my neck.

I ignored the shiver his whisper produced. Then there was the uncertainty I felt about him protecting my identity. It seemed a little excessive. I made a mental note to ask him on the way home. We followed Blaze into a quaint room the same color as her eyes. The blue-green walls were trimmed in dark mahogany. A counter housed a slew of instruments that looked more torturous than artsy.

She took a seat and indicated I take the one beside her. "What do you have in mind?"

Gavin stood behind me. His presence was like a shield. "Protection. You know, the whole evil spirits and whatnot. The usual nasties."

Her smile was lovely and illuminated her entire face. "Hmm." She reached out and clasped my hand in hers. A charge of electricity jolted through our hands on contact. My eyes widened, and I studied her face, wondering how this was helping. Didn't I just pick out a pretty design and voila, abracadabra...I got a kickass rune?

Sounded accurate enough to me.

Blaze looked at me funny. "Whoa. I wasn't expecting that. You pack quite a punch in such a little package." Who was she calling little? We were about the same height and build. She smiled, aqua eyes dazzling. "I've got just the thing for you. Let the party begin."

I wouldn't exactly call this a party...to each his or her own, I guess. There was both a bubble of excitement and a sliver of fear in my chest. The fear was mostly for the pain. Glancing at Gavin, his eyes filled with worry.

"You don't have to do this, you know," he said for like the umpteenth time.

I had to fight from rolling my eyes again. "I know. I want this. I can't explain it. This just feels right."

He nodded, a loose piece of dark hair falling on his forehead. "I understand. More than you know."

The buzzing of the liner machine vibrated behind me, a sudden reminder of what I was about to do. Straddling the chair, I lifted my shirt as I waited for her to get started. The first prick of the needle was like eh, no big deal. A few minutes later I was trying not to jump out of the chair.

I bit my lip to keep from squealing like a girl. It reminded me like a hot scratch on repeat. Eventually, the area went numb, until she hit a new nerve, then it started again. Gavin's warm hand clutched in mine helped me focus on anything but the unrelenting pain and kept me from jerking away.

Clamping my eyes shut, I concentrated on the pulsing vigor from our connected fingers. If I thought the outline was bad, the shading didn't compare. Dots of black swirled behind my eyelids. I was about to call it quits when at last the buzzing stopped. I thought my ears were deceiving me. They were still ringing.

"All done," Blaze's voice sounded from behind me.

I let a huge sigh of relief. She smoothed on an ointment before leading me to a full-length mirror, turning me so I had to look over my shoulder. I looked at the red patch on my lower back. There, just above my jean line, sat the dark lines and incandescent rainbow ink of my first act of rebellion. It was majestic, mystical, and alluring—a cross between a sun and a star. A trail of dust encircled the image. In awe, I watched as it swirled in movement.

"I love it!" I grinned, facing Blaze. It had been worth the risk, worth the pain. At the center of my back, I could feel the thumping of magic where the rune sat. "It is remarkable," I gushed.

Blaze smiled in the mirror. "It really is. One of the best I've ever done. A reinforcement of what already courses through your blood. This will heighten, guard, and guide you." Then her eyes went stony and opaque. "But the price for the darker side of magic will be increased tenfold. Choose wisely in your spells. The vector of elements suits you."

Her words struck a chord inside me, a weight of responsibility I hadn't felt before walking inside the deceiving rundown house. "Thank you," I managed in a soft and shaky voice.

Gavin, after a playboy-worthy smile to Blaze, ushered me back down the slender hallway into the main entrance. He was such a flirt, I thought to myself, but really, I didn't mind. It was adorable and harmless.

Billy the badass gave me a sly wink as we passed him heading for the door. "I'll see you soon, sweetheart. They say once you've been inked at *Divinity* you always come back for more."

Gavin placed a hand on my elbow, and his flirtatious mood vanished. I could feel the steam of jealousy radiating off him. "Don't hold your breath, tough guy," he added, spitefully. Then he ushered us into the cool wash of twilight not giving me a chance to say anything, a good thing.

The moment the door closed behind us, we were consumed by the darkness. Gavin intertwined our fingers. Sparks flamed in the air from all the pent up irritation that suddenly rolled through him. "I should go back there and give Rambo a thrashing," he growled.

I did my best not to smile.

He had been jealous. My chest bloomed.

I took a quick peek at the shabby house one last time before climbing into his car, careful to place my legs at an angle to avoid putting pressure on my back. I closed my eyes and listened to the low hum of the radio, comforted by Gavin's presence. Before I knew it we were zipping into his driveway, and I wasn't nearly ready to say good-bye.

Careful of my movements, I leaned a hip against his car and waited for him to walk around. Even with the black night, I could see his sapphire eyes lighting up like blue diamonds. "I wish this night would never end."

His answer was to pull me into his arms, exactly where I wanted to be. I squeezed and let out a contented sigh. Plastered against him, he kissed the top of my head. There was still a light sting at my lower back, nothing intolerable. He pressed his face next to mine, and his ridiculously long lashes fanned my cheek. "Goodnight, Bri."

I didn't want to leave. It had been a huge step from the way things used to be between us. No way was I ready to let that go. I was too afraid that when I woke in the morning, it would cease to be the same —to exist. There were a billion questions on the tip of my tongue— questions about us, questions about runes, and questions about that place. In the end, I was just too exhausted to expel the energy needed to process all the information. So instead I said, "'Night."

He pressed a sweet, soft kiss to my lips, and I floated on a cloud to the door on that kiss alone.

This was a night I would never forget.

Truly.

I had the tramp stamp to prove it.

CHAPTER 18

T HE FEELING OF BEING ON top of the world followed me the rest of the night. As I got ready for bed, I could still feel the warmth of his lips. I sat on the edge of the bed and pulled on my knee-high socks, unable to believe the events of the day. I touched my lips, remembering what it was like to have his mouth pressed to mine.

Everything with Gavin was always so intense. When things were good, they were cosmic. When things went sour, it destroyed my world. I doubted either of those things was healthy for a relationship, but I didn't think Gavin and I constituted a *normal* couple.

There was nothing *normal* about me anymore.

I snuggled into my pillow, lying on my side. The tingly throb on my lower back brought a small smile to my lips. It was annoyingly persistent but brought pleasant memories. I had to remember to thank Sophie for her underhanded plan. It was just the push Gavin and I needed.

I tried to force my giddiness to subside by closing my eyes. Sleep was going to be a long time coming. My fingers clutched the cool, tingling stones of the necklace dangling at my neck. Even though it didn't necessarily work with powerful witches like granny dearest, I felt more secure with it on. Maybe the added presence of my new glamour rune would protect my dreams from others, or more importantly, from me.

Sleep might not have been in my future, but my unusual dreams were. I recognized the dream for what it was...magic. The swooping feeling of being swept away from myself to a world I had yet to be able to control. The possibilities were there. I had even on occasion grabbed the reins and steered the mystical visions. It was just the instability of it all, the insecurity of my ability to control my dreams. One day soon, I was going to master these dreams.

For now, I wasn't sure who I would find waiting for me in this parallel universe I seemed to visit more often than not.

The frothy blue-green waves lapped against the foamy shore as they rose and fell. My dark auburn hair whipped against my face with the wind, blocking my sight. Sand squished in-between my bare toes. Spitting a strand of hair from my mouth, I pushed the tangling mess from my face.

There she stood on the bluff, like a dark goddess with mega self-entitlement and a streak of wickedness. She looked like she owned the world as if it was hers to command with a crook of a finger. If I thought Gavin had an ego problem, Morgana took the cake. She oozed badass.

She wore a bikini with a black sarong tied at her waist. Long, tan legs peeked through the sheer fabric. Waves upon waves of flaming dark red hair flowed with the wind, not like my snarling mess. Her purplish eyes laughed as she looked down at me, her granddaughter.

Immediately, I went on the defensive.

My head raised a notch as I met her amused gaze and arched a challenging brow.

She threw her head back and laughed. A deep, enchantress kind of laugh and there was pride in those twinkling eyes when they found mine again.

So much for the rune being able to ward against Morgana. Hmm. It might be my dream we were in, but it was her essence that wafted in the air, holding me in a dream.

Like a light switch had been flipped on inside me, I was packed with rage. I was tired of being her puppet. I was mad at myself for not being strong enough to block her. And I was angry about feeling useless.

The smug smile that danced on her lips made me want to strike her down with a bolt of lightning. I was so furious I was quaking.

"I see you still don't have a handle on your control over the weather," she taunted, knowing what buttons to push.

I'd been unaware of the storm brewing around me, lost in my fury and frustration until she pointed it out. The wind howled, gusting as lightning lit the sky and the heavens opened up in rolling clouds behind me. The blood through my veins intermixed with power. Together the two blended, changing me, giving me an unconscious strength and confidence.

I blinked, taking just a second to rein in what was begging to be released.

In just that nanosecond, Morgana was in front of me, her soft yet firm hands gripping mine. Her eyes illuminated like purple Lite-Brite pegs. "What you don't want is to let nature rule you. Remember that it is *you* who summoned her here. She is yours to control. Like a child, she must be taught to obey."

Together with our hands bound, I felt the energy between us amp up like a high voltage shock. Stunned, I gasped. Then the mother of all storms circled us but never touched us. We stood in the eye of the storm, unscathed. As quickly as it had been ignited, the vibrating hum of magic began a slow dance of recession, and with it, the storm followed. The winds died to a standstill, and the dark, ominous clouds broke apart, letting a stream of sunlight hit the beach. The thundering waves quieted to low, gentle surf.

"Wow. That was amazing." I couldn't keep the awe from my voice.

"It was, wasn't it?" Her smile was smug, eyes lively. "I'd expect nothing less than amazing from my granddaughter."

Every time she referred to me as her granddaughter, I forgot she was talking about me. It hadn't sunk in that this prevailing, beautiful, arrogant woman was part of my existence. Without her, I never would have been. It was a hard pill to swallow, considering she hadn't been the friendliest during our first encounter. Not typical grandmother material.

I was unsure of what to say or do. Like most of my dreams of her, she took the reins.

"Let's soak up some vitamin D and have a little girl time." She waved her hand in the air and poof, out sprang two wooden beach chairs. "We can chitchat about school, about magic, the boys in your life." She casually snuck in the last part.

Boys?

As in, more than one? Morgana knew more about my life than I was okay with. It was sort of creepy.

She made herself comfortable in one of the lounge chairs, and for the first time, I realized I was practically naked. I didn't consider the very skimpy red bikini and wrap as adequate clothing. It was like walking around in my unmentionables. "You put me in a bikini?" I couldn't help the outrage.

She tilted down a pair of sunglasses that hadn't been there a moment ago, amusement glittering in her eyes. "Hm. I wasn't sure about the cut, but it flatters your curves splendidly. I've seen your selection of clothing, dear. What you need is a little more pizazz in your wardrobe. That, and some sex appeal."

I choked on the sea salt air. My grandmother was giving me fashion advice. Who knew what was next—sex tips?

She studied me from behind her shades. "You're looking a little pale; magic will do that—drain you until you build up your strength. Why don't you have a seat?"

Grandma Morgana had just boarded the crazy train. She was out of her mind if she thought I was going to lie on the beach, mostly naked, and gossip.

However much it irked me, she had been right about my energy levels. I was feeling a little lightheaded and wobbly on my feet. Kicking my feet up sounded fabulous and too appealing to resist.

I sighed and joined her.

Sitting in the sunbaked chair, I fought the urge to cover myself with my arms. This was silly. What I needed was a large beach towel.

No more had the thought crossed my mind when lo and behold, a colorful striped towel appeared at my feet.

"Inventive. How about snapping us up a couple of martinis while you're at it?" Was everything to her so nonchalant? A joke? She gave me a smile filled with a thousand secrets. "One drink won't hurt. After all, you do have a fake ID. How is your newly mutated body art, anyway? Sore? Tingly? All normal, I assure you."

Wide-eyed and suspicious, I began to wonder if anything in my life would be my own ever again. She left me speechless, thriving on the element of surprise.

"Don't be so shocked. As my only granddaughter, well, only living descendant really, I've taken a special interest in your wellbeing."

Geez. Wonderful. "So what you're saying is, you're keeping tabs on me."

She tapped a black nail to her lip. "If you like. You should be more careful who you let in your house." Seriousness sparked in her violet eyes. Gone was the feisty banter. "You're in danger."

No shit. Thanks to you.

She let a sultry laugh. "Not me, sweet granddaughter but...someone close to you."

Oh crap. Had she just read my thoughts? That was scary.

Then it dawned on me. The magic I'd felt in the air on Thanksgiving came flooding back to me. "It was you," I accused, knowing without a doubt I was right. "You were at my house on Thanksgiving."

She grinned at me like a proud parent. "Took you long enough. I figured you'd recognize my...subtle hints."

Subtle? My aunt had been there. She was clueless about the madness I found myself surrounded in. "I should have," I muttered in hindsight. "Though, I would have expected something more dramatic from you."

"True, I do like things dazzling. In this case, I only wanted your attention. Instead, I got shoved out, by my granddaughter." She didn't look the least upset by it.

"What do you mean, I pushed you out?"

"You have more skill than you give yourself credit for. What you lack is self-assurance, my dear. Then you'd be unstoppable."

Unstoppable?

I shivered. I didn't want that kind of power or responsibility.

"It's yours, whether you want it or not, love," she informed, a hint of a smile on her deep cherry lips.

She did it again. "Will you stay out of my thoughts?" I growled. "How is that even possible?"

She tsked her tongue. "So young. So naive. So much promise, so much to learn. I could show you. Show you it all and more. And more... And more..." The last words echoed over and over in my head as her form begin to flicker. My time with her was coming to end as I descended out of the dream and back into the comfy fold of my bed.

My eyes popped open, and a quick glance at the red numbers on the alarm clock informed me I'd lost plenty of beauty rest. There was only an hour before school started. A dull ache took up residency behind my eyes. The side effects from these dreams were starting to suck some serious ass.

I slid out of bed, seeking a shower and aspirin, before changing into comfy clothes, careful not to have anything harsh touching the still-sensitive and sore skin at my lower back. Speaking of...I wanted one quick glimpse in the mirror. I tugged up my shirt and checked out the glimmering ink.

It was beautiful.

I was such a rebel.

And this rebel was going to be late for school if I sat here admiring my rune another minute.

CHAPTER 19

S CHOOL WAS UNEVENTFUL. JUST WHAT I needed. A bit of normalcy, allowing the pounding in my head to subside. Gavin had shown up in between each of my classes like old times, and the world felt right as rain again.

In chemistry, we took our usual seats at our table together. He stretched out his long legs. "Break any new rules since yesterday?" He shot me a sinful smile that had fireflies rocketing in my belly.

I leaned on my elbow. "I'm sticking to the straight and narrow path from now on."

He twirled the hoop in his bottom lip playfully. "And here I thought the whole *bad girl* persona suited you. I bet you still have the ID."

The corners of my mouth tipped. "Maybe I'm not ready to let it go completely. A girl can never be too prepared."

"That's what mom is always telling Sophie, but I'm pretty sure she isn't talking about fake IDs or tattoos."

I flushed a beet red. His words painted an explicit picture of the two of us in my head, and the satisfied smile on his lips said he knew exactly where my thoughts had headed. Suddenly, I wanted to be anywhere but here, in a class filled with prying eyes and a gossip mill waiting to explode.

But when he looked at me like that, the room disappeared. My body on its own accord leaned closer to him, his smoldering eyes doing funny things to my belly. There was this invisible pull between us. His thumb played with the jumping pulse on my wrist as I inhaled the unique woodsy scent that was all him.

My gaze dropped to his totally kissable lips, and an unhealthy dose of excitement hummed through my body—a mixture of magic and teenage hormones. I started to get all kinds of crazy ideas, and his grin turned downright wicked.

Just as I was thinking about covering those full lips with mine, our chemistry teacher shuffled in, balancing a stack of books and a wad of papers. The sound of chalk shrieking on the chalkboard had our little intimate bubble bursting and the chatter of the class resumed —regrettably.

Those sapphire eyes were heated like a blue flame. "After school..." he mouthed.

Yes. Yes. Yes. My body was screaming.

Then my tummy dropped, and my face fell, as I remembered I had plans for another vigorous training session with Lukas. I shook my head. "I can't today," I murmured, an apology bursting in my eyes.

The mood was broken. An unspoken understanding in his expression said he knew precisely what I was doing after school and with whom.

LUKAS WAS WAITING for me in my driveway when I pulled up. I had to wonder if he even went to his college classes as he claimed. He was always readily available. Weird.

The autumn sun picked up highlights in his hair, making him look like the perfect part for a boy band. Witch? Not so much. Holly Ridge was having an unseasonably warm December. Large, puffy, white clouds rolled above in a clear blue sky.

"Hey," I greeted, slamming the car door behind me. Tossing my bag over my shoulder, I forced a smile. My heart wasn't in practice mode, not when I couldn't get my mind off Gavin. So much time had been wasted these last few weeks. I hated the thought of losing time that could have been spent with him.

Lukas followed me inside, and I propelled my bag in the corner before heading to the kitchen for a couple of cans of Coke. Lunar wove in and out of my legs, yowling for attention, but once he caught sight of my guest, he ran from the room like a bat out of hell, nails shrieking against the floor. What a spaz.

I pushed aside Lunar's nutty behavior. "What's on the agenda today?"

Lukas popped the top on his Coke, the fizz hissing. "How about we do a little dreaming?"

I took a swig of my drink, the can cooling in my hand. "You mean dreamscaping?" I wasn't sure how I felt about going under again. My head had just recovered from last night's escapade, and I wasn't thrilled about another round. I needed rest. The more magic I used within the dream, the harder the effects hit when I woke up.

A half-smile played across his lips. "You know that you need to work on your control; this will help. Plus, you also need to learn to block other witches from pulling you in."

"You can do all that?"

His answer was a sunny grin.

I'll take that as a yes. "You suck," I added grumpily.

He was completely unaffected by my charm. "How about we change it up? This time I'll pull you into one of my dreams, that way you'll get the feel of being on the other side, the one summoned into a dream."

At least one of us was excited. I couldn't say the same. But he had a point. We took our drinks into the family room. "So how are we doing this?"

He grinned. "Assume the position, sleeping beauty." His hand swooped over the couch like it was my royal chamber.

I rolled my eyes. "Clever."

Setting the Coke on a coaster, I kicked off my shoes. Hey, if I was going to take a nap, I deserved comfort. I assumed to horizontal position on the couch, trying every which way to get relaxed. The fact that Lukas was watching me didn't help. It was weird. He knelt over me, his emerald eyes shining above me. "No funny business," I warned.

"Never," he swore, a corner of his mouth lifting in a way that did nothing to ease my nerves. "Close your eyes," he instructed.

"But how are you—?"

He put a finger on my lips, silencing me. "Don't question. Just trust me."

Trust.

Such a complex and simple concept. Why was it so hard to trust Lukas, but Gavin I trusted with my life? All these thoughts and questions tumbled into my head as I closed my eyes. I assumed Lukas did some kind of hocus pocus mojo to put us both under.

The next thing I knew, Lukas was calling my name. His voice had that underwater, muffled quality to it as if it was being overpowered by something. Time ceased to exist. It could have been seconds or minutes, but eventually, I followed the sound of his familiar voice.

A whole new world of vibrant, flashing color opened against the blackness. Music blared all around me in patterns of erratically flashing disco lights, shining on the floor under my feet.

"Took you long enough."

I whirled around at the sound of Lukas's voice, my hair flying out around me.

"Remind me to have us work on your timing. It blows." He stood in the middle of a sea of people who were bumping and grinding to club music.

There was a clear, straight path to him, like the Red Sea parting. I walked right up to him and socked him in the gut.

"Ouch," he complained, not really in pain. There was too much amusement sprinkled in his eyes.

I grinned. "At least I know you can be hurt here. And my timing does not suck."

He gave me a dry look. "Very funny. Whatever happens here can very easily affect us in the real world."

"I'll keep that in mind." I'd already learned that lesson the hard way.

I glanced around my surroundings. We were at some underground club, complete with the half-naked girls hanging from the rafters, strobe lights, and ear-deafening music. "So this is what you dream about? Figures. Typical guy." I had to admit though, it was pretty freaking cool. And so out of my league. Gaping, I could feel color staining my cheeks. The place oozed sweaty bodies, perfume, and sweet alcohol. It wasn't necessarily a bad combination.

He was unfazed by my sarcasm. Holding out a hand, he asked, "Dance?"

I bit my lip. Everyone around us was doing some form of dirty dancing. It was sex on the dance floor, a real classy joint.

"I don't bite...much. You aren't scared, are you?" he baited, knowing very well I would take the hook.

Please. "Only that I will trample your feet," I subtly warned.

He chuckled.

I put my hand in his, and we swayed with the music, but I made sure to keep a reasonable distance between us. Occasionally our bodies brushed, and I couldn't help but wonder if it was deliberate. I definitely wouldn't put it past him.

"So who are all these people?" I yelled over the pumping dubstep.

With a snap of his finger, they all vanished, leaving just him and me. "Nothing but a product of my ingenuity. None of their faces are real to me, just a part of the illusion I created."

I pulled away, needing distance. We stopped dancing.

Lukas grinned. "Playtime is over. Time to move into phase two. I summoned you here, now I want you to block my thread to your dream, pull yourself out."

I looked at him like he was speaking Greek. Here I was, in an empty underground club and he wanted me to do magic? I couldn't even think past the blazing music and the light show overhead.

After minutes of nothing but me standing there like a lost puppy, he tilted my chin up. "Push out," he stated like it was the simplest thing. He should have known better. Nothing with me was simple.

"How?" I countered, skirting near frustration.

"I'll show you. We can share magic. Give me your hands." He held out both of his. "It's easy as pie."

Nothing with magic was ever easy as pie.

Our hands clasped, on queue, a bolt of energy charged the air. I had only ever shared magic with Gavin once, and Morgana, if that counted, but immediately, I noticed something off. An edge of darkness hugged over my skin, transferring into my energy. It was addicting in a bad way. I like it too much and that scared me. There was a hint of something dark, something I couldn't put my finger on.

I shook my head and started to pull away, intending to break the connection of our magic, but Lukas's grip tightened. Everything inside me wanted to reject what we were brewing. I had to stop this.

Now.

Power surged inside of me, and I was unable to stop it. An electric shock emitted from my fingertips, loosening Lukas's hold. Somehow I found the strength to rip my hands from his, severing our connection not only to each other but the dream as well.

The whole thing happened in a matter of seconds, but my insides felt as if they were being ripped in half. Inhaling sharply, I tore open my eyes and bolted upright. I seethed with annoyance as I looked over at him in the recliner, eyes just starting to flutter. Everything all at once went to my head, dizziness overtook, and my stomach rolled.

"What the hell was that?" I demanded, hands still tingling.

He dragged in a ragged breath, eyes beaming like a glowworm. And he didn't look pleased. "You ended the dream abruptly. That doesn't come without a price."

I pulled a shaky hand through my hair, starting to feel a pressure building inside my head. Before I had the chance to bombard him with a string of questions, the doorbell rang.

My eyes immediately connected with Lukas. A feeling of panic overcame me, pushing aside the irritation. *Please don't let it be Gavin.* Snapping myself out of my internal dread, I began to walk to the front door. For a split second, I thought about ignoring whoever was on the other side, but as if on cue, the musical chime sounded a second time.

"This better be important," I growled under my breath.

I should have known. Tori stood on the porch with the sun at her back looking impatiently beautiful. Caramel golden waves framed her frowning face. "Finally. For God's sake, what took you so long?" she huffed, pushing her way inside. Tori never waited for an invitation, and really, she never needed one at my house.

"Tori, this isn't a good—"

Her hand flew to her heart, and she let out a tiny gasp. "Oh." The exasperation fled from her expression and was replaced with one of keen curiosity.

My back hit the wall as I followed her gaze.

Lukas was leaning in the hallway looking like an archangel. His dimples twinkled, and his eyes were brimming with laughter. He enjoyed seeing me ruffled. Both hands stuck into the front pockets of his jeans, his college T-shirt stretched over his taut chest, emphasizing the emerald green of his eyes.

Even I had to suppress a sigh, Tori wasn't so subtle.

Her big brown eyes zeroed in on Lukas like he was a decadent piece of cheesecake she was dying to take a bite. After she took her fill, she glanced back to me, uplifting a perfectly manicured brow in a quizzical glare. The corners of her lips twitched. "Why have you been hiding all this hotness to yourself?" she whispered. "You know it's not fair that you have two sizzling guys, and I don't have a single one. Didn't your aunt ever teach you to share?"

I elbowed her in the side, and she glowered at me.

Lukas's grin only grew.

Goodie gumdrops. How the hell was I going to explain this? I needed to think fast on my feet. I needed a lie. Of course, everyone knew that I was queen sucky at lying.

Lukas became my savior. He swaggered into the hallway, giving Tori the full swoon-worthy treatment. She looked ready to collapse.

There was nothing I could do but roll my eyes.

"You never told me you had such a beautiful friend." His voice was as smooth as honey and as lethal as a killer bee.

It was almost comical how easily she fell prey to his charm.

"I'm Tori," she purred like a sex kitten.

I tried not to giggle at her trying to be sexy.

He would have to be gay or a dunce to not pick up Tori's obvious and downright embarrassing flirting. Hell, it was even making me uncomfortable. I suddenly felt like a third wheel. Maybe I should have offered them my bedroom.

"Tori, Lukas. Lukas, Tori. Now with the introductions out of the way..." I turned to Tori. "What are you doing here?"

Her eyes were still glued to Lukas.

"Earth to Tori," I called, waving my hand in the air.

"Hm. I-I wanted to talk to you about the party," she tripped over her words, clearly flustered.

"Couldn't you have just called?" Yes, I was being rude, but she had caught me off guard. A few minutes earlier, and she could have walked into an extremely awkward and hard to explain the situation.

"You should come...to my party," Tori suggested, extending Lukas an invitation and ignoring me. She batted her eyelashes to sweeten the deal.

I wanted to gag.

And it had nothing to do with jealousy. Okay, maybe just a teeny, tiny tad of jealousy. As much as it didn't make sense, Lukas had only ever been mine. Mostly though, it was a heavy dose of *oh shit*.

I wanted to keep my witch live separate from my normal life, and I couldn't do that if Tori was making starry eyes at Lukas.

I glared at her. She feigned ignorance and was going to pay for it later when I got her alone. This was bad. Very bad. Gavin and Lukas in the same room, I internally groaned. I got that whole punched-in-the-gut feeling and nearly couldn't breathe. Hell must have frozen over.

Things between Gavin and I were finally in a good place. A great place. This party was going to be my downfall.

I could feel Lukas's gaze burning at me, trying to get a read on my reaction, which was sort of a feat in itself. Tori was holding her breath. I tried as hard as I could to keep my expression blank, but it wasn't working. My eyes were pleading with him to say no.

Begging him.

If I could have forced the thought in his head or made him say no with magic, you bet your ass I would have. I concentrated until I was blue in the face, but unlike Gavin, Lukas seemed to be able to ignore my powers of persuasion, not that I thought I had such powers. I wanted to kick myself for not getting this whole witch thing, and then I wanted to just kick Lukas. Tori, too.

Lukas gave Tori an impish, floor-dropping grin, his dimples winking on either side. "Is Brianna going to be there?" he asked Tori like I wasn't even in the room.

My mouth gaped open, and I crossed my arms over my chest. This was turning into an epic debacle. He had deliberately ignored my plea. There had been no mistaking that he knew I wanted him to say no. My eyes had practically screamed it at him.

Tori threw an arm around my shoulder. "Of course she is going to be there. She's my best friend. You have to come, it will be a blast."

Tori was about two seconds away from going into full fan-girl mode. I cringed.

Lukas's eyes twinkled. "Sounds like fun. Count me in." Much to my chagrin, he accepted.

My shoulders went lax. *No. No. No.*

I was royally screwed.

CHAPTER 20

I WAS SURPRISED TO SEE GAVIN waiting for me in my driveway the next morning. I assumed since he knew I had a training session with Lukas, our relationship would take two steps backward, but seeing him sitting on the hood of his car, my heart inflated with hope. Coping with all the uncertainty about us was wreaking havoc on my well-being.

I skipped off the porch, the wind blowing my hair off my face. The cool morning breeze heightened the color in my cheeks. When I reached his car I was feeling a little breathy, entirely his fault.

"Need a lift?" His voice sounded like a dip in the ocean after a hot summer day—refreshing.

I responded with a radiate smile.

He held the door open as I slipped in. A few moments later, the sound of his turbocharged engine tore through the quiet street as we sped to school. My butt vibrated on the seat, but it wasn't an annoying feeling, more like a gentle lull.

The question had been on the tip of my tongue since he showed up looking heart-stopping. I was confused. Why the about face? Why now? "You make my head spin," I said, breaking the silence.

That wasn't meant as an ego booster, but the deadly smirk on his lips said he thought it was the highest of compliments. "I tend to have that effect on girls."

"I just bet. But seriously, I'm confused. A few weeks ago you wouldn't talk to me. What changed?"

He shrugged. His hand skillfully turned the wheel as we rounded a corner, and then he blessed me with a killer smile. "I realized that you were worth fighting for."

My body went into shock.

I was at a loss for words. That was not the answer I had been expecting. He left me tongue-tied with my thumping heart echoing in my ears. The love-struck gleam was on my face all morning long.

By lunch, I was dying to see him. We were all sitting in the cafeteria listening to Tori rant on and on about her holiday party. The whole blasted school was invited. Little miss social butterfly felt the need to throw the party of the year as her one last act of senior year. I didn't need to mention that we barely knew or could stand half the kids in our graduating class.

She was over the moon excited.

I dreaded it like a trip to the dentist, but worse. Much worse.

My eye caught Sophie's. She was studying me like an algebra problem. Something was definitely nagging her. I was about to ask her what was up when she gave me a little shake of the head. Whatever it was, she didn't what to talk about it in front of everyone.

That could only be one thing.

Magic.

Normally, it was the kind of thing I would dwell on, but with Gavin beside me, it was hard to think of anything else.

My half-eaten chocolate chip cookie was forgotten as our fingers played under the table. I snuck a sideways glance at dark and gorgeous beside me. Our eyes locked, and a flood of heat rippled through me.

There was a pattern developing I noticed. When he looked at me like this, the world vanished and everyone in it. I was totally anti-PDA, but today there must have been something in the air. Or it was just the boy next to me. He made me want to do things that were out of character for me. I leaned into him, our fingers clutched under the table and pressed my lips to his, but he took it to another level.

What started as sweet and simple turned downright steamy in seconds. His tongue swept over mine in a game of cat and mouse, and I felt the kiss to my black-painted toes.

Sophie made a gagging noise. Austin was grinning. And Tori...well she had an opinion about everything.

"Ah. I'm so glad you guys kissed and made up, but I don't want to watch you two swap spit over lunch. It's not only unsanitary, it's depressing. The rest of us don't have hot dates. Well, yet..."

Sometimes Tori's untamed and loose tongue could be just too much. My stomach pitched. I knew what she was thinking or who she was thinking of. Her eyes got that glossy, starry look.

"Girl, you better dish," Austin demanded. "Are you seeing someone?"

I groaned.

Tori's doe eyes twinkled. "I'm working on it. Our girl Brianna has been holding out on us."

Gavin lifted a brow, suddenly more interested in what she was saying than in me.

My stomach hallowed. "I have been doing no such thing. He's a friend," I defended, my teeth clenched tight.

Austin's eyes gleamed. He thrived on drama, and I could see the wheels turning in his over-styled head. It was all the encouragement Tori needed. "This friend is yummy. I could eat off his abs. And he is coming to the party. My goal is to be feasting off those abs by the end of the night." She nudged Austin in the arm. "Sorry, I'm calling dibs."

I wanted to crawl under the table.

Hide in the darkest hole.

Sophie's eyes widened, and Gavin whispered in my ear, "Looks like I get to finally met the guy who consumes your dreams."

I gave him a dry look. That wasn't even close to being funny, and the intense flare in his sapphire eyes said he was looking forward to it, but not in a good way.

Right after lunch, Sophie pulled me aside—literally, dragging me off to a corner in the library. She scanned the deserted rows before facing me. Somehow this had become our place to *talk*, our secret meeting place.

I hoisted a seat on top one of the empty tables, letting my feet dangle over the edge. They were all empty. "What is going on with you? I swear, at lunch you were dissecting me like a lab rat."

She kept her voice low. "You have a hole in your aura."

"What!" I screeched.

She put a finger to her lips. "It's small, but a spot is missing."

"Missing?" I echoed.

"Missing. Gone. Finito."

I could tell by the puzzled expression on her face that it wasn't a good thing. "I'm assuming that's not normal."

She shook her head. "I've never seen it before."

Of course not.

"But I've heard stories," she continued. "It usually only happens when someone has been touched with dark magic. Or..."

"Or?" I prompted quickly. This wasn't the time to leave a girl hangin'.

"Or if a witch has been practicing dark magic." There was an ill omen tinged to her words.

"I haven't done either," I argued. "That I know of."

"It's so strange." She reached out a hand like she wanted to touch the missing chuck of my outline. "I can't tell if it is black or just a missing hole."

"Should I be worried?" A hint of dismay laced my voice.

She shrugged her dainty shoulders. "I'm not sure. This is out of my realm. Anyway, I think you have more than enough to stress about. Gavin and Lukas in the same house? Are you insane? We'll be lucky if the structure is still standing."

That's what I was afraid of.

The bell rang.

"We're late," I sighed.

"Here take this." A slip of paper appeared between her slim fingers.

I unfolded the piece of paper, a hall pass excusing my tardiness. How convenient. She grinned, reminding me of Gavin, mischief gleaming in her dark blue eyes.

"Thanks," I said jumping off the table. "You're as bad as your brother."

"Not quite."

NEVER BEFORE HAD I cared about what I wore. Now suddenly nothing in my closet was right. It wasn't stylish enough. Not sexy enough. It was all so boring like the old me.

The new me, she wanted to be vibrant, daring, and alive. She wanted to be noticed. And most importantly, she wanted to be noticed by Gavin.

"Austin," I said into my cell phone the instant he picked up. "I need your help. I have nothing to wear."

"Say no more. Tori and I will be there in seconds. And babygirl... don't make any decision without me. I got this."

I needed an intervention—a fashion intervention. This classified as a crisis.

I couldn't figure out if calling on the dynamic duo was going to be epic or a disaster.

Like my two personal fashion angels, Tori and Austin arrived at my house in record time. They ransacked my closet, my dresser, and under my bed, leaving no crevice unturned. Clothes were tossed everywhere. Not a corner, nook, or cranny was left untouched by their mayhem. To top it off, the outfit they pulled together had me blushing before I'd even tried it on.

"I can't wear that," I protested.

Austin shoved the clothes in my hands. "Can. And will." He steered me into my conjoining bathroom.

Closing the door behind me, I picked up the jean skirt. Was this even mine? On a heavy sigh, I wiggled the skirt over my hips and then looked to see where the rest of it was. The skirt gave a new definition to mini—it was micro-mini. I hoped I didn't drop anything, because I might end up being tonight's entertainment. And a peep show was not part of the deal.

This had to be a joke.

I held up the black top, a sheer, very off-the-shoulder number.

Pushing my arms through the sleeves, I slipped it over my head and checked myself out in the mirror.

I am going to kick their ass.

Storming out of the bathroom, I shot painful daggers at Tori who was sitting on my bed filing her nails.

She glanced up, her expression pleased. "You look freaking hawt."

I peered at myself in the full-length mirror. "I look worse than Julia Roberts in Pretty Woman." I put my hands on my scanty covered hips and faced her. "I look like a hooker."

"A smokin' hot hooker," she assured. "Here, I brought these over. You can borrow them. They're purrfect."

I took the pair of knee-high stiletto boots from her outstretched hand. "Oh yeah, right. Like I am not going to break my neck in these."

"Just put them on, you baby. I'm dying to see how they look." She was literally doing a happy dance in the middle of my bedroom floor.

What the hell.

I bent over a feat on its own, and slipped my foot into the boot, zipping them up. They had a pretty pattern on them with a peek-a-boo toe in the front and at the heel. I was sure they cost more than I made in a month.

"You got a tattoo!" Tori exclaimed, squealing from behind me. Her hand was already pulling up my shirt. "When were you going to tell me?"

Oh, shit. I'd forgotten, and this skimpy ass top gave her a bull's-eye shot of my back.

Austin popped around the corner. "Our Brianna got a tattoo? Get out of here. Let me see!" he demanded, worming his way in between us.

Feeling naked and vulnerable, I'd completely forgotten about my new body decoration. I shrugged. "It's not a big deal." I pushed my shirt back in place. The bigger problem was, this outfit left nothing for the imagination and barely covered the necessary parts.

"Are you kidding me? Does your aunt know? Of course not," Tori said, answering her question.

What on earth ever possessed me to think I'd ever be able to hide this from them? I chewed my lip. "No one knows...except Gavin, and now the two of you. And I expect to keep it that way."

"Please. My lips are sealed." Tori air-zippered her mouth shut. *Ha*, I thought. That would be the day. "Where and how? I need details. You aren't eighteen yet," Tori rambled, over-excited.

I rubbed the back of my neck. "Gavin might know someone." I waited to see if either one of them would notice anything peculiar about the tattoo, like the fact that the rainbow ink swirled in movement.

"You have a fake ID," Austin guessed. "Can he get me one?"

I rolled my eyes. Boy could he ever, which was beside the point.

Austin looked, really looked at me for the first time since I came out of the bathroom. "Girl, you are going to bring him to his knees. Look at those legs. Who would have guessed babygirl had legs like that."

"Me," chimed in Tori. "Someone is going to get lucky tonight," she sung, winking at me. God, she was worse than a guy. Every thought somehow started and ended with sex.

"Tonight is going to be unforgettable," Austin declared, pulling us in for a group hug.

I didn't doubt that.

CHAPTER 21

THE FIRST STIRRINGS OF BUTTERFLIES fluttered into my belly. I was upstairs in Tori's bedroom finishing my hair, while a swarm of people gathered below. I was taking my sweet old time, not entirely prepared to embrace my skanky side just yet. But, if Sandra Dee could do it, so could I. There is a little bit of bad girl in all of us. Maybe more in some than others.

I thought about what Sophie had told me about my aura, and the dark spot. I might have more darkness inside me than I knew. I couldn't shake the feeling that I'd done something. What if there was evil lurking inside me? What if I was capable of darkness—dark magic?

I shuddered at just the thought.

When Tori, Austin, and I left for Tori's house, I didn't leave without a fight. They forbid me to wear a sweater. Such cruelty. My aunt was on one of her routine date nights with Chad, missing the drama. He seemed good for her. At least I wouldn't have to worry about her when I was off to college.

College. I was light years behind my classmates on the whole college submissions. My mind this year had been filled with boys and magic. There hadn't been thoughts of my future. Now, with it looming in front of me, I was screwed.

And my aunt knew it, too.

Just the other day I'd woken up with an enrollment packet to UNC Wilmington, Lukas's school. It might have once been my first choice, and obviously my aunt's, but now...I wasn't so sure. I wasn't sure of anything.

My reflection scowled in the mirror as I wound the curling iron around my hair. A few more chunks and this was the best my hair was going to get. I ran my hand through the curls, shaking them out. "Here goes nothing," I muttered, taking one last look at myself.

My heels clicked on the tile floor as I weaved down the hallway. An interior designer had decked out Tori's pad in the spirit of Christmas. Lighted garland hung over the doorway arches, down the banisters, and alongside the fireplace mantels. Snowflakes hung sporadically from the high ceilings, and a Christmas tree adequate for Times Square twinkled in the corner. What was usually the music room had been cleared out for a dance floor and DJ.

Tori's dad's wallet knew no end. He pulled out all the stops for his little girl.

Leaning against the stair railing, a group of girls giggled wildly behind me.

Rianne and her posse of hoodrats.

Oh, goodie sugar plums.

"Looks like someone forgot to take the trash out," Rianne goaded with a sneer. Her eyes filled with ridicule and disdain.

"Apparently. They let you in," I grimaced. She deserved so much more. I ignored the clunking of heels as her minions trailed her down the hall. Far. Away. From. Me.

Where the hell are my sidekicks?

I was about to hunt them down when tingles skirted the back of my neck and the tattoo at the small of my back warmed. My eyes darted to the doorway.

Gavin—looking so insanely hot, my heart melted at the sight of him. He walked through the door with a rock-star swagger, gaze sliding over me from head-to-toe, lingering in some parts longer than others.

My pulse darted all over the place as I waited near the stairs. There was a flutter deep in my chest. He made my head swim, my knees tremble, and my blood boil.

My composure rocked, a small smile crept over his lips when he reached me. Mesmerized, I could barely pull my gaze from him, but his eyes traveled up at something over my head. I lifted my head. Mistletoe hung directly above us.

I blinked. "Oh." I couldn't help it. I stared at his kissable lips. The silver hoop rolled as he played with it. And I knew without a doubt he was going to kiss me.

Gripping the banister, I could do nothing but hold on as a gazillion pearls of anticipation beaded through me. He pressed his lips against mine in a feathery kiss that left me aching and starved for more. One was never enough.

My breath got stuck somewhere between my lungs and my throat. Dazed, my eyes fluttered open.

He smirked. "You look...dangerous."

I toyed with the necklace at my throat, needing something to do with my hands. They were itching to pull him back. "Thanks, I think," I managed to say in a breathy whisper.

He interlocked his fingers with mine as if it was the most natural thing ever. "She's outdone herself," he said surveying all the glitter, thousands of flickering candles, and lighted bulbs. There were people strewn around the great room, hanging out in the hallways, and gathering around the food in the kitchen.

"That's putting it politely. I thought it looked like Frosty exploded. Everything with Tori is over-the-top." Including the lack of supervision. Her dad and his barely legal wife, Mariah, were at one of their holiday events.

In my mind, they were nuts to leave us alone. It was only a matter of time before their house was trashed. Or we were trashed.

He chuckled. "Poor Frosty."

"I bet this doesn't even compare to the parties in Chicago," I said, thinking how boring our little shindig must be in Holly Ridge.

He pulled us down on a recently vacated couch. "Considering the people I hung out with...uh, they weren't exactly your run-of-the-mill teenagers. It feels good to have a little *normal* every once in a while. We need it to stay grounded." His deep blue's pointedly caught mine.

Got it. I needed some *normal*. *Easier said than done*, I thought to myself. "Tori and Austin saw my tattoo." I waited for his reaction.

He was as calm as ever—nerves of steel. "And you were worried they might notice something different about it?"

I nodded. It hadn't mattered that he had told me otherwise. "It's hard not sharing this huge part of my life with them. We've been through everything together, and not being honest with them feels in some way like I'm not being a good friend."

"I wish I could tell you that it gets easier, but I think you're doing the right thing by not telling them. Sometimes to protect those you love, you have to keep the truth hidden. I don't want to see you get hurt." There was concern in his eyes.

"I know," I sighed heavily, laying my head on his shoulder.

We sat on the couch together, our legs touching, and watched the crowd come and ago. I was content, and welcomed the calmness inside me until Gavin stiffened. The familiar prickles in the air announced another witch had arrived.

Lukas.

I didn't need to glance up to know it was him. Everything in Gavin's body language told me what I needed to know.

I moaned, suddenly feeling like I was walking on pins and needles. I was going to puke.

My head lifted just as Lukas and Tori strolled toward us. They looked striking together. Her long legs were accented by deathtrap heels and a blinding, sparkly, strapless little number. Lukas was in his college pretty-boy swag. I squeezed my fingers against Gavin's. Lukas might look like the boy next door, but it was the bad boy next to me who made my heart sputter. I was starting to realize what that meant to me.

I loved Gavin. I never doubted that love, not until Lukas had come along and blurred that line. Finding what my heart truly wanted had been an unexpected struggle.

Lukas's lips spread into a crooked grin as his eyes met mine. "Wow. I wasn't sure I'd ever see you in a dress. Wow."

I wanted to slide under the family room rug. He looked at me like I was the only girl in the room, totally disregarding Gavin's presence.

Tori, utterly clueless to the sudden tension, was glued to Lukas's side. He didn't seem to mind. She laid a hand on his arm, oblivious to my panic. "I take full credit. Our Brianna lacks fashion sense."

My mouth fell open. *Oh no, she didn't.* True, clothes weren't high on my priorities, but did she need to throw me under the bus like that? What I wouldn't give for a hoodie at this moment.

Introductions were unnecessary. From the glint in their eyes, they both knew who the other was, and I wasn't about to make an awkward situation any more awkward. The room suddenly got smaller, and the air crackled with thick tension like a radioactive experiment gone horribly wrong. I was suffocating from it. Or it could be because I stopped breathing.

Lukas's dimples twinkled. "It isn't the clothes that make a person; it's the person that makes the clothes."

I choked.

"I need a drink," Gavin grumbled in a foreign voice devoid of any emotion. He promptly stood up, and I watched him walk away. I'd been doing that a lot lately.

Austin came out of nowhere and plopped on the couch, putting his arm around me. The cushions sunk under his weight. "What crawled up his gorgeous butt?" Then his eyes roamed over Lukas like a mouth-watering piece of candy. "Oh, I see. You must be the *other* guy."

I elbowed Austin in the gut. He was not helping.

He grunted. "I'll pretend like that didn't happen." Looking up at Tori and Lukas, Austin said, "You must be Lukas. I've heard all about you." The words rolled off his tongue. Austin was in his element: drama.

"Any friend of Brianna's is a friend of mine," Lukas replied.

Austin raised a brow, already under Lukas's enchanting spell.

What this party needed was time for things to simmer down before it started to boil. After what I hoped was adequate downtime, I went on the hunt for Gavin. Somehow we all needed to co-exist.

The only place I had left to search in this massive house was the kitchen, which I'd been avoiding. It was jam-packed with bodies.

Sure enough, there in the corner of the kitchen was Rianne with *my* Gavin. Over the last few months he became mine, and I wasn't a sharing.

His back to the counter, Rianne was pressed up against him, attaching herself like a leech. There were no nice words to describe the way she was throwing herself at him. Her leopard skirt was shorter and tighter than mine. I don't even know how that was possible and still be covering anything at all.

It was like a punch in the gut, seeing them so close. She whispered in his ear, and all I saw was... red. Hot jealousy whipped through me, burning in my veins. Her sickening sweet laugh made me want to pull her tongue out. I was going to embarrass myself.

I stopped dead in my tracks. Neither one of them noticed me. A million voices talked at once, but for me, the room went silent with nothing but their voices. Power swam inside my veins, and it was very hard to rein it in, but I knew losing my control now would be detrimental.

"Where's your girlfriend tonight?" Rianne asked, walking a blood-red nail up Gavin's shirt. "I didn't think I would get you alone."

I was going to break her bloody finger. Totally eavesdropping, I waited at the tipped of the doorway holding my breath.

His eyes hardened to stone. "What girlfriend?"

Those words stung my heart worse than a thousand jellyfish. I couldn't be in that stuffy room another second, not with the storm that started to brew inside me. So I ran as far from the kitchen as possible. Hot and cold all at once, ran for the door, needing air and distance. There was a sea of people blocking me from escaping, and in my haste, my ankle twisted viciously. Pain exploded, making my eyes water.

Damn shoes.

What are all these people doing out here? I was about to have a magical mental breakdown and they were laughing, having fun.

Hobbling mostly on one foot, I seethed as I pushed people out of my way. As unreasonable as it sounded, I couldn't help but be infuri-ated by their laughter and general happiness.

The crisp rush of the night air washed over me like a blanket. Millions of stars sprayed the sky above, but my mind was too bogged down to appreciate their beauty. The cold burned my lungs as I dragged in a ragged breath. I needed to calm down. The swirling of magic vibrated in my fingertips and hummed between my ears.

I never heard Lukas come up behind me until his soft voice was whispering in my ear. "Careful, your eyes are starting to glow. And we know where that leads."

Whipping around, I glared at him. "Shut up," I hissed, in no mood for grief.

His lips twitched, holding up his hands. "Hey. I'm not the enemy here, but I pity whoever pissed you off."

My control snapped. I couldn't hold it in anymore.

Thunder snarled in the air behind me, lightning split across the yard, striking a nearby tree. The sound was deafening. Over and over again, the sky was aglow in a powerful display of light, and the ground under my feet shook with violence.

There I stood, in the middle of it all, shell-shocked.

Oops.

Lukas put a tentative hand on my shoulder, examining the destruction I caused. "Let's get you something to drink. Plus, I could really use one. Your friend has been smothering me all night."

I nodded, and let him lead back inside the house, completely numb inside.

One drink turned into two, two into three, and so forth. The shock had worn off, and I no longer felt anything.

And I was drunk as a skunk.

Like every great teenage party, someone had spiked the punch. The only difference this time was, bad girl Brianna didn't give a rat's ass. Bad girl Brianna told good girl Brianna to take the night off and go to hell.

"I'm such a light-weight," I proclaimed, flipping Tori's boots off. My feet were killing me. Lukas and I were sitting in Tori's backyard with a jug of the *good stuff*. I was having a hard time staying upright. Giggling, I fell on my back, staring at the millions of stars as they spun in dizzy circles.

"That's not such a bad thing," he assured, resting beside me on the grass.

I waved my hand in the air, playing connect the dots with the stars. "I think the world is spinning."

"I think you have reached your limit." There was amusement in his tone. "Come on. I'll drive you home."

Home. That sounded nice.

CHAPTER 22

L UKAS OFFERED ME A HAND. What a gentleman. I lifted mine to take his in fear of falling back on my ass, but a voice broke through the darkness before my hand touched Lukas's. It was sinister and filled with a promising threat.

"Don't touch her," Gavin growled.

I shivered. Whether it was from the dark scowl on his face or his presence, I didn't know. Maybe a little of both. That didn't mean I forgave him. The pain was too fresh and too deep, though the *special punch* had helped to alleviate some of those feelings.

Lukas glared over my shoulder at Gavin's overshadowing form. "Someone needs to help her. She can barely walk." He wasn't the least bit put off by the disdain dripping from Gavin. That was more than I could say for myself. I'd seen Gavin's fierce temper. He was not someone I would take lightly.

A muscle in Gavin's jaw ticked. "And I am sure you had nothing to do with that," he baited.

Lukas sneered. "Sorry. That was all you."

Gavin looked to me, questions radiating from those explosive sapphire eyes. So much was going on behind the scenes of those eyes.

Confusion. Anger. Hurt. Pain. They were all emotions reflecting inside me.

And in my current mood, I was all too glad to enlighten him. "I saw you with Rianne," I blurted.

He glanced out in the distance and sighed. "Then I am guessing you didn't wait around to hear me tell her she didn't have a chance in hell with me, and she should put her efforts elsewhere."

No, I hadn't.

I opened my mouth to speak, but Lukas beat me to it, probably not the smartest move. "That's neither here nor there. Haven't you done enough for one night?"

His muscles bunched, and I was afraid I knew what was coming next. The yard was empty, and my eyes bounced between them. This was going to turn into a royal rumble, the golden witch against the dark witch. I squeezed my eyes shut, praying that when I opened them, this would all disappear, a horrible, bad dream that my wild imagination was so well known for.

Yeah, that didn't happen.

I blinked. Lukas was gone from beside me, his body slammed up against the side of the brick house, secured by an invisible ribbon of force. Gavin. His cool eyes were tight with determined concentration. Lukas's body gave an unsettling thump as it hit hard enough to knock the daylights out of him. I winced.

All hell broke loose.

Hanging suspended, he raised his head, emerald eyes radiating like an alien. I was no expert in defensive or fighting magic, but I suspected things were about to get cosmic. In my current condition, I wasn't certain that there was anything I could do to stop it.

With a flick of his wrist, Lukas sent a bolt of neon green light sailing straight at Gavin's chest. I stumbled, my reflexes slow and clumsy, but unless I was mistaken, the beam of magic was coming at me. Gavin lunged like a predator, tackling me. He pivoted in the air, making sure he took the brunt of the fall. My breath expended in a whoosh as we hit the ground with me on his chest. It was jarring, to say the least, but we had dodged a lethal bullet.

He rolled me off him, and I fell onto the grass—blackness momentarily blinding me. Snarling, he was on his feet again, pairing up against Lukas who had been able to break free from his magical cuffs. "Are you trying to kill her?" Gavin roared.

The golden witch looked offended. "It wouldn't have touched her. My aim is accurate, you can be sure."

Gavin jeered a second before launching himself at Lukas, and the dark witch let a warrior cry bellowed through the twilight. Their bodies crashed in an array of tangled limbs, fists, and swirling colored magic. I couldn't tell who was beating who. Fists connected with flesh, groans mixed with gasps, all intermixed with the occasional shards of bold, bright magic. I sat on the cold grass in disbelief.

So the battle ensued, and I was helpless to do anything about it, except hope no one else noticed. That seemed pretty far-fetched, though I was too buzzed to care. Sitting in the blades of magic-sprinkled grass, I scrambled back up as they rolled in the glades toward me.

I'd had enough. "Knock it off!" I yelled jumping to my feet, my head seriously unhappy with me. The ground did this whole wavy thing and I stumbled again. My sheer lack of grace lessened the threat I was trying to deliver.

They ignored me like a pesky fly. Of course, that only infuriated me. Lately, I felt like a ticking bomb just waiting to go boom. And I'd reached the end of my fuse.

Forgoing magic, Gavin used the time-tested fist-to-the-face, followed by one to the stomach. They were on the grass pummeling each other in a series of blinks. I couldn't tell if the punches were being packed with magic; it all happened so fast.

I had to end this before any more bloodshed.

It started with a crackle and a flash of light. A strange and foreign feeling spread down the lengths of my arms, traveling throughout me. I gathered the whole potency of my power, and at full strength, it almost felt as if my feet weren't touching the ground. The earth trembled and the wind seemed to whisper my name, answering an unconscious call. Then I screamed. "Stop!" I threw everything I had behind that one singular word. A wave of air expelled, rippling until everything just froze.

The world stopped moving around me. Trees didn't sway with the wind, the music and laughter inside died. Everything was so silent you could hear a pin drop. I looked at the two hotheaded idiots. Neither of them made a single move.

Wow. That was a cool new trick.

I took a few cautious steps to where they were crouched and stood over them with my hands on my hips. I hated to admit that walking was a feat in itself. Damn liquor.

"You're both acting like lunatics. Are we ready to play nice?" I scolded as if they were two disobedient children. After all, they were acting like children.

Neither of them moved or said anything. I ran a hand through my frazzled curls, glaring. Lukas's lip was bleeding and Gavin would probably later be boasting a shiner. What was the point in making each other bleed?

Okay, so I managed to stop them from doing more damage, but how the hell did I release this spell?

Man, I could get myself into all kinds of pickles.

Biting my lip, I inhaled a deep breath and slowly let go of the pulsing energy inside. Degree by slow degree, the gentle hum receded, and with a swish, the world was back in motion, including the two nincompoops.

They were both rattling off insults at the same time.

I stood there and rolled my eyes.

Gavin unclenched his fists, brushing the dirt and grass off his jeans, and Lukas ran a hand through his hair, picking out pieces of grass. Neither of them looked at the other.

The fight looked over, and I was ready to go home. This party girl was exhausted.

In an unsteady voice, I demanded, "Somebody take me home." At this point, I didn't care who stepped up, just as long as this seasick feeling stopped rocking my head.

Gavin put a hand under my elbow, and I leaned on him. "Let's go," he whispered in a voice still hard as ice. He pivoted on his heels as he turned around to Lukas. I held my breath and watched as he gave Lukas the bird, then guided us through the yard toward his car.

"Mature," I slurred.

"Who said anything about being mature? He's lucky to still be standing. I should have knocked his ass to another planet."

Ugh. Boys. *Hadn't they knocked each other around enough?*

His strides were longer than mine, and I found it difficult to keep up. I faltered more than once, tripping over my own feet. Gavin sighed, sweeping me up into his arms. Under different circumstances, I would have protested, but tonight my head was spinning, and I didn't have it in me. Laying my head on his shoulder, I inhaled his unique scent, closing my eyes.

When I opened them again we were in my bedroom. He placed me on my feet, my body brushing down his. I sighed in contentment.

He took a step back. I took a step forward, moving into him slowly and deliberately. And kept moving, until my body was molded to his and my arms were twined around his neck like ropes. Where I was soft, he was hard. I brushed my lips over his neck, again and again, loving the taste of his heated skin. Then I sank my mouth into the soft warmth of his lips.

Apparently, alcohol turned me into a hussy.

He grabbed a fistful of my shirt at the small of my back, and it felt like a small victory. The room was spinning, but for entirely different reasons.

He made me forget. Forget everything. Forget who I was. He was turning me inside out.

With Gavin, I was just a girl head-over-heels in love. "Don't stop," I murmured.

"I wasn't planning on it," he murmured against my mouth.

Our lips sealed. As he deepened the kiss, my mouth slanted across his. I was thrilled to a whole new level. Every sensation was magnified. We landed on the bed without ever separating. The softness of the mattress on my back and his weight sinking on top of me was as sensual as kissing him.

I was bursting with a gazillion feelings, and suddenly I knew that I had to tell. It was probably the spiked punch talking. There was also a good chance I could get drunk off his kisses alone; they were that heady.

"Wait," I breathed, putting my heads on his chest.

He raised a brow. "Make up your mind, woman, which is it? You pull me close, you push me away." Teeth scraped over my leaping pulse.

"I love you," I murmured, breathless.

"I know." There was so much cockiness in those words.

I rested my head on his shoulder, my heart galloping in my chest as I realized what I was about to say. "I don't want to be just some girl."

He rained kisses over my eyelids, my cheeks, and my chin. "You could never be just some girl. Not to me."

"I want more. I want to be your girlfriend." I was going to curse my loose tongue in the morning.

"Are you asking me to go steady?" he asked. I was pretty sure he was laughing at me and totally killing my buzz. "Oh yeah, you're cute when you're hammered."

Great. I was a cute drunk.

A small smile curled on my lips. "Maybe," I yawned. I just needed to close my eyes for a minute.

I fell into a dreamless slumber curled into his embrace.

It was the most peaceful night I'd ever had.

CHAPTER 23

R OLLING ON MY SIDE, a stream of sunlight beamed
behind my closed lids. I groaned, putting a hand to my
temples. My head was killing me.

Hangovers blow.

"Hey, sunshine."

My eyes popped open. I wasn't alone in bed. My eyes tumbled into
a pair of stunning sapphire gems. Gavin. A rush of euphoria raced
through me. He hadn't left. I don't know why, but it touched me,
struck a chord in my heart.

He brushed a piece of hair out of my face, leaving a sprinkle of
tingles in its wake.

I rubbed my face into his hand, needing the warm contact. "You
stayed," I muttered. The sound of my voice vibrated inside my head.
Not a pleasant sensation, but it was dulled by the touch of his fingers. I
sighed at the relief.

"I was worried. You were vulnerable last night. I didn't want you to
have any unwanted guests in your dreams." He put his arm around me
and pulled me close. "Just me."

I snuggled against him, burrowing my head in his chest. "I'm glad
you did."

He gave me a saucy grin, and nothing but trouble of the mischievous kind brewed in those stormy eyes. "So you want to be my girlfriend?"

It took a moment before the flood of memories washed over me. I'd said that hadn't I? Cursing the spiked punch to hell and back, I groaned and threw the blanket over my head. He pulled it back down, and the sinful scent of woods surrounded me. "I was hoping that had been a dream," I admitted, my cheeks staining pink.

"Not a chance." He tucked me back into his embrace. "How are you feeling?"

I laid my hand on his beating heart. "Better with you here."

"I tend to have that effect on girls."

I heard the smirk spread over his lips and fought the urge to smack him. "So you've said." I would be lying if I didn't admit that there was a little bit of jealousy pouring through me at the thought of him with another girl.

"I've also been told that my hands are like —"

I covered my hand over his mouth. "Don't even finish that sentence. I don't want to know."

His lips grinned behind my hand and he kissed the inside of my palm. Chills streamed down my back. He leaned up on his elbow, staring down at me with eyes sparkling. "I don't like sharing you, so I think we should probably make this official."

"What did you just say?" I just couldn't believe this was real. It had to be a joke.

He dazzled me with a crooked grin. "You heard me."

My lips broke out in a generous, stupid smile. "I thought you'd never ask."

"Technically, you asked me last night. You might not remember, you were a little—"

I launched a pillow at his face. He evaded the missile only to capture me in his arms, pinning me with his weight, a clever maneuver.

"Maybe I should get drunk more often," I teased.

"Not a chance," he murmured against my skin. "I like the good girl Bri better." He slowly began to make his way to my lips giving me a soft kiss. "Way better." His smile was slow and full of the devil, and then he sealed that devastating mouth with mine.

He stirred my senses and tangled my head with the hot punch of his velvet kiss as I skimmed my fingers through his silky hair and sighed. He yanked me on top of him, taking us both to a dangerous edge.

His mouth sampled mine leisurely at first, like sweet, succulent candy. It wasn't long before the innocent kisses turned into mindless heat. Against his mouth my breath quickened when he trailed a finger up my inner thigh, touching lace, making my body quiver and arch into his. He did things with his mouth alone that left me writhing and my bones melting.

Our tongues tangled together, our bodies intertwined, and my hands slid up his chest, pushing the pesky material out of my way. Our lips broke apart only long enough for him to whip his shirt over his head.

This time his kiss wasn't light. He didn't tease. He devoured. He possessed.

Kissing him became a matter of self-preservation. It sounded dramatic; I swore it was true. My skin grew hot, his taste wild on my tongue.

Once upon a time, I thought I wanted the world, now I just wanted Gavin. I poured everything I had into kissing him, giving him my whole heart. Tendrils of magic slipped into my fingers, dazzling throughout me, but it wasn't just mine alone. Our hands linked.

The lights in the room flickered off and on as a surge of energy poured over the room. Us. Our magic merged and sparked like long-lost lovers. I gasped from the pure bliss of our power. I had no idea magic could be mixed in such a manner. My skin prickled where he touched me and then burned. All the while his mouth was driving me crazy. His hand slid up, skirting the edge of my shorts, and—

My phone went off on the nightstand, shrill like a fire truck. I pulled back a little, panting, and for an instant, I thought about ignoring it. Groaning, I grabbed the phone with one hand and glanced at the screen. Tori's picture flashed across the screen.

When I spoke my voice was rough. "It's Tori. She's probably

checking on me. I never did have a chance to say good-bye." The call went to voicemail and I bit my lip.

He laid his forehead on mine before kissing me on the nose. "I'll see you later, *girlfriend*," he murmured, leaving me in a delicious mess. I got all warm and fuzzy inside and watched him until he disappeared out the door.

Punching in Tori's number, I waited for her to pick up. Already, I missed him.

POURING a cup of sweet black coffee, I opened the cupboard and pulled out a box of strawberry Pop-Tarts. I nibbled on one square as I thought about last night: the party, the fight, and mostly the making-out.

I finally had gotten what I longed for. Gavin.

Eeep. I had a boyfriend. Not just any boyfriend. A sexy, hot witch who made me feel as if was the luckiest girl in the world.

Even my pounding head couldn't take away the elation I was feeling. For the first time, I didn't dread the Monday morning blues. Swallowing the last bite, I went to get ready for school.

In my knee-high socks, boxers, and a sweatshirt, I climbed the stairs to transform myself from tired, Pop-Tart addict witch to high school senior with an extremely hot boyfriend. Excited, I rushed my morning routine.

I waited impatiently downstairs for the rumbling of Gavin's engine. It had only been hours since we had last seen each other, but each minute that went by felt like days. We had spent the entire weekend shut up in my house, hanging out, kissing, watching movies, kissing, and a lot more kissing. We couldn't get enough of each other.

He greeted me with a kiss. "Hey."

"Hey, yourself." I pressed my lips to his again.

We arrived at school just as the bell rang, thanks to Gavin's amazing driving skills, and parted ways. We were going to have to cut down our morning greeting or risk being continuously late.

The day seemed to be broken up by classes and how long before I got to see Gavin again. I should have known that my day would eventually go down the crapper. Nothing this good ever lasted long.

I cringed at the voice I recognized behind me. It had been foolish to think she would have nothing to say for once. Rianne. My Holly Ridge High archenemy. Her voice alone made me cringe. There was still a lingering ribbon of hate harbored inside me from seeing her with Gavin at Tori's party.

Jealousy reared its ugly head.

Keeping my back to her, I shuffled my feet on the gym floor. Rianne and one of her robotic minions sauntered toward me. She leaned a hand against the bleachers where I was standing.

Rianne looked like a living, breathing Barbie. Her nose was always stuck in the air like her shit didn't stink. Gym pretty much sucked balls on its own. I didn't need Rianne making it unbearable, especially when we were doing a core strength unit, which meant rope climbing. Ugh. Someone shoot me now.

"Well, it isn't bizarre Brianna." Rianne was just plain cruel and took her popularity for granted enormously.

"Say whatever it is you want to say and cut the crap," I responded dryly.

"Someone has their granny panties in a wad."

She was cruisin' for a bruisin'. "Is there a point to this nonsense?" If there was one thing about Rianne, it was she liked to be in control, and she liked flare.

Rianne sneered. "You're not much fun...but Gavin is."

I should have seen this coming. She never missed the opportunity to point out that she could have any guy she wanted. "You mean *my* boyfriend?" It felt satisfying seeing the agitation in her eyes.

She recovered quickly. "For now..."

I was going to gouge her eyes out. Steam was starting to radiate off my skin.

Sitting on the mat, she stretched out her long legs. "He didn't seem to have a girlfriend when he had his hand up my shirt. Did you know his lips taste like sex?"

Her bragging was nothing but petty lies and insecurities, but it didn't make her bite any less harsh. Overcome with rage, my hands balled into fists at my side. I wanted to slam my curled hand into the center of her pretty face. My blood hummed.

I could feel it burning in my veins, whispering in my ear, promising me redemption.

"Rafferty! You're up," Ms. Jenson, our overly butch teacher, bellowed through the gymnasium.

After one last squinty glare, I broke eye contact and stepped up on the mats. Wiping my hands on my atrocious gym shorts, I got ready to make an utter fool of myself. Not exactly athletically inclined, I gripped the rope with sweaty palms. My head tilted back, and the top looked a million miles away. I contemplated taking an F for the day, but the diligent student inside me wouldn't allow it.

After five excruciating attempts to hoist myself up the rope and going nowhere, I gave up. My arms burned. Looking down the rope, the floor was just a few feet away. I dropped to the mat and dusted my hands off.

Rianne brushed past me, bumping lightly into my shoulder. "Kissing isn't the only thing I excel at. Ask your boyfriend," she said in a voice of molasses and vinegar.

"Blow it out your ass," I retorted. My teeth clenched until my jaw started to throb.

Rianne flipped her long blonde hair up in a messy ponytail, before putting both hands on the corded rope. She turned to me and flashed me a devious grin. I shot poisonous daggers at her in return, my whole body seething as images flickered in my head. Rianne wrapped around Gavin. Her hands in his silky hair. Her mouth on his lush lips.

Eventually, all I saw was red. "Bitch," I mumbled under my breath.

I watched as Rianne climbed the rope, the amethyst in my irises radiating like a cat at night. With each hand she clasped higher than the other on the twine, like a damn monkey, my magic increased. It happened like a bad dream. Every tiny detail I envisioned began to unfold. My entire body came alive, tingling with power and something more.

Different.

Darker.

It was exciting, yet terrifying. And I seemed helpless to stop what I set in motion.

Holy black caldrons.

She was about to make her descent back down when her hands, for unexplained reasons, let go of the thick rope. Rianne's curvy form fell ten feet in the air, flat on her ass. The sound of her butt hitting the gym mat was bittersweet. All the other girls loitering around gasped, a few snickered.

I'd done that. Everyone else in the gymnasium might not know what happened, but I did. And it didn't sit well in my stomach. It wasn't like me to steep so low. I was Glenda the good witch— at least that was who I was striving to be.

Embarrassed and horrified at what had happened, I realized I could have seriously hurt her. Such darkness. I could have killed her, whispered something deep inside me. No one would have been the wiser.

Rianne pushed the escaped hair out of her very red face eyes overflowing with accusations pinned me in the crowd. "You did this," she spat, like a crazy person. "You made me fall off the rope, you freak-a-zoid. You'll pay."

I could do nothing but stare.

She was right.

Ms. Jenson kneeled beside Rianne, asking her questions. She put an arm under her and helped the distraught bully hobble to the nurse. Rianne looked over her shoulder, giving me the evil eye.

Oh, joy.

CHAPTER 24

A FTER SCHOOL, I WAS IN a mood. The whole Rianne thing had me stressed out. Gavin repeatedly eyed me warily, sensing my weird behavior, and I was seriously trying to act normal. Obviously, I was failing miserably.

"Want to make-out?" He coughed. "I mean hang out?"

My lips curved. His mention of making-out got me thinking about the other night. I never had gotten the chance to ask him about the merging our magic. It had been on an entirely different plane of hot. "The other night while we were...you know, kissing."

He smirked at my discomfort.

I pressed on. "Did you know that we could share magic like that?"

He tossed an arm behind the couch, angling toward me. "I knew it was possible. I've just never done it with anyone before; never wanted to, I guess."

My stomach tightened and warmth blossomed all over me. "I had no idea."

He leaned closer. "There is a lot you don't know. And plenty more I could teach you." His lips grazed my cheekbone.

Oh, I just bet. I shifted on the couch, putting some space between us. If I didn't, I wouldn't get any answers as I was already almost at the point of distraction. "It felt so surreal. Do you think that's normal?"

His brows buried together. "Probably not. With you, it's never as I expect."

"Thanks," I mumbled, slouching lower on the couch. Flashbacks of Rianne's tumbling to the ground played on repeat in my head. What a day.

"Are you sure you're okay?" he asked, twirling the loop at his lip.

I nodded and swallowed a golf ball-sized lump. "Yeah. I just have to cram for this test and you're a disruption."

"I am?" He skirted the back of my neck with his skillful fingers.

Duh. I rolled my eyes. "You know you are. I need this class to grad-uate," I added, laying it on thick. He knew how important school was to me.

Leaning in, he pressed a light kiss on my lips. "I'll call you tonight," he promised.

I was reluctant to let him go, but I needed to sort my head out. Once he was gone, I climbed the stairs two at a time. Alone in my room, I sat cross-legged in the middle of the floor. Lunar was curled in my lap, looking at me with sad eyes. It was as if he could sense my inner turmoil.

Smart kitty.

I scratched the top of his head to comfort both him and me. I needed to get a grip on my power. One minute I was blowing out windows and freezing time, and then I'm dropping people from ten feet in the air.

No time like the present. I took a deep breath, centering myself. Magic should be fun, I reasoned. All work and no play makes Brianna a dull girl.

I blinked and called forth the light inside me. Each time it became easier and easier. Staring intently at the door leading to the hallway, I visualized the lock turning. The click sounded like a gunshot in the silent house. It gave me such an immense satisfaction—not just that I had succeeded, but using the magic was gratifying.

Easy peasy.

Now for something a little more complex. The first thing that popped into my head was the gentle glow of lights. Not just one lamp, but all of the lights, at least at my house. I didn't want to blow the city up accidentally. I wasn't going to let my power go to my head. I'm a grounded kind of gal.

Sending my concentration to the hub of electric power flowing through me, I only needed to think about what I wanted. With my luck, overthinking would blow a circuit in my brain. Slow and steady, I reminded myself. Watching in awe, all the lights in the house flicked off and on—over and over again. It was pretty cool, actually. Who needed a light switch when you had magic? When I got bored of that I moved onto something less strenuous on the eyes.

For the first time, practicing and doing spells felt less like a chore and more natural. I started to believe in myself and believed I was a witch. Not just any witch, but a kickass witch.

The doorbell rang before I let my head drift too far in the clouds. Bolting up, Lunar gave a strangled meow at being disturbed from his spot on my lap. I dashed down the stairs, sliding over the rug in front of the door before throw it opened. A beam of sunlight glared in my eyes, forcing me to squint as I focused on the figure outside my door.

Sophie.

Her dark hair shadowed over her face, a face that looked disgruntled. Her usually glittery sapphire eyes were serious and slightly lost.

I leaned a hand on the doorframe. "Hey," I said, winded. "Is everything okay?" My heart jackhammered in my chest as my thoughts strayed to Gavin. Maybe something had happened after he had left here.

Please God, no.

"I don't know. Maybe." Her eyes were scanning a circle around me. "I think so."

I smeared my sweaty hands on my jeans. "Okay, now you're freaking me out. Which is it?"

"Are you alone?" she asked, glancing behind me.

"Uh, yeah."

"Good." She strolled through the door. "We've got to talk."

I gulped. "Gavin—"

She waved an artful hand in the air, moving into the living area. "My egotistical brother is fine."

I released the breath I'd been holding, trailing behind her.

"It's you I'm worried about." Her colorful dress swirled out around her as we sat on the sofa.

"Me?" I echoed. What was she talking about?

She nodded her head, earrings jingling with the movement. "Your aura... It's—" She started, and then stopped as if she was unsure how to phrase her words. "The black hole in your aura...it's bigger."

"Bigger?" These one-word responses were getting old, but I couldn't seem to form anything articulate.

Again she nodded, crystal eyes warm with concern and uncertainty. "I did some digging and asked around, and from what I gathered, the darkness is chipping away at your aura. Weakening it."

"Come again."

"Point blank...you've been using black magic."

My mouth dropped far enough to hit the earth's crust. To say I was shocked was an understatement. "How is that possible?" But even as I spit the words, I thought about what had happened today in gym. What I had done to Rianne. It might have been satisfying, yet it had also felt wicked.

"Honestly, I don't know. Your aura is the first I've seen with these missing pieces. Maybe you've used it without knowing."

"Does it feel different...when you use black magic?"

"From what I've heard, it's like a drug. Once you've used it, there is a pull that calls to you, sucking you in for more. It's addictive in the worst way. All magic comes with a price."

None of what she said made me feel any better. I felt worse. Monumentally worse. Slumping into the corner of the cushions, I wished I could just disappear from my life. "Something happened today," I whispered, barely audible.

She didn't say anything, just waited patiently for me to go on. I hadn't figured out why I hadn't told Gavin, but I think that deep down in some cobweb part of my brain, I knew what I did wasn't good. "Today in gym I used magic to hurt someone. It wasn't like the other times—it was different. There was this soft voice inside me, egging me on. I dropped Rianne on her ass like I was swatting a fly."

"Have you told anyone?" A thoughtful look crossed her face.

"Nope. You're the only one who knows the truth."

Her lips pursed. "I just don't know. That seems more like a prank, but something doesn't add up. I can see it, yet it's not clear. The only thing I can see for certain is that you're at the center. There is this foggy mist blocking my view." She sounded frustrated and scared. "Something is telling me that there was a reason you were never told of your heritage—never told of your powers."

"Probably because I'm worse than the wicked witch of Oz. There's darkness inside me," I said, dejected.

Sophie shook her head. "These missing pieces in your aura are just splinters. The rest of you is pure, vibrant, and filled with nothing but goodness. Especially when you're not shitty on yourself."

I snorted. "Thanks."

The corners of her mouth lifted. "What are friends for? We're going to figure this out. My brother might be a bonehead, but he is relentless, and there's nothing he wouldn't do to keep the girl he loves safe."

Hearing that Gavin loved me cracked through my self-pity and sadness. It gave me hope, even if he hadn't yet said the three little words my heart was longing to hear. It gave me something to cling to, that it might just be possible for me to overcome or get through whatever this dark spot in my life was.

"Okay, so what should we do?" I asked, ready to tackle this invisible mountain.

She folded her hands in her lap and said seriously, "Simple. We find what spells trigger the blackness."

I plopped my head on the back of the couch, closed my eyes, and groaned. Simple, my scrawny butt.

CHAPTER 25

MY PHONE BLINKED WITH ANOTHER message from Lukas. This was like the umpteenth one since the party last weekend. Someone was feeling some serious regret. Good, let him stew.

You can't ignore me forever.

Sure, I can. **Really?** I sent back. This was my response after loads of dismissed messages. He was persistent. I'd give him that. And I couldn't ignore him forever, not without flushing my phone down the toilet.

He sent a text back in record time. **I'm sorry, okay? How many times do I have to say it?**

At least a hundred more. I couldn't help it. The two guys who were most important to me hated each other's guts. It tore me in half.

My phone vibrated. **Be real.**

I wasn't being fair. He hadn't been the only one involved in the whole incident at Tori's. I'd easily forgiven Gavin, why had I not yet forgiven Lukas? If I was going to be honest with myself, it was partially to do with my new relationship status. I was avoiding Lukas because I knew that I had to tell him that Gavin was my boyfriend.

I needed to firmly tell Lukas to keep the lines between us from crossing any boundaries. Friends. That's what we were. Something like this was probably better face-to-face, but I was chicken. One glimpse at those dimples and I was afraid of what I might agree to. I was taking the easy way out. Not in person, but a text was impersonal. A call seemed like a happy medium. It worked for me.

Before I lost my nerve, I hit his preloaded number on my phone and waited on the other end to hear his sunny voice.

"So does this mean I am forgiven?" No hello. Or what's up, Brianna?

I snickered. "Yeah. I guess it does, but—"

He groaned. "I hate buts."

I didn't blame him. "I wanted you to hear this from me." There was a long awkward pause, and I took a deep breath. "Look, I know things between you and Gavin are...tense, but I don't want you and my boyfriend—"

"Boyfriend?" he interrupted

Oh, right. The whole reason I called him. I thumbed the palm of my hand on my forehead. *Way to go, doofus.* I sighed. This wasn't going as well as I planned. "That's what I was trying to tell you."

Long pause. "I see."

"This doesn't change anything. Not with us. I still want to be your friend. I still want to practice with you." I rushed the words out.

"You know how I feel about you. I don't want to be just your friend. I don't know if I can do that." There was pain in his voice and anger.

Was I always destined to hurt people I cared about?

My voice was thick with tears. My throat closed. "I-I'm sorry." I hardly managed to speak.

The phone clicked in my ear.

Shit.

I don't know what I expected, but tears hadn't crossed my mind. Falling onto my pillow, a stream of tears ran down my cheeks, and like every other time my emotions got the best of me, my bedroom window pelted with the pitter-patter of raindrops.

I hated to cry, but recently, the waterworks kept coming. At some point, I would have to exhaust all my tears.

After a good, long cry, and a pint of triple chocolate ice cream drizzled with an enormous amount of chocolate syrup, I wasn't exactly feeling any better, but my conscience was clear. And now I had a bellyache. Talk about a sugar high. What I needed was something to take my mind off my life. Magic. Lukas. Black auras. The whole kit and caboodle. Drowning in junk food hadn't worked. It was Saturday night, and I was alone, wiping dry tear tracks from my cheeks, wishing I wasn't hurting, that I hadn't hurt someone else.

I spent the rest of the day on my bed, licking the spoon and wondering if what I was about to do was a stupid idea. Lord knows I was full of them.

There was one person who had the answers I sought. Morgana. I still couldn't think of her as my great grandma, nor did I understand how we communicated.

She was dead. How was it possible that I could summon her in my dreams?

I filed that under "crap I needed to remember to bring up on our next visit." And if things went the way I was starting to scheme in my brilliant, yet troublesome brain, it would be soon.

Very soon.

Setting the licked-clean bowl aside on my nightstand, I turned the volume on the TV down. With a bat of my eyes, the bedroom was immersed in darkness, except for the weak moonlight shining through the window.

Magic rocked.

Trying to relax was harder than it sounded. I snuggled on my pillow, pulled the covers to my chin, and stared at the ceiling, wondering how I was going to consciously dreamscape Morgana. All the other times I had shared dreams with Lukas, I didn't know what I was doing. Even with the practice, this time wasn't entirely the same either. I was going to be merging dreams with a dead witch, not a living person.

Closing my eyes, I tried to picture her face. The dark red hair framing her face, eyes just like the ones I saw reflected every day in the mirror, and a connection to her I could no longer deny. I thought about all this while my breathing evened, relying on my natural gift to lead the way. All I could do was cross my fingers and hope for the best.

My lower back tingled with warmth, and I felt my body go under. The next time my eyes fluttered open, a cool mist kissed my cheeks. I wasn't anywhere in particular. There wasn't anything defining the area; it was like being stuck in the clouds. A dense fog covered the air around me, not scarily, but angelic. Vapor curled under my toes, weaving in and around me. There was a fresh cleanliness with each breath in my lungs.

And I wasn't alone in this serene heaven. There was my Grams, looking like a Grecian goddess. The white of her flowing dress was striking against the long length of her crimson hair. Ribbons tangled around her bare feet and up her ankles.

I did it, I thought and did a little happy dance in my head.

"With a little help," her majestic voice broke through the silvery mist.

Thanks for stealing my thunder. I needed to learn how to do that whole read-your-thoughts trick, or at least figure how to block it. "I guess I should be glad you got the message."

"Loud and clear, dearie. So what do I owe the honor of being summoned?"

"I have some questions."

"I see you have already made the 'which boy do I choose' decision." She tapped a nail on the bottom of her lip. "What could you possibly have on your mind?"

"What, are you stalking me?" I blurted out.

She gave a throaty laugh. It suited her and her flaming hair. "I see so much of myself in you, except the whole prude thing."

My mouth dropped open. Did my great grandma just imply that I was a tease or that she was a slut? Either way, I couldn't decide which was better.

"Give that boy what he wants already." Her cherry lips rose in a sinister smile. She loved to shock me.

I coughed. By the time I regained my composure I was red-faced and pissed. "Just so you know, I am not a prude, and how did this become about me? How do you know I have a boyfriend?"

"I told you. Where you are concerned, I make it my business to know. You forget I've already met the lucky stud. Besides, I've left you little hints over the years. I wouldn't want you to think that you were alone in this world...or beyond."

"What do you mean, little hints?" Then it dawned on me. "That was you at Tori's. And here I thought I was being haunted by Casper the not-so-friendly ghost." I ran a hand through my auburn hair. "So you are stalking me."

She snorted in a very lady-like manner. "Don't flatter yourself, sweetheart."

"Why are you suddenly so interested in me? Why now?"

"You know why now. You've got magic, and you are not just any witch."

"So I've been told," I mumbled.

"No, you haven't. At least not everything, but you will find out soon enough."

What was that even supposed to mean, other than confuse me? My head was already spinning, the doubts and questions swirling in my brain. I needed to stick to one topic, answer one question at a time until I could put all the pieces of the puzzle together. The black spots on my aura were at the top of the list. "Can you see auras?"

She started to stroll through the mist, feet walking on air, the trail of the silky white material of her gown dancing in fluid movements. "I have many talents, but no. I have never dabbled with auras. I wasn't blessed with the sight. Why do you ask?"

I followed behind her, trying not to step on the train. "I have a friend who can. She says I have black marks on my aura like little slivers are missing." I didn't like the look that sprang into her violet eyes. It sent a tremor down the center of my spine, and I stumbled.

Damn these stupid ribbons bound at my ankles. It was only a matter of time before I killed myself with these things wrapped around my feet. I don't know how she walked so gracefully.

She quickly recovered her composure, putting her typical overly confident enchantress back into place. "A few black marks never hurt anyone," she sneered as if it wasn't a big deal.

What. Bull. Shit. "I don't believe you." Why had I expected her to be surprised by my defiant outburst?

She wasn't.

Lifting a thin brow, she put both of her hands on my arms, her purplish eyes flaming into mine. "Good. Trust nothing, no one but your instincts. They won't let you down. The sooner you learn that, the better witch you'll be."

Oookay. Now she was starting to scare me. "You make it seem simple."

Her grin was crafty. "When you trust in yourself, it is."

God, she sounded like a Hallmark card. I fought to not roll my eyes, however, I did pout. "Easy to say when your aura isn't being taken over by black holes that you may or may not have brought onto yourself."

Her painted lips only widened at my teenage annoyance. She was acting like a know-it-all grandparent, and I wasn't sure she'd earned the right. "Now who is being over-the-top? Looks like it runs in the family." I gave her a dry look.

"I see you've had time to be marked." She spun me around before I had a chance to protest or figure out what her intent was. The neckline on this flowing getup left my entire back exposed. If I had to guess, she was in charge of wardrobe during these dreams. Talk about an invasion of personal space. A cool finger traced the enchanted design of my rune. In my head, I knew what she saw.

Her soft chuckle blew against my hair. "It's beautiful and suits you, considering it is my symbol. Did the artist know who you were?"

Crossing my arms over my chest, I turned around and shook my head, once again caught off-guard. Would she forever be one step ahead of me? "No. We'd never met before, and I told her nothing of myself. What do you mean, it's your symbol?"

"My family crest."

"Oh." I wasn't sure how I felt about having something permanently on my body that represented something of Morgana. But it was too late for take-backs.

"Perceptive," she said, lost in thought. Her hands gripped either side of my arms, securing my attention. "Which means you need to be even more careful. If the artist could sense our connection, it won't be long before others will, as well, if they haven't already. And that, my dear, for you, would be grave. You're the last of my blood."

I opened my mouth, but my hold on the dream slipped from my grasp as thousands of questions tumbled to the tip of my tongue. Waking up, my breath came out in short, quick gasps, my heart beating double-time, and a dull throb worked into the back of my temples.

I had mentally and physically exhausted my capabilities, but it didn't stop the frustration from rising. I wanted more than anything to go back under, but I would be risking my health if I did. The last time I'd pushed myself too far, I ended up in bed for longer than I wished. I wasn't very good at being idle.

One question echoed in my mind. What was so *dangerous* about being her last living descendant?

CHAPTER 26

I F I HAD TO SAY *happy holidays* one more time, I was going
to scream. Mystic Floral was bursting with patrons getting
their Christmas poinsettias. The bell over the door jingled
relentlessly, letting a cool winter breeze into the shop. My feet were
starting to ache, my lips were tired of smiling, and I was moments
away from breaking the Christmas CD playing through the
speakers.

Checking the time on my phone for the millionth time, I sighed.
For some reason, this day was slower than molasses. I kept getting this
crept out feeling that someone was watching me. Paranoid, I know, but
I couldn't shake the feeling. The first inclination was Morgana, but I
wasn't so sure.

"Do you have plans tonight after work?" Aunt Clara asked. The
afternoon rush was over, and we had a few minutes of downtime.

She must have noticed my distractedness. I only had another hour
left of work, and already I was counting down each precious second. I
shrugged. "Not really."

"No hot plans with Gavin?" There was a hint of amusement in her
voice.

I snickered. "Speaking of hot plans, I saw someone the other night

346

steaming up the windows in the doorway with a certain tall gentleman."

She gasped. "You saw that?"

"Yep. And now I am completely scarred for life."

"Please. I'm not buying it. I've seen your boyfriend. You could probably teach me a few things."

Now it was my turn to be shocked and embarrassed. "We're so not going there," I groaned.

She pursed her lips and studied me. I didn't like the look on her face. She was going to go there. "Okay, now that we have sort of broached the subject..."

I moaned louder and put my head in my hands.

"And you have your first boyfriend, which I am glad you got straightened out. It wasn't fair to lead anyone on. We should talk about protection."

"There is so nothing to talk about."

"Still, it would make me feel better. You're often home alone and things can get...heated. I know what it is to be young and in love, and I can see it in your eyes. You're in love."

"Fine," I conceded. "I get your point, but you don't have to worry. There is no one more responsible than me."

She brushed my hair off my forehead. "Don't I know it," she said, smiling tenderly. It was just the kind of smile that reminded me of my mom.

۞

DRIVING HOME FROM THE SHOP, I couldn't help but notice how magnificent the twilight sky glimmered. There wasn't a cloud in sight, and it looked like you could see to Venus. The sun hadn't completely set. I was having a hard time keeping my mind focused on the road. It was the perfect night for stargazing and playing connect-the-dots with the constellations, not constantly checking out the rearview mirror to see if you were being followed.

Yet, I couldn't help myself. Halfway home, goosebumps spread over my arms, making my heart pick up speed. I didn't feel safe. I should call Gavin. The sound of his voice would be enough to calm this jittering, suspicious feeling pumping in my veins.

I tried to set my mind on other things. Like Christmas. It was just a few weeks away. I wasn't feeling the holiday spirit and hadn't even started my shopping. I don't know; this year, it lacked that magical ambiance. The stress of trying to find the perfect gift for Gavin was giving me an ulcer.

That was a problem for another day.

There was a giant sense of relief when I pulled into my driveway. Speaking of gifts, I was given the greatest present I could imagine: a heart-stopping Gavin sitting on the hood of his car in my driveway.

The spooky feeling forgotten, my eyes ate him up as I shut the door to my poor car. He had a silly grin pasted on his face and eyes brighter than the moon. Someone was definitely up to something.

"Well, this is a treat, not that I'm complaining. What are you doing here?" I asked, walking around the side of his car.

He pulled me between his legs and planted a kiss that made my head reel. "I missed you," he murmured, his eyes running over the planes of my face.

Fireflies frolicked in my belly. I laid my head on his chest. "Me, too." His heart beat under my ear.

I was wrapped up in Gavin's arms, content to stay there all night. Too bad fate had other plans. A shadow jumped out of the darkened trees. Strands of magic trickled in the air as a witch appeared from darkness, immediately on the attack.

I stifled a scream, my hand flying to my mouth. His face was hidden by a hood, with only his sneering mouth visible. I barely had time to register what was going on before Gavin pushed me out of the way.

"Stay behind me," he insisted. His jaw popped.

Like I could do anything else; fear froze me in place. I grabbed onto his arm as he stood protectively in front of me. His muscles under my hand bunched, readying for an attack. A surge of magic gathered in the air, building. I shivered in fear and from the iciness rolling off Gavin's body.

Instantly, he turned from a loving boyfriend to the ruthless dark witch. I knew better than anyone what his magic could do to someone. With our lives possibly at stake, it was a gamble I was willing to risk.

"My quarrel is not with you, young defender," the cloaked witch called from the trees. "I just want the girl." He began to walk toward us.

Gavin stiffened in front of me. "Sorry. She's already taken." His voice was dripping like icicles.

Without a warning, the mysterious witch cracked his neck and charged. Apparently, he hadn't liked what Gavin had to say. Magic charged through the air, burning like green acid. It sprayed the space around us like a grenade, heading right for us. Gavin, turning on the balls of his feet, engulfed me in his arms, throwing an invisible shield over us. We barely escaped the shrapnel of a searing ball of emerald fire. I wasn't familiar with fire magic, but this guy meant business. And I was pretty sure that business involved killing me.

I could only hope that Gavin was a stronger and faster witch. My bet was always on him. It didn't matter if this assassin was a seasoned witch. My faith was on the guy I loved. Gavin circled the witch-like a wolf, going into predator mode. Sleek. Lethal.

His eyes were tiny orbs of flaming sapphire, intent on only one thing—keeping me safe. "Two can play that game."

Instinct took over. With a snarl, Gavin lunged for an attack of his own. Spitting shards of metal spears, he flung them into the intruder's midst, catching him in the shoulder. Fire guy flinched for a brief second and leaped forward, the spears disappearing from their mark.

"Hmm. I might have underestimated you," hissed fire dude. "Time to correct my mishap."

The shadowy figure blinked from my sight, only to appear in front of me. My heart plummeted. Precious seconds ticked by as my life teetered on an invisible thread. Staring into the gleaming eyes of a witch, intent on taking my last breath, I could think of nothing. One-handed, he laced strong fingers over my neck, ribbons of magic crashing into my windpipe, cutting off all oxygen.

Everything happened so fast. I gasped at the loss of the substantial oxygen I needed to live. In cold fear, my brain shut down. It never occurred to me to use magic to save myself. I was too stunned to believe that this was happening. Someone actually wanted to kill me.

Why?

In those split seconds, Gavin, in a deadly arc, pivoted to face the nameless witch. The eyes I loved were like jagged slivers of ice. They showed no emotion. Turning himself off, he looked like a natural-born hunter—a killer.

Only an idiot would not fear Gavin, my dark witch. Even as the assassin's hands squeezed around my throat, I felt a quiver of fear at seeing the transformation. Gavin would never hurt me, but that still didn't mean he wasn't a formidable force to be reckoned with.

Out of thin air, a magical dagger appeared in Gavin's hand. He was just full of surprises. It was ominous and onyx in color, shimmering with colossal power. I didn't have to be told that this dagger was something to fear. It rippled in the twilight.

"Play time's over." Gavin glared in the pitch black of night.

The mysterious witch's eyes went wide right before Gavin plunged the knife into his heart. I heard the whoosh of the blade before it struck. He was so close to me that I felt the gasp of his last breath right before he exploded in front of my eyes. Glittery remains rained where he had last stood. I shrieked, turning my head away and squeezed my eyes shut. Only a moment later, I was swooped into Gavin's secure embrace. I buried my head into his chest.

So that's what happens when a witch dies. At least there wasn't a gruesome amount of blood. I couldn't have stomached that. Who he was? What he had wanted? Why me? Would this be the last attempt on my life, or was this just the beginning of things to come? So many questions I may never have answered.

There was something in the starry sky that whispered of trials I had yet to face. Things were bound to get worse before they got better.

I shivered against Gavin's chest.

"Bri, are you all right?"

I lifted my head and focused on Gavin, his midnight eyes speckling with worry. His hands ran over my body, checking for injury, cuts, and broken bones, now that our adrenaline was spiking down.

"He's dead," I whispered, still in shock.

Those dark blue eyes sought mine. "I'm sorry. I wish you hadn't seen that, seen me kill." His words were heavy on the heart, his heart. I felt him tremble.

My arms tightened around his waist as I searched for a way to ease his heart. Looking down at the pile of debris littering the ground at our feet, the wind suddenly churned, carrying it away. "At least we don't have to dispose of a body," I said, in a lame attempt at lightening the dreary mood that settled over us.

I felt a tiny smirk against my hair, and his arms settled over my shoulders, keeping me close. "Bri, I didn't have a choice, if I hadn't—" There was regret in his tone, along with vulnerability.

Pulling back, I embraced his face in my hands, needing to touch him. "You saved me. I don't know what he wanted with me, but if you hadn't been here..." I shuddered to think.

Gavin had killed another witch for me. Yes, it had been self-defense, but it didn't stop me from wondering and worrying about his soul. Would his aura be damaged now, like mine? Would he have black holes?

CHAPTER 27

S NUGGLING THE TOP OF MY HEAD, his arms came around me, keeping me close, keeping me safe. "You're okay," he sighed into my hair, a vast weight of tension leaving his body with it.

"Thanks to you."

"That jerk spoiled my plans." He sounded like a sullen two-year-old.

"What plans?" My eyes tapered, unsure my heart could handle any more surprises. I'd about reached my limit. Looking up into his face, tiny stars reflected in the pools of his blue eyes.

He blinked, his expression unreadable. "It can wait another night. I think you have had quite the evening as it is. I'm not even sure it's appropriate after what just happened."

My interest was piqued. "You can't do that to me, tease me like that. Now you have to tell me," I pleaded. "And right now I could use a distraction." I glanced up under my lashes.

Like a dam had been broken, he dropped the mask hiding his emotions and grinned like a little boy. "It's nothing, really. I just noticed the lack of Christmas at your house. The shop looks like Santa's workshop, but here it's...empty."

I sighed, looking over my shoulder at my house. There it sat in the dimness looking alone, while the other houses down the street beamed with glittering bulbs. "I know. I just haven't had the energy or the time to drag all that stuff out, and my aunt's been too busy."

He gave me a lopsided grin, trailing a finger down my nose. "You forget you're a witch. This will be a piece of cake," he assured me.

I narrowed my eyes. Judging by his devilish grin, we weren't going to be dragging out boxes from the attic, but after the night we just had, I needed a reminder of normal things, like decorating for Christmas. I chewed on my lip, meeting his beaming eyes. "Is this going to involve magic? 'Cuz I've just recently sworn off magic." Like ten minutes ago.

He rolled eyes and grabbed my hand. "Not today you haven't. Come on. Let's get started. You haven't lived until you have done an enchanted Christmas."

Oh goodie, snowflakes!

"It sounds pretty," I admitted, starting to warm up to the idea. I would be lying if I didn't admitted I was intrigued. "Okay. Where do we start?"

With a flick of his wrist and a wicked smirk, a dozen strands of lights started to trim the house in a pattern of beautiful colors. No ladder necessary. I had to admit, his way was much easier and less dangerous. "Just so we are clear, I don't want a National Lampoon's Christmas house. We don't want to piss off the neighbors." Thank goodness it was dark, and my house was pretty secluded, or we might have had some strange behavior to answer for.

Glancing at Gavin, I caught his mirthful gaze. "It's a good thing you said so now."

I rolled my eyes. "I bet Christmas at your house is like the Griswolds."

"You have no idea," he muttered, but there were love and admiration in his tone. He adored his family, and who could blame him? They were great.

With each tendril of magic we cast, the horror from earlier faded from my mind; never completely, but enough so that I was able to enjoy something as simple and traditional as decorating for Christmas.

I would be lying if I said I wasn't still a little jumpy being outside where the attack had taken place, but I didn't want to run and hide, to live in fear. And I was going to need magic to do that.

In each window, we plunked a pine wreath with a large red bow. They appeared literally out of thin air, making the house looked like something from a postcard. All the trees in the yard twinkled with blinking lights.

Standing in the middle of the yard, we admired our handiwork. Gavin draped an arm around my shoulder, and I huddled into his embrace, needing the heat from his body to chase the cool night. "It's perfect," I raved, and far more extravagant than I ever could have come up with on my own. What would I tell my aunt?

He propped his chin on my head. "It's only missing one thing."

"What else could you possibly add to this?"

The grin on his face said he was up to no good. "There is always room for more. Make it snow, Bri. It's not Christmas without it."

"It rarely snows here," I argued.

He fixed me with his playful blue eyes. "It can, if you will it, weather girl."

Hmm. He had a point. Snow would be glorious, a real white Christmas. I could already envision the treetops sprayed with ornate white flakes, and the grass covered in a blanket of snow. Powdery white carpeting the roofs and unique designs frosted to the windows. We got snow in Holly Ridge, just not buckets of it, but I could picture it so clearly in my head as if it was real.

"You're doing it," he murmured in my ear.

Opening my eyes, I tilted back my head as teeny, wet snowflakes dusted my eyelashes and tickled my nose. I laughed, throwing my arms around Gavin's neck as he lifted me off my feet, twirling us in circles with the snow falling around us. I felt like we were encased in one of those picture-perfect snow globes that someone had shaken up.

He set me back on my feet, his hands embracing either side of my cheeks. The snow glistened on his ridiculously long lashes, making the sapphire of his eyes glow like a thousand blue moons. "You look good with snow in your hair."

The way he was staring at me, and the sinfulness of his voice, had my breath catching in my throat. I could have said the same thing about him. There was such a dark and light contrast, with the flakes beading in his hair.

When I was finally able to speak, my voice was thick and gruff. "Thank you for doing this. I didn't realize how much I needed this." *Needed him*, I added silently before his lips softly brushed over mine. It was light and innocent, but I felt the zing to my boots.

There was an exhilarated rush from doing magic and kissing his lips. The combination was slow-burning, and left me spinning. His lips brushed the corner of mine before he dipped his head and kissed me again.

Intoxicating.

"You taste of strawberries," he whispered against my parted lips.

My heart beat erratically, and I willed it to slow down. It hardly cooperated. He was so fixated on my lips that he hadn't noticed the round ball of snow I produced out of nowhere. Nor did he seem to notice the gleam in my shining amethyst eyes. Even as he sent crazy, exciting, pesky fireflies in my belly, I still couldn't help myself. "Snowball fight!" I screamed right before pummeled him with a freshly packed ball of snow.

The shocked expression on his face was priceless and had me giggling. It was Polaroid perfect. "You're so going to pay for that," he warned in a voice that promised nothing less than retaliation.

I only laughed harder. Running was useless really, but instinct told me I needed distance before I got a face full of snow. I took off, my hair spinning out around me, but the snowball I was anticipating never came. Instead, I was swept off my feet by a pair of strong arms and hauled effortlessly over his shoulder.

I was laughing so hard I could barely breathe. "Is this my punishment?" I asked, gasping the words out between giggles and squirming.

"Oh no, I definitely have something in mind for you." The smile in his voice was anything but virtuous.

I shivered. But it wasn't fear his words enticed—it was anything but. I could all too well envision what kind of punishment he had in mind, and I wasn't exactly going to fight him off.

Wiggling closer to him, I gripped the back of his shirt. I loved the feel of his strength under my fingertips. He carried me into the house before depositing back to my feet. I shook off the powdery, wet flakes in the entryway and kicked off my shoes.

Decorating a tree with a witch was indeed magical, mystical, and memorable. Everything happened in a snap of a finger. Ornaments, lights, tinsel, all hung in the background until needed and just plucked from thin air.

By the time we finished, it was late. After all our hard work, which hadn't been physically hard, I was starving. My stomach was in the mood for cookies and hot chocolate, the perfect end to what had the potential of being a shitty day.

"We need cookies," I declared. "And I'm doing this the old fashioned way. No magic."

He bit the hoop at his lip to keep from grinning. "You're the boss."

"In the kitchen, you got it, buster?" I bumped the cabinet closed with my hip.

The scent of artificial pine and sugar cookies filled the house. This whole enchanted Christmas thing had woken up the holiday spirit inside me. It was possible that I could listen to Jingle Bells another gazillion times before I thought about chucking it out of the storefront window.

Gavin made me laugh. A ton. It felt as if I hadn't laughed in years. This day went on my list of the best times in my life, right under our first kiss.

While we were waiting for the cookies to finish baking, I made us some hot chocolate with the little colored marshmallows. They were fun, just like this evening had turned out. Good overruling the bad and ugly.

My aunt walked through the garage door. "I see the two of you have been busy little elves. I can't thank you both enough. The house looks wonderful. Can you believe that it's snowing?"

I couldn't hide the grin I aimed at Gavin, but I tried to cover up any weirdness by handing her a mug of steaming cocoa. She sat with us at the kitchen table and took a sip, sighing as he got off her feet.

"Just the way I like it. You're a goddess in the kitchen. What am I going to do when you leave next year for college?" Her eyes got misty.

My stomach dropped when I thought of her alone in this house. "Maybe you won't have to miss me," I said.

A beam of hope lit her mahogany eyes. "You decided to go to a school locally?"

"I'm thinking about it," I admitted, unable to disappoint her. It was true—I was considering it. I was also considering other options, like no college.

"Wherever you go, I want you to be happy...and safe," she added as an afterthought.

It wasn't that she mentioned safety that I found sort of odd, it was the way she said it. For the first time, I wondered if my aunt knew more than she let on. Was it possible that she knew about my heritage? That she had known all along and not told me?

The night ended with a sour taste lingering in my mouth, regardless that I had managed to shovel six cookies into my belly.

CHAPTER 28

"WHAT YOU NEED IS SOME defensive training." That was Gavin's solution after I finally told him about the dark spots on my aura. Then you throw in the attack from the other night, and I was a helpless sitting duck.

That wasn't all I needed, which was neither here nor there. After being tossed like a Raggedy Ann doll by one of Morgana's spells, and then strangled by another witch's weaving spell, it made me realize I needed to learn how to protect myself. It wasn't enough to just learn magic or control it. I needed to put it to good use, especially when I felt something horrible was looming on the horizon.

Instinct.

That was what Morgana had told me to trust, and every instinctual bone in my body was telling me that something wicked this way comes. I needed to be ready, prepared. Gavin couldn't have agreed more and insisted he help me with my badass fighting skills.

Who was I kidding?

Hopefully, I didn't hurt anyone in the process.

We were sitting on my couch, thigh against thigh, and I was doing everything in my power to not stare at his lips.

Fail.

Oops. Fail again.

At this rate, I was going to be the most preoccupied student. And this student was crushing hardcore on her teacher. The last week of school flew by, but there was this dark cloud over my head, preventing me from really enjoying the time I spent with Gavin. I finally caved and told him about the dream I'd had with Morgana and the whole black marks on my aura.

He took the news far better than I had. Of course, he blamed the one person he couldn't stand: Lukas. Unfortunately, I knew that Lukas hadn't made me drop Rianne from the gym ceiling. Nope. That had been all me.

"Are you sure this is a good idea? What if I hurt someone?" I asked, thinking about Rianne.

He gave me a goofy grin. "Trust me. You can't hurt anything with this."

I rolled my eyes. "Someone please pinch that oversized ego. We aren't going to end up leveling my house or something, are we?" I was remembering when I had blown out all the windows, not exactly something I was anxious to repeat.

He glared at me in exasperation. "What have you been doing in your practices?"

"You don't want to know," I mumbled.

"You're probably right." The implication behind his words was obvious and probably stemmed from jealousy. He thought more than just practicing had been going on like maybe Lukas and I were making our own kind of magic.

I crossed my arms. "It wasn't like that." I didn't want to get into it right now. Especially with the beginnings of a migraine working at my temples, and we hadn't even started yet. "There's this weird vibe with our magic. Not like the connection I feel with yours. Ours is more...intimate, personal. With Lukas..." His eyes flamed at the mention of his name, still a touchy topic. "With Lukas, it's like our magic are companions—brother and sister, somehow. Does that make sense?" I didn't even know what nonsense I was spewing.

Slowly the fire defused, and he cupped my cheek in his hand. "I get it. And I'm sorry. It just pisses me off that you share anything with him. I don't like it. And I don't trust him."

I nodded, understanding. It was exactly how I would feel if roles were reversed, except I'm not sure I would have the grace not to gouge her eyes out. "I know," I conceded.

He sighed looking over my shoulder. "Let's just get started."

I stared at his face and a cluster of fireflies swam in my belly. He could do that to me without even trying, or maybe I did it to myself. Who knew? "Okay," I agreed.

We stood facing each other, and I couldn't keep a straight face. This was supposed to be serious, but that was just it. He looked too serious. I giggled. The corners of his lips twitched, and my heart soared. I angled my head. "We could make-out first," I suggested, thinking I could stall this lesson. I don't know why, but I had a bad feeling about this, the kind that planted itself in my stomach and took root.

The look he gave me was lethal and should have been outlawed. "After. It will give you something to look forward to."

My teacher was all work and no play. "Hardass," I mumbled under my breath.

He grinned, stepping back before either of us forgot why he was here. "Okay, the goal here is to not get hit. I want you to stop the strike before it hits you, and I don't mean throw yourself in front of it."

That earned him the stink eye. "Funny. What kind of spell?"

"That's the beauty of it. You won't know until it's been cast, but I think your best shot at diffusing the spell would be a shield. It's fairly simple, but effective."

I didn't find anything remotely pretty in that. "Like what you did the other night?" Just thinking about it made fear lance through my heart.

He crossed his arms, leaning a hip on the edge of the couch. "Exactly. The spell I cast won't hurt you seriously. It might sting."

Oh great. "Just please tell me you aren't going to throw a knife at my head and expect me to stop it."

A single brow arched. "I'm not sadistic."

A girl had to ask. "Good to know."

He must have noticed the spike in my blood pressure. "Bri, every-thing is going to be fine. I promise."

How does someone make a promise like that? He couldn't possibly know our fate, but it didn't stop me from wanting to believe him. I sighed. He tugged me between his legs, rubbing his warm hands up and down my arms, sprinkling them with tingles. I stopped thinking altogether.

"Are you sure we don't have time for just one kiss?" I leaned my head on his chest, feeling it vibrate with a groan.

He tilted my chin up. "It's not rocket science. You can do this. I'll go easy on you."

I snorted. "Please. Bring it."

He gave me a patient look. "Bri, I need you to take this seriously. This could be life or death, and I want you to live. It's for your own good. You need something to motivate you. We are treating this like a real threat, no joke. I don't want to hurt you..." There was a pleading look in his eyes, asking me to understand.

I could see the struggle going on inside his eyes. "I can handle this," I assured with a boost of self-confidence.

He smiled a calm and arrogant smirk. Raising his hand, he stalked forward, sliding effortlessly into predator mode. "Remember don't hold back."

I gulped, stepping away from the furniture. In the space of a blink, the first little bolt of blue energy hit me like a wasp sting, piercing and unexpected. "Ouch, blast it," I complained frowning. "That hurt."

He sent me a humorless smile. "Don't let it touch you next time."

I stared at the guy in front of me like I didn't recognize him. His sapphire eyes were cold as ice, hard and unyielding. He looked dark and grim. I got that it was for my own good, but he was starting to scare me, and it wouldn't be long before that fear turned to anger. That was kind of how I operated.

By the third or fourth prick of magic, I wasn't laughing. I wasn't nervous, and I sure as hell wasn't cocky. If anything, I was irritated, and getting more irritated by the moment. To make matters worse, I got hit, a lot. I could throw up the shield, but he was always faster, beating me to it. By the time the shield encompassed me, some part of my body was feeling the sting of his spell.

I swore under my breath as another globe of blue light pierced through my jeans. The stuff was no joke, and the more I got hit, the more it stung.

Okay. This wasn't helping, and he was starting to get under my skin. I could feel the tingles of rage skirting below the surface, ready to break free. In my heart, I knew he didn't like this, hated that he caused me even the tiniest of pain. It went against his protective nature. I got it. This was the real deal, and I had to be able to act fast and be quick on my feet if I wanted to survive.

The next time he came at me, I was ready.

It was like flexing a muscle. Suddenly, a dizzying rush of power whipped through me, and a part of me liked it—really liked it. That scared the crap out of me. I didn't want to give into that kind of darkness, but it was right there within my fingers grasp, just a flick of my wrist. It teased me with potency, and I found myself unable to stop. Some part of me knew the kind of magic I'd conjured was bad, but it was too late.

The goal had been a protective barrier. Somewhere along the way, I forgot the plan. The magic I summoned had other ideas. No longer did I know what I was doing, only what I was feeling.

Rejuvenated.

Exhilarated.

Supreme power.

Above all things, there was this utterly intoxicating feeling filling my veins. I reveled in the sensation and closed my eyes. It was a better high than the fountain of youth. Better than sex. Well, what I thought sex would be like.

The best part was, Gavin's spell finally didn't strike me. Success. Truthfully, I had been worried I would never be faster than him. I couldn't wait to see the look on his face. I'd blown the roof off this spell.

With each second that ticked by, my strength grew, not weaken. Was that normal? When I didn't hear his voice, I became alarmed. My eyes opened and the world evaporated around me. What I expected to find was Gavin smiling and telling me that I'd done it, not him on the floor, gasping and in obvious pain. It seared straight through my heart. I immediately dropped the spell, breaking the connection it had on him.

He kneeled on the ground, face contorted in pain, and sapphire eyes gleaming. My stomach seized up, coiling in tight knots. All I could think was, I had done that to him. I had almost killed my boyfriend, the boy I loved.

Oh my God.

Dropping beside him, his face was ghostly white and a line of sweat covered his brow. "I-I almost killed you." I was mortified and in shock. Shame and outrage swarmed through me. I should be burned at the stake. "I'm sorry. I'm so sorry," I cried.

"You didn't, Bri," he gasped, struggling to speak. "I swear." His voice was rough and gravely which made what he was saying hard to believe.

"Really?" I replied, sarcastically hysterical.

"What you did wouldn't have killed me." He ran a hand through his messy dark hair, leaning against the nearest wall. Those eyes I loved glimmered with incredulity—or fear. I couldn't decide. "You were absorbing my powers."

"What?" I was beyond totally freaked out.

His head rested on the wall. "Well, more than just absorbing them, you were stealing them, draining them from within me." There was a charred hole in his shirt where my magic had hit him, sucked his essence, the soul of his magic.

I was going to pass out. Luckily, I was already sitting, there wouldn't be far to fall. I sunk against the wall beside him, careful not to touch him, and dropped my face into my hands. "What's wrong with me?"

He turned his head, staring at me. "There was probably a reason you never were told you were a witch...to protect you. Witches will kill for your kind of power, or kill to protect themselves from your power. Either way, it ends with your death. If others knew, you would be hunted nonstop."

Okay. I got it.

I was dead meat.

He looked at me gravely, meeting my frightened gaze. "You're a clàr silte."

I gulped. Why did that sound like a death sentence? "That doesn't mean anything to me," I whispered, barely audible.

"It's the rarest and oldest form of craft."

This wasn't making me feel any better. I was going to be sick. Pushing to my feet, he followed me. "This is bad isn't it?"

His hands spanned on either side of my waist and I winced. When I went to back away, he held steady and pulled me closer. "Don't." There was hurt in his voice. "Don't cringe from me."

Tears gathered in my eyes and coated my voice. "How can you be near me after I did that to you?"

"We didn't know, Bri." He cupped both hands around my face, and like a contented cat, I leaned into his touch. "I won't let this come between us. Not when I just got you. We will figure this out together. I promise." Softly and sweetly, he brushed kisses over my face before pressing them to my lips.

What had I done to deserve such a guy? Wonderful. Understanding. And hot as hell.

I vowed then that I would never take him for granted. Not. One. Single. Day. For as long as he was mine.

CHAPTER 29

T HERE WERE NO WORDS TO describe how I felt that night, the night I almost stole every ounce of magic from my boyfriend. What kind of girlfriend does that? Magic was such a huge part of Gavin that I couldn't imagine stripping him of his abilities.

But that was just what I'd started to do.

What would have happened had I not stopped, had I been unable to stop? I'd felt that addictive pull. I don't know why I stopped. That intense, mind-altering, heady feeling was still beating inside me. It was as if I had a living, pulsing piece of him within me, which was sort of cool and pretty freaky at the same time. I didn't like that I had stolen it from him without permission, but I loved the idea of a part of him would always be in me.

Pretty messed up.

Maybe seeing him withering in pain had snapped me out of it. Whatever it was, I was eternally grateful.

A clàr silte was a witch with the capabilities to strip powers from another witch, but there was a huge cost for such abilities...my soul. The more I tapped into that kind of magic, the more of my soul I lost. That's pretty much how these things work.

As far as I was concerned, I should never need to use that kind of power. My soul should be safe as long as I keep it under lock and key. Then throw that key into the vast ocean, safe from my temptation.

I could never use that kind of magic again. Ever.

My head hit the pillow like a brick of lead. Of course, I couldn't actually expect an undisturbed slumber. That would be too much to ask for. My eyes barely closed when I felt the familiar prickles and weightlessness. Exhausted mentally and physically, there wasn't a scrap of resistance left in me. I couldn't have fought it even if I'd known how.

Letting the floating feeling take me away, I waited for the transition to complete. Before I felt solid ground, I was blasted with icy wind and cool, crisp air. Snow-topped mountains stretched as far as the eye could see, and to my dismay, I was on the tiptop of the highest one. I shivered as another round of wind blew through my chilled bones. Snuggling deeper into the parka I was wearing, I turned, looking for my target.

I pounced on her the second I was grounded in the dream like a wild panther. "Why didn't you tell me?" I screamed above the howling winds. *That I can suck a witch dry*, I mentally added.

She moved with liquid grace, flowing over the rocky ground, and I envied her for it. "Well, someone is wound up this evening. Do tell, what did I fail to inform you of, dear granddaughter? Although, I think I am getting the message loud and clear."

"You know what I am talking about. That I'm a—a clàr silte." I was spitting fire. Not literally, but I was surprised the ice didn't melt.

She eyed me with almost approval as if she was a proud grandparent. "Would you believe that I hoped I never would have to?"

I gave her a dry look.

Her fur boots crunched under the packed snow. "There was always the chance that the gift wouldn't be yours. I didn't know for sure, and I wasn't going to trust a hunch."

A gift. I wasn't sure I would call stealing another witch's powers a gift.

Her purple eyes sobered. "I didn't wish this for you, or the consequences that come with it. I've grown fond of our little dreams. I will miss them, miss you."

Wow, granny was having a heart-to-heart. I wasn't sure she was capable of such feelings. Inside, I was flooded with dread. I took a step toward her. "You're leaving me? You can't. You just can't. I need you." There was no disguising the pure panic in my voice.

She shook her head. "No, not yet love, but there will be a time when our connection is severed. Until then, I will help when I can."

I looked out into the distance with a heavy heart, mixed feelings circling inside me. "I don't think I can do this," I whispered.

She turned me to face her and looked me straight in the eye. Gone was her usual supremacy. "You can. Do you hear me? There is no other choice for a witch like you. You must master your skills. It will be the only way for you to live, to defend yourself."

I couldn't move or say anything for a moment. I just stared into a pair of eyes identical to mine. Finally, I nodded. "You're right."

She tucked a strand of hair behind my ear. It was the first act of affection she had ever really shown me. "I do have some words of wisdom before you wake, young granddaughter. Two boys. One destined to be your true love, bound by more than just magic and love. The other..." she tsked her tongue. "...well, he isn't so lucky. He will destroy all the good you possess. Squash your pureness, which is also your strength. He will poison you with darkness—blacken your soul— and make you turn from all you love. The choice is yours, great-grand-daughter. Choose wisely. For it can't be undone."

I hated cryptic messages. "Can't you just tell me which one to choose?"

This time her smirk was sad. "If it was only that easy. I can do many things from beyond, but the choice will always be yours."

Ready for the conclusion to Gavin & Brianna's story?
Grab your next Gavin fix in MOONDUST the third book of the
Luminescence Trilogy!

CAN'T WAIT to meet you back in Holly Ridge!

Thank you for reading.

xoxo

Jennifer

P.S. Join my VIP Readers email list and receive a bonus scene told from Zane's POV, as well as a free copy of Saving Angel, book one in the Bestselling Divisa Series. You will also get notifications of what's new, giveaways, and new releases.

Visit here to sign up: www.jlweil.com

Don't forget to also join my Dark Divas FB Group and have some fun with me and a fabulous, fun group of readers. There is games, prizes, and lots of book love.

Join here: https://www.facebook.com/groups/1217984804898988/

You can stop in and say hi to me on Facebook night and day. I pop in as often as I can: https://www.facebook.com/jenniferlweil/ I'd love to hear from you.

PART III
MOONDUST

CHAPTER 1

The day before my life changed felt like any other day. No warning bells. No shift in the winds. No forewarning. That would have been too easy. And I was anything but that.

I'm a witch. Not just any witch, a clàr silte, whatever that means. I'm still unsure. What I did know was that it's ancient and powerful magic—and, of course, deadly. I'd almost killed the guy I loved above all else, the guy I would have died for.

Twisted.

I had almost killed the guy I was willing to die for.

Ironic.

The ocean breeze played with the ends of my auburn hair, lifting it off my face as I stared at the moon's glow reflecting onto the clear blue waters. What a magical night. It was chilly outside, but not enough to keep me locked indoors. Sweater weather, the kind of nights I loved. There was something absolutely peaceful about being at the beach during twilight, the moon washing over my skin, the sea salt air tickling my nose, and the cool sand between my toes.

Nothing called to me more than the shore. I felt some kind of affinity with nature, specifically with water. Maybe it went hand in hand with the whole weathercasting. The gentle winds seemed to caress my cheek, the moon wrapped around me like a cloak of warmth, and the soothing waves sung me a lullaby.

If only I felt as calm and serene as the star-strewn night looked above me.

Lying on the sand, I stared at the sky. The twinkling dots formed pictures for my distraction, which I desperately needed to take away the gnawing feeling in my stomach. Inside, I was a bundle of raw emotion, turning in chaotic loops.

Whenever I was troubled or feeling lost and alone, I retreated to the water's edge. The sights, sounds, and smells all offered me a comfort I could find nowhere else—the sloshing waters, the cries of birds on the hunt, and the undeniable scent of salt. Well, recently, Gavin's arms had offered that same kind of security, but I couldn't find it inside myself to run to him. Not when he was the root of my turmoil. Or more specifically, what I had done to him was.

A week had come and gone since I'd found out what kind of witch I was—since I had committed that unthinkable act to Gavin. What a week it had been. My face hurt from pretending not to be torn into pieces inside, like I wasn't scared of what I was or what was happening to me. The last thing I wanted was to alarm my aunt or my friends that something was wrong with me.

It was so much more difficult than it sounded. They were like PIs, picking up little clues or catching me staring into space with a sad frown. My appetite had vanished, along with my sense of humor. So yeah, I was doing a pretty shitty job trying to keep my sorrows under wrap.

Oh, and I hadn't practiced any magic at all since that night.

I didn't know if I wanted to, ever again. I felt tainted and ashamed. The messed up part was, I was mostly ashamed of the fact that there was a huge part of me that had liked it. The power I had felt was utopian, and the power I'd gained was still with me. I could feel the small amount of magic I'd stolen from Gavin swirling in me. His essence merged with mine in a way that was both exhilarating...and hot.

And I didn't mean like temperature warm; I meant sexy, in a hot, turned-on kind of way.

Ugh.

What was wrong with me?

Before, I'd always felt this unexplainable connection to Gavin, as if fate were pushing us together. Now, having his magic in my blood created a pull that was even greater. *Titanic* greater. When I wasn't feeling down in the dumps, I was imagining doing all kinds of wicked and sinful things with that boy and his mouth.

It was one extreme to the other. One minute I was on the verge of tears, and then the next, I was gazing at his lips like they were the most edible things on the menu. Gavin and his damn lip ring. He could have a least made it easier for me to resist and not look so drool-worthy all the time. It was maddening how much hotness he oozed.

My fingers dug into the grainy sand. Just thinking about him made me long to see him. And do a whole lot more than just look. I bit my lip, contemplating whether it would be wise to call him. Everything in my body screamed, *Yes, Yes, Yes.* But in my head, I thought that maybe it was something darker beckoning me to him, and for completely different reasons.

Magic.

My cheeks flushed against a chilly breeze as it passed over my skin. He had a way of heating my blood with just a fluttering thought. My phone vibrated in my back pocket, pulling me back down to earth. Speak of the devil. It was Gavin.

His name alone caused fireflies to flit in my belly, but as my finger hovered over the answer key, I bit my lip, contemplating. What was I going to say? Sorry? How many times could I apologize before I felt better? Before the shame stopped? I had broken a rule I had vowed never to cross: I hurt someone I loved.

Consciously or not, the result was the same. My powers were controlling me, when I should be controlling them. That made me dangerous—to everyone.

My finger slid over, hitting the ignore button, and I shoved the phone back into my pocket. Now I felt guilt—hordes of it—because I wanted nothing more than to talk to him, unload these mixed up feelings I was having.

Before he would be the person I ran to, until recently, that was. But honestly, before I didn't have problems—not like this.

Gavin wasn't the only guy in my life I'd been avoiding.

Blowing off Lukas for a week hadn't entirely been an easy feat either. Time was catching up to me, and I knew that I was going to have to face him sooner or, more preferably, later. I'd been flirting with the idea of telling him what had happened. For the past week, I'd done everything possible to forget the nightmarish thing I'd done. Working myself into exhaustion.

It hadn't worked.

Nothing worked.

Deep down, I knew that the only one person who might have been able to take away those feelings was the one I was running from.

Gavin.

It was like a double-edge sword.

God hates me.

On one hand, Gavin could offer me the solace I sought. On the other hand, he was part of what I didn't want to face, couldn't face.

So here I was, alone, trying to work through what I was.

A clàr silte.

Man, that was a mouthful. Magic so strong, it was both feared and coveted. How did a girl like me, someone so ordinary and naïve deserve that kind of power? What was I possibly to do with such supremacy at my fingertips? Every time I dipped into those powers, I lost a piece of my soul, and my aura darkened. The more of my aura I lost, the greater the risk I would lose myself in the darkness.

Black magic.

If that weren't enough to be scared shitless, then I was a fool.

And Aunt Clara didn't raise no fool... I think.

This whole thing felt unjust. Anger pumped through me at the unfairness of it all. Lately, anger and self-pity had been my best friends. I didn't want to hurt other witches. I wasn't a thief. But what if I couldn't stop it? I had seen the shock and fear in Gavin's eyes that night, even if it had just been a flicker. The pain that had radiated on his face was seared in my memory. It infuriated me that he had suffered at my hands.

I shot to my feet, open-armed, with the waters turning in front of me, and I thought I should be struck with lightning. The sky opened up with a crack of angry light and ground-shaking thunder. The air and water around me were vulnerable to my feelings and I often inadvertently lashed out with them. It was just so.

All my anger and pain splashed across the dark sky and over the almost-black waters. Tingles ran through my veins, and I threw my head back. It felt amazing to let my anger flow into the elements around me. They took away the emotions that spread through every muscle, every bone, and every pore in my body.

I sensed the connection from within me, spreading out to the world around me. Wind. Water. Lightning. A different link for each piece of Mother Nature. I realized then that this energy I was extending to the elements could help heal the wounds breaking inside me.

Walking to the shoreline, I waded ankle-deep into the freezing water. It burned through me, cutting off my magic. As I stared down at my reflection in the water, I saw that I didn't look like the girl I'd imagined I would have been when I grew up. Large, blazing, purple eyes stared back at me, and my lip trembled. On the brink of eighteen, I had wanted to be a strong, independent woman who knew what she wanted in life, not a frightened girl unsure of her future, unsure of herself. That was not who my mom would have raised me to be, and it wasn't the girl my aunt had taught me to be.

I was acting like a whiny child.

I wanted to be someone my aunt and my parents could be proud of. So why wasn't I? Why was I sitting here feeling dejected and sorry for myself?

In the end, hiding away—from the world, from my friends, and from myself— wasn't going to accomplish anything. It wasn't going to make my life all peachy and rosy again. The only person who could change the path I was headed down was me.

This was who I was. Nothing I could do or say would change it. No amount of begging, pleading, or wishing otherwise would make me normal. Did I really want *normal* if I couldn't have Gavin?

I knew what I was going to do, what I was born to do: wield magic.

I straightened my shoulders and lifted my chin. Waving my hand out in front of me, I felt the stirrings of magic pulse to life in my blood. The roaring waves stilled, the howling winds quieted, and the sky was once again clear and filled with stars, just as I commanded them.

I could almost hear Morgana laughing down at me. *That's my girl. About damn time, too.*

CHAPTER 2

By the time I resurfaced as one of the living again, Christmas break was over and I was getting ready for Monday morning classes. Glancing through the sheer white curtain covering the window, I was glad to see the sun shining, a reflection of the hopefulness I felt inside.

I snickered. Of course the sun was shining; I wasn't stuck with my head under the covers, bawling like a blubbering woe-is-me sap—hence, no rain. Kicking the covers to the end of the bed, I jumped up. The cold wooden floors chilled my toes as I ran to the adjoining bathroom with Lunar on my heels, meowing. If I didn't pick him up and show him some kind of attention each morning, he wouldn't stop the persistent crying. It only got longer and louder if I ignored him.

"Hey, you pest," I murmured, nuzzling his soft downy head under my chin. He started purring rapidly. "You're going to make me late for school." Two minutes later his blue eyes got that wild look in them, and he was zipping through my room at mach ten, bouncing off of anything his paws could touch. Why couldn't I wake up with that much energy? It took at least two cups of coffee before I could even function like a human.

I took the longest shower possible, steaming up the entire bathroom. I think it had even started to pour out from under the door. But I needed it just like I needed a little pampering to make myself feel alive and encouraged. It was the little things that made a difference. Like...my favorite foods, strawberry flavored lip-gloss, crisp, cool sheets on a winter's night, and most of all, Gavin's kisses.

Oh, yeah. I could really use one of those.

I missed them immensely. I was having withdrawals from no longer kissing Gavin's lips.

To my dismay, there hadn't been any heavy make-out sessions, none of the backseat groping, or whisperings of sweet nothings that I had envisioned during winter break. I only had myself to blame for this loss.

Well, then. I was going to have to put my fears aside and take that bold step I'd been afraid to take, because if there was one thing I was certain about, it was that I didn't want to push away the one guy who mattered most. He had made it clear to me that his feelings hadn't changed, that he wasn't afraid of me. But he should have been, because I was very much afraid; nonetheless, I wasn't going to live the rest of my life in a constant state of fear.

I wanted to live.

And that included kissing my very luscious boyfriend.

Sitting in front of my vanity, I spent more time working on my looks in that one sitting than I previously had throughout my whole life. I smeared on a sheer coat of strawberry lip-gloss and smacked my lips before applying layer after layer of mascara until my eyelashes were goopy and starting to stick together. Great. Well I never claimed to be a fashionista.

I zipped up my boots and headed downstairs for a breakfast of champions. Rummaging through the cabinet, I found what I was looking for: Strawberry Pop Tarts. Thank God. My good mood might have gone sour if there hadn't been any frosted Pop Tarts. I ate them like crack. Pouring a cup of coffee from the pot my aunt had left on the warmer for me, I broke off a corner of the Pop Tart and dunked it into the sugary black brew. Someone was going to be running on a sugar high. This was just the way I liked my mornings—until I crashed before lunch.

After a quick scratch behind Lunar's ears, I snatched my keys off the counter. No sooner had I put a foot outside than my blood started humming. I didn't have to look up to know who was there, yet it was a temptation I couldn't resist. He was leaning against the hood of his car, a sight I would gladly wake up at 6:30 a.m. every day of the week for. Talk about jump-starting my engine; I was afraid I might overheat and need to be hosed down. My cheeks turned pink and my steps faltered.

Gavin met me halfway on the driveway with a greeting that would leave any girl lightheaded. He pressed his lips to mine in a sweet and soft kiss. Just like that, all my worries, my fears, all the crap that was dogging my mind, simply faded to nothing. He had that effect on me.

Under thick, sooty lashes he stared down at me. "Hmm. It should be mandatory for us to start our mornings like this every day."

I grinned. "Deal."

He had an impish glee in his sapphire eyes. "I'm going to hold you to that."

"I hope so." Either he did a bang-up job covering his feelings, or he really wasn't scared or upset with me. It was almost too good to be true. How did I deserve such a boyfriend?

He arched a brow. "Well, someone ate their Wheaties this morning. 'Bout damn time too. I thought I was going to have to drag your butt down the stairs. It's so nice to be wrong."

I rolled my eyes. "Let's go, Romeo. I've got classes to attend." I started to wiggle out of his embrace to no avail. Looking up, I returned his raised brow with one of my own.

"I have a better idea. Since you are feeling so...feisty, how about we skip classes and do something more... fun?"

I was getting a clear picture from what kind of *fun* he was implying. The darkening of his blue eyes and his voice going all kinds of silky were dead giveaways. "Oh, yeah. Like what?" I asked, teasingly.

Was I actually flirting?

Holy crap. Maybe I should have gone to the beach earlier and had some kind of life-changing revelation. It was like suddenly everything was clear after living for years in a foggy haze. Plus, I had sass. I was digging it.

The corners of his mouth tilted upward and his hands slipped into the back pockets of my jeans. "I am sure we could think of a few ways to pass the time." And just to play unfair, he brushed his lips over my chin.

I shivered. "You suck," I pouted, seriously considering his offer. How could I not when I was staring into eyes the color of starlight? Sighing, I replied, "I can't. It's the first day back."

He wasn't deterred. "Precisely why it's the perfect day. We never do anything important on the first day after holiday break."

"Important to whom?" I countered.

He rocked back on his heels with a slight frown. "We're going to school, aren't we?"

A corner of my mouth curled. "Yep," I replied.

He looped his fingers with mine, leading us to his muscle car. Its black paint gleamed under the sunlight. Slipping behind the steering wheel, he rubbed the pad of his thumb over his bottom lip. "How do your lips always taste like strawberries?" he asked.

"It's called lip gloss, genius."

He grinned. "You should buy it in bulk."

Would everything he said make my heart do cartwheels?

January in Holly Ridge was mild, at least when I wasn't messing up the weather forecast. No one put any stock into their predications any more, which was entirely my fault. Occasionally I felt remorse, but today was not one of those days.

It was impossible to feel guilty when the sun was beating down on my face. Pine trees in a multitude of greens lined the road, littering the shoulder with needles. The ride to school was short—too short because I wanted more time alone with Gavin.

Leaning my head back on the seat, I studied his silhouette. Dark messy hair. High cheekbones. Deep blue eyes. Full lips with a silver hoop in the center. There was nothing but yummy goodness carved into his face.

Zipping into the school parking lot, he parked the car and then, with one last roar, the engine quieted. He dangled his keys on a finger, turning to face me. "We need to talk after school. I found out some stuff."

He sure knew how to drop a bomb. "Stuff? What kind of *stuff?*" I was both interested and panicky.

Twirling the hoop at his lip, he said, "We don't have time for me to divulge all the details. We have classes remember? You insisted."

I scowled. "Funny." Damn him for reminding me of what we could be doing right about now. I gazed at his lips, and then I damned myself for being such a stick in the mud.

His eyes flickered. "If you have plans with—"

"I don't," I quickly cut in.

"Still avoiding him?"

Lukas was still a touchy subject. "Maybe."

The muscle in his jaw locked up. "Well, you won't hear me complaining. He's trouble."

I socked him on the arm. It felt like connecting with steel. "Whatever." But I knew that he was serious. The two guys in my life couldn't stand each other.

It was kind of a big deal.

Getting out of the car, we walked through the front doors hand in hand, and it was like I lived a double life. There was Brianna, the average student, and then there was Brianna, the secret witch assassin. Rounding the corner to my locker, I was bombarded by a ball of energy that could rival the energizer bunny.

Tori.

A piece of her hair got caught in my mouth as she hugged me. "Miss me?" she asked, grinning.

Wow. Someone had more coffee than I did this morning.

Gavin shook his head behind her, wisps of hair partially obscuring his eyes. I don't know how he did it, but he had gotten out of the way before the Tasmanian Devil attacked. *See you later*, he mouthed and disappeared in the crowd.

I felt a tinge of disappointment at his departure. "If I miss you any more, people will think I am dating you and not Gavin," I grumbled.

She looped her arm through mine, ignoring my other-than-pleased attitude. "Where is that piece of hot ass? I swore you came in together."

I grinned. "We did. You scared him off."

Tori snorted. "Hardly. I doubt anything scares Gavin." Today, her light brown hair was woven into a knot at the nape of her neck. She had on at least three-inch heels, which made me feel shorter than usual. Despite her girly clothing choices, I had missed her.

"Well, if it isn't my two favorite biotches," Austin said, coming up between us and swinging his arms over our shoulders. He encompassed us in a sad excuse for a group hug. "What scandalous affairs did my two besties get mixed up in over break? You know you can tell me. Actually, I demand you tell me."

I laughed. I couldn't help myself. If there were any kind of scandals in Holly Ridge, I would bet my pink panties that Austin was at the heart of it. Just when I felt like I was drowning in magic with my arms flailing in the waters and my oxygen cut off, Tori and Austin would always pull me back to the surface, reminding me that I wasn't just a clueless witch struggling in a world I barely understood.

I slipped out of our threesome and started down the hall. "Sorry to disappoint. I studied." *Magic that was.* I snuck a glance over my shoulder, catching Austin making an L with his hand and holding it to his forehead. Jeesh. What a pair they were. Austin in his skinny jeans, styled hair, and wired frames, and Tori in her plaid school skirt and laughing chocolate eyes. We were misfits, but I wouldn't change them for the world.

Austin's grin faded. "Are you telling me that Tori's maid was getting more tail than the three of us? We are so pathetic."

"So B, have you heard from Lukas?" Tori asked, trying to sound nonchalant and failing, the glint of hopefulness in her gaze giving her up.

I cringed at the mention of his name. "Not really. Not since your party." I could have kicked myself for not being a little more delicate.

Her expression fell before she could mask it behind a forced smile of I-don't-care. She was bummed that the d-bag hadn't called her, which made me mad at Lukas all over again. He never should have flirted with her and given her false hope if he had no intention of following through.

What a tease.

And now that she brought up Lukas, I knew that I needed to talk to him—even if I wasn't quite ready. He was undeniably part of what I was going through. Morgana had pretty much told me that in her last cryptic message. *Two boys. One destined to be your true love, bound by more than just magic and love. The other... well, he isn't so lucky. He will destroy all the good you possess, squash your pureness, which is also your strength. He will poison you with darkness—blacken your soul, make you turn from all you love. The choice is yours Great-Granddaughter. Choose wisely, for it can't be undone.*

Grams was a freaking a poet. And now her words loomed in my head, day in and day out.

Lukas of all people knew more about my... I couldn't bring myself to call it a gift. Not after what I had done to Gavin, but it was a piece of me I still had to come to terms with, control, and maybe even embrace.

And that scared the ever-loving crap out of me, which in a round-about way brought me back to what Gavin wanted to talk about after school. The unknown had me chewing away at my lip all day.

CHAPTER 3

I met Mister Mysterious at his car after the final bell. Nibbling on my already destroyed nails, my gaze flickered upward at the tingles dancing down my spine. Gavin was sauntering through the parking lot, dodging between cars as he made his way toward me. His black, half-laced boots clopped on the blacktop.

Our eyes clashed.

There was something about this guy that made my cells go banana-nuts. Fireflies rocked inside my belly, coating over my nerves. I bit my lip, blushing.

When he reached me, he leaned his hip on his car beside me and arched a brow as I continued to stare. "You ready to blow this dump or are you too busy enjoying the view?"

Yes, to both counts.

"Shut up," I said, giving his shoulder a nudge.

His lips twitched. "I love it when you go all sassy-pants on me."

"You're beyond redemption."

"I hope so," he replied, reaching over me and opening my door. Our bodies brushed, separated by a hairsbreadth. I swear he did it on purpose.

I gasped. An electric current ran through my blood, and I felt my eyes darken. There was something going on between us that was more than just attraction. I did not get shocked with a bolt of lightning every time I came in contact with a witch—just Gavin.

And that was a puzzle for another day.

I had too many loose pieces, and no real picture of the final product.

I went to slide into the car, but he was still in my way, so I looked up under my lashes, trying to remember how to breathe. I could see the same pull I felt in the deep blue of his eyes. He ran a thumb over my jaw. "We should leave," he said in a raspy voice, staring at my lips.

I leaned in, placing a hand on his chest. If he expected me to oblige and get in the car, he was sorely mistaken. I did not have the kind of self-discipline that he did. And I very much wanted to kiss him.

His lips curled. "Hurry. Get in."

I cleared my throat and slipped into the seat before we gave the whole school a lesson in tonsil hockey, which I decided right then wasn't a bad thing—not if I were kissing those lips.

I heard him exhale as he shut the door. It gave me warm fireflies inside, knowing that I wasn't the only one struggling here. "Buckle up; you're in for a ride," he said at the same time the engine jumped to life.

I really hoped that was a metaphor for something else—something more enticing.

We made it to his house in record time, and I managed to stay in my seat and keep my hands to myself, not that it hadn't been without effort. My hands were still clenched together in my lap. Gravel crunched under the tires, sticking to the tread. I was always struck with the wonder and lure of this house. Its beauty was mesmerizing, which might have more to do with its inhabitants than the house itself. The ground trembled in magic as I stepped out of the car, a feat that was a power all on its own. I recognized it for what it was now, unlike the first time when I had been confused and more than a little in awe.

Once inside, we went to the lounging area just to the right of the entrance, instead of his bedroom. A smart idea. I couldn't promise that behind closed doors I wouldn't attack him with my mouth. Lordy Lord, my body was still vibrating from his touch.

Back to reality.

The octagonal room had floor-to-ceiling windows that overlooked the front porch. I sat on the other end of the couch, just in case my fingers decided to wander. "Okay. Tell me what you found out. The suspense has been killing me all day," I said as soon as his fantastic butt hit the cushions. Patience wasn't on my list of virtues today.

All the mischief had vanished from his eyes. "I did some inquiring, and there hasn't been a record of a clàr silte in decades."

I tensed up.

Clàr silte—a witch who strips other witches of their powers, sucking them dry and absorbing their powers into his- or herself. There was just one little itty bitty catch...the cost was the witch's soul. No biggie.

We hadn't seen each other in days and our first real conversation was going to be about the one thing I'd been dodging. "Great," I replied sarcastically. "How does this help me?" Other than making me feel even more freakish and alone, I might add.

"Well, that is not all. There have been whispers of your powers in the underground communities." He looked unsettled by this development. "They haven't put a name to the witch wielding enough power to strip all the downtown witches, but they do have a description."

Unease crept down my spine. "Wait. What? There is an underground community of witches? Is that what you are telling me?"

Scratching his chin, he replied, "Yeah. But that is not the point."

Umm. It was a big point to me. "How come you never told me about these witches? Are they part of some secret society?" I pictured a tunnel system underground filled with a bunch of homeless witches with scraggly hair and dirt on their cheeks.

I shivered.

He leaned forward, his elbows on his knees and eyes gripping mine. "Bri, you are getting sidetracked. There are witches looking for you. Powerful and dangerous ones. And they know how to stay off the grid. They aren't seen unless they want to be seen."

I narrowed my eyes. "And how did you know where to go to get this information?" I was afraid to ask, but I had to. If these witches didn't want to be found, how the heck had he known about them? What kind of trouble was he getting himself into because of me? I couldn't allow it. I wouldn't be able to forgive myself if something happened to him.

He gave me a sly grin. "I have my sources."

I rolled my eyes. "Oh. I just bet you do...or *Jared* does."

His smirk lost some of its luster.

"Who told you this? I want to talk to them," I demanded, suddenly growing lady balls.

He scoffed. "No way. It is out of the question, and don't even think about it," he said before I even opened my mouth to object. "I am not taking you with me next time."

It was slightly unnerving that he could read me so well. "There is going to be a next time?" I asked, but I already knew the answer. Of course he was going to go back, because he cared about me, and it was in his nature to protect. In his head, he was protecting me.

Silence.

I folded my arms. "I'll just take that as a yes. Why the hell not? It's me you are inquiring about." Or more like what my magic can do, but really that was just a technicality. "I should have a say," I argued.

His jaw set like stone. "Not going to happen."

"You are being impossible."

One shoulder shrugged. "You are being reckless."

I sunk back into the couch. We weren't going to get anywhere at this rate. There was no point in continuing to disagree. So I activated the silent treatment, except it only last a few heartbeats.

Gavin inched closer, pressing his thigh to mine. I stared straight ahead, pretending that I weren't suddenly overheating, or that I hadn't felt that zap on my thigh through my jeans. "How are you dealing with everything?" he asked in a gentler tone.

Who was I kidding? I couldn't stay annoyed, not when I saw the glint in his eyes. "I'm working through it," I said. Thanks to him. "But you don't need to worry about me."

He ran the back of his knuckles down the side of my cheek, looking doubtful. "Too late."

Using all of my self-control, I focused on what he was saying, which got shot to the moon when his lips kissed the hollow of my throat. "Gavin?" I pressed my face into his neck and inhaled deeply.

Sinful. Woodsy. Yumminess. He always had this outdoorsy scent that I loved.

"It's okay," he said, his mouth grazing the underside of my jaw. "No one is home. Jared's at class. My parents are at work. And who knows where Sophie is." His lips went to work again.

My eyes fluttered shut, and I sighed. Good enough for me. I snuggled against him as he brought down his lips on mine. A shudder rolled through me. I couldn't help myself, sinking into the kiss. It had been too long, and the touch of his lip ring cooled my inflamed lips. There was nothing sexier than sucking, biting, and playing with that hoop.

It felt downright naughty.

His hand slid down my arm to my waist, tugging me almost on his lap. Hooking a hand behind my leg, his hand inched higher and—

We were interrupted. Outside, a door slammed, followed by a giggle that sounded very familiar. His darkened eyes drifted to the window. Apparently he didn't like what he saw. Rigid, he shot up off the couch, and I almost face planted on the cushions at the sudden loss of stability I had from his arms. Blowing the hair out of my eyes, I glanced up. He was staring out the window, watching Sophie get out of a very sleek white car owned by none other than Declan Harris.

Dec was a rich kid who was in need of an extreme attitude adjustment—in short, he was a douche. I was more than a little surprised to see Sophie with him. I pegged her for having more class than that. By the dark frown on Gavin's face, I could tell he felt the same.

"Who was that?" he barked, grilling a smiling Sophie as she brushed past him through the front door.

"No one. Just a friend." There was a dreamy quality to her voice, her blue eyes wistful.

Just a friend, my scrawny butt. I wasn't buying it, but most importantly, Gavin was definitely not buying it. His brows slammed together as he stared down Dec the D-bag while he backed down the driveway. "I don't like him," Gavin announced.

Sophie twirled on her heels. "Then it is a good thing *you're* not dating him," she shot back.

I snickered, earning a fierce scowl from the overprotective brother.

Gavin folded his arms. "And neither will you."

Sophie tipped her chin, and her blue eyes flashed. Magic vibrated in the air.

Uh-oh.

"You don't have a say in who I decide to hang out with, let alone date." Sophie's eyes started to illuminate.

Here comes trouble.

Gavin straightened up, shoulders broad. "The hell I don't."

Thank God I never had any siblings.

I figured this was a good time to seek cover and get out of the way before I got caught in the crossfire. Gavin looked ready to go ape crazy on someone, and that someone looked like it was going to be Sophie.

Magic flew-- And by flew, I meant it was literally soaring through the air. Tendrils of white light sprang from Sophie's fingertips only to be intercepted by ribbons of red from Gavin's.

"You can't control my life," Sophie yelled.

"Well someone has to stop you from making dumb decisions," Gavin retorted, cracking his neck.

More sparkling light.

Sophie clenched her fists in aggravation. "Argh. You are such a Neanderthal." A wicked orangey-pink strand of energy flickered from Sophie's closed hands, heading straight for Gavin. He sidestepped with a grin, and suddenly I was the target of that wicked spell.

I ducked. The material sizzled behind me and was burned off like a wart. Holy crap. The smell of burnt fabric wafted in the air.

Sophie squeaked. "Oops. Sorry, Brianna." She had a hand to her lips in shock.

The look in Gavin's eyes intimidated even me, and I wasn't on the receiving end. "See, you are careless. You almost incinerated my girlfriend."

Sophie sent me an apologetic look before marching up the stairs.

I ran a hand through my hair to make sure the ends weren't fried to a crisp. "Wow. Remind me never to piss you off."

He slumped against the nearest wall with troubled eyes. "I let my emotions get the best of me. Not my finest moment."

I stood up and went to him, unable to help myself. Wrapping my arms around his neck, his arms tightened around me. "At least you don't cause a thunderstorm every time you get mad."

He chuckled. "I just don't want her to get hurt."

And that was why I loved him.

※

THAT NIGHT, as I lay in bed, I thought about family and the lengths we would go to protect those we love. I thought about my aunt, and all the lies and secrets I've had to keep during the last four months. I just seem to keep digging myself in deeper.

Sleep hasn't been my friend lately. I fought it, while others craved it. I feared it as others embraced it. In my dreams, I lost control. And I should have known that Lukas wouldn't be ignored forever. He was bound to make an appearance, and that night, he summoned me in his dreams. That night of all nights, when I was feeling conflicted, therefore leaving myself open to dream invasion.

No surprise.

I thought about rejecting the merger of dreams, but even as I thought about it, I wasn't sure that I could. Lukas had more experienced in dreamscaping, and I figured that if he really wanted, he would find a way to force himself into the realm of sleep.

Strap on your witch's hat, 'cause it is going to be a whirlwind of a ride.

CHAPTER 4

No sooner had my droopy eyes fluttered shut did I feel myself being sucked down a dark tunnel, into a void of nothingness: a space of no definition, no walls, no physically solid anything. There were no lamps, no moonlight, yet I could see clear as day. Strange. But then again, dreams were whatever we wanted them to be. They don't have to make sense, and, in most cases, they were a hodgepodge of thoughts.

It took me a few seconds to collect myself and get my bearings. Being pulled into a dream was not the same experience as summoning someone into yours. I prefer to do the summoning; it was less traumatic, and I liked choosing the destination, preferably a tropical one. This weird, empty space felt cold, emotionless, and sad.

Catching Lukas's eyes, I stared at him. He was dressed in wrinkled jeans and a UNC T-shirt. He was also barefoot and had his hands shoved into his pockets. Even though I hadn't seen him since the Christmas party, he looked exactly how I remembered. Sandy hair, sun-kissed skin, a lopsided grin, and twinkling emerald eyes that always looked like he just performed the world's biggest prank.

I really wanted not to be affected by his presence or his dang smirk, but I was. There was a light about him that shined brightly, even in the darkness. That was a huge difference between Lukas and Gavin: if Gavin had been in this same room, I knew that he would have melted into the shadows, blending with darkness.

My heart knocked inside my chest. Slowly Lukas made his way over to me, his eyes imprisoning mine. "So are you going to tell me what I am doing here?" I asked.

"Miss me, Brianna?"

Damn his dimples. "No." I wasn't going to be done in by his cute smile and his boyish charm. Nope.

"Not even a little?" He walked in a circle around me.

I kept my expression blank even as my heart squeezed. Yeah, I had missed the doofus, but I sure I wasn't going to admit it. My eyes followed his movements.

"Well, I see this is going to be a riveting conversation. I thought after a few weeks of not speaking, you might actually have something to say to me." His voice came from behind me.

My gaze slid back to him as he rounded the other side of me. "Guess you thought wrong."

Something flickered in his eyes. Impatience? Exasperation? Pain? I couldn't decode. "Come on. Don't be like this, Brianna."

I tilted my head to the side and folded my arms. "What exactly am I being like? You led on my best friend, who is now sitting at home by her phone waiting for a call or a simple text. You got into a fight with my boyfriend at my best friend's party. And you risked being seen doing magic. Do you want me to go on?"

His weight shifted to one foot. "Can you blame a guy for having a bad night? Plus, I thought you had already forgiven me for that. I know it was wrong for me to use your friend to try to make you jealous. I think we can both agree that plan backfired in my face." He glanced down. "I can't help how I feel about you."

The reminder of his feelings was like a kick in the gut. "Lukas—" It was true that I had forgiven him and hearing him say he had feelings for me just opened me up to emotions I didn't want to feel.

"Save me the sympathy speech, okay? I don't want it. Look, I get it. You don't l-o-v-e me, and you are dating the dark jerk. I'm coming to terms with it... but I miss doing magic with you."

I missed that, too. I did miss him.

Damn.

Last time we had talked, he had been filled with agony and hurt and had then hung up on me. I didn't want to continue hurting people I cared about—and that included Lukas. Would our being *just friends* hurt Lukas more in the end? Would seeing me with Gavin drive a wedge between us? Maybe it would be best if I put an end to it now. But I couldn't let him go.

I sighed. "Fine. Maybe I missed you a little."

He flashed me a wry smile. "That's because I am irresistible."

I repressed the urge to punch his arm. "Says who?"

He stepped closer. "Give me ten minutes."

I couldn't stop the grin from teasing my lips, or the spike in my blood pressure. "Only ten?" I baited. "I think you overestimate your magnetism."

"We'll see," he said, and bumped me lightly with his shoulder. "What have you learned?"

You don't want to know.

I bit my lip just as the words were about to tumble from my mouth. No one knew that I was a clàr silte except for Gavin. I promised, for my safety, that I would tell no one, but Lukas wasn't just anyone. He had been instrumental in my learning to control my dreams. It was on the tip of my tongue to tell him what had happened with Gavin, how I sucked the magic right from him without knowing what I was doing. But a promise was a promise, and I didn't want to do anything to break Gavin's trust ever again.

It had been bad enough when he found out that I was sharing dreams with Lukas.

But that meant that I had to lie to Lukas, something I'd never really done. In my defense, though, I also hadn't known he was real either. I continued to chew on my lip. If I didn't make a decision soon, I was going to be missing a chunk of my lip. There was a part of me that wanted to share this burden with someone who also shared some of my so-called gifts.

Indecision overwhelmed me. I wanted to do what was right, not just for me, but for Gavin and Lukas, too. A stronger piece of me held back. So I just shook my head. "Nothing new. I've been slacking." The lie was like sandpaper in my throat.

And I was pretty sure he didn't believe me. His eyes narrowed. "I thought your *boyfriend* would have jumped at the chance to take my place as your instructor."

It was no secret that those two didn't like each other. "Is this why you brought me here, to talk about Gavin?"

"What do you think?" he muttered.

I thought it was time to move onto safer topics, like our drab setting, before he tried to press me. I didn't trust myself not to cave and spill my guts or something worse... I stepped back. "Is this the best you can dream up?" I asked, looking up at... nothing.

He snorted, feigning outrage. "Have I taught you nothing?"

I blinked.

And during that nanosecond of blindness, Lukas moved. I could feel the heat radiating from his body, he was so close. Reaching out, he tucked a strand of auburn hair behind my ear. "Let's make magic."

Gulping, I got the impression that there was a double meaning behind his words, not to mention the one behind the spark that flashed in his eyes at my nearness. I was rooted in place, captured by the intensity of his dark green eyes.

He snapped his fingers, grinning like a loon. All around me, tiny pricks of starlight appeared, showering us from head to toe. Light spilled from the stars like liquid silver. A string of magic flew, bobbing and spinning into the star-strewn sky. The hiss of power sang with the ringing of stars. It was breathtaking.

Holy moly. Okay. So maybe Lukas knew how to dazzle dreams.

"It's mesmerizing," I said, struck in amazement.

"So are you," he murmured.

I scrunched my nose.

"Too cheesy?" he asked.

I pinched my thumb and index finger together leaving just an inch of space before they touched. "Just a tad."

He laughed. The sound was a burst of sunshine. It was refreshing. "Are we going to be able to see each other outside of our dreams?"

"As friends," I said, because I didn't want there to be any confusion about our relationship. Not to mention that inside, I was mixed up about what I was feeling, but I needed to make sure that Lukas understood. It was the only way I could ensure none of us got hurt, except maybe me.

One side of his lip tipped. "For now."

I wanted to argue, but I knew it would do no good. Lukas had it set in his thick head that he could sway my affections. And honestly, I wasn't even sure that he couldn't. That frightened me. "You just don't give up," I mumbled.

His jaw set. "Not when it comes to you. We are connected, whether you admit it or not. Our magic links us. Together, our power is endless."

It was the mention of our combined magic that made the hair on the back of my neck stand up. I wasn't a power-hungry whore. Just the opposite. I didn't want the kind of power I had at my fingertips. The things I could do scared the bejesus out of me. I thought that Lukas understood that. "Too much power isn't necessarily a good thing," I replied, feeling like the moment we had shared was gone.

And then I got the dimple treatment. "But it can't hurt, not if it can protect you. I heard what happened to you."

I arched a brow. There was no way he could have found what I am.

"You were attacked by another witch," he supplied, filling in the blank.

"Oh right. That." I shrugged.

"*That* is a big deal. You need to be able to defend yourself." His movements got animated, becoming passionate about his opinions.

Great. Now he sounded like Gavin. "It's on my to-do list," I replied.

He took my hand. "Let me help."

I angled my head, unsure. If he returned to my daytime life, it was sure to cause a ripple in the calm between Gavin and me. On the flip side, I didn't want to hurt Lukas's feelings, either. Ugh, the dilemma that was my life. "Fine. But absolutely, positively, no fighting with Gavin." Now I just had to get the same pledge from Gavin.

Thick lashes framed his eyes on a face that looked younger than he was. "You drive a hard bargain, but if it means seeing you, then deal."

I could only hope this didn't come back to bite me in the ass later.

I woke up just a few minutes before my alarm blared through the room. Lunar was stretched out beside me, purring and watching me thoughtfully. Groaning, I flung my arms out on the bed beside me.

What am I going to do?

I took a breath, squinting from the glare of sun cutting through the curtains. Seeing Lukas hadn't gone as I planned, not that I really had a plan. To think I thought I had it all figured out, sort of. Gavin was the one my heart chose, but according to Morgana, that meant Lukas would destroy me.

This sucked.

How could I choose?

I was starting to wonder if Morgana was screwing with me. Maybe there wasn't a prophecy attached to my powers. Maybe she wasn't trying to help me at all. In my gut, I didn't really believe that. Morgana was many things—including powerful, thorny, and a diva. I felt as if I were losing my ability to trust. Doubts seeped into my mind, scrambling my choices.

One was my soul mate, the other my destroyer.

No pressure.

Yesterday, I had been so sure that Gavin was the one. Today, I wasn't sure of anything, least of all my ability to make life-altering decisions.

My stomach sank.

Dragging myself out of bed, I showered and tossed on a pair of jeans and a cardigan. I dried my hair most of the way and threw it up into a messy bun. Lacking the energy for anything else, I forwent makeup. Dreamscaping, whether or not I was driving the boat, was exhausting. My body didn't get the deep sleep it needed while I was participating in dream sharing.

A quick glance in the mirror revealed that I needed to expend a little bit of magic and do something about the dark lines under my eyes. Thank God I had finally learned a spell or two to make myself look less like a haggard witch.

Hardy-har.

CHAPTER 5

I was sitting in the lunchroom at one of the round tables with Sophie, Austin, and Tori, picking at the bread on my peanut butter and jelly sandwich. Somehow we ended up on the topics of palm reading, fortune telling, and tarot cards. I think it was Sophie's fault, but once the idea was brought up, Tori latched onto it.

"I've always wanted to go," Tori said, waving her fork in the air. A piece of macaroni dive-bombed the floor.

"I heard about this lady just outside of town who is supposed to be phenomenal. We should check it out sometime," Sophie suggested offhandedly.

Internally groaning, I already knew what was coming.

Austin gave a slight shrug. "It could be fun."

Tori wiggled excitedly in her chair, doing some kind of happy dance. "Then it's settled. The four of us will check it out after school."

Okay, this is where I exit. "I think I'll pass." I had enough weird and unusual in my life. The last thing I wanted was to have my future read, only to find out what I already knew. I was going to be a witch practicing the dark arts. How was I going to explain that to Tori and Austin? Anyway, I had Sophie, so what did I need a fortune teller for? Not to mention, I trusted Sophie a whole heck of a lot more.

This sounded like a bad idea all around.

"It will be fun," Tori pleaded, giving me her pouty lip and batting her eyes. "Say you'll come, B?"

Fun was subjective. But what had me reconsidering was I didn't want my two best friends mixed up in witch affairs. Since they were dead-set on going, someone had to keep them out of trouble, because if Sophie was recommending her, then the fortuneteller was the genuine thing. I wanted to keep my "secret life" a secret. That was the whole point, but how could I refuse with Tori giving me her pouty face? "Whatever. I'll go," I conceded.

"Yeah! Field trip, bitches," she squealed.

Austin saluted us with his half-eaten pizza. "Cheers."

I leaned my elbows on the table with my chin in my palm. "Technically, field trips are during school. This is more of an afterschool extracurricular activity."

Tori stared at me like I was a purple-people-eater from outer space. Then her pink lips curled. "Road trip, hookers," she corrected.

I rolled my eyes.

"Hmm. Check out that tall drink," Austin said, rolling his tongue.

Everyone at the table watched as Gavin swaggered in. I might have sighed, but my heart certainly did a flip-flop. He was hard to overlook. Soft shadows of light highlighted the arches of his cheekbones and the sweet curve of his lips. His eyes sought mine the moment he stepped into the room. Hiking up the pierced brow, he winked at me. The entire table sighed, except Sophie, who snorted.

I fought the dumb, love-struck grin that was trying to break free on my lips.

"Hmm. Hmm. Mmm," Austin purred.

I elbowed him in side. "Hey! That one is all mine. Get your own hot guy to drool over."

Sophie's perky little nose wrinkled. "Gross. You guys do realize that you are talking about *my brother?*"

Austin gave her a once-over. "And honey, let me tell you that the genes in your family are superb."

Sophie beamed at the compliment.

Tori guzzled half her water. "I don't know about you guys, but all this talk about sexy bods has made me thirsty."

I laughed out loud. Only Tori.

❧

No sooner had I finished my final class than I found myself sandwiched between Sophie and a pile of shopping bags in the back seat of Tori's love bug. Tori had gone on a spending spree the day before and had yet to remove the fruits of her labor.

Austin fumbled with the radio, cranking the volume when Katy Perry's acoustics blew through the speakers. Gavin opted out of our little excursion—lucky jerk. I really needed to learn to say no. A yawn escaped. *Man, I would kill for a Starbucks right now.* The lack of sleep was catching up with me.

My prayers were answered as I saw the black and green sign appear up ahead on the road—a little blurry, I might add. My shortage of zzz's was affecting my eyesight. "Need caffeine," I said, meeting Tori's gaze in the rearview mirror.

"I'll say. For a second when I looked up, I thought I was in a bad episode of The Walking Dead," she said.

I squinted. "Hilarious. I just didn't sleep well. Give me a break."

Sophie peeked at me from the corner of eyes encased with enviously long lashes. I knew that look. It said, "I know what you were doing in your dreams last night." And she was right.

I was going to have to tell Gavin now.

But right now, I needed to take the heat off me. No more questions. "So, Sophie, are you going to tell us what is up with you and Declan?" It was a little underhanded of me, bringing up the other day, but I panicked, and it was her fault I was stuck going to get my palm read.

My little announcement got everyone's attention. Heads whipped toward the backseat, including the driver. Tori's car swerved off the road and when she jerked the steering wheel back in the other direction, she over-corrected her little car. I was flung from one side of the car to the other. She was going to kill us.

Austin's light green eyes stared at Sophie through his wire-rimmed glasses. "You and Dec? Girl, I thought you had better taste than that. He is dirtier than a monkey's butt."

I snickered.

"It was nothing. He just drove me home. Once," she defended, glancing at her painted nails.

"And Gavin blew a gasket," I added.

She speared me with a look of exasperation. "He overacts. It runs in the family." This started a whole new discussion on the inner workings of family and how annoying they can be.

Slumping against the seat, I stared out the window as Tori swung her car into the Starbucks drive-thru. At least this trip wouldn't be a complete waste of my time. A caramel macchiato was worth it, in my book.

The cup warmed my hands as we drove outside Holly Ridge to the border of Hampstead. I wouldn't quite call Hampstead a town, but more of a golfing community. It was nestled off of Route 17 between Jacksonville and Wilmington.

I was a little surprised when the GPS announced that we had arrived at our destination. Tori pulled her little car over to the shoulder and stuck it in park. "Well, doesn't this look quaint?" she commented as we all looked out the window at the cornflower-blue cottage-style house.

With my nose pressed to the glass, I saw a neon sign flashing the word *FORTUNES* in one of the bay windows. "What is she doing way out here? I can't imagine she gets a whole lot of business." It just seemed like a strange location for a woman trying to make a living by reading people's palms or whatever.

She was the only house on the street.

Walking up three wooden steps, I turned the handle and pushed. Wind chimes above the threshold jingled, the door squeaked, and floorboards groaned under my feet. At our entrance, the sound of a bird squawked from somewhere at the back of the house. Candles flickered in every free space available, which wasn't much. The room was cluttered with junk: glass bottles stuffed with dried herbs, crushed flowers, colored liquids, and oils. There were chunks of crystals on a wooden board with symbols charred into it. I ran my finger over the markings. All manner of magical things lived in this house.

And yep, I felt it.

My blood sang with the vibration of energy. It felt as if there were a spell encompassing the house—maybe for protection? I couldn't exactly ask Sophie.

"Hello?" Sophie called out. Her voice bounced around in the small space.

An old, round mahogany table sat in the middle of the next room, which looked like it would have been the dining room. A dark burgundy runner ran down the center of the table, along with a stack of worn cards and a cloudy crystal ball. My fingers itched to touch the ball, but the moving, milky substance in it made it feel like that was not a smart idea.

The room smelled of candle wax, dust, and perfume. Shimmering purple-gold curtains lined the walls around the room. I ran my finger down the velvety material as I walked.

"Oh—" I gasped.

A woman, with raven hair so long I swore it almost touched the ground, had suddenly appeared in front of me. Her yellow, cat-like eyes watched me, intrigued, but she said nothing. It made me uncomfortable.

"Err... We came for a reading," I said, filling in the silence. "That is, if you are open?" I rubbed the back of my neck, trying to avoid her piercing gaze. It was as if she could see right through me.

There was a gypsy quality to her. Silver rings donned on her fingers and dangling charms at her wrists. "I am always open to those who search for answers." Her voice was rich like satin, lyrical, even. She had a trance-like quality to her tone that made your ears perk up and listen.

Under her watchful eyes, I felt squeamish, like she could peel back the layers of my secrets and see my darkest fears. "Ah, good, I guess," I mumbled. My magical tattoo tingled, and I knew, looking at this woman, that the tingling meant something. She wasn't a witch, but something else... Where was Gavin when I needed him? My glaze slid to Sophie, who met my worried expression with a weak smile.

I was going to kill her later.

With a wave of her delicate hand, the woman gestured for us to sit at the round table. I scanned the room, trying to figure out where she had come from. I was the last to sit down.

"My name is Janessa. Who would like to go first?" A soft, gentle smile lay on her crimson lips, and she looked right at me as if she expected me to raise my hand. *Hardly.*

Tori's hand shot up. "Me."

Janessa paused a moment, before she pulled her gaze from mine to Tori. "What is your choice, lovely Tori? Palm, fortune, or the cards?"

Tori gasped, shocked at Janessa's calling her by name. It actually took all of us by surprise. "Fortune," Tori answered, slightly less enthusiastic.

While Janessa rambled on about Tori's future, I fumbled with the crystals at my neck, and Janessa once again captured me with her yellow eyes. She stared at the necklace around my neck, the moonstone and amethyst. I still wore the stones I had bought from the Halloween shop. Every day. Religiously.

She must have finished with Tori's fortune, because she held the deck of tarot cards in her hands, shuffling them. "Let me read your cards," she said. And before I could decline, she was flipping over a card from the tarot deck onto the table. "Hmm." The card was that of a magician in red robes. "The magician." Her heavily lined eyes narrowed. "You will become a conduit for great power. The forces of creation and destruction have always been at your hand."

I swallowed hard.

She turned over another and ran her fingers over the weathered card of what looked like a princess in a teal and gold gown. The condition of the cards made it obvious that she had done this frequently. "The high priestess. She acts as a guide to those of us willing to venture deep within ourselves, to discover the true hidden powers inside."

I shifted restlessly in my chair. *Swell.*

I wanted to tell her to stop, but at the same time, I was intrigued, pulled by the lure of her voice and my expectancy of the next card.

The subsequent card to land on the table elicited a unanimous gasp from all of us: the devil. She glanced up. "You are holding yourself back, restricting your abilities. The chains that bind the devil are loose enough that you can break free of this hold, but only if and when you believe in yourself." The last card was a soft yellow-white globe. "The moon's appearance means that not all is as it seems. That vigilance and perception will be necessary to show the hidden before it is too late."

The hidden?

What was that supposed to mean?

Why did everything involving magic and the supernatural have to be so damn mysterious? It was so blasted hair-pulling.

As I was biting my lip, her hand shot across the table, landing on top of mine. The grasp she had was so tight that I was unable to pull away. And then if that hadn't hit high enough on the freaky scale, her eyes rolled back in her head, like glowing balls of white.

For crying out loud. Now what?

I stiffened.

"There is only one thing that can save your soul from the darkness. Moondust. Seek the dust of the moon when you need light. It will bring you back from the dark."

Say what?

My friends' eyeballs popped out of their heads. Well, that was awkward. I didn't know about them, but I had to get out of there. I jerked my hands out from underneath her and stood. "Thanks," I mumbled and promptly left.

"That was like no tarot reading I've ever seen," Sophie mumbled as she slipped into the backseat. She gave me a pointed look that said, *we had to tell Gavin about what happened.*

I sighed.

She was right.

The whispers of the night fell silent the whole way home. Even Tori had nothing to say, and that was a first. I guess our little visit to wacky Janessa had us all on edge. Come tomorrow, I figured Tori and Austin would have a string of questions. They would be raving about the fortuneteller for weeks.

I just wanted to forget it.

When I got home, I was too tired to put any real thought into dinner. Aunt Clara was going to be at the shop late, so I was on my own.

Joy.

Grabbing a package of ramen, I dumped the noodles and water into a bowl and popped it into the microwave, setting the timer. I stared at my hands, wondering if I could just zap the water to boiling. My stomach growled. I was too hungry to experiment on my dinner. Storms were more my thing, anyway. I guess I could strike the soup with a bolt of lightning—likely a messy approach.

As I waited for my soup, I gazed out the kitchen window, frowning. The moon glowed white and full tonight. I loved twilight. Nightfall on the beach, with the foamy water at my feet, was nirvana.

The microwave dinged. Gripping my unhealthy bowl of sodium and noodles, I went into the small study and sat at the desk. Powering up the laptop my aunt and I shared, I slurped on the soup as I waited. There had been something nagging at me since my bizzaro reading with Janessa.

It was not as if I could ask Lukas, because then I would have to explain that I had my cards read, which would be followed by uncontrollable laughter. I mean, there had to be some things I could figure out on my own.

I pulled up Google and typed in MOONDUST. I'm not sure what I was expecting to get, but it was mostly crap about video games and actual dust from the moon. I don't think Janessa had been implying either of those things—I hoped not. Otherwise I totally got scammed. But I knew that she wasn't a fake; there are some things you can't pretend.

Quickly, I realized that I needed to be a little more specific.

Let's try this again, Google.

This time I typed MOONDUST IN SPELLS and hit enter. Skimming headline after headline, I found nothing of real use that told me what moondust was. But I did get quite acquainted with some wacky spells I contemplating trying, and then I thought better of it. I didn't want to blow up my house. Ugh. That was the last thing I needed—to be homeless.

By the time I gave up the search, my half-eaten noodles were cold and stuck together. I dropped the bowl into the sink, too drowsy to even clean it off.

Just as I was about to head to the stairs, I heard a rap on the window at the back door. For a startled moment, my heart jumped in my chest. What if it was another witch attempting to chop my head off... or worse? Was there something worse than losing your head?

Peeping around the corner, I saw a shadowy figure through the window. Panic squeezed my ribs. The figure's head glanced up, and I felt a scream bubble up in the back of my throat. My fingers clenched the wall.

Eyes like dark blue diamonds sparkled through the glass.

"Gavin," I exhaled.

CHAPTER 6

"Hey," he greeted me nonchalantly, like I hadn't just almost peed myself.

I pulled him inside by the front of his hoodie. "Damn it. You scared the crap out of me."

Gavin smirked. "Sorry," he said, though he didn't look it.

I shut the door and ran my hands up and down my arms. Brr. It was cold outside. "What are you doing here?"

"I needed to see you. I hope that's okay...?"

Um, yeah. "Do you even have to ask?" I slipped into his arms and tipped back my head. "You are not going to believe the kind of day I had."

He pressed his lips to my right temple and then to my left. "Sophie sort of filled me in. Sounded like... a typical day with my sister."

Good, because I wasn't sure I had the energy for a play-by-play of the freakish events. "Remind me to say no next time she wants to hang out."

He laughed. The sound was a dark zap to the gut—the good, tingling kind.

I yawned. A big, unholy yawn.

"You're tired. I won't stay long." He kissed the tip of my nose.

The problem was that I didn't want him to leave, but he was right about one thing: I was practically asleep on my feet—and it was entirely Lukas's fault. If Lukas needed to talk to me, he was going to have to find means besides hijacking my dreams. It was wreaking havoc on my life. My grades were slipping, and my aunt was counting on me to help out at the shop. In short, I needed my beauty rest, and Lukas was just going to have to accept that, or I would push him out if I had to.

I pulled out of Gavin's arms, stopping at the bottom of the stairs. Resting a hand on the banister, I turned around. "I was just going to bed. You coming?"

He angled his head, and then his lips stretched into a grin. "Thought you'd never ask."

I paused, waiting for him, and then I slipped my fingers through his as we climbed the stairs, hand in hand. Even as exhausted as I was, I felt giddy. Gavin, in my bedroom, alone—dream come true. And way overdue. We really hadn't had any "quality time" together, if you get my drift. I was in need of some serious lip-locking.

Pushing him inside my room, I shut the door behind us, softly clicking the lock in place. Insurance, just in case Aunt Clara decided to check on me. I kicked off my shoes. "God, it feels like forever since I've seen a bed."

Gavin backed into the room, grinning, with a wicked gleam in his eyes. "I really hope that is code for something naughty."

Gathering the ends of my sweater, I raised a brow. His blue eyes deepened, and I lifted my shirt over my head. "Not tonight, Slick," I said, the corners of my lips curving. I had a tank top on underneath. The teasing had been fun; however, there was a good chance it would backfire on me.

Forcing myself not to laugh at his down-turned lips, I climbed into bed. Gavin slipped under the covers, turning on his side to face me. I closed my eyes, breathing in his warmth. He ran a hand through my tangled hair. I normally brushed it before going to bed, but tonight I was too drained to do my nighttime routine.

When I opened my eyes, I saw that the twinkle in his eyes had faded. "You need to be more careful."

Not this speech again.

I had a pretty decent-sized bed. When it was just me, I felt like I was swimming in space and blankets, but the moment Gavin got in, it suddenly seemed small. His feet touched the edge of the bed, and Lunar was having none of this sharing. He meowed at us, raised his tail, and left for a more spacious place to doze.

I shifted, resting my head on my hands to meet his stare. "Nothing happened." *Unless you counted Janessa's creepy freak-out.*

His arms slid behind his head. "True, but it got me thinking. I should have gone with you. Nowhere is safe anymore, not with your face and stats on every witch's Most Wanted."

"There is no way for you to be by my side 24-7."

"Wanna bet?" he challenged, going He-Man on me.

I found it kind of hot, but still, his idea of being my shadow was out of the question. "I don't need a bodyguard."

A muscle in his jaw jumped. "That is exactly what you need."

I huffed. "I take it you've been giving this a lot of thought?"

"It's been on my mind a time or two, between trying to weasel information."

"And what about you? It's okay for you to go gallivanting in what is dubbed as the witches' bad part of town? Isn't your life in danger while you are digging around, asking questions about me?" I thought those were all extremely valid questions. I was a concerned girlfriend.

"I can take care of myself."

He could be so stubborn. Irritation spiked. I sat up. "And I am just a weak, uneducated witch who can barely cast a proper spell." Dry lightning cracked.

His eyes flashed like the light I created. "Now you are putting words in my mouth. You know that is not how I think of you."

How had things gotten so heated so fast? Fighting was taking more energy than I had to give. He was right. That had been a low blow. We both knew that I could do some pretty wicked magic, including the little light show that was going on outside. My eyes traveled to the window, watching the sky light up. "I'm sorry," I apologized.

Gavin ran his fingers through his dark hair, stretching the material of his cotton shirt taut over the muscles in his chest. "I don't want to argue; that wasn't my intent when I came here. I just... missed you."

What girl on any planet could possibly stay mad after that? Not me. My heart softened and went all mushy. "Me, too." I reposition myself into his arms, sighing. "Can you get the lights?"

His lips quirked up. "With my hands tied behind my back."

The room was suddenly engulfed in blackness, except for the occasional flicker of lightning. It was slowly dying, along with my temper. Lying in the dark, I asked, "What do you know about moondust?"

Twisting his head, he looked down at me. "I've never heard of it. Why do you ask?"

I shrugged. "It was just something the fortuneteller mentioned."

He exhaled, running his hand along my spine. "And you think it is important?"

I shrugged. "I don't know. It's probably nothing. I was mostly curious."

For a few minutes, a comfortable silence unfolded between us. There was a security and ease I hadn't felt in a long time that came with being wrapped in Gavin's arms. Somehow my mind and body knew that, with him sleeping beside me, my dreams would be undisturbed. And I didn't want him to leave.

Just as I was about to succumb to sleep, I felt Gavin press his lips to my forehead. "Sweet dreams, Bri."

My eyes fluttered open. I couldn't believe what I was about to say. "Stay. Don't leave." I stretched my arm over his chest, keeping him close.

"What about your aunt?" he asked, running the back of his knuckles down my cheek.

Winding my arms around his neck, I replied, "Can't you just make yourself invisible?"

He arched a brow.

"Don't worry." I tugged him closer, suddenly not feeling so sleepy. "She goes straight to bed. After the hours she works at the shop, she always falls asleep as soon as her head hits the pillow. Where is your car?"

Even in the dark, I saw his eyes glimmer with desire, doing crazy things to my belly. "On the side of the road."

I grinned. "Perfect. What about your parents?"

He nibbled on my earlobe. "Jared will cover for me," he murmured, his breath tickling my ear.

The moment our lips met, static tingled, and I jolted in shock. Our kisses were literally becoming electric. He ran the pad of his thumb over my lips. "That is wildly crazy. You pack quite a punch."

A short laugh escaped me. "Tell me about it."

His lips drifted over my cheek. "It's sexy."

My eyes wavered shut as he kissed me again, but this time it was soft, heartbreakingly so. But it didn't take long for the sweet, tender kiss to deepen. We were kissing, really kissing. The I-don't-need-oxygen kind of kissing. One of his fingers hooked into one of my belt loops, yanking me to him.

My lips parted. With the sweep of my tongue, I took it to a whole new level, evolving the kiss into an explosive hotness. Gavin's hands moved down to my hips, pulling me underneath him, leaving not even a millimeter of space between us.

His fingers slipped under my tank top, then splayed across my bare stomach. My pulse hammered, and my veins filled with magic. Gavin growled as I scraped his bottom lip with my teeth, sliding my tongue over the silver hoop on his lip.

I was going to lose a lot more than sleep, my shirt, and my sanity, if we kept attacking each other, yet I couldn't seem to make myself stop. It was a good thing Gavin had control over his hormones, because I was pretty much powerless against mine.

"I have to stop kissing you now, or I won't be able to later," he murmured.

I was having a hard time seeing through the lustful haze Gavin had induced, but I groaned because he was right. As much as I really wanted to kick this up to the next mind-blowing level, tonight wasn't the night. I wanted to be fully aware of every moment, every touch, and every sensation. I wanted to treasure the memory. "I know," I conceded, but it was hard to get my body to agree.

His eyes darkened to a color deeper than indigo. Voice thick, he said the words that made my heart jump into my throat. "I love you, Bri."

I nestled my head on his shoulder, laying my hand over his heart. "I love you more," I mumbled sleepily.

When I was in his arms, it was easy to convince myself that I was hopelessly in love with Gavin. Everything about our being together made sense and felt right—a perfect match.

CHAPTER 7

Valentine's Day—barf.

I despise mushy holidays like this one. It was overrated and another excuse to spend money on crap I didn't need. But for Mystic Floral, it was a jackpot—the busiest freaking day of the year. And I got to work an eight-hour shift. Go me. Good thing I didn't have any hot plans with my boyfriend.

My cheeks flushed as I leaned on the glass counter, daydreaming about the things he had done with his hands last night. I think I spaced out, because the next thing I knew, Aunt Clara was eyeing me over a banquet of long-stemmed roses, clearing her throat.

"Sorry?" I posed as a question, just in case I was in trouble.

She set the red buds aside, pulling out a pencil from behind her ear. "Bored?"

I shrugged. "Not really, just enjoying the quiet before the storm of chaos strikes."

"Hmm. That reminds me. Only seven days to go. We need to take a quick inventory and make sure that we are fully stocked for next week." The end of her pencil tapped on the counter.

I groaned. "Valentine's sucks."

She smiled softly at me. "Well, babe, the rest of the world adores love. And so do their wallets."

I tucked my hair back. "Do you ever get sick of flowers?"

Running a finger along the petals delicately, she got a wistful look. I guess I got my answer. "Honestly, I don't. The running the business part, sure; it can be overwhelming at times. But the moment I shut myself in the back room, and it's just me and the sweet smell of freesia, tulips, and daffodils, I forget about everything else. It calms me," she said.

"I need something like that in my life," I mumbled.

"We all do. Don't worry. I have every confidence that you will find what makes you happy."

Maybe I already had. Using magic—and the ocean—they gave me a tranquility I'd never felt. I must have gotten a goofy look on my face.

Aunt Clara laughed. "And I am not talking about a boy. No matter how magnificent his butt looks in jeans."

I made a face. "Are we talking about you or me now?"

"Umm. I'm ninety percent sure we were talking about you," she said.

Narrowing my eyes, I looked at her, really looked at her. Something was different. "Did you get your hair cut?"

"Maybe," she replied, a hand smoothing down her long hair.

It also looked extra caramel-y. "And highlights? Geez, what's the special occasion?"

She gave me a dry look even as her eyes shined.

"Oh. Is *Chad* taking you out for V-day?" I drew air-hearts when I said his name.

Aunt Clara giggled. She giggled!

Apparently someone had been struck by Cupid's arrow—in a bad way. "Possibly," she said, busying her hands with the roses.

I screwed up my face.

She shook her head, her hair falling over her shoulder. "How did I end up with such an anti-romantic niece?"

Leaning back on the stool, I replied, "It just seems like such a gigantic waste for one day. I don't need flowers, chocolates, or candles to feel loved. You should be able to feel it in the little things that cost nothing. Like a hug or a kiss..."

This earned me a grin. "I see. So I can assume then that you and Gavin don't have any romantic plans?"

I rolled my eyes. "I hope he saves us both the embarrassment."

She flicked the end of my nose. "By the way, just so I know... have you and Gavin been doing a lot of, you know... kissing?"

My cheeks flamed an ungodly shade of red. "Ugh. We are not having this talk at work, are we?"

Grabbing a pair of shears from one of the drawers, she began to trim the stems off the roses. "Hmm. I guess not. So that is a yes?"

I dropped my head into my hands.

She laughed, turning around and leaning against the counter. "So I've been meaning to ask you how things are going with Gavin and Lukas?"

My heart pitter-pattered. "Can I plead the fifth?"

"And here I was under the impression that you had that all squared away. You are dating Gavin, right?"

Technically, yes. But it is little more complex than that, Aunt Clara. You see, I am sharing dreams with one and making out with the other, but my heart is conflicted. I am mixing up love for a friend with the real thing. Got any advice for that? I smiled. "Yeah, Gavin and I are dating."

"And you and Lukas are...?" She left the sentence open for me to finish.

Somehow I knew before I even opened my mouth, my answer was going to bite me in the butt. "Friends?" That was the most pathetic response. I cringed.

Concern flickered over her pretty face. "You don't need to convince me, Brianna. You need to convince yourself."

I sighed heavily. She was right. Someday I was going to be able to make decisions without second-guessing myself. I was going to have the confidence to make the right choices—possibly when my life wasn't so complicated.

Who was I kidding?

My life was always going to be a mess. Unless, of course, I laced up my pointy boots, put on my black hat, and got this witch crap down pat. *Do I embrace it or hide from it?* I had been struggling with that decision all year.

The deeper I got in magic business, the scarier *I* became. It frightened me to think of the kind of person I might become if I fully accepted my fate as a witch. There was still this pinch of darkness inside me from when I had taken the tiniest bit of Gavin's magic.

On the other hand, if I turned away from my powers, would I risk losing Gavin? Would I lose a part of myself that I had only just found? Now that I have tapped into this part of me, I wasn't sure I could just turn it off or walk away. I had unlocked a piece that was tied to my birthright. By refusing it, I felt like I would be rejecting my parents.

The door chimed, and my aunt's face lit up. I figured it was Chad, so I didn't bother to look and kept twiddling with the pen in my hand. When I felt the undeniable tingles of a witch, my head snapped up. Gavin. I hadn't expected to see him so soon, especially since we spent the night together.

My heart somersaulted and fireflies started to prance in my belly.

"Your ears must be ringing. Brianna and I were just talking about you," Aunt Clara said as Gavin walked further into the shop.

He had a cat-caught-the-mouse grin on his lips. "Should I be worried?" he teased.

I steadied my hand on the counter. It was all I could do to keep from falling out of my chair. His dark hair was windblown and utterly sexy, and he made jeans look sinful.

Aunt Clara gathered her newly-cut roses in her arms. "Good luck with this one, Gavin. She's a cynic." Then she disappeared to her workroom to do what she did best.

I faced Gavin, sapphire eyes twinkling at me. Propping a hip against the counter, his fingers danced over my open palm, drawing circles. "So I was thinking for Valentine's D—"

I let out a long, loud groan before he even finished the word.

His brows rose. "I am guessing by the ghastly look on your face, you hate all things Valentine's."

I stood up from my seat. "See, you totally get me."

"Bri," he sighed.

I rolled my eyes. "If it makes you feel any better. I have to work all day. I promised Aunt Clara that I would close that night. She and *Chad* are going to paint the town red. She deserves it."

He twirled his lip ring with his teeth. It was dangerously hot... and distracting as hell.

Unable to resist, I walked around the counter and pressed my lips to his in a kiss that ended far too soon. "Did you just come to talk about the *V-word* or did you have something else on your mind?" I let my gaze roam to his lips.

His head dipped and—

The door chimed again. Slightly annoyed by the interruption, I looked over Gavin's shoulder, slowly letting my arms fall from around his neck. I sucked in a breath.

God hates me. That was my first thought as I watched Lukas saunter in through the door. Feeling the surge of another witch's energy signature, Gavin stiffened. Spinning around, he gave a quick jerk of his chin. I bit my lip, trying to decide how best to handle this situation. There was way too much male witch-osterone suddenly filling the small shop.

"What is *he* doing here?" Gavin asked under clenched teeth.

"How should I know?" I whispered.

"Bri," he growled.

Lukas had a carefree attitude and an air of confidence about him as he walked toward us, but he had nothing on Gavin's lethal, domineering presence.

This was going to be bad—epically bad.

Gavin's hand rested on the small of my back. The marking-my-territory move wasn't lost on any of us.

Lukas snickered. "Hey, Brianna." His emerald eyes slid to mine. "Sorry. Am I interrupting?" He didn't look all that remorseful or intimidated.

Just freaking Yankee-dandy-doo.

The last time the three of us were under the same roof, the two of them had decided to declare war on each other. I didn't want a repeat of that. Placing a hand on Gavin's arm, I felt his muscles bunch. Before I could mediate, a current of power coursed through Gavin's fingers and shot across the room, striking Lukas.

Lukas jerked back, scowling. "Cheap shot. I knew you were a tool."

And the name-calling has ensued.

I blinked, and that was all it took for Lukas to send an electric spark of his own. Gavin stepped out in front of me, making sure he was the only target. It hit him on the forearm.

Gavin hissed, shaking his arm. He cracked his neck. "I'm just glad you are finally showing your true colors so Bri can see what a douchebag you really are." His voice was full of contempt.

The two of them could not be in the same building, let alone the same room. I stepped out from behind Gavin and put myself between them. Maybe not the smartest move, but they left me with very few choices. "Look, hotheads. My aunt is the next room, and I really don't need her to come out and see the two of you throwing around spells and destroying her shop, so knock it off. I don't want to have to play nasty."

Lukas snorted.

I gave him a dry look. "Lukas, why are you here?"

His eyes were glaring over my head at Gavin. "I can see that my timing was bad." Then his gaze dropped to me, again. "I'll catch up with you later. It can wait. Maybe, tonight...while you're sleeping?"

That was low. And sneaky. I didn't like it, And neither did Gavin.

His lips thinned. "You go anywhere near her dreams, and you'll be having nightmares about what I'll do to your face."

Now that we got the threatening part out of the way, I figured I needed to defuse the situation, stat. "Lukas, I think you should go."

A flash of anger jumped behind his green eyes before he smothered it with cockiness and a smirk. "I'll talk to you later."

Gavin shove a hand through his hair after Lukas left the same way he had come—without a care in the world. "I really dislike that guy. There is something about him, something in his eyes when he looks at you."

He had made his contempt for Lukas abundantly clear. "You think he is dangerous," I supplied. Truthfully, the same could be said about Gavin. There was a purely predatory vibe about him.

His eyes softened a tad. "Just promise me you'll be careful?"

I nodded.

꧁꧂

LAST NIGHT I had sleep like crap, and for once it wasn't because I was dreamscaping, so I couldn't even blame Lukas. I had a nightmare.

The screwed up part is that *I* was the nightmare—my magic-stealing powers and me. I was still trying to convince myself it hadn't been real. In the dream, I had been a monster with a black heart, fueled by greed, blackness, and a hunger for power I never felt before. I didn't recognize myself. As I was right on the brink of consciousness, I heard a laugh—sinister, spine-chilling, and familiar.

When I woke up, I lay there, staring at the ceiling, beating myself up about letting my insecurities get to me. I hated that I let something so stupid upset me. My dreams weren't prophetic—that I knew. I didn't have to become that person. I wasn't doomed to be a bad witch.

After a long huff, I finally dragged my butt into the bathroom. I washed my wash face, brushed my teeth, and changed out of my jammies. The simple morning routine felt comforting. Twisting my second-day hair into a messy bun, I was ready to start my day.

No sooner had I stepped into the halls of Holly Ridge High than I was waylaid by an all-too-real nightmare. Unfortunately for her, this bully didn't know who she was really dealing with. If she had seen what I had in my dream, she would have run from me screaming.

"Hey, freak," a sweet and sour voice said from just over my shoulder.

Oh, goodie. Just how I like to start my mornings—going a round with Rianne.

CHAPTER 8

I told myself to keep walking, but my legs didn't obey. *Treacherous body*. Pivoting on the balls of my feet, I faced the queen bitch and shot her a look of extreme annoyance. "Is there a point in all this? Because I'm over you and your extra-large mouth."

Her amber eyes flamed. "I'm on to you. I've seen your eyes. They're not right," she spat.

For a brief moment, I contemplated the idea of body-slamming her right in the middle of the hall. "Maybe you need to get yours checked," I snapped, trying to act like I didn't know what she was talking about, but inside I was having an "oh shit" moment.

She wasn't deterred. "I know that there is something wrong with you, something abnormal. You're not human."

We were starting to attract a crowd. I caught a curious gaze from Sophie and a "do-you-have-a-death-wish" look from Austin. I knew I needed to keep my anger in check. "You don't know shit, Rianne. And if you knew what was good for you..." I took a step forward, completely forgetting about reining in my anger and got in her face. "... you would forget about me."

Her eyes gleamed in satisfaction, like she knew she was onto something. I wanted to wipe her face with the floor. And I might have, if I

419

hadn't noticed Rianne's eyes shift to someone behind me. Her pink lips curled.

The tattoo at my back tingled.

"Problem?" Lukas's voice came from beside me.

I snuck a glance from the corner of my eyes just to make sure my ears weren't playing tricks on me.

What the heck was Lukas doing in high school? At my school?

Rianne looked Lukas up and down and up again. An expression of interest shone on her heart-shaped face. "Your threats don't mean dick to me," she seethed, and then flipped her long blonde hair in my face. My fingers twitched to reach out and yank her back.

Lukas's hand closed over my wrist firmly, keeping me from moving. I could feel the pulse of my racing heart against his touch. "And who was that she-devil who was defaming your name?" he asked.

"No one worth mentioning," Austin muttered. He and Sophie had maneuvered their way to my side as the crowd began to shuffle down the halls again.

Bless his heart.

Sophie took a different approach. "That was the school hoe bag, and a general pain in the ass," she supplied.

Lukas blessed us with his dimples. All three of us were dazzled. "Oh, one of those. It's unfortunate, but every school has them. Wait until you get to college."

I picked up the messenger bag I had dropped on the floor in preparation for a possible beat-down with Rianne. "What are you doing here?" I asked, remembering that he was at my school—a place he shouldn't be.

"I came to see you," he replied.

"Oh." I knew that he was watching for my reaction. I kept my expression blank, for everyone's sake. "Now?"

His shoulder nudged mine. "School is overrated. Want to ditch?"

This was the second time in a week I was proposition to skip school. *What gives? It's not like I make a habit of it.* The last time I had skipped out on a class had been the day I met Gavin, and that triggered a little jog down Memory Lane. A small smile tugged at my lips.

"Earth to Brianna," Austin said, waving a hand in front of my face.

I blinked just as the bell buzzed.

"Are you coming?" Sophie asked, giving Lukas a disapproving glare. Her dislike was as clear as her brother's.

I shook my head. "Go ahead. I don't want to make you late."

"Are you sure?" There was hesitancy in her voice, and her cobalt eyes were filled with worry. She didn't want to leave me alone with Lukas. I couldn't figure out whether that was because she didn't trust Lukas or whether it was out of loyalty to Gavin.

It didn't matter.

Obviously Lukas needed to talk. She was just going to have to trust me.

With one last glance over her shoulder, Sophie and Austin both disappeared into the crowd. I faced Lukas now that we were almost alone. A few stragglers lingered in the halls. "What is going on? Why are you stalking me at school?"

Smugness crept across his face. "Someone's feeling feisty this morning." He took my elbow in his hand, leading me down the hall, and I let him.

"It's been a hell of a morning."

A glimmer of mystery sprang in his eyes. "Excellent, because I am about to blow your mind."

That didn't sound pleasant. "I am not positive my mind can handle that right now," I mumbled.

"I know what you can do, and what you are. I want to help you," he whispered, low enough for just my ears.

I tripped, my head snapping in his direction. Bug-eyed, I felt my mouth hit the floor. I really needed to work on masking my emotions. "W-what?" I stuttered, slumping against the nearest wall for support. No way he meant what I thought he meant, right?

He stopped, caging me by placing a hand on either side of my arms. "I take it by the goofy look on your face, that I took you by surprise. Well, I'll let you in a little secret: I've known for a while."

My eyes sharpened. I didn't like that he kept so many secrets from me. Every time I turned around, he was admitting something else. He knew I was a witch. He knew I wasn't just a dream. He knew that I could dreamscape. And apparently my darkest secret—that I was a clàr silte.

I got an uneasy tingle down my neck. "What are you talking about?" I pretended ignorance, not yet ready to reveal the truth. It was possible that we weren't talking about the same thing at all. And if Morgana was right, one of them, Gavin or Lukas, wasn't who he claimed to be but which? I was more confused than ever. Gavin already knew the horrible thing I could do. It wasn't because I trusted him more, but because he had been my first victim. Kind of unavoidable.

But Lukas...

Was it an unfair advantage that one knew and not the other? What if the only way I could figure out which one truly cared for me were to tell them both, put them on even playing fields? My heart and my head were at war with each other, but I knew that for my safety and my aunt's, I couldn't make any mistakes.

"It's okay. You can trust me," Lukas said.

My gaze fell. "I've got to get to class." I turned, but his hand shot out, preventing me from my intended slippery escape. I wanted to mull over some ideas before I said anything I couldn't take back.

"You've got this all wrong, Brianna. I want to help you harness your gift. You are extremely powerful, and there are risks—ginormous ones. But I know you can handle them."

A faint tremor went through me. What he was implying scared me to death. The small taste of power I had gotten was too alluring, like a drug. I didn't want to become addicted; there would be no stopping the monster it unleashed.

No, I didn't want it.

Shaking his arm off, I said, "I'll talk to you later."

He gave a slight nod of his head. "I think your boyfriend wants to rearrange my face. I guess you aren't the only one with trust issues."

I rolled my eyes and took off down the hall, Gavin quickly materializing at my side, matching my strides. "What did asshole want?"

I didn't know what to say, but I knew if I told him the truth, he would go ape shit. I needed time to think. "Nothing," I muttered. "He wanted to know if we're still going to practice you-know-what."

His eyes went gloomy. "And?"

"I told him that I had to think it over." I glanced at the clock hanging in the hallway. Classes had started five minutes ago.

Damn.

⚜

I RETREATED to an empty corner of the library. My schoolwork had been suffering for the last few months, and I was having a hard time concentrating, understandably. There had been a lot of crazy distractions in my life, but if I wanted to graduate, I needed to get my head back on task.

With about as much enthusiasm as I had for eating Brussels sprouts, I opened my massive trig book and prepared to fry my brain. Math has that effect on me. Flipping open my notebook, I searched the bottom of my bag for a pencil. The chair beside me scraped across the floor, and a stack of books joined mine on the table with a thump.

"So you are back to hiding out in the library?"

I lifted my lashes, spotting Sophie's angelic face and exhaling a rush of air. "It is the only way I have time to actually study, lately."

The material of her jeans rustled as she made herself comfortable in the seat next to me. "Is my brother sneaking into your room at night?"

I was pretty sure she was teasing, but my jaw dropped. Maybe we hadn't been as inconspicuous or clever as we had thought. I had one guy who slipped into my room and the other invaded my dreams. How do I get myself into these pickles?

I sat back in my chair. "Sophie, how is my aura today?" I hadn't really expected there to be a change in the dark spots that had appeared on my aura, but it was worth a shot. I believed in miracles. And I was in desperate need of one.

She tilted her head to the side, studying the outline of my profile, seeing the colored glow of my spirit. "It's a bluish-gray. You are under a lot of stress and..." She paused. "You still doubt yourself." Her eyes became sympathetic. "Regardless of what you think, you have come a long way. Magic isn't learned or controlled overnight. Don't be so hard on yourself."

If she only knew the half of it, and what I had done to her brother, then she might not be so understanding.

Sometimes it sucked that she could read me so well. I sighed. "And the spots?"

She nodded. "Still there. I can't be positive, and I didn't want to alarm you, but I think they might have spread."

I tried to keep the disappointment from my face. It made perfect sense, though. I had done unthinkable magic. "I was afraid you were going to say that."

"What are you going to do?"

The million-dollar question. I tapped my pencil on the table. "What can I do?"

She stayed with me, keeping me company as I worked on my homework. It was nice not to be alone, even if I got the impression she was looking out for me, making sure I was okay. On our way out of the library, she paused at the double doors. "Hey, how about we catch a movie sometime soon—you, Austin, Tori and me? Take your mind off all the crap."

I smiled. I liked the sound of that. "Sure."

She beamed at me and waved as we split off down the halls.

The rest of my day felt like all I did was play catch-up. I went straight home after school. Evading Gavin's dangerous smirks and the insinuations behind them had been challenging, but somehow I had managed.

Scooping up my black furball, Lunar and I headed upstairs to my room. I was thinking I needed a power nap, but first I had to take care of something. I reached into my bag and dug out my cellphone. Sending a quick text to Lukas, I waited for his reply, nuzzling my face into Lunar's silky-soft coat. A moment later he responded, and nervous knots formed in my stomach.

Have you thought any more about my offer?

Have I ever. It was all I thought about. **Yep.**

You aren't going to be cruel and leave me hangin', are you?

He texted back immediately.

My fingers danced over the keys. **I just don't know if I can trust you.**

Ouch. You wound me.

I plopped on my bed. **Whatever.**

My phone buzzed. **You know that I can help you.**

Did I? I guess it was time to lay all the cards on the table. **Fine. After school tomorrow. We'll talk.**

There. The decision was made. Now I hoped I had the gonads to go through with it, and whatever needed to be done. I knew that at the end of all this I would have to say goodbye to one of them.

I pressed my hand over my chest. The idea of losing either Gavin or Lukas gave me chest pains. Morgana better be right about this, or I was never going to forgive her for putting so much stress on my shoulders. Family or not, she'd better not be screwing with me.

And the plot of my so-called life curdles.

I felt like I was playing a dangerous game, where the stakes were higher than anything I would face in my life again. This was it. Sink or swim. I needed to figure out who I could trust. Keep your enemies closer, they say, except I didn't know who my enemies were.

I think Morgana just wanted to torment me.

Her visits had become few and far between, so why not today? It was already a pretty strange day, and I was feeling overwhelmed. Her timing was always impeccable.

CHAPTER 9

To add another layer of demented to my life, Morgana didn't call me in my sleep. She summoned me while I was still awake.

WTF?

No sooner had I sent my last text to Lukas than I started to feel a coldness wash over me. Rolling over on my back, I took a deep breath, eyes fixed on the ceiling. I knew the moment the ice touched my blood that something was going to happen. If there was one thing that I was getting good at, it was recognizing things as super-natural.

I blinked, which might have been a mistake.

A blinding white light flashed behind my eyes. The kind that leaves your vision impaired by glowing circles. *Just relax*, said a voice inside my head. *Don't fight it.* I forced my limbs to go lax, letting myself get sucked under.

It was like daydreaming on crack.

The foggy white mist began to fade from my vision and was replaced by a deep purple and orange sunset. The lines streaked across the horizon. Tall elms encased the small clearing, where I found myself with a spectacular view of a calm pond. The setting sun reflected off the water, making it appear blacker than its apparently usual crystal blue.

I shook my head. A minute ago I had been staring at the fractures in my ceiling, and now I was in paradise. Morgana stepped into the glade. Her long red hair glittered in the sunset, flowing over her bare shoulders. She had on a fluid dress that trailed behind her over the mossy grass. It was modest, compared to some of the other getups I had seen her in. For the first time, I saw a different side of her—less seductive and more saintly.

I grinned. "It's been awhile, Grams."

She made a funny face, purplish eyes twinkling. "You make me sound old."

"You are old. Like thousands of years old."

She tapped a nail on her lips, which were fuchsia today, instead of blood red. "Oh, right. But you have to admit, I look fabulous for my age."

That she did, and I bet she could make herself appear however she desired. I actually missed her. Who would have thunk? It seemed like a lifetime ago when I thought she was trying to kill me. "You summoned me, oh Mighty One."

Her lips pursed. "Hmm. I could get used to that. It has a nice ring."

I rolled my eyes. Only Morgana would take my sarcasm and turn into flattery. "I was wondering when I was going to see you again. I have only about a gazillion questions for you. It crossed my mind that maybe you abandoned me."

She tried to hide the sad look that popped into her eyes, but she wasn't quick enough; I'd seen it. Our time together would eventually come to an end, and neither of us wanted to admit that it would royally suck. "So have you figured out my little riddle yet, love?" she asked.

I tucked my hair behind my ears, trying to keep it from blowing in my face. "You mean have I decided which one is going to destroy me? The answer is no."

"Time is ticking."

I gave her a dry glare. *Thanks for the nasty reminder.*

She waved a hand in the air. "All right. Fine. Ask away."

"What exactly do you mean, *one will destroy me?*" I needed a little more clarity here. Would one of them kill me? Or was it less literal, like one will ruin my life?

She looped her arm through mine and started to stroll, her soft slippers squishing the on the grass. "It is the soul you need to concern yourself with."

"My soul," I repeated. "The blackness."

She nodded. "There is both light and dark magic inside you. Most witches are born light and turn to darkness, but our bloodline is born with both. The choice is yours."

Wow. I didn't really think it was much of a choice. Good or bad? *Duh. I choose good.*

"And you're positive this will come to pass?" I asked.

She gave a ladylike snort. "Is my name Morgana Le Fay?"

I rolled my eyes.

She paused at the water's edge, gazing out. "No daughter of mine will be claimed by darkness, not like I was. It is why I am here—to save you from enduring a fate such as mine."

God, was I doomed? If Morgana hadn't been able to resist the temptation of power, how would I? She was the strongest witch I knew, even if she were technically dead. "You gave yourself to darkness?"

She sighed, and it was the first time I saw trouble brew in her stormy eyes. "I did. And it controlled me for many, many years. It took precious time I could never get back—never make up for. That, my dear, is why I have a very special interest in your success. Before I passed onto the other side, I rectified my wrongs. I cleansed my magic, my soul. But it was too late for me. The damage was done, irreparable at that point."

"What happened?"

She raised her face into the breeze. It carried a light scent of sea and pine. "I got a taste of the most alluring magic I'd ever felt. Combine that with a hot guy and love—I was destined to sink."

I snorted. "I can't believe you were in love."

A small smirk curved the corner of her lips. "It feels like yesterday."

Scuffing my feet as we walked, I asked, "What happened to him?"

Her mouth twisted, looking dark and ill-omened. "Why, he joined me in Hell, of course."

Gulp.

Well, that just put a damper on things. "Your soul is in H-Hell?" I couldn't even get the word out. It seemed too horrible to imagine. I knew that she was capable of unthinkable things, but I had come to know her, to care about her. Hell was no place for Morgana.

She turned me to toward her, framing her hands on my face. "Don't worry for me, love. It's not so bad: I got to see you. And if it is the last act I do, I will ensure that you don't join me."

If I had any doubts about Morgana's loyalty or her motives, they were squashed. The sheer determination in her eyes and the electric current at her fingertips did the trick. "This is all just so much," I mumbled.

Straightening up to her full height, she lifted her chin. "No one said being a witch was a walk in the park." She started walking again, and I jogged to catch up, following her on a dirt path. "So how is Dark and Handsome handling your powers?" she asked.

"Like I never tried to drain him of his powers," I mumbled.

"That bothers you," she said in more of a statement than a question.

I gave a lopsided shrug.

"And the other—the dream stalker?"

The woods opened up to a rocky shore. "He doesn't know...yet," I added. The plan was to tell him tomorrow.

Her delicate brows lifted. "Hmm. Why the hesitation? I assumed by your troubled heart that you would have already spilled the beans."

My stomach tumbled over itself. "I'm afraid to trust anyone, even myself. What if I end up hurting him, or worse?" Taking witches' powers was as bad as stealing their souls. I might as well just plunge a knife in their backs.

She scoffed. "Sounds like a lame excuse."

Was it just an excuse? Was I making things so much more complex because I was letting my fear rule me? I was so afraid of this power inside me that I couldn't see clearly.

I swallowed the lump that had suddenly formed in my throat. "Sophie says that the darkness in my soul is growing."

Her violet eyes sobered. "And it will. Every time you take an ounce of magic from another witch, it will blacken your heart. You don't use that kind of magic without a hefty price, dear."

"What if I am unable to stop myself from using it?" I knew that there was panic in my eyes as I looked up at her.

She looked directly into my eyes, and it was almost like looking at my reflection. "Do not doubt yourself. There is power in belief. Trust in that. Trust in your choices. They will make you stronger."

Ugh. She made it sound like a piece of cake.

"I wish I could steal some of your confidence."

She laughed. "I think you have plenty. It's in your blood. You just need to unleash it."

My shoulders sagged. "Tell me you have a spell for that."

Her hands touched my shoulders. "Not everything can be fixed with a spell. The storm is coming, Brianna. Be prepared." Those were her final words before the white light blinded me, and I was once again staring at my ceiling.

CHAPTER 10

T he doorbell rang, and I jumped, even though I was expecting him. I thought about asking Gavin to be here with me when I told Lukas, but then I remembered that they couldn't stand each other. I didn't want my house to suffer any damage from their fireworks.

So it was just Lukas and me—and my huge secret.

Disheveled frat boy. That was my first impression when I opened the door and saw Lukas. The North Carolina sun was hidden behind gloomy clouds, as if the skies felt my nervousness, but it didn't matter. When Lukas smiled, he brought the sun.

I frowned. "Why do you look like you just won the lottery?" His cheerfulness made me leery; it felt like he had a trick up his sleeve.

Leaning his shoulder on the doorframe, he said, "I'm just happy you came to your senses."

I wrinkled my nose. "You're weird."

Unfazed, he brushed past me into the house, and I shut the door behind him. "That's not the response I usually get."

Lunar took one peek at the newcomer and bolted out of the room, nails catching on the carpet. I glanced at the fuzzball. "I bet. Lucky for you, I am anything but normal."

His eyes laughed. "It's why I like you best."

When he said stuff like that, it made me uncomfortable. My cheeks flushed, and I shook my head helplessly. "Do you even go to classes anymore? You are still in college, aren't you?" I thought about his just popping into my school the other day.

He made himself right at home, stretching out on the couch, his long legs extending under the glass coffee table. "If the mood strikes me," he replied, settling.

I bit my lip. Enough with the pleasantries. He was making me edgy. I was trying to take Morgana's advice, to find my inner confidence, so I blurted out, "What is going on with you? Lately, you don't seem yourself." I took a seat on the chair across from him, my leg bouncing.

Angling his head to the side, he looked me in the eye. "I could say the same about you."

Okay, I deserved that, because I hadn't been myself, but what was his excuse? Maybe I should have laid off the coffee this morning; I was jittery. "If you only knew," I muttered.

His eyes sharpened, his demeanor losing some of its carefreeness. "I would if you told me, instead of pretending everything is fine when it is clearly not."

Touché. I tensed up. "Well then, you might want to brace yourself. I still haven't gotten over the shock."

He crossed his arms over his grey t-shirt, legs kicked out in front of him, and a hint of a smile on his lips. "You forget. I already know."

I hadn't forgotten—not by a long shot, but I wanted to hear him say it. "How is that? I've told no one."

He didn't bat an eye. "Not even your boyfriend?"

Silence.

My protective instincts flared.

"That's what I thought." There was smugness in his voice.

I rushed into defensive mode. "It's not like you think. I didn't give him a choice." I took a deep breath and admitted what was hard for me to say. "I'm a clàr silte." After the words flew from my mouth, I waited for him to express outrage or to scramble for the door.

Emerald eyes held steady on mine, he said, "There, that wasn't so bad, was it?"

Wow. Not the reaction I had been expecting, but he had warned me. I guess deep down, I didn't believe that he really knew what I was because, if he did, I didn't understand how he could continue to be my friend. It didn't make sense to me.

My eyes narrowed. "How do you know what I only just found out?"

"It's simple, really. Our bloodlines have crossed before," he said, as if he weren't dropping another atomic bomb.

At first I thought he was kidding, but as I stared at him, I came to realize he was being serious—dead serious.

Will everything that comes out of his mouth shock me?

I gaped at him.

Upon seeing my open mouth, he continued. "Don't tell me you are that surprised. We have a connection, and I know you've felt it."

There was no denial from my lips. For as long as I could remember, I'd felt a kinship with Lukas. It was the main reason I had been so relaxed with him and so open about my life. I tried to connect the dots that were swimming around in my head. What did he mean, connection? He mentioned bloodlines... "You're related to Morgana, too?" I asked. What other kind of connection could he be talking about? I know that it had to do with our similar powers.

He made a yuck face. "Ew. That would be awkward, considering I've kissed you. No. Not to Morgana, but to her lover."

I felt like I had just been sucker-punched.

Less than 24 hours ago I had just learned that Morgana had practiced the dark arts, and that it was the guy she loved who had pushed her further and further to the darker side of magic. "How is this possible?" I demanded. Annoyance stirred inside me. I was tired of Lukas's keeping things from me. I understood why he might not blurt out that I was a witch during a dream. Anyone would have dismissed it as wacky subconscious, but everything after that... If I was supposed to trust him, why keep so many secrets? Why hadn't he just sat me down and told me the truth?

His shoulders squared. "They had a blood bond, linking their bloodlines. It is how I was able to find you."

I thrust my fingers into my hair. "This is crazy."

That hint of a smirk appeared on his lips again. "Maybe, but I think crazy is our style."

Why hadn't Morgana told me about the relation between Lukas and... I realized I didn't know who *he* was. "Explain," I insisted.

Drawing in a breath, he leaned forward, putting his elbows on his knees. "Enrec was a witch who shared many of Morgana's gifts, just as we do, but not all of them. They forged a bond of magic and blood until she ripped the magic from his soul, but the link they created lived on through the generations. Their joined blood flows through our veins."

It sounded like he was reciting from a fairytale—unbelievable. "Are you trying to tell me that our lives are entwined together?" I didn't want to believe it. I couldn't. Not that I didn't care for Lukas. I did. But what about my feelings for Gavin? Those were very real... and very intense—an intensity that I didn't feel with Lukas.

Confusion clouded my head.

I knew that I had wavered between the two for months now, but deep down in my heart, I was positive that Gavin was *the one*. If what Lukas said was true, then how could my heart be so very wrong? How could I not love Lukas in the same way I loved Gavin?

My stomach dropped.

Did I make a grave mistake? Or was this a sign not to repeat history—not to follow in Morgana's footsteps.

Lukas stood up upon seeing the bewilderment scroll through my eyes and walked to where I was. He propped a hip on the arm of the chair. "Yes," he said directly. "Would that be so horrible?" There was a soft vulnerability in his eyes I'd never seen before, like I had the power to hurt him.

I sat back against the cushions, feeling as if the ground were slipping out from underneath me. "I don't know. I'm sorry. This is all just —" my voice broke.

There was a shadow of something—pain, sadness, or anger? I couldn't decipher which, but it didn't matter. He masked it quickly. He caressed my cheek, lifted my face, and I let him. "Take as much time as you need; I'll be waiting for you."

His head dipped, and I thought he was going to kiss me. I held my breath, but he stopped short. I couldn't tell whether I was relieved or disappointed. Either way, it would have just complicated matters, and I was pretty sure I couldn't handle any more layers of complexity. I watched him stride across the room and slip out the door.

Overwhelmed, I sat there, unmoving, processing what I had learned. My feelings were all over the place, and I felt pressured now more than ever. Was it wrong that I didn't want to hurt anyone? Did I follow my heart? After my impromptu visit with Morgana, I'd had a renewed sense of confidence in my choices, but now, Lukas's little revelation knocked that assurance down a few pegs, leaving me once again confused—and vulnerable.

It sucked.

Gavin found me in the same spot a few hours later. I looked up, startled to see him. In a daze, I studied the lines of his face, the sharp angles of his cheeks. His eyes were incredibly blue. Fireflies warmed my tummy.

"Why do you look like your world is collapsing all around you?" he asked, concern lacing his dark voice.

"Because that is exactly how I feel," I grumbled, hugging one of the couch's decorative pillows.

His brow shot up, the silver hoop in it glinting off the soft glow of lamplight. He must have flipped on the lights because the darkness was gone. Taking the empty spot next to me, he lifted me into his lap.

Instantly, I rested my head on his shoulder. "There have been some new developments in my totally screwed-up life." Being in his arms felt so natural, so right. He felt right.

Brushing the hair off my neck, he produced tingles all over me with his touch. "Why do I get the feeling that I am not going to like what you are about to tell me?"

I swallowed. "I saw Lukas today," I blurted. It almost sounded painful.

He groaned, his arms tightening around me. "I really want to kick that piss-ant's ass."

My lips twitched. "He told me that our bloodlines are linked." Just as I was afraid, the muscles in his body tightened. I tilted my head back so I could look into his face.

"And you believe him?" Doubt was carved into every line of his expression.

I nodded. "I had a visit from Morgana. She told me how she gave in to the darkness, and how a guy was responsible for her downfall."

Fierce determination set in his jaw. "That won't be you. I won't let it be."

I placed my hand on his chest. "I'm counting on it, but that doesn't change that I might have some kind of link with Lukas."

Jealousy leapt into his eyes, lighting them like twin blue flames. "I don't like it. Something feels wrong. I know it in my gut. You can't trust what he says, Bri."

I envied that he was so confident about his instincts. *Clarification. That is what I need.* "And if I do have some predestined connection to Lukas, what does that mean for us?" The words felt like acid in my mouth. I hated that we were even having this discussion, and I realized that I didn't want to be linked to Lukas. If I had to be fated to end up with someone, I wanted it to be Gavin.

His hand touched my cheek. "It doesn't have to change anything. The future is still yours to decide. Don't let him get inside your head. You and I, we make sense. I won't let you go, not without a fight."

That was what I was afraid of. And if I had to let him go, what then?

I shuddered.

Anguish flickered in his darkened eyes. "Unless, of course, you don't feel—" he added.

I silenced him with a kiss. "My love for you is not in question. I wish it was you," I whispered. It was the honest-to-God truth. I loved Gavin. I was head-over-heels-crazy in love with him. No one else made me feel like he did. And if I was going to start trusting in myself, I needed to trust in my instincts, which were screaming for me to kiss him again. So I did.

I might be linked to Lukas, but that didn't mean my heart belonged to him. It was still mine to give to whomever I chose. And I picked Gavin.

Fate be damned.

CHAPTER 11

The big V-day had arrived.

Joy.

If Aunt Clara even suggested I wear red, I was going to quit, so when I strolled down the stairs dressed from head to toe in black, I waited. She glanced up from her cup of coffee and lifted her brow, but didn't say a word.

I grinned to myself and poured my own cup of caffeine and sugar. Taking the stool beside her, I let the brisk aroma rouse my senses.

"Are you ready for chaos?" she asked, sipping from her white mug. Her caramel hair was in a messy bun similar to mine, but much more stylish.

"Ask me after my third cup of coffee," I grumbled.

"Boycotting as usual?" she asked, finally commented on my funereal appearance. She knew me well.

I cast a sideways glance. "I just don't want to clash with the flowers."

She tried not to smile. "I thought since you had a *boyfriend,* you might have different feelings about heart-shaped candies and candlelit dinners."

I scrunched my nose. "So where is Chad taking you tonight?" I asked, changing the subject from me to her—a much safer topic.

This time there was no disguising the smile that spread across her lips. "Bella Donna's."

"Oooh. Chad the Stud Muffin is pulling out all the stops." Bella's was a fancy Italian restaurant right on the harbor. They had twinkling strands of lights, outdoor seating, and overpriced, but to-die-for, food. I couldn't afford half a meal from that place. Someone was looking to get lucky.

She tapped a nail against her mug, and I could see she had something on her mind beneath her excitement. "Are you sure you are okay with closing up by yourself? I can always have Chad change the reservation to later, or better yet, you could come with us?"

I had to stifle a groan. As appealing as Bella Donna's was, being a third wheel on my aunt's date was pathetic beyond anything else I could imagine. "I will be fine. Promise." I crossed my heart with my finger. "You deserve a night off. Bring me a doggie bag?"

She smiled warmly. "Always."

Finishing our coffee, I grabbed a granola bar as Aunt Clara snatched the keys. Normally we drove separately, but today we rode together. Chad was picking her up from Mystic Floral for their romantic excursion. I tried to contain the need to gag.

As expected, the shop was a madhouse. I didn't get two seconds to myself once the doors opened, but it was good for business, or so I kept telling myself. I forced a bright smile for the next customer. My face muscles were in agony, and there was a good chance that I would have a permanent creepy smile like the Joker by the time this puking pink holiday was over.

We had just made it through the lunch-hour rush when Aunt Clara's cellphone vibrated. Her face lit up as she glanced at the number flashing on her phone: Chad. She always got that goofy look when he called.

I rolled my eyes and started to restock the cases for the next rush. The entire shop smelled of roses and baby's breath. *Beats coming home reeking of greasy burgers and salty fries, I guess.* In the background I heard her bubbly whispers, and it was a reassuring sound that let me know she was happy.

I, on the other hand, was a bundle of turmoil ever since the other night, when I had come to the realization that no matter what kind of connection Lukas and I might have, it was Gavin that I was in love with. That wouldn't change. Now I just had to find the words to tell that to Lukas. I didn't want to hurt him. I didn't want to hurt either of them, but I couldn't shake the feeling that was exactly what I was going to end up doing: hurting people close to me.

Shooing Aunt Clara out the door with a dewy-eyed Chad, I took a quick look around the shop and saw that I had a moment just to myself. I knew it wouldn't last, so I closed my eyes and tried to clear my head. I felt the gentle hum of magic swirling inside me for just a moment before the door chimed, and I kissed my solitude goodbye.

I huffed, watching the gazillionth guy scramble last-minute to get his wife or girlfriend a gift. If the bells dinged one more time before we closed, I was going to rip them from the above threshold and toss them out the door.

Shifting my weight restlessly, I watched the hands on the clock. When at last nine o'clock struck, I already had the drawer counted, the shelves cleaned, and the flowers restocked. I was out the door. With the keys jingling in my hand, I turned the lock and set the security system to "active."

As I walked around the building to the back parking lot, something cold and prickly opened up inside me. I peeked over my shoulder, unable to shake the chill on my spine.

Someone was watching me; I was sure of it.

Before I had a chance to process that I was in danger, it was already upon me. Out of the shadows, a figure immerged. Cloaked in black, with a hood shielding his face, the man stood between my car and me. Panic skyrocketed in my chest. The vibrations in the air were undeniable. He was a witch, and by the ominous sneer on his mouth, the only part of his face I could really see, he wasn't here to buy flowers; he was here to kill me.

For the love of God.

I knew that my life was in danger, but it didn't really hit me until I was staring it in the face. The mystery witch faced me, and a shudder rolled through me. I took a step backward, away from the parking lot. If I could just get back into the shop...

A really stupid plan. He would catch me before I had the chance to put the key in the door, let alone unlock it. I was cornered, and the feeling sucked big time. My eyes darted around the area, looking for any means of escape. There were two lampposts buzzing above us, flicking light across the parking lot.

I sensed a tremor of power, and the parking lot went black.

Crap on a cracker.

"I have to say, you don't look like much of a threat." The sound of his voice was strained and sinister. That seemed to be a running theme.

Silence soaked up the night. I was at a loss for words as I tried to figure how I was going to get myself out of this sticky situation—alive, hopefully.

"I'm not a threat," I stated, my voice quivering. I prayed he was a reasonable witch, but I wasn't holding my breath. If it weren't for his glowing eyes, I wouldn't have been able to track his movements, or so I thought; it blows to be wrong.

Whipping a hand out to his side, sparks of magic danced along his fingertips. Cool trick. Fear aside, I was kind of envious of how quickly he conjured his power. "There have been murmurings of your rise in command." He cocked his head, the black hood falling low over his eyes. "Now that I see you, I think the forewarnings were exaggerated."

I couldn't have agreed more. It was unnerving knowing that there were witches out there talking about me, organizing my demise.

I attempted to sidestep around him, but he blocked my escape with his body. I guess the time for pleasantries had come to an end. A whitish-red light erupted from his fingers and shot straight toward me. The impact knocked me flat on my ass.

Wrong move, dude.

My fear swiftly turned to anger. I don't do well with bullies. Bad things happen when I get mad. Blowing my hair out of my face, magic trembled in the air, and this time it was mine. It gathered inside me.

Pushing to my feet, a single spear of lightning broke the darkness with a blinding white light.

"You don't want to mess with me," I warned him, in a tone I barely recognized as mine. I knew that my eyes were radiant.

A pair of boots came into my vision, and I lifted my head, prepared to protect myself. I stopped thinking and began running on pure adrenaline and reflex. Ignoring the throbbing from having been tossed across the parking lot, I centered myself, wishing I could fully see my assassin rather than a shadow with eerie eyes.

He hovered over me. "Power like yours should not exist. It's unnatural, and you have to be stopped."

I realized that he was out of his freaking gourd.

No sooner had the thought occurred to me than he struck. A green ball of energy whizzed toward me, slamming into my chest. I hit the ground—again— the air flying from my lungs. Shit, that stung like a bitch.

Stars exploded behind my eyes, and I drew in a breath, scrambling to get to my feet before he released another ball of neon ectoplasm at me. "Look, I just recently found out what I am, and I'm not out to take over the world." I kept babbling, hoping that I could somehow reach him emotionally because I was afraid I would hurt him physically. "I swear. I'm just a high school senior getting ready for college."

Static charged in his hands, radiating in a blinding green light. "It is only a matter of time before the temptation becomes too much for you. There is no stopping it."

So much for trying to be sensible. He made my life sound so hopeless. This time, when he attacked me, I was ready. I dodged to the right, and I watched his attack whirl past me. "Asshole," I muttered under my breath.

Well, he might think there was no option beyond my demise, but I was going to do my damnedest to stop him. I wasn't some weak girl, too scared to put up a fight. I was a godforsaken witch. While I was letting my magic build up inside of me, the wind around me picked up, blowing my hair out around my face. Energy crackled over my knuckles, mimicking the lightning in the sky, a daring show of heat and light.

"You don't know what my future will hold. What makes you any better, playing God with my life?" I contradicted. He must not have liked my tone, which I thought sounded very authoritative.

"I like to think of this as protecting my family's future."

Family. I had a family too—my aunt. Already, she had to deal with the loss and pain of losing my mom, her twin sister. I shuddered to think about what losing me would do to her. I was all the family she had left, and the last connection she had to her sister.

Something inside me snapped.

What about the family I would never have, if he succeeded?

A rage I'd never felt before came blistering to the surface, setting every molecule in my body on fire. In the center of my chest, a heady surge of power arose. I knew somewhere in the back of my mind that I shouldn't release the energy that was bursting to break free, but that voice of caution was overruled.

My bluish-white strand of magic hit the mysterious man right in the heart. He stumbled, his hood falling away from his face. For the first time, I got a clear view of the man trying to kill me.

He had skin paler than I'd imagined, like he didn't see much sunlight and lived among the shadows. A mixture of green and brown blended together inside his wide eyes. Short brownish hair teased his temples. There was nothing special about this man, nothing that jumped out and screamed *murderer.*

I stood above him, as he lay pinned to the ground by my spell, one that I had cast but had no clue what it was. Regardless, it was effective in paralyzing my attacker. Looking down into his eyes, I felt like a different person—detached, emotionally and physically, from my body. My other hand reached out, and this indisputable need inside me fought to be set free. It whispered in my head, begging me to release the power that was gathered at my fingertips. The voice lulled me in a sweet, tempting caress.

There might have been a split second in which I knew what I was about to do— unleash that dark part of me that I had locked away and sworn never to use—but with my life being threatened, I was willing to pay the price that came with using it. Just as my hand trembled to release the power, I hesitated.

Somewhere, through the haze of darkness, I heard a voice that was both familiar and warm. My fingers twitched, the magic trying to lure me, but the sound of Gavin's voice broke its hold.

He grounded me. I grasped that thought and, dropping my hand, the energy fizzled.

"Gavin?" I murmured.

CHAPTER 12

H e looked like he was fighting the urge to commit first-degree murder. In five ground-eating steps, he was at my side. I knew his next move was going to be epic.

The attacker at my feet moved, crawling slowly away, assessing the unexpected newcomer. I, on the other hand, was relieved to see my boyfriend. The jerk didn't get very far in his escape; Gavin's foot connected with his gut, sending the guy back to the ground, groaning. "I might have stopped the lady from killing you, but you can bet your ass we're not done here. Not by a long shot," Gavin growled.

The anonymous man winced. "You are a fool. She is wicked. You will be abetting the extinction of power."

Obviously, he didn't get the message. There was a satisfactory thud when Gavin followed his first kick with a second. This guy was glutton for punishment. Curled up on the blacktop, he began to laugh—a sick and twisted laugh that made my skin crawl.

Gavin's eyes darkened.

When I first saw him, I had assumed he was planning on blasting this guy to the next planet, but I realized that he wanted the satisfaction of hurting him with his bare hands. It must be a guy thing. He had come in, guns blazing.

Gavin paused from thrashing the other man to catch a glimpse of me and make sure I was still standing, not passed out. At least that's what I figured he was doing, when his eyes connected with mine. In that moment of distraction, a flash of light exploded in the night, and when the blinding glow faded, my mysterious assailant was gone.

And the kicker was... that meant he would probably try again.

Great. Something to look forward to.

Gavin's gaze scanned the tree line. "Looks like our *friend* didn't want to stick around. How disappointing. The fun was just beginning."

I didn't have the quite same reaction. Springing to my feet, I threw myself into his arms.

"Hey, I've got you," he murmured as I buried my face into his neck.

I was encompassed by his warmth, and then I started to babble incoherently like an idiot. Random words describing what had happened just started spewing from my mouth: incomplete thoughts, run-on sentences, made-up words, the whole nine yards. It was bad.

He listened to me, getting the gist of what I was trying to articulate. Putting me at arm's length, he helped calm me down. I don't know how it happened, but over the last few months, Gavin had become my anchor. He was able to pull me back from the darkness, but I had to wonder if there would be a point at which I would be too far gone for even him to reach me.

I prayed that never happened.

In the afterglow of the events, guilt gnawed at me, bit by bit. "Did I—?" The possibility that I had done the unthinkable plagued me.

Gavin shook his head, staring off into the darkness. "Not a drop." Facing me, his eyes surveyed my face. "Are you okay? If he hurt you—"

I swallowed. "I'm fine. Just a few scratches." I thought it would be better if I left out the details about what happened before he gallantly arrived. The last thing I wanted was for him to go off on some kind of revenge mission.

"That is one hell of a scratch," he said, stepping forward, the pad of his thumb lightly tracing the side of my cheek. I flinched. Tomorrow that would be the mother of all bruises.

Wrapping my arms around myself, I started to shake. "No. I'll be okay. I need to get the car home."

The heat from his eyes was gone now. "Don't worry about that now. I'll arrange for Jared to get it. You are no condition to drive."

Maybe he was right. Fatigue hit me like a wrecking ball. With an arm around my waist, I let him lead me to his car; summoning and using so much magic had depleted me of energy. I slid into the leather seat, thinking about how close I had come to ripping the power right from that guy's soul. It was my last thought before I crashed, exhaustion devouring me. Magic overload.

My EYELIDS FLUTTERED OPEN.

A heartbeat of time passed as I lay there, putting together the pieces of how I got *here*. Where exactly was here? The last thing I remembered was some douchebag ranting on about how I was evil and had to be stopped. Then Gavin showed up out of nowhere. Everything after that was fuzzy.

I twisted on my side. My bedroom, with its soft lavender walls, came into focus. I was stretched out on the white sheets, the sweet scent of a wild berry candle and fresh flowers filling the room. Someone had lit the candle at my dresser, its flame casting a small glow in the dark room.

Gavin.

I thought his name before I saw his face. He moved silently through my room, prowling toward me. Tingles skirted across my skin, and the tattoo at the small of my back came alive. The mattress shifted under his weight as he settled down beside me. He propped himself up on his side, using his arm to hold up his head. "Hey," he murmured, brushing a chunk of hair off my face.

"How long have I been out?" I asked, staring into his bright blue eyes.

"Not long." He played with the hoop at his lip, searching my eyes. "How are you feeling?"

Like I got tossed around in a dump truck. My clothes were torn, and there were streaks of dirt on my arms. "I'll live."

"Good, because it would really piss me off if you didn't." He placed a hand on my hip. Fireflies fluttered in response.

"What were you doing there?" I asked. Don't get me wrong; I was eternally grateful that he had been at right place at the right time.

One side of his mouth tipped up. "I wanted to surprise you. Valentine's and all..."

"Valentine's Day sucks," I grumbled.

He shoulders moved in a silent laugh. "I believe you now."

Now that I was fully awake, the griminess was getting to me. I wanted to scrub away the memories, erase them from my brain. "I need to clean up. Don't leave, okay?"

He grinned. "I wouldn't think of it."

Making haste toward the bathroom, I glanced at him over my shoulder right before I closed the door. It was a tempting sight, seeing Gavin sprawled out on my bed with all that bad boy, yummy goodness. I took the fastest shower ever known to mankind, then quickly threw on a pair of shorts and a loose T-shirt. I didn't want to give him the chance to sneak away.

Steam followed me out of the bathroom when I remerged. He was right where I had left him, and those warm fireflies returned, darting around in my belly. "I'm happy you're here," I said, climbing back into bed with a huge grin on my lips.

"And?" He had a hand behind his head.

I lifted my hand, running my fingers through his silky hair that tumbled over his brow. "Stay," I whispered. "I can't bear to be alone." I needed him. His presence was the only thing that was going to calm me. Inside, I felt icy, and Gavin was the one person who could melt that cold.

His eyes drifted shut as he leaned his forehead against mine, and my breath caught.

"You're killing me," he sighed.

A smile swept across my face.

His eyes popped open suddenly. "I didn't mean that literally."

I wrapped both my arms around his neck. "I know."

His eyes darkened and his lips brushed across mine in the most tantalizing way. "If anything had happened to you..."

"It didn't. You were there." He was always there.

In soft caresses, his fingers slowly trailed down the underside of my arm. Tiny blue sparks skimmed over the surface. It was unearthly. Then he was kissing me and his lips were cosmic, out of this world. I was transported to another galaxy—just where I needed to be: no worries, no one threatening my life, no Lukas.

His mouth was warm over mine with a hint of coolness coming from the silver hoop in his lip. My lips tingled, but it wasn't long before my entire body was sparking. What started off as tentative and sweet soon spiraled, creating a yearning inside of me. Our hearts beat heavily, quickening.

The sensations he enticed ignited something deep within me: the knowledge of what I wanted—him. I wanted Gavin. *Holy moonbeams.* I was love-struck, spellbound, hypnotized by his touch, and I wasn't alone in my feelings....

He made a guttural sound in the back of his throat as his fingers made quick work of the thin straps of my tank top. Hooking a finger under the light material, he brushed them off my shoulder, pressing a kiss where the straps had been. "If you don't stop me soon, I won't be able to."

I'm counting on it. Instead of telling him with words, I showed him. Crushing my body to his, I deepened our kiss, sweeping my tongue against his in a seductive game of tag. I was blown away, not only by the intensity of my feelings, but also by realizing that I had this strong, violent emotion inside me—love. It took me by surprise.

If someone had told me last summer that the edgiest, not to mention the hottest, boy at school would be in my bed, I would have laughed in his or her face—heck, I probably would have snorted. But a lot had changed; I had changed. Four months ago, I didn't believe in witches, and here I am today, not only believing in them, but also knowing that I am one. That was one heck of a pill to swallow.

Now I was approaching a different milestone, a much more intimate one, and I knew to the very depth of my core that I had made the right choice, fate and premonitions be damned.

I got lost in the feel of his mouth. My body was molded to his, and

I parted my lips, intoxicated by the taste of his breath. There was fire in his eyes as he pulled back. "Bri?"

I knew what he was asking, and my answer was still the same. I nibbled on his ear. "I want this," I murmured. *I want you,* I added silently—at least, I was pretty sure it had been in my head.

I trailed my tongue over his bottom lip, and Gavin growled, claiming my mouth in a branding kiss. Magic picked up inside me, flowing through my heated veins, stirring a delicious storm of need. Clothing vanished in a wink, leaving us skin to skin. *A neat trick.* Having a witch for a boyfriend definitely had its perks.

He leaned over me, my auburn hair spilling over the white sheets. Marveling at his sun-kissed skin, I ran my hands over his chest, feeling the muscles jump under my touch. I never wanted to stop. I didn't need tender words or sappy romance. All I wanted was to feel loved and safe. Gavin gave me those feelings in abundance. He would never let anyone or anything harm me, and that was damn sexy, in my book.

When we came together, I felt as if my body were a part of his, like I were burning, reaching for something. My head twisted to the side and... starbursts in all the colors of the rainbow shot through me, glorious and dreamy. I bit my lip to keep from crying out, and I lost control.

Magic tumbled from my fingertips, haloing the room in a bluish-white light. It swirled, spun up, and spun out. At the same time, dry lightning flashed across the sky outside, striking in a jagged and impressive display.

Oops.

God, I hope that doesn't happen every time we...

"Should I take that as a compliment?" Gavin asked huskily, his brow raised.

I let out a breathy giggle.

Poised above me, he brushed away some strands of hair that were stuck to my face. "Your eyes are glowing."

Imprisoned by the darkest blue eyes, I murmured, "So are yours."

Moonlight, like a blanket, spilled through the window as I snuggled into his arms. Only moments later, my eyes drifted shut.

CHAPTER 13

Sprawled on his belly, with one arm slung around my waist, Gavin appeared almost angelic in sleep. White sheets were twisted and tangled around his hips. His soft lips were relaxed, and thick black lashes fanned the tops of his cheeks. There was youthfulness to his face in sleep that made him less intimidating and dangerous.

I wanted to stay just like this for as long as possible.

I lay on the bed beside him, and, like a total creeper, I watched the rise and fall of his even breathing. A need to touch him punched inside me, and as my fingers inched toward him, he rolled, tugging me closer. Suddenly the angel looked like a disgruntle lion—adorable and lethal.

I grinned. "Morning."

He groaned.

Utterly delectable.

Placing a hand on his bare chest, his skin was hot. "If we don't get up, we are going to be late for school."

He snaked an arm around my waist, pulling me toward him. "Hmm. I think we deserve a day off."

I smacked him on the chest. "That is your answer to everything."

I received a dazzling grin. "Well, I didn't get a lot of sleep last night."

My cheeks turned an embarrassing shade of pink. "Whose fault is that?"

"Yours," he said, nuzzling my neck.

I knew that if I didn't get out of this bed very soon, I would give in to his every request, including ditching school. But with his tongue flirting with my neck, I stopped thinking altogether.

If it wasn't for my alarm, we might have very well skipped school, but the annoying buzzing didn't stop until Gavin sent it flying across the room. It hit the wall with a clatter, smashing to smithereens.

I burst out laughing.

Gavin plopped back onto the bed, his hands scrubbing at his face. "I'll be back to get you in twenty. Be ready, or I drag you back here for the rest of the day."

Jumping from the bed and out of his reach, I padded to the bathroom, grinning from ear to ear. As soon as the door clicked shut, I turned on the shower, knowing that he would make good on his warning. Not that the idea didn't sound appealing. It was because it was so darn tempting that I was ready for school in fifteen minutes flat.

His car was idling in my driveway as I rushed out of the house, a beaming grin still on my lips. I didn't think there was anything that could damper my fantastic mood. Overhead, the sun was sunny and cheerful, not a cloud in the sky.

I sunk into my chair of my first class with dopey hearts in my eyes. I could still taste Gavin on my lips.

Tori leaned over the side of her desk. "Well, aren't you bursting with good news."

"What?" I asked, cutting off my own personal swoon-fest. I only had one thing on the brain: Gavin. Gavin's lips. Gavin's abs. Gavin. He was chili pepper hot today.

Maybe it had something do with what happened between us last night, but I was even more attracted to him. My head was overflowing with all things Gavin. I'd always wanted my first time to be with someone special, someone who respected me and cared deeply for me.

Gavin hadn't disappointed. He made the memory unforgettable. The little display of fireworks might have added to its hot factor.

"Holy shit! You did *it*," Tori said.

She suddenly had my full attention, along with the half-filled classroom. There was still a minute before the bell rang to signify the start of school. I narrowed my eyes, prepared to hush her by any means and unleash holy hell if necessary.

But Austin stole my chance. He turned around from the seat in front of me. "Oh. My. Gawd, B. Dish now! Don't even think about leaving out even the teensiest detail. I want it all."

The cat was out of the bag.

There was no stopping them now.

I dropped my head into my hands, my cheeks staining red. "It's no big deal."

Tori's face fell. "That bad huh? The first time is never as glamorous as you imagine."

"No. That's not what I meant," I quickly rushed. "It was…" I struggled for the appropriate word. No matter what I said, Tori and Austin were going to gush. "…life changing," I finally decided.

Austin smile was nauseating. "Gavin's got game," he sang.

I rolled my eyes. "You have no idea."

"We would if you weren't holding out on us," Tori said, scooting to the edge of her seat.

Austin adjusted his glasses, swiping an invisible tear from the corner of his eye. "Our babygirl is all grown up."

I slid farther down in my seat, begging for Mr. Carlson to start class and shut these two up. "Can we do this later?" I begged through my teeth, lowering my voice.

"Lunch," they both said in perfect unison.

I nodded, agreeing to anything if it got them off the subject of my sex life.

Holy smokes. I have a sex life.

Still, I didn't want the details headlined in the school newspaper, which was exactly what would happen if Tori and Austin had their way. Decorum was not in their vocab. Today was the first time I did not wish to speed up time, so of course the day flew by.

Twirling a fry between my fingers, I sat at our usual round table, sandwiched between Tori and Austin. "You don't really expect me to answer that?" I said in outrage.

Two pairs of expectant eyes stared at me.

I guess that was a yes.

"I don't know who wrote the best friend code book, but this is nuts."

"Just spill, Rafferty. There is nothing to be embarrassed about," Tori scoffed.

"Did you, you know..." Austin wiggled his brows.

Good Lord. Had I ever. I didn't think it wise to tell them that I shot lightning across the sky and sent the room aglow in magic, however much that was precisely what they wanted to hear. I stared down at my burger and fries.

"OMG. She did!" Austin supplied for me, seeing my face start to turn pink.

I swear I've never blushed so much in my life as I have the last twenty-four hours. It was ridiculous.

"I knew that boy had swag." There was an envious quality to his voice.

I am sure Gavin would be glad to hear it. "Are you satisfied? The freaky deak details of my sex life are over."

A shadow fell over me. "Gross. I am going to pretend I didn't hear that," Sophie said, her pixie face contorted in pucker face. Her tray clattered on top of the table filled with a chicken Caesar salad and bottled water.

Her lunch immediately made me feel guilty, and I dropped the greasy fry that was halfway to my mouth. I rocked back in my chair. Then I remembered what I had just admitted.

Awkward times infinity.

Sneakers squeaked over the tiled floor, and the common room reeked of sweat, smoke, and burnt pizza—the joys of high school cafeteria.

And through the masses one person stood out. He couldn't help it, or maybe it was because I was hyperaware of his presence. The tattoo at my back began to hum in rhythm with the blood in my veins.

Gavin.

"Speak of the devil."

I threw a fry at Austin.

Gavin swept down, brushing a kiss across me cheek. "We've got *work* to do after school," he murmured. The way he said it made it seem like work was code for something dirty.

"Oooh," came from Austin, totally misreading, but I couldn't help think that was exactly what Gavin had intended. "I just bet you do," Austin added, watching Gavin saunter away.

I did a little eyeballing of my own.

Training day.

Someone shoot me now.

It was a perfect day for a little magic, if one actually knew what they were doing. Oh, I was getting better...at striking things with lightning. My weathercasting was as unpredictable as always and fueled by my volatile emotions.

Blue skies. A balmy breeze. The crashing of sea-foam waters. And a really hot instructor.

Gavin's backyard butted up to the beach, and he thought that would be a good spot to resume my magical defense skills, which were sorely lacking. I really hoped that I didn't kill anyone. More than a little tense, I walked down to the shore. Barefoot, sand granules squished between my toes, getting wetter the closer I got to the receding water's edge. A peace I only ever felt on the beach swirled through me.

For just a moment, I closed my eyes and breathed in the sharp smell of the ocean and listened to the intangible roar of waves.

"You look like an illusion," Gavin said, his voice rising just above the tides. "There is something here that calls to you. I can feel it shimmering in the air. Your gift responds naturally to the water. It's beautiful."

I was caught by the intensity in his eyes. "I feel it, too."

His lips twisted into a smirk. "Are you ready to kick some ass?"

I dug my foot into the sand. "You are braver than most to spar with me."

Eyes trained on me, he crooked his finger. "I trust you. It is time you did, too."

Trust had to be earned, and I needed to earn my own before I felt confident. I gave a slight tilt of my head and centered myself. It came instantaneously, the flood of energy, and surprised me. Usually it took more effort. This had been seamless.

Gavin noticed and arched a brow.

A violet light hurled from my fingers, spinning in dizzying colors at a grinning Gavin. With a flick of his wrist, he deflected the spell, sending it back toward me. I wasn't so savvy on the return, and the shimmery light hit me in the chest. On impact I fell backward, my butt thumping in the sand. It hadn't been a very dangerous conjuration, more of a stun gun.

I blew out a breath and shoved to my feet, brushing the sandy partials off my jeans. Seeing the curl of amusement on Gavin's lips sparked my annoyance. I bit the inside of my cheek, concentrating, and threw my second spell. Shards of magic glittered, slicing through the air like jagged daggers. I gasped, not meaning to unleash such a lethal spell. He spun around, his arm cutting through the charm. I watched in awe as the magical spears dissolved, raining in sparkling ash to the ground.

Show off.

I turned away to hide my burning face. "This is so stupid," I barked.

His shadow appeared over me. "And you have the patience of a two-year-old."

I scowled and kicked water at him. "I suck at magic."

He kicked some right back, laughing. "On the contrary. You are extraordinary, just not at fighting." A few minutes later, we were both soaking wet and grinning. He had taken the edge off.

I tried to wring the water out of my hair. "Again?" I asked, glancing up. Glistening droplets clung to his lashes, making his eyes incredibly blue. I swear I could see the ocean in them. My irritation dissipated, and my belly fluttered with fireflies.

His lips curled faintly. "Bring it."

"If I didn't know better, I would think you are enjoying this."

He shook the water from his hair, looking wickedly handsome. "I am."

I flung up my arms and ran my tongue over my lips. For the other spells, I had just relied on the energy inside me. This time, I extended my power to the elements around me. The winds whispered in my ear and the lapping waters answered my call. A miniature tsunami erupted in the waters behind him. Magic danced over the sea. With each roll of the waves, they climbed higher, thundering toward us.

"Bri!" he yelled, stepping backward, eyes centered on the towering wall of water. "Bri! Stop!"

CHAPTER 14

I t was wrong to play with his arrogance, but this time I actually knew what I was doing. My purple irises illuminated, and just as the massive wave reached the shoreline, threatening to sweep us both away, I threw my arms out to my sides. My head fell back.

I laughed as water sloshed around us, but never touching us. Contained, I kept the formidable surf from reaching past where we stood and sent it back into the ocean with rocky force. A light mist tickled my face. In all honesty, I really had not a clue how I had done the spell. There was nothing technical about it, my conjuring just born from feelings.

Once the water show quieted down, Gavin eyed me. "How did you do that?"

I shrugged, feeling exposed. "It's weather related. I don't have to think about it so hard, and the elements response to my emotions. Watch." The soft breeze from the ocean swirled around me, picking up pieces of my hair. Smiling, I used the warm gust as a hand, stroking the side of his cheek.

He blinked, startled. "You never fail to surprise me."

I caught my reflection in the water and gasped.

Oh God, I look like the Swamp Thing.

He gave me an appraising look. "I think we should call it quits for the day."

"Gladly," I agreed, thinking I needed a brush and a bottle of leave-in conditioner, pronto. "As long as I don't have to hurt you anymore."

He snorted. "You can't hurt steel."

That was an invitation I couldn't refuse. "Oh, really?" A bolt of lightning sliced through the air, hitting the sand a fraction from his bare feet.

He gave me a wicked grin. "See, that's what I'm talking about."

I laughed. This hadn't turned out to be such a catastrophe after all.

SCHOOL DRAGGED. The teachers all spoke Greek, and my mind was anything but focused. It was Friday, and I was ready to get my weekend on.

It had been too long since I had a night out with friends. After the recent attacks on my life, I wasn't sure it was a good idea, but when Gavin insisted, and with Sophie tagging along, I relented. We all deserved some girl time, Austin included. He would not take offense in calling it such.

"Vampires, werewolves, and witches. Sounds like a concoction for a blockbuster," Austin said, staring at the promotion for the paranormal movie premier.

We were standing in line at the ticket booth of Wilmington Theatre. It was one of those posh movie places with leather recliners, pillows, blankets, and free popcorn. Great, except the price of admission was a night's shift at Mystic Floral. But I figured my friends were worth the splurge.

"Why does Tori always pick the films?" I grumbled, eyeing the pale, jaw-droppingly handsome vampire with his teeth sunk erotically into some lucky bitch's neck on the poster.

Sophie raised her slender brows. "This should be interesting," she murmured.

I knew what she meant. We were living paranormal. A ghost of a smile touched my strawberry glossed lips. "It always is."

"What or who are we gossiping about?" Austin asked, squeezing beside me and draping an arm over my shoulder.

"You," I replied, poking him in the chest.

"Hmm. My favorite topic."

I rolled my eyes.

Austin and I walked through the doors behind Tori and Sophie who were scoping a guy who had apparently caught their eye as soon as they crossed the threshold. Boy-crazed Tori couldn't go anywhere without checking out the goods.

"And she's off," Austin whispered in my ear, causing me to laugh a little too loud.

I covered my hand over my mouth.

"I'll get the extra buttery popcorn, and you save us some seats?" Austin suggested.

Still smiling, I nodded, snagging Sophie along the way.

"It's nice to see your aura so sunny," she commented. "Your friends make you happy and carefree."

That they did.

"But you still worry about them," she added.

"I can't help it. With everything that has happened lately, I don't want them to get hurt because of what I am."

She smiled, and it lit up her pixie eyes in the dim theatre. "It's a good thing you have me. And my overprotective brother, I guess."

"I'm really lucky to have you both. I think your family are the only witches not hunting me." We climbed the stairs to the very top row, our preferred seating. The theatre was pretty much empty. "How come you aren't trying to make magical mincemeat out of me? Not that I am ungrateful, I'm curious."

"Are you planning on sucking me dry?"

I was horrorstruck. "No!" I quickly replied.

Sitting in a seat smack dab in the middle of the row, she wrinkled her nose cutely. "I was only teasing. We were raised not to judge a witch based on gifts or power, but on the pureness of their light. Plus, Gavin loves you."

I exhaled. If only love was enough. "I just don't want anyone to get hurt."

"I see your aura, and not once has there been anything that has given me alarm. I don't care what other say about the powers you possess; I know you wouldn't cause harm on purpose, but when pushed comes to shove, who wouldn't defend themselves the only way they know how, and protect the people they love?"

I propped my feet up on the empty seat in front of me. "Thanks, Sophie. I don't know what I would do without you guys." Go out of my mind crazy.

Austin and Tori stumbled their way through the dark, arms loaded with junk food. Just as soon as they planted their butts, the theatre went black and the red curtains drew back. During the movie there was some thrown popcorn, (which got stuck in my hair) uncontrollable snickering, (my gut hurt) and really bad acting, but it was the best time.

Because we had arrived, as Tori put it, fashionably late, we had to walk a few blocks to get to where we had parked the car. You'd think I could have gone down a few streets at night without bringing out the freaks.

Wrong.

Tingles crept up my spine, and my skin prickled with coldness.

We weren't alone.

Laugher exploded behind me, the haunting kind. I jumped.

"Just keep walking," Sophie muttered under her breath, looping her arm through mine.

Easier said than done. My fight-or-flight response had kicked in. And flight was winning, marginally. She was more or less dragged me down the road as I fought the urge to peek behind me.

This wasn't happening. Not now. Not with my friends. They could get hurt, and I would never forgive myself.

It took Tori and Austin a few steps to sense our uneasiness. They had been busy arguing about which werewolf had been smexier. Austin snuck a glance over his shoulder. "Oh. My. God. They are going to mug us," he hissed.

Tori chewed on her lip, securing her Michael Kors bag closer.

I jabbed him in the side. "They don't want our money, dinglebat," I quietly snapped. I needed to think, and I couldn't do that if my friends were spazzing out.

Austin's manicured brows slammed together. "And what makes you so sure?" he whispered.

He might just find out. *Dammit.*

"Walk faster," Tori barked, speeding up to a power walk.

The clomping of feet hitting the pavement increased behind us, and so did my heart rate. "Shit," I muttered, turning the corner and coming face-to-face with a witch, blocking our only escape.

Sophie and I shared a look of oh-shit-this-isn't-really-happening.

My worry spiked. I was going to vomit chunks of popcorn and gooey raisinettes. It wouldn't be pretty.

The four of us stood back to back. There were three of them. Under *normal* circumstances, we might have been able to hold our own, but the humming in my blood and the warmth radiating from my tattoo pointed that these guys were witches.

I knew what I had to do, but it didn't make my decision any easier. After this there was no going back, no backspace to erase my exposure to the two people who meant so much to me, but I was left with no other choice.

Three against two wasn't exactly fair odds. I was a novice, so I didn't even think I counted as a full witch. Tori and Austin were about to get the shock of the decade, and I wanted them out of the crossfires.

"It must be our lucky night," sneered a young woman, who was maybe in her early twenties with bright pink hair. Her eyes were trained on me, flanked by two very scary dudes.

Not very reassuring.

In a bold move, I stepped forward in front of my friends. "Do you have any idea who I am?" Stupidly, I thought maybe I could scare them off, threatening them with my magic vacuum powers.

It didn't work.

The girl with the Powerpuff hair laughed. "Why do you think we're here, bitch?"

Oh. This one had it coming.

Anger ricocheted inside me. "Good. Then you know what I am capable of."

She gave me the stink eye. "That's why I brought backup."

Her two muscles closed in. One was bald, with crazy shimmery marks on the side of his glossy head. Enchantments like the tattoo on my back. The other looked like a shaggy dog with a mean snarl.

I slanted my head. "This is your last chance to leave here intact. I suggest you take the opportunity, because I won't offer a second time."

Austin grabbed my arm. "B, are you crazy? What are you doing?"

"I second that," Tori agreed. "Let's just give them whatever they want." There was fear quivering in her voice.

"They want me." I shook Austin's off hand and glanced over my shoulder at them. "No matter what happens...stay behind me and stay close," I growled to Austin and Tori. Their eyes widened, and I knew that mine had begun to illuminate.

Obviously, reasoning with these witches wasn't going to work—I don't know why I even bothered. It was time to brew up a nice pot of kick-ass.

Sophie was at my side. "Are you thinking what I'm thinking?"

"Probably not," I muttered.

The leader of the pack cast the first strike. Sophie reached out like she was catching a ball and closed her fist around the neon pink light. When she opened her fingers, it was empty. "Nice try," Sophie said like a bad ass.

Poo hit the fan. Sparks started to fly.

Unison gasps of "holy shit" came from Tori and Austin as they got their first glimpse of magic. I couldn't believe this was happening, but I didn't have time to dwell on their reactions, not when psycho in pink had her claws out.

"I'm just getting started," she hissed, and then she let it pour.

Sophie was quick on the draw, deflecting what she tossed our way, but when I felt the air tremble with combined power of dickhead one and dickhead two, I realized I was going to have to do something.

Maybe they didn't think of Sophie as much as a threat and would be able to take me down without a fight. I was more than a little surprised myself, knowing that it was her brothers that were the fighters. Still, she wouldn't be able to ward off three witches alone.

My gaze zeroed in on rocker-wannabe-witch. I did what I did best. I weaved a mother of all storms, letting the fear of my friends feed my rage. "Why don't you give me a shot? I'm what you really want."

"With pleasure," she snarled.

The winds picked up, howling. Lightning slashed across the black night. Thunder crashed above me, in a deafening roar. And my hair thrashed around my face from the strength of the gusts. It was all a very impressive display, until a rainbow laser beam smacked me, rocking my head back in what felt like the perfect execution of an invisible bitch slap. The storm I just started to create died.

Hell bells.

I saw stars.

Blood dribbled down from my lip. I swiped it with the back of my hand, glaring at the skank responsible for my soon to be swollen mouth. She was smirking as if my pain gave her pleasure. To my right I heard the cracking of spells colliding.

Before I was able to get my bearings and throw the counterstrike I was building, she hit me again—a lash across my cheek. It stung like a muther trucker, bringing tears to my eyes.

"You're not nearly as dangerous as I anticipated, Brianna."

She knew my name. That could not be good.

Tori and Austin had gone into shellshock, frozen, with their mouths hanging open, dragging on the ground. Suddenly the pink-haired crazy was in my face, light blue eyes blazing. She reminded me of an anime with an attitude problem. I resisted the urge to back away. What in my right mind had made me think I could take on a seasoned witch?

This was turning into a disaster, and I'd had enough.

Power surged to the surface, humming though my entire body. I felt like I was electrified from head to toe. Blankets of rain fell from the dark purple sky, assaulting the witches who wished me dead, while my friends and I stood in a pocket of dry ground. Isolating the storm, I let the fierce winds keep the two lackeys at bay. There was no turning back now. Blinded by fury, fear, and protectiveness, I unfurled the darkness I promised I would never let loose again.

I latched onto the source of the girl not more than a few years my senior. "I'll show you just how dangerous I can be." A sliver of her magic trickled into me, and I closed my eyes. The arousal of such supreme power was vivid and potent in my blood.

"Your kind deserves to die," she wheezed, pain slicing across her face as she dropped to her knees, drenched.

Tight-lipped, I towered over her. "Are those your final words?"

The voice that yelled over the pounding rain wasn't hers. "Bri! Don't!"

CHAPTER 15

I didn't immediately stop ripping the magic from her soul. It took more effort than I wanted to admit, but hearing Gavin's voice reminded me of what I had done to him—what I was doing to this witch.

Around me a small monsoon still poured. I took a few long, deep breaths and quieted the elements that answered my summons. Slowly the downpour became a light drizzle. The lightning disappeared behind the dark clouds. And winds died down.

Lifting my gaze, sapphire eyes met mine.

Where the hell did he come from?

"What are you doing here?" I croaked.

Dark hair was plastered to his face, curling at the ends. His ripped jeans and dark shirt clung to his formidable form. He hadn't faired the rainstorm as well as we had. "Sophie texted me that you were in trou ble. I was a couple blocks away with Jared."

I frowned, feeling disorientated. "How did you find me?"

He stepped in front of me, eyes glued to mine. "I followed the storm."

My face tensed. "Oh." Later, when I wasn't shaken up, I was going to ask just what exactly he and Jared had been up to. Nothing good, I am sure, and probably dangerous.

"I got here as soon as I could," he said, an unspoken apology in his eyes.

But it hadn't been soon enough. I lowered my eyes and turned around, needing a few minutes to collect myself. Frenzy was swimming in my veins.

"Holy fuck!" Austin exclaimed, his eyes as large as an owl. "That. Was. Sick."

He didn't even know what 'that' was, I thought to myself.

"You really think so?" I heard Sophie ask, sounding surprised.

Excitement laced Austin's voice. "Hell, yes! What, did you guys get bit by a radioactive spider or something?" Just like Austin to think we were from a comic book.

"Or something," Gavin muttered. I could sense his eyes on me. "Bri," he called my name.

I shook my head vigorously, keeping my back to him as I tried to fight the power that consumed me. There was this bad aftertaste from stealing a witch's power. It left me feeling frazzled and hungry for more. I didn't trust myself. "Don't touch me," I warned, dark and raspy.

He didn't listen. His hand touched my shoulder.

I spun around so fast, colors swirled. "I said, *don't touch me*," I growled, eyes blazing in the darkness.

Didn't he get it? I just needed a few minutes to absorb this huge amount of energy I had stolen. *Stolen*. The word rolled around in my head. I had never stolen anything in my life. I could feel the witch's essence inside me, flowing through my veins. It was a high like no other. Euphoric. Supreme.

I was afraid that if anyone got too close, I might lose control. It was a valid worry. A growing darkness fluttered inside me, inciting me to take more. Devour them all. Once I had a taste, I felt starved. I needed time to get the craving under control. Problem was…I just didn't know how.

Damn it.

Brow arched. "You won't hurt me," he said. Reaching out, his hand brushed alongside my cheek. A spark ignited.

His touch changed everything. I sighed. The buildup of power evaporated into wisps of smoke, no longer enchanting me. Clear eyed, I shifted my gaze to the figure still lying on the ground, her wet pink hair splayed on the blacktop. A heavy weight settled inside me, knowing that I had done the unthinkable.

"What did you do to her?" Tori asked, stepping forward. "Is she dead?"

I had almost forgotten about my friends.

Gavin never took his eyes off me, but shook his head. "No. She's not dead. Bri stripped her soul of magic. Every last drop. She was a witch."

Every last drop. Those words ricocheted in my head. I thought I had stopped in time, that I hadn't taken her to the cleaners, but looking down at her pale face, I could no longer sense the tingles of magic. Her two cronies had bolted at Gavin's arrival and seeing me suck their friend dry. Lucky for them...but not for me.

They had seen my face. They knew my name. It was only a matter of time before they or others came looking for me. And that was really bad. *My aunt.* What if they stumbled upon her instead of me? What if they hurt her to get to me?

I couldn't let that happen, but what was I supposed to do?

Slurp the magic from every witch?

That was the exact thing I was trying to avoid. Using those powers was going to destroy me, but if I didn't...I was toast anyway.

Talk about being stuck between a rock and a hard place. I was too drained to think, let alone plan. The magical high was dropping fast.

"A witch?" I heard both Tori and Austin echoed, bringing me back to the present.

Right. One disaster at a time.

First I had to get through this night and the explanation of what the hell they had just witnessed. By telling them, I couldn't shake the feeling that I would be putting them smack dab in the middle of danger, but what other choice did I have, except tell them the truth.

The truth sets you free.

Well, I was about to find out if that was the case.

"Sweet," Austin added.

Only Austin would think seeing the unexplainable was cool.

Tori's eyes bounced between Gavin, Sophie, and me. "I-Is Brianna going to be okay?" she stammered, hugging her arms around herself.

Gavin raked a hand through his messy hair. "I hope so."

I couldn't help but notice that Tori stuck close to Austin side, and it made me wonder if she was afraid of *me*. I wouldn't have blamed her. Hell, I scared myself.

"What just happened? I don't understand. What is going on?" Tori demanded.

Gavin took my hand, threading our fingers together. "We'll explain, but first we need to get Bri off the streets."

"What do we do with *her*?" Sophie gestured with her eyes to the body.

His jaw worked. "I'll come back and make sure she is...okay."

Sophie narrowed her eyes. "Are you sure that is wise?"

Staring at his shoulder, I bit my lip. I didn't really believe that Gavin was going to just let her walk away into the sunset. I've seen another darker side of him, and I think Sophie and I both wondered just how far he would go to keep me safe.

Wordlessly, I walked to the car.

I was afraid to look at my friends—scared to see the condemnation and fear in their eyes. Not everyone would be so willing to accept what I was—a witch. It had taken me more than a minute to accept, so I could expect nothing less of them. As much as it would hurt me, I would give them space and time to come to terms with everything they were going to learn about me.

Tori's hand shook as she fumbled with keys, trying to unlock her car.

"You've had quite a shock, Tori. Let me drive," Sophie offered, holding out her hand.

Tori chewed on her lip before dropping the keys in Sophie's palm.

Gavin pulled me into his embrace and whispered in my ear, "Don't stress. I'll take care of it."

I nodded and tucked myself into the backseat of Tori's beetle with

Austin beside me. I got one last glimpse of Gavin before he disappeared into the shadows.

We had barely glided out of the parking space when Austin's mouth started flapping. "That was flipping awesome," he raved, like he just had a caffeine rush. "Don't get me wrong— It was some seriously messed up voodoo shit, but babygirl...that was badass."

I couldn't believe it. I just couldn't believe it. Austin didn't hang me on the spot with a noose, or burn me at the stake. "Thanks...I think."

He shifted excitedly in his seat. "So you are like a witch?"

"She isn't *like* anything. She *is* a witch," Sophie replied, peeking at us from the rearview mirror.

Tori turned around in her seat, her light brown ponytail swished through the air. "Did you always know that you were...?"

"A witch," I supplied, sensing her disbelief.

Tori fidgeted with the strap of her seatbelt. I couldn't fault her for being uncomfortable, because I was feeling pretty awkward myself.

"No. I just found out this year. Gavin told me."

"So hot and smexy is a witch too?" Austin asked.

I could only assume he was talking about Gavin. Austin looked to be rolling the idea around in his head, testing it out. I nodded. "Yup."

"Christ. That explains why he is so piping hot."

Only Austin. "I guess, but I don't really think being a witch automatically means you are guaranteed to be swoon-worthy."

He leaned forward. "I beg to differ. You. Lukas. Gavin. Sophie. I haven't met Jared, but yeah...so far everyone on that list is categorized as smokin' hot."

I rolled my eyes.

"I have so many questions. You caused that wicked storm back there, didn't you?"

Ding. Ding. Ding. Give that man a gold star. "Just one of my many talents."

He angled in his seat toward me. "Just how many more do you have?"

The list seemed to be growing. I shrugged, eyeballing a piece of fuzz on the back of Tori's seat. "I can summon dreams."

"I always knew you were a badass," he said, grinning.

I stared. He was giving me a brain freeze, and my lip was starting to throb. I tried to answer the gazillion questions Austin kept throwing at me, while Tori stay silent, just listening. It worried me. I glanced at the dash, checking out the time. My body was screaming to lie down.

"I can't believe you never told us." Hurt laced Tori's voice, and it tugged at my heart. She had been quiet most of the drive.

My eyes begged her to understand from my perspective. "I'm sorry. I just didn't know how to tell you without sounding like a total whack job."

Tori looked away, chewing on her lip. "Nothing is ever going to be the same."

Nope. Normal ended the moment I exposed myself. I struggled for something to say, but nothing would erase what she had seen, what she now knew. At least Austin had handled the truth with more vigor than I deserved.

The little car slipped lower into gear as we approached Holly Ridge. I stared out the window, losing myself in the blurring trees that crowded the sides of the road. There was lightness in my chest. I still wished the revelation of my true nature had been on my terms, when I had been ready, yet now that they knew, I was relieved.

No more lies.

No more hiding.

No more secrets.

There was only one more person left. I could just imagine that conversation.

Hey, Aunt Clara, Gavin is a witch. And so am I. Except I strip other witches of their magic, absorbing their powers. Just one small hitch, it damages my soul. No biggie. Any questions?

Yeah, that so wasn't going to go well.

I knew that I had to tell her the truth...eventually.

The sight of my house, and the little glowing light in the kitchen window warmed my heart. Sophie assured me that she would see to it that my friends got home safe. I sent her a quick text when I dragged my butt through my bedroom door, thanking her again for everything. Then I tossed my phone on the dresser and collapsed.

Alone, tears climbed up my throat. I couldn't stop thinking about what I'd done tonight. How could I look at myself in the mirror and not see a monster? The power I had, the enjoyment it gave me, and the thirst for more, all filled me with guilt.

Sleep eluded me and probably would for many nights to come. Lying on the bed, staring at nothing, I thought about invading Lukas's dreams, but I realized I wanted someone else. It wasn't that I didn't think Lukas could distract me. I just wanted a different kind of distraction; because I couldn't close my eyes without seeing the girl, with her pink hair, sprawled on the ground. It was an image I wanted burned from my memory, and maybe if I knew that she was alive, it would lesson my guilt.

Hey, if I wasn't going to get any beauty rest, then I might as well do something productive. I should have been all out of juice, but I was guessing the magic I stole rejuvenated my energy.

Just handy-dandy.

Letting my eyes drift shut, tingles mingled as I guided them into the realm of dreams. At first I stumbled around in the dark before I find the star-like lights that led to millions and millions of dreams. I pictured Gavin's masculine beauty and whispered his name, waiting...

CHAPTER 16

I refused to force my will upon him. It would be his choice to let me in...if he was asleep. By now it was well after midnight and the rest of the world was fast asleep with sugarplums dancing in their heads. Not me.

Why hadn't I done this more?

My heart skipped when I felt our dreams merge, two pieces that finally clicked.

The blackness around me was swept away in a tunnel of blurring speed. I blinked a few times, adjusting to my new surroundings.

Just like a guy to dream about being a rock star. Not that I expected unicorns and rainbows, but this...it made my lips twitch. I guess those little kid dreams still live in us all, and I could picture Gavin as a little boy rockin' out in a make-believe stadium just like this. Although I imagined it would have been packed with screaming, adoring fans, instead of empty.

Thank God he wasn't wearing tight leather pants. I might not have been able to keep it together.

The click of my heels echoed as I walked down the aisle toward center stage.

Wait. Heels?

WTF.

I glanced down at my feet, seeing silvery, cage-like high heels—emphasis on high. I'd be lucky I didn't break my neck before I got there. But that wasn't the only thing that caught my attention. I was dressed in a skintight dress that clung to my every curve.

Oh. He was funny.

I heard a chuckle, and my head snapped up. There he was, alone with just a stool and a guitar. Fireflies jetted into my belly, and I missed a step when he flashed me a sexy smirk.

Now he's done it.

Even my heart sighed at the sight of him in ripped jeans and a black t-shirt. It wasn't fair how just a glimpse could send me into cardiac arrest. And just like that my mind went blank and I forgot what I'd been running from. Mission accomplished. I got my distraction.

He had one leg propped up on the stool crossbar, with the acoustic guitar resting in his lap. "I didn't expect to see you so soon." His voice carried through the stadium.

I regained my composure and made my way up the stage. "I couldn't sleep."

Understanding crept into his eyes. "You had quite a confrontation tonight. Only makes sense that your mind would be racing."

Racing? It was running a bloody marathon. "So this is what you dream about? Classic."

He strummed a cord on the guitar with his thumb. "There is nothing classic about me."

I kicked off the strappy shoes. "Thanks for the duds by the way. They really make a statement."

His blue eyes sparkled. "It suits you."

"That's because you are a guy. I am about two seconds away from ripping this itchy dress into tiny little pieces."

Undeniable amusement sparked in his expression. "Can I watch?"

I let a out short laugh. In a just a few minutes of being in his presence, I already felt lighter, but I was about to make the atmosphere heavy again. The small curl on my lips faded. "What happened to her?"

He stood, setting aside the guitar. "I should have known that you just couldn't let it be. Do you really want the details, Bri? They will not change anything."

I might not want to hear them, but I needed to know. Maybe it will help clear my guilty conscious. "I need to know that I didn't kill that girl or screw her up for life."

His lips brushed the side of my cheek as he reached me. "You didn't."

"What I did—if she hadn't pushed me—" I couldn't finish the sentences without choking up.

"I wish I could give you the answers you are looking for, but she was gone when I went back. I'm sorry."

"Are you sure you went the right way? I mean, she looked pretty out of it."

His hand fell to his side, and he tilted his head to the side. "I might not have lived here long, but I have a sick sense of direction."

I didn't doubt his skills. My shoulders sagged. "She knew my name."

Brows drawn tight, he said, "Then someone gave it to them."

A bitter sensation had taken up residency in my belly. "That's what I was afraid of."

His hands curled at his sides and eyes flashed. "They know who you are now. You are not safe, and the attacks will only increase. I'm going to find out who has the big ass mouth and make them regret squealing."

Right. I hadn't told him that Lukas knows what I am. Now seemed like the wrong time. I wanted to talk to Lukas first. "I'm coming with you," I said. Someone had to keep him out of trouble.

His jaw set. "Not happening."

Stubborn as usual, but I had expected nothing less. I can be just as pigheaded. "You can't stop me." Sure, I had no idea where this underground community of witches was, but I could be resourceful. And he wasn't the only witch I knew. Lukas could probably get me there just as easily. I hoped.

"It is far too dangerous for you to walk right into the lion's den, because that is exactly where I'd be taking you."

I pressed my lips together. "This is my life. I think I have a right to

474

know what is going on." If witches were plotting to kill me, I wanted a heads-up.

These gangs of underground witches were starting to become a real thorn in my side. I racked my brain trying to figure out who would sell me out, unless of course the culprit wasn't a witch at all. You ask the right questions, cast the proper spells, and you could get Mother Teresa to spill her beans. Food for thought. Unfortunately, my brain wasn't hungry at the moment.

His striking features were highlighted in the waning light. "I want to protect you from getting hurt, and that means sheltering you from all the evil in the world."

The sincerity in his voice almost had me giving in. Almost. However, the desire to protect my only family and *him* overruled. "I'll wear a disguise. No one will recognize me. I can get Sophie to help me."

He wasn't convinced. "You are going to get us both in a lot of trouble."

"It wouldn't be the first time," I muttered.

Sauntering to the edge of the stage, he scanned the row upon row of empty seats, and then ran a hand through his hair. "If she got back to them and told them what happened, what you did... It will support their campaign that you are a threat and must be eliminated." He spun around, pinning me with a look. "Don't you see that?"

I understood exactly what I might walk into. Still didn't change anything. If he was going, I was going. "Fine," I huffed. "You made your point. I understand the dangers, but what about the risks you put yourself in because of me? What is the difference?"

He cocked a brow. "The difference is, I can handle myself."

Oh, no. He did not just pull that Neanderthal stunt.

My inner bitch came out. "Is that a dig because I am a girl or because you're a better witch?" My intention when I merged our dreams had not been to fight, but it looked like a fight was imminent.

Standing in front of me, he looked down, a frown on his lips. "You know that's not what I meant."

"Good. Then there isn't a problem. I'm going."

Doubt crossed his features. "If we do this, we do it my way, which means you follow *my* directions."

"I can do that." Well, at least in theory.

Warm hands framed my face, and the pupils of his blue eyes started to glow. "I'm counting on it." Ever so lightly he pressed his lips to mine in a soft kiss. My pulsed kicked up. And then he was kissing me again, but it was nothing like the first. Gone was the tenderness and in its place was a fierce unspoken promise. It broke my insecurities, my fears, my uncertainties, only to build me back up.

He grounded me. He made me stronger. Maybe that's what love did.

When I finally woke up, it was still dark and upon further investigation, I discovered it was just after three in the morning. Ugh. It was too early to get up for school, but I knew that I would not be able to go back to sleep—the undisturbed kind. My lips were still tingling.

I thought I deserved a mental health day.

AFTER A VERY FEEBLE charade at being sick, my aunt called me out of school for the day. I did a little happy dance in my room and then sent a quick text to Gavin who responded with, **hooky!**

He could make even the simplest things bad. I loved that about him. He made me feel like a rebel, when I was anything but.

I switched myself off from the world and finally caught a few hours of needed sleep. It was my growling tummy that woke me up. Throwing my hair into a crazy knot, I went in search of something to satisfy my hunger.

A quick glance at the clock told me it was more lunchtime than breakfast. I reached for the box of strawberry Pop-tarts that were ever present in our kitchen, because I couldn't live without them. I tore open the silver foil package, and breaking off a corner, I stuffed my face. I didn't even warm them up.

I was going to take advantage of having the house to myself.

My aunt had already left for the day, and I had no intention of cleaning up after myself, getting dressed, or even taking a shower. It was that kind of day. I wanted to see no one and I wanted no one to see me. It was just me and my DVR filled with bad reality TV.

Taking my breakfast/lunch to the sofa, I collapsed like a hippo getting a suntan. I wiped the crumbs off my T-shirt and licked my fingers. Today, I wanted to give my brain a break and think about nothing related to magic, witches, or being hunted like an animal.

The doorbell rang just as one nameless girl on the TV ripped the hair from another nameless girl in what was surely going to be an epic catfight. I groaned. The last thing I wanted was to move, and I laid there a moment contemplating ignoring the salesman or worse. But the ringing was followed sharply by the rapping of knuckles on wood.

Swearing under my breath, I rolled off the couch and swung open the door. I took one look at who was on the other side and started to slam it closed. A menacing Lukas shot his hand out. I knew before he even uttered a word that something was wrong. His hair was disheveled, his usual college tee was wrinkled, and he smelled like stale beer. I was in for a treat.

"You slept with him!" he exploded.

Well, damn.

Lukas. Yelled. At. Me. I was almost in as much shock at him yelling at me as I was that he knew Gavin and I had...well, done the dirty. Lukas hadn't even bothered to pose it as a question, but went straight to an accusation...meaning he already knew the answer.

I wanted to crawl into the nearest hole.

Wow. That was quite a greeting. I was taken aback. "Who told you that?"

"Are you saying it's not true?" He dared me in a growl.

The ball in my stomach grew.

I wanted to lie, and it was on the tip of my tongue to confirm that it wasn't true, but I knew that sooner or later I was going to have to make it clear that he was not my choice. Connection or not, my feelings for him were not as strong as what I felt for Gavin. I wanted to spare Lukas pain, and I had tried to warn him off, but he wouldn't listen.

Yet, I felt trapped.

And my silence was confirmation enough.

"That's what I thought," he snapped.

Hurt. Anger. Pain. Sadness.

They were all behind Lukas's emerald eyes. He made me feel like a piece of crap, and that got under my skin. "It's really none of your business," I snapped, and started to once again slam the door in his face.

He stuck his foot out, stopping the forward process and bulldozed his way into my house. "That's such bullshit." The door vibrated shut behind him, shaking the rafters of the house.

I am pretty sure I missed the episode in my life where I agreed to have Lukas approve of my every decision. "You are drunk," I said, pushing at his chest. It was like trying to move a cement wall. Hurt, I understood, even anger, but there was such a strong jealousy growing in his green eyes. It started to frighten me. It seemed so alien of his personality. I half-expected to see a circular mother-ship land in my front yard.

Beam me up, Scotty.

"With good cause." Sparks started to shoot off him.

Holy crap.

He looked like a ticking bomb ready to explode, and I was going to be hit by the shrapnel. Okay. Maybe this was the wrong approach, but he caught me off guard. I saw my lazy day drift right out the window. "Lukas. You need to calm down."

Waves of anger rolled off his body as he towering over me. "How did you think I would feel? I've waited years to be with you, and you throw it in my face."

That was a low blow, and I felt it right in the gut. "That's not fair. I didn't even know that you were real until a few months ago."

Energy crackled in the air, bouncing off the walls, leaving behind black burnt marks on my aunt's pretty paint. "But it doesn't change all that we've shared. It might have been in our dreams, but it was real."

I locked down my jaw. What he said was true. How did I tell him that I loved him, but I wasn't *in* love with him? "It was for me, too."

His hand latched onto my arm, and a severe shock jolted through me, stronger than I'd ever felt. The grip in his fingers was tight, to the point of painful. "Do you feel that?" he seethed. "It is our energies linking, responding to the other. They were meant for one other, just as *you were meant to be mine.*"

The possessiveness in his voice sent a shiver down my spine, and the magic fused to my bones. "We might be connected through magic, but that is where it stops for me. My heart belongs to another." Then I held my breath.

Eyes glowing in electric-green seared mine. "For now," he conceded, his voice strained.

Power rippled through the room. The paintings on the walls trembled, and one fell to the floor, shattering. The carpet quaked under my feet, and when Lukas finally let go of my arm, there were red imprints where his fingers had been, just like the ones I had given Rianne earlier in the school year. That suddenly felt like a lifetime ago.

Whirling around, he left the same way he had come, with sheer force, fiery temper, and uncontained magic. *What the hell just happened?* I felt like I had just taken a spin through the center of a tornado. Sinking against the wall, my whole body was shaking, and there was a ball of magic sitting in the center of my chest, waiting to be set free.

I rubbed my wrist and closed my eyes.

So much for peace and quiet. It looked like I was going to be spending the rest of the day cleaning up the destruction Lukas left behind. I despised cleaning.

CHAPTER 17

The next day at school, I sought out Tori. Unlike Austin, who thought my powers were the greatest thing since smartphones, Tori had been avoiding me since the night she found out I wasn't human. It sucked. I missed her, and it had only been a few days. I had given her space, because that was what I thought she needed, but now I needed her.

"Tori!" I called.

As my best friend, I expected her to turn around and acknowledge me. That was not what happened. Pushing my way through the crowded hall, I tried to get to Tori, but after hearing me call her name, she sped up. Stunned, I stopped walking, causing a traffic jam that resulted in some name-calling and shoving. I was hurt. I couldn't believe she had given me the cold shoulder.

It felt like the whole school was against me as I was bounced around like a basketball. When I could finally see past the hordes, Tori was gone. My stomach dropped. On the flip side, she couldn't ignore me forever. Our class schedules didn't allow it, and if I had to, I would tie her up in the locker room and make her listen to what I had to say.

Austin snuck up behind me and nudged me with his shoulder. "She'll come around."

I had thought so too, but now, I wasn't so sure. "Maybe," I muttered, a sinking feeling in my tummy.

He looped an arm through mine. "Babygirl, there is nothing you can ever do, say, or *be* that would end our friendship. You are stuck with me for life."

I gave him a sideways glance. "I have yet to decide if that is good or bad."

Smiling like a goofball, he looked adorable. "Please. My friendship is a bonafide blessing."

I knew that was an attempt to make me smile, and I gave him A for effort, but it was going to take more than his dorky charm to break through my dark cloud. "I can't believe she actually snubbed me," I mumbled.

He gave my arm a squeeze. "Don't sweat it. Come on. I'll walk you to class."

I snorted, moving my feet. "We have the same class."

He grinned and ran a hand over his sleek hair. "Can't a guy just be a gentleman?"

Not in this day and age.

Tori might be ignoring me, but I was doing some ignoring of my own. I refused to let myself dwell on what happened the other day with Lukas, when he decided to fly off the handle. My head was still spinning, and I had a hard time wrapping my mind around a side of Lukas I'd never seen.

I knew that I had wounded him by choosing Gavin, and pain makes people irrational. Though seriously, he had taken irrational to a whole new level. I had been *afraid*, a new feeling for me where Lukas was involved. And once again, I couldn't help but compare Lukas to Gavin. Even when Gavin had been hurt by me and furious with me, I still felt safe. That was where the difference lay. I couldn't help but think that Lukas hadn't needed to be such a jerkface.

He'd left behind a mess that I had to clean up, and to my annoyance, it took me more than a twitch of my nose. Five hours of my life I could never get back, but for now I put Lukas at the back of my mind. I needed to find a way to get my best friend to stop treating me like a leper.

So I became a woman on a freaking mission. Nothing was going to stand in my way. True to my word, I cornered Tori in the girl's locker room. I didn't give her a chance to refuse or walk away. As the other girls were heading to the gym in their oh-so-flattering uniforms, I snagged Tori by the arm, tugging her behind a row of lockers. She didn't precisely go with me gracefully.

Jerking out of my grasp, she kept her gaze averted, tawny hair curtaining her face. "What is your deal?"

"My deal!" I screeched. "You are the one who can't even look at me now." Helpless exasperation seeped into the air, settling over me like a murky cloud.

She sunk to the bench, resting her hands on her knees. "It's not you or...what you can do."

I put my hands on my hips. "Really? Because that is not what it feels like."

"It's the world. I don't know what kind of place we live in anymore. It scares me."

Which was code for, she was scared. But I understood all too well how she felt. Not that long ago, when I had found out what Gavin was, I had the same uncertainty. "Me too," I admitted, sitting down beside her.

When our eyes met, there was so much confusion in hers. "Why did you never tell me?"

I shrugged, running my hands over the mesh material covering my thighs. "I thought I was protecting you, and..." I owed her honesty, no matter how exposing. Swallowing the lump that suddenly formed in my throat, I barreled on. "I was afraid you would look at me differently."

Tears welled in her chocolate eyes. "And that was exactly what I did. I'm sorry, B. I don't know how you handled this by yourself."

"I didn't. I had Gavin. And you are right. I should have told you. It's me who needs to apologize. I've been a crappy friend."

She brushed aside the tears before they could roll down her cheeks. "You can never be a crappy friend. Can you forgive me for the way I reacted?"

I smiled. "Always. You're my best friend, Tori."

She threw her arms around me, nearly tumbling us off the bench. "I've missed you."

I hugged her back just as tightly. It had only been a week, but I knew what she meant. "Me, too." I let go, blinking back tears of my own.

She sniffed a very unflattering goop of snot, but hey, none of that mattered among friends. "We're late." The bell had rung a few minutes ago.

"Screw Ms. Jensen."

She laughed. It was the greatest sound.

From that point on, my day no longer sucked.

My step was a little lighter as I walked onto my porch after school. The only thing this day was lacking was Gavin. I'd seen very little of him, and man could I use some one-on-one time with the big lug. He had been as preoccupied as I had been, which was odd. Usually Gavin was attuned with my emotions and the craziness that was knocking around in my brain. Today was Friday night, and I wanted to go out on a date with my boyfriend like a *normal* teenager.

I had forgotten what normal was.

Thinking of sending him a text when I got inside, I had a naughty image conjured in my head of Gavin as I passed a black bird perched on the white porch railing. "Hey, Jared," I said mindlessly.

It squawked in return, and I paused.

Did I just talk to a bird? Had I just called it Jared?

Backing up a step, I turned toward the bird, staring into its beady eyes, and I swore it was laughing at me. Then I felt the distinctive tingles of magic and knew I was off my rocker. This bird *was* Jared. So my next question was, what was Jared doing at my house? In the form of a goddamn bird?

"What are you doing here?" I snuck a quick look around just to make sure none of my neighbors saw me talking to a bird.

Jared tilted his head to the side.

I guess I shouldn't have expected him to talk back. That would have been extreme, even for me. I'd seen a lot of weird shit, but a talking bird? Even I had to draw a line somewhere.

Before I could digest what was happening, my feathered friend's form began to swirl and shimmer. Jared was transforming. I closed my eyes. "Please God, let him be wearing clothes," I mumbled to myself, pressing a hand over my closed eyes as added protection and to resist the temptation of sneaking a peek.

As soon as I heard Jared chuckle, I knew it was my sign that it was safe to open my eyes. Knowing Jared, though, I wouldn't have put it past him to try and shock me. Peering between my fingers, I was relieved to find him mostly dressed.

He was shirtless, and I didn't doubt he was that way on purpose. But I guess if I was a guy, and I had muscles like Jared, I might walk around shirtless all the time. However, for the sanity of womankind, Jared needed to keep his abs covered.

The bigger question...what was he doing here—incognito nonetheless?

Then it hit me.

It was time. We were going underground, so to speak.

"Gavin sent me to retrieve you for our little excursion." He cracked a grin, completely at ease with his near-nakedness.

I, on the other hand, was starting to develop hot flashes, and it was becoming increasingly hard to keep my gaze focused on his face. "We're going now?" I asked, my voice just one notch below shrill.

He leaned a jean-clad hip on the rail. "Well, once Sophie is finished with you." Jared shook his head. "I don't envy you. My sister is going to do a number on you. Gavin told her to make you look like completely different person, and I think you and I both know that Soph can be over the top."

I let that sink in. Just great. "Wonderful. Lead the way." Then I realized he hadn't taken a car. "I guess I'll drive."

He gave me a wicked grin.

I sent a quick text to my aunt, telling her that I was going out with Gavin tonight and not to wait up; I was probably going to be home late. Then we climbed into my Mustang. During the short drive, the car felt cramped, with Jared's bulky presence next to me. And there were waves of anticipated excitement rolling off his muscled form, which made me antsy.

Gavin was waiting at the door when I put the car in park, killing the engine. He arched a brow at his shirtless brother. "When I asked you to get Bri, I didn't expect you to go Magic Mike."

Jared's eyes twinkled. "I couldn't resist."

Gavin faced me, leaning a shoulder on the door. "There's still time to change your mind."

I screwed up my face. "Not happening."

"I was afraid you'd say that," he grumbled, clearly displeased.

Sophie bounced out of nowhere, and grabbed my hand, dragging me upstairs. All I got from Gavin was a smirk. I didn't know which was worse, letting Sophie have full control over my makeover or sneaking into an exclusive club of witches to ask questions that would probably get us killed. I was such a shitty girlfriend.

If I really loved Gavin, I should probably let him go, because being with me was hazardous to everyone's life. But I was just too selfish and too chicken shit to face this alone. I needed and depended on him.

"I have been dying to wield my awesome skills on you since we met," she said as we climbed the stairs.

Oh, boy. She reminded me of Austin and Tori, who took every opportunity to make me their living Barbie doll. "That seems to be a running theme from people in my life," I mumbled, rounding the hall and following her into her room.

A wrought iron bed sat just under a wide window. I could hear the lapping of waves. A sheer teal canopy surrounded a bed decorated in deep purple and gold. There was a gypsy ambiance. In the corner was a dresser of rich wood, housing a display of brightly colored perfume bottles reflecting against a mirror. The room smelled distinctly female, a mix of floral and vanilla.

Sophie shut the door behind us. "That's because you don't see the potential the rest of us do."

I snorted. "Or you all suffer from some kind of eye condition like beer goggles."

She shook her head, sending her raven hair over her shoulder. "Well, when I'm done with you, you'll be unrecognizable."

"That's the plan."

"No one is going to be able to take their eyes off you."

Gulp. I definitely didn't like the sound of that. "Umm. I was hoping for something more subtle, you know, to blend in, not draw too much attention."

She gave a musical laugh. "Oh Brianna, you are in for a treat. I wish I was going to be able to see your face."

"Aren't you coming with us?" I asked as she angled her head, studying me. Under her scrutiny I started to get nervous. What I was about do, where I was about to go, finally sunk in. This shit was real.

She bit her lip, picking up the ends of my hair. "I think I'll start with whatever you call this. Hold on to your witch's brew. You're in for the shock of your life."

That was debatable. Finding out I was a clàr silte was currently the blow of the decade.

"And sadly no," she continued. "I won't be going with you. I was overruled by muscles and testosterone. It sucks being the only girl. Of course if you talked to Gavin..."

"Oh, no. I am not getting in the middle. It's probably best anyhoo. I would only blame myself if something happened to you." And I would never forgive myself, I thought silently.

Just a flicker of emotion crossed her face before she snuffed it. "A girl can try. I just hate to miss out on all the excitement."

She started to work her magic as we talked. I could feel the tingles vibrating in the air and dancing over my skin. I stood as still as possible. The last thing I wanted was to make a sudden move and end up with neon green skin or a third nipple. "Your family has a weird sense of excitement," I mumbled.

Her perky little nose wrinkled. "I never really thought about it. So how are Austin and Tori handling your heritage?"

I gave a one-shoulder shrug. "They're adjusting, one more than the other, but I think we reached a turning point today."

"Good, because the darkness on your soul—it's doubled," she informed stonily.

Sophie—the bearer of bad news. My heart leaped into my throat. "Not entirely a surprise, after what I did." All that wishful thinking flushed down the drain.

"Stop fidgeting," she scolded.

I frowned. My mind was whirling, and she was worried about my posture? The only positive side I could see to this situation was that tonight I was going to do something about it. No more sitting on the couch with my head under the covers. I couldn't spend the rest of my life shut up in my house, no matter how appealing that sounded right now.

"Smile," Sophie instructed.

I gave her a dry look, not exactly in a cheery moody.

She put a hand on her hip, shifting her weight. "I can't work with scowl lines."

Softening my lips, I tipped the corners in a pathetic smile. "Happy?" I said between clenched teeth.

"Don't stress. I know Gavin, and he will move heaven and earth to find a way to stop the darkness and he will remove every witch who stands in his way."

At what expense? And for how long? He couldn't protect me 24-7, and I needed to stand on my own two feet—as a witch and as a young woman on the edge of adulthood. There wouldn't always be someone to save me. Aunt Clara. Gavin. Lukas. My friends. Morgana. I never realized how many people I had that I cared about. I needed to do this for them. But most importantly for me.

A saucy grin spread over her soft pink lips. "My masterpiece is complete. Gavin is so going to flip his lid. At least I'll be able to see that."

My heart stuttered. I got the feeling that was a bad thing.

She put her hands on my shoulders and ordered me to close my eyes. Spinning me around, I let her guide me. Then when we weren't moving anymore, she said, "Okay, open them."

I stood in front of a full-length mirror. Starting from my toes, I was surprised to see these adorable black army booties on my feet. A sigh escaped my mouth, silently thanking Sophie for not making me trudge around in four-inch heels. This might not be so bad. My gaze tipped upward.

Then I saw the candy-striped thigh-high socks with lace detail, and I groaned. Above the top of socks was a bit of peek-a-boo flesh before the start of the barely there tutu black skirt. *Tutu?* The fun didn't stop there. Hell, no. A hot pink tank top hugged my skin with a black ripped shirt overlaid. It looked like Wolverine had taken a swipe at it. And if that wasn't enough, there were lace gloves on my hands.

I blinked.

Was that me in the reflection?

It couldn't be. Good God. I looked like a...

A freaking anime with Barney-colored purple hair and gold eyes.

I gasped, running a hand over my face. "Sophie," I growled.

CHAPTER 18

I definitely didn't look like Brianna Rafferty anymore. Snapping a quick photo of myself, I sent it to Tori and Austin. They would get a kick out of seeing a different side of me.

"What do you think?" Sophie asked in a singsong voice.

I picked my jaw off the floor. "I think you are a mad genius."

She stood behind me observing her handiwork. "That's a compliment, right?"

"Sophie!" Gavin yelled from the other side the door. "What is taking so—?"

He had opened the door, getting his first glimpse of the *new* me. His ocean-blue eyes darkened, caressing every curve of my body, until they settled on mine in the mirror. My cheeks started to turn the color of my hot pink shirt. And then he simple said, "You're not coming."

I spun around, meeting him face to face. "I did not just spend the last half hour having my entire look screwed with for nothing. I'm going. We discussed this."

He crossed his arms and assumed his I'm-not-budging-stance. "Yeah, that was before my sister decided to dress only half of you."

I rolled my eyes.

Sophie snorted, throwing her hands in the air. "Please. You are just use to seeing her in jeans. Jealous much?"

I wasn't sure if I should get in the middle, so I kind of stood in the center of the room all awkwardly. I tried to shove my hands in my pockets, only to realize I wasn't wearing pants.

He cut Sophie a droll look. "You were supposed to disguise her, not make her an invitation to every freak."

So much for keeping my mouth shut. "Can we just forget what I'm wearing? I mean seriously. I have purple hair. Sophie, why do I have grape Kool-Aid hair?"

She cracked a small smile and covered a snicker with a cough. "Trust me. No one will even think twice."

That's what I'm afraid of.

"Because my sister isn't thinking straight," Gavin said, quickly losing his patience and riling my irritation.

I brushed past Gavin without another word.

"Bri, wait!" he called, falling in step behind me.

"Smooth move," I heard Sophie before I was out of earshot.

This was not how I envisioned my evening. What started out as a PJs, movie, and popcorn kind of night quickly turned into...I couldn't even find the words to describe what was happening.

Regardless, it was time to get this sideshow on the road. I rounded the stairs with him nipping at my heels. Gavin caught me before I could step outside, and by caught, I mean his arm snaked around my waist and hauled me up against him. "Just wait a minute, will you?"

It only took a heartbeat for me to relax in his arms. I stared at the black band around his wrist, trying to avoid the tingles tiptoeing down my spine.

His voice tickled my ear. "If we are going to do this, then we can't go at odds with each other. The tension between us will be easily picked up, and the place we are going thrives on chaos."

I knew that there were going to be a variety witches there tonight able to do all kinds of magic I didn't understand. He was right. I needed to chill out. "Are you done bossing me around?" I asked.

He released a heavy sigh. "For now."

Good enough—*for now*, my thoughts echoed his words. I rested the back of my head on his chest. "I just want my life back," I whispered. He nipped at my ear. "Then let's go get it."

THE WHOLE DRIVE, I kept my eyes peeled for anyone suspicious. The problem was, my paranoia was getting the best of me and everyone looked suspicious at the moment. The car behind us must be tailing us, right? The little old lady walking her dog was a double agent, surely? I mean, Jared could turn into a bird. I transformed into a class act hooker. So that meant no one could be trusted, not even the sweet grandmas. It didn't matter what time it was, there were witches lurking everywhere, and we were walking right into the heart of a coven.

However, the highlight of the trip into Wilmington was the little boy in the car next to me. He took one look at my colorful hair and stuck his tongue out at me. It made me laugh, releasing some of the tension that lined my body.

But it returned in tenfold at the arrival of our destination. We had driven into the city and through some dicey neighbors. It occurred to me that for a Friday night, this part of town seemed eerily dead. I was used to the Riverfront, with its boisterous boardwalk, tea tree lights, and the constant music of the ocean.

Gavin greeted me at the car door, lacing his fingers with mine, and Jared flanked me on the other side. My two bodyguards—they were kind of an impressive sight. As we approached a small black building nestled between two larger ones, my pulse started hammering.

Gavin must have noticed the increase in my heart rate. "There is still time to change your mind, Bri. Jared and I can handle this."

I shook my head, and kept my gaze straight before I lost my nerve. My boots clapped on the pavement as we approached the one-story building. It was almost invisible, overshadowed by the sheer size of the others, but I think that was the point. This was a sparse part of the city, off the main strip. On the metal door was a glowing, light blue symbol that I knew was laced with enchanted ink. I didn't have to be told that only those with magic running in their blood could enter. No bouncer necessary.

"This is it?" I asked, clearly not awestruck. I had been anticipating something more intimidating, like creepy iron fences and gargoyle statues.

"What were you expecting?" Gavin asked, amused at my scrunched face.

Jared was grinning like a total shithead, loving every second of my unease. "A spooky castle with a dungeon and a dragon," Jared supplied.

Gavin glanced around me, searing his brother with a glare. "Jared, don't be a dick."

Jared rocked on his heels. "It can't be helped. It's in my nature."

I rolled my eyes, but he really wasn't that far off, not that I was going to admit it. I had expected less ordinary. "Can we just go in already?" Being on the streets made me feel exposed.

Jared's eyes twinkled. "Ladies first." The door squeaked as he swung it open.

The magic inside me kicked up as I took in my surroundings. It wasn't at all like I had imagined, just like the exterior. No black caldrons with steam brewing from them. No one was riding around on a broomstick or wearing a velvet cloak. It wasn't dark, damp, and musty, like an underground cave. I had been warned, but not prepared.

Eyes widening, I stood eyeballing the hordes of people crammed into the main room. I had to hand it to Sophie; she knew what she was doing when she gave me this wacky makeover. It looked like someone had vomited skittles. There were people—correction, there were witches—scantily dressed like me, with wild hair like me. Jared and Gavin were the ones who stood out in their jeans and rocker t-shirts. Jared might be beefier, but Gavin had a dark scowl that was more potent than any muscle could ever be.

Looking around, it was literally a damn dance club.

Music blared and lights flashed throughout the industrial styled room. Metal I-beams stretched across the ceiling, but it was the cages that caught my eye.

Color me surprised.

Jared grinned. "Normal is overrated."

That's just it. It wasn't the oddity of the people; it was that I had been here before. In a dream. A dream I had shared with Lukas during training. I bristled.

The hand around mine tightened, and Gavin leaned closed to me, whispering in my ear "What is it? Shocked?"

That's just it, I wasn't. Not as much as I should have been, because of Lukas. What did that mean? Now wasn't the time, but later, Lukas had plenty to answer for. Not for a second did I think it was a co-winky-dink that he had brought me here. I shook my head.

Looking closer, I saw little things at first glance I had missed—the shimmery glow that radiated off some of the witches—the occasional glimpse of swirling tattoos on bodies. Something furry brushed up against my legs, and my gaze dropped to the ground.

Yikes. I jumped.

Jared snickered. "Looks like you've got an admirer."

Gavin frowned.

I had a feeling that was going to be the theme of the night. "Shifter?" I assumed. "A distant cousin of yours?" I asked Jared.

Now it was Gavin's turn to snicker. "Shall we?" he said, nodding to the room in front of us.

Jared put on his game face. "Let's get this party started."

"Why did I drag him along?" Gavin mumbled, watching his brother weave into the mass of bodies on the dance floor.

"Because he knows people who know people. Don't worry. He knows that we are here for a purpose, right?"

"I wouldn't count on it."

Our fingers were still interlocked as we meandering our way through the crowds, following behind Jared. Every few steps he gave a nod to someone he recognized or a charming grin to some girl. We reached the bar, and all I could think was that I needed a drink —desperately.

"Captain and coke," I said to the bartender, sliding him my fake ID, the one Gavin had gotten me for my tattoo.

Both Jared and Gavin lifted their identical dark brows.

I stared back. "What?"

"I'll have what she's having," Jared said, turning to the dude behind the bar with neon green spiky hair. There were dark shades covering his eyes.

"Coming right up. Anything for you, handsome?" the bartender asked, slipping his sunglass down and winking at Gavin.

I couldn't stop the giggle from escaping.

"No, thanks," Gavin replied. Then he pinned Jared and I with a look, muttering, "Someone has to drive tonight." He leaned back against the bar, as we waited for our drinks, which arrived shockingly quick.

I swirled the drink with my straw, wondering if there was anything *extra* added, like some kind of magical juice, if you get my drift. My hands clasped around the iced glass. Bottoms up. I sucked down a huge gulp to both calm my nerves and rid the dryness that had settled in my mouth. The rum burned slightly as it coated my throat.

Gavin slid a hand to the small of my back, the corners of his mouth twitching. "Slow down, hoss. I don't want to have to carry you out of here."

I tugged down the hem of my uber short shirt, cursing Sophie under my breath. "One drink isn't going to send me over the edge. Anyway, aren't we supposed to be undercover?"

"You—yes. Jared and I have been here before." His brows were dark straight slashes above his serious eyes. "I am used to a more *attack first, ask questions later* approach, but with you by my side, I need to be more cautious."

"You don't need to change your tactics for me. I can hold my own."

"If you get hurt..." He glanced away, a muscle ticking in his jaw.

This was a good time to chance the subject. "So what's the plan?"

He blinked, and I tried not to be swept away by my surroundings, including the guy next to me. "We wait," he said.

Not precisely the covert operation I'd expected. "I'm going to need another drink," I muttered.

Gavin's sharp eyes kept scanning the slew of witches, darting from one end of the room to the other. I couldn't tear my gaze from him. Under disco lights, in a room filled with ribbons of magic, he never looked more ominous...or hot. Maybe it was the drink, or because I loved him, but I knew he was primed for trouble. "Are we looking for someone?" I asked, biting the end of my straw.

He didn't say anything for a moment. "Yeah. Our key into the back room."

Nothing good ever comes from the back room of a place like this. "What does he look like?"

"*She*," he corrected.

We were looking for a girl. Peachy. I tried to bank the jealousy that crawled inside me. I failed.

"Don't worry. She's not my type." He reached up and smoothed my hair back off my face. "I miss your eyes," he whispered and kissed the tip of my nose. He tucked me against his side, and his warmth was reassuring, diffusing my momentary lapse in security.

Sipping on my watered-down drink, I thought about the dream with Lukas and our dance, which was totally inappropriate, considering I was snuggled up to my boyfriend, who was willing to put his life on the line for mine. Immediately I felt guilty and banished all thoughts of Lukas from my mind. I owed Gavin that respect, and I needed to keep a clear head in case things went south.

The waiting was killing me, and the alcohol only helped a little. At any minute I waited for someone to yell, 'Look! It's Brianna Rafferty, the energy sucker. Get her!' And then all hell would rain down on us.

I was slurping down my second drink when a girl slinked up to Jared. She had silver hair that reached just past her chin in an asymmetrical bob and a killer body. I was envious. Her gray eyes were framed by bright blue lashes, the same shade as her satin dress. Jared grinned down at the girl a few years older than me, flashing his lethal dimples. "Astar. I had just about given up on you tonight."

She gave him a sultry grin. "And I thought I'd never see you again."

Jared took a swig of his drink with an air of indifference. "I like to keep things mysterious."

"I guess there's more we don't know about each other." Her cosmic blue nails tiptoed up his chest.

Jared's eyes raked over her frame. "Other than our bodies," he added.

TMI.

I almost vomited in my mouth.

Gavin put his hand at my hip and squeezed, my warning to behave. This must be who we had been waiting for—Jared's booty call. I didn't know what game they were up to, but it better pay off. We had risked too much to waste the opportunity at finding out any information. There were people conspiring to kill me.

Watching Jared work his mojo was both nauseating and bewildering, but he got the job done. Go team Jared. I got the feeling he was playing a dangerous game with this Astar. She had a gleam of naughtiness in her smoky eyes.

"You remember my brother."

She bit her bottom lip. "How could I forget?"

Gavin gave her short nod and went back to ignoring her. His body was rigid beside me. It made me wonder if he wasn't a fan of Astar.

"This is his girlfriend..." she said glancing at me.

Um, we couldn't for obvious reason use my real name. I recalled the name on my fake ID that Gavin had given me. "Britney," I supplied, trying not to cringe.

She dismissed me quickly enough, turning her full attention back to Jared. "How about the four of us go somewhere quieter?"

Finally, we were getting somewhere.

"I thought you'd never ask," Jared replied in a toe-curling voice. He had a certain flare. I'd give him that.

I stood on legs that felt weak, following Astar to a narrow hallway, past the bathrooms. The further we went, the softer the music became. Somehow I felt safer in the crowd than I did in this constricted space with only two exit points. Before we slipped behind the door at the end of the hall, I saw a flash of sandy hair and emerald eyes. It was hard to get a clear view, but I paused in the doorway, focusing. Whatever I thought I saw, it wasn't Lukas.

I breathed a sigh of relief.

"You okay?" Gavin asked from behind me, eyeing me with concern.

If Lukas were here, Gavin would go postal—probably Jared too. I nodded. "Yeah."

He rested his chin on my shoulder and whispered, "Don't worry. I won't let anything happen to you."

Inside the *back room,* as Gavin had called it, was a private VIP room. Crisp white couches lined along the walls, some occupied by what I would classify as less-than-stellar-individuals. A chill shot through me. There were some serious discussions and plotting happening in this room. In the center was a rectangular table with maps laid out on top. These weren't just any maps. Some of the lines on the paper were glowing, and at closer inspection, I knew that they all led to Holly Ridge—to me.

I swallowed thickly.

Suddenly the room became muffled, my vision blurring as the reality of where I was hit me. Jared, Gavin, and Astar moved over to a group near the table as I leaned against the wall, trying to steady myself.

Sometime during their conversation Gavin glanced at me. His eyes narrowed.

I gave a feeble smile.

"How do we know we can trust your source?" Gavin asked. I got the impression that he was rushing this along for my sake.

The guy next to Astar with turquoise hair responded. "She took out one of our witches, Lotus, confirming that he gave us the right witch. Lotus was stripped of all her powers."

I stifled a gasp, trying not to show any emotion. It was hard to take anything from a guy with peacock-colored hair seriously, which made it a little easier.

Jared stood straight, with his feet apart and arms crossed like a military lieutenant. "Is he here? We'd like to talk to him. See if we can help."

Astar nodded. "He might be. He is known to hang out here. His name is Devine. Lukas Devine."

CHAPTER 19

My mouth opened, but I didn't know what to say. A thousand denials were at the tip of my tongue, but I couldn't voice any of them. She had to be mistaken.

Gavin's faced turned dark, and he sent me a warning look. *Keep quiet.*

Suddenly, it felt like a living, breathing monster had moved into the room with us, cramming me into a corner. My stomach seized. The next thing I knew I was gasping for air. *Lukas? Lukas?* His name echoed over and over in my head. A sense of denial took over and I started shaking my head.

There was no way he would betray me. Lukas was my friend. Christ, he claimed that he cared about me, wanted to be with me. What was all the crap he was vomiting about us being destined for each other?

Was this some kind of sick, twisted attempt to hurt me because I had chosen Gavin?

My mind was whirling, but I still refused to believe that Lukas would stoop that low. He had done some pretty shitty things, like lie to me, but I had given him the benefit of the doubt. It had been to protect me. Right?

I wasn't so sure anymore. And I hated being filled with doubt. It made me weak and vulnerable, which were two things I couldn't afford in the witches den.

"I think there's something wrong with your girl," Astar commented.

I probably looked like I was having a seizure or something.

In two ground-eating strides, Gavin was in front of me. He grabbed my chin, forcing me to look at him "Hey," he crooned. "I've got you." Wrapping an arm around my waist, he started to lead me toward the door.

Thank God. I couldn't stand to be inside the club another nanosecond without feeling like I was suffocating, like I was being pulled by quicksand, drowning.

"What did you slip into her drink?" I heard someone sneer before Gavin got me out of there.

I leaned on his sturdy frame, taking comfort in his woodsy scent as he moved us through the crowded space. There were bodies everywhere, and I couldn't breathe. What a time and a place to have a freaking panic attack. Timing was never my friend. And then just to drive home just how much my timing sucked...

I saw *him*. We were about to reach the exit, and I looked back over my shoulder.

"Lukas," I hissed between gritted teeth. And before anyone could stop me, I was racing across the dance floor, zeroing in on my target. Lukas's eyes found mine. "What are you doing here?" I demanded, and somehow was able to keep my voice even. Though I already knew, but I wanted to hear him say it—admit that he had put a hit out on me.

I expected to see surprise in his eyes, not coolness. "Don't you look...different."

Oh, snap. I had forgotten about my disguise, but it didn't seem to matter. He still knew it was me underneath all the gunk. "Don't dick me around," I barked, tired of all the lies.

His eyes narrowed. "Have you been drinking?"

How dare he turn this around on me without a single bead of sweat. I was dripping with perspiration. The lights beat down on me like a sauna. "Is it true? Did you—"

A hand closed over my mouth, silencing me from blowing my cover. "Bri, now is not the time," Gavin hissed in my ear. I could feel the barely restraint anger seething from him in the arms wrapped around me. He wanted to kick Lukas's ass as much as I did.

Lukas's lips thinned in a tight line. "You are going to get yourself in serious trouble in here. They don't take kindly to fighting."

"I don't believe it." But, I was starting to. It was hard to imagine Lukas selling me out. He just wouldn't.

Yet he didn't deny or admit that he was involved, and I found his silence maddening. The longer I stared at him, begging him to tell me that they were all wrong, the more heated my blood became. That was it. I reached my boiling point.

The anger I felt just then was chart topper.

I thought about shoving my boot up his ass, but instead I punched him in the gut. It wasn't a girly kind of hit. I had packed it with magic. The air expelled from Lukas's lungs in a rush.

Jared laughed to my right. "Damn, girl."

It felt good to hit Lukas. My lips twitched in a giddy satisfaction as he groaned, which only sweetening the deal, but one taste wasn't enough to feed my anger or hurt. So I lunged forward. My fingertips tingled with power, except I never made it. I found myself plucked midair, hoisted over Gavin's shoulder, fireman style.

"I never want to see you again. Ever!" I screamed, pushing the colored hair out of my face so I could sear Lukas with glares of hate. *What an asshat.* The fact that Lukas sold me out really burned my butt.

Gavin's dark eyes flashed like blue flames. "I'll deal with you later," he growled.

Lukas cocked his head. "I'm looking forward to it."

Gavin pivoted, weeding his way toward the exit as I tried to wiggle free, but his hold was like vise grips. "I'll behave. You can let me down, now," I yelled.

"I kind of like manhandling you," he said, but put me on my feet.

Any other time, I would have appreciated the way my body glided down his. I guess I could blame Lukas for that, as well. The list of crud I could pin on Lukas was getting quite extensive.

I stomped out of the club, dying for a gulp of fresh air without all the smoke, sweat, and magic clogging my senses. Air punched my lungs as I pushed my way out the door, Gavin and Jared right behind me.

Gavin didn't say anything, just stood beside me, letting me greedily inhale the cool night's breeze. I was thankful for the quiet, just listening to the bustle of the city streets a block or two away.

It was Jared who finally broke the silence. "This was the first time a *girl* almost got us kicked out of club, little brother. That makes her practically family now." He swung an arm around my shoulder.

I think that was Jared's warped way of saying I passed the Mason initiation.

Now that my lungs could breathe easier and my anger had subsided momentarily, I started to have a whole new onset of problems. My head started to spin in dizzy circles, blurring the city lamplights in a nauseating way. I lost my balance, and if it hadn't been for Gavin's ninja reflexes, I would have face planted the ground. "I think I'm going to be sick," I moaned.

Jared took a step back. "Yep. She's all yours, bro. I'll drive."

There wasn't much talk or goofing-off as we piled into Gavin's car. He threw the keys to Jared. They both knew that I wasn't in the mood for bantering, not because my head was throbbing, but because of what I'd learned.

This night had gone to shit. I had naïvely thought that after we left the secret society, I would...

God, what had I thought?

Once I'd learned the name of the witch who had given away my identity, then what? Did I plan to storm their house and threaten them or worse? The damage was already done. My name, my face was already circling through the community like wildfire.

It was only a matter of time, and I felt as if my days were numbered.

This had been a wasteful, stupid idea. I accomplished not a darn thing and lost a friend. I couldn't afford to lose any more.

Sitting in the backseat, I was feeling like I'd been poisoned, and Jared's *The Fast and the Furious* driving wasn't helping. *God, did he think he was Dominic Toretto?* Newsflash. If we got pulled over, I would definitely be asked to walk a straight line.

Huddled in the backseat, I could do nothing but groan. I didn't protest when Gavin pulled me against him, or when I felt the tremors of magic skip on my skin. "What are you doing?" I barely managed to ask, the sound of my voice croaky.

"Just helping take the edge off. Close your eyes," he instructed.

With pleasure. When I opened them again, I was entangled by the depths of his sapphire eyes.

He rubbed his cheek against mine, the stubble tingling on my face. "Better?"

Considering the shape I had been in before, the worst of my hangover was gone. "My head still feels like a bowling ball, but I don't feel like I am going to yack all over you anymore."

"Good." He kissed my forehead.

"I don't know what I would do without you," I said, snuggling up against his side.

He sent me a mischievous grin. "I'm pretty damn awesome."

And just when I didn't think I had it in me to smile, Gavin proved me wrong.

We were almost home, I realized, as Jared took the last turn to my street. Home sweet home. The sight of my house and the giant pear tree out front almost sent me to tears. Glancing up at the second-story window of room, I could practically hear my bed screaming my name. All I wanted to do was crawl as quietly and quickly as possible to my bedroom, and lock the door, so I could do some wallowing.

Self-pity. So not cute.

Gavin walked me to the door. "Are you sure you are going to be okay tonight?"

A thrill sparked inside me. It was a miracle I could feel anything at all. I brushed my frazzled hair behind my ear. "Yeah. I just need to be alone." I sensed a part of him was leery to leave my side, but he respected my request for space, though not too much. He would be at my house at first light regardless that it was a Saturday. I didn't imagine I would be sleeping in anyway.

"Bri," he called as my hand reached the doorknob.

I glanced over my shoulder.

"Don't shed a single tear on him. He doesn't deserve them."

I gulped, my throat suddenly closing. All I could do was nod, before I disappeared inside my safe haven. I closed the door silently behind me and tiptoed into the kitchen with only thoughts of my jammies dancing in my head. Then a voice pierced through the darkness, making me jump out of my panties.

"Where have you been?" Aunt Clara demanded. She was sitting on the kitchen table in the dark.

I squealed.

Oh. My. God.

My shoulders sagged. My hand flew over my sputtering heart. "You scared me half to death. I can explain," I rushed, praying that I hadn't slurred my words or smelled like a Captain Morgan.

She wrung her fingers around a mug of hot tea. "Good, because I would love to hear it."

I scuffed my boot on the kitchen floor, wondering if I lied or told her the truth. I had known the time would come sooner or later, and I'd had enough of lies. The deceit would feel like sandpaper on my tongue.

A purple strand of hair fell over my eyes. *Shit-on-a-broomstick*. I had forgotten to say the words to remove Sophie's charms. How in hell was I going to explain this to my aunt?

Wait a second.

Why wasn't she freaking out? "You know it's me?" I asked.

She scoffed. "Of course I do. I know my niece when I see her."

That's what she thinks...

Or did she?

I scrambled for a logically explanation, but as I looked at her face, I realized that it wouldn't make a difference.

Reality was a bit sobering.

"How long have you been using magic?" she asked, staring at the tea in her cup.

Bam. I was hit with one shock after another tonight.

I froze. "You know about that?" I asked in a breathy tone.

The corners of her lips tipped in a weak smile. "I've always known what you were capable of. The gifts you inherited."

For the second time today, I had the rug swept out from underneath me. I didn't know how I was going to find my balance again. Sinking down into a chair at the end of the table, I dropped my head into my hands. "Why didn't you ever tell me?"

"I wanted to, many times, but your mom made me promise that I would not tell you. She was worried for your safety and trying to protect you. I had to honor her final wish."

I knew how hard she had taken the death of my mom, and I totally got why she had kept the truth from me. Like my mom, they both loved me and didn't want me to get hurt, but none of their efforts had changed the outcome.

She took a sip of her tea. "Are you okay?"

No. I was not okay. I was far from okay. "I don't know. It's been a roller coaster of a year, and I am still processing."

Confusion flickered over Aunt Clara's pretty face. "Are you at least going to tell me why you are dressed like that? Are you in trouble?"

Crap. I was so exhausted I kept forgetting about my trashy look. Glancing into her concern eyes, all the words—the truth about where I'd been—got ensnared in my vocal cords. Things were complicated. If I started talking, I would have to tell her about Gavin, and Lukas, and I just didn't have the energy in me tonight.

"I went to a club," I said, yawning. It was the most truth I could give at the moment.

She stood up, placing a hand on my shoulder and squeezed. "We're both tired. Let's get some sleep and we can talk in the morning."

I think I nodded. I would have agreed to anything as long as it got me into my bed. Holding onto the banister, I pulled my dragging butt upstairs and into my sanctuary. With a sense of sadness, I crossed the room and caught my reflection in the mirror. I hadn't bothered to flick on the lights, but even in darkness, I looked like a hot mess. Mascara streaked down my cheeks. I was seriously rocking the world's messiest do. And my outfit was laughable.

Screw it.

I tore off my clothes and body slammed the bed. Burying my face into the pillow, I inhaled the familiar scent of my life. Lunar came jumping up and curled into my arms, resting his little head next to mine. So many things were spinning in my head, creating a chaotic noise. I felt like I was spiraling downward, and by the time I understood what it was, there was no stopping it.

I was being summoned.

CHAPTER 20

"I didn't think you were ever going to close your eyes," Morgana's voice sounded from behind me, slightly miffed.

I spun around, facing her, and angled my head to the side. "Do you watch my every move?"

"Usually."

I gave her a bland look.

Dark waves of hair spilled over her shoulders as she looked at me with eyes that were anything but innocent. "What? There's not much to do on the other side, and you amuse me." She walked around the room, occasionally running her finger along the back of the couch or over the woodwork.

She looked so strange inside my house. Speaking of strange...I glanced down at myself and sighed. For once I wasn't dressed in some sheer flowing dress or half naked. I had on my favorite tattered jeans, my *coffee solves everything* shirt, and pink, polka-dot socks. I couldn't have been happier.

Until I remembered all that had happened.

My face fell.

"Oh, shoot. You didn't know if it was going to be me or *him* summoning you." Morgana's violet eyes missed nothing. "Grab me a drink, love. I'm parched. All this dreaming, traveling and spying stuff wears me out. And we have a lot to catch up on."

She was right. I watched as she sauntered toward the porch like she was walking the red carpet, her hips swaying. Shaking my head, I grabbed two cans of soda from the fridge and followed her outside. There was something stunningly beautiful about the sky. Reddish oranges and pinks smeared across the horizon. Hidden crickets sung from the overgrown brush and woodlands surrounding my house.

It made me miss summer, so much tranquility and quietude. The perk of a dream was you could make it any season you wished. In the real world, summer was still a few months away, which meant graduation was that much closer.

She was sitting on the old porch swing, staring off at the sky, much like I had. I sat down beside her, the wood creaking under my weight, and handed her a drink.

"I miss this the most," she said, lifting her face up to the light. "The feel of the sun."

Morgana may be many things, including sometimes a bitch, but she knew what I needed, when I needed it. She knew when to push me, when to console me, and when to be my friend or a shoulder to cry on. For the first time, I saw the woman sitting next to me as family. "I think I will miss the ocean the most."

With a flick her wrist, the porch swing started swinging on its own. "We each have an element we connect with. It is no surprise that yours is water. Do you plan on going somewhere, dear?"

My brows scrunched together in confusion. "No."

"You said *will* miss, not would."

My feet stopped swinging over the side.

She took a sip of her drink and winced. "How do you stand this stuff?" Waving her hand over the drink, I felt the swirling of magic. "There. If Jesus can turn water into wine, I can turn whatever this into something just as sweet."

The idea of alcohol turned my stomach.

A secret grin appeared on her lips as if she knew that just a small whiff would have me puking over the edge. "You think because of what happened last night that you are doomed, is that it?"

Did I?

There just seemed to be so many strikes against me. If I managed to live and survive the attacks on my life, my soul still had shards of darkness, and they weren't getting any smaller. If anything, they were growing, and it would only be a matter of time before the light was snuffed out.

"I am here to tell you that there is still hope."

She was able to cut through my bleak thoughts. "How?" I asked.

Hesitating, her expression sobered. "When the darkness becomes too much, you will find reprieve in the one thing you keep close."

That was eerily familiar, like I'd heard it before. I turned toward her, twisting the moonstone necklace in my fingers. "What is that supposed to mean? For once, could you just spell it out for me?" The guessing games were getting on my nerves.

Her crimson nails tapped on the aluminum can. "Ah, if only the universe worked that way. I have every confidence that you will figure it out. You are of my blood, after all."

I rolled my eyes. If that was what she was banking on, then we were both in deep poo-poo. "Your blood or not, I have a giant target on my back. And as much as I wanted you to be wrong about Lukas and Gavin, you were very much right. One of them betrayed me." Just thinking about Lukas brought on a fresh wave of pain that sliced across my heart. Water gathered at the corner of my eyes.

"Boys, can't live with them, can't live without—Well, that's not really true, as I haven't had a man in centuries. Come to think of it, the male species has always proven to be just a pain in my ass."

Morgana oozed independence. She didn't need to depend on a guy or rely on one to protect her. She was a get-shit-done kind of witch. I wanted to be more like that. I wanted to exude badass confidence, woman empowerment. Maybe her mojo would rub off on me, the longer we were together. "We're cursed when it comes to men."

"There is probably truth to that. Although, haven't you already chosen your prince charming?"

My eyes widened. "You weren't watching the other night..." I couldn't say it.

She winked. "I never kiss and tell."

Gross. "I'm going to pretend I didn't hear that," I muttered.

Her laugh was silky. "I see the truth has revealed itself to you. Yet you shed a tear for the traitor?"

I sighed, my chest squeezing. "He hurt me, deeply," I whispered. And now that I'd had a moment to digest what Lukas had done, my heart splintered. "Why did he do it?"

"Because he is a d-bag," she stated matter-of-factly.

I let a short, unflattering giggle that was almost a snort. The fact that she knew what a d-bag was shouldn't have surprised me. Morgana was not your usual grandma. Hell, she didn't even look like a grandma, not a single gray hair in sight. "Total douchebag," I agreed.

It was so unbelievably normal, having a cold drink with my great-grandma on a sweltering summer night, swaying on an old white wicker porch swing, and bashing men. I almost laughed, because the conversation was anything but ordinary. One bright spark in the otherwise black misery of my life gave me hope.

"And why are you grinning?" she asked, suspiciously.

I shrugged, twirling the cola in my hands. "I was just thinking how normal this is, us sitting here watching the sunset."

"Hmm," she pursed her lips. "We better enjoy it, because it won't last."

That's comforting.

A faint glimmer of sunlight shaded the outline of her form. "Let me give you one last piece of advice. As mouthwatering as your choice may be, I am not ready just yet to be a great, great, great—you get the picture. Use caution and your head. Don't let your hormones rule your life."

I turned shades of pink. "Uh, sure," I said awkwardly.

How did this turn into such an awkward conversation?

We sat on the porch talking about nonsense until the sun set. It could have been hours or minutes, time was irrelevant. My problems forgotten, we sipped on our drinks and got to know one another on a different level. She was relaxed in a way I'd never witnessed. It made her more human. When I woke up, Lunar was purring in my face, his whiskers tickling my cheek.

CHAPTER 21

It was Saturday. Someone please tell that to my body. Ugh. I had awakened at an indecent hour, so of course the first thing I did was reach for my phone. After checking my emails, stalking Twitter, and opening every app on my IPhone, I finally gave into what I had wanted to do since I opened my eyes.

He answered the phone on the third ring in an inaudible grumble that had fireflies fluttering in my belly. "Hey," I said.

"Hey yourself, sunshine," he said, his voice gravelly and deep.

I adored the grogginess in his voice. "Did I wake you?" I asked, though I knew that I had. No one said my brain was functioning intelligently this early.

"I'm glad you did. I missed you. Even in sleep."

Dear God. His sleepy voice was the sexiest thing on earth. I might be sneaking into his room at five o'clock in the morning. My heart skipped. "I saw Morgana last night," I blurted, and then face-palmed my forehead. I had wanted to tell him about the dream, but I hadn't planned for it to be the first thing out of my mouth.

"What did she say?" He instantly lost the hot gruffness and became golden retriever alert. I could picture him bolting straight up in bed, shirtless, with the covers gathered at this waist and a hand shoved in his hair.

What an image.

My mouth watered.

I needed a cold shower...or something.

It was no secret that my boyfriend and my grandma hadn't gotten off on the right foot. They hadn't exactly made up, either. "She told me that craziness in my life isn't over..." I replied, checking my hormones.

He made some kind of low growl in the back of his throat.

"And she told me that she approved of my choice." I smiled into the phone.

"About?" he prompted.

I had never told him about her cryptic messages regarding my love life. "Picking you over d-bag. Her words, not mine."

"I knew I liked that crazy bat."

"Hey!"

"At least she has good instincts." There was a smirk coming through loud and clear from his side of the phone

I snuggled into my pillow. "There is that."

"And so do you," he added.

I wanted to kiss him just then—full-on dirty girl. "That's debatable."

"Since you got me out of bed, do you want me to come over?" His voice was husky.

It was on the tip of my tongue to tell him to hurry, but then I remembered my aunt. I groaned. "Crap," I swore. "I almost forgot. My aunt knows I'm a witch."

There was a pause, then a sigh. "I can't leave you alone for five minutes."

I could always count on him to make me laugh, even in the most ridonkulous situations. "Tell me about it. She was waiting up for me last night when I got home, and I thought at first I was being busted for curfew." Not that I really had one. "Then I realized that I was still dressed incognito."

He snickered. "I would have loved to have been there to see your face."

Speaking of, my eyes flew down, scoping out my hair. I exhaled in relief as I stared down at my drab auburn hair. "Trust me. It wasn't pretty," I mumbled.

I heard him shift on the bed. "So Aunt Clara has a few skeletons of her own."

"It appears so." I nibbled on one of my fingernails. "We didn't really get a chance to hash out the how's and why's. I was still a little woozy."

"I just bet you were."

If we had been in the same room, I would have thrown something at this head. "Whatever. I'll see you tonight?"

"Wouldn't miss it," he said.

Immediately I missed the sound of his voice as I hung up, but I had more pressing matters than my longing heart. Flopping onto my back with oomph, my body was too jazzed to stay in bed. So I swung my legs over the side and decided I needed some fresh air. Last night I watched the sunset with Morgana, this morning I would take in the North Carolina sunrise, alone.

Discarding my cell phone on the nightstand, I went to toss on some clothes and brush my teeth. Ten minutes later, I sat in the middle of my backyard, soaking up the sun. It was the perfect temperature. Warm enough in just leggings and a shirt, without any sticky humidity, and a gentle breeze that always carried the scent of the sea. All morning I thought about my dream with Morgana. How could I not? On top of everything, a part of me was afraid that I would not see her again.

Inside, my aunt was still snoring, so very unlike her to sleep in, even on a Saturday. I figured maybe it had something to do with what I put her through last night. She needed her beauty rest, and we needed to have a heart to heart.

But it could wait.

Stretching out on the plaid blanket, I opened a book that I had brought with me, a mindless story about someone else's life, what a perfect diversion. Halfway into chapter three, I heard the soft crunch of grass. Startled, I looked up just in time to see Aunt Clara sit down next to me.

She handed me a mug filled with black coffee, her hair pulled back off her face. "You were up early," she said.

I took a long whiff of the bitter aroma. God, she was a lifesaver. "I've been having unsettling dreams."

She crossed her legs at her ankles. The sunbeams picked up the dark blonde highlights in her hair. "I bet. Do you want to tell me about them?"

Impatient, I took a sip from my cup and was rewarded with a burnt tongue. I wondered just how much she knew about my powers. I gathered that she knew I was a witch, that I wielded magic, but did she know just what kind of power? Or how dangerous I could be? I smiled sheepishly. "This is so surreal," I admitted. "I thought by hiding this part of myself from you, I was protecting *you*."

Never had she ever looked at me with anything but love—even now —her eyes glistened with pride. "It looks like we both had the same idea. You don't have to hide who you are from me."

Averting my eyes, I glanced down at the steam rising from my coffee. "I might have also been the teeniest bit afraid that you would kick me to the curb." Being rejected and homeless at one time had been a real fear, although realistically, my aunt wasn't the type of person to abandon family.

She snorted. "You are the only family I have, Brianna. There is nothing that will change that. Nothing. You can't get rid of me that easy."

I manufactured a smile. "What about Chad?"

"You've been mine since you were five. No one is as important to me as you," she said, lightly brushing the hair off my shoulder.

Inhaling, I asked, "So you knew that my dad was...a witch?"

A wistful look passed over her expression. "I did. Your mom told me everything. And I mean *everything*. She didn't know what TMI meant."

I laughed. "How did you keep such a big secret?" It had been less than a year since I found out what I was, and keeping such a gargantuan secret had eaten me up inside. The people who meant the most— Tori, Austin, and my aunt—had been the ones I wanted to confide in.

She looked me directly in the eyes. "I wanted to tell you almost every day."

Because I could relate, I found that I wasn't angry she hadn't told me sooner. Essentially we had been doing the same thing—shielding each other. "I know the feeling," I muttered. "Why did you decide to bring it up last night, besides the fact that I came home looking like Sideshow Bob?"

Her smile was quick. "You gave me a heart attack. Don't. Ever. Do that again," she added.

"Duly noted."

"I noticed changes in you this last year, little things at first. Then when I noticed the stress and the worry you've been under...I knew that something was wrong. And I realized the time had come—your safety depended on it." A shadow passed over her eyes. "Are you in danger?"

I blinked. "It's nothing that I can't handle." I hoped.

She didn't look convinced, but then again, I had done a crappy job trying to be assuring. "I might not be able to turn a frog into a prince, but if you let me, I can help you."

"My life is a mess." I don't know if anyone could help me.

Setting aside her coffee in the grass, she said, "Tell me about your dreams."

Where did I start? "I met Morgana Le Fey," I said.

Her eyes bugged out. Finally, a reaction I expected. "*The* Morgana?"

I nodded. "The one and only. She's my great, great, great, great grandma." I think that was right.

She chewed on her lip for a moment. "Your father failed to mention that little tidbit."

"I'm not sure he knew. Morgana came to warn me, and I think it was the first time she has reached out. Our p-powers are almost parallel." I tripped over the word, finding strange to be saying it out loud in front of my aunt.

"Warn you about what?" she asked, eyes narrowing.

Damn. So much for not telling her about the dangers in my life. This was a fresh wound, and it still hurt. My gaze flickered. "That someone close to me would betray me."

She put the pieces together. "And that was what last night was about?"

"Yeah." My voice dropped. "Lukas turned out to be someone he's not."

She stiffened. "A witch?"

It was more than just that. "And not a friend," I grumbled.

Her brows drew together, making her pretty face fierce. "He hurt you?"

"Not physically," I said just in case she was confused. "But yes. I thought he was my friend."

"People suck."

A sad chuckle tumbled from my lips. "I hit him."

There was a spark of fire in her eyes. "Good for you. Now tell me about your gifts?" She pulled her legs up, sitting Indian-style across from me.

I shrugged. "I'm still learning, but I have affinities with the weather and with dreams. I can call upon storms and invade dreams." I dragged my eyes back to the cup in my hands. *Here goes nothing.* I had a sneaky suspicion that she knew about my supernatural boyfriend. "Shortly after meeting Gavin at the beginning of the school year, he told me what I was capable of—showed me that I had magic."

She smiled at me encouragingly.

I wasn't done just yet, leaving the jaw-dropper for last. "And recently, I discovered that I can steal power from other witches."

A small gasp leapt from her mouth. "Your father talked about witches with the abilities to take the powers from others. Are you sure?" She tried to keep the worry out of her tone, but I heard it.

Nodding, my unease soared. I couldn't bring myself to tell her why I was so positive. Stealing from your boyfriend wasn't something I was proud of, not to mention the witch I left powerless.

"Oh, Brianna," she sighed. "I did not wish for that kind of responsibility on you, and I know that your parents didn't either."

I twiddled with a blade of grass I'd plucked. "I'm dealing with it."

She gave me a sappy look. "Your parents would be so proud of the person you have become. I know I am."

Damn. She was going to make me cry. I swallowed back the tears that threatened, because with tears came rain, and I really didn't want to get wet.

She dabbed at her lower lashes, one eye at a time. "No more secrets, deal?"

That I could agree on. Nothing good ever came from hiding the truth. "Deal."

"Well, I've procrastinated long enough. I've got to go into the shop, make sure Salena hasn't burnt it to the ground. Are you coming in?"

Salena was one of the part-time employees who helped out. I shook my head. "Not yet."

"Call me at the shop if you need *anything*." She captured my chin between her fingers and tipped my face up. "Got that?"

I smiled. "I will," I assured, hugging her. She was surprised at first, and then she relaxed, wrapping her arms around me and squeezing me tightly. I watched her walk inside, thinking I was the luckiest witch in the world to have someone who cared unconditionally for me. And a few minutes later I listened to the gentle hum of her engine as she backed down the driveway.

It did feel like a weight had been lifted off my shoulders, by being open and honest with my aunt. I was still dogged with problems, but it was one less obstacle I had to hurdle. And that felt pretty damn good.

Sitting there alone with Mother Nature, I mindlessly called forth my magic to pass time and keep myself from dwelling on what I planned to do about Lukas. He wasn't a hurdle I had to deal with; he was a freaking planet-sized obstacle. And knowing Lukas, he would be searching for me sooner than later. I wanted the time and place to be on my grounds—my terms.

I should have known that nothing goes as smoothly as intended— at least not in my life.

Normally when my emotions were scattered and running wild like today, I caused wicked storms. Instead I decided I needed a less volatile approach. Something less dramatic and more subdued. Something magical and happy. No tears I told myself. So I made it rain a rainbow of petals. Coral. Garnet. Canary. Fuchsia. All around me, vibrant colors fell and swirled in the winds. I plucked them off trees, from the bushes, and swept them from the ground, uplifting them into the air. It was stunningly beautiful and filled the area with a sweet perfume.

"This isn't exactly the kind of skills I had hoped to teach you."

I went perfectly still. The petals dropped to the ground, strewn over the green grass like blood droplets. There were a few stuck in my hair, but I didn't care. Seeing Lukas had drained all the color from my face.

CHAPTER 22

I stopped breathing, partly because I didn't know how I was going to react. There was a good chance that I would hit him again. Maybe a black eye this time, keep him on his toes. I jumped to my feet, with my hands clenched at my side, and stared at him.

The wind had tousled his hair, separating the strands. Green flecks sparkled in his eyes from the sun beating down upon us. There was no remorse in his typical carefree expression. Even his dimples flashed at the center of his cheeks.

I don't know what he was so amused with, but it fueled my anger. So I swung. In truth, I didn't think I would get the jump on him a second time. He sidestepped out of the way, my fist connecting with nothing but air.

His lips curled as he stared down at me. "Is this going to be the way you greet from now on?"

"What are you doing here?" I demanded.

The dark blue shirt he wore stretched across his chest. "We need to talk. Or rather, you need to listen."

I scoffed. How dare he come to my house and order me about. "I don't want to hear anything you have to say." *Asshole.* I spun on my heel with every intention of leaving him to eat my dust. I only got one step before a hand grabbed my arm.

"Brianna," he said, spinning me back around to face him. He kept his hand glued to my arm, preventing him from the escape I sought. "Just wait."

But the thing was, I didn't want to wait. I wanted nothing from him. I wanted to be far away from him until I could get myself under control and form an intelligent thought. I grimaced. "Let go of me."

His face was forbidding. "Not until you agree to give me a chance to explain myself."

I jerked my arm free. "You don't deserve the time of day."

He pinched the bridge of his nose. "You sound like a crazy person."

Did he just call *me* crazy? I'll show him every color of crazy. "That is rich, coming from you."

"You and I. We're the same."

My stomach soured. "I am nothing like you," I spat, but deep down, I was afraid that I was worse than Lukas. He might not be who I believed he was, but I knew who I was. The realization that maybe we were alike in some aspects turned my stomach, but that didn't mean I was going to give Lukas the pleasure of admitting it, especially after he betrayed me.

He was damn lucky I didn't fry his ass here and now, because I felt the familiar pull—the one that whispered in my ear. Urging me to take —to feed the darkness—satisfy this craving. The fact that we were talking at all was a miracle, since my first instinct was to cause him bodily harm.

He stepped forward invading my personal bubble. "I never pegged you for a liar."

I quenched the impulse to back up, not wanting him to think he was intimidating me, which was exactly what he wanted. "I guess there is a lot we don't know about each other."

"I thought you understood. I love you, Brianna. It was the only way I could get you to stand up, to show them you wouldn't be cast aside. All I did was force your hand a little. I did it for us."

Dumbstruck, I just stared at him. He was shitting me, right? Putting a massive spotlight on my head was helping me? "What you did to me was not out of love," I said flatly. "You put me in danger, Lukas—life-threatening, never-ending danger."

"But I knew that you would be able to handle it—*we* could handle it. You have the kind of power that is limitless, and others need to know that you won't live your life in fear. Why should you hide who you are? They have no right to decide your fate."

His reasoning was horseshit. How was it any different than those trying to zap me into orbit? I wasn't about to go in, gung-ho with guns blazing, and demand everyone pledge their allegiance to me or else... "That is not what I want. You knew that. I barely had gotten used to the idea of being a witch. Lukas, using that kind of power is dangerous, and it changes you, forever."

"Dark magic isn't evil. It is stronger. Potent. Pure. People are naturally afraid of what they can't control."

Uh. I beg to differ. Everyone knew that white magic trumped black magic, ten out of ten times. Apparently Lukas had drunk the cuckoo Kool-Aid.

I shot him a level look. "If you were really my friend, you never would have put me in such a position or tried to make me into something I'm not. I don't want to use my gifts to make people fear me. I don't want supreme control. I don't want people thinking that I am better than they are. I want to be treated as an equal."

He looked crestfallen. "But you aren't," he argued. "You are so much more. *We* are so much more. Together, we are unstoppable." The tips of his fingers began to spark with magic.

Just great. Lukas was on a power trip. "There is no *we*," I insisted.

Static crackled under my shirt. If I had to, I would defend myself, but I didn't want to hurt him. And that fear was all too real, because I knew that I was capable of doing worse than just hurting him as he had hurt me. I could destroy him. And in the process, probably destroy myself. There was a good chance that if I used that kind of dark magic again, it would tip me over the edge—the point of no return. My poor soul could only handle so much darkness, and after my last talk with Sophie, I wasn't very optimistic.

"I *will* have you, Brianna. You were meant to be mine. If you just give us a chance, I know that you will feel it too."

Not likely.

"I've already given myself to someone else," I said, crossing my fingers. The sooner he got that through his thick skull, the sooner I could skedaddle.

"You weren't supposed to fall for that douchebag. You are mine," Lukas growled.

Warning, my internal "oh shit" alarm went off. I needed to send out a SOS. I had a sinking feeling about this. There was no one around and essentially I was so screwed that it wasn't even funny. "But I did fall for Gavin. I love him, Lukas."

Green rage flashed into his irises. "That guy is such a putz."

Something told me that I needed to tread lightly. We were strolling into dangerous territory, and Lukas was unstable, quickly shifting toward the point of no return. One wrong move, one slip of the tongue, and he would turn on me. My body trembled with certainty. I guess a witch knew when another was threatening her. The sizzle of magic might have been a dead giveaway.

I needed distance. As slowly as possible, I started to take tiny steps backward, all while trying to keep Lukas focused on my face, not my movements. Obviously mentioning Gavin enraged him, so I needed to steer this conversation to safer ground. "Why are you doing this?" I didn't try to hide the quiver from my voice, thinking if he knew that he was frightening me, he would back down.

Yeah. It backfired.

A twisted smile curved on his lips. "I want power. And with you at my side, there wouldn't be a witch around stupid enough to mess with us." His greed hung heavy in the air.

For the first time, I saw Lukas in a new light—and it was a frightening image. Gone was the smoke of charm he hid behind, and in its place was something truly terrifying. My stomach clenched up in knots. "Let me get this straight. You want me to let the darkness consume my soul?" Sounded like a suicide mission.

He cocked his head. "Like I said, we're two peas in a pod. I know that you like the taste of power—the high it gives after you've squeezed a witch dry."

We were day and night. Light to dark. I might be capable of both, but I choose light. The aftereffects of being a clàr silte were alluring—they were downright addicting, but the consequences were more than I was willing to wager. "You are out of your freaking gourd."

Crap.

Did I say that out loud?

That would be a big fat affirmative. I might have just fed the beast, because there was nothing human about the way Lukas was glaring at me. My heart threw itself against my ribs so hard it hurt. If I could just get close enough to the house I might be able to make it inside, but a quick peek from the corner of my eye told me I'd never make it.

"That wasn't very nice," he growled.

Screw this.

I ran, my flight response kicking in. It was human nature to run away from danger. And Lukas was flipping oozing the black stuff.

But I didn't get far. With a low snarl, his had hand shot out, grabbing my hair and yanked. "That was a bad move," he warned in my ear.

I'll say.

Emerald eyes glowing like some kind of cracked-out demon, he spun me to face him, and I seared him with a shut-up-or-die look. "I won't give you what you want," I said, my teeth clenched.

His fingers dug into my arms, and I winced. The worst part was, I felt his desire for me—lust— like sweaty palms on my skin. Revulsion swept through me, rising up to the back of my throat. But it was my gift he coveted more than my body, I was certain. He didn't love *me...* he loved power.

The storm I had just barely begun to weave started to take life. Born from my fear and my rage, winds howled around me, darkening the sky to a dusty gray. Sooty clouds took shape in wrathful forms. Violent thunder cracked, trembling the ground at my feet. Bolts of lightning speared above our heads, brightly flashing in fury.

"I always knew you were a hothead," he taunted.

I had on my rage face. "If you don't let me go, I will shove a broomstick up your ass. Don't test me."

"It's that fire I want. It is why you are my perfect match." He shook me, rattling brain matter.

I threw up a little in my mouth.

"I want it all. Your body. Your soul. Your magic."

Dry lightning fissured around us, and storm clouds gathered not only in the skies but also in my eyes. Hoping I knew what the hell I was doing, I closed my eyes and sent a bolt of light at his feet. He jumped, just as I hoped, and it was the distraction I banked on. With a jerk, I was able to break out of his hold and put distance between the lunatic and me. "This is your last chance. I'm warning you, Lukas. Leave now, before things get messy."

I saw the choice in his eyes and my heart plummeted. "I enjoy getting dirty."

I just bet he did.

So be it.

It was time for the showdown of the century. Lukas and I—a battle of wills. May the best witch remain standing.

I just prayed that witch was me.

He gave me no warning. I blinked, and in the split hair of a second, he threw a ball of neon energy with blinding force. Before my eyes, I watched the mesmerizing light break apart into millions of shimmering dots. As pretty as it was, I knew that those dots were lethal. No friendly fire.

A scream lodged into my throat that would have made a banshee proud. At the last second, before I became a magical pincushion, I cast what I prayed to God was a shield, and then just in case, I turned, covering my arms over my face and braced myself.

He laughed. It was a troubling sound. "See what you are capable of, with your back pushed to the wall?"

I didn't die after all. The winds tangled my hair. *My turn, asshole.* "Maybe you're right," I muttered. Magic thrummed through my veins, and I took my best shot. It was measly at most. Fighting wasn't my forte, but slurping magic like a cherry slushy was right up my alley.

I was out of my league going toe-to-toe with Lukas, but he didn't give me a choice. Strands of a purplish glow shot from my fingertips, sailing at him. I had no idea what it would do if it actually hit him. It could melt his flesh or turn him into a blue-spotted leopard for all I knew. But it was a fruitless effort. He squashed my spell like faerie dust with just a closing of his fist.

Frustration growled inside me. I opened my mouth to tell him to stop this nonsense and felt an invisible slap across my cheeks. My head lobbed to the side, and I stumbled. Black spots darkened my vision. There was no time to even catch my breath. Ribbons of magic folded me in a cage, tightening around my neck and stomach. Within seconds my windpipes were struggling for air. My hands flew to my neck, trying to rid the energy that was squeezing the life out of me. Wide-eyed, I realized that I wasn't the only clàr silte out there.

Lukas was stealing my power.

I gasped, but no sound came out.

"I crave what you have. And I am insatiable," he whispered in my ear.

He was getting what he wanted after all—my magic. And there was not a damn thing I could do about it. Lukas made me his bitch. There was nothing pleasant or euphoric about having my power ripped from me. It felt as if he was carving out pieces of my internal organs, and then tearing them from my body. The pain brought me to my knees and tears filled my bright eyes.

I might have given up right then and there if it hadn't been for a familiar voice that sounded in my head. *Don't just sit there and take it like you don't have a backbone. Fight back.*

Morgana.

I don't know how she was able to get in my head, and I long since stopped questioning how she did anything. Hearing her snarky voice filled me with relief. I wasn't alone.

You are tougher than he is. Your bloodline is stronger. Now get to your feet. Push back your fear and focus on the source that gives you power. Don't let him take what is yours by birthright.

She gave me the shove I needed, the spark of fight. I did as told and pushed against the bonds that held clutched me. On my feet, my legs wobbled like a baby doe, my body weakened and imprisoned from his spell. But little good any of it did me. No sooner did I have both feet on the ground, when my knees buckled, sending me back down. Defeat raced through me, squashing the shred of hope Morgana's presence had instilled.

About damn time, I heard her grumble in my head.

I had exhausted all my energy. Whatever had her all fired up was at the very bottom of my shit-I-should-be-concerned-about list.

Then I felt it—the tingles of another witch. Lifting my head, the tattoo at my back hummed with recognition.

Gavin.

CHAPTER 23

"Bri!" he yelled.

I heard my name in the distance. It was washed out by the roaring in my head and Morgana's voice coaxing me not to give up. I wasn't the only one startled by Gavin's appearance. Lukas actually looked horror-struck.

Gavin hit him like a freaking NFL linebacker, knocking them both to the ground. They rolled, severing the link he had on my energy. I sucked in a sharp breath of invigorating air and coughed. My entire body was still radiating with magic and relief. He hadn't been able to wipe me clean. No surprise, since I had an excessive amount. There was a little of Gavin flowing through my veins and all of Lotus. I had more than enough to go around, which made me all that more dangerous. In theory.

Sucking every last drop of my magic was going to be difficult, and no way in hell was I going to lie down and make it a cinch for him. Not an option. But now that Gavin was here and in the line of fire, it changed the rules. And Lukas was playing a game without rules.

Their forms swirled crazy fast, combining the colored lights of magic with punches. It was unnatural the way they fought each other.

My blurred vision and labored breathing only made it that much harder to keep track of their movements, spiking my fear.

Lukas' head jerked to the side when Gavin's fist hit him in the jaw. And so the beat down ensued. They took turns pummeling each other as I tried to regain my strength. I could barely wrap my head around what was happening. It still seemed so unreal, like I was dreaming, and any minute I would wake. But the pain in my chest was all too real, and the blood gushing from the side of Gavin's temple was not a figment of my imagination.

My worst fear came true. Lukas kicked Gavin in the back of the shin, sending Gavin to the floor. Then Lukas pounced, securing him with invisible bonds as he had done me. I scrambled to feet, ignoring the way my head spun.

With a sadistic twist of his lips, Lukas's eyes flicked to mine. I let a startled gasp. His green irises illuminated in a ruthless chill. "Don't do this—" I pleaded, but before I could get the words out, Lukas tossed me like a beanbag.

What a colossal asshole.

Apparently I was nothing but baggage in his way to get what he truly wanted. The knowledge hurt almost as my landing. I crashed to the ground with such a jarring impact that my teeth shook. Gavin's growl bellowed over the surging storm, breaking the binds that held him. With his hands free, he threw a flaming ball at Lukas's chest, but the sly devil was able to step back at just the last second. Fire exploded at his feet. How long could the three of us tear into each other? I never in a gazillion years thought my life would come to this.

My boyfriend.

Me.

And the guy I'd known most of my life.

Fighting on opposing sides. My judgment of character was seriously deranged. How had I let Lukas fool me for so long? He was unhinged, and frankly, he scared the ever-loving crap out of me.

One wrong move and it was all over.

Hasta la vista baby.

Do something before he makes mincemeat out of your boyfriend, Morgana goaded in my head. *Or worse.*

I had forgotten about her. The *"or worse"* stopped my heart. Instinct propelled me into action. I might have been a little slow on the uptake, but I shot to my feet. On sturdier feet, I shoved my ratty hair out of my face. The storm above me was still aggressive, moving in a whirlwind around me. I reigned in the winds, allowing me to get a clearer sight of the two of them.

"Bri, run! Get out of here," Gavin yelled, taking a hit to his left shoulder.

And leave him? Not on his life. "I can't," I snapped, suddenly fighting angry tears. Drops of rain started to pelt from the sky. Seeing him with blood on his lip, swollen knuckles, and the determination of a mule, I was on the verge of losing my shit.

Gavin ducked. "You have a choice to make, Bri. Make it now," he prodded, dodging yet another beam of blazing gunk.

Tears blinded me, but I blinked them away. He was right. I threw my arms out on either side of me, and power rippled in the air surrounding me. If I didn't do this, Lukas was going to rip the magic from not only me, but also Gavin. If I did, then there was no going back. The darkness would increase tenfold, and the desire for more would triple. My soul for Gavin's life...

Because I was sure that Lukas was out for blood and playing for keeps.

It seemed like a fair trade in the heat of the moment. Unlike Lukas, I didn't enjoy the daunting task or look forward to the agony I was about to cause. *Don't be a wuss*, I ordered myself. "I'm sorry," I choked, no longer fighting the tears. And then I let the power gather inside me, ready to unleash at my command.

Gavin saw the decision in my face. Understanding and regret swam in his eyes. He would save me from this formidable deed if he could. I watched as he struggled with his need to protect me and my soul. We both knew there was no other way. I had to stop Lukas—not just today, but any future attempts as well—and this was the only way I knew how.

Now that I had made the choice, the witch inside was in a hurry to get it over with. I stepped forward.

Lukas's dark green eyes drifted over me suddenly, looking like the boy in my dreams. "Brianna. Don't. What I did, I did for your own good. You can't handle your powers."

Gavin smashed his fist into the center of his gut. "Shut up," he roared.

In any other situation, I might have laughed.

But it didn't matter what pleas Lukas emitted—it was too late. He threatened me—and what was mine. I gathered all that I had, and with sad eyes, I hurled my light, my darkness, my power. It struck Lukas in the heart, blinding me. Lightness and darkness swirled, for I had both.

The first taste of his magic was idyllic—a high with no equivalent —the sweetest forbidden nectar. I let the stream of his energy flow into me, pumping my veins with a sensation like nothing I'd ever felt. I didn't need to be a sorceress or a rocket scientist to realize that I was being pumped full of dark magic.

Lukas had more than dabbled in the darkness.

Like a dam bursting, I was flooded with so much power it bordered on painful. I panicked and almost broke the connection. It was Morgana who gave me the last bit of strength I needed. Her shimmery form stood beside me, offering her light—her guidance. She placed a hand on my shoulder, and I lifted my chin.

Pushing past my anguish, I held on, praying that when this was over, I wouldn't be an utter basket case. Morgana's outline flickered, signaling that her spirit in this plane would not last much longer. We both knew that this was it—our final goodbye. Everything seemed to be coming down on me at once. When it rains, it pours. I was losing so much in just a blink.

A friend.

A grandma.

My soul.

On one last raspy gasp, the link I had to Lukas fractured. A bitter flamed burned inside me, spreading from the very tips of my toes to the split ends in my hair. I wouldn't have been surprised if my hair was floating in the air like I'd been given the world's biggest noogie with a balloon.

Oh man. Ohmanohmanohman.

I had done the unspeakable—again.

Experience taught me that in the aftermath, I operated on a no-touch policy. I was numb to the core. What I had done would cost me dearly. Lukas had been powerful, and his magical roots an deep. There would be a steep pricing for stripping him naked—leaving him human.

I felt it crawl inside me—pure evil.

What an odd thing it was to be powerless one moment and a witch on steroids the next. That's how it felt...like I had become a witch overnight.

"It will pass," Morgana said, suddenly in front of me. The black dress she wore was faded gray, and her form was sheer. I could see right through her. There were so many emotions swimming in her violet eyes. "And when it does, you must find a way to counter the stains on your soul. You won't have long."

I choked on a sob, not knowing how to say all the words that were running through my head. "I wish we had more time," I whispered. There was still so much I didn't know, so many uncertainties. What if I wasn't able to fight the blackness?

She brushed a piece of hair out of my face, her touch a warm glow. "Blessed be, granddaughter. You did well." With one last lash of the wind, she was gone, and the cold carved deep in my bone.

I fell to my knees. Sweat soaked me. Fire and ice flowed through my veins in a waging war against each other. Footsteps trotted behind me. Gavin sunk down beside me, but was careful not to touch me. "How did you know?" I asked in a weak voice. My energy was depleted, and my throat scratchy.

His gaze searched my face. "Because no one can make a storm like you can."

My lips curved in a feeble smile. "For once, I'm glad."

Brows drawn tight, he said, "I just wish I had been here sooner—"

I put a finger to his lips, trying to avoid the cut, silencing him. "Don't. You got here. That's all that matters."

The moon's glow dusted over his face. His closeness in itself gave me comfort. "I'll find a way to save you. I promise," he vowed.

There was such determination in his voice and eyes, that I even believed him. "Lukas?" I asked, wondering if he was okay. He would never forgive me, but I was okay with that. At least he wouldn't be able to hurt me anymore, or anyone else, for that matter. He needed to be humbled, and I thanked God I had Gavin as my anchor, or I might have ended up as power- hungry as Lukas.

Gavin glanced over his shoulder to where Lukas' body had been. "He's gone."

My shoulders slumped.

Suddenly I was crying—an ugly cry. Maybe it was the residual adrenaline from the fight, or that I had just stolen magic from someone I once considered a friend. Gavin gathered me in his arms, shielding me from the rain the drizzled down on us.

CHAPTER 24

"No way am I leaving you alone. And I'm not asking you, I am telling you that you're spending the night with me." Gavin shoved his hands into his back pockets, glowering.

Under any other circumstances, I would have jumped at the chance to be in his bed. I opened my mouth, but I was too weary to argue. Lukas hadn't disappeared off my worry radar, and it was obvious that Gavin felt the same. Now that I had a moment to breathe, I didn't want to be alone.

I exhaled. "Let me grab a quick bag and text my aunt." The slightest movements, even one as small as breathing, ached. I hurt in places I didn't know could be sore. It was a strange feeling. I was engorged with power, but I had no outlet to release it. My body couldn't keep up with the tornado going on inside me. It shocked my system.

Gavin was also worse for wear. His shirt was torn at the hem and had blood dribbles down the front. A purplish-yellow bruise had started to form at the apple of his left cheek and just under the eye.

I reached for his hand, the cuts over his knuckles catching my eye. Seeing him like this made me wish I had the ability to heal. I pressed a soft kiss to his hand. "Thank you for always being here."

He cracked a smile. "I love a good bashing now and again."

My throat constricted. I couldn't ask someone to love me more. "Good. I think I am the kind of girl that has trouble following her everywhere."

Wrapping his arm over my shoulder, he replied, "I know you are."

He helped me to my feet, and together we more or less wobbled into the house. Lunar, happy to see anyone, started weaving in and out of our legs as we tackled the stairs. He was such an attention hog, but I couldn't resist picking him up and nuzzling the little fuzz-ball.

The first thing I noticed when I entered my room was the beams of light struggling to break through my white curtains. I took it as a sign. The storm had passed, and things could always be worse—no one died. Looking at the room of my childhood, I knew things could never go back to how they used to be. I had to look toward the future and come to terms with my decisions, no matter how harsh they might seem now.

Taut lines appeared at the corners of Gavin's mouth. "You okay?"

I stretched up, securing my arms around his neck. "I am now."

He lowered his head, resting his chin on my shoulder. Letting my eyes fall shut, minutes passed with only the sound of the whistling winds and the occasionally dripping of water. His heart beat strong and steady against mine. That's what he meant to me—strong and steadfast.

His arms tightened.

Regrettably, I stepped out of his embrace and went to my dresser. Opening the drawer, my hands shook slightly—not completely okay after all, but I would get there. I tossed random crap into a beach bag in record time. The sooner we got out of here, the better. I wanted... I didn't know what I wanted, but I knew that I wanted to be away from here—at least for the time being. The wounds were still raw, and a change in scenery might do me some good.

Gavin leaned against the wall, waiting patiently, and when I stopped fluttering around the room, he asked, "Ready?"

I bit my lip and nodded.

On the car ride to Gavin's house, I sent my aunt a text telling her that I was spending the night at Sophie's. Her short response back lifted the little bit of guilt I was feeling. She was going to be staying the night at Chad's. Her first sleepover. I tried not to make a big deal out of it. You would have thought that I was the parent here—worrying obsessively, but knowing she wouldn't be alone made all the difference.

The what-ifs would always haunt me. What if I can't be saved? What if Gavin decided I was hazardous? What if I hurt someone? My soul might forever be hellbound.

By the time Gavin pulled into his driveway, I had worked myself up to the point that I felt like I was going to hurl. There was no telling what was going to happen.

There was a warm, inviting aroma of cinnamon and spice when we walked into his house. A candle burned on the dining room table, and there were soft voices coming from the back porch—female laughter—Sophie and her mom.

Soundlessly, he tugged me upstairs, shutting the door to his room behind us. "I thought before the hordes get a look at us, we should change," he said at the same time he yanked his shirt over his head.

My mouth went dry.

He lifted a brow. "You can use the bathroom first."

I tore my eyes from his abs. "W-what?" My mind had gone blank, and I hadn't processed anything he'd said.

Gavin grinned, eyes twinkling. "I said, you take the bathroom first. There are fresh towels in the closet."

"Oh." I might have stared another minute or two before hiking my bag higher on my shoulder and moving into the plush bathroom.

Behind closed doors, I refused to fall apart, so I washed my, ran a brush through my matted hair and threw it into a messy knot on my head. I would win no beauty pageants, but I no longer looked like death. Slipping into a pair of sweats and a tank, I shoved my old ones into the bag and made a mental note to burn them later.

I reemerged feeling almost human again—and alone. Gavin was nowhere in sight. Curiously, I traced my finger along the edge of his bed, walking toward the open balcony door. The breeze from the ocean was flapping the stone-colored curtains. I stepped outside and inhaled deeply, loving the fresh scent of sea and sand.

The view was breathtaking, nothing but the lapping of foamy waves. I could lose myself in the beauty of the endless ocean. My tattoo began to tingle, and I didn't need to turn around to know that Gavin had joined me. I welcomed his warmth as his arms circled my waist from behind.

I leaned against his chest. He rested his face against mine, propping his chin on my shoulder. Strands of his wet hair tickled my cheeks. "I had to board up the door to keep Sophie from barging in," he murmured.

Just the deep timbre of his voice had the fireflies in my belly making an appearance. "Is it okay that I am here?"

"Sophie isn't the only one who is concerned." Keeping an arm secured at my hip, he reached for something behind him on the ledge. "My mom ordered me to have you drink this." He handed me a clear glass with a yellow substance.

I took the swirling opaque fluid. Concoctions always made me leery, especially when they had a magical mist emitting from them. It wasn't that I didn't trust Gavin's mom, because I did, but I was a picky eater, and this bordered into the strange and unusual food group.

He smirked at my hesitation. "I promise it tastes better than it looks. It will just ease the aches and pains."

Now that he mentioned it, all the small cuts and bruising was gone from his face. His mom was handy to have around. Regardless of what he said, I braced myself for the nasty aftertaste. Surprisingly, there was none. It was tasteless.

"Are you hungry?" he asked, releasing me and leaned against the porch rail.

I shook my head, turning around to face him. There was no way I could eat, not with my stomach twisting and turning. I might not eat again. "Morgana was there," I blurted, out of the blue.

His eyes narrowed. "What did that *witch* say?"

The way he said "witch", implied that he was calling her a foul name. I imagined she would have gotten a kick out of it. Suddenly, my heart felt heavy—burdened. "She said goodbye."

The whole demeanor on his face changed. Sympathy glistened in his eyes. "That must have been hard."

"It was. I never thought I would end up caring about her so much." She had, in her own way, saved me.

Shifting his weight, he crossed one leg over another. "Love works in mysterious ways."

That it did—mysterious and sometimes demented ways. Lukas's so-called claim that he loved me was proof. A bitter taste filled the back of my throat. "I tore the magic right from his soul." Tears welled up and spilled down my cheeks before I could stop them.

He grabbed my hand. "Bri, you did what you had to do."

It sounded reasonable, but did I? Was there not any other way? My control slipped. This whole time I had convinced myself that I would never use dark magic, but when it came down to it, at the first sign of trouble, that was exactly what I had done. And the worst part was, I would do it again. If it meant protecting Gavin, I wouldn't blink. "I'm a monster," I whispered.

"What?" Disbelief laced his tone. "How can you think that?"

"Did you see what I did to him?"

He placed his hands on my shoulders, his brows wrinkled in concern. "And if you hadn't, Lukas would have done worse, to you and me both. The difference is, you used your powers to protect. You acted out of self-defense. Lukas used them for greed and personal gain."

I dragged a lungful of air. "It's hard to admit out loud, but I would do it again. If anyone threatened you or my aunt, I wouldn't hesitate."

He made a sound in the back of his throat, and then pulled me into his arms. The tears came. My shoulders shook as I purged myself, over-come with guilt. Gavin held me close, rocking me, rubbing my back. When the tears stopped, he pulled back, grasping my face in his hands. "You look like you are about to drop dead on your feet."

I gave a wet snort. "Is that your way of telling me I look like crap?"

There was a glimmer of a smirk on his lips, not the full, heart-stop-ping kind, but it still touched me. "Hardly. In my eyes, you could never look anything but beautiful. I know you are good inside, and no spell is going to tell me otherwise."

I laughed. "That was so cheesy."

He kissed the tip of my nose. "You loved it."

I did, because I loved him. His words, all teasing aside, wrapped around me, filling me with warmth. He might not be able to wash away all my fears, or the guilt weighing inside me, but for the moment, they were what I needed.

His hands trailed down my bare arms. "You should lie down, or I could carry you..."

Clearly, I was going to get off my feet, one way or the other. The question was whether or not he was going to have to force me. "Only if you come with me," I countered, knowing he was right. I was feeling pale and lightheaded.

His answer was to twine our fingers.

Wordlessly, I climbed on the bed and scooted over, making room for him. He slid under the covers, tucking me into his arms. I rested my head on his chest, just under his chin and felt him brush his lips against my hair.

We lay there, talking about nothing and everything, passing the time. He made me laugh when I didn't think I could, taking my mind off the heavy stuff. Our arms and legs were tangled together. The sun had gone down, and it was nearing midnight when I let a yawn.

A wicked glint lit in his eyes. "I know what you need." His hand traveled over my hip, then dipped at the waist. The mischief in his smoky blue eyes told me just what he had in mind.

I held my breath. "Oh yeah, and what might that be?" I drew a heart with my finger over his heart.

He ran his finger down my cheek. "I think it's better if I show you," he said in a sinful tenor, easing me gently on my back.

I beamed. "What are you waiting for?" I was impatient to lose myself in what he offered.

Grinning, he bent down and took my mouth, slanting his head to get the perfect fit. My eyes fluttered shut, and the fireflies in my belly went wacko. I ran my fingers into the still slightly damp hair that curled at the nape of his neck. A faint spark jumped from my skin to his.

Turned out, he meant kissing and stuff. I needed a little bit of both.

I moved, throwing my leg over his. I flicked my tongue across his silver hoop, sending us both into frenzy. He growled, deepening the kiss and emptying my brain. Every inch of my skin was sensitive to his touch, heating and glimmering as his fingertips teased me. From there things went to sauna hot. Clothing bunched up. Sheets pushed aside.

My lips felt swollen from his silky kisses. God, he was just so damn good at it.

Squeezing a hand at my hip, his tongue swirled in my mouth, and my heart slammed against my ribs.

Holy awesome sauce.

"Make me forget, if just for a night," I murmured. My voice broke as he nipped at my lip.

Thick, long lashes hooded eyes like the color of the ocean's floor—dark and blue. "I can do that," he whispered.

I shivered.

In the background, waves splashed in a romantic melody, singing in harmony with the sounds of nature. It was like one of those relaxation CDs my aunt pumped through the shop's speakers.

Sliding his lips from mine, he briefly nuzzled my ear, and then at the hollow of my neck. Not even the cool breeze from the sea could give my flushed body relief. I was burning from the inside out. The weight of him did wicked things to my thoughts.

Hubba hubba.

I balled my hands into the sheets, gripping tight in an attempt to keep myself from flying off the bed. Just like the first time, it was sweet, ignitable, and dazzling. Not once did I think about Lukas, my deteriorating soul, or the fact that Gavin's mom was somewhere in the house.

But something was different. Me.

Inside my head, I could hear a dark voice whispering—enticing. I couldn't make out the words, however the intent was crystal clear—it was vile. My head shook from side to side on the pillow. I had to stop. I couldn't be with Gavin. Not with this gloominess flowing in my veins. I had a harder time convincing my body to pull away. It thrived under his touch, curving into the hard planes of his torso. But my body wasn't alone in its desire, my magic also responded—humming at the surface.

But as long as the darkness was poisoning my soul, I couldn't risk his wellbeing. I would never in a thousand years forgive myself if I hurt him. And my instincts told me that I wasn't out of the woods yet. Not by a long shot.

Finding a bit of resilience, I pushed at his chest, breaking off our kiss. "I can't," I muttered, my breathing uneven.

His eyes were iridescent in the twilight as he glanced down into my face. "What's wrong?" he asked in a raspy voice.

How did I tell him what was happening to me, when I didn't know? "I can't be with you like this," I said, fumbling with the sheets. The words got stuck in my throat. Bringing up Lukas's name while we were in bed signaled all kinds of red flags, but I owed him honesty. "Not while the darkness of his magic is swirling around in my blood. It is trying to mess with my head. I won't let it. I refuse to let it touch you."

He pushed the hair away from my face. "What can I do?" There was a glint at frustration that even now Lukas had found a way to get between us, but the softness of his fingers told me that he wasn't upset with me.

"Just hold me," I said, suddenly feeling my blood turn to ice.

Pressing a tender kiss to my lips, he tucked me at his side, securing his arms around me. "You're worried," he said.

I played with the ends of his hair, loving the silky texture between my fingers. I wasn't the only one who enjoyed it. Gavin's eyes were closed, and like a giant cat, he stretched out beside me. I swear he practically purred—a rumbling in the back of his throat.

Hell, yes, I was worried. How could I not be? So much was still at stake for me. I didn't want to ruin the ending to what had started as a horrific night. He had been able to override the memory of what was worst night of my life with something extraordinary, and then I go and ruin it. I squeezed him hard. "I am."

"It's going to be okay."

I wanted to believe him, to trust in his confidence. Sometimes it felt as if he knew me better than I knew myself. Snuggling up against him, it would have taken an army of witches to pry me away from him.

He settled in, his leg brushing mine. I flattened my hand over his chest, entranced by the electric current still flowing between us.

Settling in for what was sure to be a long and restless night, I closed my eyes. I couldn't have been more wrong. Sleep overtook me within seconds. No dreams. There was no one left to invade them. No Lukas. No Morgana.

CHAPTER 25

I woke up with eye boogers at the corner of my eyes, and Gavin's arm draped over me. It was a nice place to be. The air in his room smelled of sea and pine. Soft whips of wind pattered through the opened balcony door. I felt invigorated.

Unfortunately that wasn't the only thing I felt. Along with the rejuvenation of a dreamless night (which was bittersweet) there was a heavy shadow that grew inside me. Trapped, it clawed and spread like fog over my magic, overtaking the good, bit by bit.

It was the realization that today I was going to have to face the consequences of my actions...and the awkward morning after.

Err. I'd never woken up at a boy's house before. How was I supposed to react? *Play it cool. Be natural.*

If only I knew how to play it cool.

Carefully, I slid out from under his arm and turned on my side. I wasn't ready to leave his bed just yet. It had become a sanctuary, a place free of the demons I didn't want to face. A place where if only for a little while I was able to pretend that everything was fine and we were just a boy and girl hopelessly in love.

Lying on my hands, I studied the sharp planes of his cheekbones, the curve of his lip, and how the silver hoop at the center caught the morning light. It might have been silly, but having Gavin hold me had kept my fears at bay.

He had a boyish peacefulness to his face that wasn't there when he was awake. I smiled to myself. A stray curl hung over his forehead. Unable to resist the urge, I brush the straggler aside.

Then I caught the scent of coffee. It enticed me in a pull I couldn't ignore. Tiptoeing like a lame ninja from his room, I followed the bitter roasting smell. One whiff had awakened my caffeine addiction like a wild beast.

"Oh, boy," Sophie said when she got a glimpse of me. "Rough night?"

I walked straight to the brewing pot with nothing but coffee on the brain. There were a few mugs lined up on the counter next to it. Mrs. Mason thought of everything. Before I could think about uttering anything coherent, I needed my caffeine fix. Pouring a generous cup, I plopped down onto a stool beside her, and it wasn't until after my first sip that I mumbled, "You could say that."

"You're one of those girls," Sophie said, smiling and nodded to the cup clutched in my hand as if I was afraid someone was going to snatch it.

With half-lidded eyes, I noticed that she had already showered and was wearing one of her hippy-type dresses in jewel tones. *I hate her.* When I wake up, I look like a zombie munched on my hair. Sophie looked like she had just spent the entire day at the spa. "And you're one of those girls," I shot back, blowing the steam from my mug.

She laughed, and it was a pleasant sound to hear in the morning. "I might know a spell or two. I could teach you."

"Will it eliminate me having to stick a bristle brush near my eye? If so, when do we start?"

Her smile bloomed. "I always wondered what it would be like to have a sister. I kind of like the idea, as long as it is you."

"Umm. Thanks...I think." If we were going to get into the emotional-heavy-stuff, then I was going to need another cup of coffee, and a piece of that French toast that was staring me in the face.

"There is something different about you this morning," Sophie commented.

But before I could reply, Gavin sauntered in with a massive grin on his face and took the seat next to me. "We didn't get much sleep."

My skin tingled, and I couldn't take my eyes off him. Even in black sweats and a T-shirt, he made my heart somersault. I tried not to let the implication of his tone embarrass me.

I failed.

Sophie plucked a strawberry from her plate and tossed it at his head. "Gross. That's not what I meant, you bonehead."

There was no avoiding it. I flushed the same color as the bowl of strawberries on the counter.

Sophie made an icky face. "If you start dishing all the gory details about your sexual prowess, I might lose my breakfast." She slid us both a plate and passed down a heaping piling of French toast.

Gavin mouthed, *sexual prowess?*

I shrugged, forking a piece on my plate. Gavin snatched what was left on the serving plate, and I lifted my brows. He had almost an entire loaf of bread in front of him.

He winked. "I worked up an appetite."

I rolled my eyes.

Sophie gagged. "I'm going to be sick."

I could get used to this. There was such a sense of a family between Gavin and Sophie; even when they were bickering, they were a tight-knit unit. Before finding out that I was a witch, when I thought about my future, I imagined having a family like his. Big. Lively. Trustworthy. It was hard to see that dream move further from my reach, because more than ever, I wanted that with him. And that meant I had to save myself first.

Smothering the golden pieces of toast in melted butter and Aunt Jemima syrup, I took another bite. "What did you mean, something is different about me?" I asked Sophie, swallowing a whopping bite of goodness. Then I got momentarily distracted. Food had the that effect on me. I don't know what they did to their French toast, but it was heavenly.

Ah, the little things in life.

Sophie stabbed a strawberry and met my gaze. "You don't have a soul anymore."

My mouth hit the floor.

Gavin's fork stopped midair, dripping syrup on his plate.

The waves quieted. The wind stopped whistling. And the world went silent. "Come again?" I said densely.

"Sophie," he growled. "Couldn't you have at least waited until after I ate?"

I gave him a little jab in the side.

Her eyes were wide with fear, but it wasn't directed at me. It was fear for me. "I can't see your aura. All of your usual colors are gone. There's nothing but blackness surrounding you."

"Nothing?" Gavin repeated, his hunger forgotten.

Sophie squinted, focusing on my outline. It made me want to squirm in my seat. "There might be just a fraction of murkiness, but it won't be long until it's wiped out completely. Whatever you did...it's bad."

Gavin gave Sophie a shortened version of yesterday's events, while I made hearts in my remaining syrup with my fork. Everything about yesterday seemed chaotic and surreal. The evil, it was all through me. It was in my blood. I checked out of the conversation, having no inclination to relive it. Sophie had been right about one thing...I was in deep shit.

I felt a wave of injustice and anger rise up in me. Darkness roared in pleasure, fanning the flames of my rage in its desire for chaos. The other part of me that recognized the threat fought. A sharp pain shot through my skull, and I winced, my hand flying to my temple.

"Bri, are you alright?" Gavin asked.

The pain had passed, leaving behind a dull ache. They both looked at me with worry in their eyes, watching me carefully. I cleared my throat. "I'm okay now."

His face tightened, because none of us believed that. I was miles from fine.

CHAPTER 26

I looked out the window, staring at the spot where my not-so-friendly encounter with Lukas had gone down. My eyes narrowed and focused on the tree line. I couldn't help but wonder if I would ever see him again.

I'd already lost so much.

Lukas.

Morgana.

My soul.

How much more could I possible lose?

Everything. The answer frightened me. If anything happened to my aunt, my friends, or Gavin, let's just say that losing my shit didn't even come close to how I would react.

A dull ache spread in my chest, becoming a physical pain. I rubbed my hand over the spot.

"Are you ready for school?" Aunt Clara asked from the doorway of my bedroom.

I turned around, feeling not quite like myself. Sure I was wearing my "comfy" clothes, my favorite lip-gloss, and a spritz of perfume, but none of those things changed how I felt on the inside. "Only five weeks left."

She groaned. "Don't remind me. It is hard picturing this room without you in it every night. Who is going to make the coffee in the morning?"

Oh no. Not again.

Lately, she had been having little emotional breakdowns whenever she brought up college. I had bigger problems on my mind. Not to mention, I hadn't had the heart to tell her that I was thinking of deferring for a year. With everything going on, and all that has happened to me the last year, I just needed some time to uncover the answers I needed. My future was nothing if I couldn't save my soul. Nada. Zilch. Doomed. I figured, in the meantime, I could help out at the shop more while I did the whole self-discovery thing, then I could dedicate myself to a higher education.

Plus, I hadn't even applied to a single school.

I sucked.

"I'm going to be late," I replied, dodging the question. I snatched my book bag from the corner and brushed past her before the tears started. It was way too early for tears.

When I got to school, it was hardly better. Austin and Tori were all over me like white on rice. There must be something in the air today, and it didn't help that I was feeling the height of bitchiness.

Thank you, Lukas, and your freaking magic.

It was impossible to not think about my shadowy soul, so much so that I couldn't concentrate in my classes. I was on the verge of an emotional explosion. My time was running short, and the prospect of losing my soul was racking on nerves.

Shuffling toward my locker to ditch my books before going to the cafeteria, I was bookended by the dynamic due—Tori and Austin. We hadn't spent much time together since they found out the truth about me. My fault, not theirs.

Austin eyed me through his wire-rimmed glasses. "So what is the dealio on our little witch?"

I elbowed him in the side, and hissed, "Can we not talk about this here?"

"What crawled up your butt and died?" Tori grumbled. She had such elegance for words.

I wanted to pinch her. We had reached my locker, and I started to fumble with the combination. "You wouldn't believe me."

She leaned on the locker next to mine, her blonde hair falling over her shoulders. "Please. At this point, if you told me that aliens were real, I'd believe you."

"Are they?" Austin asked, standing beside Tori.

I shoved my massive trig textbook into my locker, relieved at losing the extra five pounds. "What, aliens? How do I know?"

They both stared at me, expectantly.

Rolling my eyes, I slammed the door to my locker shut. "No, aliens aren't real...I don't think."

"So tell us the dilemma. We can help, you know? Just cause we don't have magical mojo doesn't mean we are helpless," Tori said in a can-do-attitude.

At least she didn't hate my guts and wasn't afraid of me anymore. There was that. "It's *my* problem. Not yours." I did not want the two of them mixed up in this. They already knew too much.

"So what, did someone try to kill you again?" Austin asked, hitting the nail on the head.

I glanced around just to make sure no one was listening. "Lukas," I whispered, rubbing my hands over my arms. A chill went through when I said his name.

Tori's eyes got saucer-size big.

"Are you saying that Lukas tried to—" Austin finished the sentence with the slit-your-throat hand gesture.

I sunk against the lockers. "I don't want to talk about it, okay?"

Of course they didn't listen. I never should have said anything.

Austin's light green eyes lit up. "Oh, no, he didn't."

"He wouldn't!" Outraged marked Tori's expression.

"He did," I said, unenthusiastically.

Tori grabbed my arm. "You have to tell us everything."

Today was not the day to manhandle me. In my defense, I didn't know that I was doing anything until it was too late. I just reacted. A surge of energy bolted through me.

"Ouch!" Tori squealed. "You zapped me."

"Don't touch me," I said, the panic I'd felt suddenly gone. Regrettably, the words came out harsher than I intended. I rubbed the side of my head, feeling a stab of pain radiate across my temple.

Austin started on a rant roll. "Girl, you are trippin' today? Someone flip your bitch switch? Was it Rianne? Because if that skank is spreading rumors with her lizard lips again—"

"No," I snapped. "It's no one. I just—" I shut my trap not wanting to involve them. They would only worry and the pain was intensifying. "Look, I'm sorry. I'm not feeling myself."

"Someone forgot to take their meds," Tori mumbled under her breath.

I shot her the stink eye. I needed to leave before I did any permanent damage to our friendship. Nothing would ever be normal again, not with this darkness chopping away at my soul. "I'll see you guys later. I need to find Gavin." Pronto.

As I walked away, I felt their eyes at my back as they wondered what was going on with their wacky friend.

I didn't blame them.

"Gavin!" I called, spotting him just outside the cafeteria.

He turned around at the sound of my voice. The smile that had started to curl his lips, fell. "What's wrong?" he asked, when I stopped in front of him.

I rubbed the back of my neck. "I just fried my best friend with magic."

"Which one? Because Tori might benefit from a good shock."

"This isn't funny. It's getting harder and harder to not lash out." With each word my tone got louder.

His eyes sobered. "Come on." He took my hand and led me to the south exit. With strides much longer than mine, I practically had to run to keep up. Pushing through the double doors, we exited to the back of the building.

I took a huge gulp of air, letting it smooth the burning in my lungs. This part of the school was usually where the burnouts loitered, smoking or worse.

Gavin scowled at a small group huddled against the bricks. "Scram." The way he said the single word left no room for argument. They dropped their little white sticks to the ground and scattered. The moment we were alone, Gavin crushed their still-lit cigarettes with his boot.

"Charming," I said dryly.

He arched a brow, the silver stud glinting. "I could say the same for your little outburst in the hall. You just need to hang on for a little longer."

"Does that mean you are close to figuring out how to stop it?"

"Not exactly."

His words sunk in slowly. "It's hopeless."

He flashed in front of me. "This is exactly what you can't do. Give up. The dark inside will take advantage of any weakness it senses. You can't afford to let it gain even an inch."

I forced a casual shrug. "Oh, is that all," I fired back, a buzzing in my ear. I was being a bitch, and I knew, but I couldn't help it.

"I know this isn't easy, but I refuse to lose you."

"You might not have a choice."

He boxed me in, placing a hand on either side of the brick wall. "Your pity party isn't helping."

Sparks radiated at my fingers. "Don't push me." My voice had a technetronic quality to it. Freaky.

He wasn't intimidated. "I'm not trying to be a dick, Bri. I'm trying to get you to be reasonable—to fight back."

My eyes narrowed. "All you're doing is pissing me off." I was pumped with magic.

"Good. Then at least you aren't feeling sorry for yourself. That fire will keep the dark from spreading."

Oh, God. He was right. With a lot more effort than it should have taken, I closed my fists, calling back the energy bursting to break free. It screamed inside me, begging to be released. I closed my eyes, evening out my breathing. "I don't know how much longer I can do this. It is eating me up inside," I said, my eyes opening.

He saw my struggle. "I will find a way to counteract the darkness from absorbing that asshole's magic. I promise."

I rubbed the end of my nose. "Do you have ideas?"

"Not yet, but if I ever get my hands on him..."

No other words were necessary. The menacing scowl on his face said it all. He would kill him. If Lukas knew what was best for him, he'd never show his face in Holly Ridge again. Hell, crossing the state line of North Carolina might not be far enough. Gavin had a ruthless determination, and regardless of what happened to me, Lukas was going to be Gavin's number one target.

Morgana's warning echoed in my memory. It was one I'd likely never forget.

Two boys. One destined to be your true love, bound by more than just magic and love. The other...well, he isn't so lucky. He will destroy all the good you possess. Squash your pureness, which is also your strength. He will poison you with darkness—blacken your soul. And make you turn from all you love. The choice is yours, great-granddaughter. Choose wisely. For it can't be undone.

Well. She had pinned the donkey on the butt. Lukas had definitely poisoned me, but it was of my own doing. I made the choice to take his magic. And if we didn't find a solution soon, I was likely to lose all those that I loved.

CHAPTER 27

T ime passed. Weeks turned into a month. Graduation loomed right around the corner, and I isolated myself from all those I loved. The magic breathing inside me continued to spread like a nasty virus.

I snapped at my friends for no reason.

I pushed Gavin further and further away.

I snarled at my aunt when she was only concerned.

The list of cruel things that came out of my mouth the last few weeks could fill a book. It was embarrassing, and so out of character for me, but nothing I did, no matter how hard I tried, I could not hold back the darkness from swallowing me.

And while I was wallowing in the dark, fighting every day to win this internal battle, Gavin was spending every waking moment trying to find a way to save me. He never gave up, which was more than I deserved.

I secluded myself in school, was unusually quiet at home, and I lacked pizzazz at work (not that I'd had a lot to begin with). Looking at myself in the mirror, I didn't recognize the person who stared back. Her eyes were sunken—lackluster. Her clothes were baggier than they should have been, thanks to my lack of appetite. And I didn't need Sophie to tell me that a shroud of darkness surrounded me.

Turning away from my reflection, I did what I could to make my appearance as normal as possible, but I fooled no one.

Downstairs, Aunt Clara was washing off her breakfast plate. "I can't believe this is your last week of high school," she said when she saw me, drying her hands.

My heart sunk. One more week. I might cry. Big. Blubbering. Sobs. Not because high school was coming to end, but because my time here in this house, living with my aunt, was coming to end. I finally came to the decision that for her safety...I had to leave. After graduation just seemed like the appropriate time. I didn't see the point in lingering. It would only make the choice harder by prolonging my departure, and every day that the darkness became stronger, my resilience weakened.

"Don't cry," I said, seeing her eyes well up. "I just applied this makeup, and I don't have another twenty minutes to fix it."

She laughed, shaking her head and sniffing. "Don't expect a no-tear policy at graduation," she warned, dabbing at her wet eyes.

I tried to hide my sadness. "You can bawl like a baby."

"I will," she assured, smiling. "So what do you have planned on your final Saturday before freedom?"

God, if she only knew. It was better she didn't. I took a seat. "Nothing special. I thought I would go to the beach later."

She stood behind the counter across from me and folded her hands. "You have always loved going to the beach, even as a baby. Your entire face would light up."

Threading my fingers through my hair, I smiled. "Some things never change." Like my love for her, the woman who raised me alone. She was the strongest person I knew.

I didn't have any idea how to write a goodbye letter, but I had to have everything in order, because immediately after graduation, I was out of here. Time was running out, and we were no closer to finding a way to stop the evil from winning.

How did I say goodbye to the two most important people in my life? The one who was in every memory of my past, and the other who was in all of my dreams for the future.

But to stay was a risk I was unwilling to take, not until I found a way to save myself, because the day darkness ruled me was swiftly approaching. They weren't safe while I was around and unstable.

I know that they would both feel hurt and betrayed by my leaving. I could only hope in time they would see it was for them—that there was no other way.

She tweaked my nose. "I am so proud of you."

I drank in the sight of her, searing it to memory. One week wasn't long enough. "Well, you only have yourself to thank. You taught me to be the person I am."

Her eyes filled with sentiment. "Oh, now you've done it." She wiped at her cheeks.

Jumping off the stool, I walked around the counter and gave her a hug. It was harder to pull away than I bargained for. I drew a sharp breath, suppressing the thick emotions that were clogging the back of my throat. "I'm meeting Gavin; I should probably go," I said, struggling to keep my voice even.

"Don't forget a sweater. It's cooler by the water," she said, the motherly instinct always there. She had been more mother than aunt to me, so it was fitting.

I nodded and walked toward the garage. If I stayed another minute, I was going to lose the hold on my emotions. I took one last glimpse over my shoulder before I left.

The tears broke free once I saw the house I loved in my rearview mirror. My chest tightened, but I squared my shoulders and focused ahead. Pointing my car the direction of the beach, I took a deep breath. There was still one more person I needed to say goodbye, and this one would take all my strength, all my sheer will, and an act of God.

Today I would tell Gavin goodbye.

In my own way.

I sat cross-legged on the beach. Waves crashed like cannon fire, the earth shook, and the water swirled. My emotions were going haywire.

Oh dear Mary, mother of God. My heart splintered, shattering into a billion fragments of sorrow, pain, regret, anger, longing. The range of feelings just kept piling on. I was wigging out. One minute I was confident I could do this—that I must to do this—for his protection. The next I was whimpering, on my knees, begging for a miracle—a cure to this madness choking me.

I had to get this over with. The anxiety was enough to kill me. I couldn't go another week with this weight on my chest. He would do everything in his power to stop me, which was why I wasn't precisely telling him my plans. Yes, I was saying goodbye without actually saying the words, but after I was gone, he would know.

His appearance brought forth conflicted feelings, but love overshadowed them all. My fingers shifted in the sand. "Hey," I greeted, watching him plop down next to me.

"I take it you are having a bad day?" Gavin asked, nodding to the turbulent waters churning.

I knew he was worried about me, and who could blame him? The whole reason I was here was because I had become someone else. The Brianna he knew had changed, and I didn't know how to get her back.

I wasn't *her*. Not anymore.

I had avoided his gaze until now, because I knew that once our eyes collided, I wouldn't be able to look away from his brilliant blue eyes. "I've had better."

His boots dug into the sand. "I'm not giving up, and neither should you."

"Our window is closing, Gavin. And it's no one's fault but my own. If I had found another way—"

"You can't blame yourself for things that are outside your control. We don't pick the gifts bestowed upon us. We are given only what we can handle, so someone must think that you have it inside you to overcome. I believe in you."

If only that was enough. Too bad my life wasn't a fairytale.

What he said was true, but it didn't change my decision. We sat together, talking and listening to the sounds of the beach. There was no one here but us. Being with him was so easy. It was effortless and that was what I loved about us.

I fumbled with the chain of my necklace, my first real item of magic. Not always effective, but I had kept it with me.

Gavin inched closer. "Holy shit."

He startled me. "What?" I was clueless, but it was obvious by the expression on his face that it was important.

He ran a hand through his raven hair, eyes meeting mine. "I think I figured it out, how to keep the darkness at bay."

Say what?

I did a double take, thinking my ears deceived me. "Oh," I said. I had nothing else. It seemed unreal, and I wasn't getting my hopes up. My heart couldn't take it.

Twirling the stones at my neck, his fingers grazed against my skin. I waited expectantly as he worked through whatever theory was running through his head. Twenty seconds ticked by.

Was he going to tell me or torture me by keeping me in suspense?

He tugged the hoop on his lip. "It was right in my face the whole time. How did I not guess sooner?"

I still had no idea what he was referring to, and now I was getting annoyed. I turned my body to face him, my knees in the sand. "Are you going to tell me what you are talking about or just keep speaking in circles?"

He arched a brow, the corner of his lips tipping. "It's your necklace."

"How is my necklace going to save me?" I asked, thinking he had lost his freaking mind.

Exasperation posed on his face. "Not the necklace, but the moonstone."

Right that made perfect sense. Not. The doubt was written all over my expression. A cloud passed over the sun, and the temperature seemed to have dropped. "I'm still not following."

A small smile pulled at his lips, and I saw the beginnings of excitement shining in his eyes. "It's an ancient remedy, no longer practiced. Crystals were never my thing, but my mom, being a healer, it's part of her craft. Crushed moonstone has properties that purify a soul."

Something clicked. "Moondust." The voice of the tarot card reader echoed in my head. *You keep it close to you.* I didn't realize she meant literally.

He nodded. "Moondust."

"How?" It was impossible to believe that my cure was so simple. There had to be a catch.

His hands grasped the sides of my cheeks. "I'll show you." He held out his hand.

I took a breath. With slightly shaky hands, I fumbled with the clasp at the back of my neck, removing the necklace and dropping into his waiting palm.

Without a second of hesitation, he closed his fist over the stone, whispered words that sounded foreign on the tongue. My expression grew incredulous. The blue in his eyes illuminated as bright as the stars. I was transfixed by his power, by his words, by him. Drawn by the shimmering of magic pouring from his hands, the milky-blue stone started to glow in his clench. When the spell was completed and he opened his palm, his eyes meet mine.

This was it.

Sink or swim.

I blinked. The once-solid crystal was a bluish-white power in his hand. I watched in amazement. The dust was still glowing. It was spell-binding.

Holy smokes.

"Now what?" I asked in a voice just over a whisper.

His lashes lowered, and he brought his handful of moondust up to his mouth. Then before I knew what his intentions were, he blew the magical dust over me. I gasped. The ever-present dark ribbons inside me roared as the sparkles floated down upon me.

Time moved in slow motion. I could see the diamond-like dust in the air, swirling. It landed on my skin, in my hair, and I breathed it in. Tilting my head back, I drank in the salty air infused with magic, letting the wind and the sun wash over my skin. I closed my eyes. My heart felt lighter. My magic purer. My soul repaired. I felt like myself.

And I owed it all to Gavin.

He waited patiently, expectantly, for me to say something. No words came. So I grinned, and threw my arms around his neck.

His arms tightened, and he buried his face in the hollow of my neck. "Does this mean it worked?" he murmured.

I swallowed. "I never should have doubted."

"Damn right," he responded.

I laughed, pulling back to look into his face, unable to comprehend that he had found a way to counteract the use of such dark magic. "What did you say, the words to the spell?" I asked, still hardly able to believe I was free of the darkness. My entire body felt cleansed.

"To sea. To sky. To night," he whispered.

It was beautiful.

And he was breathtaking.

Gavin slipped his arm around me as I leaned into him. He kissed my temple. And I sat with him while the storm shifted out to sea, the thunder quieted, and the whips of rain and wind turned to soft patters.

"So you think we are meant to be?" I asked with a grin in my voice.

A wealth of emotion shone in his dazzling blue eyes. "I know it."

"How?"

He angled his head. "You know why? That charge of energy you get whenever we touch, it's not coincidental."

That was twice this year that two different guys claimed that I was destined to be theirs, except this time...I believed him.

I grinned in embarrassment. "I'm glad it's you."

He smirked, eyes twinkling. "There was never another choice for me, Bri. It was always you." Then he swept me off my feet.

CHAPTER 28

On the afternoon of graduation, Tori stood in my bedroom, twirling a medium-sized curling wand through my hair. I fidgeted in front of the mirror. "Are you almost done?" I complained.

She grinned. "Shut up and sit there. You'd think I was killing you."

"It feels like it," I grumbled.

Austin spun in the desk chair, facing us, his brown hair slicked back and his bottle green eyes twinkling. "Babygirl, what are you going to do without us?"

"Use a spell."

The two of them looked at each other and then started laughing. "Why didn't you just say so?" Tori asked, waving the curling wand behind my head.

I met her reflection in the mirror. "Because this might be the last time you do my hair."

She put her hand over her heart, her eyes watering. "That is so sweet."

Austin coughed. "B, sweet? What has the world come to?"

I socked him in the arm. "I have my moments," I defended, tears stinging my eyes. I had a feeling it was going to be a day full of them.

Tori put down the wand and wiped at her eyes. "Thank God we haven't started our makeup yet."

I groaned. "I think I'll take the easy way out."

"Me too?" Tori asked.

"You better not leave me out," Austin chimed in.

Surprised, I nodded. My friends wanted me to use magic on them! I adored them to death. "As if I could forget about you."

Calling forth my magic, no longer tainted, it flowed through my veins like warm silk. A violet mist swirled around us as I recalled the words to a spell that Sophie had taught me. It was a simple one to enhance one's natural beauty. Smooth wrinkles, vanish blemishes, enhance the eyes, refresh the skin, it was like spending hours in a fancy spa, bottled in a spell.

"There," I said grinning. "Voilà."

They both rushed to my full-length mirror. "You are kickass to have around," Austin smiled, catching my eye in his reflection.

Tori puckered her rosy lips. "Screw all those expensive bottles in my bathroom. You are so much cheaper."

I stretched out my legs. "Thanks, I think."

Tori spun around, giggling, her short black dress flaring with her movements. "I can't believe we are graduating today."

Austin went to the side of my bed, rummaging through a bag he had brought with him. "And now that you aren't witch-a-saurus anymore, I think a toast is in order." He pulled out a green bottle of what looked like champagne.

I should have been totally offended, but I wasn't. I had been a complete and utter bitch the last few weeks. "Where did you get that?" I asked.

Tori grinned like she got caught eating the last Krispy Kreme at a cop convention. "It was a gift from my dad."

I shook my head. "He does realize you are only graduating high school, not college?"

She shrugged. "It's free booze. Who cares? We deserve it."

"Here, here!" Austin chanted.

The three of us held our glass flutes in the air. "I love you guys. You are the best friends a girl could have."

Austin clucked his tongue. "After the shit you put us through this year, your skinny ass better love us."

We clinked our glasses together. "Cheers," we said in unison, grinning.

I took a sip and immediately made a not-so-pretty face.

Austin had drained his glass. "Let's graduate, bitches."

"STOP FIDGETING," Gavin whispered.

"I can't. This gown is itchy." I tugged at the collar of my god awful purple and gold robe. Whoever designed these things should be shot. Haven't they ever heard of comfort?

He chuckled.

My entire graduation class was sitting in the football field, with our parents and loved ones in the stands, crying, smiling, and cheering our accomplishment. We had survived high school. For me, that was almost a bigger triumph than passing my classes. With Gavin at my side, we waited for the principal to call our names.

I twirled my hair around my fingers nervously. I glanced over at him and shielded my eyes from the sun.

Gavin elbowed me playfully. "What now, Bri?" he asked about the future.

Did he really expect me to answer that big of a question right now? I didn't know what I was doing this afternoon, let alone at the end of summer. I gave a small shrug. "I don't know, college?" He was always altering my plans, but this time it had been in a good way.

He smirked. "You just name the school...I'll take care of the rest."

I snorted. *By take care of*, he meant magic. Spelling my way into college hadn't exactly crossed my mind. But it wasn't the worst idea I'd ever heard.

Principal Les called my name over the microphone, and I froze. Gavin gave my butt a little pat, spurring me into motion. I glared over my shoulder at him, scowling. He flashed me a quick, saucy grin. The whole way to the front, I prayed I wouldn't trip.

When it was all over and the entire class had their diplomas, we threw those weird square caps in the air. My aunt was waiting for me in the crowd. She looked lovely in her simple summer dress, with a bouquet of flowers in her arms, of course.

She handed me the colorful arrangement. "I wish your mom and dad could see you," she sniffed, blotting a tissue under her eyes.

Oh, Lord. Here come the waterworks. "Me, too," I said, hugging her.

She clung, and I let her. Tears burned the back of my throat. Man, I sort of wanted to start bawling. "Thank you for always being there for me," I said.

"Always and forever," she whispered. "You were born from magic. Don't forget your roots."

"I won't," I promised.

As we separated, another pair of arms immediately bombarded me. "Congratulations," Sophie said, hugging me. "I can't believe I have another year," she groaned.

As always, Sophie came in like a whirlwind. "Don't worry. It will fly by," I assured her.

Austin and Tori joined us. "We did it," Austin sang, and I was smooched between my two best friends.

If I did any more hugging, I might be sick. "High school was a lot harder than I anticipated," I mumbled.

The three of them laughed. "Maybe more so for some than others," Sophie said, winking at me.

That was when Aunt Clara pulled out the camera. She snapped pictures of Tori, Austin and I, some with Sophie, and finally, Gavin and me. She got all teary-eyed again. Just when I thought she was finished, she would take another and another. It was almost more than I could stand, but I let her fuss.

I was surrounded by people I loved.

Although the sun was shining in my eyes, I could have sworn I caught a glimpse of sandy hair and emerald eyes. It brought on the memory of the first time I saw Lukas in the farmer's market. Acute sadness and sharp regret soared inside me. I stood on my tiptoes, trying to get a better view.

He wouldn't possibly show his face at my graduation, right? He wouldn't take the risk. Why would he? He wouldn't be so stupid, unless he had a death wish.

But it didn't stop that seed of possibility from spreading... until it was all I could think about. Stretching on my toes, I looked through the crowds, trying to see if my eyes had tricked me.

I found not a trace of Lukas in the sea of people, and I couldn't decide if it was relief or disappointment I was feeling. Regardless, it didn't last long, because a flutter of fireflies replaced all other feelings.

Gavin had come up behind me and rested his chin on my shoulder. "You okay? You look like you've seen a ghost."

A small giggle bubbled out, but before he could question my sanity, I turned in his arms, facing him. Sometimes, like now, when I was staring up at his face, I regretted that it had taken me as long as it did to realize that he was the only one. I wish that I had been as confident in us as he had been. I felt like, for him, it had been instantaneous. "I love you," tumbled from my mouth, coming straight from the bottom of my heart.

His arms squeezed around me, tingling with magic. "I love you." The words sounded devastatingly perfect coming from him

My heart tripped. A burst of light encompassed every cell in my body. Delight fluttered through my belly. Our love did that. There was hope in our future. There was our acceptance of each other—the good, the bad, and the ugly.

We kissed, and everything about him felt familiar. I know exactly how we fit together—perfectly, his arms around my waist, my hands tied at his neck, the pressure of his lips over mine. No doubts. Not about him. Not about me. And certainly not about us.

The future?

Well, that is another story. One that I can honestly say I am looking forward to.

THE END

Ready for the a bonus short novel of Gavin & Brianna's story?
Grab your next Gavin fix in <u>DARKMIST</u> the bonus book of the
Luminescence Trilogy!

CAN'T WAIT to meet you back in Holly Ridge!
Thank you for reading.
xoxo
Jennifer
P.S. Join my VIP Readers email list and receive a bonus scene told
from Zane's POV, as well as a free copy of Saving Angel, book one in
the Bestselling Divisa Series. You will also get notifications of what's
new, giveaways, and new releases.

Visit here to sign up: <u>www.jlweil.com</u>

Don't forget to also join my Dark Divas FB Group and have some
fun with me and a fabulous, fun group of readers. There is games,
prizes, and lots of book love.

Join here: <u>https://www.facebook.com/groups/1217984804898988/</u>

You can stop in and say hi to me on Facebook night and day. I pop
in as often as I can: <u>https://www.facebook.com/jenniferlweil/</u> I'd love to
hear from you.

PART IV
DARKMIST

CHAPTER 1

T humbing through the pages of my astronomy textbook, I lifted my head. Only nine minutes had passed since I sat down, and all I could think was, *why the hell had I taken astronomy?*

Maybe because the idea of taking a biology class made me want to hurl. I mean, I had to dissect a frog in high school. God only knew what they were going to make me dismember in college. Gross. Ick. That's why I was sitting in room 103 of the Natural Science building at the University of North Carolina.

The ten-minute hike across campus was convenient, as was living in the dorms, especially since I was a stickler for time management. No way was I getting stuck sitting in the front row.

Wouldn't it be easier to live here at home? Aunt Clara's voice filtered into my thoughts.

Accessibility hadn't been the only reason I'd chosen to stay in the dorms. I'd wanted the full college experience, a fragment of freedom to discover myself. It had taken a bit of convincing for Aunt Clara to agree to the co-ed dorms, particularly because my edible boyfriend's room was down the hall.

Gavin Mason.

He was not the kind of guy I ever pictured myself dating. Dark. Mysterious. Edgy. Dimples that made his blue eyes twinkle devilishly. And he was a witch...like me.

I still wasn't sure what he saw in me, but living under the same roof definitely had its perks. Gavin had taken a slightly different approach to college than I had. Where I was laser focused on my studies, he was motivated by the next party.

Austin and Gavin had become frat brothers in the sense they'd found a shared love of Alpha Beta Delta or whatever weird Greek name their fraternity. It was kind of a surprise. I never would have pegged my boyfriend as a frat boy. He was more of a loner. And that made me think he was up to something. He always had an agenda.

The question was, what?

I extended my legs under the seat in front of mine and glanced at the clock above the door. Ugh. If this was how my day was going to go, then I was in trouble. My eyes wandered about the classroom, checking out the other dorks that were dumb enough to sign up for this course.

There was a girl with cinnamon and spice hair a few seats diagonal from where I was. It wasn't her fiery hair that captured my wandering gaze, but what she was doing with her pen. The two of us should have been taking notes on the lecture Professor Burns so snoringly delivered, yet...

I had no excuse, but this girl, she was concentrating intently on the slim silver pen hovering in the air an inch or two from her face. Nothing was touching it. No fingers. No string. No trick. Except magic.

I felt the tremble of power dance in the air, and she suddenly had my undivided attention. *WTF.* She was openly using magic in the middle of class. I was flabbergasted. My mouth fell open. Did she have no regard for the safeguard of the craft?

I mean, I was still an apprentice in a manner of speaking, but even as a novice, I knew the rules. There was no doubt, this girl was a witch, but the difference between us was, I didn't flaunt my gifts. I didn't openly splash magic where others could see.

But as my eyes swept over the room, I realized no one else noticed anything amiss. *A cloaking charm?* It was the only explanation my mind could come up with. *I* could see through the spell, given the extent of my powers.

There was nothing ordinary about the magic I was born with. Nothing at all. My power was feared by most witches and coveted by the darker ones. I'd learned to accept who I was—the descendant of Morgana Le Fey—a clàr silte.

It wasn't as cool as it sounded.

The CliffNotes version was, I sucked the magic from other witches. I was the Dementor of enchantresses. Of course, there were repercussions for such power. I couldn't just go around slurping magic from every witch I encountered like they were ninety-nine cent cherry Slurpee's. The price for using magic of that magnitude left blemishes on my soul—the sort of marks that turned your soul dark.

And I'd rather punt-kick myself in the face than losing myself to dark magic. I didn't like who I turned into, or the little voices in my head, baiting me to take more. One taste led to an insatiable appetite.

To date, I'd only stripped one witch of his power. Lukas Devine. I hadn't seen or heard from him since that day. It was probably for the best. Lukas had nefarious plans where I was concerned. It was still hard to believe I'd mistaken his feelings toward me as affection, when in fact he wanted my power and what I could do with it.

Gavin, if given the chance, would love to go a round or two with Lukas, to screw up his pretty boy face, as he would say. I shuddered at the thought of them running into each other. Bloodbath.

As I stared the redheaded witch, she must have sensed my eyes on her. Her head angled, meeting my disapproving gaze dead on, but she never dropped the spell. Actually, the minx smiled at me, and not in a friendly sort of way. It was menacing and made my skin prickle with unease. There was something off about her.

I tapped my pencil on the blank paper in front of me and bit my lip.

She lifted her brow when I continued to stare. It was a challenge. The pen floating parallel to her slender nose began to spin. Then with a flick of her marshmallow painted fingernail, she sent the pen sailing through the air, directly at Professor Burns.

I froze.

The length of the pen whizzed past his ear and the tip sunk into the corkboard bulletin behind him with a *thump*. I made a loud audible gasped.

Holy shitsnacks.

Professor Burns brushed at the side of his head, but other than that, he didn't miss a beat in his lecture. However, my disruptive gasp of horror was a different story. Numerous heads turned my way, giving me the side-eye reserved for public spectacles.

My face flamed an ugly shade of pink. Dipping down, I let my hair fall forward, curtaining my face as my gripped tightened on my pencil. If there was one thing I hated more than being embarrassed, it was bullies. Silently, cursing a string of swear words that would have made my aunt blush, I peeked up from under my lashes.

The *witch* was laughing at me.

Swirls of magic gathered at my fingertips. I wanted to show this witch what real magic was. These parlor tricks were high school compared to what I could do.

But noooo. That's not why I was here, I reminded myself. Sometimes it just plain sucked being the good girl.

For the remaining of class, I avoided looking at her. I didn't want to play her games.

As soon as Professor Burns dismissed the class, I shot out of my seat like I was racing for the last cup of coffee. I made it to the double doors without tripping or mowing anyone down. Bursting out of the science building, I lifted my head up and breathed in the warm afternoon sun. There was a hint of sea in the air, but I didn't stop to smell the roses. My legs kept moving. I wanted to put as much distance as I could between the mysterious witch and me. She struck a chord inside me. And not in a good way.

"You're a witch," a dark seductive voice stated.

I stopped in my tracks. The multi-hued ginger was sitting on a bench just outside the brick library, twirling a piece of her hair.

How the hell had she gotten here before me? The library was adjacent to my dorm, a win-win in my book. "I don't know what you're talking about," I replied. This girl was a stranger to me, and I surely didn't owe her an explanation.

"You saw me in there. I know you did." She crossed her legs over an expensive pair of designer jeans. "I can feel your power, you know. It's pointless to lie."

Most witches could sense another of their kind. "I saw you showing off with a juvenile spell."

The smirk on her lips tightened. "I'd be careful who you piss off, rookie."

"I'm not looking for trouble," I said, before I said something she'd regret.

Her cherry lips puckered. "That's too bad. Trouble is way more fun. I'm Amara, by the way."

"Brianna," I replied, shifting the strap of my bag higher up on my shoulder.

She batted her heavily mascara-framed cat green eyes and stood up, pulling a slim card out from her back pocket. "Here. If you're interested, there's a party tonight at my sorority house. It's not your typical sorority, and I think you'd fit right in. I'm the house advisor."

I took the business card, but I doubted this *so-called sorority*, was approved by the school board, or if it was, a dab of magic had been involved. Last I checked there wasn't a major for witchcraft. "I'll pass," I answered, trying to keep the distain from my voice. "I have a full load this semester and hadn't really thought about rushing."

She shrugged. "Suit yourself. If you change your mind, you know where to find me, Brianna. My number's on the card." Twitching her butt, she turned back toward me after only a step or two. She popped a pair of shades over her eyes. "Hope to see you tonight."

A cold chill passed over me as I watched her saunter down the sidewalk like she was on the red carpet.

Geez.

I flipped the card over in my hand. Kappa Zeta Gamma. *If you can't fly with the big girls, get off the broom.*

Catchy. And not too subtle.

Under the tagline was her name. Amara Sanders. There was also the sorority logo. KZG. And no joke, there was a little wooden broom going through the monogram.

Wow. And to think I thought I wasn't going to make any friends. I hadn't thought I would meet a witch, or that I would accuse of her misusing magic. What a way to make a first impression. New city. New school. And I managed to muck it up in less than thirty minutes. Could be a personal record.

CHAPTER 2

Dropping my enormous astronomy book on my desk, I flopped on my dorm bed, staring at the twinkle lights dangling across the ceiling. My roommate was an interior decorator major who was obsessed with Pinterest.

Kylie was a petite brunette with skin that was golden year round and a sparkling personality. Her wardrobe reflected her flare for design, and would have made Tori green with envy.

It was strange not having Tori here, but university wasn't for her. She was furthering her education at Elite School of Beauty. I didn't doubt I was going to end up being her guinea pig on her journey to become a beautician. I only hoped that I would have hair left by the time she graduated. My only comfort was that any damage she caused could be fixed with a little bit of magic.

I missed her, especially after today.

Twirling the card between my fingers, I did something I never thought I would do. I considered joining a sorority, or the very least, checking out the house. The way I saw it, I had two choices: I could go to this party tonight and maybe meet a few cool people, or I could climb into bed, turn off all the lights, and pull the covers over my head. I so wanted to indulge myself in a good pity party, but my curiosity got the best of me. I hadn't busted my butt working all those summers at Mystic Floral, saving money for college, and taking on the additional expense of living on campus, just so I could shut myself up in my room. *The whole experience, remember.* And that included parties.

I nibbled on my nail, contemplating.

Forget it.

If I had to think this hard, it wasn't worth it. Maybe meeting other witches wasn't a good idea. Who knows what might happen. Honestly, I had better things to do with my time than get wasted with a bunch of uppity sorority sisters.

Like writing a paper for Composition I. Unwilling to give Amara and her sorority another thought, I pulled out my English textbook. My classes were finished for the day, but my run-in with Amara had interrupted my plans. I had intended to head over to the financial building after my astronomy class to fill out an application for a campus job. At eighteen credit hours, I had a full schedule, but if I was going to continue living on campus, I would need money, and a job on campus seemed like the best route.

I was going to have to make time tomorrow.

Tonight, I was going to attack my homework with a vengeance. And I did for a few hours, before I felt the fireflies flutter in my belly. There was only one person who enticed those warm flurries. Gavin. A rush of excitement whirled inside me.

My eyes lifted. He was leaning in the doorway, his startling blue eyes were vibrant and alive, a stark contrast against his midnight hair. The cool metal hoop at the center of his lip twitched as they curved. Gavin was gorgeous in a way that made me feel giddy and reckless.

Climbing off the bed, I jumped into his arms and buried my face into the alcove between his shoulder and neck. I inhaled the light scent of his cologne. Bedazzling. He smelled good and safe. A head taller than me, his strong arms wrapped around my waist, keeping me close.

"I'm glad to see you, too," he murmured into my hair.

I pulled back so I could look into his eyes. Unable to help myself, I pressed my lips to his. My fingers weaved into his silky hair. It still surprised me that even though I saw him daily, my heart yearned for him. "I missed you," I whispered against his lips, his hoop scraping lightly over my mouth.

He brushed away a strand of hair that had drifted into my face. "If I'd known you were going to attack me, I would have come by much sooner."

I grinned, rolling my eyes. "Are you going somewhere?" I asked. He was dressed in distressed jeans and a dark shirt, his hair intentional styled to look as if he just gotten out of bed.

"We are," he replied. "Get dressed." Then he proceeded to give me a swat on the butt.

I squeaked. "I am dressed."

He flashed me a grin. "As much as I love you in your Harley Quinn mile-high socks and little red shorts, I'd rather not get into a fight tonight."

"They're knee-high socks," I argued, wiggling my toes, although I was impressed he knew who Harley Quinn was. But he was right. I couldn't actually go out wearing this. I'd been so busy studying that I had forgotten what I looked like. "And where is it you think you're dragging me to?"

"A party, and before you argue, I am not letting you spend your Friday night alone in your room."

Flopping back down on my bed, I frowned. "I can't go out tonight. I have an assignment to finish for English and a quiz to study for." I'd already turned down one party.

He pushed my textbook aside and sat down next to me. "You work too hard, always pushing yourself. If you don't take a breath and have a little fun, your entire college experience will have passed you by."

Okay, I didn't know what he had up his sleeve, but as much as I needed to lighten up, there was something fishy going on. My brows knitted together. "Why do you really want to go to this party? I'm not buying that you've suddenly turned into a frat douche."

An amused expression settled on his striking face. "Fine. I actually hate frat parties, but there is supposedly a coven of witches on campus. I want to check them out. See if they're going to be a problem."

The words *problem* and *witches* in the same sentence had my internal alarm picking up. My thoughts automatically turned to Amara. "Where did you hear this tip?"

He shrugged. "Jared."

Oh wow. That's a reliable source. Except this time, Gavin's brother might be onto something. I tapped my finger on my leg. "Fine, give me five minutes to change."

Not entirely enthusiastic about my evening plans, I started rummaging around my room, looking for something clean to wear. Laundry was not any more fun to do in college. I found a semi-clean pair of jeans and started to shimmy out of my shorts. Then I remembered Gavin was still in the room. "What are you doing?"

He was kicked back on my bed, an arm propped behind his head. "I like watching you get dressed."

I rolled my eyes, tugging the pair of jeans over my hips. "I bet you do. Should I get you some popcorn for the show?"

He chuckled as I managed to squeeze my butt into the jeans and loop the button. "What's this?" he asked.

I turned my head to the side to see him holding the card Amara had given me between his fingers. "You're not the only one who got invited to a party," I grumbled.

He lips turned down. "Why didn't you tell me?"

I shrugged. "Because I had no intention of going."

His eyes ran over the card. "Who gave you this?"

"A girl in my astronomy class. What makes you think there is something corrupt about these witches?" I asked.

Watching me with a crocked smile on his lips, his gaze roamed lazily over my body. "Just a girl...or a witch?"

If he kept looking at me like that, we were never going to make it to this party. As much as I would rather stay home with Gavin and his blessed lips, my curiosity was peaked. "Why do I get the feeling you already know the answer?"

Shift to his side, he slipped his hand into his back pocket and pulled out a little card identical in size as mine. "Because I got one as well."

My eyes narrowed. "Well, isn't that dandy?"

All of sudden, Gavin was sitting upright on the bed, his eyes sharpening. "What happened?"

"Why must something have happened?"

"You hate parties, and you're biting your lip."

"That's not true," I replied, and then dragged my bottom lip into my mouth with my front teeth. As soon as I realized what I was doing, I stopped.

He arched a brow, the twinkling lights overhead catching the glint of silver from the stud. My boyfriend had more piercings than I did.

Sighing, I found the top I'd been searching for under a stack of notebooks. "Okay. I met this girl in class today. She's a witch." I snatched the purple crop top out from under the pile heavy enough to throw my arm out.

"And..." he prompted.

I grabbed the ends of my tank and tugged it over my head. "I don't know. She gave me bad mojo." I yanked on the shirt and shook my hair out.

He looked disappointed. "Why didn't you say anything?"

I took a seat in my desk chair, sliding my feet into a pair of flip-flops. "I was going to, but I saw you standing in my doorway and it slipped my mind. Then you started ordering me about."

Lips curved, he swung his legs over the bed. "That's hilarious. As if you ever do anything I ask." He looped a finger into the waistband of my jeans and tugged me forward so I was in between his legs.

My fingers entwined through his hair. "I do if you ask nicely." I leaned down, staring at his lips and...

Austin's voice carried through the hall and into my room. "Hey, babygirl, where you at?"

Gavin pressed his forehead into my belly, and sighed. "I forgot. I invited Austin."

"You didn't," I grumbled.

My best friend from high school poked around the door. His brown hair was slicked back and his bottle green eyes were bright with excitement. "Get your hot ass out here. We got witches to hunt."

I took a step back and glanced at Gavin, my lips turned down. "If anything happens to him, I'm holding you responsible. I can't believe you told him."

He winced. "What could possibly happen with us by his side?" Gavin and Austin were roomies. And knowing Austin, he viewed this party as a game, like Clue.

I lifted my brows. Gavin and I both knew the kind of shenanigans I could get into.

Getting my friends mixed up with this part of my life was still hard to accept. I wanted to protect them. I knew all magic wasn't bad, but my experience was limited. All I had to go on was what I'd seen.

CHAPTER 3

The university campus was beautiful and historic. Trees lined the walkways. White pillars decorated the entrances. Fresh, clean air, the ocean breeze, and everything you needed was in walking distance. There was a peacefulness about the place, with the warm glow of lights illuminating the dormitories.

Our dorm was on the west side of campus, Cornerstone Hall. Hiking it to the other side of the postcard-worthy grounds, we entered what was known as sorority row. Instead of the apartment-like structures freshmen lived in, here quad houses sat side by side. Each had a covered porch full of college students. The chatter of laughter and fun carried over the road. A couple of guys were tossing around a football in the yard. Half-empty bottles of beer were scattered on the stoop and porch ledge.

Shoving my hands into my back pockets, I walked up the stairs and into the house, Gavin and Austin flanking me on either side.

Holy crap.

The house was jam-packed. There was a mean game of beer pong going on in the side room. Music pumped through the house, the bass rumbling under my feet. People were everywhere: crowding the kitchen, lounging on the couch, hanging out in the garage.

Austin's eyes scanned the room. "So what are we looking for? Pointy shoes? Black hats? Warts?"

I jabbed him in the gut. "Have you ever seen me with anyone of those things?"

"Uh, there was the one time in ninth grade. You had this thing growing on—"

"Do you want me to turn you into a toad?" I threatened in a level tone.

He shot me a shit-eating grin. "I was kidding. You look all uptight. Relax, ho." He squeezed my hand.

Easier said than done. I was uptight by nature.

"Try to have fun," Gavin said. "And whatever you do, don't set anything on fire. I'm going to get us drinks."

Frowning, Gavin meandered his way through the crowd toward the back of the house. *Maybe this wasn't such a good idea.* Call it intuition or a premonition, but I couldn't shake the feeling something was going to happen. I squeezed passed a girl who could barely stand up as Austin pulled me across the room.

He dropped an arm over my shoulder. "Let's own this party."

I let a nervous giggle. *He was joking, right?*

There was a high-pitched squeal behind us, and I turned around and came face to face with Amara. She had a grin plastered on her heart-shaped face. "I was beginning to give up on you," she said, acting like we were BFFs. The dress she wore made me want to cover my eyes.

I had the shittiest luck known to man.

She wasn't alone. There were two other girls with her, one on either side of her. Witches. The glimmer of magic shimmered in the air around the three of them, and if I had the ability to see auras, theirs would radiate as only a witch's could.

The one on Amara's right had ultra-shiny black hair in a pixie cut. She was tall and slender, with a meekness in her soft smile. She didn't look like a girl who would be friends with someone like Amara, with her dominating personality.

The other wasn't rail thin or looking like she was dying for a box of Krispy Kremes, but the few extra pounds looked good on her. She had a pretty face, framed by straight, caramel-colored hair with blonde highlights.

I assumed they were sorority sisters.

I gave Amara a bland look. "You're not the only one surprised," I remarked.

"Hmm. I didn't take you as a party girl," she said, flipping her ponytail off her shoulder.

By the end of the night, I had a feeling I would be ready to chop her crimson ponytail off. She rubbed me the wrong way, and I immediately regretted coming. "I'm not."

"Yet, here you are. Does this mean you're reconsidering my offer to join my sorority?"

Austin cleared his throat. "Bri? In a sorority?" He proceeded to laugh. Loudly.

"A friend of yours?" Amara asked, her eyes sliding to Austin.

I was torn between wanting to smack him on the back of the head or rush him to the dorm and tuck him safely in bed. I didn't want to introduce him to Amara. "Austin, this is Amara. We have Astronomy together."

"It's such a blow-off class," she said. The two girls at her side giggled. "Willow and Ophelia, this is Brianna, the KZG's newest member, as soon as we convince her to rush next week."

The mere thought of rush week made me scrunch my nose in a not-so-pretty way.

Austin opened his mouth, but I conveniently stepped on his foot. He frowned. The last thing I wanted was for him to slip up and tell Amara more than I wanted her to know. Some things were better left a secret.

My powers were one of them.

"Like I said before, I appreciate the offer, but I just don't have time for any...extra activities," I answered.

Amara wasn't deterred. "I'll wear you down, eventually."

Austin leaned in and muttered from the corner of his mouth, "What is she talking about?"

"It's not important," I mumbled.

Amara and her two minions turned to whisper among themselves.

Something or someone had caught their attention. I searched the room for Gavin, wondering why he hadn't returned with our drinks.

"Six o'clock, ladies. Check the dimples on that one," I heard Amara purr. "Hmm, and he's headed this way."

Ophelia, who I thought was the rounder one, sucked in a breath as she zeroed in on their target. "Ooooh. He's scrumptious, all yummy and bad."

Amara pursed her red-hot lips. "And if my radar is on point, he's not your typical frat boy. It's about damn time this school gets a guy with a bit more spark."

The three of them giggled.

Amara leaned forward so her hip was popped out, emphasizing her model curves. It was natural to be jealous of someone who looked like Amara. Flawless. Her confidence only added to her sexiness. "Watch me work my magic, girls." Then she giggled at her own poorly said pun. With a flirtatious swagger I'd never have, Amara walked in front of me, strutting her stuff.

I frowned.

Austin's eyes widened, and he snickered under his breath.

I dragged my gaze from Austin and looked to see what poor sap she planned to make her next victim. Amara didn't strike me as the type of her girl who took relationships seriously. Deep in my gut, I already knew who the target was. It was Gavin. As far as I could tell, he was the only guy here with magical abilities.

I saw him in the sea of people walking toward me. He was utterly clueless about what was about to cross his path. With two bottles in one and a red solo cup in the other, his eyes collided with mine. He lifted a brow at my scowling face, but my gaze flickered over him and zeroed back on Amara. Crossing my arms, I shot her a look that was all kinds of dirty.

"Whoa, he's even better up close," Willow giggled.

My head snapped in her direction. "He's my boyfriend."

Willow and Ophelia had twin looks of shock. "Awkward," they sang in unison.

My heart did a series of acrobatics as Amara's hand touched Gavin's arm. The simple action sent me into a tizzy. Magic roared to my fingertips. "I'm going to zap her to Pluto," I muttered.

"Oh shit, Bri," Austin said, seeing my eyes start to glow violet. "Take a chill pill."

I watched her press her chest right up against him and smile seductively. Thunder roared in my ears. My gaze honed in on one redheaded witch with a death wish. "That witch," I seethed.

Austin shook his head. "Oh no—"

But it was too late. Whatever else he said was lost on me, because I was pushing my way through the crowd. Anger rolled off me in waves. Who did this girl think she was? In the distance, thunder cracked and the sky lit up, beaming through the windows. *That...that tramp.*

Gavin's eyes sought out mine. If a storm was coming, he knew nine out of ten times it was my fault. "What's going on?" he asked, handing me the red cup.

I didn't care what was in, taking a long swig.

Austin rubbed the back of his neck, sensing the sudden rise in tension. He clung onto the neck of the glass bottle. I hadn't realized he was right behind me. "Drama," he serenaded.

"Nothing," I said dryly, taking another gulp of my drink, eyes stuck on Amara.

Her red-painted lips twisted into a sneer. "Are you guys related?"

Bitch please.

Gavin was looking at me with concern when he answered. "She's my girlfriend."

My chin tipped.

She batted her long, lush lashes. "Huh. You don't look like his type."

Oh, and Amara was? That was it.

Austin said my name again, but I was beyond hearing. My face felt like it was on fire. I didn't even remember throwing my drink in her face. One minute I was shooting daggers at her, the next Amara was dripping wet and covered in rum and coke. Chunks of ice fell at her feet.

There was a uniform gasp that rang from the surrounding group.

Gavin's lips twitched. Austin's hand flew to his mouth as he barely restrained bouts of laughter.

In a shriek that could shatter glass, Amara leaped. From the look of pure outrage on her face, I was going to pay for that. She barreled into me, and we both went sailing through the air, her fist clenching a wad of my hair.

I landed on my side with a whack.

So much for this being an uneventful party. The entertainment had just arrived. A small group had gathered around Amara and me, some watching with interest, others jeering on a chick fight. I'd hate to disappoint.

She grabbed hold of my arm, zapping me with a sharp bolt of electricity. The shock of it made my hair sizzle. I yelped. Of course Amara was the kind of girl who fought dirty, using not only a physical attack but also magic.

Two could play this game. I rolled, taking her with me, until I was on top.

"*Jesus Christ*," I heard Gavin swear. "Bri," he warned.

But in the haze of red cloudy my vision, I ignored him. "My turn," I hissed between my teeth. With my free hand, I snatched her wrist and sent a stream of power right back. Except the moment I touched her, I could feel her magic, pulsating on the surface. My anger mixed with the tremor of her power—a volatile cocktail.

Gavin jumped up, throwing his arms around my waist, all amusement gone. "Calm down," he whispered softly in my ear, tearing me away from Amara. "Your eyes."

I pulled against his hold, but I didn't make it far. Lowering my hands, I balled them into fists at my side. People were staring at us, but I managed to keep myself from going all glow-eyes.

"You...you," Amara sputtered. She flipped the loose pieces of wet hair that had fallen in her face. "You're going to regret that," she seethed.

"Try me," I barked, seriously thinking about hitting someone for the first time in my life.

"I swear by the stars and the moons, I will destroy you."

Oh, goodie.

CHAPTER 4

T hat bitch.

I don't know who she thought she was messing with, but she had another thing coming if she thought she could intimidate me.

Gavin had his hand under my elbow, guiding me out into the street. Night reigned, the moon hemorrhaging overhead, dripping in crimson and gold. A blood moon was never a good omen.

As soon as we were outside, Austin threw his head back and laughed. "Holy shit, Bri, that was..."

"Reckless, stupid," Gavin interjected.

A frown pulled at my lips. He was right, but anger was still clouding my common sense.

"I was going to say really hot," Austin informed. He was more or less bouncing down the street alongside us. "I knew you were a tiger, but way to unleash your tigress."

My blood was still sizzling, but I let the evening breeze wash over my face and sucked in a breath of the crisp air. It helped. "I guess the party's over."

Gavin chuckled, weaving his fingers through mine. "Good grief, I can't leave you alone for five minutes. But at least we got what we wanted."

"And much more," Austin added, smirking. "A drink and a show. It's more than what I get on a first date."

I let a short laugh. "Sorry. I hope I didn't ruin your night."

"Are you kidding? That's the most fun I've had all week."

"Glad one of us enjoyed ourselves," I said, rubbing the side of my head, making sure I didn't have a bald spot. Amara had one hell of a grip.

Gavin's gaze snapped to mine, a slash of menace in the shadows. "I'm not even going to ask what happened back there, but stay clear of her, Bri. I know a witch with a vendetta, and that one has it out for you."

Unbidden, I took a step closer to him. There was something in the air, about this whole night that had me on edge. "What else is new?"

"Hold up. I know a shortcut." Austin forcible changed my direction.

Unease pricked down my spine. "A graveyard? Are you kidding me?"

"Wuss," Austin persisted, taking a step toward the cemetery. "Don't tell me you're superstitious?"

When Gavin didn't object, I wet my lips. "I'm a witch. Obviously, I'm superstitious, you idiot."

Austin grimaced.

A dark mist drifted over the uneven ground, blanketing the grass and marked graves. Austin filled the silence with nonsense chatter, reliving how I so expertly threw my drink in Amara's face. I just wanted to forget this night ever happened.

I was cursing Amara when something tight and inexorable tangled around my ankle and I stumbled. *Thump.* I went down with a scream, falling on my hands and knees. Clumps of dirt pitted under my fingernails. A few seconds went by before I got my bearings and realized the dark hole I was staring into was an open grave. The dirt was freshly turned over, as if someone had recently dug it.

A bone-chilling thought.

"What the heck," I mumbled.

Heart racing, I pushed the hair out of my face and lifted my head.

Gavin helped me to my feet, and I brushed the dirt and dust from my hands. At this rate, if I kept falling, I was going to be black and blue tomorrow.

Could this night get any worse?

Why yes, it could.

A moaning erupted a few feet from where I'd taken my less than graceful tumble. Gavin and I glanced at each other for a second, silently asking the other if they felt the sudden drop in temperature. If I thought I was cold before, now I could see the breath gather and freeze in front of my face.

His starlight eyes darkened. "Bri, we have a problem."

No shit, Sherlock. I was tired, achy, crabby, and so cold I thought my tits were going to freeze off. My teeth were starting to chatter as I looked up and saw a form emerging from the evening fog. The smell of rotting flesh wafted through the crisp air. I wrinkled my nose.

What the—

A twig snapped as a man trudged into a ray of moonlight. His clothes were dirty and ripped, eyes sunken and sagging, and his skin the color of toothpaste. Mud, leaves, and debris were scattered into his matted, stringy hair. I swear a chunk of his scalp was missing, but it could have been the light.

And then it hit me.

This dude was really, really dead.

I sucked in a breath, pushing to my feet. "Gavin?" My voice trembled slightly.

"Is this a joke?" Austin said backing up. "This better be a joke."

There was no time to process the surreal fact that this guy was a monster, and it wasn't a hallucination, because more bodies were climbing out of the ground.

Oh, God. This was a nightmare, right? Nope, this was the end of me, of us. There was no way we could fight so many. And my eyes were still having a hard time believing what I was seeing.

"Move!" Gavin railed.

The three of us spun around to go back the way we came, but ended up staring directly into the faces of four moaning monsters, their bones brittle and eroded.

"Shit," Gavin spat, eloquent as always.

Monsters. Monsters. And more monsters. They closed in around us, here, there, everywhere. A clammy sheen of fear slicked over my skin, mixed with the taste of acid in my mouth. Breathe in...breathe out...

"Bri, get behind me," Gavin ordered, always trying to be the hero. "And try not to get killed," he added.

Killed? I was just trying to avoid a panic attack. The thing was, there were too many for him to singlehandedly dispatch. He knew it. I knew it. Hell, even Austin knew it.

"Guys?" Austin said, quivering. His back touched mine.

Panting like I'd run a mile, I flipped out my hand, calling forth my power. "I guess running is off the table." I needed to be brave. It was easier to tell yourself to be something than actually *be* it.

When it came down to my friends, to those I cared about, I knew what had to be done. These things had to die. The wind picked up, howling like a pissed off banshee. Throwing my hand forward, I had a straight shot. A burst of bluish-white light exploded from my fingertips and body-slammed into one of the walking dead.

Black goo oozed from where I'd hit him, and the smell of burning corpse filled the air. Then to my great relief, the monster teetered on his rocky feet and fell to the ground. In what could only be magic, a black mist drifted over his body and it disintegrated into dirt. I didn't have time to appreciate how kickass that had felt.

"Bri!" Gavin roared.

"What?" I yelled, hardly believing he was going to scold me at a time like this.

His blue eyes were shining with magic. "I told you to stay out of the way."

The putrid stench of death was everywhere, burning my nostrils. "We don't have time to argue. I'm doing this." I didn't claim to be an all-knowing witch, but with Gavin's help, I'd been able to learn a thing or two about using magic for other means. This was what I'd been trained for, to fight magic with magic. I could do this.

When he didn't argue, I let my power build inside me, holding nothing back. I arched, giving my arms more space. Gavin's green light streamed alongside mine as we sent blast after blast, sending the monsters back into the ground where they belonged. In dizzying intervals, the tiny light particles shimmered through the air, hitting the monsters, one after another. They weren't fast or smart, which helped.

Much to my shock, the three of us stood in the center of the graveyard, alone once again. Other than my scratched knees, no one got hurt. The dark mist faded, taking the quiver of magic with it. I rubbed my hands up and down my arms, attempting to chase the icy cold that had taken up residency. Strange.

I couldn't help thinking that the fight had been too easy.

Something to contemplate later, I supposed. After we got out of here.

"What was in that drink?" Austin asked hoarsely.

My fingers were humming with the aftereffects of using so much magic. I couldn't seem to stop staring at the ground. Two fingers pressed under my chin, forcing my head up.

"You okay?" Gavin's voice softened, edged with concern.

I swallowed. "Yeah."

Dark hair toppled over his forehead. "Amara is a necromancer."

CHAPTER 5

"Anecromancer?" I echoed, the second we were inside the dorms safe and sound, thanks to a protection spell. "You're shitting me!"

"I wish," Gavin said. Thick lashes shielded his eyes, but from the strain in his voice, it wasn't good.

"You mean like dark magic?"

He nodded. "She can raise the dead."

Crap on a graham cracker. "I didn't even know that was possible."

"There is a lot you still have to learn."

I moved my fingers, the tingles of magic finally ebbing off. "What makes you think it was her?" Don't get me wrong, I wasn't Amara's biggest fan, but it seemed biased to assume she was the witch responsible. Yes, she had a reason to get back at me, but she didn't strike me as someone smart enough to pull off the kind of spell required to raise the dead.

The dorm was quiet for a Friday night. Austin had gone up to his room. Too much excitement, he proclaimed. Gavin raked a hand through his hair. "Remember how I've said that magic has a distant signature? It's kind of like a scent or a stamp. Like Sophie can see auras, I can see Amara's autograph all over those guys. It was her. I got a quick glimpse of her magic when she zapped you earlier."

"Ugh, don't remind me," I said, sinking down onto my bed and kicking off my flip-flops. College no longer seemed like the safest place. If she could raise the dead, what else could this witch do?

Nothing good came to mind.

"Geez, all I did was throw my drink on her." I couldn't imagine what the repercussions would have been if I'd done something truly wicked. She clearly hadn't been joking about destroying me.

Gavin jammed his hands into his pockets. "It's the darkness. It feeds into a witch's emotions, twisting the mind. She's more dangerous than she appears. Don't let her fool you. And keep your guard up around that one. I have a feeling tonight was only a warning. She's showing us what she can do."

"I get it. She's the big witch on campus. I'm not looking to get her way or be part of her little coven. I've never been a groupie." The frustration was evident in my tone.

Gavin stared at me, his jaw curving. "You know, Austin was right."

Tiling my head back and forth, I worked out the stress kinks in my neck. My brow crinkled. "About what?" I asked.

A glimmer of mischief crossed his expression. "It was hot."

I rolled my eyes. "You're warped."

"And you're cute when you're all worked up."

"If you think that was cute, just wait until you see what I have planned next."

He tugged on the ends of my hair, rocking back on his heels. "Honestly, I don't know if I should be intrigued or scared shitless."

"Probably a little of both." I noticed the empty bed on the other side of the room. My roommate, Kylie, was out for the night. She had a boyfriend a few floors above. The chances of her coming home tonight were slim. "Did you put that protection spell on your room?" I asked.

Gavin cast a sideway glance. "Um, of course."

"Good. I don't want to have to worry about Austin." Something came over me. Maybe it was the near death experience. I more or less tackled Gavin, throwing myself at him. "Stay," I whispered, raining kisses over his cheeks and chin.

His eyes roamed over my face in a slow perusal. "What took you so long?" he whispered, backing me into a wall and making me gasp. His gaze centered on my lips, before he closed the little distance between us.

My pulse exploded. So hot, his kiss short-circuited my brain. I wasn't thinking of anything but him in that moment. Amara and her monsters was the furthest thing from my mind.

Wonderfully dazed, I couldn't get close enough. His lips meshed against mine, his tongue sliding into my mouth. Sweeping his arms around my waist, we landed on my bed. Our legs tangled as his body pressed into me, and somehow my hands ended up under his shirt, my nails marking his skin. Shivers raced up and down my spine, and I clung to him like ivy.

He pushed the sleeve down my collarbone, exposing my skin and pressed his lips to my shoulder. "Promise me you'll be careful," he murmured.

"I can take care of myself," I assured. There was no need for him to worry. He taught me to be cautious, and how to use magic to defend myself.

"I know you can, but it only takes one careless mistake. Don't make a mistake."

My fingers dug into his shirt. "I don't want to talk about her. Actually, I don't want to talk at all."

Gavin brushed my hair back, his fingers lingering over my cheeks. "What did she say to piss you off?"

"It was stupid," I said, lowering my lashes.

"That wasn't an answer," he insisted.

"I saw her hitting on you and...I lost it."

He leaned forward, sweeping his lips over mine. "You're amazing."

My mouth tingled from his kisses, making my belly flipped. "That's what I've been telling you."

He chuckled against my mouth. "What am I going to do with you?"

"I can think of a few things," I replied, twisting in his embrace and placing a soft kiss on his lips. He ran his fingers lightly over my hip, returning the kiss. There was a tenderness that made me ache.

But the thing with Gavin, he always left me breathless. One minute he was sweet and gentle and the next, my hands were captive over my head as he changed angles, deepening the kiss. He left me no choice but to meet him heat for heat. The weight of him was delicious.

Growing impatient, I wanted the feel of him against me, skin to skin, no barriers, nothing getting in the way. I sat up and raised my arms. Gavin didn't hesitate. Bunching his fingers at the hem of my shirt, he lifted it over my head. His was next, joining mine on the floor.

With nothing standing in our way, his hands roamed everywhere, along my slender neck, down the curve of my shoulder, over the dip of my stomach. I sucked in a sharp breath and bit my lip as he followed each touch with a whisper of a kiss. The metal of his lip ring cooled my scorched flesh.

I was positive that at this point in my life, there was no other moment as perfect as this. Maybe it was the walking corpses. Maybe it was Amara. Maybe it was the thought of losing him.

Regardless of the reasons that propelled me, all that mattered was that he was here, with *me*. "I love you," I whispered.

His eyes were radiating, casting a starry light into the darkness. "Not as much as I love you."

I wound my arms around his neck, reaching for him. "Don't think about stopping," I said in case he had any ideas.

He flashed me a grin, his head dipping. "I wouldn't dream of it." Then he was kissing me again.

My body flushed, and my heart was pounding too fast. I could feel his beating with mine.

This was true love.

This was magic.

CHAPTER 6

I was in line at the small coffee shop on campus, rocking a pair of dark shades to cover the circles under my eyes. The last few nights had been restless. Even with Gavin lying beside me, I hadn't gotten much sleep—if any.

I spent the weekend holed up in the dorm, catching up on homework and binge watching Netflix with Austin and Gavin. But no matter how much drama there was on TV, it paled in comparison to my real life. I was hiding out, not only because I didn't want to have a run-in with Amara, but also because I was embarrassed by my behavior.

What had come over me?

Jealousy was an exhausting emotion, and one I wasn't proud of acting out on. My anger had always been a trigger for me, evoking my powers before I even knew I had them. It had made for a very interesting childhood.

Sometimes it was hard to ignore how effortless it would be to simply extract Amara's magic. Why did it always require more effort to be good than to be bad? Knowing Amara used black magic made me want to stop her. That kind of power was no joke. I knew firsthand the consequences and allure dark magic had. Like a drug, it was addictive to the point of self-destruction.

Or in my case, soul destruction.

As I waited for my caramel macchiato, I thought about skipping astronomy. The prospect of seeing Amara's face gave me hives, in no small part because I was afraid of what I might do. As much as I practiced control, I wasn't feeling extremely confident today in my ability to resist the urge. If she provoked me, I was afraid I would strike back in the one way I knew would truly stop her.

"Brianna," the barista called my name.

I grabbed my cup of joe and glanced at the clock. There was still twenty minutes before class started, so I found an empty seat in the corner. Digging out my phone, I passed the time scrolling through my Facebook feed. Sophie had posted a silly picture from Homecoming.

I sipped my drink, feeling a bit nostalgic. Seeing her face made me think of home and Aunt Clara. I made a mental note to call her tonight, to check in and make sure she was remembering to eat.

"Bippity-boppity-boo," a voice sang behind me.

My fingers tightened around the warm paper cup and I closed my eyes. *For the love of God.* I lifted my head, meeting Amara's cool light green eyes. "Are you stalking me?" I accused. Probably not the best way to start a conversation, but this chick was trying my patience.

Her dark denim jeans were painted on as she slid into the empty seat across from me. "You wish."

My hands flattened on the table. "Since you're not drinking coffee, what is it you want, Amara?"

She giggled, clearly taking sick pleasure in tormenting me. "Did you enjoy the party?"

Yep. She got her rocks off screwing with me. What a witch. And that wasn't a compliment. "Honestly, it was kind of *stiff*." Like those walking dead bodies, I added silently.

The fake-ass smile on her lips flinched ever so slightly. "I'm a little surprised. I sort of thought you'd be the kind of witch who would dabble on the other side. You're not exactly Glenda the Good Witch, are you?"

Unease rose swiftly, snaking its way inside me. "What are you talking about? Why would you think that?"

"Call it a talent. You might look like peaches and cream on the outside, but inside, you're not as innocent as you portray."

I pressed my knees together under the table. My palms were beginning to sweat. "I don't screw with the dark arts," I said, keeping my voice low. "And if you knew what's good for you, you wouldn't either. But then again, you don't strike me as the wisest wand in the shop."

She crossed her legs and leaned back in the chair. The soft pendant light from the coffee shop picked up the sheen from her satin shirt. "If you say so, but the craft doesn't lie, Brianna. Humans do, but magic, it doesn't discriminate."

Amara was more perceptive than I'd given her credit for. Gavin was right. I needed to be very, very cautious around her. Already, I got the impression she knew more than I was comfortable with. And don't even get me started about the way the girl dressed. Who the hell wore spiked heels and tight jeans to an 8:00 a.m. class? She looked insanely hot, which burned my butt. I was lucky if I swept a coat of mascara over my eyes. Forget about doing my hair. I was rocking a fashion-forward messy bun. "What's your deal? I thought you wanted to destroy me."

Her lips thinned. "Oh, I still do. But...I also admire a girl who doesn't take shit."

"Look, I don't want to upset your throne. I get it. You're some big shot on campus. Just so we're straight, I don't use my gifts to manipulate people."

A flash of silver popped in her eyes. I was getting to her, not necessarily a good thing. "You don't know the first thing about me."

"I know enough to not want to join your sorority." Glancing at the clock, I had less than five minutes to get to class. Time to wrap this riveting conversation up. "Is there a point to this visit, or are you here to annoy me?"

Her long nails rapped over the tabletop. "Both. Annoying you is just a bonus, an entertaining one. But there is something I want."

My mouth dried. "Oh, and what might that be?" I asked, but was afraid I already knew.

"As cute as your boyfriend is, I'm more interested in you."

My mouth nearly hit the table. "You want me?" I squeaked. I didn't know whether I should be flattered or completely freaked out. "I think it's pretty clear I don't play for the other side. I have a boyfriend."

She laughed, sexy and husky. I could never pull off a laugh like that. "You're not my type either, doll."

All I could do was lift my brows. I was at a loss for words.

"I want you in my sorority," she replied.

I choked. "In your coven," I corrected. "One minute you're trying to kill me, and the next you're trying to recruit me. I think you need to get your head examined."

A bitter laugh snuck out. "Sarcastic and funny. You're like a triple threat."

"Except, I'm not a threat." *Yet*...I added to myself.

"Listen, Brianna, I got a taste of the amount of power you keep in check. I can help, you know, tap into all that power. There is more to magic than gimmicks and hexes. I can show you." There was an undeniable eagerness in her voice.

"I already have a mentor," I said dryly.

She tipped her head, copper curls falling to one side. "Your boyfriend, as hot as he is, doesn't have the amount of juice you do. His abilities are limited. I, on the other hand, can show you magic you've never imagined."

"Thanks, but I'll take my chances with Gavin." I trusted him. We'd been through some serious crap together. Amara, I barely knew, and not to mention, she had unleashed a group of walking corpses on me. I wouldn't call that exactly trustworthy.

"You're making a huge mistake," she insisted.

Man, I was starting to think this witch didn't understand the word no. "It's mine to make. Why would you want to help me? What's in it for you?" I shot back.

"As sisters, we support each other. Our circle makes us stronger. Haven't you ever heard of camaraderie?"

My stomach tumbled over. I tried to swallow, but a god-awful lump formed in the back of my throat. "I don't get along well with others."

Fire crackled in her eyes. "I've heard some pretty lame excuses, but yours take the cake."

"Okay, how about this. No. Is that plain enough for you?" I gathered my books and drink. Amara and I were done here. I had nothing else to say to her.

"I don't take no. Eventually, I'll wear you down."

I jerked my head up. "How? By threatening me?"

She shrugged. "I'm used to getting what I want."

"I don't know what you think you'll gain from having me in your coven, but I promise you, there is nothing you can do or say that will change my mind. I'm not here to gain power or join a coven. I just want a degree." I stood and started for the door.

"We'll see about that. I can be very persuasive," she said, following me out the door and across the yard to the science building.

I said nothing as I power-walked. She was hot on my heels. Throwing open the door, I briefly contemplated casting a quick spell to lock the double doors, but she'd probably undo it faster than I could conjure.

Her bombshell-red lips curled. "You can run, Brianna, but you can't escape your destiny."

"I've already meet my destiny," I replied coldly, turning the handle to room 103.

Everyone turned to look as Amara and I burst into the classroom, making enough noise to start a stampede. I wanted to duck under a table. I could feel my cheeks starting to burn. Being the center of attention sucked. Amara however, seemed to thrive on disruptive nature.

"Ladies, is there a problem?" Professor Burns asked, as we had walked in on his lecture. Class had started.

All I could think as I slinked to my seat was, *only one. Amara.*

CHAPTER 7

A dark cluster of clouds moved in front of the moon, mirroring my current mood: glum and despondent. North Carolina was having unseasonably cold weather for this time of year. I hunkered down in my UNCW hoodie as the wind whipped around me. Gold and rust colored leaves fell from the trees, spiraling to the ground.

Austin let out a stream of hot air. "Christ, it's colder than an Eskimo pie."

I shivered. "Don't even think about suggesting another shortcut," I warned him.

"I can't believe I let you talk me into going to the library."

I matched our footsteps, keeping my arms wrapped around me. "Do you want to actually pass a class?"

"Why do you think I am trudging it across campus in this kind of weather? If I don't pass *all* my classes, you can kiss my sorry ass goodbye."

His parents were stickler about grades. If he didn't hold at least a 3.0 GPA, he would be paying for college out of his own pocket.

Austin pulled his Neff beanie down over his ears. "Can't you do something about the weather? I mean, this is ridiculous."

I frowned. "I am doing something."

Tipping his head back, he glanced up at the sky. "Wow, Bri, what the heck is up your butt?"

"You know I can't always control it."

"Well, whatever it is, can you hurry up and get happy? I want to see the sun. And I really hate knowing you're in a rut. Do you want a hug?" Whether I did or not, Austin didn't give me a choice. His arms wiggled through mine. "Or maybe a big, fat slice of warm apple pie with a scoop of vanilla ice cream? It works for me."

I leaned my head on his shoulder. His body heat chased the chill. "I wish it were that simple. I miss Aunt Clara and Tori. I know it's only an hour away, but lately it feels like I'm living on the other side of the universe."

"I know what you mean. We should take ourselves on a little road trip this weekend," he suggested.

I nodded. He was right. I really needed a weekend at home, in my own bed.

"Maybe we can even get that slice of pie."

I laughed.

In spite of the weirdness that was my life, I felt at peace the moment I stepped into the library. Books of every shape, size, and color lined the walls. Dusty ones or new books with their seams still intact, it didn't matter, I loved them all. There was this little breath of happiness that filled me, taking a way a sliver of the homesickness.

The library was deader than Amara's corpses, just the way I liked it. Despite Austin's procrastination and grumbling, we got to work. His study ethics were very different than mine. Earbuds in, he repeatedly tapped the end of his pencil with the beat of his playlist.

"How do you retain any information like that?" I whispered.

"Huh?" he answered in a volume louder than his inside voice.

"Sshh," I scolded, putting my finger to my lips.

His eyes widened in understanding, and he pulled out the cord from his ears. "Oh yeah, like there is anyone to disturb."

"There's me," I said drily.

"That's because you're the only idiot dumb enough to traipse around in this kind of weather, and I'm the moron who agreed to go with you."

I rolled my eyes.

"So, where's hotpants at?" Austin asked, referring to Gavin.

My lips twitched at the corners. "I would pay to see you call him that to his face."

He drummed his pencil against his lips, contemplating. "It might be worth the risk of being zapped by magic."

I grinned. "He's meeting Jared to see if they can dig up any info on necromancers and Amara's sorority."

"Boy is paranoid, but again, he has a right to be. Seen any corpses wandering around campus lately?"

I exhaled. "No, thank God." "The one time was enough for me."

"Does hotpants still think it was she-who-may-not-be-named?"

"For sure. I just can't figure what her angle is. She's wants my power, but for what? That's what has got Gavin on edge."

"Which is precisely why I'm sticking to you like white on rice, girlfriend."

My gaze tapered. "Did Gavin ask you to come with me today?" I inquired, suspecting that my overprotective boyfriend didn't want me to be left alone. This had his signature all over it.

Austin turned his head to the side, running his hand along the back of his neck. "I know nothing about that."

I pursed my lips. "Uh-huh."

The two seats across the table were suddenly no longer empty. Willow and Ophelia occupied the seats, making themselves comfortable in their matching KZG hoodies. Austin and I looked at each other with the same WTH glances.

I cleared my throat.

Smiling slightly, Ophelia dropped her backpack on the floor. "Hey."

"Hey," I replied. "Ophelia, right? We meet at the party the other night."

She nodded. "Yeah, when you dumped your drink over Amara."

I had a feeling, that one incident was going to follow me through all four years of college. "Um, that was sort of a misunderstanding."

Her shoulders gave a shrug. "We get it. Amara can be a bitch sometimes."

"Sometimes?" I repeated, unable to keep the disbelief from my voice.

"Okay, maybe once or twice a day," Willow amended.

"Or more like every hour," Austin mumbled, eyes staring down at his open textbook.

"True, she isn't the easiest person to get along with, but she'll be the first one to stick up for you."

Austin nudged me with his elbow. "Sounds like someone else I know."

I scowled, more or less ignoring him. "Let me guess. She sent you guys here to convince me to join your sorority?"

Willow winked. "That obvious, huh?"

Amara had warned me she was relentless. "I'm pretty sure nothing Amara does is subtle."

Willow put up a hand. "Before you say no, all we ask is that you come by and check out the house, meet some of the girls, see what we're all about before you make up your mind about KZG. I'm sure you have this preconceived notion of what you think our sorority is like. We'd like you to give us the chance to show you we're not a cult. We're sisters. A family. We help each other. We support one another."

I believed Willow and Ophelia truly believed that, and maybe it was true, but I'd gotten a glimpse of the darker side of Amara. She had a game plan. I wouldn't be surprised if the whole sorority was part of a larger scheme. My gut was telling me not to trust Amara.

They read the doubt on my face. "No parties. Just the sorority sisters," Ophelia added.

"You guys have a really strange way of recruiting members," Austin rebutted. "Unleashing an army of—"

I kicked him under the table. Austin, Gavin, and I knew what Amara had done in the graveyard, but I wasn't sure if her sorority sisters knew the kind of magic she conjured. "What Austin is trying to say is that Amara and I haven't exactly gotten off on the right foot."

"Well, you must have done something to impress her. She's never works this hard to get someone into the cov...sorority," Willow corrected.

Clearly, they weren't sure how much Austin knew of my world. "I hope Amara appreciates the friends she has, and I'm sorry you wasted your Saturday."

"There's nothing we can do to change your mind?" Ophelia asked, one last attempt to get me to change my mind.

I gritted my teeth and shoved my books into my bag. "Austin, let's go."

CHAPTER 8

R ush week.
Someone shoot me now.
It was hard to ignore all the house colors every other student wore, and the clutter of streamers and flyers being handed out at the dorms.

But I was doing my damnedest.

The only way Amara was going to get me into house KZG was kicking and screaming. Now that the thought crossed my mind, I wouldn't put it past her. I glanced over my shoulder to make sure no one was following me as I exited the math building.

Paranoid much?

Any anxiety I was feeling dissipated the moment I set eyes on Gavin. He was lazily leaning against the brick building, looking so content. Faint traces of stubble shadowed his jaw as he lifted his head up, and when he looked at me like that, his eyes most definitely twinkled. He had a disheveled-from-sleep sexiness I couldn't resist. You would think that after a year, I wouldn't get giddy and excited every time he looked at me. I did. Fireflies zoomed in my belly, warm and charged.

My lips curved. I stood on my toes and pressed my lips to his. "Is it your turn to babysit me?"

Gavin tipped his head down, smirking. "First off, wanting to spend time with my girlfriend is not babysitting."

My arms went around his neck. "You know, nothing has happened since the night of the party. Maybe she isn't up to anything. Maybe she was just feeling slighted and vindictive that night."

He kissed the tip of my nose. "Maybe hell has frozen over."

I looped my arm through his, doing a mental eye roll. "Fine. I get it. You're still skeptical."

Putting an arm around my shoulder, he tucked me into his side as we started walking to the dorm. "Give her time. She'll dig her own grave."

The warmth of him quickly seeped into my bones. I smacked him on the chest. "Funny. Maybe you should quit school and become a comedian."

His sapphire eyes sparkled under the waning light. "Who would keep you out of trouble?"

He had a point. It felt good to be nestled up against him, safe, after I'd slogged through two classes today. "Trouble does seem to find me no matter where I hide. Have you figured what she's up to?" Like many of our conversations, we someone how circled back to Amara.

He shook his head. "Not yet."

I made my steps match his long strides as he ate up the ground. "That's a good thing, right?"

Brows knitting, a bothered expression settled on his face. "Not necessarily."

The wind whined and groaned in the distance. *Wait, what?* It wasn't even windy. If the wind wasn't making those noises, then...

I stiffened, jerking to a halt. "Did you hear that?"

The muscle at his jaw ticked. "Yeah, but I'm really hoping it was some drunk frat douche."

I snuggled closer to him. "Me, too."

The moan sounded again, but this time was followed by a high-pitch scream.

Shit.

Every inch of Gavin's body went on high alert. I placed a hand on his arm, needing to touch him. "Drunk or not, someone is screaming in fear," I said, knowing I couldn't stand here and pretend I didn't here them. I spun around. The air was stale in my lungs as I listened to pinpoint which direction it was coming from.

My eyes brightened, narrowing in the direction of the grassy section behind the library, toward the...

You've got to be kidding me. The cemetery! Again!

Now I positively knew what those groans were—the dead being raised.

My eyes were large as saucers when I turned back to Gavin, peering at him. "We need to do something."

His gaze was steely. "Yeah, we do. I need to get you out of here."

"Gavin!" I protested when his fingers wrapped around mine, tugging me down the path away from the screams.

"Hell, no. You're not running straight into a graveyard filled with zombies."

I dug my heels in and planted my weight, refusing to take another step in the wrong direction. "You're going to have to drag me, then."

"That can be arranged." Stealth-mode Gavin appeared. "You're going to the dorm."

"I'm not leaving," I shouted. Little good it did.

He moved. His shoulder dipped as he placed his hands on my hips to hoist me over his shoulder. "Why do you always insist on arguing with me? Just once, will you do as I ask?"

Not today. "I'm not leaving you alone. We both know you can't walk away," I said, dangling in the air. I grabbed onto his shirt, my hair flying in my face.

"I didn't think so," he answered himself, and took a step or two away from the cries.

"It could be someone we know. It could be Austin."

He paused, and I knew I'd won. Then he huffed, his chest rising and falling heavily underneath me. "What are we waiting for?" he grumbled, sounding resigned. His fingers ran up to my hips.

"Thank you," I said a soon as my feet touched the ground. If there had been time, I would have kissed him.

He angled his head at me, eyeing me with disbelief. "You know, you won't always get your way."

My lips twitched. That was debatable. My amusement was short-lived. Another long and tortured scream rang, louder and more frantic. "Hurry. We've got to stop them before they hurt someone!"

"If they haven't already," he said grimly.

And that was probably what Amara wanted. I had a bad, bad feeling about this. We were walking into a trap, but what else could we do? We couldn't let those things run around. If we didn't stop them, there was no telling how many people might get hurt...or worse.

It was always the *or worse* that made me prickly.

CHAPTER 9

I wasn't fond of the dead....or the cemetery, for that matter.
Together we raced toward the cries. As I ran, I conjured my magic, preparing for the worse. When I reached the edge of the hill, I stumbled and came to a dead stop, Gavin skidding beside me.

It was almost too much to take in. The entire lot not far from the school campus was covered with about a dozen monsters, with more scratching and clawing out of the ground. And in the middle of monster mash pit was... I craned my neck, trying to get a better look without drawing attention our way. The dead hadn't noticed the arrival of two witches, and it would be in our best interest to keep it that way, get the jump on them.

To my utter relief, it wasn't Austin being cornered by the dead. It was Willow. *Seriously.*

There was no time to process the surreal fact that Amara put one of her own sorority sisters in danger. Then again, it shouldn't have surprised me.

Right now, I had to fight, to put the skills Gavin had taught me to good use. I couldn't allow Gavin to deal with the monsters himself. For a panicked moment, I realized I didn't have a weapon, and then I remembered: I was a witch; magic was my sword.

Breathe...in...breathe...out.

The therapeutic exercise didn't really help.

While I was having a semi-breakdown, Gavin jumped right in. When he fought using magic, it was as if he became a different person—a different version of himself. The one standing in front of me now was fierce and cold, a warrior. It was a calculated move, putting himself in the line of fire and giving me time to collect myself.

He conjured a bow, equipped with glowing green arrows. He extended the bow and launched an arrow straight for Willow. At the last second, the monster surged ahead in the direct path of the arrow. It sliced across its throat, spraying bits of flesh. The entire creature's body shuddered, and then he just sort of stopped, his body exploding in darkmist that spread over the ground. The dust hadn't even settled, and Gavin was locking and loading for round two.

A moan sounded from behind me. It was my time to shine. I whirled. Two monsters decided to join the massacre bash and another one was digging himself out of his grave. Lighting up my hands, I tossed an electric ball of power at the closest one. His black orbs glazed before he gave a feral howl and burst into mist. One down, and more than we could handle left.

These things had to die.

I took a deep breath, steadying myself and launched forward. My fist went through the air, packed with magic as the next one reached me. On contact, a wave of energy fizzled through my veins and the monster went kaboom.

It felt good.

Apparently, I could do this.

I arched back, giving my power time to rejuvenate before slamming my palm into the next creature's nose. This was a female, except the bitch didn't disintegrate. *What the hell.* The creature grabbed me, latching onto my arms, scratching me with its jagged, dirty claws. Panic set in.

I twisted, kicked, and bucked, basically anything I could think of to loosen this thing's grasp. One of my blows landed in the creature's stomach, propelling her backward. She went to the ground, but another one took her place. It would only be a minute before she was back on her feet and going for my throat.

Hands extended, the walking dead snarled and hissed inaudible noises that reminded me of tortured animals.

Like a puff of hot air, I blasted a sphere of magic, not wanting another up close and personal encounter. Not only did these things smell to high heaven, they were faster than they were previously. Then again, it was magic giving them life.

Taking a second to find Gavin, I was relieved to see he was up and fighting. He moved with fluid grace, bending out of the way when a creature lunged, only to circle around and blast them from behind.

He had made his way to Willow, and was trying to keep the monsters off of them both. But the moment they had a clear path, Willow took off, darting into the woods. And that left Gavin and I in the thick of it.

Typical. That's the thanks we get for saving her life.

As soon as I made it out of here alive, I was going to march down to that stupid witchcraft sorority house and give Willow the tongue lashing of a lifetime. What a dick move, leaving us there.

But the battle raged on. The more we fought, the more excited they seemed to become. The faster my heart pounded, the faster they moved. It was an endless cycle.

But I had to survive.

I had to stop Amara, and there was only one way I knew how. All I had to do was make my way to her, and to do that, I needed to battle my way through the army of monsters she called upon.

"Why don't you fight me yourself?" I yelled into the air. Instead she sent her bony and decayed goons.

Her response was the converging of four monsters.

I backed up, shooting a series of blasts—a glow here, a glow there. Grunts and moans came from all around me.

One of the monsters snuck up behind me and managed to shackle my ankle with his skeletal fingers. Unbelievable. His grip was so strong, I couldn't break free, and he tugged me to the ground, but not before I blasted the last of the group with a beam of magic.

As soon as I hit the ground, I was kicking and twisting, doing whatever I could to free myself. But no matter how hard I struggled, I couldn't break away. It was just one monster, but it was as though he had the strength and weight of a thousand. I fought and fought and fought as the thing clawed at my face and ripped at my clothes. He barred his teeth, trying to take a chunk out of my neck.

I screamed.

An instant later, Gavin was behind the bastard. He reached around, flattening his palm over the monster's heart. A green light erupted between them, so it intense it was blinding.

I blinked. Gavin was hovering over me, and we were both panting and sweating. "Stay quiet," he whispered, carefully securing his hands under my upper arms and hauling me to my feet.

I glanced at him. It was not surprising that he fared far better than I had, with only a nick on his cheek and a bruise.

"Are you okay?" he asked. He was still holding me, making sure I wasn't going to crumble back to the ground.

I nodded. "I'm fine." A tremor moved down my spine. But I couldn't say the same about Amara, when I got my paws on her. The longer I stood there leaning on Gavin, seeing the pain and destruction she caused, for no good reason, the more my blood boiled. "I'm going to kill her," I rasped, eyes burning violet.

Gavin's gaze narrowed. "I agree she needs to be stopped, but I don't think we have to resort to murder."

"You know what I mean. I'm not going to literally kill her." It was a proclamation I meant to keep.

"Oh, good. Just so were clear." Concern rightfully clouded his eyes. "Are you sure you want to do that?"

We stared at each other, the ground littered with the darkmist of the dead. What I was proposing wasn't to be taken lightly. There would be consequences if I took Amara's power—serious-no-take-back repercussions, but she had to be stopped. It became clear raising the dead wasn't a one-time thing for Amara. I needed to make sure tonight was the last time, and I would deal with the fallout once I knew she was no longer a threat.

I looked him in the eyes. "Yeah. I have to."

He might not like my choice, but he would support me. Always. "Well, let's go get us a witch."

I stepped back, more than ready to blow this dead zone. My fingers were intertwined with Gavin's as I swung around, giving him a tug, but something stopped him, his body firm.

Bri!" Gavin screamed.

My head whipped around at the sound of the sheer panic in his voice. There was a flare of fireworks sparking in front of my eyes. Beautiful. Mesmerizing. Bright.

I blinked.

And before my brain could compute what was happening, blackness descended.

CHAPTER 10

I woke up tied to a chair, with music blaring in the background, no doubt to mask my screams. The bindings that held me weren't chains or loops of rope, but the magical kind, paralyzing my hands behind the chair and bolting my feet to the floor. Icy fear trickled down my spine.

Is that Madonna?

The pop acoustics of Material Girl pumped through the room at volumes that I hadn't attempted since I was thirteen.

Wow. Someone had a weird complex for Eighties music.

As my eyes adjusted to the candlelit room, I took stock of my surroundings, anything to keep my mind from panicking over the fact I was restrained. The first thing I noticed was that the room was windowless, with no natural light to tell me how long I'd been unconscious. There was a damp coolness to the air, like the room was a basement or partially underground.

I looked down at my feet, willing them to move. Nothing happened. Fear and frustration tore through me, and I shuddered. I looked for something I could use, anything to aid my escape, when I noticed something unusual.

Runes.

They were charred into the hardwood floors, symbols I didn't recognize. I knew they were runes, but what kind. Protection? Traps? Summoning? My knowledge of runes and the ability of them were extremely lacking. I'd only just recently learned of the magical symbols —tools of the craft. There was so much to learn. Just when I thought I was wrapping my head around this witch stuff, I discovered I had barely broken the surface.

Red pillar candles flickered around the circle, with me tied in the center. At least I knew the properties of burning red candles. Danger. Channeling. Strength.

And then I saw it. Or him. A body lay just to the right of my eyesight within the circle from me, unmoving and pale as a ghost. I wasn't all that shocked Amara had a dead dude in her house; it was the green misty glow surrounding his body from head to toe that gave me pause for concern. A spell. But what kind of spell?

If I had to guess...a preservation charm. A spell that preserved the body after someone had died and their soul had moved on.

My throat felt as if it was going to close up. The picture was suddenly becoming crystal clear in my head. Amara was channeling the power of her sorority sisters to try to bring someone back from the dead. All those zombies had been practice, but to restore more than a body, she would need an exuberant amount of power.

Oh God, please let me be wrong. If that was Amara's end game, then I understood what she needed me for. She needed more power. And I had enough to blow the roof off this place.

Forget regulating my breathing. It was coming out in short, hard pants that I couldn't seem to control. The scent of melting wax and expensive perfume filtered through the room, burning my nose.

"Good. You're awake."

My body locked up at the sound of the familiar voice. I tried to twist in the chair so I could see her with my own eyes, but the invisible knots on my hands and feet prevented it.

"How are you feeling?" Amara asked. She came into my eyesight, candlelight flickering shadows on the side of her face.

I blinked, focusing on the belittling curve on her lips. "I'd feel a whole lot better if I wasn't tied to a seat."

She crossed her arms and put a single finger to her lips. "It does seem a bit extreme, but in my defense, I did try to get you here without the theatrics. You didn't make it easy."

"Relentless," I laughed, the freaked-out-scared-shitless-shrilly kind of laugh. "I guess you weren't kidding."

She blinked, and the look she gave me sent chills up my back. "I have plans for you, little witch. Big plans. You're the last piece I need... what I've been waiting for. And to think when I'd lost all hope, you practically fell at my feet."

"Plans? What plans?" My voiced was pitched high with fear.

"You'll see," she announced, a demented excitement in her voice. "Don't worry. You'll be fine. I'm not a serial killer or anything."

Her words did nothing to ease the terror seizing me. "Good to know."

She walked the rim of the circle. "The other girls will be here soon, and then before you know it, this will all be over. Nothing but a memory, and you can trot back home to your boyfriend."

Gavin? Oh, my God. He'd been with me when I'd lost consciousness. "Where is he? What did you do with him?" I demanded, the fear I was feeling turned to anger, making my tone gravelly. If she'd hurt him...

Well, she didn't want to find out what I would do to her if one hair were harmed on his body.

"Your boy toy is fine, at least he was when we left him comatose in the cemetery," her green eyes focused on mine. "I'm sure my loyal minions are taking good care of him. His head might be throbbing, and he could be a little disoriented when he wakes up, but other than that, he'll live."

I fought against the bands of magic, but it was pointless. They didn't give, and I hadn't expected them to. "If you're lying," I seethed, nearly foaming at the mouth.

She lifted her chin. "Everything I've told you has been the truth."

"But not the whole truth," I interjected. "Whatever you're planning to do, Amara, I won't let you."

She smiled in a not so friendly way. "You don't have a choice."

The hell I didn't. There was always a choice. Amara had no idea who she was dealing with, or the kind of witch I was. These binds might physically hold me, but it wouldn't contain my magic. She had another thing coming if she thought I was going to stand by and be a puppet in her spell.

I let out a shaky breath. "I have more power than you know."

She made a dismissive gesture, like I was nothing but an annoying fly buzzing in her ear. "That's what I'm counting on. You're not the only one who would do anything for someone you love. I understand the lengths you're willing to go, to protect Gavin. More than you know."

"I understand love, and how hard it must be losing someone you love. Who was it you lost?" I asked.

"No one that concerns you," she barked. "That's all you need to know."

Holy crap. I knew in my gut, I was right. The pieces fell into place. She was going to try and bring someone back from the dead. One thing I learned was, just because magic could do all sorts of phenomenal things, doesn't mean it was right. "I see a guy in my crystal ball," I replied, part smartass, part investigator.

"Enough!" she snapped, clenching her fists. The candles in the room flickered before the flame shot up, quadrupling in size and washing the room in burning glow. Someone had an anger management problem. That I understood.

I flinched before the candles returned to normal soft light, darkening the room.

After a calming breath, her gaze jerked to the corner of the room. As far as I could tell, nothing was there, but when her eyes began to glimmer in the dark, I knew things were about to get real. "The moon is high and full. It's time," she said, more to herself than me.

Time for what? It looked like I was about to find out.

She spun around, and footsteps sounded behind me. One by one, her fellow sorority sisters and witches came into the room, include Ophelia and Willow. If I wasn't tied to this chair, I would have flown out of the seat, straight at Willow, for her part in this shenanigan. Sitting around the drawn circle, they joined hands, beginning and ending with Amara.

An electric shock trembled in the air as soon as the circle was complete. The room was swathed in a reddish light, and within seconds, the temperature in the room went to subzero. A chill radiated over my body. My blood pressure accelerated, and the tightening in my chest couldn't be a good sign.

Power gripped me, and my head tipped back. Frustration bounced around inside my already tightened gut. I was unable to stop it. I pulled against my binds, to no avail. *What a bunch of cuckoo witches*, I added silently to myself.

Amara and her followers began the chant to what I recognized as a channeling spell. They were allowing Amara to borrow their gifts. Tonight was one of those times it sucked to be right. The other girls had power, but it was mediocre. Amara herself had more than the lot of them put together, but not as much as I had. I had given her a chance to be reasonable, and she was a fool if she thought her magic would hold me.

Forcing my body to relax, I took control of my gift, trying to calm the spark that begged to be unleashed. A boom of thunder crackled outside. "If you think using magic is the answer, then you're a bigger fool than I took you for. All of you," I ranted in a last desperate attempt make them see the mistake they were about to embark. "Dark magic comes with a price. It's dangerous and destructive. Whoever you're trying to bring back, this isn't the way. It's not natural. Not even magic can reverse death."

"Thanks for the buzzkill," Amara snarled. "Now keep quiet so I can concentrate. I wouldn't want to screw up the spell and hurt someone." Her insinuation was clear. If I didn't cooperate, Gavin would pay the price. "I'm only going to borrow a bit of magic. No harm done. You'll only be a bit tired. I'd prescribe lots of rest for the next few days."

Her sarcasm was stale. "You can breathe life into a dead body, Amara, but you can't give him his soul back."

She closed her eyes, ignoring me, as she channeled power from her circle. The other girls were as still as statues. Again, I felt her magic weave its way into me. This was it. I had to do something. Now. Before it was too late and I lost myself to the dark pull. "Listen to me closely, Amara. Stop this spell and close the circle."

Her voice only grew louder and stronger as she pushed the spell forward.

I'd given her a shot. One was all she got, and it was evident, she wanted to do this the hard way. I was going to siphon her dry. Every. Last. Magical. Drop.

All I had to do was touch her. *How hard could that be?*

I was about to find out.

Do it. Before it's too late. Do it now. A pulse of energy nudged me forward as I called forth my power. It accompanied the darkness egging me on, begging me to take her source. That was part of the burden of being a clàr silte. I had to fight harder than other witches to keep my magic pure, and it was nearly impossible when the power I absorbed was dark. Although, good or bad, any magic I stole, left blemishes on my soul.

The magic inside scared me, but I push aside all fears. To do what must be done, I needed to be strong and confident. The second I made the decision to take her power, my own leapt with excitement and anticipation. It roared to the surface, my eyes glowing like polished amethyst. Solely concentrating on my hands and feet, I felt the binds snap, and my body was trembling with the power that granted my freedom.

Eyes closed, the circle was oblivious that their host of power was about to break the chain. My knees and legs were a bit shaky as I pushed slowly to my feet. Amara was directly in front of me, only a few feet of space between us. Once I made contact, there was nothing she could do to stop it. I was stronger.

Careful not to even breathe, I reached out, my hand circling her wrist. "I didn't want to have to do this, Amara, but you leave me no choice."

Her eyes popped open at the sound of my voice. "There's nothing you can do to me that I can't counter." The room blanketed with dark-mist, the same I'd seen in the cemetery. Nothing good ever followed the darkmist.

"That's what you think," I replied, releasing the magic humming in my veins. Thanks to the changeling spell, it was right there at the surface, ready to do my bidding. "I'm not your average witch. You should have gotten to know me before you decided to threaten my life and the life of the people I care about."

The center of her orbs went wide as she felt the first tendrils of my power weave around hers like a vine. I could see the reflection of my vibrant eyes in her glassy ones. Amara's expression was bright with fear, and I was luminous with sovereignty. Her body shuddered from the force and shock of my energy.

Everything happened faster than I expected. Either I was getting better at this, or my power was growing. Regardless, it didn't sit well in my stomach. The moment I released her, Amara fell to the ground just outside the circle. I had to wonder if any of the girls knew what they were about to do, or if they'd all been under Amara's incantation. The others glanced back and forth to each other, eyes shifting over the room, clarity beginning to break through the cloudy haze.

Except Amara. She looked like she was going to chop me up into bits and feed me to a pack of dogs. That was usually the response I got when sucking the magic from a witch. I'd expected nothing short of rage. "You bitch!" she screamed.

Gavin came flying down the stairs just as Amara lunged herself at me. "Bri!" he cried in part relief, part worry.

I didn't have time to respond, because I was sailing through the air with Amara's hands on my throat.

Oh, for the love of God...

CHAPTER 11

She didn't have any magic, whereas I was supercharged. I waited until my back hit the ground, the impact jarring my head, but I managed to keep it from smacking the ground, and then I threw my hands out.

Sparks fluttered.

Amara was suspended in the air, arms and legs spread out. She was glaring down above me, practically spitting in my face with anger. "You're the devil!" she screamed.

I angled my head. "Not quite. I'm a clàr silte. I warned you."

"Adam," she whispered, her eyes darting to the spot where her boyfriend had been. He was nothing but charred ash. The moment I'd taken her magic, all her spells dismantled.

Gavin reached me, murmuring my name.

I sat up, wincing. My body had been hammered to the ground one too many times in a single day. His hands tenderly cupped my cheeks, sliding across my skin in the most delicious way. Moving slowly, his eyes savored my face before he pressed his lips to mine. "Don't ever do that again," he murmured.

"I don't plan on it,"

"What does a guy have to do to keep you safe?"

I shrugged, a barely-there smile on my lips. "Lock me in a tower?" I jokingly suggested.

But by the look in his dark blue eyes, he appeared to be contemplating the ridiculous notion.

"Never going to happen," I said, before he took the idea a step past only thinking. "What did she do to you?" I asked, softly running my fingers over his cheek.

His eyes glittered like diamonds as he recalled the events in the cemetery. I knew that look. He wanted to make someone pay for hurting me, but had no one on whom to unleash his anger. "Amara used a spell to knock us out."

Dark magic could often be stronger than pure magic. Unless you were like me...a bit of both. "And you still managed to find me." I took a moment to appreciate that we were both alive, and how good it felt to be in his arms.

"Nothing would stop me finding you. Not the dead. Not a spell."

It was good to have someone who never gave up, who loved me as much as he did, who would fight until the end of time alongside me. I wanted to keep it that way. "I was so worried that she'd—"

He pressed a finger to my lip silencing me. "Don't even think it. I'm fine. We're fine."

I nodded and wrapped my arms around his neck, pressing my face against his. "She wanted to channel my power to bring back someone she lost."

"What are you going to do about her?" His eyes moved upward.

Good question. I couldn't leave her dangling in the air, however tempting. I pulled back, glancing at Amara, still floating in the air. But first, we needed to take care of her sorority sisters. They all had that WTF look on their faces. "You handle them, while I take care of her?"

We couldn't just let them go, not after what they knew about me. I wasn't a killer, so there was only one option left. We needed to wipe their memories. The deal was, though, that there was always the chance the other witches could find a way to recover the lost memories, but Amara, being only human now, would have to find another witch to regain hers. Of course, she would also have to remember a witch had taken them.

It was imperative that my identity stayed hidden, for my safety and others.

The moment he stood up and turned around, the silent room erupted into squeals and shrills as the circle broke and scrambled. Gavin cut them off at the bottom of the stairs, blocking their only escape. "Not so fast, ladies." And before anyone twitched their finger, Gavin fabricated the spell to extract memories. The swirl of green and blue mist interwove among the other girls. All it took was a whiff, and time lapsed to the exact moment before the coven had joined the circle.

They might be fuzzy and disoriented for the day, but there would no long term affects. I couldn't say the same for myself. Already, mere minutes after taking Amara's magic, I sensed the darkness she wielded, flowing through my veins.

I would be a fool not to feel some apprehension. And a fool I was not.

Understanding quickly dawned in Amara's eyes when I angled my head to look up at her. "This won't hurt; I promise," I mocked.

"Don't touch me!" she screamed.

I should have thought about sealing her mouth closed.

Her green eyes went wild as I fed the spell into the air, watching it gather around her pretty face. "You should have listened to me, but I guess like the saying goes, hindsight is twenty-twenty."

For Amara, I had a special spell. It was more than memory wiping. I was also implanting a new ending. Once I had her enthralled, all remembrance of me taking her powers gone, I carefully set her on her feet and stared in her eyes. "I'm sorry, Amara, but something went terribly wrong. The spell didn't work. Adam is gone. Forever. Do you understand?"

Big, fat tears welled in her eyes. "Gone," she sobbed. She shook her head in disbelief.

"Gone. He's in a better place now," I told her. "The spell did something to your magic. You're no longer a witch."

"What?" she gasped, her voice thick with emotion.

I know I was piling on a lot of heavy stuff, but there was no other way. "You're going to be okay. You're a strong person. You have the sorority to lean on."

She nodded, sniffing. "I do."

"They're waiting for you upstairs," I said, softening my tone.

"Why are you being so nice to me?"

Good question. I wanted to roll my eyes, but after I thought on it, I realized it was simple. "Because I know what it's like to lose someone. I know what it's like to miss someone so much, you'd give anything to see them again. I know what it's like to feel alone."

She gave one last glance at the center of the circle, her eyes running over the chair I'd be confined to, and the place where Adam had been. Without an argument, Amara walked numbly to the stairs. In a sad way, she reminded me of the dead she raised—lost and empty.

Strong arms circled me from behind. "Think you can walk out of here, or do you need me to carry you?"

I leaned back, relaxing for the first time in what felt like weeks. Turning in his arms, I pressed my face into his chest. "I'm fine."

"Do you feel good enough for this?" he rasped, leaning down and brushing his lips across mine. The most amazing scent drifted from him. Crisp and fresh, like a walk in the woods on an autumn morning. But most of all, he smelled familiar.

I nipped the ring at his bottom lip. "As soon as you get me out of here. This place has gone far past giving me the heebie-jeebies."

He chuckled softly.

I knew college wouldn't be easy, but *deadly* hadn't crossed my mind.

⚜

THE DOOR JINGLED as I walked into Madame Cora's shop. It seemed like a lifetime ago, the last time I'd been here with Tori and Austin. I felt a sense of déjà vu. Then I hadn't known what I was or what I was capable of. It was a different experience walking into the mystical shop now. I recognized the ripple of magic. I sensed the importance of the items she sold, from crystals to books—each had a purpose.

As did I.

Already, I could feel the darkmist of Amara's magic spreading on my soul. There was only one way to cure the scar left behind from taking the magic from a witch, especially a witch who practiced dark magic.

Moondust.

THE END

READ MORE BY J. L. WEIL

Black Crow
Soul Symmetry

BEAUTY NEVER DIES CHRONICLES
(Teen Dystopian Romance)
Slumber
Entangled
Forsaken

NINE TAILS SERIES
(Teen Paranormal Romance)
First Shift
Storm Shift
Flame Shift
Time Shift

SINGLE NOVELS
Starbound
(Teen Paranormal Romance)
Dark Souls
(Runes KindleWorld Novella)
Casting Dreams
(New Adult Paranormal Romance
Ancient Tides
(New Adult Paranormal Romance

For an updated list of my books, please visit my website: www. jlweil.com

Join my VIP email list and I'll personally send you an email reminder as soon as my next book is out! Click here to sign up: www.jlweil.com

ABOUT THE AUTHOR

USA TODAY bestselling author J. L. Weil lives in Illinois where she writes teen and new adult paranormal romances about spunky, smart-mouthed girls who always wind up in dire situations. For every sassy girl, there is an equally mouthwatering, overprotective guy. Of course, there is also lots of kissing. And stuff.
An admitted addict to Love Pink clothes, raspberry mochas from Starbucks, and Jensen Ackles, she loves gushing about books and *Supernatural* with her readers.
She is the author of the international bestselling Raven and Divisa series.

Stalk Me Online
www.jlweil.com
jenniferlweil@gmail.com

Made in the USA
Middletown, DE
12 July 2021